STEPHEN KING
OMNIBUS

The Eyes of the Dragon

•

Firestarter

LITTLE, BROWN AND COMPANY

A Little, Brown Book
This edition first published in Great Britain by Little, Brown in 2000
Copyright © Stephen King 2000

The Eyes of the Dragon Copyright © Stephen King 1987
Firestarter Copyright © Stephen King 1980

The moral right of the author has been asserted.

A CIP catalogue record for this book
is available from the British Library.

ISBN 0 316 85517 0

Printed and bound in Spain

Little, Brown and Company (UK)
Brettenham House
Lancaster Place
London WC2E 7EN

The Eyes of the Dragon

nce, in a kingdom called Delain, there was a King with two sons. Delain was a very old kingdom and it had had hundreds of Kings, perhaps even thousands; when time goes on long enough, not even historians can remember everything. Roland the Good was neither the best nor the worst King ever to rule the land. He tried very hard not to do anyone great evil and mostly succeeded. He also tried very hard to do great works, but, unfortunately, he didn't succeed so well at that. The result was a very mediocre King; he doubted if he would be remembered long after he was dead. And his death might come at any time now, because he had grown old, and his heart was failing. He had perhaps one year left, perhaps three. Everyone who knew him, and everyone who observed his grey face and shaking hands when he held court, agreed that in five years at the very

most a new King would be crowned in the great
plaza at the foot of the Needle . . . and it would only
be five years with God's grace. So everyone in the
Kingdom, from the richest baron and the most fop-
pishly dressed courtier to the poorest serf and his
ragged wife, thought and talked about the King in
waiting, Roland's elder son, Peter.

And one man thought and planned and brooded
on something else: how to make sure that Roland's
younger son, Thomas, should be crowned King
instead. This man was Flagg, the King's magician.

Although Roland the King was old – he
admitted to seventy years but was surely older than
that – his sons were young. He had been allowed to
marry late because he had met no woman who
pleased his fancy, and because his mother, the great
Dowager Queen of Delain, had seemed immortal to
Roland and to everyone else – and that included her.
She had ruled the Kingdom for almost fifty years
when, one day at tea, she put a freshly cut lemon in
her mouth to ease a troublesome cough that had been
plaguing her for a week or better. At that particular
teatime, a juggler had been performing for the
amusement of the Dowager Queen and her court.
He was juggling five cunningly made crystal balls.
Just as the Queen put the slice of lemon into her

mouth, the juggler dropped one of his glass spheres. It shattered on the tiled floor of the great East Court-room with a loud report. The Dowager Queen gasped at the sound. When she gasped, she pulled the lemon slice down her throat and choked to death very quickly. Four days later, the coronation of Roland was held in the Plaza of the Needle. The juggler did not see it: he had been beheaded on the execu-tioner's block behind the Needle three days before that.

A King without heirs makes everybody ner-vous, especially when the King is fifty and balding. It was thus in Roland's best interest to marry soon, and to make an heir soon. His close advisor, Flagg, made Roland very aware of this. He also pointed out that at fifty, the years left to him in which he could hope to create a child in a woman's belly were only a few. Flagg advised him to take a wife soon, and never mind waiting for a lady of noble birth who would take his fancy. If such a lady had not come into view by the time a man was fifty, Flagg pointed out, she probably never would.

Roland saw the wisdom of this and agreed, never knowing that Flagg, with his lank hair and his white face that was almost always hidden behind a hood, understood his deepest secret: that he had never met the woman of his fancy because he had never really fancied women at all. Women worried him. And he had never fancied the act that puts babies in the bellies of women. That act worried him, too.

But he saw the wisdom of the magician's advice, and six months after the Dowager Queen's funeral, there was a much happier event in the Kingdom –

the marriage of King Roland to Sasha, who would become the mother of Peter and Thomas.

Roland was neither loved nor hated in Delain. Sasha, however, was loved by all. When she died giving birth to the second son, the Kingdom was plunged into darkest mourning that lasted a year and a day. She had been one of six women Flagg had suggested to his King as possible brides. Roland had known none of these women, who were all similar in birth and station. They were all of noble blood but none of royal blood; all were meek and pleasant and quiet. Flagg suggested no one who might take his place as the mouth closest to the King's ear. Roland chose Sasha because she seemed the quietest and meekest of the half-dozen, and the least likely to frighten him. So they were wed. Sasha of the Western Barony (a very small barony indeed) was then seventeen years old, thirty-three years younger than her husband. She had never seen a man with his drawers off before her wedding night. When, on that occasion, she observed his flaccid penis, she asked with great interest: 'What's that, Husband?' If she had said anything else, or if she had said what she said in a slightly different tone of voice, the events of that night – and this entire history – might have taken another course; in spite of the special drink Flagg had given him an hour before, at the end of the wedding feast, Roland might simply have slunk away. But he saw her then exactly as she was – a very young girl who knew even less about the baby-making act that he did – and observed her mouth was kind, and began to love her, as everyone in Delain would grow to love her.

'It is King's Iron,' he said.

'It doesn't look like iron,' said Sasha, doubt-fully.

'It is before the forge,' he said.

'Ah!' said she. 'And where is the forge?'

'If you will trust me,' said he, getting into bed with her, 'I will show you, for you have brought it from the Western Barony with you but did not know it.'

The people of Delain loved her because she was kind and good. It was Queen Sasha who created the Great Hospital, Queen Sasha who wept so over the cruelty of the bearbaiting in the Plaza that King Roland finally outlawed the practice, Queen Sasha who pleaded for a Remission of King's Taxes in the year of the great drought, when even the leaves of the Great Old Tree went grey. Did Flagg plot against her, you might ask? Not at first. These were relatively small things in his view, because he was a real magician, and lived hundreds and hundreds of years.

He even allowed the Remission of Taxes to pass, because the year before, Delain's navy had smashed the Anduan pirates, who had plagued the Kingdom's southern coast for over a hundred years. The skull of the Anduan pirate-king grinned from a spike outside the palace walls and Delain's treasury was rich with recovered plunder. In larger matters, matter of state, it was still Flagg's mouth which was closest to King Roland's ear, and so Flagg was at first content.

Although Roland grew to love his wife, he never grew to love the activity which most men consider sweet, the act which produces both the lowliest cook's 'prentice and the heir to the highest throne. He and Sasha slept in separate bedrooms, and he did not visit her often. These visits would happen no more than five or six times in a year, and on some of those occasions no iron could be made at the forge, in spite of Flagg's ever more potent drinks and Sasha's unfailing sweetness.

But, four years after the marriage, Peter was made in her bed. And on the one night, Roland had no need of Flagg's drink which was green and foaming and which always made him feel a little strange in his head, as if he had gone crazy. He had been hunting that day in the Preserves with twelve of his men. Hunting was the thing that Roland had always loved most of all – the smell of the forest, the crisp tang of the air, the sound of the horn, and the feel of the bow as an arrow left on a true, hard course. Gunpowder was known but rare in Delain, and to hunt game with an iron tube was considered low and contemptible in any case.

Sasha was reading in bed when he came to her, his ruddy, bearded face alight, but she laid her book on her bosom and listened raptly to his story as he told it, his hands moving. Near the end, he drew back to show her how he had drawn back the bow and had let Foe-Hammer, his father's great arrow, fly across the little glen. When he did this, she laughed and clapped and won his heart.

The King's Preserves had almost been hunted out. In these modern days it was rare to find so much as a good-sized deer in them, and no one had seen a dragon since time out of mind. Most men would have laughed if you had suggested there might still be such a mythy creature left in that tame forest. But an hour before sundown on that day, as Roland and his party were about to turn back, that was just what they found . . . or what found them.

The dragon came crashing and blundering out of the underbrush, its scales glowing a greenish copper colour, its soot-caked nostrils venting smoke. It had not been a small dragon, either, but a male just before its first moulting. Most of the party were thunderstruck, unable to draw an arrow or even to move.

It stared at the hunting party, its normally green eyes went yellow, and it fluttered its wings. There was no danger that it could fly away from them – its wings would not be well developed enough to support it in the air for at least another fifty years and two more moultings – but the baby-webbing which holds the wings against a dragon's body until its tenth or twelfth year had fallen away, and a single flutter stirred enough wind to topple the head huntsman backward out of his saddle, his horn flying from his hand.

Roland was the only one not stunned to utter movelessness, and although he was too modest to say so to Sasha, there was real heroism in his next few actions, as well as a sportsman's zest for the kill. The dragon might well have roasted most of the surprised party alive, if not for Roland's prompt action. He gigged his horse forward five steps, and nocked his great arrow. He drew and fired. The arrow went straight to the mark – that one gill-like soft spot under the dragon's throat, where it takes in air to create fire. The worm fell dead with a final fiery gust, which set all the bushes around it alight. The squires put this out quickly, some with water, some with beer, and not a few with piss – and, now that I think of it, most of the piss was really beer, because when Roland went a-hunting, he took a great lot of beer with him, and he was not stingy with it, either.

The fire was out in five minutes, the dragon gutted in fifteen. You still could have boiled a kettle over its steaming nostrils when its tripes were let out upon the ground. The dripping nine-chambered heart was carried to Roland with great ceremony. He ate it raw, as was the custom, and found it delicious. He only regretted the sad knowledge that he would almost certainly never have another.

Perhaps it was the dragon's heart that made him so strong that night. Perhaps it was only his joy in the hunt, and in knowing he had acted quickly and coolheadedly when all the others were sitting

stunned in their saddles (except, of course, for the head huntsman, who had been lying stunned on his back). For whatever reason, when Sasha clapped her hands and cried, 'Well done, my brave Husband!,' he fairly leaped into her bed. Sasha greeted him with open eyes and a smile that reflected his own triumph. That night was the first and only time Roland enjoyed his wife's embrace in sobriety. Nine months later – one month for each chamber of the dragon's heart – Peter was born in that same bed, and the Kingdom rejoiced – there was an heir to the throne.

5

You probably think – if you have bothered to think about it at all – that Roland must have stopped taking Flagg's strange green drink after the birth of Peter. Not so. He still took it occasionally. This was because he loved Sasha, and wanted to please her. In some places, people assume that only men enjoy sex, and that a woman would be grateful to be left alone. The people of Delain, however, held no such peculiar ideas – they assumed that a woman took normal pleasure in that act which produced earth's most pleasurable creatures. Roland knew he was not properly attentive to his wife in this matter, but he resolved to be as attentive as he could, even if this meant taking Flagg's drink. Only Flagg himself knew how rarely the King went to his Queen's bed.

Some four years after the birth of Peter, on New Year's Day a great blizzard visited Delain. It was the greatest, save one, in living memory – the other I'll tell you of later.

Heeding an impulse he could not explain even to himself, Flagg mixed the King a draught of double strength – perhaps it was something in the wind that urged him to do it. Ordinarily, Roland would have made a grimace at the awful taste and perhaps put it aside, but the excitement of the storm had caused the annual New Year's Day party to be especially gay, and Roland had become very drunk. The blazing fire on the hearth reminded him of the dragon's final explosive breath, and he had toasted the head, which was mounted on the wall, many times. So he drank the green potion off at a single gulp, and an evil lust fell upon him. He left the dining hall at once and visited Sasha. In the course of trying to love her, he hurt her.

'Please, Husband,' she cried, sobbing.

'I'm sorry,' he mumbled. 'Huzzz . . .' He fell heavily asleep beside her and remained insensible for the next twenty hours. She never forgot the strange smell that had been on his breath that night. It had been a smell like rotten meat, a smell like death. Whatever, she wondered, had he been eating . . . or drinking?

Roland never touched Flagg's drink again, but Flagg was well satisfied, nevertheless. Nine months later, Sasha gave birth to Thomas, her second son. She died bringing him forth. Such things happened, of course, and while everyone was saddened, no one was really surprised. They believed they knew what had happened. But the only people in the Kingdom who really knew the circumstances of Sasha's death were Anna Crookbrows, the midwife, and Flagg, the King's magician. Flagg's patience with Sasha's meddling had finally run out.

·P·eter was only five when his mother died, but he remembered her dearly. He thought her sweet, tender, loving, full of mercy. But five is a young age, and most of his memories were not very specific. There was one clear memory which he held in his mind, however – it was of a reproach she had made to him. Much later, the memory of this reproach became vital to him. It had to do with his napkin.

Every first of Five-month, a feast was held at court to celebrate the spring plantings. In his fifth year, Peter was allowed to attend for the first time. Custom decreed that Roland should sit at the head of the table, the heir to the throne at his right hand, the Queen at the foot of the table. The practical result of this was that Peter would be out of her reach during the meal, and so Sasha coached him carefully beforehand on how he should behave. She wanted him to show up well, and to be mannerly. And, of course, she knew that during the meal he would be on his own, because his father had no idea of manners at all.

Some of you may wonder why the task of instructing Peter on his manners fell to Sasha. Did the boy not have a governess? (Yes, as a matter of fact he had two.) Were there no servants whose service was dedicated wholly to the little prince? (Battalions of them.) The trick was not to get these people to take care of Peter but to keep them away. Sasha wanted to raise him herself, at least as much as she could. She had very definite ideas about how her son should be raised. She loved him dearly and wanted to be with him for her own selfish reasons. But she also realized that she had a deep and solemn responsibility in the matter of Peter's nurture. This little boy would be King someday, and above all else, Sasha wanted him to be good. A good boy, she thought, would be a good King.

Great banquets in the King's Hall were not very neat affairs, and most nannies wouldn't have been very concerned about the little boy's table manners. *Why, he is to be the King!* they would have said, a little shocked at the idea that they should correct him in such piddling matters. *Who cares if he spills the gravy boat? Who cares if he dribbles on his ruff, or even wipes his hands on it? Did not King Alan in the old days sometimes vomit into his plate and then command his court jester to come nigh and 'drink this nice hot soup'? Did not King John often bite the heads of live trout and then put the flopping bodies into the bodices of the serving girl's dresses? Will not this banquet end up, as most banquets do, with the participants' throwing food across the table at each other?*

Undoubtedly it would, but by the time things degenerated to the food-throwing stage, she and Peter would long since have retired. What concerned

Sasha was that attitude of *who cares*. She thought it was the worst idea anyone could ever plant in the head of a little boy destined to be King.

So Sasha instructed Peter carefully, and she observed him carefully on the night of the banquet. And later, as he lay sleepy in his bed, she talked to him.

Because she was a good mother, she first complimented him lovingly on his behaviour and manners – and this was right, because for the most part they had been exemplary. But she knew that no one would correct him where he went wrong unless she did it herself, and she knew she must do it now, in these few years when he idolized her. So when she was finished complimenting him, she said:

'You did one thing wrong, Pete, and I never want to see you do it again.'

Peter lay in his bed, his dark blue eyes looking at her solemnly. 'What was that, Mother?'

'You didn't use your napkin,' said she. 'You left it folded by your plate, and it made me sorry to see it. You ate the roast chicken with your fingers, and that was fine, because that is how men do it. But when you put the chicken down again, you wiped your fingers on your shirt, and that is not right.'

'But Father . . . and Mr. Flagg . . . and the other nobles . . .'

'Bother Flagg, and bother all the nobles in Delain!' she cried with such force that Peter cringed back in his bed a little. He was afraid and ashamed for having made those roses bloom in her cheeks. 'What your father does is right, for he is the King, and what you do when you are King will always be right. But Flagg is not King, no matter how much he would like to be, and the nobles are not Kings, and you are not King yet, but only a little boy who forgot his manners.'

She saw he was afraid, and smiled. She laid her hand on his brow.

'Be calm, Peter,' she said. 'It is a small thing, but still important – because you'll be King in your own time. Now run and fetch your slate.'

'But it's bedtime –'

'Bother bedtime, too. Bedtime can wait. Bring your slate.'

Peter ran for his slate.

Sasha took the chalk tied to the side and carefully printed three letters. 'Can you read this word, Peter?'

Peter nodded. There were only a few words that he could read, although he knew most of the Great Letters. This happened to be one of the words. 'It says GOD.'

'Yes, that's right. Now write it backward and see what you find.'

'Backward?' Peter said doubtfully.

'Yes, that's right.'

Peter did so, his letters staggering childishly across the slate below his mother's neat printing. He was astounded to find another of the few words he could read.

'DOG! Mamma! It says DOG!'

'Yes. It says dog.' The sadness in her voice quenched Peter's excitement at once. His mother pointed from GOD to DOG. 'These are the two natures of man,' she said. 'Never forget them, because someday

you will be King and Kings grow to be great and tall
– as great and tall as dragons in their ninth moultings.'

'Father isn't great and tall,' objected Peter.
Roland was, in fact, short and rather bowlegged.
Also, he carried a great belly in front of him from all
the beer and mead he had consumed.

Sasha smiled.

'He is, though. Kings grow *invisibly*, Peter, and
it happens all at once, as soon as they grasp the sceptre
and the crown is put on their heads in the Plaza of
the Needle?'

'They do?' Peter's eyes grew large and round.
He thought that the subject had wandered far from
his failure to use his napkin at the banquet, but he
was not sorry to see such an embarrassing topic lost
in favour of this tremendously interesting one.
Besides, he had already resolved that he would never
forget to use his napkin again – if it was important
to his mother, then it was important to him.

'Oh yes, they do. Kings grow most *awfully* big,
and that's why they have to be specially careful, for
a very big person could crush smaller ones under his
feet just taking a walk, or turning around, or sitting
down quickly in the wrong place. Bad Kings do such
things often. I think even good Kings cannot avoid
doing them sometimes.'

'I don't think I understand –'

'Then listen a moment longer.' She tapped the
slate again. 'Our preachers say that our natures are
partly of God and partly of Old Man Splitfoot. Do
you know who Old Man Splitfoot is, Peter?'

'He's the devil.'

'Yes. But there are few devils outside of made-up stories, Pete – most bad people are more like dogs than devils. Dogs are friendly but stupid, and that's the way most men and women are when they are drunk. When dogs are excited and confused, they may bite; when men are excited and confused, they may fight. Dogs are great pets because they are loyal, but if a pet is all a man is, he is a bad man, I think. Dogs can be brave, but they may also be cowards that will howl in the dark or run away from danger with their tails between their legs. A dog is just as eager to lick the hand of a bad master as he is to lick the hand of a good one, because dogs don't know the difference between good and bad. A dog will eat slops, vomit up the part his stomach can't stand, and then go back for more.'

She fell silent for a moment, perhaps thinking of what was going on in the banqueting hall right now – men and women roaring with goodnatured drunken laughter, flinging food at each other, and sometimes turning aside to vomit casually on the floor beside their chairs. Roland was much the same, and sometimes this made her sad, but she did not hold it against him, nor did she tax him with it. It was his way. He might promise to reform in order to please her, and he might even do it, but he would not be the same man afterwards.

'Do you understand these things, Peter?'

Peter nodded.

'Fine! Now, tell me.' She leaned toward him. 'Does a dog use a napkin?'

Humbled and ashamed, Peter looked down at the counterpane and shook his head. Apparently the conversation hadn't wandered as far as he had thought. Perhaps because the evening had been very full and because he was now very tired, tears rose in his eyes and spilled down his cheeks. He struggled against the sobs that wanted to come. He locked them in his chest. Sasha saw this and admired it.

'Don't cry over an unused napkin, my love,' said Sasha, 'for that was not my intention.' She rose, her full and pregant belly before her. The delivery of Thomas was now very near. 'Your behaviour was otherwise exemplary. Any mother in the Kingdom would have been proud of a young son who behaved himself half so well, and my heart is full with admiration for you. I am the mother of a prince. That is sometimes hard, but it cannot be changed, and i' truth, I would not change it if I could. But remember that someday lives will depend on your every waking motion; lives may even depend on dreams which come to you in sleep. Lives may not depend on whether or not you use your napkin after the roast chicken . . . but they may. They may. Lives have depended on less, at times. All I ask is that in everything you do, you try to remember the civilized side of your nature. The good side – the God side. Will you promise to do that, Peter?'

'I promise.'

'Then all is well.' She kissed him lightly. 'Luckily, I am young and you are young. We will talk of these things more, when you have more understanding.'

They never did, but Peter never forgot the lesson: he always used his napkin, even when those around him did not.

So Sasha died.

She has little more part in this story, yet there is
one further thing about her you should know: she
had a doll's house. This doll's house was very large
and very fine, almost a castle in miniature. When the
time of her marriage came round, Sasha mustered as
much cheer as she could, but she was sad to be leaving
everyone and everything at the great house in the
Western Barony where she had grown up – and she
was a little bit nervous, too. She told her mother, 'I
have never been married before and do not know if
I shall like it.'

But of all the childish things she left behind, the
one she regretted most was the doll's house she had
had ever since she was a little girl.

Roland, who was a kind man, somehow discovered this, and although he was also nervous about his
future life (after all, he had never been married
before, either), he found time to commission Quentin Ellender, the greatest craftsman in the land, to
build his new wife a new doll's house. 'I want it to
be the finest doll's house a young lady ever had,' he
told Ellender. 'I want her to look at it once and forget
about her old doll's house forever.'

As you'll no doubt realize, if Roland really
meant this, it was a foolish thing to say. No one ever
forgets a toy that made him or her supremely happy
as a child, even if that toy is replaced by one like it
that is much nicer. Sasha never forgot her old doll's

house, but she was quite impressed with the new one. Anyone who was not a total idiot would have been. Those who saw it declared it was Quentin Ellender's best work, and it may have been.

It was a country house in miniature, very like the one Sasha had lived in with her parents in rolling Western Barony. Everything in it was small, but so cunningly made you would swear it must really work . . . and most things in it did!

The stove, for instance, really got hot and would even cook tiny portions of food. If you put a piece of hard coal no bigger than a matchbox in it, it would burn all day . . . and if you reached into the kitchen with your clumsy big-person's finger and happened to touch the stove while the coal was burning, it would give you a burn for your pains. There were no faucets and no flushing toilets, because the Kingdom of Delain did not know about such things – and doesn't even to this day – but if you were very careful, you could pump water from a hand pump that stood not much taller than your pinkie finger. There was a sewing room with a spinning wheel that really spun and a loom that really wove. The spinet in the parlour would really play, if you touched the keys with a toothpick, and the tone was true. People who saw this said it was a miracle, and surely Flagg must have been involved somehow. When Flagg heard such stories, he only smiled and said nothing. He had not been involved in the doll's house at all – he thought it a silly project, in truth – but he also knew it was not always necessary to make claims and tell people how wonderful you were to achieve greatness. Sometimes all you had to do was look wise and keep your mouth shut.

In Sasha's doll's house were real Kashamin rugs, real velvet curtains, real china plates; the cold cabinet really kept things cold. The wainscoting in the receiving parlour and the front hall was of cherished ironwood. There was glass in all the windows and a many-coloured fanlight over the wide front doors.

All in all it was the jolliest doll's house any child ever dreamed of. Sasha clapped her hands over it with real delight at the wedding party when it was unveiled, and thanked her husband for it. Later she went to Ellender's workshop and not only thanked him but curtsied deeply before him, an act that was almost unheard of – in that day and age, Queens did not curtsy to mere artisans. Roland was pleased and Ellender, whose sight had failed noticeably in the course of the project, was deeply touched.

But it did not make her forget her old dear doll's house at home, as ordinary as it seemed when compared with this one, and she did not spend as many rainy afternoons playing with it – rearranging the furniture, lighting the stove and watching the chimneys smoke, pretending that there was a high tea going on or that there was to be a great dinner party for the Queen – as she had before, even as an older girl of fifteen and sixteen. One of the reasons was very simple. There was no fun making ready for a pretend party at which the Queen would be in attendance when she was the Queen. And maybe that one reason was really all the reasons. She was a grown-up now, and she discovered that being a grown-up was not quite what she had suspected it would be when she was a child. She had thought then that she would make a conscious decision one day to simply put her toys and games and little make-believes away. Now she discovered that was not what happened at all. Instead, she discovered, interest simply faded. It became less and less and less, until a dust of years drew over the bright pleasures of childhood, and they were forgotten.

Peter, a little boy who would someday be King, had dozens of toys – no, if I am to tell you the truth, he had *thousands* of toys. He had hundreds of lead soldiers with which he fought great battles, and dozens of play horses. He had games and balls and jacks and marbles. He had stilts that made him five feet high. He had a magical spring-stick on which he could bounce, and all the drawing paper he wanted in a time when paper was extremely hard to make and only wealthy people could afford to have it.

But of all the toys in the castle, the one he loved the best was his mother's doll's house. He had never known the one in the Western Barony, and so to him that was the doll's house of doll's houses. He would sit before it for hours on end when the rain poured down outside, or when the winter wind shrieked out of a blue throat filled with snow. When he fell ill with Children's Tattoo (a disease which we call chicken pox), he had a servant bring it to him on a special table that went over his bed and played with it almost ceaselessly until he was well.

He loved to imagine the tiny people that would fill the house; sometimes they were almost so real he could see them. He talked for them in different voices and invented them all. They were the King family. There was Roger King, who was brave and powerful (if not very tall, and slightly bowlegged), and who had once killed a dragon. There was lovely Sarah King, his wife. And there was their little boy, Petie, who loved and was loved by them. Not to mention, of course, all the servants he invented to make the beds, stoke the stove, fetch the water, cook the meals, and mend the clothes.

Because he was a boy, some of the stories he made up to go with the house were a little more bloodthirsty than the stories Sasha had made up to go with hers as a little girl. In one of them, the Anduan pirates were all around the house, wanting to get in and slaughter the family. There was a famous fight. Dozens of pirates were killed, but in the end they were too many. They made to attack for the final time. But just before they did, the King's Own Guard – this part was played by Peter's lead soldiers – arrived and killed every one of those rotten Anduan sea-dogs. In another story, a nest of dragons burst out of a nearby wood (usually the nearby wood was under Sasha's sofa by the window), meaning to burn up the house with their furious breath. But Roger and Petie rushed out with their bows and killed every one. 'Until the ground was black with their icky old blood,' Peter told his father the King that night at dinner, and this made Roland roar with approval.

After Sasha died, Flagg told Roland that he did not believe it was right for a boy to be playing with doll's houses. It might not make him a sissy, Flagg said, but then again, it might. Certainly it would not sound well, if the tale got out to the general population. And such stories always did. The castle was full of servants. Servants saw everything, and their tongues wagged.

'He's only six,' Roland said, uneasy. Flagg, with his white, hungry face far back in his deep hood and his magical spells, always made him uneasy.

'Six is old enough to train a boy in the way he should go, Sire,' Flagg said. 'Think you well on it. Your judgment will be right in this, as in all things.'

Think you well on it, Flagg said, and that was just what King Roland did. In fact, I should think it fair to say that he never thought on anything so hard during his entire twenty-some-year reign as King of Delain.

That probably sounds strange to you, if you have thought of all the duties a King has – weighty matters such as putting taxes on some things or ending them on others, whether or not to declare war, whether to pardon or condemn. What, you might say, was a decision over whether or not to allow a little boy to play with a doll's house next to those other things?

Maybe nothing, maybe much. I will let you make up your mind on that. I *will* tell you that Roland was not the smartest King who had ever ruled in Delain. Thinking well had always been very hard work for him. It made him feel as if boulders were rolling around in his head. It made his eyes water and his temples throb. When he thought deeply, his nose got stuffed up.

As a boy, his studies in composition and mathematics and history had made his head ache so badly that he had been allowed to give them up at twelve and do what he did best, which was to hunt. He tried very hard to be a good King, but he had a feeling that he could never be good enough, or smart enough, to solve the Kingdom's problems or to make many decisions the right way, and he knew if he made them the wrong way, people would suffer for it. If he had heard Sasha telling Peter about Kings after the banquet, he would have agreed completely. Kings really *were* bigger than other people, and sometimes – a lot of times – he wished he were smaller. If you have ever in your life had serious questions about whether or not you were good enough for some task, then you will know how he felt. What you may not know is that such worries start to feed on themselves after awhile. Even if that feeling that you aren't good enough to get the job done isn't true at first, it can become true in time. This had happened to Roland, and over the years he had come to rely more and more on Flagg. He was sometimes troubled by the idea that Flagg was King in all but name – but these worries came only late at night. In the daytime he was only grateful for Flagg's support.

If not for Sasha, Roland might have been a much worse King than he really was, and that was because the little voice he sometimes heard in the night when he couldn't sleep held much more of the truth than his daytime gratitudes. Flagg really *was* running the Kingdom, and Flagg was a very bad man. We will have to speak more of him later, unfortunately, but we'll let him go for now, and good riddance.

Sasha had broken Flagg's power over Roland a little. Her own advice was good and practical, and it was much more kind and just than the magician's. She never really liked Flagg – few in Delain did, and many shuddered at his very name – but her dislike was mild. Her feelings might have been much different if she had known how carefully Flagg watched her, and with what growing, poisonous hate.

Once Flagg really *did* set out to poison Sasha. This was after she asked Roland to pardon a pair of army deserters whom Flagg had wanted beheaded in the Plaza of the Needle. Deserters, he had argued, were a bad example. If one or two were allowed to get away without paying the full penalty, others might try it. The only way to discourage them, he said, was to show them the heads of those who had already tried it. Other would-be deserters would look at those flyblown heads with their staring eyes and think twice about the seriousness of their service to the King.

Sasha, however, had discovered facts about the case from one of her maids that Roland didn't know.

The mother of the older boy had fallen gravely ill. There were three younger brothers and two younger sisters in the family. All might have died in the bitter cold of the Delain winter if the boy hadn't left his encampment, gone home, and chopped wood for his mother. The younger boy had gone because he was the older's best friend, and his sworn blood brother. Without the younger boy, it might have taken two weeks to chop enough wood to keep the family through the winter. With both of them working at top speed, it had taken only six days.

This was putting it in a different light. Roland had loved his own mother very much, and would gladly have died for her. He made inquiries and found out that Sasha had the right of the story. He also found out that the deserters had left only after a sadistic sergeant major had repeatedly refused to relay their requests for compassionate leave to their superior, and that as soon as four cords of wood had been chopped, they had gone back, although both had known they must be court-martialled and face the headsman's axe.

Roland pardoned them. Flagg nodded, smiled, and said only: 'Your will is Delain's will, Sire.' Not for all the gold in the Four Kingdoms would he have allowed Roland to see the sick fury that rose in his heart when his will was balked. Roland's pardon of the boys was greatly praised in Delain, because many of Roland's subjects also knew the true facts and those who didn't know them were quickly informed by the rest. Roland's wise and compassionate pardon of the two was remembered when other, less humane decrees (which were, as a rule, also the magician's ideas) were imposed. All of this made no difference to Flagg. He had wanted him killed, and Sasha had interfered. Why could Roland not have married another? He had known none of them, and cared for women not at all. Why not another? Well, it didn't matter. Flagg smiled at the pardon, but he swore in his heart then that he would attend Sasha's funeral.

On the night Roland signed the pardon, Flagg went to his gloomy basement laboratory. There he donned a heavy glove and took a deathwatch spider from a cage where he had kept her for twenty years, feeding her newborn baby mice. Each of the mice he fed the spider was poisoned and dying; Flagg did this to increase the potency of the spider's own poison, which was already potent beyond belief. The spider was blood red and as big as a rat. Her bloated body quivered with venom; verom dripped from her stinger in clear drops that burned smoking holes in the top of Flagg's worktable.

'Now die, my pretty, and kill a Queen,' Flagg whispered, and crushed the spider to death in his glove, which was made of a magical steel mesh which resisted the poison – yet still that night, when he went to bed, his hand was swollen and throbbing and red.

Poison from the spider's crushed, twisted body gushed into the goblet. Flagg poured brandy over the deadly stuff, then stirred the two together. When he took the spoon from the glass, its bowl was twisted and misshapen. The Queen would take one sip and fall dying on the floor. Her death would be quick but extremely painful, Flagg thought with satisfaction.

Sasha was in the habit of taking a glass of brandy each night, because she often had trouble falling asleep. Flagg rang for a servant to come and take the drink to her.

Sasha never knew how close she came to death that night.

Moments after brewing the deadly drink, before the servant knocked, Flagg poured it down the drain in the centre of his floor and stood listening to it hiss and bubble away into the pipe. His face was twisted with hate. When the hissing had died away, he flung the crystal goblet into the far corner with all his force. It shattered like a bomb.

The servant knocked and was admitted.

Flagg pointed to where the shards glittered. 'I've broken a goblet,' he said. 'Clean it up. Use a broom, idiot. If you touch the pieces, you'll regret it.'

10

He poured the poison down the drain at the last moment because he realized he might well be caught. If Roland had loved the young Queen just a little less, Flagg would have chanced it. But he was afraid that Roland, in his wounded fury at the loss of his wife, would never rest until he found the killer and saw his head on the spike at the very tip of the Needle. It was the one crime he would see avenged, no matter who had committed it. And would he find the murderer?

Flagg thought he might.

Hunting, after all, was the thing Roland did best.

So Sasha escaped – that time – protected by Flagg's fear and her husband's love. And in the meantime, Flagg still had the King's ear in most matters.

Concerning the doll's house, however – in that matter, you could say Sasha won, even though Flagg had by then succeeded in ridding himself of her.

Not long after Flagg made his disparaging comments about doll's houses and royal sissies, Roland crept into the dead Queen's morning room unseen and watched his son at play. The King stood just inside the door, his brow deeply furrowed. He was thinking much harder than he was used to thinking, and that meant the boulders were rolling around in his head and his nose was stuffy.

He saw that Peter was using the doll's house to tell himself stories, to make believe, and that the stories he made up were not sissy stories at all. They were stories of blood and thunder and armies and dragons. They were, in other words, stories after the King's own heart. He discovered in himself a wistful desire to join his son, to help him make up even better tales in which the doll's house and all its fascinating contents and its make-believe family figured. Most of all, he saw that Peter was using Sasha's doll's house to keep Sasha alive in his heart, and Roland approved of this most of all, because he missed his wife sorely. Sometimes he was so lonely he almost cried. Kings, of course, do not cry . . . and if, on one or two occasions after Sasha had died, he awoke with the case on his pillow damp, what of that?

The King left the room as silently as he had come. Peter never saw him. Roland lay awake most of that night, thinking deeply about what he had seen, and although it was hard for him to endure Flagg's disapproval, he saw him the next morning in a private audience, before his resolve could weaken, and told him he had thought the matter over carefully and decided Peter should be allowed to play with the doll's house as long as he wished. He said he believed it was doing the boy no harm.

With that out, he settled back uneasily to wait for Flagg's rebuttal. But no rebuttal came. Flagg only raised his eyebrows – this Roland barely saw in the deep shadow of the hood Flagg always wore – and said, 'Your will, Sire, is the will of the Kingdom.'

Roland knew from the tone that Flagg thought his decision was a bad one, but the tone also told him Flagg would not dispute it further. He was deeply relieved to be let off so cheaply. Later that day, when Flagg suggested that the farmers of the Eastern Barony could stand higher taxes in spite of the drought that had killed most of their crops the year before, Roland agreed eagerly.

In truth, having the old fool (for so Flagg

thought Roland to be in his deeper thoughts) go against his wishes in the matter of the doll's house seemed a very minor thing to the magician. The rise in taxes for the Eastern Barony was the important thing. And Flagg had a deeper secret, one which pleased him well. In the end he had succeeded in murdering Sasha, after all.

12

In those days, when a Queen or any woman of royal birth was taken to bed to deliver a child, a midwife was called in. The doctors were all men, and no man was allowed to be with a woman when she was about to have a child. The midwife who delivered Peter was Anna Crookbrows, of the Third South'ard Alley. She was called again when Sasha's time with Thomas came around. Anna was past fifty at the time when Sasha's second labour began, and a widow. She had one son of her own, and in his twentieth year he contracted the Shaking Disease, which always killed its victims in terrible pain after some years of suffering.

She loved this boy very much, and at last, after every other idea had proved useless, she went to Flagg. This had been ten years before, neither prince yet born and Roland himself still a royal bachelor. He received her in his dank basement rooms, which were near the dungeons – during their interview the

uneasy woman could sometimes hear the lost
screams of those who had been locked away from
the sun's light for years and years. And, she thought
with a shudder, if the dungeons were near, then the
torture chambers must also be near. Nor did Flagg's
apartment itself make her feel any easier. Strange
designs were drawn on the floor in many colours
of chalk. When she blinked, the designs seemed to
change. In a cage hung from a long black manacle, a
two-headed parrot cawed and sometimes talked to
itself, one head speaking, the other head answering.
Musty books frowned down at her. Spiders spun in
dark corners. From the laboratory came a mixture of
strange chemical smells. Yet she stammered out her
story somehow and then waited in an agony of suspense.

'I can cure your son,' he said finally.

Anna Crookbrow's ugly face was transformed
into something near beauty by her joy. 'My Lord!'
she gasped, and could think of no more, so she said
it again. 'Oh, my Lord!'

But in the shadow of his hood, Flagg's white
face remained distant and brooding, and she felt
afraid again.

'What would you pay for such a miracle?' he
asked.

'Anything,' she gasped, and meant it. 'Oh my
Lord Flagg, anything!'

'I ask for one favour,' he said. 'Will you give it?'

'Gladly!'

'I don't know what it is yet, but when the time
comes, I shall.'

She had fallen on her knees before him, and now

he bent toward her. His hood fell back, and his face was terrible indeed. It was the white face of a corpse with black holes for eyes.

'And if you refuse what I ask, woman . . .'

'I shall not refuse! Oh my Lord, I shall not! I shall not! I swear it on my dear husband's name!'

'Then it is well. Bring your son to me tomorrow night, after dark.'

She led the poor boy in the next night. He trembled and shook, his head nodded foolishly, his eyes rolled. There was a slick of drool on his chin. Flagg gave her a dark, plum-coloured potion in a beaker. 'Have him drink this,' he said. 'It will blister his mouth, but have him drink every drop. Then get the fool out of my sight.'

She murmured to him. The boy's shaking increased for a moment as he tried to nod his head. He drank all of the liquid and then doubled over, screaming.

'Get him out,' Flagg said.

'*Yes, get him out!*' one of the parrot's two heads cried.

'*Get him out, no screaming allowed here!*' the other head screamed.

She got him home, sure that Flagg had murdered him. But the next day the Shaking Disease had left her son completely, and he was well.

Years passed. When Sasha's labour with Thomas began, Flagg called for her and whispered in her ear. They were alone in his deep rooms, but even so, it was better that such a dread command be whispered.

Anna Crookbrows's face went deadly white, but she remembered Flagg's words: *If you refuse . . .*

And would not the King have two children? She had only one. And if the King wanted to remarry and have even more, let him. In Delain, women were plentiful.

So she went to Sasha, and spoke encouragingly, and at a critical moment a little knife glittered in her hand. No one saw the one small cut she made. A moment later, Anna cried: 'Push, my Queen! Push, for the baby comes!'

Sasha pushed. Thomas came from her as effortlessly as a boy zipping down a slide. But Sasha's lifeblood gushed out upon the sheet. Ten minutes after Thomas came into the world, his mother was dead.

And so Flagg was not concerned about the piffling matter of the doll's house. What mattered was that Roland was growing old, there was no meddling Queen to stand in his way, and now he had not one son to choose from but two. Peter was, of course, the elder, but that did not really matter. Peter could be gotten out of the way if time should prove him unsuitable for Flagg's purposes. He was only a child, and could not defend himself.

I have told you that Roland never thought longer or harder on any matter during his entire reign than he did on this one question – whether or not Peter should be allowed access to Sasha's doll's house, cunningly crafted by the great Ellender. I have told you that the result of his thought was a decision that ran against Flagg's wishes. I have *also* told you that Flagg considered this of little importance.

Was it? That you must decide for yourself, after you have heard me to the end.

13

Now let many long years pass, all in a twinkling – one of the great things about tales is how fast time may pass when not much of note is happening. Real life is never that way, and it is probably a good thing. Time only passes faster in histories, and what is a history except a grand sort of tale where passing centuries are substituted for passing years?

During those years, Flagg watched both boys carefully – he watched them over the ageing King's shoulder as they grew up, calculating which should be King when Roland was no more. It did not take him long to decide it should be Thomas, the younger. By the time Peter was seven, he knew he did not like the boy. When Peter was nine, Flagg made a strange and unpleasant discovery; he feared Peter, as well.

The boy had grown up strong and straight and handsome. His hair was dark, his eyes a dark blue that is common to people of the Western Barony. Sometimes, when Peter looked up quickly, his head cocked a certain way, he resembled his father. Otherwise, he was Sasha's son almost entirely in his looks and ways. Unlike his short father with his bow-legged walk and his clumsy way of moving (Roland was graceful only when he was horsed), Peter was tall and lithe. He enjoyed the hunt and hunted well, but it was not his life. He also enjoyed his lessons – geography and history were his particular favourites.

His father was puzzled and often impatient with jokes; the point of most had to be explained to him, and that took away all the fun. What Roland liked was when the jesters pretended to slip on banana peels, or knocked their heads together, or when they staged pie fights in the Great Hall. Such things were about as far as Roland's idea of good fun extended. Peter's wit was much quicker and more subtle, as Sasha's had been, and his rollicking, boyish laughter often filled the palace, making the servants smile at each other approvingly.

While many boys in Peter's position would have become too conscious of their own grand place in the scheme of things to play with anyone not of their own class, Peter became best friends with a boy named Ben Staad when both children were eight. Ben's family was not royalty, and though Andrew Staad, Ben's father, had some faint claim to the High Blood of the kingdom on his mother's side, they could not even rightly be called nobility. 'Squire' was probably the kindest term one could have applied to Andy Staad, and 'squire's son' to his boy. Even so, the once-prosperous Staad family had fallen upon hard times, and while there could have been queerer choices for a Prince's best friend, there couldn't have been many.

They met at the annual Farmers' Lawn Party when Peter was eight. The Lawn Party was a yearly ritual most Kings and Queens viewed as tiresome at best; they were apt to put in a token appearance, drink the quick traditional toast, and then be away after bidding the farmers enjoy themselves and thanking them for another fruitful year (this was also part of the ritual, even if the crops had been poor). If Roland had been that sort of King, Peter and Ben would never had gotten the chance to know each other. But, as you might have guessed, Roland *loved* the Farmers' Lawn Party, looked forward to it each year, and usually stayed until the very end (and more than once was carried away drunk and snoring loudly).

As it happened, Peter and Ben were paired in the three-legged sack-race, and they won it . . . although it ended up being much closer than at first it seemed it would be. Leading by almost six lengths, they took a bad spill and Peter's arm was cut.

'I'm sorry, my prince!' Ben cried. His face had gone pale, and he may have been visualizing the dungeons (and I know his mother and father, watching anxiously from the sidelines, were; if it weren't for bad luck, Andy Staad was fond of growling, the Staads would have no luck at all); more likely he was just sorry for the hurt he fancied he had caused, or was amazed to see that the blood of the future King was as red as his own.

'Don't be a fool,' Peter said impatiently. 'It was my fault, not yours. I was clumsy. Hurry and get up. They're catching us.'

The two boys, made into a single clumsy three-legged beast by the sack into which Peter's right leg and Ben's left one had been tightly tied, managed to get up and lurch on. Both had been badly winded by the fall, however, and their long lead had been cut to almost nothing. Approaching the finish line, where crowds of farmers (not to mention Roland, standing among them without the slightest feeling of awkwardness, or of being somewhere he shouldn't) were cheering deliriously, two huge, sweating farm boys began to close in. That they would overtake Peter and Ben in the last ten yards of the race seemed almost inevitable.

'*Faster, Peter!*' Roland bellowed, swinging a huge mug of mead with such enthusiasm that he poured most of it onto his own head. In his excitement he never noticed. '*Jackrabbit, son! Be a jackrabbit! Those clod-busters are almost up your butt and over your back!*'

Ben's mother began to moan, cursing the fate that had caused her son to be paired up with the prince.

'If they lose, he'll have our Ben thrown into the deepest dungeon in the castle,' she moaned.

'Hush, woman,' Andy said. 'He'd not. He's a good King.' He believed it, but he was still afraid. Staad luck was, after all, Staad luck.

Ben, meanwhile, had begun to giggle. He couldn't believe he was doing it, but he was. 'Be a jackrabbit, did he say?'

Peter also began to giggle. His legs ached terribly, blood was trickling down his right arm, and sweat was flooding his face, which was starting to

turn an interesting plum colour, but he was also unable to stop. 'Yes, that's what he said.'

'Then let's *hop!*'

They didn't look much like jackrabbits as they crossed the finish line; they looked like a pair of strange crippled crows. It was really a miracle they didn't fall, but somehow they didn't. They managed three ungainly leaps. The third one took them across the finish line, where they collapsed, howling with laughter.

'Jackrabbit!' Ben yelled, pointing at Peter.

'Jackrabbit yourself!' Peter yelled, pointing back.

They slung their arms about each other, still laughing, and were carried on the shoulders of many strong farmers (Andrew Staad was one of them, and bearing the combined weight of his son and the prince was something he never forgot) to where Roland slipped blue ribbands over their necks. Then he kissed each of them roughly on the cheek and poured the remaining contents of his mug over their heads, to the wild cheers and huzzahs of the farmers. Never, even in the memory of the oldest gaffer there that day, had such an extraordinary race been run.

The two boys spent the rest of the day together and, it soon appeared, would be content to spend the rest of their lives together. Because even a boy of eight has certain duties (and if he is to be the King someday he has even more), the two of them could not be together all they wanted to be, but when they could be, they were.

Some sniffed at the friendship, and said it wasn't right for the King in waiting to be friends with a boy

who was little better than a common barony clod-
buster. Most, however, looked upon it with
approval; it was said more than once over deep cups
in the meadhouses of Delain that Peter had gotten
the best of both worlds – his mother's brains and his
father's love of the common folk.

There was apparently no meanness in Peter. He
never went through a period when he pulled the
wings of flies or singed dogs' tails to see them run.
In fact, he intervened in the matter of a horse which
was to be destroyed by Yosef, the King's head
groom . . . and it was when this tale made its way
to Flagg that the magician began to fear the King's
oldest son, and to think perhaps he did not have as
long to put the boy out of the way as he had once
thought. For in the affair of the horse with the broken
leg, Peter had displayed courage and a depth of
resolve which Flagg did not like at all.

14

Peter was passing through the stableyard
when he saw a horse tethered to the hitching rail just
outside the main barn. The horse was holding one of
its rear legs off the ground. As Peter watched, Yosef
spat on his hands and picked up a heavy maul. What
he meant to do was obvious. Peter was both frightened and appalled. He rushed over.

'Who told you to kill this horse?' he asked.

Yosef, a hardy and robust sixty, was a palace fixture. He was not apt to brook the interference of a snot-nosed brat easily, prince or no. He fixed Peter with a thunderous, heavy look that was meant to wilt the boy. Peter, then just nine, reddened, but did not wilt. He seemed to see a look in the horse's mild brown eyes which said, *You're my only hope, whoever you are. Do what you can, please.*

'My father, and his father before him, and his father before *him*,' Yosef said, seeing now that he was going to have to say something, like it or not. '*That's* who told me to kill it. A horse with a broken leg is no good to any living thing, least of all to itself.' He raised the maul a little. 'You see this hammer as a murder weapon, but when you're older, you'll see it for what it really is in cases such as these . . . a mercy. Now stand back, so you don't get splashed.'

He raised the maul in both hands.

'Put it down,' Peter said.

Yosef was thunderstruck. He had *never* been interfered with in such a way.

'Here! Here! What are you a-saying?'

'You heard me. I said *put that hammer down.*' As he said these words Peter's voice deepened. Yosef suddenly realized – really, really realized – that it was the future King standing here in this dusty stable-yard, commanding him. If Peter had actually *said* as much – if he had stood there in the dust squeaking, *Put that down, put it down, I said, I'm going to be King someday, King, do you hear, so you put that down!*, Yosef would have laughed contemptuously, spat, and ended the broken-legged horse's life with one hard swing of his deeply muscled arms. But Peter did not have to say any such thing; the command was clear in his voice and eyes.

'Your father shall hear of this, my princeling,' Yosef said.

'And when he hears it from you, it will be for the second time,' Peter replied. 'I will let you go about your work with no further complaint, Lord High Groom, if I may put a single question to you which you answer yes.'

'Ask your question,' Yosef said. He was impressed with the boy, almost against his will. When he had told Yosef that he, Peter, would tell his father of the incident first, Yosef believed he meant what he said – the simple truth shone in the lad's eyes. Also, he had never been called Lord High Groom before, and he rather liked it.

'Has the horse doctor seen this animal?' Peter asked.

Yosef was thunderstruck. 'That is your question? *That?*'

'Yes.'

'Dear creeping gods, *no!*' he cried, and, seeing Peter flinch, he lowered his voice, squatted before the boy, and attempted to explain. 'A horse with a broken leg is a goner, y'Highness. Always a goner. Leg never mends right. There's apt to be blood poisoning. Turrible pain for the horse. *Turrible* pain. In the end, its poor heart is apt to burst, or it takes a brain fever and goes mad. Now do you understand what I meant when I said this hammer was mercy rather than murder?'

Peter thought long and gravely, with his head down. Yosef was silent, squatting before him in an almost unconscious posture of deference, allowing him the full courtesy of time.

Peter raised his head and asked: 'You say everyone says this?'

'Everyone, y'Highness. Why, my father –'

'Then we'll see if the horse doctor says it, too.'

'*Oh . . . PAH!*' the groom bellowed, and threw the hammer all the way across the courtyard. It sailed into a pigpen and struck head down in the mud. The pigs grunted and squealed and cursed him in their piggy Latin. Yosef, like Flagg, was not used to being balked, and took no notice of them.

He got up and stalked away. Peter watched him, troubled, sure that he must be in the wrong and knowing he was apt to face a severe whipping for this little piece of work. Then, halfway across the yard, the head groom turned, and a reluctant grim little smile hit across his face like a single sunray on a grey morning.

'Go get your horse doctor,' he said. 'Get him yourself, son. You'll find him in his animal surgery at the far end of Third East'rd Alley, I reckon. I'll give you twenty minutes. If you're not back with him by then, I'm putting my maul into yon horse's brains, prince or no prince.'

'Yes, Lord Head Groom!' Peter yelled. 'Thank you!' He raced away.

When he returned with the young horse doctor, puffing and out of breath, Peter was sure that the horse must be dead; the sun told him three times twenty minutes had passed. But Yosef, curious, had waited.

Horse doctoring and veterinary medicine were

then very new things in Delain, and this young man was only the third or fourth who had practised the trade, so Yosef's look of sour distrust was far from surprising. Nor had the horse doctor been happy to be dragged away from his surgery by the sweating, wide-eyed prince, but he became less irritated now that he had a patient. He knelt before the horse and felt the broken leg gently with his hands, humming through his nose as he did so. The horse shifted once as something he did pained her. 'Be steady, nag,' the horse doctor said calmly, 'be oh so steady.' The horse quieted. Peter watched all this in an agony of suspense. Yosef watched with his maul leaning nearby and his arms folded across his chest. His opinion of the horse doctor had gone up a little. The fellow was young, but his hands moved with gentle knowledge.

At last the horse doctor nodded and stood up, dusting stableyard grime from his hands.

'Well?' Peter asked anxiously.

'Kill her,' the horse doctor said briskly to Yosef, ignoring Peter altogether.

Yosef picked up his maul at once, for he had expected no other conclusion to the affair. But he found no satisfaction in being proved correct; the stricken look on the young boy's face went straight to his heart.

'Wait!' Peter cried, and although his small face was full of distress, that deepness was in his voice again, making him sound much, much older than his years.

The horse doctor looked at him, startled.

'You mean she'll die of blood poisoning?' Peter asked.

'What?' the horse doctor asked, eyeing Peter with a new care.

'She'll die of blood poisoning if she's allowed to live? Or her heart will burst? Or she will run mad?'

The horse doctor was clearly puzzled. 'What are you talking about? Blood poisoning? There is no blood poisoning here. The break is healing quite cleanly, in fact.' He looked at Yosef with some disdain. 'I have heard such stories as these before. There is no truth in them.'

'If you think not, you have much to learn, my young friend,' Yosef said.

Peter ignored this. It was now his turn to be bewildered. He asked the young horse doctor, 'Why do you tell the head groom to kill a horse which may heal?'

'Your Highness,' the horse doctor said briskly, 'this horse would need to be poulticed every day and every night for a month or more to keep any infection from settling in. The effort might be made, but to what end? The horse would always limp. A horse that limps can't work. A horse that limps can't run for idlers to bet on. A horse that limps can only eat and eat and never earn its provender. Therefore, it should be killed.'

He smiled, satisfied. He had proved his case.

Then, as Yosef started forward with his hammer again, Peter said; '*I'll* put on the poultices. If a day should come when I can't, then Ben Staad will. And she'll be good because she'll be my horse, and I'll ride her even if she limps so badly she makes me seasick.'

Yosef burst out laughing and clapped the boy on his back so hard his teeth rattled. 'Your heart is kind as well as brave, my boy, but lads promise quick and regret at leisure. You'd not be true to it. I reckon.'

Peter looked at him calmly. 'I mean what I say.'

Yosef stopped laughing all at once. He looked at Peter closely and saw that the boy did indeed mean it . . . or at least thought he did. There was no doubt in his face.

'Well! I can't tarry here all day,' the horse doctor said, adopting his former brisk and self-important manner. 'I've given you my diagnosis. My bill will be presented to the Treasury in due course . . . Perhaps you'll pay it out of your allowance, Highness. In any case, what you decide to do is not my business. Good day.'

Peter and the head groom watched him walk out of the stableyard, trailing a long afternoon shadow at his heels.

'He's full of dung,' Yosef said when the horse doctor was out the gate, beyond earshot, and thus unable to contradict his words. 'Mark me, y'Highness, and save y'self a lot o' grief. There never was a horse what busted a leg and didn't get blood poisoning. It's God's way.'

'I'll want to talk to my father about this,' Peter said.

'And so I think you must,' Yosef said heavily . . . but as Peter trudged away, he smiled. He thought the boy had done right well for himself. His father would be honour-bound to see the boy was whipped for interfering with his elders, but the head groom knew that Roland set a great store by both of his sons in his old age – Peter perhaps a bit more than

Thomas – and he believed that the boy would get his horse. Of course, he would also get a heartbreak when the horse died, but, as the horse doctor had quite rightly said, that was not his business. He knew about the training of horses; the training of princes was best left in other hands.

Peter *was* whipped for interfering in the head groom's affairs, and although it was no solace to his stinging bottom, Peter's mind understood that his father had afforded him great honour by administering the whipping himself, instead of handing Peter over to an underling who might have tried to curry favour by making it easy on the boy.

Peter could not sleep on his back for three days and was not able to eat sitting down for nearly a week, but the head groom was also right about the horse – Roland allowed Peter to keep her.

'It won't take up your time for long, Peter,' Roland advised him. 'If Yosef says it will die, it will die.' Roland's face was a bit pale and his old hands were trembling. The beating had pained him more than it had pained Peter, who really was his favourite . . . although Roland foolishly fancied no one knew this but himself.

'I don't know,' Peter said. 'I thought that horse-doctoring fellow knew what he was talking about.'

It turned out that the horse-doctoring fellow had. The horse did not take blood poisoning, and it did not die, and in the end its limp was so slight that even Yosef was forced to admit it was hardly noticeable. 'At least, when she's fresh,' he amended. Peter was more than just faithful about putting on the poultices; he was nearly religious. He changed old for new three times a day and did it a fourth time before he went to bed. Ben Staad did stand in for Peter from time to time, but those times were few. Peter named the horse Peony, and they were great friends ever after.

Flagg had most assuredly been right about one thing on the day he advised Roland against letting Peter play with the dollhouse: servants were everywhere, they see everything, and their tongues wag. Several servants had witnessed the scene in the stable-yard, but if every servant who later claimed to have been there really had been, there would have been a mob of them crowded around the edges of the stable-yard that hot summer day. That had, of course, not been the case, but the fact that so many of them found the event worth lying about was a sign that Peter was regarded as an interesting figure indeed. They talked about it so much that it became something of a nine days' wonder in Delain. Yosef also talked; so, for that matter, did the young horse doctor. Everything that they said spoke well for the young prince – Yosef's word in particular carried much weight, because he was greatly respected. He began to call Peter 'the young King', something he had never done before.

'I believe God spared the nag because the young King stood up for her so brave-like,' he said. 'And he worked at them poultices like a slave. Brave, he is; he's got the heart of a dragon. He'll make a King someday, all right. Ai! You should have heard his voice when he told me to hold the maul!'

It was a great story, all right, and Yosef drank on it for the next seven years – until Peter was arrested for a hideous crime, judged guilty, and sentenced to imprisonment in the cell atop the Needle for the rest of his life.

15

Perhaps you are wondering what Thomas was like, and some of you may already be casting him in a villain's part, as a willing co-schemer in Flagg's plot to snatch the crown away from its rightful owner.

That was not really the case at all, although to some it always seemed so, and of course Thomas did play a part. He did not seem, I admit, to be a really good boy – at least, not at first glance. He was surely not a good boy in the way that Peter was a good boy, but *no* brother would have looked really good beside Peter, and Thomas knew it well by the time he was four – that was the year after the famous sack-race, and the one in which the famous stableyard incident took place. Peter rarely lied and never cheated. Peter was smart and kind, tall and handsome. He looked like their mother, who had been so deeply loved by the King and the people of Delain.

How could Thomas compare with goodness like *that*? A simple question with a simple answer. He couldn't.

Unlike Peter, Thomas was the spitting image of his father. This pleased the old man a little, but it didn't give him the pleasure most men feel when they have a son who carries the clear stamp of their features. Looking at Thomas was too much like looking into a sly mirror. He knew that Thomas's fine blond hair would grey early and then begin to fall out; Thomas would be bald by the time he was forty. He knew that Thomas would never be tall, and if he had his father's appetite for beer and mead, he would be carrying a big belly before him by the time he was twenty-five. Already his toes had begun to turn in, and Roland guessed Thomas would walk with his own bowlegged swagger.

Thomas was not exactly a good boy, but you must not think that made him a bad boy. He was sometimes a sad boy, often a confused boy (he took after his father in another way, as well – hard thinking made his nose stuffy and his head feel like boulders were rolling around inside), and often a jealous boy, but he wasn't a bad boy.

Of whom was he jealous? Why, of his brother, of course. He was jealous of Peter. It wasn't enough that Peter would be King, Oh no! It wasn't enough that their father liked Peter best, or that the *servants* liked Peter best, or that their *teachers* liked Peter best because he was always ready at lessons and didn't need to be coaxed. It wasn't enough that *everyone* liked Peter best, or that Peter had a best friend. There was one more thing.

When anyone looked at Thomas, his father the King most of all, Thomas thought he knew they were thinking: *We loved your mother and you killed her in your coming. And what did we get out of the pain and death you caused her? A dull little boy with a round face*

*that has hardly any chin, a dull little boy who couldn't
make all fifteen of the Great Letters until he was eight.
Your brother Peter was able to make them all when he was
six. What did we get? Not much. Why did you come,
Thomas? What good are you? Throne insurance? Is that
all you are? Throne insurance in case Peter the Precious
should fall off his limping nag and crack his head open? Is
that all? Well, we don't want you. None of us want you.
None of us want you . . .*

The part Thomas played in his brother's imprisonment was dishonourable, but even so he was not
a really bad boy. I believe this, and hope that in time
you will come to believe it, too.

Once, as a boy of seven, Thomas spent a
whole day labouring in his room, carving his father
a model sailboat. He did it with no way of knowing
that Peter had covered himself with glory that day
on the archery range, with his father in attendance.
Peter was not, ordinarily, much of a bowman – in
that area, at least, Thomas would turn out to be far
superior to his older brother – but on that one day,
Peter had shot the junior course of targets like one
inspired. Thomas was a sad boy, a confused boy, and
he was often an unlucky boy.

Thomas had thought of the boat because sometimes, on Sunday afternoons, his father liked to go

out to the moat which surrounded the palace and float a variety of model boats. Such simple pleasures made Roland extremely happy, and Thomas had never forgotten one day when his father had taken him – and *just* him – along. In those days, his father had an advisor whose only job was to show Roland how to make paper boats and the King had conceived a great enthusiasm for them. On this day, a hoary old carp had risen out of the mucky water and swallowed one of Roland's paper boats whole. Roland had laughed like a boy and declared it was better than a tale about a sea monster. He hugged Thomas very tight as he said so. Thomas never forgot that day – the bright sunshine, the damp, slightly mouldy odour of the moat water, the warmth of his father's arms, the scratchiness of his beard.

So, feeling particularly lonely one day, he had hit on the idea of making his father a sailboat. It would not be a really great job, and Thomas knew it – he was almost as clumsy with his hands as he was at memorizing his lessons. But he also knew that his father could have any craftsman in Delain – even the great Ellender himself, who was now almost completely blind – make him boats if he so desired. The crucial difference, Thomas thought, would be that Roland's own son had taken *a whole day* to carve him a boat for his Sunday pleasure.

Thomas sat patiently by his window, urging the boat out of a block of wood. He used a sharp knife, nicked himself times without number, and cut himself quite badly once. Yet he kept on, aching hands or no. As he worked he daydreamed of how he and his father would go out on Sunday afternoon and sail the boat, just the two of them all alone, because Peter would be riding Peony in the woods or off playing with Ben. And he wouldn't even mind if that same carp came up and ate his wooden boat, because then his father would laugh and hug him and say it was better than a story of sea monsters eating Anduan clipper ships whole.

But when he got to the King's chamber Peter was there and Thomas had to wait for nearly half an hour with the boat hidden behind his back while his father extolled Peter's bowmanship. Thomas could see that Peter was uncomfortable under the unceasing barrage of praise. He could also see that Peter knew Thomas wanted to talk to their father, and that Peter kept trying to tell their father so. It didn't matter, none of it mattered. Thomas hated him anyway.

At last Peter was allowed to escape. Thomas approached his father, who looked at him kindly enough now that Peter was gone. 'I made you something, Dad,' he said, suddenly shy. He held the boat behind his back with hands that were suddenly wet and clammy with sweat.

'Did you now, Tommy?' Roland said. 'Why, that was kind, wasn't it?'

'Very kind, Sire,' said Flagg, who happened to be idling nearby. He spoke casually but watched Thomas with bright interest.

'What is it, lad? Show me!'

'I remembered how much you liked to have a boat or two out on the moat Sunday afternoons, Dad, and . . .' He wanted desperately to say, *and I wanted you to take me out with you again sometime, so I made this*, but he found he could not utter such a thing. '. . . and so I made you a boat . . . I spent a whole day . . . cut myself . . . and . . . and . . .' Sitting in his window seat, carving the boat, Thomas had made up a long, eloquent speech which he would utter before bringing the boat out from behind his back and presenting it with a flourish to his father, but now he could hardly remember a word of it, and what he could remember didn't seem to make any sense.

Horribly tongue-tied, he took the sailboat with its awkward flapping sail out from behind his back and gave it to Roland. The King turned it over in his big short-fingered hands. Thomas stood and watched him, totally unaware that he had forgotten to breathe.

At last Roland looked up. "Very nice. Very nice, Tommy. Canoe, isn't it?'

'Sailboat.' *Don't you see the sail?* he wanted to cry. *It took me an hour alone just to tie the knots, and it isn't my fault one of them came loose so it flaps!*

The King fingered the striped sail, which Thomas had cut from a pillowcase.

'So it is . . . of course it is. At first I thought it was a canoe and this was some Oranian girl's washing.' He tipped a wink at Flagg, who smiled vaguely at the air and said nothing. Thomas suddenly felt he might vomit quite soon.

Roland looked at his son more seriously, and beckoned for him to come close. Timidly, hoping for the best, Thomas did so.

'It's a good boat, Tommy. Sturdy, like yourself, a bit clumsy like yourself, but good – like yourself.

And if you want to give me a really *fine* present, work hard in your own bowmanship classes so you can take a first-class medal as Pete did today.'

Thomas *had* taken a first in the lower-circle bowmanship courses the year before, but his father seemed to have forgotten this in his joy over Peter's accomplishment. Thomas did not remind him; he merely stood there, looking at the boat in his father's big hands. His cheeks and forehead had flushed to the colour of old brick.

'When it was at last down to just two boys – Peter and Lord Towson's son – the instructor decreed they should draw back another forty koner. Towson's boy looked downcast, but Peter just walked to the mark and nocked an arrow. I saw the look in his eyes, and I said to myself "He's won! By all the gods that are, he hasn't even fired an arrow yet and he's won!" And so he had! I tell you, Tommy, you should have been there! You should have . . .'

The King prattled on, putting aside the boat Thomas had laboured a whole day to make, with barely a second look. Thomas stood and listened, smiling mechanically, that dull, bricklike flush never leaving his face. His father would never bother to take the sailboat he had carved out to the moat – why should he? The sailboat was as pukey as Thomas felt. Peter could probably carve a better one blindfolded, and in half the time. It would look better to their father, at least.

A miserable eternity later, Thomas was allowed to escape.

'I believe the boy worked very hard on that boat,' Flagg remarked carelessly.

'Yes, I suppose he did,' Roland said. 'Wretched-looking thing, isn't it? Looks a little like a dog turd with a handkerchief sticking out of it.' *And like something I would have made when I was his age*, he added in his own mind.

Thomas could not hear *thoughts* . . . but a hellish trick of acoustics brought Roland's *words* to him just as he left the Great Hall. Suddenly the horrible green pressure in his stomach was a thousand times worse. He ran to his bedroom and was sick in a basin.

The next day, while idling behind the outer kitchens, Thomas spied a half-crippled old dog foraging for garbage. He seized a rock and threw it. The stone flew to the mark. The dog yipped and fell down, badly hurt. Thomas knew his brother, although five years older, could not have made such a shot at half the distance – but that was a cold satisfaction, because he also knew that Pete never would have thrown a rock at a poor, hungry dog in the first place, especially one as old and decrepit as this one obviously was.

For a moment, compassion filled Thomas's heart and his eyes filled with tears. Then, for no reason at all, he thought of his father saying, *Looks a little like a dog turd with a handkerchief sticking out of it.* He gathered up a handful of rocks, and went over to where the dog lay on its side, dazed and bleeding from one ear. Part of him wanted to let the dog alone, or perhaps heal it as Peter had healed Peony – to make it his very own dog and love it forever. But part of him wanted to hurt it, as if hurting the dog would ease some of his own hurt. He stood above it, undecided, and then a terrible thought came to him:

Suppose that dog was Peter?

That decided the case. Thomas stood over the old dog and threw stones at it until it was dead. No one saw him, but if someone had, he or she would have thought: *There is a boy who is bad . . . bad, and perhaps even evil.* But the person who saw only the cruel murder of that dog would not have seen what happened the day before – would not have seen Thomas throwing up into a basin and crying bitterly as he did it. He was often a confused boy, often a sadly unlucky boy, but I stick to what I said – he was never a bad boy, not really.

I also said that no one saw the stoning of the mongrel dog behind the outer kitchens, but that was not quite true. Flagg saw it that night, in his magic crystal. He saw it . . . and was well pleased by it.

17

Roland . . .   Sasha . . .   Peter . . . Thomas. Now there is only one more we must speak of, isn't there? Now there is only the shadowy fifth. The time has come to speak of Flagg, as dreadful as that may be.

Sometimes the people of Delain called him Flagg the Hooded; sometimes simply the dark man – for, in spite of his white corpse's face, he was a dark man indeed. They called him well preserved, but they used the term in a way that was uneasy rather than complimentary. He had come to Delain from Garlan in the time of Roland's grandfather. In those days he had appeared to be a thin and stern-faced man of about forty. Now, in the closing years of Roland's reign, he appeared to be a thin and stern-faced man of about fifty. Yet it had not been ten years, or even twenty, between then and now — it had been seventy-six years in all. Babies who had been sucking toothlessly at their mother's breasts when Flagg first came to Delain had grown up, married, had children, grown old, and died toothlessly in their beds or their chimney corner. But in all that time, Flagg seemed to have aged only ten years. It was magic, they whispered, and of course it was good to have a magician at court, a *real* magician and not just a stage conjurer who knew how to palm coins or hide a sleeping dove up his sleeve. Yet in their hearts, they knew there was *nothing* good about Flagg. When the people of Delain saw him coming, with his eyes peeking redly out from his hood, they quickly found business on the far side of the street.

Did he really come from Garlan, with its far vistas and its purple dreaming mountains? I do not know. It was and is a magical land where carpets sometimes fly, and where holy men sometimes pipe ropes up from wicker baskets, climb them, and disappear at the tops, never to be seen again. A great many seekers of knowledge from more civilized lands like Delain and Andua have gone to Garlan. Most disappear as completely and as permanently as those strange mystics who climb the floating ropes. Those who do return don't always come back changed for the better. Yes, Flagg might well have come to Delain from Garlan, but if he did, it was not in the reign of Roland's grandfather but much, much earlier.

He had, in fact, come to Delain often. He came under a different name each time, but always with the same load of woe and misery and death. This time he was Flagg. The time before he had been known at Bill Hinch, and he had been the King's Lord High Executioner. Although that time was two hundred and fifty years past, his was a name mothers still used to frighten their children when they were bad. 'If you don't shut up that squalling. I reckon Bill Hinch will come and take you away!' they said. Serving as Lord High Executioner under three of the bloodiest Kings in Delain's long history, Bill Hinch had made an end to hundreds – thousands, some said – of prisoners with his heavy axe.

The time before *that*, four hundred years before the time of Roland and his sons, he came as a singer named Browson, who became a close adviser to the King and a Queen. Browson disappeared like smoke after drumming up a great and bloody war between Delain and Andua.

The time before *that* . . .

Ah, but why go on? I'm not sure I could if I wanted to. When times are long enough, even the storytellers forget the tales. Flagg always showed up with a different face and a different bag of tricks, but two things about him were always the same. He always came hooded, a man who seemed almost to have no face, and he never came as a King himself, but always as the whisperer in the shadows, the man who poured poison into the porches of Kings' ears.

Who was he, really, this dark man?

I do not know.

Where did he wander between visits to Delain?

I do not know that, either.

Was he never suspected?

Yes, by a few — by historians and spinners of tales like me, mostly. They suspected that the man who now called himself Flagg had been in Delain before, and never to any good purpose. But they were afraid to speak. A man who could live among them for seventy-six years and appear to age only ten was obviously a magician; a man who had lived for ten times as long, perhaps longer than that . . . such a man might be the devil himself.

What did he want? That question I think I can answer.

He wanted what evil men always want: to have power and use that power to make mischief. Being a King did not interest him because the heads of Kings all too often found their way to spikes on castle walls when things went wrong. But the advisors to Kings . . . the spinners in the shadows . . . such people usually melted away like evening shadows at dawning as soon as the headsman's axe started to fall. Flagg was a sickness, a fever looking for a cool brow to heat up. He hooded his actions just as he hooded his face. And when the great trouble came — as it always did after a span of years — Flagg always disappeared like shadows at dawn.

Later, when the carnage was over and the fever had passed, when the rebuilding was complete and there was again something worth destroying, Flagg would appear once more.

*T*his time, Flagg had found the Kingdom of Delain in exasperatingly healthy condition. Landry, Roland's grandfather, was a drunken old fool, easy to influence and twist, but a heart attack had taken him too soon. Flagg knew by then that Lita, Roland's mother, was the last person he wanted holding the sceptre. She was ugly but good-hearted and strong-willed. Such a Queen was not a good growth medium for Flagg's brand of insanity.

If he had come earlier in Landry's reign, there would have been time to put Lita out of the way, as he expected to put Peter out of the way. But he'd had only six years, and that was not long enough.

Still, she had accepted him as an advisor, and that was something. She did not like him much but she accepted him – mostly because he could tell wonderful fortunes with cards. Lita loved hearing bits of gossip and scandal about those in her court and her Cabinet, and the gossip and scandal were doubly good because she got to hear not only what *had* happened but what *would* happen. It was hard to rid yourself of such an amusing diversion, even when you sensed that a person able to do such tricks might be dangerous. Flagg never told the Queen any of the darker news he sometimes saw in the cards. She wanted to know who had taken a lover or who had had words with his wife or her husband. She did not want to know about dark cabals and murderous plans. What she wanted from the cards was relatively innocent.

During the long, long reign of Lita, Flagg was chagrined to find his main accomplishment was to be not turned out. He was able to maintain a foothold but to do little more than that. Oh, there were a few bright spots – the encouragement of bad blood between two powerful squires in the Southern Barony and the descrediting of a doctor who had found a cure for some blood infections (Flagg wanted no cures in the Kingdom that were not magical – which is to say, given or withheld at his own whim) were examples of Flagg's work during that period. It was all pretty small change.

Under Roland – poor bowlegged, insecure Roland – things marched more quickly toward Flagg's goal. Because he did have a goal, you know, in his fuzzy, malevolent sort of way, and this time it was grand indeed. He planned nothing more nor less than the complete overthrow of the monarchy – a bloody revolt that would plunge Delain into a thousand years of darkness and anarchy.

Give or take a year or two, of course.

19

In Peter's cool gaze he saw the very possible derailment of all his plans and careful work. More and more Flagg came to believe that getting rid of Peter was a necessity. Flagg had overstayed in Delain this time and he knew it. The muttering had begun. The work so well begun under Roland – the steady rises in taxes, the midnight searches of small farmers' barns and silage sheds for unreported crops and foodstuffs, the arming of the Home Guards – must continue to its end under Thomas. He did not have time to wait through the reign of Peter as he had through that of his grandmother.

Peter might not even wait for the mutterings of the people to come to his ears; Peter's first command as King might well be that Flagg should be sent eastward out of the Kingdom and forbidden ever to come again, on pain of death. Flagg might murder an advisor before he could give the young King such advice, but the hell of it was, Peter would *need* no advisor. He would advise himself – and when Flagg saw the cool, unafraid way the boy, now fifteen and very tall, looked at him, he thought that Peter might already have given himself that advice.

The boy liked to read, and he liked history, and in the last two years, as his father grew steadily greyer and frailer, he had been asking a lot of questions of his father's other advisors, and of some of his teachers. Many of these questions – *too* many – had to do either with Flagg or with roads which would lead to Flagg if followed far enough.

That the boy was asking such questions at fourteen and fifteen was bad. That he was getting comparatively honest answers from such timid, watchful men as the Kingdom's historians and Roland's advisors was much worse. It meant that, in the minds of these people, Peter was already almost King – and that they were glad. They welcomed him and rejoiced in him, because he would be an intellectual, like them. And they also welcomed him because, *unlike* them, he was a brave boy who might well grow into a lionhearted King whose tale would be the stuff of legends. In him, they saw again the coming of the White, that ancient, resilient, yet humble force that has redeemed humankind again and again and again.

He had to be put out of the way. *Had* to be.

Flagg told himself this each night when he retired in the blackness of his inner chambers, and it was his first thought when he awoke in that blackness the next morning.

He must be put out of the way, the boy must be put out of the way.

But it was harder than it seemed. Roland loved and would have died for either of his sons, but he loved Peter with a particular fierceness. Smothering the boy in his cradle, making it look as if the Baby Death had taken him, would have once perhaps been possible, but Peter was now a healthy teen-ager.

Any accident would be examined with all the raging scrutiny of Roland's grief, and Flagg had thought more than once that the final irony might be this: Suppose Peter really *did* die an accidental death, and he, Flagg, was somehow blamed for it? A small miscalculation while shinnying up a drainpipe . . . a slip while crawling around on a stable roof playing Dare You with his friend Staad . . . a tumble from his horse. And what would the result be? Might not Roland, wild in his grief and growing senile and confused in his mind, see wilful murder in what was *really* an accident? And might his eye not turn on Flagg? Of course. His eye would turn to Flagg before it turned to anyone else. Roland's mother had mistrusted him, and he knew that, deep down, Roland mistrusted him as well. He had been able to hold that mistrust in check with mingled fear and fascination, but Flagg knew that if Roland ever had reason to think Flagg had caused, or even played a part in, the death of his son –

Flagg could actually imagine situations where he might have to interfere on Peter's behalf to keep the boy safe. It was damnable. Damnable!

He must be put out of the way. Must be put out of the way! Must!

As the days and weeks and months passed, the drumbeat of this thought in Flagg's head grew ever more urgent. Every day Roland grew older and weaker; every day Peter grew older and wiser and thus a more dangerous opponent. What was to be done?

Flagg's thoughts turned and turned and turned on this. He grew morose and irritable. Servants, especially Peter's butler, Brandon, and Brandon's son, Dennis, gave him a wide berth, and spoke to each other in whispers of the terrible smells that sometimes came from his laboratory late at night. Dennis in particular, who would someday take the place of his good old da' as Peter's butler, was terrified of Flagg, and once asked his father if he might say a word about the magician. 'To make him safe, is all I'm thinking,' Dennis said.

'Not a word,' Brandon said, and fixed Dennis,

who was only a boy himself, with a forbidding look. 'Not a word will you say. The man's dangerous.'

'Then is that not all the more reason – ?' Dennis began timidly.

'A dullard may mistake the rattle of a Biter-Snake for the sound of pebbles in a hollow gourd and put out his hand to touch it,' Brandon said, 'but our prince is no dullard, Dennis. Now fetch me another glass of bundle-gin, and say no more on't.'

So Dennis did not speak of it to Peter, but his love of his young master and his fear of the King's hooded adviser both grew after that short exchange. Whenever he saw Flagg sweeping up one of the corridors of the castle in his long hooded robe he would draw aside, trembling, thinking: *Biter-Snake! Biter-Snake! Watch for him, Peter! And listen for him!*

Then, one night when Peter was sixteen, just as Flagg had begun to believe that there really might not be any way to put an end to the boy without unacceptable risk to himself, an answer came. That was a wild night. A terrible autumn storm raged and shrieked around the castle, and the streets of Delain were empty as people sought shelter from the sheets of chilly rain and the battering wind.

Roland had taken a cold in the damp. He took cold more and more easily these days, and Flagg's medicines, potent as they were, were losing their power to cure him. One of these colds – perhaps even the one he was hacking and wheezing with now – would eventually deepen into the Wet Lung Disease, and that would kill him. Magic medicines were not like doctors' medicines, and Flagg knew that one of the reasons the potions he gave the old King were now so slow to work, was that he, Flagg, no longer really *wanted* them to work. The only reason he was keeping Roland alive was that he feared Peter.

I wish you were dead, old man, Flagg thought with childish anger as he sat before a guttering candle, listening to the wind shriek without and his two-headed parrot mutter sleepily to itself within. *For a row of pins — a very short row at that — I'd kill you myself for all the trouble you and your stupid wife and your elder son have caused me. The joy of killing you would almost be worth the ruin of my plans. The joy of killing you —*

Suddenly he froze, sitting upright, staring off into the darkness of his under-ground rooms, where the shadows moved uneasily. His eyes glittered silver. An idea blazed in his mind like a torch.

The candle flared a brilliant green and then went out.

'*Death!*' one of the parrot's two heads shrieked in the darkness.

'*Murder!*' shrieked the other.

And in that blackness, unseen by anyone, Flagg began to laugh.

Of all the weapons ever used to commit regicide – the murder of a King – none has been as frequently used as poison. And no one has greater knowledge of poisons than a magician.

Flagg, one of the greatest magicians who ever lived, knew all the poisons that we know – arsenic; strychnine; the curare, which steals inward, paralyzing all the muscles and the heart last; nicotine; belladonna; nightshade; toadstool. He knew the poison venoms of a hundred snakes and spiders; the clear distillation of the clànah lily which smells like honey but kills its victims in screaming torments; Deadly Clawfoot which grows in the deepest shadows of the Dismal Swamp. Flagg did not know just dozens of poisons but dozens of dozens, each worse than the last. They were all neatly ranked on the shelves of an inner room where no servant ever went. They were in beakers, in phials, in little envelopes. Each deadly item was neatly marked. This was Flagg's chapel of screams-in-waiting – agony's antechamber, foyer of fevers, dressing room for death. Flagg visited it often when he felt out of sorts and wanted to cheer himself up. In this devil's marketplace waited all those things that humans, who are made of flesh and are so weak, dread: hammering headaches, screaming stomach cramps, detonations of diarrhoea, vomiting, collapsing blood vessels, paralysis of the heart, exploding eyeballs, swelling, blackening tongues, madness.

But the worst poison of all Flagg kept separate

from even these. In his study there was a desk. Every drawer of this desk was locked . . . but one was triple-locked. In it was a teak box, carved all over with magical symbols . . . runes and such. The lock on this box was unique. Its plate seemed to be a dull orange steel, but very close inspection showed it was really some sort of vegetable matter. It was, in fact, a kleffa carrot, and once a week Flagg watered this living lock with a tiny spray bottle. The kleffa carrot also seemed to have some dull species of intelligence. If anyone tried to jemmy the kleffa lock open, or even if the wrong someone tried to use the right key, the lock would scream. Inside this box was a smaller box, which opened with a key Flagg wore always around his neck.

Inside this second box was a packet. Inside the packet was a small quantity of green sand. Pretty, you would have said, but nothing spectacular. Nothing to write home to Mother about. Yet this green sand was one of the deadliest poisons in all the worlds, so deadly that even Flagg was afraid of it. It came from the desert of Grenh. This huge poisoned waste lay even beyond Garlan, and was a land unknown in Delain. Grenh could be approached only on a day when the wind was blowing the other way, because a single breath of the fumes which came from the desert of Grenh would cause death.

Not instant death. That was not the way the poison worked. For a day or two – perhaps even three – the person who breathed the poison fumes (or even worse, swallowed the grains of sand) would feel fine – perhaps better than ever before in his life. Then, suddenly, his lungs would grow red-hot, his skin would begin to smoke, and his body would shrivel like the body of a mummy. Then he would drop dead, often with his hair on fire. Someone who breathed or swallowed this deadly stuff would burn from the inside out.

This was Dragon Sand, and there was no antidote, no cure. What fun.

On that wild, rainy night, Flagg determined to give a bit of Dragon Sand to Roland in a glass of wine. It had become Peter's custom to take his father a glass of wine each night, shortly before Roland turned in. Everyone in the palace knew it, and commented on what a loyal son Peter was. Roland enjoyed his son's company as much as the wine he brought, Flagg thought, but a certain maiden had caught Peter's eye and he rarely stayed longer than half an hour with his father these days.

If Flagg came one night after Peter had left, Flagg did not think the old man would turn down a second glass of wine.

A very special glass of wine.

A hot vintage, my lord, Flagg thought, a grin dawning on his narrow face. *A hot vintage indeed, and why not? The vineyard was right next door to hell, I think, and when this stuff starts working in your guts, you'll think hell is where you are.*

Flagg threw back his head and began to laugh.

Once his plan was laid – a plan that would rid him of both Roland and Peter forever – Flagg wasted no time. He first used all his wizardry to make the King well again. He was delighted to find that his magic potions worked better than they had for a long, long time. It was another irony. He earnestly wanted to make Roland better, so the potions worked. But he wanted to make the King better so he could kill him and make sure everyone knew it was murder. It was really quite funny, when you stopped to think it over.

On a windy night less than a week after the King's hacking cough had ceased, Flagg unlocked his desk and took out the teak box. He murmured, 'Well done,' to the kleffa carrot, which squeaked mindlessly in reply, and then lifted the heavy lid and took out the smaller box inside. He used the key around his neck to open it, and took out the packet that contained the Dragon Sand. He had bewitched this packet, and it was immune to the Dragon Sand's terrible power. Or so he thought. Flagg took no chances, and removed the packet with a small pair of silver tweezers. He laid it beside one of the King's goblets on his desk. Sweat stood out on his forehead in great round drops, for this was ticklish work indeed. One little mistake and he would pay for it with his life.

Flagg went out into the corridor that led to the dungeons and began to pant. He was hyperventilating. When you breathe rapidly, you fill your whole body with oxygen, and you can hold your breath for a long time. During the critical stage of his preparations, Flagg did not mean to breathe at all. There would be no mistakes, big or little. He was having too much fun to die.

He took a final great gasp of clean air from the barred window just outside the door to his apartment and reentered his rooms. He went to the envelope, took his dagger from his belt, and delicately slit it open. There was a flat piece of obsidian, which the magician used as a paperweight, on his desk – in those days, obsidian was the hardest rock known. Using the tweezers again, he grasped the packet, turned it upside down, and poured out most of the green sand. He saved back a tiny bit – hardly more than a dozen grains, but this bit of extra was extremely important to his plans. Hard as the obsidian was, the rock immediately began to smoke.

Thirty seconds had passed now.

He picked up the obsidian, careful that not a single grain of Dragon Sand should touch his skin – if it did, it would work inward until it reached his heart and set it on fire. He tilted the stone over the goblet and poured it in.

Now, quickly, before the sand could begin to eat into the glass, he poured in some of the King's favourite wine – the same sort of wine Peter would be taking his father about now. The sand dissolved immediately. For a moment the red wine glimmered a sinister green, and then it returned to its usual colour.

Fifty seconds.

Flagg went back to his desk. He picked up the flat rock and took his dagger by its handle. Only a few grains of Dragon Sand had touched the blade when he slit through the paper, but already they were working their way in, and evil little streamers of smoke rose from the pocks in the Anduan steel. He carried both the stone and the dagger out into the hallway.

Seventy seconds, and his chest was beginning to cry for air.

Thirty feet down the hallway, which led to the dungeon if you followed it far enough (a trip no one in Delain wanted to make), there was a grating in the floor. Flagg could hear gurgling water, and if he had not been holding his breath, he would have smelled a foul stench. This was one of the castle's sewers. He dropped both the rock and the blade into it and grinned at the double splash in spite of his pounding chest. Then he hurried back to the window, leaned far out, and took breath after gasping breath.

When he had his wind back, he returned to his study. Now only the tweezers, the packet, and the glass of wine stood on the desk. There was not so much as a grain of sand on the tweezers, and the bit of sand left inside the bewitched packet could not harm him as long as he took reasonable care.

He felt he had done very well indeed so far. His work was by no means done, but it was well begun. He bent over the goblet and inhaled deeply. There was no danger now; when the sand was mixed with a liquid, its fumes became harmless and undetectable. Dragon Sand made deadly vapours only when it touched a solid, such as stone.

Such as flesh.

Flagg held the goblet up to the light, admiring its bloody glow.

'A final glass of wine, my King,' he said, and laughed until the two-headed parrot screamed in fear. 'Something to warm your guts.'

He sat down, turned over his hourglass, and began to read a huge book of spells. Flagg had been reading from this book – which was bound in human skin – for a thousand years and had gotten through only a quarter of it. To read too long of this book, written on the high, distant Plains of Leng by a madman named Alhazred, was to risk madness.

An hour . . . just an hour. When the top half of his hourglass was empty, he could be sure Peter would have come and gone. An hour, and he could take Roland this final glass of wine. For a moment, Flagg looked at the bone-white sand slipping smoothly through the waist of the hourglass, and then he bent calmly over his book.

22

Roland was pleased and touched that Flagg should have brought him a glass of wine that night before he went to bed. He drank it off in two large gulps, and declared that it had warmed him greatly.

Smiling inside his hood, Flagg said: 'I thought it would, your Highness.'

23

Whether it was fate or only luck that caused Thomas to see Flagg with his father that night is another question you must answer for yourself. I only know that he *did* see, and that it happened in large part because Flagg had been at pains over the years to make a special friend of this friendless, miserable boy.

I'll explain in a moment – but first I must correct a wrong idea you may have about magic.

In stories of wizardry, there are three kinds that are usually spoken of almost carelessly, as if any second-class wizard could do them. These are turning lead into gold, changing one's shape, and making oneself invisible. The first thing you should know is that real magic is never easy, and if you think it is, just try making your least favourite aunt disappear the next time she comes to spend a week or two. Real magic is *hard*, and although it is easier to do evil magic than good, even bad magic is tolerably hard.

Turning lead into gold *can* be done, once you know the names to call on, and if you can find someone to show you exactly the right trick of splitting the loaves of lead. Shape changing and invisibility, however, are impossible . . . or so close to it that you might as well use the word.

From time to time Flagg – who was a great eavesdropper – had listened to fools tell tales about young princes who escaped the clutches of evil genies by uttering a simple magic word and popping out of sight, or beautiful young princesses (in the stories they were always beautiful, although Flagg's experience had been that most princesses were spoiled rotten and, as the end products of long, inbred family lines, ugly as sin and stupid in the bargain) who tricked great ogres into becoming flies, which they then quickly swatted. In most stories, the princesses were also good at swatting flies, although most of the princesses Flagg had seen wouldn't have been able to swat a fly dying on a cold windowsill in December. In *stories* it all sounded easy; in *stories* people changed their shapes or turned themselves into walking windowpanes all the time.

In *truth*, Flagg had never seen either trick done. He had once known a great Anduan magician who believed he had mastered the trick of changing his shape, but after six months of meditation and nearly a week of incantations in a series of agonizing body postures, he uttered the last awesome spell and succeeded only in making his nose nearly nine feet long and driving himself insane. And there had been fingernails growing out of his nose. Flagg remembered with a grim little smile. Great magician or not, the man had been a fool.

Invisibility was likewise impossible, at least as far as Flagg himself had been able to determine. Yet it was possible to make oneself . . . *dim*.

Yes, *dim* – that was really the best word for it, although others sometimes came to mind: *ghostly, transparent, unobtrusive*. Invisibility was out of his reach, but by first eating a pizzle and then reciting a number of spells, it was possible to become *dim*. When one was *dim* and a servant approached along a passageway, one simply drew aside and stood still and let the servant pass. In most cases, the servant's eyes would drop to his own feet or suddenly find something interesting to look at on the ceiling. If one passed through a room, conversation would falter, and people would look momentarily distressed, as if all were having gas pains at the same time. Torches and wall sconces grew smoky, Candles sometimes blew out. It was necessary to actually hide when one was *dim* only if one saw someone whom one knew well – for, whether one was *dim* or not, these people almost always saw. *Dimness* was useful, but it was not invisibility.

On the night Flagg took the poisoned wine to Roland, he first made himself *dim*. He did not expect to see anyone he knew. It was after nine o'clock now, the King was old and unwell, the days were short, and the castle went to bed early. *When Thomas is King,* Flagg thought, carrying the wine swiftly through the corridors, *there will be parties every night. He already has his father's taste for drink, although he favours wine rather than beer or mead. It should be easy enough to introduce him to a few stronger drinks . . . After all, am I not his friend? Yes, when Peter is safely out of the way in the Needle and Thomas is King, there will be great parties every night . . . until the people in the alleys and the Baronies are choked enough to rise in bloody revolt. Then there will be one final party, the greatest of all . . . but I don't think Thomas will enjoy it. Like the wine I'm bringing his father tonight, that party will be extremely hot.*

He did not expect to see anyone he knew, and he didn't. Only a few servants passed him, and they drew away from the place where he stood almost absently, as if they felt a cold draught.

All the same, someone saw *him*. Thomas saw him through the eyes of Niner, the dragon his father had killed long ago. Thomas was able to do this because Flagg himself had taught him the trick.

The way his father had rejected the gift of the boat had hurt Thomas deeply, and after that he tended to keep clear of his father. All the same, Thomas loved Roland and badly wanted to make him happy the way Peter made him happy. Even more than that, he wanted to make his father love him the way he loved Peter. In fact, Thomas would have been happy if their father had loved him even half as much.

The trouble was, Peter had all the good ideas first. Sometimes Peter tried to share his ideas with Thomas, but to Thomas the ideas either sounded silly (until they worked) or else he feared he wouldn't be able to do his share of the work, as when Peter had made their father a set of Bendoh men three years ago.

'I'll give Father something better than a bunch of stupid old game pieces,' Thomas had said haughtily, but what he was *really* thinking was that if he couldn't make his father a simple wooden sailboat, he would never be able to help make something as difficult as the twenty-man Bendoh army. So Peter made the game pieces alone over a period of four months – the infantry men, the knights, the archers, the Fusilier, the General, the Monk – and of course Roland had loved them even though they were a bit clumsy. He had immediately put away the jade Bendoh set the great Ellender had carved for him forty years before and put the one Peter had made for him in its place. When Thomas saw this, he crept away to his apartments and went to bed, although it was the middle of the afternoon. He felt as if someone had reached into his chest and cut off a tiny piece of his heart and made him eat it. His heart tasted very bitter to him, and he hated Peter more than ever, although part of him still loved his handsome older brother and always would.

And although the taste had been bitter, he had liked it.

Because it was his heart.

Now there was the business of the nightly glass of wine.

Peter had come to Thomas and said, 'I was thinking it would be nice if we brought Dad a glass of wine every night, Tom. I asked the steward, and he said he couldn't just give us a bottle because he has to make an accounting to the Chief Vintner at the end of each sixmonth, but he said we could pool some of our money and buy a bottle of the Barony Fifth Vat, which is Father's favourite. And it's really not expensive. We'd have lots of our allowances left over. And –'

'I think that's the stupidest idea I ever heard!'

Thomas burst out. '*All* the wine belongs to Father, all the wine in the Kingdom, and he can have as much of it as he wants! Why should we spend *our* money to give Father something he owns anyway? We'll enrich that fat little steward, that's all we'll do!'

Peter said patiently, 'It will please him that we spent our money on him, even if it's something he owns anyway.'

'How do you know *that*?'

Simply, maddeningly, Peter replied: 'I just do.'

Thomas looked at him, scowling. How could he tell Peter that the Chief Vintner had caught him in the wine cellar, stealing a bottle of wine, just the month before? The fat little pig had given him a shaking and threatened to tell his father if Thomas didn't give him a gold piece. Thomas had paid, tears of rage and shame standing in his eyes. *If it had been Peter, you would have turned the other way and pretended not to see, you slug*, he thought. *If it had been Peter, you would have turned your back. Because Peter is going to be King someday soon, and I'll just be a prince forever.* It also occurred to him that Peter never would have tried to steal wine in the first place, but the truth of this thought only made him angrier at his brother.

'I just thought –' Peter began.

' "You just thought, you just thought," ' Thomas mimicked savagely. 'Well, go think somewhere else! When Father finds out you paid the Chief Vintner for his own wine, he'll laugh at you and call you a fool!'

But Roland hadn't laughed at Peter, hadn't called him a fool – he had called him a good son in a voice that was unsteady and almost weepy. Thomas

knew, because he had crept after when Peter took
their father the wine that first night. He watched
through the eyes of the dragon and saw it all.

·I·f you had asked Flagg straight out why
he had shown Thomas that place and the secret passageway which led to it, he would have been able
to give you no very satisfactory answer. That was
because he didn't exactly *know* why he had done it.
He had an instinct for mischief in his head, just as
some people have a way with numbers or a clear
sense of direction. The castle was very old, and there
were many secret doors and passages in it. Flagg
knew most of them (no one, not even he, knew all of
them), but this was the only one he had ever shown
Thomas. His instinct for mischief told him that this
one might cause trouble, and Flagg simply obeyed
his instinct. Mischief, after all was Flagg's cake and
pie.

Every now and then he would pop into Thomas's room and cry, 'Tommy, you look glum! I've
thought of something you might like to see! Want to
go and have a look?' He almost always said *you look
glum, Tommy* or *you look a bit in the dumps, Tommy* or
you look like you just sat on a pinchbug, Tommy because
he had a knack of showing up when Thomas was
feeling particularly depressed or blue. Flagg knew

that Thomas was afraid of him, and Thomas would find an excuse not to go with him unless he particularly needed a friend . . . and felt so low and unhappy he wouldn't be particular about which friend it was. Flagg knew this, but Thomas himself did not – his fear of Flagg ran deep. On the surface of his mind, he thought Flagg was a fine fellow, full of tricks and fun. Sometimes the fun was a bit mean, but that often suited Thomas's disposition.

Do you think it strange that Flagg would know something about Thomas that Thomas didn't know about himself? It really isn't strange at all. People's minds, particularly the minds of children, are like wells – deep wells full of sweet water. And sometimes, when a particular thought is too unpleasant to bear, the person who has that thought will lock it into a heavy box and throw it into that well. He listens for the splash . . . and then the box is gone. Except it is not, of course. Not really. Flagg, being very old and very wise, as well as very wicked, knew that even the deepest well has a bottom, and just because a thing is out of sight doesn't mean it is gone. It is still there, resting at the bottom. And he knew that the caskets those evil, frightening ideas are buried in may rot, and the nastiness inside may leak out after awhile and poison the water . . . and when the well of the mind is badly poisoned, we call the result insanity.

If the magician showed him scary things in the castle sometimes, he did it because he knew that the more frightened of him Thomas was, the more power he would gain over Thomas . . . and he knew he could have that power, because he knew something I've already told you – that Thomas was weak and often neglected by his father. Flagg wanted Thomas to be afraid of him, and he wanted to make sure that, as the years passed, Thomas had to throw many of those locked boxes into the darkness inside him. If Thomas were to go insane at some point after he became King, well, what of that? It would make it easier for Flagg to rule; it would make his power all the greater.

How did Flagg know the right times to visit Thomas, and take him on these strange tours of the castle? Sometimes he saw what had happened to make Thomas sad or angry in his crystal. More often, he simply felt an urge to go to Thomas and heeded it – that instinct for mischief rarely led him wrong.

Once he took Thomas high into the eastern tower – they climbed stairs until Thomas was panting like a dog, but Flagg never seemed to lose his breath. At the top was a door so small that even Thomas had to crawl through it on his hands and knees. Beyond was a dark, rustling room with a single window. Flagg had led him to that window without a word, and when Thomas saw the view – the entire city of Delain, the Near Towns, and then the hills which stood between the Near Towns and the Eastern Barony marching off into a blue haze – he thought that the sight had been worth every stair his aching legs had climbed. His heart swelled with the beauty of it, and he turned to thank Flagg – but something about the white blur of the magician's face inside his hood had frozen the words on his lips.

'Now watch *this*!' Flagg said, and held up his hand. A spurt of blue flame rose from his index

finger, and the rustling sound in the room, which Thomas had first taken for the sound of the wind, turned to a rising whir of leathery wings. A moment later Thomas was screaming and beating the air above his head as he blundered blindly back toward the tiny door. The little round room at the top of the castle's eastern tower had the best view in Delain save for the cell at the top of the Needle, but now he understood why no one visited it. The room was infested with huge bats. Disturbed by the light Flagg had raised, they whirled and swooped. Later, after they were out and Flagg had quieted the boy – Thomas, who hated bats, had been in hysterics – the magician insisted it was just a joke meant to cheer him up. Thomas believed him . . . but for weeks after he awoke screaming with nightmares in which bats flapped around his head, got caught in his hair, and ripped at his face with their sharp claws and ratty teeth.

On another excursion, Flagg took him to the King's treasure room and showed him the mounds of gold coins, tall stacks of gold bars, and the deep bins marked EMERALDS, DIAMONDS, RUBIES, FIREDIMS, and so on.

'Are they really full of jewels?' Thomas asked.

'Look and see,' Flagg said. He opened one of the bins and pulled out a handful of uncut emeralds. They sparkled wildly in his hand.

'My father's *name!*' Thomas gasped.

'Oh, that's nothing! Look over here! Pirate treasure, Tommy!'

He showed Thomas a pile of booty from the encounter with the Anduan pirates some twelve years ago. The Delain Treasury was rich, the few treasure-room clerks old, and this particular heap hadn't been sorted yet. Thomas gasped at heavy swords with jewelled hilts, daggers with blades that had been crusted with serrated diamonds so they would cut deeper, heavy killballs made of rhodochrosite.

'All this belongs to the Kingdom?' Thomas asked in an awed voice.

'It all belongs to your *father*,' Flagg replied, although Thomas had actually been correct. 'Someday it will all belong to Peter.'

'And me,' Thomas said with a ten-year-old's confidence.

'No,' Flagg said, just the right tinge of regret in his voice, 'just to Peter. Because he's the oldest, and he'll be King.'

'He'll share,' Thomas said, but with the slightest tremor of doubt in his vocie. 'Pete *always* shares.'

'Peter's a fine boy, and I'm sure you're right. He'll *probably* share. But no one can *make* a King share, you know. No one can *make* a King do anything he doesn't want to do.' He looked at Thomas to guage the effect of this remark, then looked back at the deep, shadowy treasure room. Somewhere, one of the aged clerks was droning out a count of ducats. 'Such a lot of treasure, and all for one man,' Flagg remarked. 'It's really something to think about, isn't it, Tommy?'

Thomas said nothing, but Flagg had been well pleased. He saw that Tommy *was* thinking about it, all right, and he judged that another of those poisoned caskets was tumbling down into the well of Thomas's mind — *ker-splash!* And that was indeed so. Later, when

Peter proposed to Thomas that they share the expense of the nightly bottle of wine, Thomas had remembered the great treasure room – and he remembered that all the treasure in it would belong to his brother. *Easy for you to talk so blithely of buying wine! Why not? Someday you'll have all the money in the world!*

Then, about a year before he brought the poisoned wine to the King, on impulse, Flagg had shown Thomas this secret passage . . . and on this one occasion his usually unerring instinct for mischief might have led him astray. Again, I leave it for you to decide.

26

Tommy, you look down in the dumps!' he cried. The hood of his cloak was pushed back on that day, and he looked almost normal.

Almost.

Tommy *felt* down in them. He had suffered through a long luncheon at which his father had praised Peter's scores in geometry and navigation to his advisors with the most lavish superlatives. Roland had never rightly understood either. He knew that a triangle had three sides and a square had four; he knew you could find your way out of the woods when you were lost by following Old Star in the sky; and that was where his knowledge ended. That was where Thomas's knowledge ended, too, so he felt that luncheon would never be done. Worse, the meat was just the way his father liked it – bloody and barely cooked. Bloody meat made Thomas feel almost sick.

'My lunch didn't agree with me, that's all,' he said to Flagg.

'Well, I know just the thing to cheer you up,' Flagg said. 'I'll show you a secret of the castle, Tommy my boy.'

Thomas was playing with a buggerlug bug. He had it on his desk and had set his schoolbooks around it in a series of barriers. If the trundling beetle looked as if he might find a way out, Thomas would shift one of the books to keep him in.

'I'm pretty tired,' Thomas said. This was not a lie. Hearing Peter praised so highly always made him feel tired.

'You'll like it,' Flagg said in a tone that was mostly wheedling . . . but a little threatening, too.

Thomas looked at him apprehensively. 'There aren't any . . . any bats, are there?'

Flagg laughed cheerily – but that laugh raised gooseflesh on Thomas's arms anyway. He clapped Thomas on the back. 'Not a bat! Not a drip! Not a draught! Warm as toast! And you can peek at your father, Tommy!'

Thomas knew that peeking was just another way of saying spying, and that spying was wrong – but this had been a shrewd shot all the same. This next time the buggerlug bug found a way to escape between two of the books, Thomas let it go. 'All right,' he said, 'but there better not be any bats.'

Flagg slipped an arm around the boy's shoulders. 'No bats, I swear – but here's something for

you to mull over in your mind, Tommy. You'll not
only see your father, you'll see him through the eyes
of his greatest trophy.'

Thomas's own eyes widened with interest.
Flagg was satisfied. The fish was hooked and landed.
'What do you mean?'

'Come and see for yourself,' was all he would
say.

He led Thomas through a maze of corridors.
You would have become lost very soon, and I probably would have gotten lost myself before long, but
Thomas knew this way as well as you know your
way through your own bedroom in the dark – at least
he did until Flagg led him aside.

They had almost reached the King's own apartments when Flagg pushed open a recessed wooden
door that Thomas had never really noticed before.
Of course it had always been there, but in castles
there are often doors – whole wings, even – that have
mastered the art of being *dim*.

This passage was quite narrow. A chambermaid
with an armload of sheets passed them; she was so
terrified to have met the King's magician in this slim
stone throat that it seemed she would happily have
shrunk into the very pores of the stone blocks to
avoid touching him. Thomas almost laughed
because sometimes he felt a little like that himself
when Flagg was around. They met no one else at all.

Faintly, from below them, he could hear dogs
barking, and that gave him a rough idea of where he
was. The only dogs inside the castle proper were
his father's hunting dogs, and they were probably
barking because it was time for them to be fed. Most

of Roland's dogs were now almost as old as he was, and because he knew how the cold ached in his own bones, Roland had commanded that a kennel be made for them right here in the castle. To reach the dogs from his father's main sitting chamber, one went down a flight of stairs, turned right, and walked ten yards or so up an interior corridor. So Thomas knew they were about thirty feet to the right of his father's private rooms.

Flagg stopped so suddenly that Thomas almost ran into him. The magician looked swiftly around to make sure they had the passageway to themselves. They did.

'Fourth stone up from the one at the bottom with the chip in it,' Flagg said. 'Press it. Quick!'

Ah, there was a secret here, all right, and Thomas loved secrets. Brightening, he counted up four stones from the one with the chip and pressed. He expected some neat little bit of jiggery-pokery – a sliding panel, perhaps – but he was quite unprepared for what did happen.

The stone slid in with perfect ease to a depth of about three inches. There was a click. An entire section of wall suddenly swung inward, revealing a dark vertical crack. This wasn't a wall at all! It was a huge door! Thomas's jaw dropped.

Flagg slapped Thomas's bottom.

'Quick, I said, you little fool!' he cried in a low voice. There was urgency in his voice, and this wasn't simply put on for Thomas's benefit, as many of Flagg's emotions were. He looked right and left to verify that the passage was still empty. 'Go! Now!'

Thomas looked at the dark crack that had been

revealed and thought uneasily about bats again. But one look at Flagg's face showed him that this would be a bad time to attempt a discussion on the subject.

He pushed the door open wider and stepped into the darkness. Flagg followed at once. Thomas heard the low flap of the magician's cloak as he turned and shoved the wall closed again. The darkness was utter and complete, the air still and dry. Before he could open his mouth to say anything, the blue flame at the tip of Flagg's index finger flared alight, throwing a harsh blue-white fan of illumination.

Thomas cringed without even thinking about it, and his hands flew up.

Flagg laughed harshly. 'No bats, Tommy. Didn't I promise?'

Nor were there. The ceiling was quite low, and Thomas could see for himself. No bats, and warm as toast . . . just as the magician had promised. By the light of Flagg's magic finger-flare, he could also see they were in a secret passage which was about twenty-five feet long. Walls, floor, and ceiling were covered with ironwood boards. He couldn't see the far end very well, but it looked perfectly blank.

He could still hear the muffled barking of the dogs.

'When I said be quick, I meant it,' Flagg said. He bent over Thomas, a vague, looming shadow that was, in this darkness, rather batlike itself. Thomas drew back a step, uneasily. As always, there was an unpleasant smell about the magician – a smell of secret powders and bitter herbs. 'You know where the passage is now, and I'll not be the one to tell you not to use it. But if you're ever *caught* using it, you must say you discovered it by accident.'

The shape loomed even closer, forcing Thomas back another step.

'If you say *I* showed it to you, Tommy, I'll make you sorry.'

'I'll never tell,' Thomas said. His words sounded thin and shaky.

'Good. Better yet if no one ever sees you using it. Spying on a King is serious business, prince or not. Now follow me. And be quiet.'

Flagg led him to the end of the passageway. The far wall was also dressed with ironwood, but when Flagg raised the flame that burned from the tip of his finger, Thomas saw two little panels. Flagg pursed his lips and blew out the light.

In utter blackness, he whispered: 'Never open these two panels with a light burning. He might see. He's old, but he still sees well. He might see something, even though the eyeballs are of tinted glass.'

'What —'

'*Shhhh!* There isn't much wrong with his ears, either.'

Thomas fell quiet, his heart pounding in his chest. He felt a great excitement that he didn't understand. Later he thought that he had been excited because he knew in some way what was going to happen.

In the darkness he heard a faint sliding sound, and suddenly a dim ray of light — torchlight — lit the darkness. There was a second sliding sound and a second ray of light appeared. Now he could see Flagg again, very faintly, and his own hands when he held them up before him.

Thomas saw Flagg step up to the wall and bend a little; then most of the light was cut out as he put his eyes to the two holes through which the rays of light fell. He looked for a moment, then grunted and stepped away. He motioned to Thomas. 'Have a look,' he said.

More excited than ever, Thomas cautiously put his eyes to the holes. He saw clearly enough, although everything had an odd greenish-yellow aspect – it was as if he were looking through smoked glass. A sense of perfect, delighted wonder rose in him. He was looking down into his father's sitting room. He saw his father slouched by the fire in his favourite chair – one with high wings which threw shadows across his lined face.

It was very much the room of a huntsman; in our world such a room would often be called a den, although this one was as big as some ordinary houses. Flaring torches lined the long walls. Heads were mounted everywhere: heads of bear, of deer, of elk, of wildebeest, of cormorant. There was even a grand featherex, which is the cousin of our legendary bird the phoenix. Thomas could not see the head of Niner, the dragon his father had killed before he was born, but this did not immediately register on him.

His father was picking morosely at a sweet. A pot of tea steamed near at hand.

That was all that was really happening in that great room that could have (and at times had) held upward of two hundred people – just his father, with a fur robe draped around him, having a solitary after-

noon tea. Yet Thomas watched for a time that seemed endless. His fascination and his excitement with this view of his father cannot be told. His heart-beat, which had been rapid before, doubled. Blood sang and pounded in his head. His hands clenched into fists so tight that he would later discover bloody crescent moons imprinted into his palms where his fingernails had bitten.

Why was he so excited simply to be looking at an old man picking halfheartedly at a piece of cake? Well, first you must remember that the old man wasn't just *any* old man. He was Thomas's father. And spying, sad to say, has its own attraction. When you can see people doing something and they don't see you, even the most trivial actions seem import-ant.

After awhile, Thomas began to feel a little ashamed of what he was doing, and that was not really surprising. Spying on a person is a kind of stealing, after all – it's stealing a look at what people do when they think they are alone. But that is also one of its chief fascinations, and Thomas might have looked for hours if Flagg had not murmured, 'Do you know where you are, Tommy?'

'I –' *don't think so*, he was going to add, but of course he did know. His sense of direction was good, and with a little thought he could imagine the reverse of this angle. He suddenly understood what Flagg meant when he said he, Thomas, would see his father through the eyes of Roland's greatest trophy. He was looking down at his father from a little more than halfway up the west wall . . . and that was where the greatest head of all was hung – that of Niner, his father's dragon.

He might see something, even though the eyeballs are of tinted glass. Now he understood that, too. Thomas had to clap his hands to his mouth to stifle a shrill giggle.

Flagg slid the little panels shut again . . . but he, too, was smiling.

'No!' Thomas whispered. 'No, I want to see more!'

'Not this afternoon,' Flagg said. 'You've seen enough this afternoon. You can come again when you want . . . although if you come too often, you'll surely be caught. Now come on. We're going back.'

Flagg relit the magic flame and led Thomas down the corridor again. At the end, he put the light out and there was another sliding sound as he opened a peephole. He guided Thomas's hand to it so he would know where it was, and then bade him look.

'Notice that you can see the passageway in both directions,' Flagg said. 'Always be careful to look before you open the secret door, or someday you will be surprised.'

Thomas put one eye to the peephole and saw, directly across the corridor, an ornate window with glass sides that angled slightly into the passageway. It was much too fancy for such a small passageway, but Thomas understood without having to be told that it had been put here by whoever had made the secret passageway. Looking into the angled sides, he could indeed see a ghostly reflection of the corridor in both directions.

'Empty?' Flagg whispered.

'Yes,' Thomas whispered back.

Flagg pushed an interior spring (again guiding Thomas's hand to it for future reference), and the door clicked open. 'Quickly now!' Flagg said. They were out and the door was shut behind them in a trice.

Ten minutes later, they were back in Thomas's rooms.

'Enough excitement for one day,' Flagg said. 'Remember what I told you, Tommy: don't use the passageway so often that you'll be caught, and if you *are* caught' – Flagg's eyes glittered grimly – 'remember that you found that place by accident.'

'I will,' Thomas said quickly. His voice was high and it squeaked like a hinge that needed oil. When Flagg looked at him that way, his heart felt like a bird caught in his chest, fluttering in panic.

27

Thomas heeded Flagg's advice not to go often, but he *did* use the passageway from time to time, and peeked at his father through the glass eyes of Niner – peeked into a world where everything became greeny-gold. Going away later with a pounding headache (as he almost always did), he would think: *Your head aches because you were seeing the way dragons must see the world – as if everything was dried out and ready to burn.* And perhaps Flagg's instinct for mischief in this matter was not so bad at all, because, by spying on his father, Thomas learned to feel a new thing for Roland. Before he knew about the secret passage he had felt love for him, and often a sorrow that he could not please him better, and sometimes fear. Now he learned to feel contempt, as well.

Whenever Thomas spied into Roland's sitting room and found his father in company, he left again quickly. He only lingered when his father was alone. In the past, Roland rarely had been, even in such rooms as his den, which was a part of his 'private apartments.' There was always one more urgent matter to be attended to, one more advisor to see, one more petition to hear.

But Roland's time of power was passing. As his importance waned with his good health, he found himself remembering all the times he had cried to either Sasha or Flagg: 'Won't these people ever leave me alone?' The memory brought a rueful smile to his lips. Now that they did, he missed them.

Thomas felt contempt because people are rarely at their best when they are alone. They usually put their masks of politeness, good order, and good breeding aside. What's beneath? Some warty monster? Some disgusting thing that would make people run away, screaming? Sometimes, perhaps, but usually it's nothing bad at all. Usually people would just laugh if they saw us with our masks off – laugh, make a revolted face, or do both at the same time.

Thomas saw that his father, whom he had always loved and feared, who had seemed to him the greatest man in the world, often picked his nose

when he was alone. He would root around in first
one nostril and then the other until he got a plump
green booger. He would regard these with solemn
satisfaction, turning each one this way and that in the
firelight, the way a jeweller might turn a particularly
fine emerald. Most of these he would then rub under
the chair in which he was sitting. Others, I regret to
say, he popped into his mouth and munched with an
expression of reflective enjoyment on his face.

He would have only a single glass of wine at
night – the glass which Peter brought him – but after
Peter left, he drank what seemed to Thomas huge
amounts of beer (it was only years later that Thomas
came to realize that his father hadn't wanted Peter to
see him drunk), and when he needed to urinate, he
rarely used the commode in the corner. Most times
he simply stood up and pissed into the fire, often
farting as he did so.

He talked to himself. He would sometimes walk
around the long room like a man who was not sure
where he was, speaking either to the air or to the
mounted heads.

'I remember that day we got you, Bonsey,' he
would say to one of the elk heads (another of his
eccentricities was that he had named every one of the
trophies). 'I was with Bill Squathings and that fellow
with the great lump on the side of his face. I remember how you come through the trees and Bill let
loose, and then that fellow with the lump let loose,
then *I* let loose –'

Then his father would demonstrate how he had
let loose by raising his leg and farting, even as he
mimed drawing back a bowstring and letting fly.

And he would laugh an old man's shrill, unpleasant cackle.

Thomas would slide the little panels back after awhile and slink down the corridor again, his head pounding and an uneasy grin on his face – the head and grin of a boy who has been eating green apples and knows he may be sicker by morning than he is now.

This was the father he had always loved and feared?

He was an old man who farted out stinking clouds of steam.

This was the King his loyal subjects called Roland the Good?

He pissed into the fire, sending up more clouds of steam.

This was the man who made his heart break by not liking his boat?

He talked to the stuffed heads on his walls, calling them silly names like Bonsey and Stag-Pool and Puckerstring; he picked his nose and sometimes ate the boogers.

I don't care for you anymore, Thomas would think, checking the peephole to make sure the corridor was empty and then creeping back to his room like a felon. *You're a filthy, silly old man and you're nothing to me! Nothing at all! No!*

But he *was* something to Thomas. Some part of him went on loving Roland just the same – some part of him wanted to go to his father so his father would have something better to talk to than a bunch of stuffed heads on the walls.

Still, there was that other part of him that liked spying better.

*T*he night that Flagg came to King Roland's private rooms with the glass of poisoned wine was the first occasion in a very long time that Thomas had dared spy. There was a good reason for this.

One night about three months before, Thomas found himself unable to sleep. He tossed and turned until he heard the keep watchman cry eleven. Then he got up, dressed, and left his rooms. Less than ten minutes later, he was looking down into his father's den. He had thought his father might be asleep, but he was not. Roland was awake, and very, very drunk.

Thomas had seen his father drunk many times before, but he had never seen him in anything remotely like his current state. The boy was flabber-gasted and badly frightened.

There are people much older than Thomas was then who harbour the idea that old age is always a gentle time – that an old person may exhibit gentle wisdom, gentle crabbiness or craftiness, perhaps the gentle confusion of senility. They will grant these, but find it hard to credit any real fire. They have an illusion that by the seventies, any real fire must have faded to coals. That may be true, but on this night Thomas discovered that coals may sometimes flare up violently.

His father was striding rapidly up and down the length of his sitting room, his fur robe flying out behind him. His nightcap had fallen off; his remaining hair hung down in tangled locks, mostly about his ears. He was not staggering, as he had done on other nights, moving tentatively with one hand out to keep from running into the furniture. He was rolling like a sailor, but he was not staggering. When he did happen to run into one of the high-backed chairs which stood near the walls beneath the snarling head of a lynx, Roland threw the chair aside with a roar that made Thomas cringe. The hairs on his arms prickled. The chair flew across the room and hit the far wall. Its ironwood back splintered down the middle – in this bitter drunkenness, the old King had regained the strength of his middle years.

He looked up at the lynx head with red, glaring eyes.

'*Bite me!*' he roared at it. The raw hoarseness in his voice made Thomas cringe again. '*Bite me, are you afeard? Come down out of that wall, Craker! Jump! Here's my chest, see?*' He tore open the robe, revealing his scrawny chest. He bared his few teeth at Craker's many, and lifted his head. '*Here's my neck! Come on, jump! I'll do you with my bare hands! I'LL RIP YOUR STINKING GUTS OUT!*'

He stood for a moment, chest out and head up, looking like an animal himself – an ancient stag, perhaps, that has been brought to bay and can now hope for nothing better than to die well. Then he whirled away, stopping at a bear's head to shake a fist at it and roar a string of curses at it – curses so terrible that Thomas, cringing in the dark, believed that the bear's outraged spirit might swoop down, reanimate the stuffed head, and tear his father open while he watched.

But Roland was away again. He seized his mug, drained it, then whirled with brew dripping from his chops. He hurled the silver mug across the room, where it struck a stone angle of the fireplace hard enough to leave a dent in the metal.

Now his father came down the room toward him, throwing another chair out of the way, then kicking a table aside with his barefoot. His eyes flicked up . . . and met Thomas's own. Yes – they met his own eyes. Thomas felt their gazes lock, and a grey, swooning terror filled him like frozen breath.

His father stalked toward him, his yellowed teeth bared, his remaining hair hanging over his ears, beer dripping from his chin and the corners of his mouth.

'You,' Roland whispered in a low, terrible voice. 'Why do you stare at me? What do you hope to see?'

Thomas could not move. *Found out*, his mind gibbered, *found out, by all the gods that ever were or shall be, I am found out and I will surely be exiled!*

His father stood there, his eyes fixed on the mounted dragon's head. In his guilt, Thomas was sure his father had spoken to him, but this was not so – Roland had only spoken to Niner as he had spoken to the other heads. Yet if Thomas could see out of the tinted glass eyeballs, then his father could see in, at least to some degree. If Thomas hadn't been utterly paralyzed with fear, he would have run away in a panic – even if he had summoned enough presence of mind to hold his ground, his *eyes* surely would have moved. And if Roland had seen the eyes of the dragon move, what might he have thought? That the dragon was coming to life again? Perhaps. In his drunken state, I even think that likely. If Thomas had so much as blinked his eyes on that occasion, Flagg would have needed no poison later. The King, old and frail in spite of the temporary potency the drink had given him, would almost surely have died of fright.

Roland suddenly leaped forward.

'*WHY DO YOU STARE AT ME?*' he shrieked, and in his drunkenness it was Niner, Delain's last dragon, that he shrieked at, but of course, Thomas did not know that. '*WHY DO YOU STARE AT ME SO? I'VE DONE THE BEST I COULD, ALWAYS THE BEST I COULD! DID I ASK FOR THIS? DID I ASK FOR IT? ANSWER ME, DAMN YOU! I DID THE BEST I COULD AND LOOK AT ME NOW! LOOK AT ME NOW!*'

He pulled his robe wide open, showing his naked body, its grey skin blotchily flushed with drink.

'*LOOK AT ME NOW!*' he shrieked again, and looked down at himself, weeping.

Thomas could take no more. He slammed shut the panels behind the dragon's glass eyes at the same moment his father took his eyes from Niner to look down at his own wasted body. Thomas crashed and blundered down the black corridor and slammed full force into the closed door, braining himself and falling in a heap. He was up in a moment, unaware of the blood pouring down his face from a cut in his forehead, pounding at the secret spring until the door popped open. He rushed out into the corridor, not even thinking to check if anyone was there to see him. All he could see was his father's glaring, blood-shot eyes, all he could hear was his father screaming *Why do you stare at me?*

He had no way of knowing that his father had already fallen into a sleep of deep drunkenness. When Roland woke up the next morning, he was still on the floor, and the first thing he did, in spite of his fiercely aching head and his throbbing, bruised body (Roland was far too old for such strenuous revels), was to look at the dragon's head. He rarely dreamed when he was drunk – there was only an interval of sodden darkness. But last night a terrible dream had come to him: the glass eyes of the dragon's head had moved and Niner came to life. The worm breathed its deadly breath down on him, and although he could not see that fire, he could feel it deep down inside him, hot and getting hotter.

With this dream still lingering fresh in his mind, he dreaded what he might see when he looked up. But all was as it had been for years now. Niner snarled his fearsome snarl, his forked tongue lolled between teeth almost as long as fence pickets, his green-gold eyes stared blankly across the room. Ceremoniously crossed above this fabulous trophy were Roland's great bow and the arrow Foe-Hammer, its tip and shaft still black with dragon blood. He mentioned this terrible dream once to Flagg, who only nodded and looked more thoughtful than usual. Then Roland simply forgot it.

Forgetting was not so easy for Thomas.

He was haunted for weeks by nightmares. In them, his father stared at him and shrieked, '*See what you've done to me!*' and threw his robe open to display his nakedness – old puckered scars, drooping belly, sagging muscles – as if to say this too had all been Thomas's fault, that if he hadn't spied . . .

'Why do you never want to see Father anymore?' Peter asked him one day. 'He thinks you're mad at him.'

'That *I'm* mad at *him*?' Thomas was astounded.

'That's what he said at tea today,' Peter said. He looked at his brother closely, observing the dark circles under Thomas's eyes, the pallor of Thomas's cheeks and forehead. 'Tom, what's wrong?'

'Maybe nothing,' Thomas said slowly.

The next day he took tea with his father and brother. Going took all of his courage, but Thomas *did* have courage, and he sometimes found it – usually when his back was to the wall. His father gave him a kiss and asked him if anything was wrong. Thomas muttered that he hadn't been feeling well, but now he felt fine. His father nodded, gave him a rough hug, then went back to his usual behaviour – which consisted mostly of ignoring Thomas in favour of Peter. For once, Thomas welcomed this – he didn't want his father looking at him any more than necessary, at least for a while. That night, lying awake for a long time in bed and listening to the wind moan outside, he came to the conclusion that he had had a very close shave . . . but that he had somehow gotten away with it.

But never again, he thought. In the weeks after, the nightmares came less and less frequently. Finally they stopped altogether.

Still, the castle's head groom, Yosef, was right

about one thing: boys are sometimes better at pledging vows than they are at keeping them, and Thomas's desire to spy on his father at last grew stronger than both his fears and his good intentions. And that is how it happened that on the night Flagg came to Roland with the poisoned wine, Thomas was watching.

When Thomas got there and slid aside the two little panels, his father and his brother were just finishing *their* nightly glass of wine together. Peter was now almost seventeen, tall and handsome. The two of them sat by the fire, drinking and talking like old friends, and Thomas felt the old hate fill his heart with acid. After some little time, Peter arose and took courteous leave of his father.

'You leave earlier and earlier these nights,' Roland remarked.

Peter made some demurral.

Roland smiled. It was a sweet, sad smile, mostly toothless. 'I hear,' said he, 'that she is lovely.'

Peter looked flustered, which was uncommon with him. He stammered, which was even less common.

'Go,' Roland interrupted. 'Go. Be gentle with her, and be kind . . . but be hot, if there is ardour in you. Later years are cold years, Peter. Be hot while your years are green, and fuel is plentiful, and the fire may burn high.'

Peter smiled. 'You speak as if you are very old, Father, but you still look strong and hale to me.'

Roland embraced Peter. 'I love you,' he said.

Peter smiled with no awkwardness or embarrassment. 'I love you, too, Dad,' he said, and in his lonely darkness (spying is always lonely work, and the spyer almost always does it in the dark), Thomas pulled a horrible face.

Peter left, and for an hour or more not much happened. Roland sat morosely by the fire, drinking glass after glass of beer. He did not roar or bellow or talk to the heads on the walls; there was no destruction of furniture. Thomas had almost made up his mind to leave, when there was a double rap at the door.

Roland had been looking into the fire, almost hypnotized by the flicker-play of the flames. Now he roused himself and called, 'Who comes?'

Thomas heard no response, but his father rose and went to the door as if *he* had. He opened it, and at first Thomas thought his father's habit of talking to the heads on the walls had taken a queer new turn – that his father was now inventing invisible human company to relieve his boredom.

'Strange to see *you* at this hour,' Roland said, apparently walking back toward the fire in the company of no one at all. 'I thought you were always at your spells and conjurations after dark.'

Thomas blinked, rubbed his eyes, and saw that someone was there after all. For a moment he couldn't rightly make out who . . . and then he wondered how he could possibly have thought his father was alone when Flagg was right there beside him. Flagg was carrying two glasses of wine on a silver tray.

'Wives' tale, m'Lord – magicians conjure early as well as late. But of course we have our darksome image to keep up.'

Roland's sense of humour was always improved by beer – so much so that he would often laugh at things that weren't funny in the least. At this remark he threw back his head and bellowed as if it was the greatest joke he had ever heard. Flagg smiled thinly.

When Roland's fit of laughing had passed, he said: 'What's this? Wine?'

'Your son is barely more than a boy, but his deference toward his father and his honour of his King have shamed me, a grown man,' Flagg said. 'I brought you a glass of wine, my King, to show you that I, too, love you.'

He passed it to Roland, who looked absurdly touched.

Don't drink it, Father! Thomas thought suddenly – his mind was full of an alarm he couldn't understand. Roland's head came up suddenly and tilted, almost as if he had heard.

'He's a good boy, my Peter,' Roland said.

'Indeed,' Flagg replied. 'Everyone in the Kingdom says so.'

'Do they?' Roland asked, looking pleased. 'Do they, indeed?'

'Yes – so they do. Shall we toast him?' Flagg raised his glass.

No, Father! Thomas shouted in his mind again,

but if his father had heard his first thought, he didn't hear this one. His face shone with love for Thomas's elder brother.

'To Peter, then!' Roland raised the glass of poisoned wine high.

'To Peter!' Flagg agreed, smiling. 'To the King!'

Thomas cringed in the dark. *Flagg's making two different toasts! I don't know what he means, but . . . Father!*

This time it was Flagg who turned his darkly considering gaze toward the dragon's head for a moment, as if *he* had heard the thought. Thomas froze, and in a moment Flagg's gaze turned back to Roland.

They clinked glasses and drank. As his father quaffed the glass of wine, Thomas felt a splinter of ice push its way into his heart.

Flagg made a half-turn in his chair and threw his glass into the fire. 'Peter!'

'Peter!' Roland echoed, and threw his own. It smashed against the sooty brickwork at the back of the fireplace and fell into the flames, which for a moment seemed to flare an ugly green.

Roland raised the back of his hand to his mouth for a moment, as if to stifle a belch. 'Did you spice it?' he asked. 'It tasted . . . almost mulled.'

'No, my Lord,' Flagg said gravely, but Thomas thought he sensed a smile behind the mask of the magician's gravity, and that splinter of ice slipped further into his heart. Suddenly he wanted no more of spying, not ever. He closed the peepholes and crept back to his room. He felt first hot, then cold, then hot again. By morning he had a fever. Before he was well again, his father was dead, his brother imprisoned in the room at the top of the Needle, and he was a boy King at the age of barely twelve – Thomas the Light-Bringer, he was dubbed at the coronation ceremonies. And who was his closest advisor?

You guess.

When Flagg left Roland (the old man was feeling sprightlier than ever by then, a sure sign the Dragon Sand was at work in him), he went back to his dark basement rooms. He got out the tweezers and the packet containing the remaining few grains of sand and put them on his huge old desk. Then he turned his hourglass over and resumed reading.

Outside, the wind screamed and gobbled – old wives cringed in their beds and slept poorly and told their husbands that Rhiannon, the Dark Witch of the Coos, was riding her hateful broom this night, and wicked work was afoot. The husbands grunted, turned over, told their wives to go back to sleep and leave them alone. They were dull fellows for the most part; when an eye is wanted to see straws flying in the wind, give me an old wife any day.

Once a spider skittered halfway across Flagg's book, touched a spell so terrible not even the magician dared use it, and turned instantly to stone.

Flagg grinned.

When the hourglass was empty, he turned it over again. And again. And again. He turned it over eight times in all, and when the eighth hour's worth of sand was nearly gone, he set about finishing his work. He kept a large number of animals in a dim room down the hall from his study, and he went there first. The little creatures skittered and cringed when Flagg came near. He did not blame them.

In the far corner was a wicker cage containing half a dozen brown mice – such mice were everywhere in the castle, and that was important. Down here there were also huge rats, but it was not a rat Flagg wanted tonight. The Royal Rat upstairs had been poisoned; a simple mouse would be enough to make sure the crime came home to the Royal Ratling. If all went well, Peter would soon be as tightly locked up as these mice.

Flagg reached into the cage and removed one. It trembled wildly in his cupped hand. He could feel the rapid thrumming of its heart, and he knew that if he simply held it, it would soon die of fright.

Flagg pointed the little finger of his left hand at the mouse. The fingernail glowed faintly blue for a moment.

'Sleep,' the magician commanded, and the mouse fell on its side and went to sleep on his open palm.

Flagg took it back into his study and laid it on his desk, where the obsidian paperweight had rested earlier. Now he went into his larder and drew a little mead from an oaken barrel into a saucer. He sweetened it with honey. He put it on his desk, then went out into the corridor and breathed deeply at the window again.

Holding his breath, he came back in and used the tweezers to pour all but the last three or four grains of Dragon Sand into the honey-sweetened mead. Then he opened another drawer of his desk and removed a fresh packet, which was empty. Then, reaching all the way to the back of this drawer, he brought out a very special box.

The fresh packet was bewitched, but its magic was not very strong. It would hold the Dragon Sand safely only for a short while. Then it would begin to work on the paper. It would not set it alight, not inside the box; there would not be air enough for that. But it would smoke and smoulder, and that would be enough. That would be fine.

Flagg's chest was thudding for air, but he still spared a moment to look at this box and congratulate himself. He had stolen it ten years ago. If you had asked him at the time why he took it, he would have known no more than he knew why he had shown Thomas the secret passage that ended behind the dragon's head – that instinct for mischief had told him to take it and that he would find a use for it, so he had. After all those years in his desk, that useful time had come.

PETER was engraved across the top of the box.

Sasha had given it to her boy; he had left it for a moment on a table in a hallway when he had to run down the hallway after something or other; Flagg came along, saw it, and popped it into his pocket. Peter had been grief-stricken, of course, and when a prince is upset – even a prince who is only six years old – people take notice. There had been a search, but the box had never been found.

Using the tweezers, Flagg carefully poured the last few grains of Dragon Sand from the original packet, which had been wholly enchanted, into the packet which had been only incompletely enchanted. Then he went back to the window in the corridor to draw fresh breath. He did not breathe again until the fresh packet had been laid in the antique wooden box, the tweezers laid in there beside it, the top of the box slowly closed, and the original packet disposed of in the sewer.

Flagg was hurrying now, but he felt secure enough. Mouse, sleeping; box, closed; incriminating evidence safely latched inside. It was very well.

Pointing the little finger of his left hand at the mouse lying stretched out on his desk like a fur rug for pixies, Flagg commanded: 'Wake.'

The mouse's feet twitched. Its eyes opened. Its head came up.

Smiling, Flagg wiggled his little finger in a circle and said: 'Run.'

The mouse ran in circles.

Flagg wiggled his finger up and down.

'Jump.'

The mouse began to jump on its hind legs like a dog in a carnival, its eyes rolling wildly.

'Now drink,' Flagg said, and pointed his little finger at the dish holding the honey-sweetened mead.

Outside, the wind gusted to a roar. On the far side of the city, a bitch gave birth to a litter of two-headed pups.

The mouse drank.

'Now,' said Flagg, when the mouse had drunk enough of the poison to serve his purpose, 'sleep again.' And the mouse did.

Flagg hurried to Peter's rooms. The box was in one of his many pockets – magicians have many, many pockets – and the sleeping mouse was in another. He passed several servants and a laughing gaggle of drunken courtiers, but none saw him. He was still *dim*.

Peter's rooms were locked, but that was no problem for one of Flagg's talents. Three passes with his hands and the door was open. The young prince's rooms were empty, of course; the boy was still with his lady friend. Flagg didn't know as much about Peter as he did about Thomas, but he knew enough – he knew, for instance, where Peter kept the few treasures he thought worth hiding away.

Flagg went directly to the bookcase and pulled out three or four boring textbooks. He pushed at a wooden edging and heard a spring click back. He then slid a panel aside, revealing a recess in the back of the case. It was not even locked. In the recess was a silk hair-ribbon his lady had given him, a packet of letters she had written him, a few letters from him to her which burned so brightly he did not dare to send them, and a little locket with his mother's picture inside it.

Flagg opened the engraved box and very carefully shredded one corner of the packet's flap. Now it looked as if a mouse had been chewing at it. Flagg closed the lid again and put the box in the recessed space. 'You cried so when you lost this box, dear

Peter,' he murmured. 'I think you may cry even more when it's found.' He giggled.

He put the sleeping mouse beside the box, closed the compartment, and put the books neatly back in place.

Then he left, and slept well. Great mischief was afoot, and he felt confident that he had moved as as he liked to move – behind the scenes, seen by no one.

31

For the next three days, King Roland seemed healthier, more vigorous, and more decisive than anyone had seen him in years – it was the talk of the court. Visiting his ill and feverish brother in his apartments, Peter remarked to Thomas in awe that what remained of their father's hair actually seemed to be changing colour, from the baby-fine wispy white it had been for the last four years or so to the iron grey it had been in Roland's middle years.

Thomas smiled, but a fresh chill raced through him. He asked Peter for another blanket, but it wasn't really a blanket he needed; he needed to unsee that final strange toast, and that, of course, was impossible.

Then, after dinner on the third day, Roland complained of indigestion. Flagg offered to have the court physician summoned. Roland waved the suggestion away, saying that he felt fine, actually, better than he had in months, in years –

He belched. It was a long, arid, rattling sound. The convivial crowd in the ballroom fell silent with wonder and apprehension as the King doubled over. The musicians in the corner ceased playing. When Roland straightened up, a gasp ran through those present. The King's cheeks were aflame with colour. Smoking tears ran from his eyes. More smoke drifted from his mouth.

There were perhaps seventy people in that great dining hall – rough-dressed Riders (what we would call knights, I suppose), sleek courtiers and their ladies, attendants upon the throne, courtesans, jesters, musicians, a little troupe of actors in one corner who had been going to put on a play later, servants in great numbers. But it was Peter who ran to his father; it was Peter they all saw going to the doomed man, and this did not displease Flagg at all.

Peter. They would remember it had been Peter.

Roland clutched his stomach with one hand and his chest with the other. Smoke suddenly poured out of his mouth in a grey-white plume. It was as if the King had learned some amazing new way of telling the story of his greatest exploit.

But it was no trick, and there were screams as smoke poured not only from his mouth but from his nostrils, ears, and the corners of his eyes. His throat was so red it was nearly purple.

'*Dragon!*' King Roland shrieked as he collapsed into his son's arms. '*Dragon!*'

It was the last word he ever spoke.

The old man was tough – incredibly
tough. Before he died he was throwing off so much
heat that no one, not even his most loyal servants,
could approach closer to his bed than four feet.
Several times they threw buckets of water on the
poor dying King when they saw the bedclothes
beginning to smoulder. Each time, the water turned
instantly to steam that billowed through his bedchamber and out into the sitting room where courtiers and Riders stood in numb silence and ladies
clustered, weeping and wringing their hands.

Just before midnight, a jet of green flame shot
from his mouth and he died.

Flagg went solemnly to the door between the
bedchamber and the sitting room and announced the
news. There followed an utter silence that stretched
out for more than a minute. It was broken by a single
word which came from somewhere in the gathered
crowd. Flagg did not know who spoke that one
word, and he did not care. It was enough that it had
been spoken. Indeed, he would have bribed a man to
speak it if such could have been done with no danger
to him.

'Murder!' this someone said.

There was a universal gasp.

Flagg raised a solemn hand to his mouth to hide
a smile.

33

The court physician amplified one word to three: *Murder by poison*. He did not say *Murder by Dragon Sand*, for the poison was unknown in Delain, except to Flagg.

The King died shortly before midnight, but by dawn the charge was rife in the city and spreading outward toward the far reaches of the Eastern, Western, Southern, and Northern Baronies: *Murder, regicide, Roland the Good dead by poison*.

Even before then, Flagg had organized a search of the castle, from the highest point (the Eastern Tower) to the lowest (the Dungeon of Inquisition, with its racks and manacles and squeezing boots). Any evidence bearing on this terrible crime, he said, must be searched out and reported at once.

The castle rang with the search. Six hundred grimly eager men combed through it. Only two small areas of the castle were exempt; these were the apartments of the two princes, Peter and Thomas.

Thomas was barely aware of this; his fever had worsened to the point where the court physician had become deeply alarmed. He lay in a delirium as dawn's first light fingered its way into his windows. In his dreams, he saw two glasses of wine raised high, heard his father say again and again: *Did you spice it? It tasted mulled.*

Flagg had ordered the search, but by two in the morning, Peter had recovered enough of his wits to take charge of it. Flagg let him. These next few hours would be terribly important, a time when all could be won or lost, and Flagg knew it. The King was dead; the Kingdom was momentarily headless. But not for long; this very day, Peter would be crowned King at the foot of the Needle, unless the crime was brought home to the boy quickly and conclusively.

Under other circumstances, Flagg knew, Peter would have been under suspicion at once. People *always* suspect those who have the most to gain, and Peter had gained a great deal by his father's death. Poison was horrible, but poison might have won him a kingdom.

But in this case, the people of the Kingdom spoke of the boy's loss rather than the boy's gain. Of course, *Thomas* had lost his father, too, they might add after a pause – almost as if they were ashamed of the momentary lapse. But Thomas was a sullen, sulky, awkward boy who had often argued with his father. Peter's affection and respect for Roland, on the other hand, were known far and wide. And why, people would ask – if the monstrous idea was even raised, and so far it had not been – why would Peter kill his father for the crown when he would surely inherit it in a year, or three, or five?

If evidence of the crime were to be found in a secret place that only Peter knew, however – a place in the prince's own rooms – the tide would turn quickly. People would begin to see a murderer's face beneath a mask of affection and respect. They would point out that, to the young, a year may seem like three, three like nine, five like twenty-five. Then they would point out that the King had seemed, in the last few days of his life, to be coming out of a long, dark time – had seemed to be growing hale and vigorous again. perhaps, they would say, Peter had believed his father was entering a long, healthy Indian summer, had panicked and done something as foolish as it was monstrous.

Flagg knew something else; he knew that people have a deep and instinctive distrust of all Kings and princes, for these are people who may order their deaths with a single nod, and for crimes as petty as dropping a handkerchief in their presence. Great Kings are loved, lesser Kings are tolerated; Kings-to-be represent a scary unknown quantity. They might come to love Peter if given a chance, but Flagg knew they would also condemn him quickly if shown enough evidence.

Flagg thought such evidence would be forth-coming soon.

Nothing more than a mouse. Small . . . but big enough in its way to shake a kingdom to its foun-dations.

34

·I·n Delain there were only three stages of being: childhood, half-manhood or -womanhood, and adulthood. These 'half-years' lasted from four-teen to eighteen.

When Peter entered half-manhood, the scolding nannies were replaced with Brandon, his butler, and

Dennis, Brandon's son. Brandon would be Peter's butler for years yet, but probably not forever. Peter was very young, and Brandon was nearing fifty. When Brandon was no longer able to buttle, Dennis would take over. Brandon's family had buttled high royalty for nearly eight hundred years, and were justifiably proud of the fact.

Dennis rose each morning at five o'clock, dressed, laid out his father's suit, and shined his father's shoes. Then he wandered blearily into the kitchen and ate breakfast. At quarter to six, he set out from the family's home on the west side of the castle keep and entered the castle proper by the Lesser West Door.

Promptly at six o'clock he would reach Peter's rooms, let himself quietly in, and go about the early chores – building a fire, making half a dozen breakfast muffins, heating water for tea. Then he would quickly circle the three rooms, setting them to rights. This was usually easy, because Peter was not a messy boy. Last of all, he would return to the study and lay out breakfast, for the study was where Peter liked to eat the meals he took in his rooms – usually at his desk by the east windows, with a history book open before him.

Dennis didn't like getting up early, but he liked his job very much, and he liked Peter, who was always patient with him, even when he made a mistake. The only time he had ever raised his voice to Dennis was when Dennis had brought him a light lunch and had neglected to put a napkin on the tray.

'I'm very sorry, y'Highness,' Dennis had said on that occasion. 'I just never thought –'

'Well next time, *do* think!' Peter said. He was not shouting, but it was a close thing. Dennis had never neglected to put a napkin on Peter's tray again – and sometimes, just to be safe, he put on two.

Morning chores done, Dennis faded into the background and his father took over. Brandon was every bit the perfect butler, with his cravat neatly knotted, his hair pulled tightly back and rolled in a bun at the nape of his neck, his coat and breeches without a speck, his shoes shined to a mirror gloss (a mirror gloss Dennis was responsible for). But at night, with his shoes off, his coat hung in the closet, his cravat loosened, and a glass of bundle-gin in his hand, he looked to Dennis a much more natural man.

'Tell you something to always be remembrun, Denny,' he had said to his son on many occasions while in this comfortable state. 'There may be as many's a dozen things in this world which last, but surely no more, and may be less. Passey-o-nut love of a woman don't last, and a runner's wind don't last, nor does a braggart's wind, nor does haytime in the summer or sugartime in spring thaw. But two things that do last is one, royalty, and another, service. If you stick with your young man until he's an old man, and if you take care of him proper, he'll take care of you proper. You serve him an' he'll serve you, if you take the turn o' my mind. Now pour me another glass, and take a drop for yourself, if you like, but no more than a drop or your mother'll skin us both alive.'

Undoubtedly, some sons would quickly have grown bored with this catechism, but Dennis did not. He was the rarest of sons, a boy who had reached twenty and still thought his father wiser than himself.

On the morning after the King's death, Dennis hadn't had to force himself blearily out of bed at five o'clock; he had been awakened at three by his father, with the news of the King's death.

'Flagg's rared up a search party,' his father said, eyes full of bloodshot distress, 'and that's right enough. But my master will be leading it soon enough, I'll warrant, and I'm off to help him hunt for the fiend who done it, if he'll have me.'

'Me, too!' Dennis cried, grabbing for his breeches.

'Not at all, not at all,' his father said with a hard sternness that made Dennis subside at once. 'Things'll go forrad here just as they always have, murder or no – the old ways must be kept to now more than ever. My master and your master will be crowned King at noon, and that's well enough, although he comes to the crown in a bad time. But the death of a King by violence is always an evil thing if it comes not on the field of battle. The old ways will hold, doubt it not, but there may be trouble in the meantime. What's best for you, Dennis, is to go about your work just the same as always.'

He was gone before Dennis could protest.

And when five o'clock came, Dennis told his mother what his father had said and told her he should get about his morning round, even though he knew Peter would be gone. Dennis's mother was more than agreeable. She was dying for news. She told him to go, of course . . . go and then come back to her no later than eight of the clock, and tell her all he heard.

So Dennis went to Peter's rooms, which were utterly deserted. Nevertheless, he observed his regular routine, finishing by setting breakfast in the prince's study. He looked ruefully at the plates and glasses, the jams and jellies, reflecting that surely none of those things would be used that morning. Still, going about his ordered course had made him feel better for the first time since his father had turned him out of bed, for he now understood that, for better or worse, things were never going to be the same again. Times had changed.

He was preparing to leave when he heard a sound. It was so muffled he couldn't rightly tell where it was – only the general area from which it came. He looked toward Peter's bookcase, and his heart leaped in his chest.

Tendrils of smoke were drifting from between the loosely shelved books.

Dennis leaped across the room and began pulling books out by double handfuls. He saw that the smoke was issuing from cracks at one side of the bookcase's back. Also, that sound was clearer with the books gone. It was some sort of animal, squeaking in pained distress.

Dennis clawed and pawed at the bookcase, his fright spiralling toward panic. If there was one thing people were afraid of in that time and place, it was fire.

Soon enough his fingers happened on the secret spring. Flagg had foreseen this, too – after all, the secret panel wasn't really very secret – enough to amuse a boy, but not much more. The back of the bookcase slid to the right a bit, and a puff of grey smoke wafted out. The smell that escaped with the smoke was extremely unpleasant – a mixture of cooking meat, frying fur, and smouldering paper.

Not thinking, Dennis swept the panel all the way open. Of course, when he did that, more air got in. Things which had been only smouldering before now showed the first winks of flame.

This was the crucial point, the one place where Flagg had to be content not with what he was sure would happen but with his best guess of what would *probably* happen. All his efforts of the last seventy-five years now swung upon the fragile hinge of what a butler's son might or might not do in the next five seconds. But the Brandons had been butlers since time out of mind, and Flagg had decided he must depend on their long tradition of impeccable behaviour.

If Dennis had frozen in horror at the sight of those blossoming flames, or if he had turned and run for a pitcher of water, all of Flagg's carefully planted evidence might have burned in greenish tinted flames. The murder of Peter's father would never have been laid at Peter's door and he would have been crowned King at noon.

But Flagg's judgment was right. Instead of freezing or going for water, Dennis reached in and beat the flames out with his bare hands. It took less than five seconds, and Dennis was barely singed. The doleful squeaking went on, and the first thing he saw when he had waved the smoke aside was a mouse, lying on its side. It was in its death agonies. It was only a mouse, and Dennis had killed dozens of them in the line of duty without the slightest feeling of pity. Yet he felt sorry for this poor little bugger. Something terrible, something he could not even begin to understand, had happened to it and was still happening to it. Smoke rose from its fur in fine ribbons. When he touched it, he drew his hand back with a hiss – it was like touching the side of a tiny stove, such as the one in Sasha's doll house.

More smoke drifted lazily from an engraved wooden box with its lid slightly ajar. Dennis lifted the lid a little. He saw the tweezers, the packet. A number of brownish spots had flowered on the packet and it smouldered sluggishly, but had not burst into flame . . . nor did it now. The flames had come from Peter's letters, which were, of course, not enchanted at all. It was the mouse that had set these alight with its fearfully hot body. Now there was only the sullenly smouldering packet, and something warned Dennis not to touch it.

He was afraid. There were things here that he didn't understand, things he was not sure he *wanted* to understand. The one thing he knew for sure was that he badly needed to speak to his father. His father would know what to do.

Dennis took the ash bucket and a small shovel from beside the stove and went back to the secret panel. He used the shovel to pick up the smoking body of the mouse and drop it into the ash bucket. He wet the charred corners of the letters once more, just be be sure. Then he closed the panel, replaced the books, and left Peter's apartments. He took the ash bucket with him, and now he did not feel like

Peter's loyal servant but like a thief – his booty was a poor mouse that died even before Dennis got back out the West Gate of the castle.

And before he had even reached his house on the far side of the castle keep, a horrible suspicion had dawned in his mind – he was the first in Delain to feel this suspicion, but he would not be the last.

He tried to push the thought out of his head, but it kept coming back. What sort of poison, Dennis wondered, had killed King Roland, anyway? Exactly what sort of poison had it been?

By the time he got back to the Brandon house, he was in a bad state indeed, and he would answer none of his mother's questions. Nor would he show her what was in the ash bucket. He told her only that he must see his father the moment he came in – it was dreadfully important. Then he went into his room and wondered exactly what sort of poison it had been. He only knew one thing about it, but that one thing was enough. It had been something hot.

Brandon arrived just before ten o'clock,
short-tempered, exhausted, and in no mood for foolishness. He was dirty and sweaty, there was a thin
cut across his forehead, and cobwebs flew from his
hair in long strings. They had found no sign of the
assassin at all. His only news was that preparations
for Peter's coronation were going full speed ahead in
the Plaza of the Needle, under the direction of Anders
Peyna, Delain's Judge-General.

His wife told him of Dennis's return. Brandon's
brow darkened. He went to the door of his son's
room and rapped not with his knuckles but with a
closed fist. 'Come 'ee out here, boy, and tell us why
you come back with the ash bucket from your
master's study.'

'No,' Dennis said. 'You come in here, Dad – I
don't want Mother to see what I've got, and I don't
want her to hear what we say to each other.'

Brandon barged in. Dennis's mother waited
apprehensively by the stove, expecting it was some
sort of semi-hysterical foolishness which the boy had
thought up, some ill-advised monkeyshine, and that
very soon she would hear Dennis's wails as her tired
and distraught husband, who must begin today at
noon to buttle not a prince but a King, took out all
his fears and frustrations on the boy's backside. She
hardly blamed Dennis; everyone in the keep seemed
hysterical this morning, running around like crazy
people just let out of bedlam, repeating a hundred

false rumours, then taking them back in order to repeat a hundred new ones.

But there were no raised voices from behind Dennis's door, and neither of them came out for more than an hour. When they did, a single look at her husband's white face made the poor woman feel like fainting dead away. Dennis scurried along at his father's heels like a scared puppy.

Now Brandon was carrying the ash bucket.

'Where are you going?' she asked timidly.

Brandon said nothing. It seemed that Dennis *could* say nothing. He only rolled his eyes at her and then followed his father out the door. She saw neither of them for twenty-four hours, and became convinced that both were dead – or even worse, that they were suffering in the Dungeon of Inquisition below the castle.

Her dire thoughts were not so unlikely, either, for those were a terrible twenty-four hours in Delain. The day mightn't have seemed so terrible in some places, places where revolt and upheaval and alarms and midnight executions are almost a way of life . . . there really are such places, although I wish I didn't have to say so. But Delain had for years – and even centuries – been an ordered and orderly place, so perhaps they were spoiled. That black day really began when Peter was *not* crowned at noon and ended with the stunning news that he was to be tried in the Hall of the Needle for the murder of his father. If Delain had had a stock market, I suppose it would have crashed.

Construction on the dais where the coronation was to take place began at first light. The platform would be a jury-rigged affair of plain boards, Anders Peyna knew, but he also knew that enough flowers and bunting would cover the rude spots. They had had no warning of the King's passing, because murder isn't a thing that can be predicted. If it could be, there would be no murders, and the world would almost certainly be a happier place. Besides, pomp and circumstance wasn't the point – the point was to make the people feel the continuity of the throne. If the citizens got the feeling that everything was still all right in spite of the terrible thing that had happened, Peyna didn't care how many flower girls got splinters.

But at eleven o'clock, construction abruptly ceased. The flower girls were turned away – many of them in tears – by the Home Guards.

At seven that morning, most of the Home Guards had begun dressing in their gorgeous red ceremonial uniforms and their tall grey Wolf-Jaw shakos. They were, of course, to form the ceremonial double line, an aisle down which Peter would walk to be crowned. Then, at eleven, they received new orders; strange unsettling orders. The ceremonial uniforms came off in a blazing hurry and their dull, dun-coloured combat uniforms went on instead. The showy but clumsy ceremonial swords were replaced with the lethal shortswords which were everyday equipment. Impressive but impractical Wolf-Jaw shakos were cast aside in favour of the squat leather helmets that were normal battle dress.

Battle dress – the very term was distressing. *Is there such a thing as* normal *battle dress? I do not think* so. Yet soldiers in battle dress were everywhere, their faces stern and forbidding.

Prince Peter has committed suicide! That was the most common rumour which went flying about the castle keep.

Prince Peter has been murdered! That one ran a close second.

Roland was not dead; it was a mistaken diagnosis, the physician has been beheaded, but the old King is insane and no one knows what to do. That was a third.

There were many others, some even more foolish.

No one slept as darkness stole over the confused, sorrowing castle keep. All the torches in the Plaza of the Needle were lit, the castle blazed with lights, and every house in the keep and on the hills below showed candles and lanterns, as frightened people gathered to talk about the day's events. All agreed wild work was afoot.

The night was even longer than the day. Mrs Brandon kept watch for her men in terrible loneliness. She sat at the window, but for the first time in her life, the air was rife with more gossip than she wanted to hear. Yet for all that, could she stop listening? She could not.

As the small hours of the morning stretched out endlessly toward a dawn that she felt would never come, a new rumour began to supplant all the old ones – it was incredible, unbelievable, and yet it was asserted with more and more assurance until even the guards at their posts were repeating it to one another in undertones. This new rumour terrified Mrs Brandon most of all, because she remembered – too well!

– how white poor Dennis's face had been when he had come in with the prince's ash bucket. There had been something inside, something that smelled sick and burnt, something he wouldn't show her.

Prince Peter's been taken in custody for the murder of his father, this awful rumour went. *He's been taken . . . Prince Peter's been taken . . . the prince has murdered his own father!*

Shortly before dawn, the distracted woman laid her head in her arms and wept. After a bit, her sobbing faded as she fell into a troubled sleep.

Now tell me what's in that bucket, and be quick about it! We want no fooling, Dennis, d'you understand me?' was the first thing Brandon said when he entered Dennis's room and closed the door behind him.

'I'll show you, Dad,' Dennis said, 'but first, answer me one question: what sort of poison was it that killed the King?'

'No one knows.'

'What were its ways?'

'Show me what's in the bucket, boy. Do it now.' Brandon balled a great hard fist. He did not shake it; he only held it up. That was enough. 'Show me now or be knocked aside.'

Brandon looked at the dead mouse for a long

time, saying nothing. Dennis watched, scared, as his dad's face grew paler, graver, greyer. The mouse's eyes had burned until they were nothing but charred black cinders. Its brown fur had been crisped black. Smoke still rose from its tiny ears, and its teeth, visible in its death grimace, were a sooty black, like the teeth in the grate of a stove.

Brandon made as if to touch it, and then pulled his hand back. He raised his face to his son and spoke in a hoarse whisper. 'Where did you find this?'

Dennis began to stammer out bundles of phrases which didn't mean a thing.

Brandon listened a moment and then squeezed his son's shoulder.

'Draw you a deep breath and put your thoughts all in a row, Denny,' he said. 'I'm on yer side in this, as I am in all else, yer know. Yer did right to keep the sight of this poor thing from yer mom. Now tell me how you found it, and where you found it.'

Eased and reassured, Dennis was able to tell his father the story. His telling was a bit shorter than mine, but it still look several minutes. His father sat in a chair, one knuckle digging into his forehead, shading his eyes. He asked no questions, did not even grunt.

When Dennis had finished. His father muttered four words in an undertone. Just four words – but they froze the boy's heart into a cold blue cake – or so it felt to him at the time. 'Just like the King.'

Brandon's lips were trembling with fright, but he seemed to be trying to smile.

'Do you suppose yonder animal was a King of Mice, Denny?'

'Dad . . . Daddy, I . . . I . . .'

'There was a box, you said.'

'Yes.'

'And a packet.'

'Yes.'

'And the packet was charred, but not burned.'

'Yes.'

'And tweezers.'

'Yes, like Mamma uses to pluck the hairs from out'n her nose –'

'Shh,' Brandon said, and dug his knuckle into his forehead again. 'Let me think.'

Five minutes went by. Brandon sat motionless, almost as if he had gone to sleep, but Dennis knew better. Brandon did not know that Peter's mother had given him the engraved box or that Peter had lost it when he was small; both of those things had happened long before Peter entered his half-man-hood and Brandon came into his service. He did know about the secret panel; he had happened on this in the very first year he had served Peter (and not very far into that year, either). As I may have said, it wasn't really a very secret compartment, as those things went – just enough to satisfy such an open boy as Peter. Brandon knew about it, but had never looked into it after that first time, when it had con-tained nothing more than the glorified junk that any boy calls his treasures – a Tarot deck with a few cards missing, a bag of marbles, a lucky coin, a braided bit of hair from Peony's mane. If a good butler under-stands anything, he understands that quality we call discretion, which is a respect for the borders of other people's lives. He had never looked in that compartment again. It would have been like stealing.

At last Dennis asked: 'Should we go over, Father, so you can look in the box?'

'No. We must go to the Judge-General with this mouse, and you must tell your story to him just as you've told it to me.'

Dennis sat down heavily on his bed. He felt as if he had been punched in the belly. Peyna, the man who ordered jail terms and beheadings! Peyna, with his white, forbidding face and his tall, waxy brow! Peyna, who was, below the King himself, the greatest authority in the Kingdom!

'No,' he whispered at last. 'Dad, I couldn't . . . I . . . I . . .'

'You must,' his father said sternly. 'This is a turrible business – the most turrible business I've ever known of, but it must be reckoned with and set right. You'll tell him just as you've told me, and then it'll be in his hands.'

Dennis looked in his father's eyes and saw that Brandon meant it. If he refused to go, his father would lay hold of the scruff of his neck and drag him to Peyna like a kitten, twenty years old or no.

'Yes, Dad,' he said miserably, thinking that when Peyna's cold, calculating eyes fell on him, he would simply drop dead of a heart attack. Then (with rising panic) he remembered that he had stolen an ash bucket from the prince's rooms. If he didn't die of fright the moment Peyna commanded him to speak, he would probably spend the rest of his life in the castle's deepest dungeon for theft.

'Be easy in your mind, Denny – easy as you

can be, anyway. Peyna's a hard man, but he's fair. You've done nothing to be ashamed of. Just tell him as you've told me.'

'All right,' Dennis whispered. 'Are we going now?'

Brandon got out of the chair and onto his knees. 'First we'll pray. Get here beside me, son.'

Dennis did.

27

Peter was tried, found guilty of regicide, and ordered imprisoned for life in the cold two rooms at the top of the Needle. All of this was done in only three days. It will not take long to tell you how neatly the jaws of Flagg's cruel trap closed around the boy.

Peyna did not order the preparations for the coronation stopped at once – in fact, he thought that Dennis must be mistaken, that there must be a reasonable explanation for all of this. Just the same, the condition of the mouse, so like the condition of the King, was impossible to ignore, and the Brandon family had a long and valued reputation for honesty and levelheadedness in the Kingdom. That was important, but there was something else of far greater importance: when Peter was crowned, there must not be a single stain on his reputation.

Peyna heard Dennis out and then summoned

Peter. Dennis really might have died of fright at the sight of his master, but he was mercifully allowed to go into another room with his father. Peyna gravely explained to Peter that a charge had been levelled against him . . . a charge that Peter himself might have played a part in the murder of Roland. Anders Peyna was not a man to mince words, no matter how much those words might hurt.

Peter was stunned . . . flabbergasted. You must remember that he was still trying to cope with the idea that his beloved father was dead, killed by a cruel poison that had burned him alive from the inside out. You must remember that he had been leading the search all night, had had no sleep, and was physically exhausted. Most of all, you must remember that, although he had a man's height and breadth of shoulder, he was only sixteen. This stunning news on top of all else caused him to do a very natural thing, but it was a thing he should have avoided at all costs under Peyna's cold and assessing eyes: he burst into tears.

If Peter had hotly denied the charge, or if he had expressed his shock and exhaustion and grief by laughing wildly at such an absurd idea, the whole thing might have ended right there. I'm sure *that* possibility never entered Flagg's mind, but one of Flagg's weaknesses was a tendency to judge others according to what was in his own black and murky heart. Flagg regarded everyone with suspicion, and believed everyone had hidden reasons for the things they did.

His mind was very complex, like a hall of mirrors with everything reflected twice at different sizes.

The track of Peyna's thoughts was not convoluted but very straightforward. He found it very difficult – almost impossible – to believe that Peter could have poisoned his father. If he had raged or laughed out loud, things probably would have ended without even a trip to investigate the supposed box with his name carved on it, or the packet and tweezers it supposedly held. Tears, however, looked very bad. Tears looked like an expression of guilt coming from a boy old enough to commit murder but not old enough to hide what he had done.

Peyna decided he must investigate further. He hated to do this, because it meant taking guards, and that meant some word, some whisper, of these momentary suspicions would leak out, to taint the first weeks of Peter's reign.

Then he reflected that perhaps even this could be avoided. He would take half a dozen Home Guards, no more. He could leave four stationed outside the door. After this ridiculous business had blown over, all of them could be shipped off to the remotest part of the Kingdom. Brandon and his son would also have to be sent away, Peyna thought, and that was a pity, but tongues had a way of wagging, especially when liquor loosened them, and the old man's liking for bundle-gin was well known.

So Peyna ordered work on the coronation platform temporarily suspended. He felt confident that work could begin again in less than half an hour, with the labourers sweating and cursing and hurrying to make up for lost time.

Alas –

The box, the packet, and the tweezers were there, as you know. Peter had sworn on his mother's name he had no such engraved box: his heated denial now looked very foolish. Peyna picked up the charred packet carefully with the tweezers, peered in, and saw three flecks of green sand. They were so small they could barely be seen, but Peyna, mindful of what had befallen both great King and humble mouse, put the packet back in the box and closed the lid. He ordered two of the four Home Guards still in the hall to step in, realizing reluctantly that the matter was steadily growing more serious.

The box was put carefully on Peter's desk, little wisps of smoke escaping from it. One of the guards was sent after the man who knew more about poisons than anyone else in the Kingdom.

That man, of course, was Flagg.

I had nothing to do with this, Anders,' Peter said. He had recovered himself, but his face was still pale and wretched, his eyes a deeper blue than the old Judge-General had ever seen them.

'The box *is* yours, then?'

'Yes.'

'Why did you deny that you had such a box?'

'I forgot. I haven't seen this box in probably eleven years or more. My mother gave it to me.'

'What happened to it?'

He's not calling me 'm'Lord' or 'your Highness' anymore, Peter thought with a chill. *He's not calling me by any term of respect at all. Can all of this really be happening, I wonder? Father poisoned? Thomas terribly ill? Peyna standing here and doing everything but accusing me of murder? And my box — where in the name of gods did it come from, and who put it in the secret compartment behind the books?*

'I lost it,' Peter said slowly. 'Anders, you don't really believe I murdered my father, do you?'

I did not . . . but now I wonder, Anders Peyna thought.

'I loved him dearly,' Peter said.

I always thought so . . . but now I wonder about that, too, Anders Peyna thought.

40

'**F**lagg bustled in and, without even looking in Peyna's direction, began immediately to bombard the numbed, frightened, outraged prince with questions about the search. Had any trace been found of the poison or the poisoner? Any sign of a plot uncovered? He himself was of the opinion that it might have been a single individual, almost surely insane. He had spent the whole morning before his crystal, Flagg said, but the crystal remained stubbornly dark. He didn't care, though, he could do more than shake bones and peer into crystals. He craved action, not spells. Anything the prince wanted him to do, any dark corner he wanted explored –

'We did not call you here to listen to you babble like your own parrot, with both heads talking at once,' Peyna said coldly. He did not like Flagg. As far as Peyna was concerned, the magician had been demoted to the position of Court Nobody at the moment of Roland's death. He might be able to tell them what those evil green flecks in the packet were, but that was the extent of his usefulness.

Peter'll have no truck with this weasel when he's crowned, Peyna thought. He got just that far, and then his thoughts derailed in dismay, because the chances of Peter's being crowned seemed to be growing slimmer.

'No,' Flagg said, 'I don't suppose you did.' He looked at Peter and said, 'Why am I summoned, my King?'

'*Don't call him that!*' Peyna exploded, deeply shocked in spite of himself. Flagg saw this shock on Peyna's face, and although he affected to look puzzled, he understood perfectly what it meant and was satisfied. A worm of suspicion was working its way toward the centre of the Judge-General's chilly heart. Good.

Peter turned his pale face away from both of them and looked out across the city, once more struggling for control of his emotions. His fingers were laced tightly together. His knuckles were white. He looked much older than sixteen just then.

'Do you see the box on the desk?' Peyna asked.

'Yes, Judge-General,' Flagg said in his stiffest, most formal voice.

'Inside is a packet which appears to be slowly charring. Inside the packet are what look like grains of sand. I would like you to examine them and see if you can tell me what they are. I urge you very strongly not to touch them. I believe that the substance in the packet may have caused King Roland's death.'

Flagg allowed himself to look worried. To tell the truth, he was feeling very fine. Playing a part always made him feel that way. He liked to act.

He picked up the packet, using the tweezers. He peered into it. His gaze sharpened.

'I want a piece of obsidian,' he said. 'I want it right now.'

'I have a piece in my desk,' Peter said dully, and brought it out. It was not as big as the one Flagg had used and then disposed of, but it was thick. He handed it to one of the Home Guards, who handed it to Flagg. The magician held it toward the light, frowning a little . . . but inside his heart, a little man was jumping excitedly up and down, turning cartwheels, and doing somersaults. The obsidian was much like his own, but one side was broken and jagged. Ah, the gods were smiling on him! Indeed, indeed, indeed they were!

'I dropped it a year or two ago,' Peter said, seeing Flagg's interest. He was unaware – as was Peyna, at least for the moment – that he had added another layer of bricks to the wall that was a-building around him. 'The half you're holding landed on my rug, which cushioned its fall. The other half landed on the stones, and shattered into half a hundred pieces. Obsidian is hard, but very brittle.'

'Indeed, my Lord?' Flagg said gravely. 'I've never seen such stone, although I've of course heard of it.'

He put the obsidian on Peter's desk, upended the packet over it, and poured the three grains of sand onto it. In a moment, little tendrils of smoke began to rise from the obsidian. All present could see that each grain was slowly sinking into the pockmark it was creating in the world's hardest known stone. The guards murmured uneasily at the sight.

'*Be silent!*' Peyna roared, whirling on them. The guards drew back, faces long and white with terror. This seemed more and more like witchcraft to them.

'I believe I know what these grains are, and how to test my idea,' Flagg said, rapping the words out. 'But if I'm right, the test must be performed as quickly as possible.'

'Why?' Peyna demanded.

'I believe these are grains of Dragon Sand,' Flagg said. 'I had a very small quantity once, but it disappeared, alas, before I could study it closely. It may well have been stolen.'

Flagg did not miss the way Peyna's eyes flicked toward Peter at this.

'I have been uneasy about it off and on ever since,' he went on, 'because it is reputed to be one of the deadliest substances on earth. I did not have a chance to test its properties and so doubted, but I see much of what I was told proved here, already.'

Flagg pointed at the obsidian. The dimples in which the three specks of green sand rested were each now nearly an inch deep – smoke rose from each like smoke from a tiny campfire. Flagg guessed that each grain had eaten through half the thickness of the stone.

'Those three specks of sand are working their way rapidly through a piece of the hardest rock we know,' he said. 'Dragon Sand is reputed to be so corrosive that it will eat through any solid – any solid at all. And it produces fearsome heat. You! Guard!'

Flagg pointed at one of the Home Guards. He stepped forward, not looking happy to have been chosen.

'Touch the side of the rock,' Flagg said, and as the guard reached a tentative hand forward to touch the paperweight, he added sharply: 'Just the side! Don't get your hand near those holes!'

The guard touched the paperweight and drew his hand back with a gasp. He stuck his fingers in his mouth, but not before Peyna had seen the blisters rising there.

'Obsidian conducts heat very slowly, I've heard,' Flagg said, 'but that piece is as hot as the top of a stove . . . all from three grains of sand that would fit on the moon of your pinkie fingernail, with room left over! Touch the prince's desk, Lord Judge-General!'

Peyna did. He was distressed and amazed by the heat under his hand. Soon the heavy wood must begin to blister and char.

'So we must act quickly,' Flagg said. 'Soon the desk itself will catch fire. If we breathe the fumes – always assuming the stories I've been told are true – all of us will die within days. But, to be sure, another test –'

At this, the Home Guards looked more uneasy than ever.

'All right,' Peyna said. 'What is this test? Be quick, man!' He detested Flagg more than ever now, and if he had ever felt it would not do to underestimate him, he felt that doubly now. Five minutes before, Peyna had been ready to dismiss the man as the Court Nobody. Now it seemed that their lives – and Peyna's case against Peter – depended on him.

'I propose to fill a bucket with water,' Flagg said, speaking more rapidly than ever. His dark eyes gleamed.

The Home Guards and Peyna stared at those small black holes in the obsidian, at those tiny ribbons of steam, with the evil fascination of birds hypnotized by a nest of weaving pythons. How deep into the obsidian now? How close to the wood? Impossible to tell. Even Peter was looking, although the tired mixture of sorrow and confusion had not left his face.

'Water from the prince's pump!' Flagg shouted at one of the guards. 'We want it in a bucket, or a deep pot or pan. Now! Now!'

The guard looked at Peyna.

'Do it,' Peyna said, trying not to sound frightened – but he *was* frightened, and Flagg knew it.

The guard went. In moments, they heard water

being pumped into a bucket he had found in the butler's cupboard.

Flagg was speaking again.

'I propose to dip my finger into this bucket and let a drop of water fall into one of those holes,' he said. 'We'll watch this closely, Lord Judge-General. We must see if the water which goes into the hole turns momentarily green. It's a sure sign.'

'And then?' Peyna asked tautly.

The Home Guard returned. Flagg took the bucket, set it on the desk.

'Then I'll put drops very carefully into the other two holes,' Flagg said. He spoke calmly, but his normally pallid cheeks were flushed. 'Water won't stop Dragon Sand, it's told, but it'll hold it.' This was making things quite a bit worse than they were, but Flagg wanted them frightened.

'Why not just douse it?' one of the guards blurted.

Peyna favoured this upstart with a horrible glare, but Flagg answered the question calmly as he dipped his pinkie finger into the bucket.

'Would you like me to wash those three grains of sand out of the holes they've made in the rock and somewhere onto the lad's desk?' he asked, almost jovially. 'We could leave you in here to put out the fire when the water dried up, sirrah!'

The guard said no more.

Flagg drew his dripping finger out of the bucket.

'Water's warm already,' he said to Peyna, 'just from sitting on the desk.'

He carefully brought his finger, from which a single drop of water hung, over one of the holes.

'Watch closely!' Flagg said sharply, and to Peter he sounded at that moment like a cheap peddler about to perform some monstrously deceiving trick. But Peyna bent close. The Home Guards craned their necks. That single drop of water hung from Flagg's finger, for a moment catching all of Peter's room behind it in perfect curved miniature. It hung . . . elongated . . . and dropped into the hole.

There was a spatting *hisss*, like the sound of grease dropped onto a hot iron skillet. A tiny geyser of steam arose from the hole . . . but before it did, Peyna clearly saw a cat's-eye flash of green. In that moment, Peter's fate was sealed.

'Dragon Sand, by the gods!' Flagg whispered hoarsely. '*Don't, for pity's sake, breathe that steam!*'

Anders Peyna's courage was as hard as his reputation, but he was afraid now. To him that single wink of green light had seemed inexpressibly evil.

'Put out the other two,' he said hoarsely. 'Now!'

'I told you,' Flagg said, calmly dipping his pinkie again and staring at the obsidian. 'They can't be put out – well, there is one way, the tales say, but only one. You wouldn't like it. Yet we can hold them, and then get rid of them. I think.'

He carefully plinked a drop into each of the other two holes. Each time there was a sullen green flash of light, and a plume of steam.

'We're all right for a bit, I think,' Flagg said. One of the Home Guards sighed in gusty relief. 'Bring me gloves . . . or folded cloths . . . anything I can use to pick up this rock. It's as hot as fury, and those drops of water will be boiled away in no time.'

Two hot pads from the butler's closet were

brought quickly. Flagg used them to grasp the obsidian. He lifted it, careful to keep it level, then dropped it into the bucket. As the obsidian sank to the bottom, all of them clearly saw the water turn a momentary light green.

'Now,' Flagg said expansively, 'that is well. One of these guards must take this bucket out of the castle, and to the large pump by the Great Old Tree in the middle of the keep. There you must draw a large basin of water, and put the bucket in the basin. The basin must be taken to the middle of Lake Johanna, and sunk in the middle. The Dragon Sand may heat up the lake in a hundred thousand years, but let those that come in that time – if any do – worry about that, I say.'

Peyna paused for just a moment, biting his lip in uncharacteristic indecision, and then he said: 'You and you and you. Do as he says.'

The bucket was removed. The Home Guards carried it like men carrying a live bomb. Flagg was amused, for all of this was, in large part, magician's foolery, as Peter himself had momentarily suspected. The single drops of water he had allowed to fall into the holes had not been enough to stop the corrosive effect of the sand – at least not for long – but he knew that the water in the bucket would damp it well. Even less liquid would have served for more of the sand . . . a goblet of wine, say. But let them believe what they would; in time they would turn against Peter with that much more fury.

When the guards had gone, Peyna turned to Flagg. 'You said there was one way the effect of Dragon Sand could be neutralized.'

'Yes – the stories say that if it is taken into a living being, that living being will burn in agony until it is dead . . . and when it is over – the dying – the power of the Dragon Sand also dies. I had meant to test it, but before I could do it, my sample disappeared.'

Peyna was staring at him, white around the lips. 'And on what sort of living being did you intend to test this damned stuff, Magician?'

Flagg looked at Peyna with bland innocence. 'Why, on a mouse, my Lord Judge-General, of course.'

At three that afternoon, a strange meeting took place in the Royal Court of Delain at the base of the Needle – a great room which, over the years, had become known simply as 'Peyna's Court'.

Meeting – I don't like that word. It's too tame and small to describe the momentous decision that was arrived at that afternoon. I cannot call it a hearing or a trial, because that gathering had no legal meaning at all, but it was very important, as I think you will agree.

The room was large enough to hold five hundred, but there were only seven there that afternoon. Six of them huddled close together, as if it made them nervous to be so few in a place meant for so many.

The royal arms of the Kingdom – a unicorn spearing a dragon – hung on one of the circular stone walls, and Peter found his gaze returning to this again and again. Besides himself, Peyna was there, and Flagg (it was Flagg, of course, who sat slightly apart from the others), and four of the Kingdom's Great Lawyers. There were ten Great Lawyers in all, but the other six were at various farflung places in Delain, hearing cases. Peyna had decided he couldn't wait for them. He knew he had to move fast and decisively, or the Kingdom might bleed. He knew it, but it galled him to know he would need the help of this cool young murderer to avert such bloodshed.

That Peter *was* a murderer was something Anders Peyna had now decided in his own heart. It wasn't the box, the green sand, or even the burning mouse that had decided him. It was Peter's tears. Peter, to do him credit, looked neither guilty nor weak now. He was pale but calm, completely in charge of himself again.

Peyna cleared his throat. The sound echoed dully back from the forbidding stone walls of the court chamber. He pressed a hand to his forehead and was not entirely surprised to find a sheen of cold sweat there. He had heard testimony in hundreds of great and solemn cases; he had sent more men than he cared to remember beneath the headsman's axe. But never had he thought he would have to attend a 'meeting' such as this, or the trial of a prince for the murder of his royal father . . . and such a trial would surely follow if all went as he hoped this afternoon. It was right, he thought, that he be sweating, and right that the sweat should be cold.

Just a meeting. Nothing legal here; nothing official; nothing of the Kingdom. But none of them – not Peyna, not Flagg, not the Great Lawyers, not Peter himself – were fooled. This was the real trial. This meeting. The power was here. That burning mouse had set a great course of events in motion. That course would either be turned here, as a great river may be turned near its source when it is still a brook, or it would be allowed to run onward, gathering power as it went, until no force on earth could turn it or stand before it.

Just a meeting, Anders Peyna thought, and wiped more sweat from his forehead.

42

Flagg watched the proceedings with a lively eye. Like Peyna, he knew that all would be decided here, and he felt confident.

Peter's head was up, his gaze firm. He met the eyes of each member of this informal jury in turn.

The stone walls frowned down on all seven. The spectators' benches were empty, but Peyna seemed to feel the weight of phantom eyes, eyes that *demanded* justice be rendered in this terrible matter.

'My Lord,' Peyna said at last, 'the sun made you King three hours ago.'

Peter looked at Peyna, surprised but silent.

'Yes,' Peyna said, as if Peter *had* spoken. The

Great Lawyers were nodding, and they looked dreadfully solemn. 'There has been no coronation, but a coronation is only a public event. It is, for all its solemnity, show and not substance. God, the law, and the sun make a King, not the coronation. You are King at this very minute, legally able to command me, all of us here, the entire Kingdom. This puts us in a terrible dilemma. Do you understand what it is?'

'Yes,' Peter said gravely. 'You think your King is a murderer.'

Peyna was a little surprised by this bluntness, but not entirely unhappy with it. Peter had always been a blunt boy; it was a pity that his surface bluntness had concealed such depths of calculation, but the important thing was that such bluntness, probably the result of a boy's stupid bravado, would speed things up.

'What we believe, my Lord, doesn't matter. Guilt or innocence is for a court to determine – so I've always been taught, so I believe with my most sincere heart. There is only one exception to this. Kings are above the law. Do you understand?'

'Yes.'

'*But –*' Peyna raised his finger. '*But* this crime was committed before you were King. So far as I know, this terrible situation has never come before a court of Delain before. The possibilities are terrible. Anarchy, chaos, civil war. To avert all of these things, my Lord, we must have your help.'

Peter looked at him gravely. 'I will help if I can,' he said.

And I think – I pray – you will agree to what I am

about to propose, Peyna thought. He was conscious of fresh sweat on his forehead, but he didn't wipe if off this time. Peter was only a boy, but he was a bright boy – he might take it as a sign of weakness. *You'll say you're agreeing for the good of the Kingdom, but a boy who could have the monstrous, twisted courage to kill his own father is also, I hope, a boy who cannot help believing he will get away with it. You believe we will help you cover this up, but oh my Lord, you are so wrong.*

Flagg, who could almost read these thoughts, raised his hand to his mouth to cover a smile. Peyna hated him, but Peyna had become his number-one helper without even knowing it.

'I want you to put aside the crown,' Peyna said.

Peter looked at him with grave surprise. 'Renounce the throne?' he asked. 'I . . . I don't know, my Lord Judge-General. I should have to think about that before I said yes or no. That might be hurting the Kingdom by trying to help it – as a doctor may kill a sick man by giving him too much medicine.'

The lad's clever, Flagg and Peyna thought together.

'You misunderstand me. It's not a renunciation of the throne I ask for. Only that you put the crown aside until this matter has been decided. If you are found innocent of your father's murder –'

'As I will be,' Peter said. 'If my father had ruled until I was old and toothless, it would have made me perfectly happy. I wanted only to serve him and support him and love him in all I did.'

'Yet your father *is* dead, and you stand accused by circumstance.'

Peter nodded.

'If you are found innocent, you would resume the crown. If you are found guilty –'

The Great Lawyers looked nervous at this, but Peyna did not flinch.

'If you are found guilty, you would be taken to the top of the Needle, where you would spend the rest of your life. None of the royal family may be executed; that law is a thousand years old.'

'And Thomas would become King?' Peter asked thoughtfully. Flagg stiffened slightly.

'Yes.'

Peter frowned, deep in thought. He looked terribly tired, but not confused or afraid, and Flagg felt a faint stirring of fear.

'Suppose I refuse?'

'If you refuse, then you become King in spite of terrible charges which have not been answered. Many of your subjects – most, in light of the evidence – will believe they have come to be ruled by a young man who murdered his own father to gain the throne. I think there will be revolt and civil war, and that those things will come before much time has passed.

'As for myself, I would resign my post and set out toward the west. I am old to begin over, but I should have to try to do so just the same. My life has been the law, and I could not serve a King who has not knelt to the law in such a matter as this.'

There was silence in the chamber, a silence that seemed very long. Peter sat with his head bowed, the heels of his hands planted against his eyes. They all watched and waited. Now even Flagg felt a thin film of sweat on his brow.

Finally Peter raised his head and took his hand from his eyes.

'Very well,' he said. 'Here is my command as King. I will put the crown aside until I am cleared of my father's murder. You, Peyna, will serve Delain as Chancellor during the time it is without a royal head. I would that the trial should take place as soon as may be – tomorrow, even, if that is possible. I will be bound by the decision of the court.

'But you will not try me.'

They all blinked and sat up straighter at this dry note of authority, but Yosef of the stables would not have been surprised by it; he had heard that tone in the boy's voice before, when Peter was only a stripling.

'One of these other four will do that,' Peter continued. 'I'll not be tried by the man who will hold power in my place . . . a man who, by his look and manner, already feels in his heart that I have committed this terrible crime.'

Peyna felt himself flush.

'One of these four,' Peter reiterated, turning to the Great Lawyers. 'Let four stones, three black and one white, be put in a cup. The one who draws the white stone shall preside at my trial. Do you agree?'

'My Lord, I do,' Peyna agreed slowly, hating the flush which even now wouldn't leave his cheeks.

Again, Flagg had to raise a hand to his mouth to cover a small smile. *And that, my little doomed Lord, is the only command you will ever give as King of Delain,* he thought.

43

The meeting which began at three o'clock was over by quarter past the hour. Senates and parliaments may drone on for days and months before deciding a single issue – and often the issue is never decided at all in spite of all the talk – but when great things happen, they usually happen fast. And three hours later, as dark was coming down, something happened which made Peter realize that, mad as it seemed, he was going to be found guilty of this terrible crime.

He was escorted back to his apartments by unsmiling, silent guards. His meals, Peyna said, would be brought to him.

Supper was fetched by a burly Home Guardsman with a heavy stubble of beard on his face. He was holding a tray. On it were a glass of milk and a large, steaming bowl of stew. Peter stood up as the guardsman came in. He reached for the tray.

'Not yet, my Lord,' the guardsman said, the sneer in his voice apparent. 'It needs seasoning, I think.' And with that he spat into the stew. Then, grinning, showing a mouthful of teeth and gaps like an ill-tended picket fence, he held the tray out. 'Here.'

Peter made no motion to take it. He was utterly astonished.

'Why did you do that? Why did you spit in my stew?'

'Does a child who murders his father deserve any better, *my Lord?*'

'No. But one who has not even been tried for the crime does,' Peter said. 'Take that out and bring me a fresh tray. Bring it in fifteen minutes, or you'll sleep tonight below Flagg in the dungeons.'

The guardsman's ugly sneer faltered for a moment and then returned. 'I think not,' he said. He tilted the tray, first just a little, then more, then more. The glass and bowl shattered on the flagstones. Thick stew splattered in ropes.

'Lick it up,' the guardsman said. 'Lick it up like the dog you are.'

He turned to go. Peter, suddenly blazing, leaped forward and slapped the man. The sound of the blow rang in the room like a pistol shot.

With a bellow, the scruffy guardsman pulled out his short-sword.

Smiling humourlessly, Peter lifted his chin and bared his neck. 'Go ahead,' he said. 'A man who would spit in another man's soup is perhaps also the sort of man who would cut an unarmed man's throat. Go ahead. Pigs also do God's bidding, I believe, and my shame and my grief are very great. If God wills me to live, I must, but if God wills me to die and has sent such a pig as you to do the killing, that is very well.'

The Home Guardsman's anger melted into confusion. After a moment he sheathed his sword.

'I'll not dirty my blade,' he said, but his words were almost a mumble, and he was not able to meet Peter's eye.

'Bring me fresh food and drink,' Peter said quietly. 'I don't know who you have been talking to, guardsman, and I don't care. I don't know why you are so eager to condemn me for my father's murder when no testimony has yet been heard, and I don't care about that, either. But you will bring me fresh meat and drink, and a napkin to go with them, and you will do this before the clock strikes half past six, or I will ring for Peyna, and you will sleep below Flagg tonight. My guilt is not proved, Peyna is yet mine to command, and I swear what I say is true.'

During this the Home Guardsman grew paler and paler, because he saw Peter did speak the truth. But this was not the only reason for his pallor. When his mates had told him the prince had been caught red-handed, he had believed them – he had *wanted* to believe them – but now he wondered. Peter did not look or speak like a guilty man.

'Yes, my Lord,' he said.

The soldier went out. A few moments later, the captain of the guard opened the door and looked in.

'I thought I heard some disturbance,' he said. His eye fell on the broken glass and crockery. 'Has there been trouble here?'

'No trouble,' Peter said calmly. 'I dropped the tray. The guardsman has gone to fetch me a fresh meal.'

The captain nodded and left.

Peter sat on his bed for the next ten minutes and thought deeply.

There was a brief knock on the door. 'Come,' Peter said.

The bearded, gap-toothed guard came in with a fresh tray. 'My Lord, I wish to apologize,' he said with awkward stiffness. 'I've never behaved so in my whole life, and I don't know what came over me. For my life I do not. I –'

Peter waved it away. He felt very tired. 'Do the others feel as you do? The other guards?'

'My Lord,' the guardsman said, carefully setting the tray on Peter's desk, 'I'm not sure *I* still feel the way I did.'

'But do the others feel that I am guilty?'

There was a long pause, and the soldier nodded.

'And is there some one reason they tell against me most of all?'

'They speak of a mouse that burned . . . they say you wept when Peyna confronted you . . .'

Peter nodded grimly. Yes. Weeping had been a bad mistake, but he hadn't been able to help it . . . and it was done.

'But most all they only say you were caught, that you wanted to be King, that it must be so.'

'That I wanted to be King and so it must be so,' Peter echoed.

'Yes, my Lord.' The guardsman stood looking at Peter miserably.

'Thank you. Go now, please.'

'My Lord, I apologize –'

'Your apology is accepted. Please go. I need to think.'

Looking as if he wished he had never been born, the Home Guardsman stepped out the door and closed it behind him.

Peter spread his napkin over his knees but didn't eat. Any hunger he might have felt earlier was now gone. He plucked at the napkin and thought of his mother. He was glad – very glad indeed – that she wasn't alive to see this, to see what he had come to. All of his life he had been a lucky boy, a blessed boy, a boy to whom, it sometimes seemed, no bad luck ever came. Now it seemed that all the bad luck which should have been his over the years had only been stored up to be paid at once, and with sixteen years of interest.

But most of all they say you wanted to be King and it must be so.

In some deep way he understood. They wanted a good King they could love. But they also wanted to know they had been saved by only a hair's breadth from a bad one. They wanted blackness and secrets; they wanted their fearful tale of rotten royalty. God only knew why. *They say you wanted to be King, they say it must be so.*

Peyna believes it, Peter thought, *and that guardsman believed it; they will all believe it. This is not a nightmare. I have been accused of my father's murder, and not all my good behaviour and my obvious love for him will dismiss the charge. And part of them* wants *to believe I did it.*

Peter carefully refolded his napkin and laid it over the top of the fresh bowl of stew. He could not eat.

44

There was a trial, and it was a great wonder, and there are histories of the event if you care to read them. But here's the root of the matter: Peter,

son of Roland, was brought before the Judge-
General of Delain by a burning mouse; tried in a
meeting of seven which was not a court; convicted
by a Home Guardsman who delivered his verdict by
spitting into a bowl of stew. That is the story, and
sometimes stories tell more than histories, and more
quickly, too.

45

When Ulrich Wicks, who drew the
white stone and took Peyna's place on the bench,
announced the verdict of the court, the spectators –
many of whom had sworn for years that Peter would
make the best King in Delain's long history –
applauded savagely. They rose to their feet and
surged forward, and if a line of Home Guards with
their swords drawn had not held them back, they
might well have overturned the sentence of lifelong
imprisonment and exile at the top of the Needle and
lynched the young prince instead. As he was led
away, spittle flew in a rain, and Peter was well
covered by it. Yet he walked with his head up.

A door to the left of the great courtroom
led into a narrow hallway. The hallway stretched
perhaps forty paces, and then the stairs began. They
wound up and up, around and around, all the way
to the top of the Needle, where the two rooms
Peter would live in henceforth, until the day he

died, awaited him. There were three hundred stairs in all. We will come to Peter at the top, in his rooms, and in good time; his story, as you will see, is not done. But we will not climb with him, because it was a climb of shame, leaving his rightful place as King at the bottom and marching, shoulders back and head erect, toward his place as prisoner of the Kingdom at the top – it would not be kind to follow him or any man on such a walk.

Let us instead think of Thomas for a while, and see what happened when he recovered his wits and discovered that he was King of Delain.

'No,' Thomas whispered in a voice that was utterly horrified.

His eyes had grown huge in his pale face. His mouth trembled. Flagg had just told him that he was King of Delain, but Thomas did not look like a boy who has been told he is the King; he looked like a boy who has been told he is to be shot in the morning. 'No,' he said again. 'I don't want to be King.'

It was true. All his life he had been bitterly jealous of Peter, but one thing he had never been jealous of was Peter's coming ascension to the throne. That was a responsibility Thomas had never in his wildest dreams wished for. And now one nightmare was piled on top of another. It seemed it wasn't enough

that he had awakened to the news that his brother
had been imprisoned in the Needle for the murder of
their father, the King. Now here was Flagg, with the
appalling news that *he* was King in Peter's place.

'No, I don't want to be King, I *won't be* King.
I . . . I refuse! *I UTTERLY REFUSE!*'

'You can't refuse, Thomas,' Flagg said briskly.
He had decided this was the best line to take with
Thomas: friendly but brisk. Thomas needed Flagg
more now than he had ever needed anyone in his
whole life. Flagg knew this, but he also knew that he
was uniquely at Thomas's mercy. He would be wild
and skittish for a time, apt to do anything, and care
would have to be taken to establish a firm hold over
the boy here at the outset.

*You need me, Tommy, but it would be a very bad
mistake for me to tell you that. No, you must say it to me.
There must be no question about who is in charge. Not
now, not ever.*

'*Can't* refuse?' Thomas whispered. He had
jerked upright on his elbows at Flagg's awful news.
Now he fell weakly back on his pillows again. '*Can't?*
I feel weak again. I think the fever's coming back.
Send for the doctor. I might need to be bled. I –'

'You're fine,' Flagg said, standing up. 'I've
filled you full of good medicine, your fever's gone,
and all you want is a little fresh air to finish the
job. But if you need a doctor to tell you the
same thing, Tommy' (Flagg let the smallest note of
reproach creep into his voice), 'then you need only
to pull the bell.'

Flagg pointed at the bell and smiled a little. It
was not a terribly kind smile.

'I understand your urge to hide in your bed, but I wouldn't be your friend unless I told you that any refuge you sense in your bed or in trying to stay sick, is a false refuge.'

'False?'

'I advise you to get up and begin working at getting your strength back. You're to be crowned with royal pomp and ceremony in three days' time. Being carried up the aisle in your bed to the platform where Peyna will stand with the crown and sceptre would be a humiliating way to start a kingly reign, but if it comes to that, I assure you they will do it. Headless kingdoms are uneasy kingdoms. Peyna means to see you crowned as soon as possible.'

Thomas lay on his pillows, trying to absorb this information. He was rabbit-eyed with fear.

Flagg grabbed his red-lined cloak from the bed-post, swirled it over his shoulders, and hooked its gold chain at his neck. Next he took a silver-headed cane from the corner. He flourished it, crossed his waist with it, and made a large bow in Thomas's direction. The cloak . . . the hat . . . the cane . . . these things scared Thomas. Here had come a terrible time when he needed Flagg more than he had ever needed him before, and Flagg looked dressed for . . . for . . .

He looks dressed for travelling.

His panic of a few moments ago was only a minor scare in comparison with the frightful cold hands which seized Thomas's heart now.

'And now, dear Tommy, I wish you a healthy disposition all of your life, all the cheer your heart can stand, a long, prosperous reign . . . and goodbye!'

He started for the door and had actually begun to think the boy was so utterly paralyzed with panic that he, Flagg, would have to think of some stratagem for returning to the little fool's bedside on his own, when Thomas managed a single, strangled word: 'Wait!'

Flagg turned back, an expression of polite concern on his face. 'My Lord King?'

'Where . . . where are you going?'

'Why . . .' Flagg looked surprised, as if it hadn't occurred to him until now to think Thomas would even care. 'Andua to start with. They are great sailors, you know, and there are many lands beyond the Sea of Tomorrow I've never seen. Sometimes a captain will take a magician on board for good luck, to conjure a wind if the ship is becalmed, or to tell the weather. If no one wants a magician – well, I am not as young as I was when I first came here, but I can still run a line and unfurl a sail.' Smiling, Flagg mimed the action, never dropping his cane.

Thomas was up on his elbows again. 'No!' he nearly screamed. 'No!'

'My Lord King –'

'*Don't call me that!*'

Flagg crossed to him, now allowing an expression of deeper concern to fill his face. '*Tommy*, then. Dear old Tommy. Whatever's wrong?'

'What's wrong? *What's wrong?* How can you be so *stupid?* My father's dead by poison, Peter's in the Needle for the crime, I must be King, you are planning to leave, and you want to know *what's wrong?*' Thomas uttered a wild, shrieky little laugh.

'But all these things must be, Tommy,' Flagg said gently.

'I can't be King,' Thomas said. He seized Flagg's arm, and his nails sank deeply into the magician's strange flesh. 'Peter was meant to be King, Peter was always the smart one, I was stupid, I *am* stupid, I can't be King!'

'God makes Kings,' Flagg said. *God . . . and sometimes magicians*, he thought with an inward titter. 'He has made *you* King, and mark me, Tommy, you *will* be King. Either you'll be King or there will be dirt shovelled over you.'

'Let it be dirt, then! I'll kill myself.'

'You'll do no such thing.'

'Better to kill myself than to be laughed at for a thousand years as the prince who died of fright.'

'You'll make a King, Tommy. Never fear. But I must go. These days are cold, but the nights are colder. And I want to be clear of the city before dusk falls.'

'No, stay!' Thomas clutched wildly at Flagg's cloak. 'If I must be King, then stay and advise me, as you advised my father! Don't go! I don't know why you want to go, anyway! You've been here forever!'

Ah, finally, Flagg thought. *This is good – in fact, this is RICH.*

'It *is* hard for me to go,' Flagg said gravely. 'Very hard. I love Delain. And I love *you*, Tommy.'

'Then stay!'

'You don't understand my situation. Anders Peyna is a powerful man – an *extremely* powerful man. And he doesn't like me. I should think it fair to say he probably hates me.'

'Why?'

Partly because he knows how long – how very long – I have been here. More, I think, because he senses exactly what I mean to Delain.

'It's hard to say, Tommy. I suppose it has to do with the fact that he is a very powerful man, and powerful men usually resent other men who are as powerful as themselves. People like a King's closest advisor, perhaps.'

'As you were my father's closest advisor?'

'Yes.' He picked up Thomas's hand and squeezed it for a moment. Then he let go of it and sighed mournfully. 'A King's advisors are much like the deer in a King's private park. Such deer are cosseted and petted and fed by hand. Both advisors and tame deer have pleasant lives, but I've all too often seen a tame park deer end up on the King's table when the King's Preserves wouldn't yield up a wild buck for that night's deer steaks or venison stew. When a ruling King dies, the old advisors have a way of disappearing.'

Thomas looked both angry and alarmed. 'Has Peyna threatened you?'

'No . . . he has been very good,' Flagg said. 'Very patient. I have read his eyes, however, and I know that his patience will not last forever. His eyes tell me that I might find the climate in Andua healthier.' He rose with another swirl of cape. 'So . . . as little as I like to go . . .'

'Wait!' Thomas cried again, and in his pinched, pallid face, Flagg saw all his ambitions about to be fulfilled. 'If you were protected when my father was King, because you were *his* advisor, wouldn't you be protected now that I am King, if you were *my* advisor?'

Flagg appeared to think deeply and gravely. 'Yes . . . I suppose . . . if you made it very clear to Peyna . . . *very* clear indeed . . . that any move made against me would be looked upon with royal disfavour. Very *great* royal disfavour.'

'Oh, I would!' Thomas said eagerly. 'I would! So will you stay? Please? If you go, I really will kill myself! I don't know anything about being a King, and I really will!'

Flagg still stood with his head down, his face deep in shadow, apparently thinking solemnly. He was, in fact, smiling.

But when he raised his head, his face was grave.

'I have served the Kingdom of Delain almost all of my life,' he said, 'and I suppose that if you commanded me to stay . . . to stay and serve you to the best of my abilities . . .'

'I do so command you!' Thomas cried in a quivering, febrile voice.

Flagg sank to one knee. 'My Lord!' he said.

Thomas, sobbing with relief, threw himself into Flagg's arms. Flagg caught him and held him.

'Don't cry, my little Lord King,' he whispered. 'All will be well. Yes, all will be very well for you and me and the Kingdom.' His grin widened, showing very white, very strong teeth.

*T*homas couldn't sleep a wink the night before he was to be crowned in the Plaza of the Needle, and in the early-morning hours of that dread day he was seized by a terrible fit of vomiting and diarrhoea brought on by nervousness – it was stage fright. Stage fright sounds both silly and comic, but there was nothing either silly or comic about this. Thomas was still only a little boy, and what he felt in the night, when we are all most alone, was an extremity of fear so great that it would not be wrong to call it mortal terror. He rang for a servant and bade him fetch Flagg. The servant, alarmed by Thomas's pallor and the smell of vomit in the room, ran all the way and hardly waited to be given entry before bursting in and telling Flagg that the young prince was very ill indeed, might even be dying.

Flagg, who had an idea of what the trouble was, told the servant to go and tell his master he would be with him shortly, and to fear nothing. He was there in twenty minutes.

'I can't go through with it,' Thomas moaned. He had vomited in his bed, and the sheets stank of it. 'I can't be King, I can't, please, you have to stop it from happening, how can I go through with it when I may vomit in front of Peyna and all of them, vomit or . . . or . . .'

'You'll be fine,' Flagg said calmly. He had mixed a brew which would both soothe Thomas's stomach and temporarily cement his bowels shut. 'Drink this.'

Thomas drank it.

'I'm going to die,' he said, putting the glass aside. 'I won't have to kill myself. My heart will just burst from fear. My father said that sometimes rabbits die that way in snares, even if they aren't badly hurt. And that's what I am. A rabbit in a trap, dying of fear.'

You're partly right, dear Tommy, Flagg thought. *You're not dying of fear as you think, but you are indeed a rabbit in a trap.*

'You will change your mind about that, I think,' Flagg said. He had been mixing a second potion. It was cloudy pink – a restful colour.

'What's that?'

'Something to calm your nerves and let you sleep.'

Thomas drank it. Flagg sat by his bedside. Soon Thomas was sleeping deeply – so deeply that if the servant had seen him at that moment, he might have believed his prediction had come true and Thomas was dead. Flagg took the boy's sleeping hand in his own and patted it with something like love. In his own way he *did* love Thomas, but Sasha would have known Flagg's love for what it was: the love of a master for his pet dog.

He is so much like his father, Flagg thought, *and the old man never knew it. Oh, Tommy, we will have wonderful times, you and I, and before I am done the Kingdom will run with royal blood. I'll be gone, but I won't go far, at least not at first. I'll come back in disguise just long enough to see your flyblown head on a spike . . . and to*

*open your brother's chest with my dagger, and rip his heart
from his chest, and eat it raw, as his father ate the heart of
his precious dragon.*

Smiling, Flagg left the room.

48

The coronation went off with no trouble
or complications at all. Thomas's servants (he had no
butler, being too young, but this would be provided
for soon) dressed him for the occasion in fine clothes
of black velvet which were strewn with jewels (*All
mine*, Thomas thought with wonder – and with
dawning greed – *These are all mine now*) and high
black boots of finest kid leather. When Flagg
appeared promptly at eleven-thirty and said, 'It is
time, my Lord King,' Thomas was far less nervous
than he had expected. The sedative the magician had
given him the night before was still working in him.

'Take my arm then,' he said, 'in case I stumble.'

Flagg took Thomas's arm. In the years to come,
it was a posture the inhabitants of the court city
would become very familiar with – Flagg appearing
to bear the boy King up as if he were an old man
instead of a healthy youngster.

They walked out together into bright wintry
sunshine.

A cheer so great it was like the sound of surf
breaking against the long, desolate strands of the

Eastern Barony greeted their coming. Thomas looked around, amazed at the sound, and his first thought was: *Where is Peter? Surely this must be for Peter!* Then he remembered that Peter was in the Needle and realized the cheering was for him. He felt a dawning pleasure . . . and I must tell you that the pleasure was not just in knowing the cheers were for him. He knew that Peter, locked in his lonely tower rooms, must hear the cheering, too.

What does it matter now that you were always best in lessons? Thomas thought with a mean happiness that pricked him even as it warmed him. *What does it matter now? You are locked in the Needle and I . . . I am to be King! What does it matter that you brought him a glass of wine every night and —*

But this last thought caused a strange, greasy sweat to rise on his forehead, and he put it away from him.

The cheers rose again and again as he and Flagg walked first to the Plaza of the Needle and then under the arch formed by the upraised ceremonial swords of the Home Guard, dressed again in their fine red ceremonial uniforms and their tall Wolf-Jaw shakos. Thomas began to positively enjoy himself. He raised a hand in salute, and his subjects' cheers became a storm. Men threw their hats in the air. Women wept for joy. Cries of *The King! The King! Behold the King! Thomas the Light-Bringer! Long live the King!* rose in the air. Thomas, who was only a boy, thought they were for him. Flagg, who had perhaps never been a boy, knew better. The cheers were because the time of unease was past. They were cheering the fact that things could go on as they always had, that the shops

could be reopened, that grim-eyed soldiers in tight leather hats would no longer stand watches around the castle in the night, that everyone could get drunk following this solemn ceremony and not worry about waking to the sounds of confused midnight revolt. No more than that, no less than that. Thomas could have been anyone, anyone at all. He was a figurehead.

But Flagg would see that Thomas never knew that.

Not, at any rate, until it was too late.

The ceremony itself was short. Anders Peyna, looking twenty years older than the week before, officiated. Thomas answered *I will, I shall*, and *I swear* in all the right places, as Flagg had coached him. At the end of the ceremonies, which were conducted in such solemn silence that even those at the farthest edges of the huge crowd could hear them clearly, the crown was placed on Thomas's head. Cheers rose again, louder than ever, and Thomas looked up – up and up the smooth, rounded stone side of the Needle, to the very top, where there was but one window. He couldn't see if Peter was looking down, but he hoped Peter was. He hoped Peter was looking down and biting his lips in frustration until the blood flowed down his chin, as Thomas had often bitten his own lips – bitten them until there was a fine white network of scars there.

Do you hear that, Peter? he shrilled in his mind. *They're cheering for* ME! *They're cheering for* ME! *They're finally cheering for* ME!

49

On his first night as King, Thomas the Light-Bringer awoke straight up and staring in bed, his face stark and horrified, his hands crammed against his mouth as if to stifle a scream. He had just had a terrible nightmare, one even worse than those in which he relived the awful afternoon in the Eastern Tower.

This dream had been a kind of reliving, too. He was in the secret passage again, spying on his father. It was the night his father had been so drunk and furious, striding around the room and shrilling defiance at the heads on the walls. But when his father came to the head of Niner, the things he said were not the same.

Why do you stare at me? his father shrieked in the dream. *He's killed me and I suppose you couldn't stop that, but how could you see your brother imprisoned for it? Answer me, damn you! I did the best I could, and look at me! Look at me!*

His father began to burn. His face turned the dull red of a well-banked fire. Smoke burst from his eyes, his nose, his mouth. He doubled over in agony and Thomas saw that his father's hair was on fire. That was when he woke up.

The wine! he thought now, in horror. *Flagg brought him a glass of wine that night! Everyone knew that Peter brought him wine every night, so everyone thought Peter poisoned the wine! But Flagg brought him wine that night, too, and he never did before! And the poison came from Flagg! He said it was stolen from him years ago, but . . .*

He would not allow himself to think of such things. He would *not*. Because if he *did* think of such things –

'He would kill me,' Thomas whispered, horrified.

You could go to Peyna. Peyna doesn't like him.

Yes, he could do that. But then all his old dislike and jealousy of Peter returned. If he told, Peter would be let out of the Needle and would take *his* place as King. Thomas would be no one again, just a bumbling prince who had been King for one day.

It had taken only one day for Thomas to discover he could *like* being King – he could like it very much, especially with Flagg to help him. Besides, he didn't really *know* anything, did he? He only had an idea. And his ideas had always been wrong.

He's killed me and I suppose you couldn't stop that, but how could you see your brother imprisoned for it?

Never mind, Thomas thought, it must be wrong, it *has* to be wrong, and even if it isn't, it serves him right. He turned over on his side, determined to go back to sleep. And after a long time, sleep came.

In the years ahead, that nightmare sometimes came again – his father accusing his hidden, spying son and then doubling over, smoking, his hair on fire. In those years, Thomas discovered two things: guilt and secrets, like murdered bones, never rest easy; but the knowledge of all three can be lived with.

If you had asked him, Flagg would have said with smiling contempt that Thomas could keep a secret from no one except a person who was mentally enfeebled, and perhaps not even from such a one as that. Certainly he could not keep a secret, Flagg would have said, from the man who had engineered his rise to the throne. But men like Flagg are full of pride and confidence in themselves, and although they may see much, they are sometimes strangely blind. Flagg never guessed that Thomas had been behind Niner that night, and that he had seen Flagg given Roland the glass of poisoned wine.

That was a secret Thomas kept.

Above the jubilee of the coronation, at the top of the Needle, Peter stood at a small window, looking down. As Thomas had hoped, he had seen and heard everything, from the first cheers when Thomas appeared on Flagg's arm to the last as he disappeared back into the palace itself, also on Flagg's arm.

He stood at the window for nearly three hours after the ceremony was over, watching the crowds.

They were loath to break up and go home. There was much to discuss and much to relive. This-One had to tell That-One just where he had been when he heard the old King was dead, and then they both had to tell T'other-One. The women had a final good cry over Roland and exclaimed over how *fine* Thomas had looked, and how *calm* he had seemed. The children chased each other and pretended *they* were Kings and rolled hoops and fell down and skinned their knees and screamed and then laughed and chased each other again. The men clapped one another on the back and told each other that they guessed all would be well now – it had been a terrible week, but now all would be well. Yet through all of this there ran a dull yellow thread of unease, as if they realized that all was *not* well, that the things which had gone so wrong when the old King had been murdered were not right yet.

Peter, of course, could tell none of this from his high, lonely perch in the Needle, but he sensed something. Yes, something.

At three o'clock, three hours early, the mead-houses opened, supposedly in honour of the new King's coronation, but mostly because there was business to be had. People wanted to drink and celebrate. By seven that night, most of the population of the city was reeling through the streets, drinking the health of Thomas the Light-Bringer (or brawling with each other). It was nearly dark when the revellers finally began to disperse.

Peter left the window, went to the one chair in his 'sitting room' (*that* name was a cruel joke), and simply sat there with his hands folded in his lap. He

saw and watched the room darken. His dinner came
– fatty meat, watery ale, and coarse bread so salty it
would have stung his mouth if he had eaten any. But
Peter did not eat the meat or bread, nor did he drink
the ale.

Around nine o'clock, as the carousing in the
streets began again (this time the crowds were much
more boisterous . . . almost riotous), Peter went
into his prison's second room, stripped to his singlet,
washed with water from the basin, knelt by his bed,
and prayed. Then he got into bed. There was only a
single blanket, although the little bedroom was very
cold. Peter pulled it to his chest, laced his hands
together in back of his head, and looked up into the
darkness.

From outside and below came screams and
cheers and laughter. Now and then there was the
sound of firecrackers, and once, near midnight, there
was an explosive gunpowder flatulence as a drunken
soldier set off a blank charge (the following day, the
unfortunate soldier was sent as far east as the Kingdom of Delain stretched, for his drunken salute to
the new King – gunpowder was rare in Delain, and
jealously hoarded).

Sometime after one in the morning, Peter at
last closed his eyes and slept.

The next morning, he was up at seven. He knelt,
shivering in the cold, his breath puffing white from
his mouth, goosebumps on his bare arms and legs,
and prayed. When his prayers were done, he dressed.
He went into the 'sitting room' and stood by the
window silently for nearly two hours, watching the
city come to life below him. That coming alive was

slower and crankier than usual; most of the adults in
Delain woke with drink-swollen heads. They stumbled to their jobs slowly, and in a foul temper. Many
of the men went to their tasks blistered by angry
wives who had no sympathy with their aching heads
(Thomas also had an aching head – he had drunk too
much wine the night before – but at least he was
spared the lecturing wife).

Peter's breakfast came, Beson, his Chief Warder
(who had a hangover of his own), fetched him plain
bran cereal with no sugar, watery milk that was
rapidly souring, and more of the coarse, salty bread.
This was a bitter contrast to the pleasant breakfasts
Peter had enjoyed in his study, and he ate none of it.

At eleven, one of the Lesser Warders fetched it
silently away.

'Young princeling means to starve, thinks I,' he
said to Beson.

'Good,' Beson replied indifferently. 'Spare us
the trouble of keeping him.'

'Maybe he fears poison,' the Lesser Warder ventured, and in spite of his aching head, Beson laughed.
The jest was a good one.

Peter spent most of his day in the 'sitting-room'
chair. In the later part of the afternoon, he stood
at the window again. The window was not barred.
Unless you were a bird there was nowhere to go but
straight down. No one, not Peyna, not Flagg, not
Aron Beson, worried that the prisoner might somehow climb down. The Needle's curving stone wall
was utterly smooth. A fly might have done it, but
not a man.

And if he grew depressed enough to jump,

would anyone care? Not much. It would save the state the expense of feeding and housing a blue-blooded murderer.

As the sun began to move across the floor and up the wall, Peter sat and watched it. His dinner – more fatty meat, watery ale, and salty bread – came. Peter did not touch it.

When the sun was gone, he sat in the dark until nine, and then went into the bedroom. He stripped to his singlet, knelt, and prayed with small white puffs coming from his mouth. He got into bed, laced his hands behind his head, and lay on his back, staring up into the darkness. He lay there thinking about what had become of him. Around one o'clock in the morning, he slept.

So he was on the second day.

And the third.

And the fourth.

For a full week Peter ate nothing, spoke nothing, and did nothing but stand at his sitting-room window or sit in his chair, watching the sun crawl across the floor and then up the wall to the ceiling. Beson was convinced that the boy was in an utter blackness of guilt and despair – he had seen such things before, especially among royalty. The boy would die, he thought, like a wild bird that was never meant to be caged. The boy would die, and good riddance to him.

But on the eighth day, Peter sent for Aron Beson and gave him certain instructions . . . and he did not give them like a prisoner.

He gave them like a King.

Peter *did* feel despair . . . but it was not as deep as Beson believed. He spent that first week in the Needle carefully thinking out his position, and trying to decide what he should do. He had fasted to clear his head. Eventually it *did* clear, but for a while he felt terribly lost, and the weight of his situation pressed down on his head like a blacksmith's anvil. Then he remembered one simple truth: *he* knew he hadn't killed his father, even if everyone else in the Kingdom thought he had.

During the first day or two, he grappled with useless feelings. The childish part of him kept crying out, *Not fair! This is not fair!* And of course it *wasn't*, but that sort of thinking got him no place. As he fasted, he began to regain control of himself. His empty belly peeled the childish part of him away. He began to feel cleaner, husked out, empty . . . like a glass waiting to be filled. After two or three days of eating nothing, the growlings in his stomach subsided, and he began to hear his *real* thoughts more clearly. He prayed, but part of him knew that he was doing more than praying; he was talking to himself, listening to himself, wondering if there was a way out of this prison in the sky where he had been so neatly put.

He had not killed his father. That was the first thing. Someone had blamed it on him. That was the second thing. Who? There was only one person who *could* have, of course; only one person in all of Delain who could have had such an awful poison as Dragon Sand.

Flagg.

It made perfect sense. Flagg knew he would have no place in a kingdom ruled by Peter. Flagg had been careful to make Thomas his friend . . . and to make Thomas fear him. Somehow, Flagg had murdered Roland and then arranged the evidence which had sent Peter here.

He was this far by the third night of Thomas's reign.

Then what was he to do? Simply accept? No, he wouldn't do that. Escape? He *couldn't* do that. No one had ever escaped from the Needle.

Except . . .

A glimmer came to him. This was on the fourth night, as he looked at his dinner tray. Fatty meat, watery ale, salty bread. A plain white plate. No napkin.

Except . . .

The glimmer grew brighter.

There might be a way to escape. There *might*. It would be horribly dangerous, and it would be long. At the end of much work, he might only die in spite of all his efforts. But . . . there might be a way.

And if he did escape, what then? Was there a way to bring the murder home to the magician? Peter did not know. Flagg was a wily old serpent – he would have left no evidence of what he had done to damn him later on. Could Peter worm a confession out of the magician? He *might* be able to, always assuming Peter could lay hands on him in the first place – Peter guessed that Flagg might disappear like smoke if he heard that Peter had escaped the Needle. Would anyone *believe* Flagg's confession, even if Peter could get one out of him? *Oh yes, he confessed to the murder of Roland*, people would say. *Peter, the escaped father-killer, had a sword to his throat. In a fix like that, I might confess to anything, even the murder of God!*

You might be tempted to laugh at Peter, turning such things over in his mind while he was still imprisoned three hundred feet in the sky. You might say he had gotten the cart quite a bit forward of the horse. But Peter had seen a way he might escape. It might, of course, only be a way to die young, but he thought it had a chance of working. Still . . . was there any reason to go through all the work if in the end it could come to nothing? Or, worse still, if it were to cause the Kingdom fresh harm in some way he did not see now?

He thought about these things and prayed over them. The fourth night passed . . . the fifth . . . the sixth. On the seventh night, Peter came to this conclusion: it was better to try than not to try; better to make an effort to right the wrong even if he died trying to do so. An injustice had been done. He discovered a strange thing — the fact that the injustice had been done to *him* didn't seem half so important as the fact that it had been done at all. It ought to be righted.

On the eighth day of Thomas's reign, he sent for Beson.

53

Beson listened to the speech of the imprisoned prince with incredulity and mounting rage. Peter finished and Aron Beson let loose a gutter flood of obscenity that would have made a horse drover blush.

Peter stood before it, impassive.

'You murdering snot-nosed hound!' Beson finished, in a tone that was close to wonder. 'I guess you think yer still livin in the bloody lap o luxury, with yer sairvants to run scurrying every time you lift one o yer perfoomed little fingers. But it ain't like that in here, my young prince. No, *sir*.'

Beson leaned forward from the waist, scruffy chin jutting, and although the stench of the man – sweat and thick cheap wine and great grey scales of dirt – was nearly overpowering, Peter did not give ground. There were no bars between them; Beson had yet to fear a prisoner, and certainly he felt no fear of this young whelp. The Chief Warder was fifty, short, broad of shoulder, deep in the gut. His greasy hair hung in tangles around his cheeks and down the back of his neck. When he had come into Peter's room, one of the Lesser Warders had locked the door behind them.

Beson balled his left hand into a fist and shook it under Peter's nose. His right hand slid into the pouch pocket of his shirt and closed around a smooth cylinder of metal. One hard smash with that loaded fist would break a man's jaw. Beson had done it before.

'You take your *requests*, and you jam them up

your nose with the rest of the boogers, my dear little prince. And the next time you call me in here for any such royal rubbage as *this*, you'll bleed for it.'

Beson started away towards the door, short and hunched over and almost troll-like. He travelled in his own tight little cloud of stink.

'You are in danger of making an extremely bad mistake,' Peter said. His voice was soft but grim, and it carried.

Beson turned back to him, his face incredulous. '*What* did you say?'

'You heard me,' Peter said. 'And when you speak to me next, you stinking little turnip, I think you had better remember you are speaking to royalty, don't you? My lineage did not change when I climbed those steps.'

For a moment Beson could not reply. His mouth opened and closed like the mouth of a fish yanked out of the ocean – although any fisherman catching something as ugly as Beson would surely have thrown it back. Peter's cool requests – requests delivered in a tone which made it clear that they were in reality demands not to be refused – made Beson's head buzz with fury. One of the requests had been that of either an utter sissy or an outright lunatic. That one Beson had dismissed at once as nonsense and tomfoolery. The other, however, had to do with his meals. That, combined with the firm resolute look in Peter's eye, suggested that the young prince had thrown off his despair and meant to live.

The future prospects for idle days and drunken nights had looked bright. Now they had dimmed again. This young boy looked very healthy, very strong. He might live a long time. Beson might very well have to look at the young murderer's face for the rest of his own life – *there* was a thought to set a man's teeth on edge! And –

Stinking turnip? Did he actually call me a stinking turnip?

'Oh, my dear little prince,' Beson said, 'I think you are the one who has made the mistake . . . but I can promise you'll never make it again.' His lips split open in a grin, revealing a few blackened stumps of teeth. Now, about to attack, he moved with surprising grace. His right hand came out of the pouch pocket, wrapped around the bar of metal.

Peter took a step backward, his eyes moving from Beson's fisted hands to Beson's face and then back to his fists. Behind Beson, the tiny barred window in the middle of Peter's door was opened. Two of the Lesser Warders were crammed there cheek to stubbly cheek, grinning and waiting for the fun to start.

'You know that royal prisoners are to be given some consideration in smaller matters,' Peter said, still backtracking and circling. 'That is tradition. And I have asked you for nothing untoward.'

Beson's grin widened. He imagined he heard fear in Peter's voice. He was mistaken. This error would shortly be brought home to him in a way to which he was unaccustomed.

'Such traditions are paid for, even among the royalty, my little prince.' Beson rubbed his left thumb and finger together. His right fist remained tightly balled around the chunk of metal.

'If you mean you wish an odd bit of cash from

time to time, that might be arranged,' Peter said, continuing to circle away. 'But only if you drop this foolish behaviour of yours right now.'

'Afraid, are you?'

'If anyone should be afraid here, I think it is you,' Peter said. 'You apparently mean to attack the brother of the King of Delain.'

This shot struck home, and for a moment Beson faltered. His eyes grew uncertain. Then he glanced towards the open window in the door, saw the faces of his Lesser Warders, and his own face darkened again. If he drew back now, he would have trouble with them – nothing he couldn't handle, of course, but still more annoyance than this little stinker was worth.

He moved forward in a rush and swung the weighted fist. He was grinning. The prince's screams as he fell to the stone floor with his smashed and squirting nose clutched in his hands would be, Beson thought, shrill and babyish.

Peter moved back easily, his feet moving as gracefully as if in a dance. He seized Beson's fist and was not surprised in the least by its weight – he had seen the gleam of metal between Beson's swelled fingers. Peter pulled with a wiry strength that Beson would not have believed five minutes ago. He spun through the air and hit the curving inner wall of Peter's 'sitting room' with a crash that rattled the few teeth remaining in his jaws. Stars exploded in his head. The metal cylinder flew from his fist and rolled across the floor. And before Beson could even begin to recover, Peter had sprung after it and seized it. He moved with the simple, pure liquidity of a cat.

This can't be happening, Beson thought with dawning dismay and stupid surprise. *This absolutely can't be happening*.

He had never feared entering the two-room prison at the top of the Needle, because there had never been a prisoner here, not of noble blood, not of royal blood, who could best him. Oh, there had been some famous fights up here, but he had taught them all who was boss. Perhaps they ruled the roost down below, but up here he was the boss, and they came to respect his dirty, compact power. But now this stripling of a *boy* . . .

Bellowing with rage, Beson came off the wall, shaking his head to clear it, and charged Peter, who had folded the cylinder of metal into his own right hand. The Lesser Warders stood staring at this unexpected development with stupid wonder. Neither thought of interfering; they could believe what was happening no more than Beson himself.

Beson ran at Peter with his arms outstretched. Now that the prince had gotten his fist weight away from him, Beson had no more interest in the sort of free-for-all swinging and hitting he thought of as 'boxing'. He meant to close with Peter, grapple with him, drive him to the floor, land on top of him, and then choke him unconscious.

But the space where Peter had been emptied with magical suddenness as the boy stepped aside and dropped into a crouch. As the squat, troll-like Chief Warder went past, trying to turn, Peter hit him three times with his right fist, which was closed around the metal cylinder. *Hardly fair*, Peter thought, *but, then, it wasn't I that brought this piece of metal into it, was it?* The blows did not look hard at all. If Beson had been watching a fight and had seen those three quick, fluttering punches thrown, he would have laughed and called them 'sissy punches'. Beson's idea of a real man's punch was a roundhouse blow that made the air whistle.

But they weren't sissy punches at all, no matter what the likes of Beson might have thought. Each was driven out from the shoulder, just as Peter's boxing instructor had taught him in their twice-weekly classes over the last six years. The punches were economical, they didn't make the air whistle, but Beson felt as if he had been kicked three times in rapid succession by a very small pony with very big hoofs. There was a flare of agony across the left side of his face as his cheekbone broke. To Beson, it sounded as if a small branch had snapped inside his head. He was driven into the wall again. He hit it like a rag doll and bounced back buckle-kneed. He stared at the prince with obvious dismay.

The Lesser Warders peering through the hole in the door were agog with surprise. Beson, being beaten by a *boy?* It was as unbelievable as rain would have been coming down from a clear blue sky. One of them now looked at the key in his hand, thought briefly of going in there, then thought better of it. A man could get hurt in there. He slipped the key into his pocket, where he could later claim to have forgotten it.

'Are you ready to talk reasonably now?' Peter wasn't even out of breath. 'This is silly. I require only two small favours of you, favours for which you can count on being well and amply repaid. You –'

With a roar, Beson flung himself at Peter again. This time Peter was not expecting an attack, but he managed to pull back anyway, the way a matador pulls back from a bull which charges unexpectedly – the matador may be surprised, perhaps even gored, but he rarely loses his grace. Peter did not lose his, but he *was* wounded. Beson's nails were long, ragged, and filthy – more like animal claws than human nails – and he liked to tell his Lesser Warders (on dark winter's nights when a gruesome tale seemed required) about the time he had slit a prisoner's neck from ear to ear with one of those thumbnails.

Now one drew a bloody line down Peter's left cheek as Beson flailed his way by. The cut zigzagged from temple to jawline, missing Peter's left eye by hardly half an inch. Peter's cheek fell open in a flap, and all his life he would bear the scar of his encounter with Beson there.

Peter grew angry. All the things that had happened to him over the last ten days seemed to slam together in his head, and for a moment he was almost – not quite, but *almost* – angry enough to kill the brutish Chief Warder instead of just teaching him a lesson he would never, never forget.

As Beson turned, he was rocked by left hooks and right jabs. The jabs would ordinarily have done little damage, but the pound and a half of metal in Peter's fist turned them into torpedoes. His knuckles sprung Beson's jaw. Beson roared with pain and again tried to close with Peter. This was a mistake. There was a crunch as his nose broke and blood flooded over his mouth and chin. It dripped on to his filthy jerkin. Then a bright flare of pain as that heavy right hand smashed his lips back. Beson spat a tooth onto the floor and tried to circle away. He had forgotten that his Lesser Warders were watching, afraid to interfere. Beson had forgotten his anger at the young prince's attitude, had lost his former desire to teach the young prince a lesson.

For the first time in his tenure as Chief Warder, he had forgotten everything but a blind desire to survive. For the first time in his tenure as Chief Warder, Beson was afraid.

Nor was it the fact that Peter was now punching him at will that frightened him. He had taken bad beatings before, although never at the hands of a prisoner. No, it was the look in Peter's eyes that had so terrified him. *It is the look of a King. Gods protect me, it is the face of a King – his fury blazes almost with the heat of the sun.*

Peter drove Beson against the wall, measured the distance to Beson's chin, and then drew back his weighted right fist.

'Do you need more convincing, turnip?' Peter asked grimly.

'No more,' Beson replied groggily, through his rapidly puffing lips. 'No more, my King, I cry your mercy, I cry your mercy.'

'What?' Peter asked, flabbergasted. 'What did you call me?'

But Beson was sliding slowly down the curved stone wall. When he had called Peter *my King*, he had done so as unconsciousness stole over him. He would not remember saying it, but Peter never forgot.

Beson was unconscious for over two hours. If not for his thick, snoring breaths, Peter would have been afraid that perhaps he really *had* killed the Chief Warder. The man was a gross, vicious, underhanded pig . . . but for all of that, Peter had no wish to kill him. The Lesser Warders took turns staring in the little window in the oaken door, their eyes wide and round – the eyes of small boys looking at the man-eating Anduan tiger in the King's Menagerie. Neither made any effort to rescue their superior, and their faces told Peter that they expected him to leap on the unconscious Beson at any moment and tear his throat out. Perhaps with his teeth.

Well, why shouldn't they think such things? Peter asked himself bitterly. *They think I killed my own father, and a man who would do such a thing might stoop to any low act, even that of killing an unconscious opponent.*

Finally Beson began to moan and stir. His right eye fluttered and came open – the left *couldn't* open, and wouldn't completely for some days.

The right eye looked at Peter not with hate, but with unmistakable alarm.

'Are you ready to speak reasonably?' Peter asked.

Beson said something Peter couldn't understand. It sounded like mush.

'I don't understand you.'

Beson tried again. 'You could have killed me.'

'I've never killed anyone,' Peter said. 'The time may come when I'll have to, but if it ever does, I hope I don't have to start with unconscious warders.'

Beson sat against the wall, looking at Peter with his one open eye. An expression of deep thought, absurd and a little frightening on his swelled and battered features, settled over his face.

At last he managed another mushy phrase. Peter thought he understood this one, but wanted to be absolutely sure.

'Repeat that, please, Mr Chief Warder Beson.'

Beson looked startled. As Yosef had never been called Lord High Groom before Peter, so Beson had never been called Mr Chief Warder.

'We can do business,' he said.

'That is very well.'

Beson struggled slowly to his feet. He wanted no more to do with Peter, at least not today. He had other problems. His Lesser Warders had just watched him take a bad beating at the hands of a boy who hadn't had anything to eat for a week. Watched – and no more, the cowardly sots. His head ached, and he might well have to whip those poor fools into line before he could slink off to bed.

He had started out when Peter called to him.

Beson turned back. That turning was really all it took. Both of them knew who was in charge here. Beson had been beaten. When his prisoner told him to wait, he waited.

'I have something I want to say to you. It will be good for both of us if I do.'

Beson said nothing. He only stood and watched Peter warily.

'Tell *them*' – Peter jerked his head towards the door – 'to close the spyhole.'

Beson stared at Peter for a moment, then turned towards the staring warders and gave the command.

The Lesser Warders currently jammed cheek to cheek into the opening, stood there staring, not understanding Beson's blurred words . . . or pretending not to. Beson ran his tongue over his blood-flecked teeth and spoke more clearly, obviously with some pain. This time the peephole was swung shut and bolted from the outside . . . but not before Beson had heard the contemptuous laughter of his underlings. He sighed wearily – yes, they would have to be taught some hard lessons before he could go home. Cowards learned quickly, though. This prince, whatever else he might be, was surely no coward. He wondered if he really wanted to do any business at all with Peter.

'I want to give you a note to take to Anders Peyna,' Peter said. 'You'll come back for it tonight, I hope.'

Beson said nothing, but he was trying very hard to think. This was the most unsettling twist yet. Peyna! A note to Peyna! He had had a cold moment when Peter reminded him that he was the brother of the King, but it had been nothing compared with this. Peyna, by the gods!

The more he thought of it the less he liked it.

King Thomas might not much care if his older brother was roughed up in the Needle. The older brother had murdered their father, for one thing; Thomas probably didn't feel much brotherly love right now. And more important, Beson felt little or no fright when the name of King Thomas the Light-Bringer was invoked. Like almost everyone else in Delain, Beson had already begun to view Thomas with a certain contempt. But Peyna, now . . . Peyna was different.

To the likes of Beson, Anders Peyna was more frightening than a whole marching regiment of Kings, anyway. A King was a distant sort of being, bright and mysterious, like the sun. It didn't matter if the sun went behind the clouds and froze you, or came out all hot and white to bake you alive – either way you only accepted, because what the sun did was far beyond the ability of mortal creatures to understand or to change.

Peyna was a more earthly being. The sort of being Beson could understand . . . and fear. Peyna with his narrow face and his ice-blue eyes, Peyna with his high-collared judge's robes, Peyna who decided who would live and who would go under the headsman's axe.

Could this boy really command Peyna from his cell here at the top of the Needle? Or was it only a desperate bluff?

How can it be a bluff if he means to write him a note I shall myself deliver?

'If I were King, Anders Peyna would serve me in any way I commanded,' Peter said. 'I am not a King now, only a prisoner. Still, not long ago I did him a favour for which I think he is very grateful.'

'I see,' Beson replied, as noncommittally as he could.

Peter sighed. Suddenly he felt very weary, and wondered what sort of foolish dream he was pursuing here. Did he really believe he was taking the first few steps on the road to freedom by beating up this stupid warder and then bending him to his will? Did he have any real guarantee that Peyna would do even the smallest thing for him? Perhaps the concept of a favour owed was only in Peter's own mind.

But it had to be tried. Hadn't he decided, on his long, lonely nights of meditation as he grieved for both his father and himself, that the only real sin would be in not trying?

'Peyna is not my friend,' Peter went on. 'I won't even try to tell you that he is. I've been convicted of murdering my father, the King, and I shouldn't think I have a friend left in all of Delain, from north to south. Would you agree, Mr Chief Warder Beson?'

'Yes,' Beson said stonily. 'I would.'

'Nevertheless, I believe that Peyna will undertake to provide you with the bit of cash you are used to receiving from your inmates.'

Beson nodded. When a noble was imprisoned in the Needle for any length of time, Beson would commonly see that the prisoner got a better grade of food than the fatty meat and watery ale, fresh linen once a week, and sometimes a visit from a wife or a sweetheart. He did not do this free, of course. Imprisoned nobles almost always came from rich families, and there was always someone in those families willing to pay Beson for Beson's services, no matter what the crime had been.

This crime was of an exceptionally terrible nature, but here was this boy, saying that no less a one than Anders Peyna might be willing to provide the bribe.

'One other thing,' Peter said softly. 'I believe Peyna will do this because he is a man of honour. And if anything were to happen to me – if you and several of your Lesser Warders were to rush in here tonight, and beat me in revenge for the beating I have given you, for example – I believe that Peyna might take an interest in the matter.'

Peter paused.

'A *personal* interest in the matter.'

He looked closely at Beson.

'Do you understand me?'

'Yes,' Beson said, and then added: 'my Lord.'

'Will you provide me with pen, inkpot, blotter, and paper?'

'Yes.'

'Come here.'

With some trepidation, Beson came.

The Chief Warder's stink was tremendous, but Peter did not draw away – the stink of the crime with which he had been accused had almost inured him to the smell of sweat and dirt, he had discovered. He looked at Beson with a hint of a smile.

'Whisper in my ear,' Peter said.

Beson blinked uneasily. 'What shall I whisper, my Lord?'

'A number,' Peter said.

After a moment, Beson did.

One of the Lesser Warders brought Peter the writing implements he had asked for. He gave Peter the wary look of an alley cat that has been often kicked, and skittered away before he could receive a helping of the anger that had been heaped on Beson's head.

Peter sat down at the rickety table by the window, breath puffing out in the deep cold. He listened to the restless whine of the wind around the tip of the Needle and looked down at the lights of the city.

Dear Judge-General Peyna, he wrote, and then stopped.

Will you see who this is from, crumple it in your hand, and throw it into the fire unread? Will you read it and then laugh contemptuously at the fool who murdered his father and then dared to expect help from the Judge-General of the land? Will you, perhaps, even see through the scheme, and understand what it is I'm up to?

Peter was in a cheerier frame of mind that evening, and thought the answer to all three questions would probably be no. His plan might well fail, but it was unlikely to be foreseen by such an orderly and methodical man as Peyna. The Judge-General would be as apt to imagine himself donning a dress and dancing a hornpipe in the Plaza of the Needle at the full of the moon as he was to guess what Peter was up to. *And what I'm asking is so little*, Peter thought. That ghost of a smile touched his lips again. *At least I hope and believe it will seem so . . . to him.*

Bending forward, he dipped the quill pen in the inkpot and began to write.

56

On the following evening, shortly after nine had struck, Anders Peyna's butler answered an unaccustomedly late knock and looked down his long nose at the figure of the Chief Warder standing on the doorstep. Arlen – that was the butler's name – had seen Beson before, of course; like Arlen's master, Beson was a part of the Kingdom's legal machinery. But Arlen did not recognize him now. The beating Peter had given Beson had had a day to set, and his face was a sunset of reds and purples and yellows. His left eye had opened a little, but was still little more than a slit. He looked like a dwarvish ghoul, and the butler began to swing the door shut almost at once.

'Wait,' Beson said in a hard growl that made the butler hesitate. 'I come with a message for your master.'

The butler hesitated for a moment and then began to swing the door closed again. The man's sullen, swollen face was frightening. *Could* he actually be a dwarf, down from the north country? Supposedly the last of those wild, fur-clad tribes had either died or been killed off in his grandfather's time, but still . . . one never knew . . .

'It is from Prince Peter,' Beson said. 'If you close this door, you will hear hard things later from your marster, thinks I.'

Arlen hesitated again, torn between closing the door against the ghoul and the power the name of Prince Peter still held. If this man came from Peter, he must be the Needle's Chief Warder. Yet –

'You don't *look* like Beson,' he said.

'You don't look like your father, neither, Arlen, and it's made me wonder more than once where your mother may have been,' the lumpish ghoul retorted rudely, and stuck a smudged envelope through the crack still open in the door. 'Here . . . take it to 'im. I'll wait. Close the door if you want, although it's devilish cold out here.'

Arlen didn't care if it was twenty below. He didn't intend to have the horrible-looking fellow toasting his feet in front of the fire in the servants' kitchen. He snatched the envelope, shut the door, bolted it, started away . . . then returned and double-bolted it.

57

Peyna was in his study, staring into the fire and thinking long thoughts. When Thomas had been crowned the moon had been new; it was not yet at the half, and already he did not like the way things were going. Flagg – that was the worst. Flagg.

The magician already wielded more power than in the days of Roland's reign. Roland had at least been a man, full of years, no matter how slow his thinking might have been. Thomas was only a boy, and Peyna feared that Flagg might soon control all Delain in Thomas's name. That would be bad for the Kingdom . . . and bad for Anders Peyna, who had never concealed his dislike of Flagg.

It was pleasant here in the study, before the crackling fire, but Peyna thought he nonetheless felt a cold wind around his ankles. It was a wind which might rise and blow away . . . everything.

Why, Peter? Why, oh why? Why couldn't you wait? And why did you have to seem so perfect on the outside, like a rose-red apple in autumn, and be so rotten below the skin? Why?

Peyna didn't know . . . and would not admit to himself, even now, that doubts as to whether or not Peter really *had* been rotten were beginning to nibble at his heart.

There was a knock at the door.

Peyna roused himself, looked around, and called out impatiently: 'Come! And it better be damned good!'

Arlen came in, looking ruffled and confused. He held an envelope in one hand.

'Well?'

'My Lord . . . there's a man at the door . . . at least, he *looks* like a man . . . that is, his face is most awfully puffed and swelled, as if he had gotten a terrible beating . . . or . . .' Arlen's voice trailed away.

'What's that to do with me? You know I don't

receive this late. Tell him to go away. Tell him to go
to the devil!'

'He says he's Beson, my Lord,' Arlen said, more
flustered than ever. He raised the smudged envelope,
as if to use it as a shield. 'He brought this. He says
it's a message from Prince Peter.'

Peyna's heart leaped at that, but he only frowned
more strenuously at Arlen.

'Well, is it?'

'From Prince Peter?' Arlen was almost gibbering now. His usual composure was utterly lost, and
Peyna found this interesting. He wouldn't have
believed Arlen would lose his composure come fire,
flood, or invasion of ravaging dragons. 'My Lord, I
would have no way of knowing . . . That is, I . . .
I . . .'

'Is it *Beson*, you idiot?'

Arlen licked his lips – actually *licked his lips*. This
was utterly unheard of. 'Well, it might be, my
Lord . . . it looks a bit like him . . . but the fellow on
the doorstep is most awfully bruised and lumpy . . .
I . . .' Arlen swallowed. 'I thought he looked like a
dwarf,' he said, bringing out the worst and then trying to soften it with a lame smile.

It IS Beson, Peyna thought. *It's Beson and if he
looks as if he's been beaten it's because Peter administered
the beating. That's why he brought the message. Because
Peter beat him and he was afraid not to. A beating's the
only thing that convinces his sort.*

There came a sudden feeling of exultation in
Peyna's heart: he felt as one might feel in a dark cave
when a light suddenly shines out.

'Give me the letter,' he said.

Arlen did. He then made as if to scuttle out, and this was also something new, because Arlen did not scuttle. *At least*, Peyna thought, his mind lawyerly as always, *I have never KNOWN him to scuttle.*

He let Arlen get as far as the study door, as a veteran fisherman will let a hooked fish run, and then pulled him up short. 'Arlen.'

Arlen turned back. He looked braced, as if to receive a reprimand.

'There are no more dwarves. Did your mother not tell you so?'

'Yes,' Arlen said reluctantly.

'Good for her. A wise woman. These dreams in your head must have come from your father. Let the Chief Warder in. To the servants' kitchen,' he added hastily. 'I have no wish to have him in here. He stinks. But let him into the servants' kitchen so he may warm himself. The night is cold.' Since the death of Roland, Peyna reflected, all the nights had been cold, as if in reproach for the way the old King had burned, from the inside out.

'Yes, my Lord,' Arlen said with marked reluctance.

'I'll ring for you shortly and tell you what to do with him.'

Arlen went out, a humbled man, and closed the door behind him.

Peyna turned the envelope over in his hands several times without opening it. The dirt was no doubt from Beson's own greasy fingers. He could almost smell the villain's sweat on the envelope. It had been sealed shut with a blot of common candle wax.

He thought, *I would do better, perhaps, to throw*

this directly into the fire, and think of it no more. Yes, throw it into the fire, then ring Arlen and tell him to give the little hunched-over Chief Warder – he really DOES *look like a dwarf, now that I think of it – a hot toddy and send him away. Yes, that is what I should do.*

But he knew that he wouldn't. That absurd feeling – that feeling that here was a ray of light in hopeless darkness – would not leave him. He put his thumb under the flap of the envelope, broke the seal, took out a brief letter, and read it by firelight.

58

Peyna,
I have decided to live.

I had read only a little about the Needle before I actually found myself in the place, and although I had heard a bit more, most of it was only gossip. One of the things I heard was that certain small favours might be purchased. It seems this really is so. I of course have no money, but I thought you might perhaps defray my expenses in this matter. I did you a favour not long ago, and if you were to pay the Chief Warder a sum of eight guilders – such sum to be paid anew at the beginning of each year I spend in this unhappy place – I would consider the favour repaid. This sum, you will notice, is very small. That is because I require only two things. If you will arrange for Beson to 'wet his beak' so that I may have them, I'll trouble you no more.

I am aware that you would be put in a bad light if it

came out that you have helped me, even in a small way. I
suggest that you make my friend Ben your go-between, if you
decide to do as I ask. I have not spoken to Ben since my arrest,
but I think and hope he remains true to me. I would ask him
rather than you, but the Staads are not well off, and Ben
has no money of his own. It shames me to ask money from
anyone, but there is no other to whom I may turn. If you feel
you cannot do as I request, I will understand.

I did not murder my father.

Peter

59

Peyna looked at this amazing letter for
quite some time. His eyes kept returning to the first
line, and the last.

I have decided to live.
I did not murder my father.

It did not surprise him that the boy continued to
protest – he had known criminals to go on for years
and years protesting their innocence of crimes of
which they were patently guilty. But it was not like
a guilty man to be so bald in his own defence. So . . .
so commanding.

Yes, that was what bothered him most about
the letter – its tone of command. A true King, Peyna
felt, would not be changed by exile; not by prison;
not even by torture. A true King would not waste

time justifying or explaining. He would simply state his will.

I have decided to live.

Peyna sighed. After a long time, he drew his inkpot to him, took a sheet of fine parchment from his drawer, and wrote upon it. His note was even shorter than Peter's had been. It took him less than five minutes to write it, blot it, sand it, fold it, and seal it shut. With that done, he rang for Arlen.

Arlen, looking much chastened, appeared almost at once.

'Is Beson still here?' Peyna asked.

'I think so, sir,' Arlen said. In fact he *knew* Beson was still there, because he had been peeking through the keyhole at the man, watching him lurch back and forth restlessly from one end of the servants' kitchen to the other with a cold chicken leg clutched like a club in one hand. When the meat on the leg was all gone, Beson had crunched the bones – horrible splintering sounds they made – and sucked contentedly at the marrow.

Arlen was still not utterly convinced the man was not a dwarf . . . perhaps even a troll.

'Give him this,' Peyna said, handing Arlen the note, 'and this for his trouble.' Two guilders clinked into Arlen's other hand. 'Tell him there may be a reply. If so, he's to bring it at night, as he did this one.'

'Yes, my Lord.'

'Don't linger and chat with him, either,' Peyna said. It was as close as he was able to come to making a joke.

'No, my Lord,' Arlen said glumly, and went

out. He was still thinking of the crunching sounds the chicken bones had made when Beson bit through them.

60

'**H**ere,' Beson said grumpily when he came into Peter's cell the next day, thrusting the envelope at Peter. In truth, he *felt* grumpy. The two guilders handed to him by Arlen had been an unexpected windfall, and Beson had spent most of the night drinking it up. Two guilders bought a great lot of mead, and today his head felt large and very painful. 'Damned messenger boy is what I'm turning into.'

'Thank you,' Peter said, holding the envelope.

'Well? Ain'tcher going to open it?'

'Yes. When you leave.'

Beson bared his teeth and clenched his fists. Peter simply stood there, looking at him. After a moment, Beson lowered his fists. 'Damned messenger boy, is all!' he repeated, and went out, slamming the heavy door behind him. There was the thud of iron locks being turned, followed by the sliding sound of bolts – three of them, each as thick as Peter's wrist – being slid into place.

When the sounds had stopped, Peter opened the note. It was only three sentences long.

I am aware of the long-standing customs of which you speak. The sum you mentioned could be arranged. I will

*do so, but not until I know what favours you expect to buy
from our mutual friend.*

Peter smiled. Judge-General Peyna was not a sly
man – slyness was not at all in his nature, as it was in
Flagg's – but he was exceedingly careful. This note
was the proof of that. Peter had expected Peyna's
condition. He would have felt wary if Peyna had
not asked what he wanted. Ben would be the go-
between, Peyna would cease to actually be a part of
the bribe very shortly, but still he walked carefully,
as a man might walk on loose stones which might
slide out from under his feet at any moment.

Peter went to the door of his cell, rapped, and
after some conversation with Beson, was given the
inkpot and dirty quill pen again. Beson did more
muttering about being nothing but a damned messenger boy, but he was not really unhappy about the
situation. There might be another two guilders in
this for him.

'If them two write back and forth long enough,
I guess I could get rich arter it,' he said to no one at
all, and roared laughter in spite of his aching head.

61

Peyna unfolded Peter's second note and
saw that this time the prince had left off both of their
names. That was very well. The boy learned fast. As
he read the note itself, his eyebrows shot up.

Perhaps your request to know my business is presump-
tuous, perhaps not. It matters little, since I am at your
mercy. Here are the two things your eight guilders per year
are to purchase:

    1. I want to have my mother's doll's house. It always
took me to pleasant places and pleasant adventures, and I
loved it much as a boy.

    2. I would like to have a napkin brought with my
meals — a proper royal napkin. The crest may be removed,
if you like.

    These are my requests.

Peyna read this note over and over again before
throwing it into the fire. He was troubled by it
because he did not understand it. The boy was up to
something . . . or was he? What could he want with
his mother's doll's house? So far as Peyna knew, it
was still in storage somewhere in the castle, gathering dust under a sheet, and there could be no reason
not to give it to him – not, that was, if a good man
was charged with going through it carefully first, to
make sure all the sharp things – tiny knives and such
– were removed from it. He remembered quite well
how enchanted Peter had been with Sasha's doll's
house as a very young boy. He also remembered –
vaguely, very vaguely – that Flagg had protested that
it was hardly fitting for a boy who would someday
be King to be playing with dolls. Roland had gone
against Flagg's advice that time . . . wisely, Peyna
thought, for Peter had given the doll's house up, all
in good time.

    Until now.

    Has he gone mad, then?

    Peyna did not think so.

The napkin, now . . . that he could understand. Peter had always insisted upon a napkin at every meal, always spread it neatly on his lap like a small tablecloth. Even when on camping trips with his father, Peter had insisted on a napkin. So oddly like Peter not to ask for better food than the normal poor prison rations, as almost any other noble or royal prisoner would have done before asking for anything else. No, he had asked for a napkin instead.

That insistence on always being neat . . . on always having a napkin . . . that was his mother's doing. I'm sure of it. Do the two go together, somehow? But how? Napkins . . . and Sasha's doll's house. What do they mean?

Peyna did not know, but that absurd feeling of hope remained. He kept remembering that Flagg had not wanted Peter to have the doll house as a little boy. Now, years later, here was Peter asking to have it again.

There was another thought wrapped up inside this, as neatly as filling is wrapped up in a tart. It was a thought Peyna hardly dared to entertain. If – just *if* – Peter had not murdered his father, who did that leave? Why, the person who had originally owned that hideous poison, of course. A person who would have been nothing in the Kingdom if Peter had followed his father . . . a person who was nearly *everything* now that Thomas sat on the throne in Peter's place.

Flagg.

But this thought was hideous to Peyna. It suggested that justice had somehow gone wrong, and that was bad. But it also suggested that the simple logic in which he had always prided himself had been washed away in the revulsion he had felt at the sight of Peter's tears, and this idea – the idea that he had made the single most important decision of his career on the basis of emotion rather than fact – was much worse.

What harm can there be in his having the doll's house, as long as the sharp things are removed?

Peyna drew his writing materials to him and wrote briefly. Beson had another two guilders to drink up – already he had been paid half the sum he would receive for the prince's little favours each year. He looked forward to more correspondence, but there was no more.

Peter had what he wanted.

62

As a child Ben Staad had been a slim, blue-eyed boy with curly blond hair. The girls had been sighing and giggling over him since he was nine years old. 'That'll stop soon enough,' Ben's father said. 'All the Staads make handsome enough lads, but he'll be like the rest of us when he gets his growth, I reckon – his hair'll darken to brown and he'll go around squintin' at everything and he'll have all the luck of a fat pig in the King's slaughtering pen.'

But neither of the first two predictions came true. Ben was the first Staad male in several generations to remain as blond at seventeen as he had been at seven, and who could tell a brown hawk from an auger hawk at four hundred yards. Far from developing a nearsighted squint, his eyes were amazingly keen . . . and the girls still sighed and giggled over him as much now, at seventeen, as they had when he was nine.

As for his luck . . . well, that was another matter. That most of the Staad men had been unlucky, at least for the last hundred years or so, was beyond argument. Ben's family thought that Ben might be the one to redeem them from their genteel poverty. After all, his hair hadn't darkened and his eyes hadn't grown dim, so why should he not escape the curse of bad luck as well? And after all, Prince Peter was his friend, and Peter would someday be King.

Then Peter was tried and convicted of his father's murder. He was in the Needle before any of the bewildered Staad family could get their minds around what had happened. Ben's father, Andrew, went to Thomas's coronation, and he came home with a bruise on his cheek – a bruise his wife thought it might be prudent not to speak of.

'I'm *sure* Peter's innocent,' Ben said that night at supper. 'I simply refuse to believe –'

The next moment he was sprawling on the floor, his ear ringing. His father was towering over him, pea soup dripping from his moustache, his face so red it was almost purple, and Ben's baby sister, Emmaline, was crying in her high chair.

'Don't mention the murdering whelp's name again in this house,' his father said.

'Andrew!' his mother cried. 'Andrew, he doesn't understand –'

His father, normally the kindest of men, turned his head and stared at Ben's mother. 'Be quiet, woman,' he said, and something in his voice made her sit down again. Even Emmaline stopped crying.

'Father,' Ben said quietly, 'I can't even remember the last time you struck me. It's been ten years, I think, maybe longer. And I don't think you ever struck me in anger, until now. But it doesn't change my mind. I don't believe –'

Andrew Staad raised one warning finger. 'I told you not to mention his name,' he said, 'and I meant it, Ben. I love you, but if you say his name, you'll be leaving my house.'

'I'll not say it,' Ben replied, getting up, 'but because I love you, Da'. Not because I'm scared of you.'

'Leave off!' Mrs Staad cried, more frightened than ever. 'I won't have the two of you bickering this way! Do you want to drive me insane?'

'No, Mother, don't worry, it's over,' Ben said. 'Isn't it, Da'?'

'It's over,' his father said. 'You're a good son in all things, Ben, and always have been, but mention him not.'

There were things Andy Staad felt he couldn't tell his son – although Ben was seventeen, Andy still saw him as a boy. He would have been surprised if he'd known that Ben understood his reasons for striking out quite well.

Before the unfortunate turn of events of which you now know, Ben's friendship with the prince had already begun changing things for the Staads. Their Inner Baronies farm had once been very large. Over the last hundred years, they had been forced to sell the land off, a piece at a time. Now fewer than sixty reels remained, most of that mortgaged.

But over the last ten years or so, things had gradually improved. Bankers who had been threatening first became willing to extend the outstanding mortgages, and to even offer new loans at interest rates so cheap they were unheard of. It had hurt Andrew Staad bitterly to see the land of his ancestors whittled away reel by reel, and it had been a happy day for him when he was able to go to Halvay, the owner of the next farm over, and tell him that he had changed his mind about selling him the three reels Halvay had wanted to buy for the last nine years. And he knew who he had to thank for these wonderful changes, too. His son . . . his son who was a close friend of the prince who also happened to be the King-in-waiting.

Now they were only the unlucky Staads again. If that had been all, only a case of things going back to the way they had been, he could have stood up under it without striking his son at the dinner table . . . an act of which he was already ashamed. But things *weren't* going to go back to the way they had been. Their position had worsened.

He had been lulled when the bankers had started behaving like sheep instead of wolves. He had borrowed a great deal of money, some to buy back land which he had already sold, some to install things like the new windmill. Now, he felt sure, the bankers would take off their sheepskins, and instead of losing the farm a piece at a time, he might lose it all at once.

Nor was that all. Some instinct had told him to forbid any of his family members to go to Thomas's coronation and he had listened to that inner voice. Tonight he was glad.

It had happened after the coronation, and he supposed he should have expected it. He went into a meadhouse to have a drink before starting home. He was very depressed by the whole sorry business of the King's murder and Peter's imprisonment; he felt that he needed a drink. He had been recognized as Ben's father.

'Did yer son help his friend do the deed, Staad?' one of the drunks had called, and there had been nasty laughter.

'Did he hold the old man while the prince poured the burnin' pizen down his thrut?' one of the others called out in turn.

Andrew had put his mug down half empty. This was not a good place to be. He would leave. Quickly.

But before he could get out, a third drunk – a giant of a man who smelled like a pile of mouldy cabbages – pulled him back.

'And how much did *you* know?' this giant had asked in a low, rumbling voice.

'Nothing,' Andrew said. 'I know nothing about this business, and neither does my son. Let me pass.'

'You'll pass when – and *if* – we decide to *let* yer pass,' the giant said, and shoved him backward into the waiting arms of the other drunks.

The pummelling then began. Andy Staad was pushed from one to the next, sometimes slapped, sometimes elbowed, sometimes tripped. No one quite dared to go as far as punching him, but they came close; he had seen in their eyes how badly they had wanted to. If the hour had been later and they had been drunker, he might have found himself in very serious trouble indeed.

Andrew was not tall, but he was broad-shouldered and well muscled. He calculated that he might be able to dust off any two of these idlers in a fair fight – with the exception of the giant, and he thought that perhaps he could give even *that* fellow a run for his money. One or two, possibly even three . . . but there were eight or ten there in all. If he had been Ben's age, full of pride and hot blood, he still might have had a go at them. But he was forty-five, and did not relish the thought of creeping home to his family beaten within an inch of his life. It would hurt him and frighten them, and both things would be to no purpose – it was just the Staad luck come home with a vengeance, and there was nothing to do but endure it. The barkeeper stood watching it all, doing nothing, not attempting to put a stop to it.

At last they had let him escape.

Now he feared for his wife . . . his daughter . . . and most of all for his son Ben, who would be the prime target for bullies such as those. *If it'd been Ben in there instead of me*, he thought, *they would have used their fists, all right. They would have used their fists and beaten him unconscious . . . or worse.*

So, because he loved his son and was afraid for him, he had struck him and threatened to drive him from the house if Ben ever mentioned the prince by name again.

People are funny, sometimes.

63

What Ben Staad didn't already understand abstractly about this strange new state of affairs he discovered very concretely the next day.

He had driven six cows to market and sold them for a good price (to a stockman who didn't know him, or the price mightn't have been so good). He was walking toward the city gates, when a bunch of loitering men set upon him, calling him murderer and accomplice and names even less pleasant.

Ben did well against them. They beat him quite badly in the end – there were seven of them – but they paid for the privilege with bloody noses, black eyes, and lost teeth. Ben picked himself up and went home, arriving after dark. He ached all over, but he was, all things considered, rather pleased with himself.

His father took one look at him and knew exactly what had happened. 'Tell your mother you fell down,' he said.

'Aye, Da',' Ben said, knowing his mother would not believe any such story.

'And after this, I'll take the cows to market, or the corn, or whatever we have to take to market . . . at least until the bankers come an' take the place out from under us.'

'No, Da',' Ben said, just as calmly as he had said *Aye*. For a young man who had taken a bad beating, he was in a very strange mood indeed – almost cheerful, in fact.

'What do you mean, telling me no?' his father asked, thunderstruck.

'If I run or hide, they'll come after me. If I stand my ground, they'll grow tired soon enough and look for easier sport.'

'If someone draws a knife from his boot,' Andrew said, voicing his greatest fear, 'you'll never live to see them grow tired of it, Benny.'

Ben put his arms around his father and hugged him tight.

'A man can't outsmart the gods,' Ben said, quoting one of Delain's oldest proverbs. 'You know that, Da'. And I'll fight for P . . . for him you'd not have me mention.'

His father looked at him sadly and said, 'You'll never believe it of him, will you?'

'No,' Ben said steadfastly. 'Never.'

'I think you've become a man while I wasn't looking,' his father said. 'It's a sad way to have to become a man, scuffling in the streets of the market with gutter louts. And these are sad times that have come to Delain.'

'Yes,' Ben said. 'They are sad times.'

'Gods help you,' Andrew said, 'and gods help this unlucky family.'

Thomas had been crowned near the end
of a long, bitter winter. On the fifteenth day of his
reign, the last of that season's great storms fell on
Delain. Snow fell fast and thick, and long after dark
the wind continued to scream, building drifts like
sand dunes.

At nine o'clock on that bitter night, long after
anyone sensible should have been out, there was a
fist began to fall on the front door of the Staad house.
It was not light or timid, that fist; it hammered
rapidly and heavily on the stout oak. *Answer me and
be quick*, it said. *I haven't all night.*

Andrew and Ben sat before the fire, reading.
Susan Staad, wife of Andrew and mother of Ben, sat
between them, working at a sampler which would
read GOD BLESS OUR KING when finished. Emmaline had long since been put to bed. The three of them
looked up at the knock, then around at each other.
There was only curiosity in Ben's eyes, but both
Andrew and Susan were instantly, instinctively
afraid.

Andrew rose, putting his reading glasses in his
pocket.

'Da'?' Ben asked.

'I'll go,' Andrew said.

*Let it only be some traveller, lost in the dark and
seeking shelter*, he hoped, but when he opened the
door a soldier of the King stood there on the stoop,
stolid and broad-shouldered. A leather helmet – the

helmet of a fighting man – clung to his head. There
was a shortsword in his belt, near to hand.

'Your son,' he said, and Andrew felt his knees
buckle.

'Why do you want him?'

'I come from Peyna,' the soldier said, and
Andrew understood that this was all the answer he
was to have.

'Da'?' Ben asked from behind him.

No, Andrew thought miserably, *please, this is too
much bad luck, not my son, not my son –*

'Is that the boy?'

Before Andrew could say no – useless as that
would have been – Ben had stepped forward.

'I am Ben Staad,' he said. 'What do you want
with me?'

'You must come with me,' the soldier said.

'Where?'

'To the house of Anders Peyna.'

'*No!*' his mother cried from the doorway of their
small living room. 'No, it's late, it's cold, the roads
are full of snow –'

'I have a sleigh,' the soldier said inexorably, and
Andrew Staad saw the man's hand drop to the shaft
of his shortsword.

'I'll come,' Ben said, getting his coat.

'Ben –' Andrew began, thinking: *We'll never see
him again, he's to be taken away from us because he knew
the prince.*

'It will be all right, Da',' Ben said, and hugged
him. And when Andrew felt that young strength
embracing him, he could almost believe it. But, he

thought, his son had not learned fear yet. He had not learned how cruel the world could be.

Andrew Staad held his wife. The two of them stood in the doorway and watched Ben and the soldier break their way through the drifts toward the sleigh, which was only a shadow in the dark with lanterns glowing eerily on either side. Neither of them spoke as Ben climbed up on one side, the soldier on the other.

Only one soldier, Andrew thought, *that's something. Maybe it's only for questioning that they want him. Pray it's only for questioning that they want my son!*

The Staads stood in silence, membranes of snow blowing around their ankles, as the sleigh pulled away from the house, the flames in the lanterns jiggling, the sleigh bells jingling.

When they were gone, Susan burst into tears.

'We'll never see him again,' she sobbed. 'Never, never! They've taken him! Damn Peter! Damn him for what he's brought my son to! Damn him! Damn him!'

'Shh, mother,' Andrew said, holding her tightly. 'Shh. Shh. We'll see him before morning. By noon at the latest.'

But she heard the quiver in his voice and cried all the harder. She cried so hard she woke little Emmaline up (or maybe it was the draught from the open door), and it was a very long time before Emmaline would go back to sleep. At last Susan slept with her, the two of them in the big bed.

Andy Staad did not sleep all that night.

He sat up by the fire, hoping against hope, but in his heart he believed he would never see his son again.

Ben Staad stood in Anders Peyna's study an hour later. He was curious, even a little awed, but not afraid. He had listened closely to everything Peyna said, and there had been a muted chink as money changed hands.

'You understand all of this, lad?' Peyna asked in his dry courtroom voice.

'Yes, my Lord.'

'I would be sure. This is no child's business I send you on. Tell me again what you are to do.'

'I am to go to the castle and speak to Dennis, son of Brandon.'

'And if Brandon interferes?' Peyna asked sharply.

'I am to tell him he must speak to you.'

'Aye,' Peyna said, settling back in his chair.

'I am not to say "Tell no one of this arrangement."'

'Yes,' Peyna said. 'Do you know why?'

Ben stood thoughtfully for a moment, head down. Peyna let him think. He liked this boy; he seemed coolheaded and unafraid. Many others brought before him in the middle of the night would have been gibbering with terror.

'Because if I said such a thing, he would be quicker to tell than if I said nothing,' Ben said finally.

A smile touched Peyna's lips. 'Good,' he said. 'Go on.'

'You've given me ten guilders. I'm to give two to Dennis, one for himself and one for whoever finds the doll house that belonged to Peter's mother. The other eight are for Beson, the Chief Warder. Whoever finds the doll's house will deliver it to Dennis. Dennis will deliver it to me. I will deliver it to Beson. As for the napkins, Dennis himself will take them to Beson.'

'How many?'

'Twenty-one each week,' Ben replied promptly. 'Napkins of the royal house, but with the crest removed. Your man will engage a woman to remove the royal crests. From time to time you will send someone to me with more money, either for Dennis or for Beson.'

'But none for yourself?' Peyna asked. He had already offered; Ben had refused.

'No. I believe that's everything.'

'You are quick.'

'I only wish I could do more.'

Peyna sat up, his face suddenly harsh and forbidding. 'You must not and you shall not,' he said. 'This is dangerous enough. You are procuring favours for a young man who has been convicted of committing a foul murder – the second-foulest murder a man may do.'

'Peter is my friend,' Ben said, and he spoke with a dignity that was impressive in its simplicity.

Anders Peyna smiled faintly, and raised one finger to point at the fading bruises on Ben's face. 'I would guess,' he said, 'that you are already paying for that friendship.'

'I would pay such a price a hundred times

over,' Ben said. He hesitated just a moment and then went on boldly: 'I don't believe he killed his father. He loved King Roland as much as I love my own da'.'

'Did he?' Peyna asked, apparently without interest.

'He did!' Ben cried. 'Do *you* believe he murdered his father? Do you *really* believe he did it?'

Peyna smiled such a dry and ferocious smile then that even Ben's hot blood was cooled.

'If I didn't, I should be careful who I said it to,' he said. 'Very, very careful. Or I should soon feel the headsman's blade go through my neck.'

Ben stared at Peyna silently.

'You say you are his friend, and I believe you.' Peyna sat up straighter in his chair and levelled a finger at Ben. 'If you would be a true friend, do just the things I have asked, and no more. If you see any hope for Peter's eventual release in your mysterious summons here – and I see by your face that you do – you must give that hope up.'

Rather than ring for Arlen, Peyna saw the boy out himself – out the back way. The soldier who had brought him tonight would be on his way to the Western Barony tomorrow.

At the door, Peyna said, 'Once more: do not stray from the things we've agreed upon *so much as one solitary bit*. The friends of Peter are not much cared for in Delain now, as your bruises prove.'

'I'd fight them all!' Ben said hotly. 'One at a time or all at once!'

'Aye,' Anders Peyna said with that dry,

ferocious smile. 'And would you ask your mother to do the same? Or your baby sister?'

Ben gaped at the old man. Fear opened in his heart like a small and delicate rose.

'It will come to that, if you do not exercise all your care,' Peyna said. 'The storms are not over in Delain yet, but only beginning.' He opened the door; snow swirled in, driven by a black gust of wind. 'Go home now, Ben. I think your parents will be happy to see you so soon.'

This was an understatement of some size. Ben's parents were waiting at the door in their nightclothes when Ben let himself in. They had heard the jingle of the approaching sleigh. His mother hugged him close, weeping. His father, red-faced, unaccustomed tears standing in his eyes, wrung Ben's hand until it ached. Ben remembered Peyna saying *The storms are not over but only beginning*.

And still later, lying in bed with his hands behind his head, staring up into the darkness and listening to the wind whistle outside, Ben realized that Peyna had never answered his question – had never said whether or not he believed Peter to be guilty.

66

'**O**n the seventeenth day of Thomas's reign, Brandon's son, Dennis, brought the first lot of twenty-one napkins to the Needle. He brought

them from a storeroom that neither Peter nor
Thomas nor Ben Staad nor Peyna himself knew
about – although all would become aware of it before
the grim business of Peter's imprisonment was done.
Dennis knew because he was a butler's son from a
long line of butlers, but familiarity breeds contempt,
so they say, and he thought nothing much about the
storeroom from which he fetched the napkins. We'll
speak more of this room later; let me tell you now
only that all would have been struck with wonder at
the sight of it, and Peter in particular. For had he
known of this room which Dennis took completely
for granted, he might have attempted his escape as
much as three years sooner . . . and much, for better
or for worse, might have been changed.

The royal crest was removed from each
napkin by a woman Peyna had hired for the quick-
ness of her needle and the tightness of her lips. Each
day she sat in a rocker just outside the doorway of
the storeroom, picking out stitches that were very
old indeed. When she did this her lips were tight
for more reasons than one; to unmake such lovely
needlework seemed to her almost a desecration, but
her family was poor, and the money from Peyna was
like a gift from heaven. So there she sat, and would
sit, for years to come, rocking and plying her needle

like one of those weird sisters of whom you may have heard in another tale. She spoke to no one, not even her husband, about her days of unmaking.

The napkins had a strange, faint smell – not of mildew but of must, as if from long disuse – but they were otherwise without fault, each of them twenty rondels by twenty, big enough to cover the lap of even the most dedicated eater.

There was a bit of comedy attached to the first napkin delivery. Dennis hung about Beson, expecting a tip. Beson let him hang about a while because he expected that sooner or later the dimwitted lad would remember to tip *him*. They both came to the conclusion that neither was going to be tipped at the same time. Dennis started for the door, and Beson helped him along with a kick in the seat of the pants. This caused a pair of Lesser Warders to laugh heartily. Then Beson pretended to wipe his bottom with the handful of napkins for the Lesser Warders' further amusement, but he was careful only to pretend – after all, Peyna was in this business somewhere, and it was best to tread lightly.

Perhaps Peyna would not be around a great deal longer, however. In the meadhouses and wineshops, Beson had begun to hear whispers that Flagg's shadow had fallen on the Judge-General, and that if Peyna was not very, very careful, he might soon be watching the proceedings at court from an even more commanding angle than the bench upon which he now sat – he might be looking in the window, these wags said behind their hands, from one of the spikes atop the castle walls.

On the eighteenth day of Thomas's reign, the first napkin was on Peter's breakfast tray when it was delivered in the morning. It was so large and the breakfast so small that it actually covered the meal completely. Peter smiled for the first time since he had come to this cold, high place. His cheeks and chin were shadowed with the beginnings of a beard which would grow full and long in these two draughty rooms, and he looked quite a desperate character . . . until he smiled. The smile lit his face with magical power, and made it strong and radiant, a beacon to which one could imagine soldiers rallying in battle.

'Ben,' he muttered, picking the napkin up by one corner. His hand shook a bit. 'I knew you'd do it. Thank you, my friend. Thank you.'

The first thing Peter did with his first napkin was to wipe away the tears that now ran freely down his cheeks.

The peephole in the stout wooden door popped open. Two Lesser Warders appeared again like the two heads of Flagg's parrot, packed into the tiny space cheek to scruffy cheek.

'Hope that baby won't forget to wipe his chin-ny-chin!' one cried in a cracked, warbling voice.

'Hope that baby won't forget to wipe the eggy off his shirty!' the other cried, and then both screamed with derisive laughter. But Peter did not look at them, and his smile did not fade.

The warders saw that smile and made no more jokes. There was something about it which forbade joking.

Eventually they closed the peephole and left Peter alone.

A napkin came with his lunch that day.

With his dinner that night.

The napkins came to Peter in his lonely cell in the sky for the next five years.

he doll's house arrived on the thirtieth day of Thomas the Light-Bringer's reign. By then modils, those first harbingers of Spring (which we call bluets) were coming up in pretty little roadside bunches. Also by then Thomas the Light-Bringer had signed into Law the Farmers' Tax Increase, which quickly became known as Tom's Black Tax. The new joke told in the meadhouses and wineshops was that the King would soon be changing his royal name to Thomas the Tax-Bringer. The increase was not eight per cent, which might have been fair, or eighteen per sent, which might have been bearable, but eighty per cent. Thomas had had some doubts about it at first, but it hadn't taken Flagg long to convince him.

'We must tax them more on what they admit they own, so we can collect at least some of what's due us on all they hide from the tax collector,' Flagg said. Thomas, his head fuddled by the wine that now flowed constantly in the court chambers of the castle, had nodded with what he hoped was a wise expression on his face.

For his part, Peter had begun to fear that the doll's house had been lost after all these years – and that was almost the truth. Ben Staad had commissioned Dennis to find it. After several days of fruitless searching, Dennis had confided in his good old da' – the only person he dared trust with such a serious matter. It had taken Brandon another five days to find the doll's house in one of the minor storage rooms on the ninth floor, west turret, where its cheerful pretend lawns and long, rambling wings were hidden under an ancient (and slightly moth-eaten) dustcloth that was grey with the years. All of the original furnishings were still in the house, and it had taken Brandon and Dennis and a soldier handpicked by Peyna three more days to make sure all the sharp things were removed. Then, at last, the doll's house was delivered by two squire boys, who toiled up the three hundred stairs with the heavy, awkward thing spiked to a board between them. Beson followed closely behind, cursing and threatening terrible reprisals if they should drop it. Sweat rolled down the boys' faces in rivers, but they made no reply.

When the door of Peter's prison opened and the doll's house was brought in, Peter gasped with surprise – not just because the doll's house was finally here, but because one of the two boys carrying it was Ben Staad.

Give not a sign! Ben's eyes flashed.

Don't look at me too long! Peter's flashed back.

After the advice he had given, Peyna would have been stunned to see Ben here. He had forgotten that the logic of all the wise old men in the world cannot often stand against the logic of a boy's heart, if the boy's heart is large and kind and loyal. Ben Staad's was all three.

It had been the easiest thing in the world to exchange places with one of the squires meant to carry the doll's house to the top of the Needle. For a guilder – all the money Ben had in the world, as a matter of fact – Dennis had arranged it.

'Don't tell your father of this,' Ben cautioned Dennis.

'Why not?' Dennis had asked. 'I tell my old da' almost everything . . . don't you?'

'I *did*,' Ben said, remembering how his father had forbidden him to mention Peter's name any more in the house. 'But when boys grow up, I think that sometimes changes. However that may be, you mustn't tell him this, Dennis. He might tell Peyna, and then I'd be in a hot pot on a high fire.'

'All right,' Dennis promised. It was a promise he kept. Dennis had been cruelly hurt when his master, whom he had loved, had been first accused and then convicted of murder. In the last few days, Ben had gone a long way towards filling the empty place in Dennis's heart.

'That's good,' Ben said, and punched Dennis playfully on the shoulder. 'I only want to see him a minute, and refresh my heart.'

'He was your best friend, wasn't he?'

'Still is.'

Dennis had stared at him, amazed. 'How can you claim a man who murdered his own father as your best friend?'

'Because I don't believe he did it,' Ben said. 'Do you?'

To Ben's utter amazement, Dennis burst into wretched tears. 'All my heart says the same, and yet –'

'Listen to it, then,' Ben said, and gave Dennis a large rough hug. 'And dry off your mug before someone sees you bawling like a kid.'

'Put it in the other room,' Peter said now, distressed at the slight tremble in his voice. Beson didn't notice; he was too busy cursing the two boys for their slowness, their stupidity, their very existence. They carried the doll's house into the bedroom and set it down. The other boy, who had a very stupid face, dropped his end too quickly and too hard. There was the tiny sound of something breaking inside. Peter winced. Beson cuffed the boy – but he smiled as he did it. It was the first good thing that had happened to him since these two lads had appeared with the accursed thing.

The stupid boy stood up, wiping the side of his face, which was already starting to swell, and staring at Peter with frank wonder and fear, his mouth wide open; Ben remained on his knees a moment longer. There was a small rattan mat in front of the house's front door – what we would call a welcome mat, I suppose. For just a moment Ben allowed his thumb to move over the top of this, and his eyes met Peter's.

'Now get out!' Beson cried. 'Get out, both of you! Go home and curse your mothers for ever

bringing such slow, clumsy fools as yourselves into
the world!'

The boys passed Peter, the loutish one shrinking
away as if the prince might have a disease he could
catch. Ben's eyes met Peter's once more, and Peter
trembled at the love he saw in his old friend's gaze.
Then they were gone.

'Well, you have it now, my good little princeling,' Beson said. 'What shall we be bringing you
next? Little ruffly dresses? Silk underpants?'

Peter turned slowly and looked at Beson. After
a moment, Beson dropped his eyes. There was something frightening in Peter's gaze, and Beson was
forced to remember again that, sissy or not, Peter
had beaten him so badly that his ribs had ached for
two days and he had had dizzy spells for a week.

'Well, it's your business,' he muttered. 'But
now that you have it, I could find a table for you to
put it on. And a chair to sit in while you . . .' He
grimaced. 'While you play with it.'

'And how much would this cost?'

'A mere three guilders, I should think.'

'I have no money.'

'Ah, but you know powerful people.'

'No more,' Peter said. 'I traded a favour for a
favour, that's all.'

'Sit on the floor, then, and get chilblains on your
arse, and be damned to you!' Beson said, and strode
from the room. The little flood of guilders he had
enjoyed since Peter came to the Needle had apparently dried up. It put Beson in a foul mood for days.

Peter waited until he had heard all the locks and
bolts go rattling home before lifting the rattan mat

Ben had rubbed with his thumb. Beneath he found a square of paper no larger than the stamp on a letter. Both sides had been written on, and there were no spaces between the words. The letters were tiny indeed – Peter had to squint to read them, and guessed that Ben must have made them with the aid of a magnifying glass.

Peter – Destroy this after you have read it. I don't believe you did it. Others feel the same I am sure. I am still your friend. I love you as I always did. Dennis does not believe it, either. If I can ever help get to me through Peyna. Let your heart be steadfast.

As he read this, Peter's eyes filled with warm tears of gratitude. I think that real friendship always makes us feel such sweet gratitude, because the world almost always seems like a very hard desert, and the flowers that grow there seem to grow against such high odds. 'Good old Ben!' he whispered over and over again. In the fullness of his heart, he couldn't think to say anything else. 'Good old Ben! Good old Ben!'

For the first time he began to think that his plan, wild and dangerous as it was, might have a chance of succeeding.

Next he thought of the note. Ben had put his life on the line to write it. Ben was noble – barely – but not royal; thus not immune from the headsman's axe. If Beson or one of his jackals found this note, they would guess that one or the other of the boys who had brought the doll's house must have written it. The loutish one looked as if he couldn't read even the large letters in a child's book, let alone write such tiny ones as these. So they would look for the other boy, and from there to the chopping block might be a short trip for good old Ben.

He could think of only one sure way to get rid of it, and he didn't hesitate; he crumpled the little note up between the thumb and forefinger of his right hand and ate it.

70

By now I am sure you have guessed Peter's plan of escape, because you know a good deal more than Peyna did when he read Peter's requests. But in any case, the time has come to tell you straight out. He planned to use linen threads to make a rope. The threads would come, of course, from the edges of the napkins. He would descend this rope to the ground and so escape. Some of you may be laughing very hard at this idea. *Threads from napkins to escape a tower three hundred feet high?* you could be saying. *Either you are mad, Storyteller, or Peter was!*

Nothing of the sort. Peter knew how high the Needle was, and he believed he must never be greedy about how many threads he took from each napkin. If he unravelled too much, someone might become very curious. It didn't have to be the Chief Warder; the laundress who washed the napkins might be the one to notice rather a lot of each one was gone. She might mention it to a friend . . . who could mention it to another friend . . . and so the story would spread . . . and it wasn't really Beson Peter was worried about, you know. Beson was, all things said, a fairly stupid fellow.

Flagg was not.

Flagg had murdered his father –

– and Flagg kept his ear to the ground.

It was a shame Peter never stopped to wonder about that vague smell of must about the napkins, or to ask if the person hired to remove the royal crests had been let go after removing a certain number, or if that person was still at work – but, of course, his mind was on other things. He could not help noticing that they were very old, and this was certainly a good thing – he was able to take a great many more threads from each than he ever would have guessed in even his most optimistic moments. How many more than *that* he could have taken he came to know only in time.

Still, I can hear some of you saying, *threads from napkins to make a rope long enough to reach from the window of the Needle's topmost cell to the courtyard? Threads from napkins to make a rope strong enough to support one hundred and seventy pounds? I still think you are joking!*

Those of you who think so are forgetting the doll's house . . . and the loom within, a loom so tiny that the threads of napkins were perfect for its tiny shuttle. Those of you who think so are forgetting that everything in the doll's house was tiny, but worked perfectly. The sharp things had been removed, and that included the loom's cutting blade . . . but otherwise it was intact.

It was the doll's house about which Flagg had had vague misgivings so long ago which was now Peter's only real hope of escape.

I would have to be a much better story-teller than I am, I think, to tell you how it was for Peter during the five years he spent at the top of the Needle. He ate; he slept; he looked out the window, which gave him a view to the west of the city; he exercised morning, noon, and evening; he dreamed his dreams of freedom. In the summer his apartment sweltered. In the winter it froze.

During the second winter he caught a bad case of the grippe which almost killed him.

Peter lay feverish and coughing under the thin blanket on his bed. At first, he was only afraid he would lapse into delirium and rave about the rope that was hidden in a neat coil under two of the stone blocks on the east side of his bedroom. As his fever grew worse, the rope he had woven with the tiny doll house loom came to seem less important, because he began to think he would die.

Beson and his Lesser Warders were convinced of it. They had, in fact, begun to wager on when it would happen. One night, about a week after the onset of his fever, while the wind raged blackly outside and the temperature dropped down to zero,

Roland appeared to Peter in a dream. Peter was convinced that Roland had come to take him to the Far Fields.

'I'm ready, Da'!' he cried. In his delirium he didn't know if he had spoken aloud or only in his mind. 'I'm ready to go!'

Ye'll not be dying yet, his father said in this dream . . . or vision . . . or whatever it was. *Ye've much to do, Peter.*

'*Father!*' Peter shrieked. His voice was powerful, and below him, the warders – Beson included – quailed, thinking that Peter must be seeing the smoking, murdered ghost of King Roland, come to take Peter's soul to hell. They made no more wagers that night, and in fact one of them went to the Church of the Great Gods the very next day and embraced his religion again, and eventually became a priest. This man's name was Curran, and I may tell you of him in another story.

Peter really *was* seeing a ghost in a way – although whether it was the actual shade of his father or only a ghost born in his fever-struck brain, I cannot say.

His voice lapsed into a mutter; the warders did not hear the rest.

'It's so cold . . . and I am so hot.'

My poor boy, his glimmering father said. *You've had hard trials, and there are more of them ahead, I think. But Dennis will know . . .*

'Know what?' Peter gasped. His cheeks were red, but his forehead was as pale as a wax candle.

Dennis will know where the sleepwalker goes, his father whispered, and was gone.

Peter lapsed into a faint that quickly became a deep, sound sleep. In that sleep, his fever broke. The boy who had made it his practice over the last year to do sixty push-ups and a hundred sit-ups each day awoke the next morning too weak to even get out of bed . . . but he was lucid again.

Beson and the Lesser Warders were disappointed. But after that night, they always treated Peter with a kind of awe, and took care never to go too close to him.

Which, of course, made his job that much easier.

All that is an easy enough tale to tell, though it would no doubt be better if I could say for sure that the ghost was there or that it was not. But like other matters in the larger tale, you'll have to make up your own mind about it, I suppose.

But how am I to tell you about Peter's endless, drudging work at that tiny loom? That tale is beyond me. All the hours spent, sometimes with frosty breath pluming from his mouth and nose, sometimes with sweat running down his face, always in fear of discovery; all those long hours alone, with nothing but long thoughts and almost absurd hopes to fill them. I can tell you some things, and will, but to convey such hours and days of slow time is impossible for me, and might be impossible for anyone except one of the great storytellers whose race is long vanished. Perhaps the only thing that even vaguely suggests how much time Peter spent in those two rooms was his beard. When he came in, it was only a shadow on his cheeks and a smudge under his nose – a boy's beard. In the 1,825 days which followed, it grew long and luxuriant; by the end it reached the middle of his chest, and although he was only twenty-one, it was shot with grey. The only place it did not grow was along the length of the jagged scar left by Beson's thumbnail.

Peter dared pluck only five threads from each napkin the first year – fifteen threads each day. He kept them under his mattress, and at the end of each week, he had one hundred and five. In our measure, each thread was about twenty inches long.

He wove the first batch a week after he received the doll's house, working carefully with the loom. Using it was not as easy at seventeen as it had been at five. His fingers had grown; the loom had not. Also, he was horribly nervous. If one of the warders caught him at his work, he could tell them he was using the loom to weave errant threads from the old napkins for his own amusement . . . *if* they believed it. And *if* the loom worked. He wasn't sure that it would until he saw the first slim cable, perfectly woven, emerging from the loom's far end. When Peter saw this, his nervousness abated somewhat and he was able to weave a little faster, feeding the threads in, tugging them to keep them straight, operating the foot pedal with his thumb. The loom squeaked a little at first, but the old grease soon limbered up and it ran as perfectly as it had in his childhood.

But the cable was terribly thin, not even a quarter of an inch through the centre. Peter tied off the ends and tugged experimentally. It held. He was a little encouraged. It was stronger than it looked, and he thought it *should* be strong. They were royal napkins, after all, woven from the finest cotton thread in the land, and he had woven tightly. He pulled

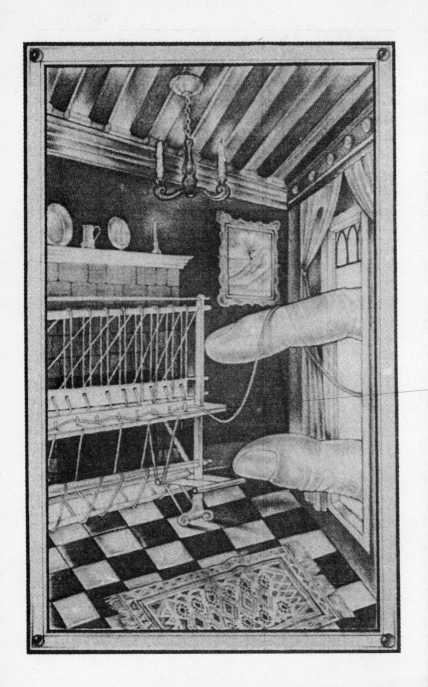

harder, trying to guess how many pounds of strain he was putting on the slim cotton cable.

He pulled even harder, the rope still held, and he felt more hope come stealing into his heart. He found himself thinking about Yosef.

It had been Yosef, head of the stables, who told him about that mysterious and terrible thing called 'breaking strain'. It was high summer, and they had been watching huge Anduan oxen pull stone blocks for the plaza of the new market. A sweating, cursing drover sat astride each ox's neck. Peter had then been no more than eleven, and he thought it better than a circus. Yosef pointed out that each ox wore a heavy leather harness. The chains that pulled the dressed blocks of stone were attached to the harness, one on each side of the animal's neck. Yosef told him the cutters had to make a careful estimate of just how much each block of stone weighed.

'Because if the blocks are too heavy, the oxen might hurt themselves trying to pull them,' Peter said. This wasn't even a question, because it seemed obvious to him. He felt sorry for the oxen, dragging those great blocks of rock.

'Nay,' Yosef said. He lit a cigarette made of cornshuck, almost burning off the end of his nose, and drew deeply and contentedly. He always liked the young prince's company. 'Nay! Oxen aren't stupid – people only think them so because they are large and tame and helpful. Says more about the people than about the oxen, if you ask me, but leave that b'hind, leave that b'hind.

'If an ox can pull a block, he'll pull it; if he can't, why, he'll try twice and then stand with 'is head down. And he'll stand so, even if a bad master whups his hide to ribbons. Oxen look stupid, but they ain't. Not a bit.'

'Then why do the cutters have to guess at the weight of the blocks they cut, if the ox knows what he can pull and what he can't?'

'T'ain't the blocks; it's the *chains*.' Yosef pointed to one of the oxen, which was dragging a block that looked to Peter almost as big as a small house. The ox's head was down, its eyes fixed patiently ahead, as its drover sat astride it and guided it with little taps of his stick. At the end of the double length of chain, the block moved slowly along, goring a furrow in the earth. It was so deep that a small child would need to work to climb out of it. 'If an ox can pull a block, he will, but an ox don't know nothing about chains, or about the breaking strain.'

'What's that?'

'Put a thing under enough of a tug, and it'll snap,' Yosef said. 'If yonder chains were to snap, they'd fly around something turrible. You wouldn't want to be a witness to what can happen if a heavy chain lets go when it's under such a tug as those oxen can put on. It's apt to fly anywhere. Back'rds, mostly. Apt to hit the drover and tear him apart, or cut the legs from under the beast itself.'

Yosef took another drag at his makeshift cigarette and then tossed it in the dirt. He fixed Peter with a shrewd, friendly glare.

'Breaking strain,' he said, 'is a good thing for a prince to know about, Peter. Chains break if you put on enough of a tug, and people do, too. Keep it in mind.'

He kept it in mind now, as he pulled at his first cable. How much of a 'tug' was he putting on? Five rull? At least. Ten? Perhaps. But maybe that was only wishful thinking. He would say eight. No, seven. Better to make a mistake on the pessimistic side, if a mistake was to be made. If he miscalculated . . . well, the cobblestones in the Plaza of the Needle were very, very hard.

He tugged harder still, the muscles on his arms now beginning to stand out a little. When the first cable finally snapped, Peter guessed he might be applying as much as fifteen rull – almost sixty-four pounds – of tug.

He was not unhappy with this result.

Later that night, he threw the broken cable out of his window, where the men who cleaned the Plaza of the Needle daily would sweep it up with the rest of the rubbish the following day.

Peter's mother, seeing his interest in the dollhouse and the little furnishings inside, had taught him how to weave cables and braid them into tiny rugs. When we have not done a thing for a long period, we are apt to forget exactly how that thing was done, but Peter had nothing but time, and after some experimentation, the trick of braiding came back to him.

'Braiding' was what his mother had called it and so that was how he thought of it, but braiding was not really the right word for it; a braid, precisely speaking, is the hand-weaving of two cables. *Wrapping*, which is how rugs are made, is the hand-weaving of three or more cables. In wrapping, two cables are placed apart, but with their tops and bottoms even. The third is placed between them, but lower, so its end sticks out. This pattern is carried on as length after length is added. The result looks a little bit like Chinese finger-pullers . . . or the braided rugs in your favourite grandmother's house.

It took Peter three weeks to save enough threads to try this technique, and most of a fourth to remember exactly how the over-and-under pattern of wrapping had gone. But when he was done, he had a real rope. It was thin, and you would have thought him mad to entrust his weight to it, but it was much stronger than it looked. He found he could break it, but only by wrapping its ends firmly around his hands and pulling until the muscles bulged on his arms and chest and the cords stood out on his neck.

Overhead in his sleeping chamber were a number of stout oak beams. He would have to test his weight from one of these, when he had a rope long enough. If it snapped, he would have to start all over again . . . but such thoughts were useless and Peter knew it – so he just got to work.

Each thread he pulled was about twenty inches long, but Peter lost roughly two inches in the weaving and wrapping. It took him three months to make a rope of three strands, each strand consisting of a hundred and five cotton threads, into a cable three feet long. One night, after he was sure all of the warders were drunk and at cards below, he tied this pigtail to a rope over one of the beams. When it had been looped over and tied in a slipknot, less than a foot and a half hung down.

It looked woefully thin.

Nevertheless, Peter seized it and hung from it,

mouth tightened to a grim white line, expecting the threads to let go at any moment and spill him to the floor. But they held.

They held.

Hardly daring to believe it was happening, Peter hung there from a rope almost too thin to see. He hung there for almost a full minute, and then he stood on his bed to pull the slipknot free. His hands trembled as he did it, and he had to fumble at the knot twice, because his eyes kept blurring with tears. He didn't believe his heart had been so full since reading Ben's tiny note.

72

He had been keeping the rope under his mattress, but Peter realized this would not do much longer. The Needle was three hundred and forty feet high at the peak of its conical roof; his window was just about three hundred feet above the cobblestones. He was six feet tall and believed he would dare to drop as much as twenty feet from the end of his rope. But even at best, he would eventually have to hide two hundred and seventy feet of rope.

He discovered a loose stone on the east side of the bedroom floor, and cautiously pried it up. He was surprised and pleased to find a little space beneath. He couldn't see into it properly so he reached in and felt around in the darkness, his whole body stiff and tense as he waited for something down there in the dark to crawl over his hand . . . or bite it.

Nothing did, and he was just about to withdraw it, when one of his fingers brushed something – cold metal. Peter brought it out. It was, he saw, a heart-shaped locket on a fine chain. Both locket and chain looked to be made of gold. Nor did he think, by its weight, that the locket was false gold. After some poking and feeling, he found a delicate catch. He pushed it and the locket sprang open. Inside were two pictures, one on each side – they were as fine as any of the tiny paintings in Sasha's doll house; even finer, perhaps. Peter stared at their faces with a boy's frank wonder. The man was very handsome, the woman very beautiful. There was a faint smile on the man's lips and a devil-may-care look in his eyes. The woman's eyes were grave and dark. Part of Peter's wonder came from the fact that this locket must be very old, judging by what he could make out of their dress, but only part of it. Most came from the fact that these two faces looked eerily familiar. He had *seen* them before.

He closed the locket and looked on the back. He thought there were initials entwined there, but they were too flounced and curlicued for him to read.

On impulse, he delved into the hold again. This time he touched paper. The single sheet of foolscap he brought out was ancient and crumbling, but the writing was clear and the signature unmistakable. The name was Leven Valera, the infamous Black Duke of the Southern Barony. Valera, who might someday have been King, had instead spent the last twenty-five years of his life in the room at the top of the Needle for the murder of his wife. No wonder the pictures in the locket looked familiar! The man was Valera; the woman was Valera's murdered wife, Eleanor, about whose beauty ballads were still sung.

The ink Valera had used was a strange rusty black, and the first line of his note chilled Peter's heart. The note *entire* chilled his heart, and not only because the similarity between Valera's position and his own seemed too great for coincidence.

> *To the Finder of the Note —*
> *I write with my own Blood, drawn from a vayne I have opened in my left Forearm, my pen the Shaft of a Spune which I have sharpened long and long upon the stones of my Bedchamber. Nearly a quarter of a Centurie I have spent here in the skie; I came here a Young Man and now am I Old. The Coughing Spells and Fayver have come on me again, and this time I think I shall not survive.*
>
> *I did not kill my Wyfe. Nay, though all the Evidence say otherwise, I did not kill my Wyfe. I did love her and love her still, although her dear Face has grown misty in my treacherous Mind.*
>
> *I believe 'twas the King's Magician who killed Eleanor, and arranged Matters to see me put asyde, for I stood in his Way. It seems his Plans have worked and he has prospered; yet I believe there are Gods who punish Wickedness in the end. His Day shall come, and I have come to feel more and more strongly as my own Death approaches that he shall be brought down by One who comes to this Place of Dispair, One who finds and reads this Letter written in my Blood.*
>
> *If 'tis so, I cry out to you; Avenge, Avenge, Avenge! Ignore me and my lost Years if you must, but never, never,*

never ignore my dear Eleanor, murdered as she slept in her Bed! It was not I who poisoned her Wine; I write the name of the Murderer here in Blood: Flagg! 'Twas Flagg! Flagg! Flagg!

Take the Locket, and show it to him the instant before you relieve this the World of Its greatest Scoundrel – show him so that he may know in that Instant that I have been a part of his Downfall, even from beyond my unjust Murderer's Grayve.

Leven Valera

Perhaps now you can understand the true source of Peter's chill; perhaps not. Perhaps you will understand it better if I remind you that, although he looked to be a man in a hale and hearty middle age, Flagg was really very old.

Peter had read about the supposed crime of Leven Valera, yes. But the books in which he had read of it were histories. *Ancient* histories. This crumbling, yellowed parchment first spoke of the King's magician, and then spoke of Flagg by name. *Spoke* his name? Cried it, shrieked it – in blood.

But Valera's supposed crime had happened in the reign of Alan II –

– and Alan II had ruled Delain four hundred and fifty years ago.

'God, oh great God,' Peter whispered. He staggered back to his bed and sat down on it heavily, just before his knees would have unhinged and spilled him to the floor. 'He's done it all before! He's done it all before, and in exactly the same way, *but he did it over four centuries ago!*'

Peter's face was deadly white; his hair was standing on end. For the first time he realized that Flagg, the King's magician, was in reality Flagg the monster, loose in Delain again now, serving a new King — serving his own young, confused, easily led brother.

73

Peter at first entertained giddy thoughts of promising Beson another bribe to take the locket and the crumbling sheet of foolscap to Anders Peyna. In his initial flush of excitement, it seemed to him that this note must point the finger of guilt at Flagg and set him, Peter, free. A little reflection convinced him that while that might happen in a storybook, it would not happen in real life. Peyna would laugh and call it a forgery. And if he took it seriously? That might mean the end of both the Judge-General and the imprisoned prince. Peter's ears were sharp, and he listened closely to the gossip of the meadhouses and the wineshops as it was passed back and forth between Beson and the Lesser Warders. He had heard of the Farmers' Tax Increase, had heard the bitter joke which suggested that Thomas the Light-Bringer should be renamed Thomas the Tax-Bringer. He had even heard that some few daring wags had renamed his brother Foggy Tom the Constantly Bombed. The headsman's axe had swung with the regularity of a clock's pendulum since Thomas had ascended Delain's throne, only *this* clock called out *treason-*

sedition, treason-sedition, treason-sedition with a regularity that would have been monotonous, had it not
been so frightening.

By now Peter had begun to suspect Flagg's goal:
to bring the ordered monarchy of Delain to an utter
smash. Showing the locket and the note would only
get him laughed at or cause Peyna to take some sort
of action. And that would undoubtedly get them
both killed.

In the end Peter put the locket and foolscap back
where they had come from. And with them he put
the little three-foot pigtail it had taken him a month
to weave. On the whole, he did not feel too bitter
about the evening's work – the rope had held, and
the finding of the locket and foolscap after more than
four hundred years proved at least one thing – the
hiding place was not apt to be discovered.

Still, he had much food for thought, and he lay
long awake that night.

When he slept, he seemed to hear Leven Valera's
dry, stony voice whispering in one ear: *Avenge!
Avenge! Avenge!*

74

Time, yes, time – Peter spent a great deal
of time at the top of the Needle. His beard grew long,
save for where that white scar streaked his cheek like
a lightning bolt. He saw many changes from his win-

dow, as it grew. He heard of more terrible changes yet. The headsman's pendulum had not slowed down but actually speeded up: *treason-sedition, treason-sedition*, it sang, and sometimes half a dozen heads rolled in the course of but a single day.

During Peter's third year of imprisonment, the year in which Peter was first able to do thirty chin-ups in a single effort from his bedchamber's central beam, Peyna resigned his post as Judge-General in disgust. It was the talk of the meadhouses and wine-shops for a week, and the talk of Peter's keepers for a week and a day. The warders believed that Flagg would have Peyna jailed almost before the heat of the old man's bum had left the judge's bench, and that soon after the citizens of Delain would find out once and for all if there was blood or ice water in the Judge-General's veins. But when Peyna remained free, the talk died down. Peter was glad Peyna had not been arrested. He bore him no ill will, in spite of Peyna's willingness to believe that he had murdered his father; and he knew that the arrangement of the evidence had been Flagg's doing.

Also during Peter's third year in the Needle, Dennis's good old da', Brandon, died. His passing was simple but dignified. He had finished his day's work in spite of a terrible pain in his chest and side and came slowly home. He sat down in the little living room, hoping the pain would pass. Instead it grew worse. He called his wife and son to his side, kissed them both, and asked if he might have a glass of bundle-gin. This was provided. He drank it off, kissed his wife again, and then sent her from the room.

'You must serve your master well now, Dennis,' he said. 'Ye're a man now, with a man's tasks set before you.'

'I'll serve the King as well as I may, Da',' Dennis said, although the thought of taking over his father's responsibilities terrified him. His good, homely face was shiny with tears. For the last three years, Brandon and Dennis had battled for Thomas, and Dennis's responsibilities had been much the same as before, with Peter; but it had never been the same, somehow – never even *close* to the same.

'Thomas, aye,' Brandon said, and then whispered: 'But if the time comes to do yer first master a service, Dennis, you mustn't hesitate. I have never –'

At that moment, Brandon clutched the left side of his chest, stiffened, and died. He died where he would have wanted to die, in his own chair, in front of his own fire.

In Peter's fourth year of imprisonment – his rope below the stones growing steadily longer and longer – the Staad family disappeared. The throne possessed itself of what little there remained of their lands, as it had done when other noble families disappeared. And as Thomas's reign progressed, there were more and more disappearances.

The Staads were only one item of meadhouse gossip in a busy week that included four beheadings, an increased levy against shopkeepers, and the imprisonment of an old woman who had for three days walked back and forth in front of the palace, screaming that her grandson had been taken and tortured for speaking against the previous year's Cattle Levies. But when Peter heard the Staad name in the warders' conversation, his heart had stopped for a moment.

The chain of events leading to the disappearance of the Staads was one familiar to everyone in Delain by now. The tick-tocking pendulum of the headsman's axe had thinned the numbers of the nobility terribly. Many of these nobles died because their families had served the Kingdom for hundreds – or thousands – of years, and they could not believe such an unjust fate would or could fall on them. Others, seeing bloody handwriting on the wall, fled. The Staads were among these.

And the whispering began.

Tales were told behind cupped hands, tales suggesting that these nobles had not simply scattered to the four winds but had gathered together somewhere, perhaps in the deep woods at the northern end of the Kingdom, to plan an overthrow of the throne.

These stories passed to Peter like the wind through his window, the draughts beneath his door . . . They were dreams of a wider world. Mostly he worked on his rope. During the first year, the rope grew longer by eighteen inches every three weeks. At the end of that year, he had a slim cable that was twenty-five feet long – a cable that was, theoretically at least, strong enough to bear his weight. But there was a difference between dangling from a beam in his bedroom and dangling above a drop of three hundred feet, and Peter knew it. He was, quite literally, staking his life on that slim cord.

And twenty-five feet a year was perhaps not enough; it would take more than eight years before he could even try, and the rumblings he heard at second hand had grown loud enough to be disturbing. Above all else, the Kingdom must endure – there must be no revolt, no chaos. Wrongs must be put right, but by law, not by bows and slings and maces and clubs. Thomas, Leven Valera, Roland, he himself, even Flagg paled into insignificance next to that. There must be law.

How Anders Peyna, growing old and bitter by his fire, would have loved him for that!

Peter determined that he must make his effort to escape as soon as possible. Accordingly he made long calculations, doing the figures in his head so as to leave no trace. He did them again and again and again, proving to himself that he had made no mistake.

In his second year in the Needle, he began to pluck ten threads from each napkin: in his third year fifteen; in his fourth year, twenty. The rope grew. Fifty-eight feet long after the second year; a hundred and four after the third; a hundred and sixty after the fourth.

The rope at that time would still have fetched up a hundred and forty feet from the ground.

During his last year, Peter began to take thirty threads from each napkin, and for the first time his robberies showed clearly – each napkin looked frayed on all four sides, as if mice had been at it. Peter waited in agony for his thefts to be discovered.

75

But they were not discovered then, or ever. There was not so much as a question ever raised. Peter had spent endless nights (or so they seemed to him) wondering and worrying when Flagg would hear some wrong thing, some wrong note, and so get wind of what he was up to. He would send some underling, Peter supposed, and the questions would begin. Peter had thought things out with agonizing care, and he had made only one wrong assumption – but that one led to a second (as wrong assumptions so often do) and that second was a dilly. He had assumed that there was some finite number of napkins – perhaps a thousand or so in all – and that they were being used over and over again. His thinking on the subject of the napkin supply never went much further than that. Dennis could have told him differently and saved him perhaps two years of work, but Dennis was never asked. The truth was simple but staggering. Peter's napkins were not coming from a supply of a thousand, or two thousand, or twenty thousand; there were nearly *half a million of these old, musty napkins in all.*

On one of the deep levels below the castle was a storeroom as big as a ballroom. And it was filled with napkins . . . napkins . . . nothing but napkins. They smelled musty to Peter and that wasn't surprising – most of them coincidentally or not, dated from a time not long after the imprisonment and death of Leven Valera, and the existence of all those napkins

– coincidentally or not – was, indirectly at least, the work of Flagg. In a queer sort of way, he had created them.

Those had been dark times indeed for Delain. The chaos Flagg so earnestly wished had almost come upon the land. Valera had been removed; mad King Alan had ascended the throne in his place. If he had lived another ten years, the Kingdom surely would have drowned in blood . . . but Alan was struck down by lightning while playing cubits on the back lawn in the pouring rain one day (as I told you, he was mad). It was lightning, some said, sent by the gods themselves. He was followed by his niece, Kyla, who became known as Kyla the Good . . . and from Kyla, the line of succession had run straight and true down through the generations to Roland, and the brothers to whose tale you have been listening. It was Kyla, the Good Queen, who brought the land out of its darkness and poverty. She had nearly bankrupted the Royal Treasury to do it, but she knew that currency – hard currency – is the life's blood of a kingdom. Much of Delain's hard currency had been drained away during the wild, weird reign of Alan II, a King who had sometimes drunk blood from the notched ears of his servants and who had insisted that he could fly; a King more interested in magic and necromancy than profit and loss and the welfare of his people. Kyla knew it would take a massive flow of both love and guilders to set the wrongs of Alan's reign right, and she began by trying to put every able-bodied person in Delain back to work, from eldest to youngest.

Many of the older citizens of the castle keep had

been set to making napkins – not because napkins were needed (I think I have already told you how most of Delain's royalty and nobility felt about them), but because *work* was needed. These were hands that had been idle for twenty years or more in some cases, and they worked with a will, weaving on looms exactly like the one in Sasha's doll's house . . . except in the matter of size, of course!

For ten years these old people, over a thousand of them, made napkins and drew hard coin from Kyla's Treasury for their work. For ten years people only slightly younger and a little more able to get about had taken them down to the cool, dry store-room below the castle. Peter had noticed that some of the napkins brought to him were moth-eaten as well as musty-smelling. The wonder, although he didn't know it, was that so many of them were still in such fine condition.

Dennis could have told him that the napkins were brought, used once, removed (minus the few threads Peter plucked from each), and then simply thrown away. After all, why not? There were enough of them, all told, to last five hundred princes five hundred years . . . and longer. If Anders Peyna had not been a merciful man as well as a hard one, there really might have been a finite number of nap-kins. But he knew how badly that nameless woman in the rocking chair needed the work and the pittance it brought in (Kyla the Good had known the same, in her time), and so he kept her on, as he continued to see that Beson's guilders went on flowing after the Staads were forced to flee. She became a fixture outside the room of the napkins, that old woman with her needle for unmaking rather than making. There she sat in her rocker, year after year, removing tens of thousands of royal crests, and so it was really not surprising that no word of Peter's petty thievery ever reached Flagg's ears.

So you see that, except for that one mistaken assumption and that one unasked question, Peter could have gotten about his work much faster. It *did* sometimes seem to him that the napkins were not shrinking as rapidly as they ought to have done, but it never occurred to him to question his basic (if vague) idea that the napkins he used were being regularly returned to him. If he had asked himself that one simple question – !

But perhaps, in the end, all things worked for the best.

Or perhaps not. That is another thing you must decide for yourself.

76

Eventually Dennis got over his fright of being Thomas's butler. After all, Thomas ignored him almost completely, except to sometimes berate him for forgetting to put out his shoes (usually Thomas himself had left his shoes somewhere else, then forgotten where) or to insist Dennis have a glass of wine with him. The wine always made Dennis feel sick to his stomach, although he had come to enjoy a wee drop of bundle-gin in the evenings. He drank it nonetheless. He did not need his good old da' around to tell him one did not refuse to drink with the King when asked. And sometimes, usually when he was drunk, Thomas would forbid Dennis to go home but insist that he spend the night in Thomas's apartments instead. Dennis supposed – and rightly – that these were nights on which Thomas simply felt too lonely to bear his own solitary company. He would give long, besotted, rambling sermons on how difficult it was to be King, how he was trying to do the best job he could and be fair, and how everyone hated him for some reason or other just the same. Thomas often wept during these sermons, or laughed wildly at nothing, but usually he just fell asleep halfway through some mangled defence of one tax or another. Sometimes he staggered off to his bed, and Dennis could sleep on the couch. More often, Thomas fell asleep – or passed out – on the couch, and Dennis made his uncomfortable bed on the cooling hearth. It was perhaps the strangest existence any King's butler had ever known, but, of course, it seemed normal enough to Dennis because it was all he had ever known.

Thomas mostly ignoring him was one thing. *Flagg* ignoring him was another, even more important thing. Flagg had, in fact, entirely dismissed Dennis's part in his scheme to send Peter to the Needle. Dennis had been no more than a tool to him – a tool which had served its purpose and could be put aside. If he *had* thought of Dennis, it would have seemed to him that the tool had been well rewarded: Dennis was the King's butler, after all.

But on an early winter's night in the year when Peter was twenty-one and Thomas sixteen, a night when Peter's thin rope was finally nearing completion, Dennis saw something which changed everything – and it is with the thing Dennis saw that cold night that I must begin to narrate the final events in my tale.

It was a night much like those during the terrible time just before and after Roland's death. The wind shrieked out of a black sky and moaned in the alleys of Delain. Frost lay thick in the pastures of the Inner Baronies and on cobbles of the castle city. At first, a three-quarters moon chased in and out of the rushing clouds, but by midnight the clouds had thickened enough to obscure the moon completely, and by two in the morning, when Thomas awoke Dennis by rattling the latch of the door between his sitting room and the corridor outside, it had begun to snow.

Dennis heard the rattling and sat up, grimacing at the stiffness in his back and the pins and needles in his legs. Tonight Thomas had fallen asleep on the couch instead of lurching his way to bed, so it had been the hearth for the young butler. Now the fire was almost out. The side of him which had been lying closer to it felt baked; the other side of him felt frozen.

He looked towards the rattling sound . . . and

for a moment terror froze his heart and vitals. For
that one moment he thought there was a ghost at the
door, and he almost screamed. Then he saw it was
only Thomas in his white nightshirt.

'M-My Lord King?'

Thomas took no notice. His eyes were open,
but they were not looking at the latch; they were
wide and dreaming and they looked straight ahead at
nothing. Dennis suddenly guessed that the young
King was sleepwalking.

Even as Dennis decided this, Thomas seemed to
realize that the reason the latch wouldn't work was
that the bolt was still on. He drew it and then passed
out into the hall, looking more ghostlike than ever
in the guttering light of the corridor sconces. There
was a swirl of nightshirt hem, and then he was gone
on bare feet.

Dennis sat stock-still on the hearth for a
moment, cross-legged, his pins and needles forgotten, his heart thumping. Outside, the wind hurled
snow against the diamond-shaped panes of the sitting-room window and uttered a long banshee howl.
What should he do?

There was only one thing, of course – the young
King was his master. He must follow.

Perhaps it was the wild night which had brought
Roland so vividly to Thomas's mind, but not necess-
arily – in fact, Thomas thought of his father a great
deal. Guilt is like a sore, endlessly fascinating, and
the guilty party feels compelled to examine it and
pick at it, so that it never really heals. Thomas had
drunk far less than usual but, strangely, had seemed
drunker than ever to Dennis. His sentences had been

broken and garbled, his eyes wide and staring, showing too much of the whites.

   This was, to a large extent, because Flagg was
gone. There had been rumours that the renegade
nobility – Staads among them – had been seen gathered together in the Far Forests at the northern
reaches of the Kindom. Flagg had led a regiment of
tough, battle-hardened soldiers in search of them.
Thomas was always more skittish when Flagg was
gone. He knew it was because he had come to depend
completely on the dark magician . . . but he had
come to depend on Flagg in ways he did not fully
understand. Too much wine was no longer
Thomas's only vice. Sleep is often denied to those
with secrets, and Thomas was afflicted with severe
insomnia. Without knowing it, he had become
addicted to Flagg's sleeping potions. Flagg had left a
supply of the drug with Thomas when he led the
soldiers north, but Flagg had expected to be gone
only three days – four at the most. For the last three
days, Thomas had slept badly, or not at all. He felt
strange, never quite awake, never quite asleep.
Thoughts of his father haunted him. He seemed to
hear his father's voice in the wind, crying out *Why
do you stare at me? Why do you stare at me so?* Visions of
wine . . . visions of Flagg's darkly cheerful face . . .
visions of his father's hair catching fire . . . these
things drove sleep away and left him wide-eyed in
the long watches of the night while the rest of the
castle slept.

   When Flagg had still not returned on the eighth
night (he and his soldiers were even then camped
fifty miles from the castle and Flagg was in a foul

mood; the only trace of the nobles they found had been frozen hoofprints that might have been days or weeks old), Thomas sent for Dennis. It was later that night, that eighth night, that Thomas arose from his couch and began to walk.

*S*o Dennis followed his lord and master the King down those long, draughty stone corridors, and if you have come this far, I think you must know where Thomas the Light-Bringer finished up.

Late stormy night had passed into early stormy morning. No one was abroad in the corridors — at least, Dennis saw no one. If anyone *had* been abroad, he or she might well have fled in the other direction, perhaps screaming, believing he or she had seen two ghosts walking, the one leading in a long white nightshirt that could easily have been mistaken for a shroud, the other following in a plain jerkin, but with bare feet and a face pale enough to have been mistaken for the face of a corpse. Yes, I believe any-one who saw them would have fled, and told long prayers before sleeping . . . and even many prayers might not have kept the nightmares at bay.

Thomas stopped in the middle of a corridor that Dennis had seldom been down, and he opened a recessed door which Dennis had never really noticed at all. The boy King stepped into another corridor (no chambermaid passed them with an armload of sheets, as one had once passed Thomas and Flagg when Flagg had brought the prince this way some years before; all good chambermaids were long since in their beds), and partway down it, Thomas stopped so suddenly that Dennis almost ran into him.

Thomas looked around, as if to see if he had been followed, and his dreaming eyes passed directly over Dennis. Dennis's skin crawled, and it was all he could do to keep from crying out. The sconces in this almost forgotten hallway guttered and stank foully of *das* oil; the light was faint and gruesome. The young butler could feel his hair trying to clump up and push out in spikes as those empty eyes – eyes like dead lamps lit only by the moon – passed over him.

He was there, standing right there, but Thomas did not see him; to Thomas, his butler was *dim*.

Oh, I must run, part of Dennis's mind whispered distractedly – but inside his head, that distracted little whisper was like a scream. *Oh, I must run, he has died, he has died in his sleep and I am following a walking corpse!* But then he heard the voice of his da', his own dear, dead da', whispering: *If the time ever comes to do yer first master a service, Dennis, you mustn't hesitate.*

A voice deeper than either told him that the time for that service had come. And Dennis, a lowly servant boy who had changed a kingdom once by discovering a burning mouse, perhaps changed it again by holding his place, in spite of the terror which froze his bones and pushed his heart into his throat.

In a strange, deep voice that was nothing at all like his usual voice (but to Dennis that voice sounded weirdly familiar), Thomas said: 'Fourth stone up from the one at the bottom with the chip in it. Press it Quick!'

The habit of obedience was so ingrained in Dennis that he had actually begun to move forward before realizing that Thomas, in his dream, had commanded himself in the voice of another. Thomas pushed the stone before Dennis could move more than a single step. It slid in perhaps three inches. There was a click. Dennis's jaw dropped, as part of the wall swung inward. Thomas pushed it farther, and Dennis saw there was a huge secret door here. Secret doors made him think of secret panels, and secret panels made him think of burning mice. Again he felt an urge to run and fought it down.

Thomas went in. For a moment he was only a glimmering nightshirt in the dark, a nightshirt with no one inside it. Then the stone wall closed again. The illusion was perfect.

Dennis stood there, shifting from one cold bare foot to the other cold bare foot. What should he do now?

Again, it was his da's voice he seemed to hear, impatient now, brooking no refusal. *Follow, you paltry boy! Follow, and be quick! This is the moment! Follow!*

But Da', the dark —

He seemed to feel a stinging slap, and Dennis thought hysterically: *Even when you're dead you got a strong right hand, Da'! All right, all right, I'm going!*

He counted up four from the chipped stone and pushed. The door swung about four inches inward on darkness.

There was a tiny clittering sound in the awesome silence of the corridor – a sound like mice made of stone. After a moment Dennis realized that sound was his own teeth, chattering together.

Oh Da;, I'm so scared, he mourned . . . and then followed King Thomas into the darkness.

79

·**F**·ifty miles away, rolled into five blankets against the bitter cold and the roaring wind, Flagg cried out in his sleep at the precise moment Dennis followed the King into the secret passageway. On a knoll not far distant, wolves howled in unison with that cry. The soldier sleeping nearest Flagg on the left died instantly of a heart attack, dreaming that a great lion had come to gobble him up. The soldier sleeping on Flagg's right woke up in the morning to discover he was blind. Worlds sometimes shudder and turn *inside* their axes, and this was such a time. Flagg felt it, but did not grasp it. The salvation of all that is good is only this – at times of great import, evil beings sometimes fall strangely blind. When the King's magician awoke in the morning, he knew that he had had a bad dream, probably from his own long-forgotten past, but he did not remember what it had been.

The darkness inside the secret passage was utter and complete, the air still and dry. In it, coming from somewhere ahead, Dennis heard a terrible, desolate sound.

The King was weeping.

At that sound, some of Dennis's fear left him. He felt a great wonder, and a great pity for Thomas, who always seemed so unhappy, and who had grown fat and pimply as King – often he was pallid and shaky-handed from too much wine the night before, and his breath was usually bad. Already Thomas's legs were beginning to bow, and unless Flagg was with him, he had a tendency to walk with his head down and his hair hanging in his face.

Dennis felt his way forward, his hands held out in front of him. The sound of weeping grew closer in the dark . . . and then, suddenly, the dark was no longer complete. He heard a faint sliding noise and then he could see Thomas faintly. He was standing at the end of the corridor, and faint amber light was coming in from two small holes in the dark. To Dennis, those holes looked strangely like floating eyes.

Just as Dennis began to believe that he would be all right, that he would probably survive this strange night walk, Thomas shrieked. He shrieked so loudly it seemed that his vocal cords must split open. The strength ran out of Dennis's legs and he fell to his knees, hands clapped over his mouth to stop his own screams, and now it seemed to him that this secret way was filled with ghosts, ghosts like strange flapping bats that might at any moment snare themselves in his hair; oh yes, the place seemed filled with the unquiet dead to Dennis, and perhaps it was; perhaps it was.

He almost swooned . . . almost . . . but not quite.

Somewhere below him, he heard barking dogs and realized they were above the old King's kennels. The few of Roland's dogs still alive had never been moved outside again. They were the only living beings – besides Dennis himself – that had heard those wild shrieks. But the dogs were real, not ghosts, and Dennis held on to that thought the way a drowning man might hold on to a floating mast.

A moment or two later, he realized that Thomas was not *just* shrieking – he was crying out words. At first Dennis could make out only a single phrase, howled out again and again: *'Don't drink the wine! Don't drink the wine! Don't drink the wine!'*

81

Three nights later, a light knock came at the closed sitting-room door of a farm in one of the Inner Baronies, a farm quite close to where the Staad family had lived not so long ago.

'Come!' Anders Peyna growled. 'And it better be damned good, Arlen!'

Arlen had aged in the years since Beson had appeared at Peyna's door with Peter's note. The changes in him, however, were slight when compared with the changes in Peyna. The former Judge-General's hair was almost all gone. His spareness of frame had become gauntness. The loss of hair and weight were very little, however, when compared with the changes in his face. Formerly he had been stern. Now he was grim. Dark-brown hollows floated below his eyes. The stamp of despair was clear on his face, and there was a good reason for this. He had seen the things he had spent his life defending brought to ruin . . . and this ruin had been accomplished with shocking ease, and in a shockingly brief period of time. Oh, I suppose all men of intelligence know how fragile such things as Law and Justice and Civilization really are, but it's not a thing they think of willingly, because it disturbs one's rest and plays hob with one's appetite.

Seeing his life's work knocked casually apart like a child's tower of blocks was bad enough, but there was another thing which haunted Peyna these last four years, something that was even worse. This was the knowledge that Flagg had not achieved all the dark changes in Delain alone. Peyna had helped him. For who else had seen Peter brought to a trial which was perhaps *too* speedy? Who else had been so convinced of Peter's guilt . . . and not so much by the evidence as by a young boy's shocked tears?

Since the day Peter had been led to the top of the Needle, the chopping block in the Plaza of the Needle had been stained a sinister rusty colour. Not even the hardest rain could wash it clean. And Peyna thought he could detect that sinister red stain spreading out from the block – spreading out to cover the Plaza, the market streets, the alleys. In his troubled dreams Peyna saw rills of fresh blood washing in bright, accusing threads between the cobblestones and running down the gutters in streamlets. He saw the redans of Castle Delain gleaming bloody in the sun. He saw the carp in the moat floating belly-up, poisoned by the blood which poured out of the sewers in floods and which rose from the springs in the earth itself. He saw the blood rising everywhere, staining the fields and forests. In these unhappy dreams even the sun began to look like a bloodshot, dying eye.

Flagg had let him live. In the meadhouses, people whispered behind their hands that he had reached an agreement with the magician – that he had perhaps given Flagg the names of certain traitors, or that perhaps Peyna 'had something' on Flagg, some secret that would come out if Peyna died suddenly. This was of course, ridiculous. Flagg was not a man to be threatened – not by Peyna, not by anyone. There were no secrets. There had been no agreements or deals. Flagg had simply let him live . . . and Peyna knew why. Dead, he would perhaps have been at peace. Alive, he was left to twist on the rack of his own bad conscience. He was left to watch the terrible changes Flagg had wrought on Delain.

'Well?' he asked irritably. 'What is it, Arlen?'

'A boy has come, my Lord. He says he must see you.'

'Send him away,' Peyna said moodily. He reflected that, even a year ago, he would have heard a knock at the front door, but it seemed that he became more deaf with every passing day. 'I see no one after nine, you know that. Much has changed, but not that.'

Arlen cleared his throat. 'I know the boy. It is Dennis, son of Brandon. It is the King's butler who calls.'

Peyna stared at Arlen, hardly believing what he had heard. Perhaps he was growing deaf even faster than he had thought. He asked Arlen to repeat, and it came out sounding just the same.

'I'll see him. Send him in.'

'Very good, my Lord.' Arlen turned to leave.

The similarity to the night Beson had come with Peter's note – even down to the cold wind screaming outside – came strongly to Peyna now. 'Arlen,' he called.

Arlen turned back. 'My Lord?'

The right corner of Peyna's mouth quirked the smallest bit. 'Are you quite sure it's not a dwarf-boy?'

'Quite sure, my Lord,' Arlen replied, and the *left* corner of his own mouth twitched the tiniest bit. 'There are no dwarves left in the known world. Or so my mother told me.'

'Obviously she was a woman of good sense and clear discernment, dedicated to raising her son properly and not to be held responsible for any inherent flaws in the material she had to work with. Bring the boy here directly.'

'Yes, my Lord.' The door closed.

Peyna looked into his fire again and rubbed his old, arthritis-crippled hands together in a gesture of unaccustomed agitation. Thomas's butler. Here. Now. Why?

But there was no sense in speculating; the door would open in a moment and the answer would come walking through it in the form of a man-boy who would be shaking with the cold, perhaps even frostbitten.

Dennis would have found it a good deal easier to reach Peyna if Peyna had still been at his fine house in the castle city, but his house had been sold from beneath him for 'unpaid taxes' following his resignation. Only the few hundred guilders he had put away over the course of forty years had allowed him to buy this small, draughty farmhouse and continue to pay Beson. It was technically in the Inner Baronies, but he was still many miles west of the castle . . . and the weather had been very cold.

In the hallway beyond the door, he heard the murmur of approaching voices. Now. Now the answer would come through the door. Suddenly that absurd feeling – that feeling of hope, like a ray of strong light shining in a dark cave – came back to him. *Now the answer will come through the door*, he thought, and for a moment he found himself believing that was really true.

As he drew his favourite pipe from the rack beside him. Anders Peyna saw that his hands were trembling.

The boy was really a man, but Arlen's use of the word was not unjustified – at least not on this night. He was cold, Peyna saw, but he also knew that the cold alone does not make anyone shudder as Dennis was shuddering.

'Dennis!' Peyna said, sitting forward sharply (and ignoring the twinge in his back the sudden movement caused). 'Has something happened to the King?' Dreadful images, awful possibilities suddenly filled Peyna's old head – the King dead, either from too much wine, or possibly by his own hand. Everyone in Delain knew that the young King was deeply moody.

'No . . . that is . . . yes . . . but no . . . not the way you mean . . . the way I think you mean . . .'

'Come in here close to the fire,' Peyna snapped. 'Arlen, don't just stand there gawking! Get a blanket! Get two! Wrap this boy up before he shakes himself to death like a buggerlug bug!'

'Yes, my Lord,' Arlen said. He had never gawked in his life – he knew it, and Peyna did, too. But he recognized the gravity of this situation and left quickly. He stripped the two blankets from his own bed – the only other two in this glorified peasant's hut were the ones on Peyna's – and brought them back. He took them to where Dennis crouched as close to the fire as he could without bursting into flames. The deep frost which had covered his hair had begun to melt and to run down his cheeks like tears. Dennis wrapped himself in the blankets.

'Now, tea. Strong tea. A cup for me, a pot for the boy.'

'My Lord, we only have half a canister left in the whole – '

'Bugger how much we have left! A cup for me, a pot for the boy.' He considered. 'And make a cup for yourself, Arlen, and then come in here and listen.'

'My Lord?' Even all of his breeding could not keep Arlen from looking frankly astounded at this.

'Damn!' Peyna roared. 'Would you have me believe you're as deaf as I've become? Get about it!'

'Yes, my Lord,' Arlen said, and went to brew the last tea in the house.

83

Peyna had not forgotten everything he had ever known about the fine art of questioning; in point of fact, he had forgotten damned little of that, or anything else. He had had long sleepless nights when he wished that he *could* forget some things.

While Arlen made the tea, Peyna went about the task of putting this frightened – no; this *terrified* – young man at his ease. He asked after Dennis's mum. He asked if the drainage problems which had so plagued the castle of late had improved. He asked Dennis's opinion on the spring plantings. He steered clear of any and all subjects which might be dangerous . . . and little by little, as he warmed, Dennis calmed.

When Arlen served the tea, hot and strong and steaming, Dennis slurped half the cup at a gulp, grimaced, then slurped the rest. Impassive as ever, Arlen poured more.

'Easy, my lad,' Peyna said, lighting his pipe at last. 'Easy's the word for hot tea and skittish horses.'

'Cold. Thought I was going to freeze coming out here.'

'You *walked*?' Peyna was unable to conceal his surprise.

'Yes. Had my mother leave word with the lesser servants that I was home with the grippe. That'll hold all for a few days, it being so catching this time of year . . . or should do. Walked. Whole way. Didn't dare ask a ride. Didn't want to be remembered. Didn't know it was quite this far. If I'd known, I might have taken a ride after all. I left at three of the clock.' He struggled, his throat working, and then burst out: 'And I'm not going back, not ever! I seen the way *he* looks at me since he come back! Narrow and on the side, his eyes all dark! *He* never used to look at me that way – never used to look at me at all! *He* knows I seen something! Knows I heard something! *He* don't know what, but *he* knows there's something! He hears it in my head, like I'd hear the bell ringin' out from the Church of the Great Gods! If I stay, *he'll* get it out of me! I know he will!'

Peyna stared at the boy under furrowed brows, trying to sort out this amazing flood of declaration.

Tears were standing in Dennis's eyes. 'I mean
F–'

'Softly, Dennis,' Peyna said. His voice was
mild, but his eyes were not. 'I know who you mean.
Best not to speak his name aloud.'

Dennis looked at him with dumb, simple gratitude.

'You'd better tell me what you came to say,'
Peyna told him.

'Yes. Yes, all right.'

Dennis hesitated for a moment, trying to get
himself under control and to arrange his thoughts.
Peyna waited impassively, trying to control his rising excitement.

'You see,' Dennis began at last, 'three nights
ago Thomas called me to come and stay with him,
as he sometimes does. And at midnight, or sometime
thereabouts –'

Dennis told what you have already heard,
and to his credit, he did not try to lie about his own terror, or gloss it over. As he spoke, the wind whined outside and as the fire burned low Peyna's eyes burned
hotter and hotter. Here, he thought, were worse things
than he ever could have imagined. Not only had Peter
poisoned the King, *Thomas had seen it happen.*

No wonder the boy King was so often moody

and depressed. Perhaps the rumours that passed in the meadhouses, rumours that had Thomas more than half mad already, were not so far-fetched as Peyna had thought.

But as Dennis paused to drink tea (Arlen refilled his cup from the bitter lees of the pot), Peyna drew back from that idea. If Thomas had witnessed *Peter* poisoning Roland, why was Dennis here now . . . and in such deadly terror of *Flagg?*

'You heard more,' Peyna said.

'Aye, my Lord Judge-General,' Dennis said. 'Thomas . . . he raved quite some time. We were closed up in the dark together long.'

Dennis struggled to be clearer, but found no words to convey the horror of that closed-in passage-way, with Thomas shrieking in the darkness before him and the dead King's few surviving dogs barking below them. No words to describe the *smell* of the place – a smell of secrets which had gone rancid like milk spilled in the dark. No words to tell of his growing fear that Thomas had gone mad while in the grip of his dream.

He had screamed the name of the King's magician over and over again; had begged the King to look deep into the goblet and see the mouse that simultaneously burned and drowned in the wine. *Why do you stare at me so?* he had shrieked. And then: *I brought you a glass of wine, my King, to show you that I, too, love you.* And finally he had shrieked out words that Peter himself would have recognized, words better than four hundred years old: *'Twas Flagg! Flagg! 'Twas Flagg!*

Dennis reached for his cup, got it halfway to his

mouth, and then dropped it. The cup shattered on the hearthstones.

The three of them looked at the shards of crockery.

'And then?' Peyna asked, in a deceptively gentle voice.

'Nothing for a long, long time,' Dennis said in a halting voice. 'My eyes had . . . had gotten used to the darkness, and I could see him a little. He was asleep . . . asleep at those two little holes, with his chin on his breast and his eyes closed.'

'And he remained so for how long?'

'My Lord, I know not. The dogs had all quietened again. And perhaps I . . . I . . .'

'Dozed a bit yourself? I think it is likely, Dennis.'

'Then, later, he seemed to wake. His eyes opened, at any rate. He closed the little panels and all was dark again. I heard him moving and I drew my legs back so he would not trip over them . . . his nightshirt . . . it brushed my face . . .'

Dennis grimaced as he remembered a feeling like cobwebs drawn in a whisper over his left cheek.

'I followed him. He let himself out . . . I followed still. He closed the door so that it looked like only plain stone wall again. He went back to his apartments and I followed him.'

'Did you meet anyone?' Peyna rapped so sharply that Dennis jumped. 'Anyone at all?'

'No. No, my Lord Judge-General. No one at all.'

'Ah.' Peyna relaxed. 'That is very well. And did anything else happen that night?'

'No, my Lord. He went to bed and slept like a dead man.' Dennis hesitated and then added, 'I didn't sleep a wink, meself, and haven't slept many since, either.'

'And in the morning he –?'

'Remembered nothing.'

Peyna grunted. He steepled his fingers and looked at the dying fire through the little finger-building he had built.

'And did you go back to that passageway?'

Curiously, Dennis asked: 'Would you have gone back, my Lord?'

'Yes,' Peyna said dryly. 'The question is, did *you*?'

'I did.'

'Of course you did. Were you seen?'

'No. A chambermaid passed me in the hallway. The laundry is down that way, I think. I smelled lye soap, like my mum uses. When she was gone, I counted up four from the chipped stone and went in.'

'To see what Thomas had seen.'

'Aye, my Lord.'

'And did you?'

'Aye, my Lord.'

'And what was it?' Peyna asked, knowing. 'When you slid aside those panels, what did you see?'

'My Lord, I saw King Roland's sitting room,' Dennis said. 'With all them heads on the walls. And . . . my Lord . . .' In spite of the heat of the dying fire, Dennis shuddered. 'All of them heads . . . they seemed to be *looking* at me.'

'But there was one head you *didn't* see,' Peyna said.

'No, my Lord, I saw them a –' Dennis stopped,

eyes widening. 'Niner!' He gasped. 'The peepholes –'
He stopped his eyes now almost as big as saucers.

Silence fell again inside. Outside, the winter wind
moaned and whined. And miles away, Peter, rightful
King of Delain, hunched over a tiny loom high in the
sky and wove a rope almost too fine to see.

At last, Peyna fetched a deep sigh. Dennis was
looking up at him from his place on the hearth plead-
ingly . . . hopefully . . . fearfully. Peyna bent forward slowly and touched his shoulder.

'You did well to come here, Dennis, son of
Brandon. You did well to make a reason for your
absence – quite a plausible one, I think. You'll sleep
here with us tonight, in the attic, under the eaves.
It'll be cold, but I think you'll sleep better than you
have of late. Am I wrong?'

Dennis shook his head slowly once, and a tear
spilled from his right eye and ran slowly down his
cheek.

'And your mum knows naught of your reason
for needing to be away?'

'No.'

'Then the chances are very good she'll not be
touched by it. Arlen will take you up. Those are his
blankets, I think, and you'll have to return them. But
there's straw above, and it's clean.'

'I'll sleep just as well with only one blanket, my
Lord,' Arlen said.

'Hush! Young blood runs hot even in its sleep,
Arlen. Your blood has cooled. And you may want
your blankets . . . in case dwarves and trolls come
in your dreams.'

Arlen smiled a little.

'In the morning, we'll talk more, Dennis – but you may not see your mum for a bit now; I must tell you that, although I suspect you already know it might not be healthy for you to go back to Delain, by the look of you.'

Dennis tried to smile, but his eyes were shiny with fear. 'I had thoughts of more than the grippe when I came here, and that's the honest truth. But now I've put your own health in danger as well, haven't I?'

Peyna smiled dryly. 'I'm old, and Arlen is old. The health of the old is never very strong. Sometimes that makes them more careful than they should be . . . but sometimes it makes them dare much.' *Especially*, he thought, *if they have much to atone for.* 'We'll speak more in the morning. In the meantime, you deserve your rest. Will you light his way upstairs, Arlen?'

'Yes, my Lord.'

'And then come back to me.'

'Yes, my Lord.'

Arlen led the exhausted Dennis from the room, leaving Anders Peyna to brood before his dying fire.

85

When Arlen came back, Peyna said quietly: 'We have plans to make, Arlen, but perhaps you'll draw us a drop of wine. It would be well to wait until the boy is asleep.'

'My Lord, he was asleep before his head touched the hay he had gathered for his pillow.'

'Very well. But draw us a drop of wine anyway.'

'A drop is all there is to draw,' Arlen said.

'Good. Then we'll not have to set out with big heads tomorrow, will we?'

'My Lord?'

'Arlen, we leave here tomorrow, the three of us, for the north. I know it, you know it. Dennis says there's grippe in Delain – and so there is; one who would grip us if he could, anyway. We go for our *health*.'

Arlen nodded slowly.

'It would be a crime to leave that good wine behind us for the tax man. So we'll drink it . . . and then take ourselves off to bed.'

'As you say, my Lord.'

Peyna's eyes glinted. 'But before *you* go to bed, you'll mount to the attic and get the blanket you left with the boy, against my strict and specific instructions.'

Arlen gaped at Peyna. Peyna mocked his gape with uncanny aptness. And for the first and last time in his service as Peyna's butler, Arlen laughed out loud.

86

Peyna went to bed but could not sleep. It wasn't the sound of the wind that kept him awake, but the sound of cold laughter coming from inside his own head.

When he could stand that laughter no longer, he got up, went back into the sitting room, and sat before the cooling fireplace ashes, his white hair floating in small clouds over his skull. Unaware of his comic look (and if he *had* been aware of it, he would have been unmindful), he sat wrapped in his blankets like the oldest Indian in the universe and looked into the dead fire.

Pride goes before a fall, his mother had told him when he was a child, and Peyna had understood that. *Pride's a joke that'll make the stranger inside you laugh sooner or later*, she had also told him, and he hadn't understood that . . . but he did now. Tonight the stranger inside was laughing very hard indeed. Too hard for him to be able to sleep, even though the next day was apt to be long and difficult.

Peyna was fully able to appreciate the irony of his position. All his life, he had served the idea of the law. Ideas like 'prison break' and 'armed rebellion' horrified him. They still did, but certain truths had to be faced. That the machinery of revolt had come to exist in Delain, for instance. Peyna knew that the nobles who had fled to the north called themselves 'exiles', but he also knew that they were edging ever closer to calling themselves 'rebels'. And if he were to keep that revolt from happening, he might well have to use the machinery of rebellion to help a prisoner break out of the Needle. *That* was the joke the stranger inside was laughing at, laughing too loudly for sleep to be even a remote possibility.

Such actions as the ones he was now thinking about went against the grain of his whole life, but he would go ahead anyway, even if it killed him (which

it just might). Peter had been falsely imprisoned.
Delain's true King was not on the throne, but locked
in a cold two-room cell at the top of the Needle. And
if it took lawless forces to put things right again, so
it must be. But . . .

'The napkins,' Peyna muttered. His mind circled back to them and back to them. 'Before we
resort to force of arms to free the rightful King and
see him enthroned, the business of the napkins
should be investigated. He'll have to be asked.
Dennis . . . and the Staad boy, perhaps . . . aye . . .'

'My Lord?' Arlen asked from behind him. 'Are
you unwell?'

Arlen had heard his master rise, as butlers almost
always do.

'I am unwell,' Peyna agreed gloomily. 'But it's
nothing my physician can fix, Arlen.'

'I'm sorry, my Lord.'

Peyna turned to Arlen, and fixed his bright,
sunken eyes upon the butler.

'Before we become outlaws, I want to know
why he asked for his mother's doll's house . . . and
for napkins with his meals.'

87

'**G**o back to the castle?' Dennis asked the
next morning, in a hoarse voice that was almost a
whisper. 'Go back to where *he* is?'

'If you feel you can't, I'll not press you,' Peyna said. 'But you know the castle well enough, I think, to stay out of *his* way. If, that is, you know a way to get in unnoticed. To be noticed would be bad. You look much too lively for a boy who is supposed to be home sick.'

The day was cold and bright. The snow on the long, rolling hills of the Inner Baronies threw back a diamond dazzle which made the eyes water before long. *I'll probably be snowblind by noon, and it'll serve me right*, Peyna thought grumpily. The stranger inside seemed to find this prospect hilarious indeed.

Castle Delain itself could be seen in the distance, blue and dreaming on the horizon, its walls and towers looking like an illustration in a book of fairy stories. Dennis, however, did not look like a young hero in search of adventure. His eyes were full of fear, and his face bore the expression of a man who has escaped from a den of lions . . . only to be told he's forgotten his lunch, and must go back in and get it, even though he's lost his appetite.

'There might be a way to get in,' he said. 'But if *he* smells me, how I get in or where I hide won't matter. If he smells me, he'll run me down.'

Peyna nodded. He did not want to add to the boy's fear, but in this situation, nothing less than the truth could serve them. 'What you say is true.'

'But you still ask me to go?'

'If you can, I still ask it.'

Over a meagre breakfast, Peyna had told Dennis what he wanted to know, and had suggested some ways Dennis might go about getting the information. Now Dennis shook his head, not in refusal but in bewilderment.

'Napkins,' he said.

Peyna nodded. 'Napkins.'

Dennis's fearful eyes went back to that distant fairy-tale castle dreaming on the horizon. 'When he was dying, my da' said if I ever saw a chance to do a service for my first master, I must do it. I thought I'd done it coming here. But if I must go back . . .'

Arlen, who had been busy, closing up the house, now joined them.

'Your house key, please, Arlen,' Peyna said.

Arlen handed it to him, and Peyna handed it to Dennis.

'Arlen and I go north to join the' – Peyna hesitated and cleared his throat – 'the exiles,' he finished. 'I've given you Arlen's key to this house. When we reach their camp, I'll give mine to a fellow you know, if he be there. I think he will be.'

'Who's that?' Dennis asked.

'Ben Staad.'

Sunshine broke on Dennis's gloomy face. 'Ben? Ben's with them?'

'I think he may be,' Peyna said. In truth, he knew perfectly well that the entire Staad family was with the exiles. He kept his ear firmly to the earth, and his ears had not grown so deaf that he was not able to hear many movements in the Kingdom.

'And you'd send him down here?'

'If he'll come, aye, I mean to,' Peyna replied.

'To do what? My Lord, I'm still not clear about that.'

'Nor am I,' Peyna said, looking cross. He felt

more than cross; he felt bewildered. 'I've spent my whole life doing some things because they were logical and not doing others because they were not. I've seen what happens when people act on intuition, or for illogical reasons. Sometimes the results are ludicrous and embarrassing; more often they are simply horrible. But here I am, just the same, behaving like a crackbrained crystal gazer.'

'I don't understand you, my Lord.'

'Neither do I, Dennis. Neither do I. Do you know what day this is?'

Dennis blinked at this sudden change in direction, but answered readily enough. 'Yes – Tuesday.'

'Tuesday. Good. Now I'm going to ask you a question that my cursed intuition tells me is very important. If you don't know the answer – even if you are not sure – for the gods' sake, say so! Are you ready for the question?'

'Yes, my Lord,' Dennis said, but he wasn't sure that he really was. Peyna's piercing blue eyes under the wild tangle of his white brows had made him very nervous. The question was apt to be very difficult indeed. 'That is, I think so.'

Peyna asked his question, and Dennis relaxed. It didn't make much sense to him – it was only more nonsense about the napkins, as far as he could see – but at least he knew the answer, and gave it.

'You're sure?' Peyna persisted.

'Yes, my Lord.'

'Good. Then here is what I want you to do.'

Peyna spoke to Dennis for some time, as the three of them stood in the chilly sunshine in front of the 'retirement cottage' where the old judge would never come again. Dennis listened earnestly, and when Peyna demanded that he repeat the instructions back, Dennis was able to do it quite neatly.

'Good,' Peyna said. 'Very, very good.'

'I'm glad I've pleased you, sir.'

'Nothing about this business pleases me, Dennis. Nothing at all. If Ben Staad is with those unfortunate outcasts in the Far Forests, I mean to send him away from relative safety and into danger because he *may* be of some use to King Peter. I'm sending you back to the castle because my heart tells me there's something about those napkins he asked for . . . and the doll's house . . . *something*. Sometimes I think I almost have it, and then it dances out of my grasp again. He did not ask for those things idly, Dennis. I'd wager my life on that. But I don't *know*.' Peyna abruptly slammed his fist down on his leg in frustration. 'I am putting two fine young men into terrible danger, and my heart tells me I am doing the right thing, but I . . . don't . . . know . . . *WHY!*'

And inside the man who had in his heart once condemned a boy because of that boy's tears, the stranger laughed and laughed and laughed.

88

The two old men parted from Dennis. They shook hands all around; then Dennis kissed the Judge's ring, which bore the Great Seal of Delain on its face. Peyna had given up his Judge-General's bench, but had not been able to part with the ring, which to him summed up all the goodness of the law. He knew he had made mistakes from time to time, but he had not allowed them to break his heart. Even over this last and greatest of mistakes, his heart did not break. He knew as well as we in our own world do that the road to hell is paved with good intentions – but he also knew that, for human beings, good intentions are sometimes all there are. Angels may be safe from damnation, but human beings are less fortunate things, and for them hell is always close.

He protested Dennis's act of kissing his ring, but Dennis insisted. Then Arlen shook Dennis's hand and wished him speed o' the gods. Smiling (but Peyna could still see the fear lurking in Dennis's eyes), Dennis wished them the same. Then the young butler turned east, toward the castle, and the two old men headed west, toward the farmstead of one Charles Reechul. Reechul, who raised Anduan huskies for a living, paid the grinding taxes the King had imposed without complaint, and was thus considered loyal . . . but Peyna knew that Reechul was sympathetic to the exiles encamped in the Far Forests, and had helped others reach them. Peyna had never expected to need Reechul's services himself, but the time had come.

The farmer's eldest daughter, Naomi, drove Peyna and Arlen north on a sled pulled by twelve of the dogger's strongest huskies. By Wednesday night, they reached the edge of the Far Forests.

'How long to the camp of the exiles?' Peyna asked Naomi that night.

Naomi cast the thin, evil-smelling cigar she had been smoking into the fire. 'Two more days if the skies keep fair. Four more days if it snows. Maybe never, if it blizzards.'

Peyna turned in. He drifted off to sleep almost at once. Logic or illogic, he was sleeping better than he had in years.

The weather kept clear the next day, and on Friday as well. At dusk of that day – the fourth since Peyna and Arlen had parted from Dennis – they reached the small huddle of tents and makeshift wooden huts for which Flagg had searched in vain.

'Ho! Who comes, and can you say the password?' a voice called. It was strong, sturdy, cheerful, and unafraid. Peyna recognized it.

'It's Naomi Reechul,' the girl called, 'and the password two weeks ago was "tripos". If it's not that now, Ben Staad, then put an arrow through me and I'll come back and haunt you!'

Ben appeared from behind a rock, laughing. 'I'd not dare meet you as a ghost, Naomi – you're fearsome enough alive!'

Ignoring this, she turned to Peyna. 'We've come,' she said.

'Yes,' Peyna said. 'So I see.'

And I believe it's well that we have . . . because something tells me that time has grown short . . . very short indeed.

89

Peter had the same feeling.

By Sunday, two days after Peyna and Arlen reached the camp of the exiles, his rope would still, by his calculations, finish up thirty feet short of the ground. This meant that when he dangled from the end of it with his arms fully extended, he would face a drop of at least twenty-one feet. He knew that he would be wiser by far to go on with his rope for another four months – even another two. If he dropped from the rope, fell badly, and broke both of his legs so that the Plaza guards found him groaning on the cobbles when they made their round-o'-the-clock, he would have wasted more than four years, simply because he did not have the patience to pursue his labour another four months.

This was logic Peyna could have appreciated, but Peter's feeling that he must now hurry was much stronger. Once Peyna would have snorted at the idea that feelings could be more trustworthy than logic . . . but now he might have been less sure.

Peter had been having a dream – for almost a week running now it had played over and over, gradually becoming more distinct. In it, he saw Flagg, bent over some bright and glowing object – it lit the magician's face a sickly greenish-yellow. In this dream, there always came a point when Flagg's eyes first widened, as if in surprise, and then narrowed to cruel slits. His brows pulled down; his forehead darkened; a grimace as bitter as a crescent moon twisted his mouth. In this expression, the dreaming Peter read one thing and one thing only: death. Flagg said only one word as he leaned forward and blew upon the brightly glowing object, which whiffed out like a candle when the magician's breath touched it. Only one word, but one was enough. The word from Flagg's mouth was Peter's own name, uttered in tones of angry discovery.

The night before, Saturday night, there had been a fairy-ring around the moon. The Lesser Warders thought it would soon snow. Examining the sky this afternoon, Peter knew they were right. It was his father who had taught Peter to read the weather and, standing at the window, Peter felt a pang of sadness . . . and a renewed spark of cold, quiet anger . . . the need to make things right again.

I'll make my try under cover of darkness and under cover of storm, he thought. *There'll even be a bit of snow to cushion my fall.* He had to grin at that idea – three inches of light, powdery snow between him and the cobbles would do precious little one way or the other. Either his perilously thin rope would hold . . . or it would break. Assuming it held, he would take the drop. And his legs would either take the impact . . . or they wouldn't.

And if they do take it, where will you go on them? a little voice whispered. *Any who might have shielded you or helped you . . . Ben Staad, for instance . . . have long since been driven from the castle keep . . . from the very Kingdom itself, for all you know.*

He would trust to luck, then. King's luck. It was a thing his father had often talked about. *There are lucky Kings and unlucky. But you'll be your own King and you'll have your own luck. M'self, I think you'll be very lucky.*

He had been King of Delain – at least in his own heart – for five years now, and he thought his luck had been the kind which the Staad family, with its famous bad luck, would have understood. But perhaps tonight would make up for all.

His rope, his legs, his luck. Either all would hold or all would break, quite possibly at the same time. No matter. Poor as it had been, he would trust to his luck.

'Tonight,' he murmured, turning from the window . . . but something happened at supper which changed his mind.

It took Peyna and Arlen all day Tuesday to make the ten miles to the Reechul farm, and they were nearly done in when they arrived. Castle Delain was twice as far, but Dennis probably could have been knocking at the West Gate – if he had actually been mad enough to do such a thing – by two that afternoon, in spite of his long walk the day before. Such is the difference, of course, between young men and old men. But what he *could* have done really didn't matter, because Peyna had been very clear in his instructions (especially for a man who claimed not to have the slightest idea of what he was doing), and Dennis meant to follow them to the letter. As a result, it would be some time yet before he entered the castle.

After covering not quite half the distance, he began to look for a place where he could hole up for the next few days. So far he had met no one on the road, but noon had passed and soon there would be people returning from the castle market. Dennis wanted no one to see him and mark him. He was, after all, supposed to be home, sick in bed. He did not have to look long before he found a place that suited him well enough. It was a deserted farmstead, once well kept but now beginning to fall into ruin. Thanks to Thomas the Tax-Bringer, there were many such places on the roads leading to the castle keep.

Dennis remained there until late Saturday afternoon – four days in all. Ben Staad and Naomi were already on their way back from the Far Forests to Peyna's farm by then, Naomi pushing her team of huskies for all they were worth. The knowledge would have eased Dennis a bit if he had known – but of course he did not, and he was lonely.

There was no food at all upstairs, but in the cellar he found a few potatoes and handful of turnips. He ate the potatoes (Dennis hated turnips, always had, and always would), using his knife to cut out the rotten places – which meant he cut away three-fourths of every potato. He was left with a handful of white globes the size of pigeons' eggs. He ate a few, looked toward the turnips in the vegetable bin, and sighed. Like them (he didn't) or hate them (he did), he supposed he would be reduced to eating them by Friday or so.

If I'm hungry enough, Dennis thought hopefully, *maybe they'll taste good. Maybe I'll just gobble those old turnips up and beg for more!*

He finally did have to eat a number of them, although he managed to hold out until Saturday noon. By then, they actually had begun to *look* good, but as hungry as he was, they still *tasted* terrible.

Dennis, who suspected the days ahead might be very hard, ate them anyway.

91

Dennis also found an old pair of snow-shoes in the basement. The straps were far too large, but he had plenty of time to shorten them. The lacings had begun to rot, and there was nothing Dennis could do about that, but he thought they would serve the purpose. He wouldn't need them for long.

He slept in the cellar, fearing surprise, but during the daylight hours of those four long days, Dennis spent most of his time in the parlour of the deserted farmstead, watching the traffic pass to and fro – what little there was began around three o' the clock and had mostly ceased by five, when early-winter shadows began to cover the land. The parlour was a sad, empty place. Once it had been a cheery spot in which the family had gathered to discuss the day just done. Now it belonged only to the mice . . . and to Dennis, of course.

Peyna, after hearing Dennis declare that he could read and write 'pretty well for a fellow in service' and seeing him draw his Great Letters (this had been over breakfast on Tuesday – the last real meal Dennis had had since his own lunch on Monday, a meal he looked back on with understandable nostalgia), had provided him with several sheets of paper and a lead pencil. And during most of the hours he spent in the deserted house, Dennis laboured earnestly over a note. He wrote, scratched out, rewrote, frowned horribly as he reread, scratched his head, resharpened his pencil with his knife, and wrote again. He was ashamed of his spelling, and terrified he would forget some crucial thing Peyna had told him to put in. There were several times, times when his poor frazzled brain could make no more progress, when he wished Peyna had stayed up an hour longer on the night Dennis had come and written his own damned note, or called it aloud to Arlen. Most times, however, he was glad of the job. He had worked hard his whole life, and idleness made him nervous and uneasy. He would rather have worked his sturdy young man's body than his not-so-sturdy young man's brains, but work was work, and he was glad to have it.

By Saturday noon, he had a letter he was pretty well satisfied with (which was good, since he had worked his way down to the final two sheets of notepaper). He looked at it with some admiration. It covered both sides of the paper, and was by far the longest thing he had ever written. He folded it to the size of a medicine tablet, and then peeked out the sitting-room window, waiting impatiently for it to be dark enough to leave. Peter saw the gathering clouds from his own poor sitting room atop the Needle, Dennis from the sitting room of this deserted house; but both had been taught by their fathers – one a King and the other a butler to that King – to read the sky, and Dennis also thought there would be snow tomorrow.

By four, the long, blue shadow of the house had begun to creep out from the foundations, and Dennis no longer felt so eager to go. It was danger ahead . . . deadly danger. He was to go where Flagg was perhaps even now brooding long over his infernal magics, perhaps even now checking upon a certain sick butler. But how he felt did not really matter, and he knew it – the time had come to do his duty, and as every butler in his family line had done for centuries and centuries, Dennis would do his best.

He left the house in the bleak sunset hour, donned the snowshoes, and struck off across the field on a direct line toward the castle keep. The idea of wolves occurred to his uneasy mind, and he could only hope there would be none, and if there were, that they would leave him alone. He hadn't the slightest idea that Peter had decided to make his dangerous escape attempt the following night, but like Peyna – and Peter himself – he felt a need to hurry; it seemed to him that there were mackerel-scale clouds laid across his heart as well as the sky.

As he trudged through the snow-desolate fields, Dennis's thoughts turned to how he might enter the castle without being seen and challenged. He thought he knew how it could be done . . . if, that was, Flagg did not smell him.

He had no more than thought the magician's name when a wolf howled somewhere out in the still white wastes. In a dark room below the castle, Flagg's own sitting room, the magician sat bolt upright suddenly in his chair, where he had fallen asleep with a book of arcane lore open on his stomach.

'Who speaks the name of Flagg?' the magician whispered, and the two-headed parrot shrieked.

Standing in the centre of a long and desolate field of white, Dennis heard that voice, as dry and scabrous as a spider's scuttle, in his own head. He paused, his breath indrawn and held. When he finally let it go, it plumed frosty from his mouth. He was cold all over, but hot drops of sweat stood out on his forehead.

From his feet he heard dry snapping noises – *Pouck! Pouck! Pouck!* – as several of the snowshoes' rotted cross-lacings let go.

The wolf howled in the silence. It was a hungry, heartless sound.

'No one,' Flagg muttered in the sitting room of his dark apartments. He was rarely sick – could remember being sick only three or four times in all of his long life – but he had caught a bad cold in the north, sleeping on the frozen ground, and although he was improving, he was still not well.

'No one. A dream. That's all.'

He took the book from his lap, closed it, and set it on a side table – the surface of this table had been handsomely dressed in human skin – and settled back in his chair. Soon he slept again.

In the snowy fields west of the castle, Dennis slowly relaxed. A single drop of stinging sweat ran into his eye and he wiped it away absently. He had thought of Flagg . . . and somehow Flagg had *heard* him. But now the dark shadow of the magician's thought had passed over him, as the shadow of a hawk may pass over a crouching rabbit. Dennis let out a long, shaky sigh. His legs felt weak. He would try – oh, with all his heart he would try – to think of the magician no more. But as the night came on and the moon with its ghostly fairy-ring rose in the sky, that was a thing easier resolved upon than done.

92

At eight of the clock, Dennis left the fields and entered the King's Preserves. He knew them well enough. He had been a squireen for Brandon when his da' buttled the old King in the fields of the hunt, and Roland had come here often, even in his old age. Thomas came less often, but on the few occasions when the boy King did come, Dennis had, of course, been required to come with him. Soon he struck on a trail he knew, and just before midnight he reached the verge of this toy forest.

He stood behind a tree, looking out at the castle wall. It was half a mile away over open, snow-covered ground. The moon was still shining, and Dennis was all too aware of the sentries who walked the castle parapet. He would have to wait until Prince Ailon had driven his silvery chariot over the edge of the world before crossing that open space. Even then he would be horribly exposed. He had known from the first that this would be the riskiest part of the whole adventure. Parting from Peyna and Arlen, with the good sun shining down, the risk had seemed acceptable. Now it seemed utterly mad.

Go back, a cowardly voice inside him begged, but Dennis knew he couldn't. His father had laid a charge on him, and if the gods meant him to die trying to fulfil it, then he would die.

Faint and yet clear, like a voice heard in a dream, came the call of the Crier, drifting out to him from the castle's central tower: '*Twelve o'clock and all's well . . .*'

Nothing's well, Dennis thought miserably. *Not one single thing.* He drew his thin coat more tightly around him and began the long job of waiting down the moon.

Eventually it left the sky, and Dennis knew he had to move. Time had grown short. He stood, said a brief prayer to his gods, and began to walk across the open space as rapidly as he could, expecting a hail of *Who goes there?* from the castle walls at every moment. The hail did not come. The clouds had thickened across the night sky. All below the castle wall was one dark shadow. In less than ten minutes, Dennis had reached the edge of the moat. He sat on its low bank, the snow crunching under his bottom, and took the snowshoes off. He slid down onto the moat itself, which was frozen and covered with more snow.

Dennis's thundering heart slowed down. He was in the shadow of the bulking castle wall now, and would not be seen unless a sentry happened to look straight down, and most probably not even then.

Dennis was careful not to go all the way across the moat – not yet – because the ice close to the castle wall would be rotted and thin. He knew why this was so; the reason for the thin ice and the unpleasant smell here and the mossy wetness on the huge stones of the outer wall was his hope of entering the castle secretly. He moved carefully to the left, ears listening for the noise of running water.

At last he heard it, and looked up. There, at eye

height, was a round black hole in the solid castle wall.
Fluid ran from it in listless streams. It was a sewer
outflow pipe.

'Now for it,' Dennis muttered. He drew back
five paces, ran, and leaped. As he did, he felt the ice,
rotted by the constant outflow of warm waste from
the pipe, give under his feet. Then he was clinging
to the mossy lip of the pipe. It was slick, and he had
to clutch hard to keep from falling. He pulled himself
up, digging for purchase with his feet, and finally
yanked himself inside. He paused for a moment, trying to get his breath back, then began to crawl along
the pipe, which slanted steadily upward. He and
several of his playmates had found these pipes when
they were children, and had been quickly warned off
by their parents, partly because they might become
lost, mostly because of the sewer rats. Still, Dennis
thought he knew where he would come out.

An hour hater, in a deserted corridor of the
castle's east wing, a sewer grating moved – was still
– then moved again. It was shoved partway aside,
and a few moments later a very dirty (and very
smelly) butler named Dennis pulled himself out of a
hole in the floor and lay panting on the cold cobbles.
He could have used a longer rest, but someone might
come along, even at this unearthly hour. So he
replaced the grating and looked around.

He did not recognize the hallway at once, but this
in no way upset him. He started down it toward the T-
intersection at the far end. At least, he reflected, there
had been no rats in the warren of sewer pipes below the
castle. That had been a great relief. He had been prepared
for them, not just because of the gruesome tales his da'

had told him, but because there *had* been rats on a few occasions when he and his mates had ventured with fearful screeches of laughter down into the pipes as children – the rats had been part of the scary, dare-you adventure of it.

Probably there were just a few mice, and your memory's exaggerated them into rats, Dennis thought now. This was not the truth, but Dennis would never know it. His memory of the rats in the sewers was a true one. The pipes had been infested with great, disease-bearing rodents since time out of mind. It had only been for the last five years that they had ceased to teem in the sewers. They had been wiped out by Flagg. The magician had rid himself of both a piece of stone and his own dagger by means of a sewer grating similar to the one from which Dennis had emerged on this early Sunday morning. He had rid himself of them, of course, because there were a few flecks of the deadly green Dragon Sand on each. The fumes from those few grains had killed the rats, burning many of them alive even as they paddled through the scummy water in the pipes, suffocating all the others before they could flee. Five years later, the rats had still not come back, although most of the poisonous fumes had dissipated. Most, but not all. If Dennis had entered one of the sewer pipes a bit closer to Flagg's apartments, he might well have died himself. Perhaps it was luck that saved him, or fate, or those gods he prayed to; I'll not take a stand on the matter. I tell tales, not tea leaves, and on the subject of Dennis's survival, I leave you to your own conclusions.

93

He reached the junction, peered around the corner, and saw a sleepy young Guard o' the Watch passing farther up the way. Dennis pulled back. His heart was thumping hard again, but he was satisfied – he knew where he was. When he looked back, the guard was gone.

Dennis moved quickly, up this corridor, down that flight of stairs, across t'other gallery. He moved with speedy sure-footedness, for he had spent his whole life in the castle. He knew it well enough, certainly, to find his way from the east wing, where he had come out of the sewers, to the lower west wing, where the napkins were stored.

But because he dared not be seen – not by anyone – Dennis went by the most obscure corridors he knew, and at the sound of every footfall (either real or imagined, and I do think quite a few of them were imagined), he withdrew into the nearest cranny or niche. In the end, it took him over an hour.

He thought he had never been so hungry in his life.

Never mind your cussed belly now, Dennis – take care of your master first, your belly later.

He was standing far back in a shadowy doorway. Faintly, he heard the Crier call four o'clock. He was about to move forward when slow, echoing footfalls came down the hallway . . . a clank of steel-and-scabbard – a creak of leather leggings.

Dennis pushed himself farther back into the shadows, sweating.

A Guard o' the Watch paused just in front of the thinly shadowed doorway where Dennis hid. The fellow stood for a moment rooting in his nose with his little finger, and then leaned over to blow a stream of snot between his knuckles. Dennis could have reached out and touched him, and felt certain that any moment the guard would turn . . . his eyes would widen . . . he would draw his shortsword . . . and that would be the end of Dennis, son of Brandon.

Please, Dennis's frozen mind whispered. *Please, oh, please* –

He could smell the guard, could smell the old wine and burned meat on his breath, and the sour sweat coming out of his skin.

The guard started to move on . . . Dennis began to relax . . . then the guard stopped and began rooting in his nose again. Dennis could have screamed.

'I have a girrul name of Marchy-Marchy-Melda,' the guard began to sing in a low-pitched, droning voice, rooting in his nose all the while. He produced a large green something, examined it thoughtfully, and flicked it onto the wall. *Splat*. 'She's got a sister named Es-a-merelda . . . I would sail the seven seas . . . Just to kiss her dimply knees! Tootie-sing-tay, sing-tiy, and pass me a bucket-da wine.'

Something exceedingly horrible was now happening to Dennis. His nose had begun to itch and tickle in a way which was unmistakable. Very soon he would sneeze.

Go! he screamed in his mind. *Oh, why don't you go, you stupid fool?*

But the guard seemed to have no intentions of going. He had apparently struck a rich lode up in the left nostril, and he meant to mine it.

'I have a girrul name of Darchy-Darchy-Darla. . . . She's got a sister named Red Headed Carla. . . . I would take a thousand sips . . . From her pretty pretty lips. . . . Tootie-sing-tay, sing-tiy, and pass me a bucket-da wine.'

I'll hit you over the HEAD with a bucket of wine, you fool! Dennis thought. *Move ON!!* The itch in his nose grew steadily worse, but he did not dare even touch it, for fear the guard would see the movement from the corner of his eye.

The guard frowned, bent over, blew his nose between his knuckles again, and finally moved on, still singing his droning song. He was barely out of sight before Dennis threw his arm over his own nose and mouth and sneezed into the crook of his elbow. He waited for the clash of metal as the guard drew his sword and whirled back, but the fellow was half asleep, and still half drunk from whatever party he had been at before his tour of duty commenced. Once, Dennis knew, such a slovenly creature would have been quickly discovered and sent to the farthest reaches of the Kingdom, but times had changed. There was a click of a latch, the *scree-eeee* of hinges as a door was drawn open, and then it boomed closed, cutting off the guard's song just as he reached the chorus again. Dennis sagged back in his niche for a moment, eyes closed, cheeks and forehead on fire, his feet twin blocks of ice.

*For a few minutes there I didn't think of my belly at
all!* he thought, and then had to slam both hands over
his mouth to stifle a giggle.

He peeked out of his hiding place, saw no one
about, and moved to a doorway down the corridor
and on his right. He knew this doorway very well,
although the empty rocker and the needlework case
outside it were new to him. The door led to the room
where all of those napkins had been stored since the
time of Kyla the Good. It had never been locked
before, and was not now. Old napkins were apparently not considered worth locking up. He peered
inside, hoping that his answer to Peyna's key question still held true.

Standing there in the road on that bright morning five days ago, Peyna had asked him this: *Do you
know when they take fresh stores of napkins to the Needle,
Dennis?*

This seemed like a simple question indeed to
Dennis, but you may have noticed that all questions
seem simple if you know the answers, and most horribly difficult if you don't. That Dennis knew the
answer to this one was a testament to his honesty and
honour, although those traits were so deeply
ingrained in his character that he would have been
surprised if someone had told him this. He had taken
money – Anders Peyna's money, in fact – from Ben
Staad to make sure those napkins were delivered.
Only a guilder, true, but money was money and pay
was pay. He had felt honour-bound to make sure,
from time to time, that the service was continuing.

He told Peyna about the big storeroom (Peyna
was flabbergasted to hear of it) and how each Satur-

day night around seven o'clock, a maid took twenty-one napkins, shook then, ironed them, folded them, and set them in a stack on a small wheeled cart. This cart stood just inside the room's doorway. Early on Sunday morning – at six o'clock, less than two hours from right now – a servant boy would pull the cart to the Plaza of the Needle. He would rap at the bolted door at the base of the ugly stone tower, and one of the Lesser Warders would pull the cart inside and place the napkins on a table, where they would be doled out, meal by meal, through the week.

Peyna had been satisfied.

Dennis now hurried forward, feeling inside his shirt for the note he had written at the farmhouse. He had a bad moment or two when he couldn't find it, but then his fingers closed over it and he sighed with relief. It had only slipped a little to one side.

He lifted the Sunday breakfast napkin. Sunday lunch. For a moment he almost passed over Sunday supper as well, and if he had done that, my tale would have had a very different ending – better or worse I cannot say, but surely different. In the end, however, Dennis decided three napkins deep was safe enough. He had found a pin in a crack between two boards in the farmhouse living room and had nipped it into one shoulder strap of the rough linsey camisole he wore as underwear (and if he had been thinking a little better, he would have nipped the note to his underwear with it in the bargain, and spared himself that bad moment, but as I may have told you, Dennis's brains were sometimes a little lacking). Now he retrieved the pin and carefully attached the note to an inner fold of the napkin.

'Let it find you, Peter,' he murmured in the ghostly silence of that storeroom, piled high with napkins made in another age. 'Let it find you, my King.'

Dennis knew he must lie low now. The castle would be waking up soon; stableboys would be stumbling out to the barns, washerwomen would be moving to the laundries, cook's apprentices would be stumbling puffy-eyed and sleepy to their fires (thinking of the kitchens made Dennis's belly rumble anew – by now even the hateful turnips would have tasted quite nice – but food, he reckoned, would have to wait).

He worked his way farther back into the big room. The stacks were so high, the ways so zigzagging and irregular, that it was like working his way into a maze. The napkins gave off a sweet, dry, cottony smell. He finally reached one of the far corners, and here he reckoned he could be safe. He overspilled a stack of the napkins, spread them out, and took another handful for a pillow.

It was by far the most luxurious mattress he had ever lain upon and, hungry as he was, he needed sleep much more than food after his long walk and the frights of the night. He was asleep in no time at all, and he was troubled by no dreams. We leave him now, with the first part of his job well and bravely accomplished. We will leave him turned upon his side, right hand curled under his right cheek, sleeping on a bed of royal napkins. And I would like to make a wish for you, Reader – that your sleep this night be as sweet and as blameless as his was all that day.

94

On Saturday night, as Dennis was standing in the horror of that wolf's howl and feeling the shade of Flagg's thought pass over him, Ben Staad and Naomi Reechul were encamped in a snowy hollow thirty miles north of Peyna's farm . . . or what had *been* Peyna's farm before Dennis showed up with his story of a King who walked and talked in his sleep.

They had made the sort of rough camp people make when they mean to spend only a few hours and then push on. Naomi had seen to her beloved huskies while Ben put up a small tent and built a roaring fire.

Shortly, Naomi joined him at the fire and cooked deer meat. They ate in silence, and then Naomi went to check the dogs again. All were sleeping except for Frisky, her favourite. Frisky looked at her with almost human eyes, and licked her hand.

'A good pull today, m'dear,' Naomi said. 'Sleep, now. Catch a moon rabbit.'

Frisky obediently put her head down on her paws. Naomi smiled and went back to the fire. Ben sat before it, his knees pulled up to his chest and his arms around them. His face was sombre and thoughtful.

'Snow's coming.'

'I can read the clouds as well as you, Ben Staad. And the fairies have made a ring around Prince Ailon's head.'

Ben glanced at the moon and nodded. Then he looked back at the fire. 'I'm worried. I've had dreams of . . . well, dreams of one it's better not to name.'

She lit a cigar. She offered the little package, which was wrapped in muslin to prevent drying, to Ben, who shook his head.

'I've had the same dreams, I think,' she said. She tried to make her voice casual, but was betrayed by a slight tremor.

He stared around at her, eyes wide.

'Aye,' she said, as if he had asked. 'In them, he looks into some bright glowing thing and speaks Peter's name. I've never been one of your skittish little girls who screeches at the sight of a mouse or a spider in its web, but I wake from that dream wanting to scream aloud.'

She looked both ashamed and defiant.

'How many nights have you had it?'

'Two.'

'I've had it four a-running. Mine's just the same as yours. And you needn't look like I'm going to laugh at you or call you Little Nell Weeping at the Well. I also wake up wanting to scream.'

'This bright thing . . . at the end of my dreams, he seems to blow it out. Is it a candle, do you think?'

'No. You know it's not.'

She nodded.

Ben considered. 'Something far more dangerous than a candle, I think . . . I'll take that cigar you offered, if I may.'

She gave him one. He lit it from the fire. They sat a while in silence, watching the sparks rise toward the dark wind which trawled nets of powdery field snow through the sky. Like the light in the dream they'd shared, the sparks blew out. The night seemed very black. Ben could smell snow in that wind. A great deal of snow, he thought.

Naomi seemed to read his thought. 'I think such a storm as the old folks tell about may be on the way. What do you think?'

'The same.'

With a hesitation utterly unlike her usual forthright manner, Naomi asked: 'What does the dream mean, Ben?'

He shook his head. 'I can't tell. Danger to Peter, that much is clear. If it means anything else – anything I can ken – it's that we must hurry.' He looked at her with an urgent directness that made her heart speed up. 'Can we reach Peyna's farm tomorrow, do you think?'

'We should be able to. No one but the gods can say that a dog won't break a leg or that a killer bear who can't sleep his winter sleep won't come out of the woods and kill us all, but aye . . . we *should* be able to. I exchanged all the dogs I used on the run up, except for Frisky, and Frisky's almost tireless. If the snow comes early it'll slow us down, but I think it will hold off . . . and off . . . and for every hour it does, it'll be that much worse when it finally comes. Or so I think. But if it *does* hold off, and if we take turns jumping off the sledge and running alongside, I think we can make it. But what can we do except sit there, unless your friend the butler returns?'

'I don't know.' Ben sighed and rubbed a hand over his face. What good, indeed? Whatever it was the dreams foretold, it would happen at the castle, not at the farm. Peyna had sent Dennis to the castle, but how did Dennis mean to get in? Ben didn't know, because

Dennis hadn't told Peyna. And if Dennis did gain
entry undetected, where would he hide? There were a
thousand possible places. Except . . .

'Ben!'

'What?' Jerked out of his thoughts, he turned to
her.

'What did you think of just now?'

'Nothing.'

'Yes, *something*. Your eyes gleamed.'

'Did they? I must have been thinking of pies. It's
time you and I turned in. We'll want to be off at first
light.'

But in the tent, Ben Staad lay awake long after
Naomi had gone to sleep. There were a thousand
places in the castle to hide, yes. But he could think
of two rather special ones. He thought he might well
find Dennis in one . . . or the other.

At last he fell asleep . . .

. . . and dreamed of Flagg.

Peter began that Sunday as he always did,
with his exercises and a prayer.

He had awakened feeling fresh and ready. After
a quick look at the sky to gauge the progress of the
coming storm, he ate his breakfast.

And, of course, he used his napkin.

96

By Sunday noon, everyone in Delain had come out of his or her house at least once to look worriedly toward the north. Everyone agreed that the storm, when it came, would be one to tell stories about in later years. The clouds rolling in were a dull grey, the colour of wolf pelts. Temperatures rose until the icicles hanging beneath the eaves of the alleys began to drip for the first time in weeks, but the old-timers told each other (and anyone else who would listen) that they were not fooled. The temperature would plummet quickly, and hours later – perhaps two, perhaps four – the snow would begin. And, they said, it might fall for days.

By three o'clock that afternoon, those farmers of the Inner Baronies fortunate enough to still have livestock to watch out for had gotten their animals into the barns. The cows went mooing their displeasure; the snow had melted enough for them to crop last fall's dry grasses for the first time in months. Yosef, older, greyer, but still lively enough at seventy-two, saw that all the King's horses were stabled. Presumably there was someone else to take care of all the King's men. Wives took advantage of the mild temperatures to attempt to dry sheets which otherwise simply would have frozen on the lines, and then took them in as the daylight lowered toward an early, storm-coloured dark. They were disappointed; their washing had not dried. There was too much moisture in the air.

Animals were skittish. People were nervous. Wise meadhouse keepers would not open their doors. They had observed the falling mercury in their barometric glasses, and long experience had taught them that low air pressure makes men quick to fight.

Delain battened down for the coming storm, and everyone waited.

97

Ben and Naomi took turns running beside the sledge. They reached the Peyna farm at two o'clock that Sunday afternoon – at about the same time Dennis was stirring awake on his mattress of royal napkins and Peter was beginning his meagre lunch.

Naomi looked beautiful indeed – the flush of her exercise had coloured her tanned cheeks the pretty dusky red of autumn roses. As the sledge pulled into Peyna's yard, the dogs barking wildly, she turned her laughing face to Ben.

'A record run, by the gods!' she cried. 'We've made it three – no, *four!* – hours earlier than I would have believed when we left! And not one dog has burst its heart! *Aiy,* Frisky! *Aiy!* Good dog!'

Frisky, a huge black-and-white Anduan husky with grey-green eyes, was at the head of the tether. She was jumping in the air, straining against the traces. Naomi unhooked her and danced with her in the snow. It was a curious waltz, both graceful and barbaric. Dog and mistress seemed to laugh at each other in a powerful shared affection. Some of the other dogs were lying down on their sides now, panting hard, obviously exhausted, but neither Frisky nor Naomi seemed even slightly winded.

'*Aiy*, Frisky! *Aiy*, my love! Good dog! You've led a famous chase!'

'But for what?' Ben asked glumly.

She released Frisky's paws and turned to him, angry . . . but the dejection on his face robbed her of her anger. He was looking toward the house. She followed his gaze and understood. They were here, yes, but where was *here*? An empty farmhouse, that was all. What in the world had they come so far and so fast *for*? The house would have been just as empty an hour . . . two hours . . . four hours from now. Peyna and Arlen were in the north, Dennis somewhere in the depths of the castle. Or in a prison cell or a coffin awaiting burial, if he had been caught.

She went to Ben and put a hesitant hand on his shoulder. 'Don't feel so bad,' she said. 'We've done all we could do.'

'Have we?' he asked. 'I wonder.' He paused, and sighed deeply. He had taken off his knitted cap and his golden hair gleamed mellowly in the dull afternoon light. 'I'm sorry, Naomi. I don't mean to snap at you. You and your dogs have done wonders. It's just that I feel we're very far from where we could give any real aid. I feel helpless.'

She looked at him, sighed, and nodded.

'Well,' he said, 'let's go in. Maybe there'll be

some sign of what we're to do next. We'll at least be out of the blow when it comes.'

There were no clues inside. It was just a big, draughty, empty farmhouse that had been quit in a hurry. Ben prowled restlessly from room to room and found nothing at all. After an hour, he collapsed unhappily beside Naomi in the sitting room . . . in the very chair where Anders Peyna had sat when he listened to Dennis's incredible story.

'If only there was a way to track him,' Ben said.

He looked up to see her staring at him, her eyes bright and round and full of excitement.

'There might be!' she said. 'If the snow holds off –'

'What are you talking about?'

'*Frisky!*' she cried. 'Don't you see? *Frisky* can track him! She has the keenest nose of any dog I've ever known!'

'The scent would be days old,' he said, shaking his head. 'Even the greatest tracking dog that ever lived could not . . .'

'Frisky may *be* the greatest tracking dog that ever lived,' Naomi replied, laughing. 'And tracking in winter's not like tracking in summer, Ben Staad. In summer, trace dies quickly . . . it rots, my da' says, and there are a hundred other traces to cover the one the dog seeks. Not just of other people and other animals, but of grasses and warm winds, even the smells that come on running water. But in the winter, trace *lasts*. If we had something that belonged to this Dennis . . . something that carried his scent . . .'

'What about the rest of your team?' Ben asked.

'I should open the shed over there' – she pointed at it – 'and leave my bedroll in it. If I show them where it is and then free them, they'll be able to forage for their own food – rabbits and such – and they'll also know where to come for shelter.'

'They won't follow us?'

'Not if they're told not to.'

'You can do that?' He looked at her with some awe.

'No,' Naomi said matter-of-factly. 'I don't speak Dog. Nor does Frisky speak Human, but she understands it. If I tell Frisky, she'll tell the others. They'll hunt what they need, but they won't range far enough to lose the scent of my bedroll, not with the storm coming. And when it starts, they'll go to shelter. It won't matter if their bellies are hungry or full.'

'And if we had something that belonged to this boy Dennis, you really believe Frisky could track him?'

'Aye.'

Ben looked at her long and thoughtfully. Dennis had left this farm on Tuesday; it was now Sunday. He didn't believe any scent could last that long. But there *was* something in the house which would bear Dennis's scent, and perhaps even a fool's errand would be better than only sitting here. It was the pointless *sitting* more than anything else that grated on him, the hours ahead when things of grave importance might be happening elsewhere, while they sat and twiddled their thumbs here. Under other circumstances, the possibility of being snowbound with a girl as beautiful as Naomi would have delighted him, but not while a kingdom might be won and lost twenty miles to the east . . . and his best friend might be living or dying with only that confounded butler to help him.

'Well?' she asked eagerly 'What do you think?'

'I think it's crazy,' he said, 'but worth a try.'

She grinned. 'Do we have something with his scent strong upon it?'

'We do,' he said, getting up. 'Bring your dog in, Naomi, and lead her upstairs. To the attic.'

98

Although most humans don't know it, scents are like colours to dogs. Faint scents have faint colours, like pastels washed out by time. Clear scents have clear colours. Some dogs have weak noses, and they read scents the way humans with poor eyes see colours, believing this delicate blue may actually be a grey, or that dark brown may actually be a black. Frisky's nose, on the other hand, was like the eyesight of a man with the gaze of a hawk, and the scent in the attic where Dennis had slept was very strong and very clear (it may have helped that Dennis had been some days without a bath). Frisky sniffed the hay, then sniffed the blanket THE GIRL held for her. She scented Arlen upon it, but disregarded the scent; it was weaker, and not at all the scent she had found on the hay. Arlen's smell was lemony and tired, and

Frisky knew at once that it was the smell of an old man. Dennis's smell was more exciting and vital. To Frisky's nose, it was the electric blue of a summer lightning stroke.

She barked to show that she knew this smell and had put it safely away in her library of scents.

'All right, good girl,' THE TALL-BOY said. 'Can you follow it?'

'She'll follow it,' THE GIRL said confidently. 'Let's go.'

'It'll be dark in an hour.'

'That's so,' THE GIRL said, and then grinned. When THE GIRL grinned that way, Frisky thought her heart might just burst with love of her. 'But it isn't her *eyes* that we want, is it?'

THE TALL-BOY smiled. 'I guess not,' he said. 'You know, I must be crazy, but I think we're going to pick up these cards and play them.'

'Course we are,' she said. 'Come on, Ben. Let's use what little daylight's left – it'll be dark soon enough.'

Frisky, her nose full of that bright-blue scent, barked eagerly.

Peter's supper came promptly at six o'clock that Sunday night. The storm clouds hung heavy over Delain and the temperature had begun to drop, but the winds hadn't yet begun to blow and not a snowflake had fallen. On the far side of the Plaza, shivering in stolen cook-boy's whites, Dennis stood anxiously, drawn back into the deepest shadow he could find, staring at the single square of pale-yellow light at the top of the Needle – Peter's candle.

Peter, of course, knew nothing of Dennis's vigil – he was filled with the wonder of the idea that, live or die, this would be the last meal he would ever eat in this damned prison cell. It was just more tough, salty meat, half-rotted potatoes, and watery ale, but he would eat it all. For the last three weeks he had eaten little and spent all the waking time he did not spend working at the tiny loom exercising, readying his body. Today, however, he had eaten everything brought to him. He would need all his strength tonight.

What will happen to me? he wondered again, sitting down at the little table and grasping the napkin that lay over his meal. *Where exactly will I go? Who will take me in? Anyone? All men, it's said, must trust in the gods . . . but Peter, you are trusting so much it's ridiculous.*

Stop. What'll be is what'll be. Now eat, and think no more of –

But that was where his restless thoughts broke off, because as he shook the napkin out, he felt a small stab, like the prick of a nettle.

Frowning, he looked down and saw that a tiny bead of blood had seeped up on the ball of his right forefinger. Peter's first thought was of Flagg. In the fairy tales, it was always a needle that bore the poison. Perhaps he had been poisoned now, by

Flagg. That was his first thought, and not such a silly one, at that. After all, Flagg had used poison before.

Peter picked the napkin up, saw a tiny folded object with black, smudgy marks on it . . . and flipped the napkin back down at once. His face remained calm and peaceful, giving away none of the wild excitement that had burst up inside him at the sight of the note pinned inside the napkin.

He glanced casually towards the door, suddenly afraid he would see one of the Lesser Warders – or Beson himself – staring suspiciously in at him. But there was no one. The prince had been a great object of curiosity when he first came to the Needle, stared at as avidly as a rare fish is stared at in a collector's tank – some of them had even smuggled their lady-loves up to look at the murdering monster (and they would have been imprisoned for it themselves, if they had been caught). But Peter was a model prisoner, and he had palled quickly. No one was looking at him now.

Peter forced himself to eat his entire meal, although he no longer wanted it. He wanted to take not the slightest chance of rousing suspicions – now more than ever. He had no idea who the note might be from, or what it might say, or why it had aroused such a fever in him. But for a note to come now, only hours before he planned to make his try to escape, seemed an omen. But of what?

When his meal was finally eaten, he glanced towards the door again, made sure the spyhole was closed, and walked to his bedrom with his napkin still held casually in one hand, almost as if he had forgotten that he held it at all. In the bedroom, he unpinned the note (his hands were trembling so badly he pricked himself again) and unfolded it. It was written closely on both sides in letters which were rusty and a bit childish, but readable enough. His glance went first to the signature . . . and his eyes widened. The note was signed *Dennis – your Friend and Servant For-Ever.*

'Dennis?' Peter muttered, so flabbergasted he was unaware that he had whispered aloud. *'Dennis?'*

He turned back then, and the letter's opening was enough to shock his heartbeat into a fast drum-roll. The salutation was *My King.*

100

*M*y King,

As you may Noe, for the last 5 Yeres I have Buttled in Service to your Brother, Thomas. In just this last Week I have found out that You did not Murther you Father Roland the Good. I Noe who Did, and Thomas Noes as Well. You would Noe the name of this Black Killer if I dared to Rite it, but I do Not. I went to Peyna. Peyna has gone to join the Exiles with his Butler, Orlon. He has commanded I come to the Castle, and Rite to you this note. Peyna says that the Exiles may soon become Rebels and this must not Be. He thinks you may have some sort of Plan, but what he Noes Not. He commands that I be of Service to You, and my Da commanded it too, before He Dyed, and my Heart commands it, for our Famly has always served the King and you are the Right King. If you have a Plan, I will aid you in Any Way I can, even if it means my Death. As you read this, I am across the Platza in the shadows looking at the Needle where you are Pent Up. If you have a Plan, come I pray You and stand at the Window. If You have something on which You can rite, then throe down a Note and I will try to retreeve It late this Night. Wave twyce if you will try this idea.

Your friend Ben is with the Exiles. Peyna said He would send Him. I Noe were He (Ben) will be. If You say I should fetch Him (Ben) I can, in a Day. Or perhaps Two if there is Snoe. I Noe that throwing down a Note might be Riskee, but I feel Time is short. Peyna feels the Same Way. I will be Watching and Praying.
Dennis

Your Friend and Servant For-Ever

101

It was a long time before Peter would put his whirling thoughts in order. His mind kept circling back to one question: What had Dennis seen to change his mind so radically and completely? What, in the names of all the gods, could it have been?

Little by little he came to realize that it didn't matter – Dennis had seen *something*, and that was enough.

Peyna. Dennis had gone to Peyna, and Peyna

had sensed . . . well, the old fox had sensed *some-thing*. *He thinks you may have some sort of Plan, but what he Noes Not*. Old fox indeed. He had not forgotten Peter's request for the doll's house, and the napkins. He hadn't known exactly what those things meant, but he had sensed something in the wind. Aye, well and truly.

Then what was Peter to do?

Part of him – a very large part – wanted to go ahead just as he had planned. He had worked his courage up to this desperate adventure; now it was hard to let it go for nothing but more waiting. And there were the dreams, urging him on, as well.

You would Noe the name of this Black Killer if I dared to rite It, but I do Not. Peter knew just the same, of course, and it was that more than anything else that convinced him Dennis really had stumbled on to something. Peter felt that Flagg might soon awake to this new development – and he wanted to be gone before that happened.

Was a day too long to wait?

Perhaps. Perhaps not.

Peter was torn in an agony of indecision. Ben . . . Thomas . . . Flagg . . . Peyna . . . Dennis . . . they whirled in his brain like figures seen in a dream. What should he do?

In the end, it was the appearance of the note itself – not what was in it – that persuaded him. For it to come this way, pinned to a napkin on the very night he meant to try his rope made of napkins . . . it meant he should wait. But only for a night. Ben would not be able to help.

Could *Dennis* help him, though? What could he do?

And suddenly, in a flash of light, an idea came to him.

Peter had been sitting on his bed, hunched over the note, his brows furrowed. Now he straightened up, his eyes alight.

His eyes fell on the note again.

If You have something on which You can rite, then throe down a Note and I will try to retreeve It late this Night.

Yes, of course, he had something to write on. Not the napkin itself, because it might be missed. Not Dennis's note, either, because it was written on both sides, from side to side and top to bottom.

But Valera's parchment was not.

Peter went back into his sitting room. He glanced at the door and saw that the spyhole was closed. Dimly he could hear the warders at cards below. He crossed to the window and waved twice, hoping that Dennis was really out there somewhere, and could see him. He would just have to hope so.

Peter went back to the bedroom, pulled up the loose stone, and after some reaching and fumbling, retrieved the locket and the parchment. He turned the parchment over to the blank side . . . but what was he to do for ink?

After a moment the answer came to him. The same thing Valera had done, of course.

Peter worked at his thin straw mattress, and after some tugging opened a seam. The stuffing was of straw, and before long, he had found a number of good long stalks that would serve as pens. Then he opened the locket. It was in the shape of a heart, and the point at the bottom was sharp. Peter closed his eyes for a moment and said a brief prayer. Then he opened them and drew the point of the locket across his wrist. Blood welled up at once – much more than had come from the pinprick earlier. He dipped the first straw in his blood and began to write.

102

Standing in the cold darkness across the Plaza, Dennis saw Peter's shape come to the small window at the top of the Needle. He saw Peter raise his arms over his head and cross them twice. There would be a message, then. It doubled – no, trebled – his risk, but he was glad.

He settled in to wait, feeling numbness slowly creep over his feet and kill the feeling in them. The wait seemed very long. The Crier called ten . . . then eleven . . . finally twelve o' the clock. The clouds had hidden the moon, but the air seemed strangely light – another sign of a coming storm.

He was beginning to think that Peter must have forgotten him, or changed his mind, when that shape came to the window again. Dennis straightened up, wincing at a pain in his neck, which had been cocked upward for the last four hours. He thought he saw something arc out . . . and then Peter's shape left the high window. A moment later, the light up there was extinguished.

Dennis looked left and right, saw no one, took all of his courage in his hands, and ran out into the Plaza. He knew perfectly well that there might be someone – a more alert Guard o' the Watch than last night's tuneless singer, for instance – whom he *hadn't* seen, but there was nothing to be done about that. He was also gruesomely aware of all the men and women who had been beheaded not far from here. What if their ghosts were still around, lurking –?

But thinking about such things did no good, and so he tried to put them from his mind. Of more immediate concern was just finding the thing that Peter had thrown. The area at the foot of the Needle below Peter's window was a featureless white snowfield.

Feeling horribly exposed, Dennis began to cast about like an inept hunting dog. He wasn't sure what he had seen glimmering in the air – it had been there only for a second – but it had looked solid. That made sense; Peter would not have thrown a piece of paper, which might have fluttered anywhere. But what, and where was it?

As the seconds ticked by, turning into minutes, Dennis began to feel more and more frantic. He dropped to his hands and knees and began to crawl about, peering into footprints which had melted to the size of dragon prints earlier that day and which were now refreezing, hard and blue and shiny. Sweat coursed down his face. And he began to be devilled by a recurring idea – that a hand would fall on his shoulder, and when he turned he would see the grinning face of the King's magician inside his dark cowl.

A little late for hide and seek, isn't it, Dennis? Flagg would say, and although his grin would widen, his eyes would burn a baleful, hellish red. *What have you lost? Can I help you find it?*

Don't think his name! For the gods' sake, don't think his name!

But it was hard to stop. Where was it? Oh, where was it?

Back and forth Dennis crawled, his hands now as numb as his feet. Back and forth, back and forth. Where was it? Bad enough if *he* was unable to find it. Worse still if the snow held off until morning light and someone else did. Gods knew what it might say.

Dimly, he heard the Crier call one o' the clock. He was now covering ground he had already covered before, becoming more and more panicky.

Stop, Dennis. Stop, boy.

His da's voice, too clear in his head to be mistaken. Dennis had been on his hands and knees, his nose almost on the ground. Now he straightened up a little.

You're not SEEING *anything anymore, boy. Stop and close your eyes for a moment. And when you open 'em, look around. Really look around.*

Dennis closed his eyes tight and then opened them wide. This time, he looked around almost casually, scanning the whole snowy, tracked area around the foot of the Needle.

Nothing. Nothing at –

Wait! There! Over there!

Something glimmered.

Dennis saw a curve of metal, barely poking half an inch out of the snow. Beside it, he could see a round track made by one of his knees – he had almost crawled over the thing during his frantic hunt.

He tried to pluck it from the snow and on his first try only pushed it farther in. His hand was almost too numb to close. Digging in the snow for the metal object, Dennis realized that if his knee had come down on it instead of beside it, he would have driven it more deeply into the snow without even feeling it – his knees were as numb as the rest of him. And then he never would have seen it at all. It would have remained buried until the spring thaws.

He touched it, forced his fingers to close, and brought it out. He looked at it wonderingly. It was a locket – a locket which might be gold, in the shape of a heart. There was a fine chain attached to it. The locket was shut – but caught in its jaws was a folded piece of paper. Very old paper.

Dennis pulled the note free, closed his hand gently over the old paper, and slipped the locket's chain over his head. He got creakily to his feet and ran back towards the shadows. That run was, in a way, the worst part of the whole business for him. He had never felt so exposed in his whole life. For every step he ran, the comforting shadows of the buildings on the far side of the Plaza seemed to recede a step.

At last he reached comparative safety and stood in the shadows for a while, panting and shuddering. When he had gotten his breath, he returned to the castle, slinking along the Fourth Alley in the shadows and entering by Cook's Way. There was a Guard of the Watch at the doorway leading into the castle proper, but he was as sloppy about his duties as his mate had been the night before. Dennis waited, and eventually the guard wandered off. Dennis darted inside.

Twenty minutes later, he was safely back in the storeroom of the napkins. Here he unfolded the note and looked at it.

One side was closely writ in an archaic hand. The writer had used a strange rust-coloured ink and Dennis could make nothing of it. He turned the note over and his eyes widened. He recognized the 'ink' that had been used to write the short message on *this* side easily enough.

'Oh, King Peter,' he moaned.

The message was smeared and blurry – the 'ink' had not been blotted – but he could read it.

Meant to try Escape tonight. Will wait I night. Dare wait no longer. Don't go for Ben. No time. Too dangerous. I have a Rope. Thin. May break. Too short. Will be a drop in any case. 20 feet. Midnight tomorrow. Help me away if you can. Safe place. May be hurt. In the hands of the gods. I love you my good Dennis. King Peter.

Dennis read this note three times and then burst into tears – tears of joy. That light Peyna had sensed was now shining brightly in Dennis's own heart. That was well, and soon all would be well.

His eyes returned again and again to the line *I*

love you my good Dennis, written in the King's own
blood. He had not needed to add that for the message
to make sense . . . and yet, he had.

    Peter, I would die a thousand deaths for you, Dennis
thought. He put the note inside his jerkin, and lay
down with the locket still around his neck. It was a
very long time before sleep found him this time. And
he had not slept long before he snapped wide awake.
The door of the storeroom was opening – the low
creak of its hinges seemed an inhuman shriek to
Dennis. Before his sleep-fuddled mind even had time
to realize he had been found, a dark shadow with
burning eyes swept down on him.

103

The snow began at around three o' the
clock that Monday morning – Ben Staad saw the first
flakes go skating past his eyes as he and Naomi stood
at the edge of the King's Preserves, looking out
towards the castle. Frisky sat on her haunches, panting. The humans were tired, and Frisky was tired as
well, but she was eager to go – the scent had grown
steadily fresher.

    She had led them easily from Peyna's farm to
the deserted house where Dennis had spent some
four days, eating raw potatoes and thinking sour
thoughts about turnips which turned out to be as
sour as the thoughts themselves. In that empty Inner

Baronies farmstead, the bright-blue scent she had followed this far had been everywhere – she had barked excitedly, running from room to room, nose down, tail wagging cheerfully.

'Look,' Naomi said. 'Our Dennis burnt something here.' She was pointing at the fireplace.

Ben came and looked, but he could make out nothing – there were only bundles of ash which fell apart when he poked at them. Of course, they were Dennis's early tries at his note.

'Now what?' Naomi asked. 'He went to the castle from here, that's clear. The question is, do we follow or spend the night here?'

It had then been six o'clock. Outside it was already dark.

'I think we had better go on,' Ben said slowly. 'After all, it was you who said we wanted Frisky's nose, not her eyes . . . and I, for one, would testify before the throne of any King in creation that Frisky has a noble nose.'

Frisky, sitting in the doorway, barked as if to say she knew it.

'All right,' Naomi said.

He looked at her closely. It had been a long run from the camp of the exiles, with little rest for either of them. He knew they should stay . . . but he was nearly frantic with urgency.

'*Can* you go on?' he asked. 'Don't say you can if you can't, Naomi Reechul.'

She put her hands on her hips and looked at him haughtily. 'I could go on a hundred koner from the place where you dropped dead, Ben Staad.'

Ben grinned. 'You may get your chance to

prove it, too,' he said. 'But first we'll have a bite to eat.'

They ate quickly. When the meal was finished, Naomi knelt by Frisky and quietly told her that she must take up the scent again. Frisky didn't have to be asked twice. The three of them quit the farm-house, Ben with a large pack on his back, Naomi with one only slightly smaller.

To Frisky, Dennis's scent was a blue mark in the night, as bright as a wire glowing with an electric charge. She began to follow at once, and was con-fused when THE GIRL called her back. Then it came to her; if Frisky had been human, she would have slapped her forehead and groaned. In her impatience to be off, she had started sniffing up Dennis's back-trail. By midnight she would have had them back at Peyna's farmhouse.

'That's all right, Frisky,' Naomi said. 'Take your time.'

'Sure,' Ben said. 'Take a week or two, Frisky. Take a month, if you want.'

Naomi cast a sour glance Ben's way. Ben shut up – prudently, perhaps. The two of them watched Frisky nose back and forth, first across the dooryard of the deserted farm, then across the road.

'Has she lost it?' Ben asked.

'No, she'll pick it up in a minute or two.' *I think*, Naomi didn't say aloud. 'It's just that she's found a whole tangle of scents in the road and she has to sort them out.'

'Look!' Ben said doubtfully. "She's off into the field there. That can't be right, can it?'

'I don't know. Would he have taken the road to the castle?'

Ben Staad *was* human, and he *did* slap his forehead. 'No, of course not. I'm a dolt.'

Naomi smiled sweetly and said nothing.

In the field, Frisky had paused. She turned towards THE GIRL and THE TALL-BOY and barked impatiently for them to follow. Anduan huskies were the tame descendants of the great white wolves the residents of the Northern Barony had feared in earlier times, but tame or not, they were hunters and trackers before they were anything else. Frisky had isolated that bright-blue thread of scent again, and was in a fever to be off.

'Come on,' Ben said. 'I just hope she's found the right scent.'

'Of course she has! Look!'

She pointed, and Ben was just able to make out long, shallow tracks in the snow. Even in the dark Ben and Naomi knew the tracks for what they were – snowshoes.

Frisky barked again.

'Let's hurry,' Ben said.

By midnight, as they began to draw close to the King's Preserves, Naomi began to regret the crack she'd made about how she could go on a hundred koner from the place where Ben dropped dead, because she had begun to feel as if that might soon happen to her.

Dennis had made the trip in better time, but Dennis had set out after four days of rest, Dennis had had snowshoes, and Dennis had not been following a dog who sometimes lost the scent and had to cast about for it again. Naomi's legs felt hot and rubbery. Her lungs burned. There was a stitch in her left side. She had taken a few mouthfuls of snow, but they could not slake her raging thirst.

Frisky, who was not burdened by a pack and who could run lightly along the snow crust, was not tired at all. Naomi was able to walk on the crust for short distances, but then she would strike a rotten spot and plunge through the crust into soft snow up to her knees . . . and on several occasions, up to her hips. Once she plunged in waist-deep and floundered about in a tired fury until Ben worked his way over and pulled her out.

'Wish . . . sled,' she panted now.

'. . . wishes . . . horses . . . beggars'd ride,' he panted back, grinning in spite of his own weariness.

'Funny,' she gasped. 'Ha-ha. Ought to be a court jester, Ben Staad.'

'King's Preserves up there. Less snow . . . easier.'

He bent over, hands on his knees, and gasped for breath. Naomi suddenly felt that she had been selfish and unkind, thinking about how she herself felt, when Ben must be even closer to the point of exhaustion – he was much heavier than she, especially with the weight of the larger pack he carried added into the bargain. He had been breaking through the snow crust on almost every step, leaping through the long fields like a man running in deep water, and yet he had not complained or slowed.

'Ben, are you all right?'

'No,' he wheezed and grinned. 'But I'll make it, pretty child.'

'I am not a child!' she said angrily.

'But you *are* pretty,' he said, and put his thumb to the tip of his nose. He wiggled his fingers at her.

'Oh, I'll get you for that –'

'Later,' he panted. 'Race you to the woods. Come on.'

So they raced, with Frisky chasing along the scent ahead of them, and he beat her, and that made her madder than ever . . . but she admired him, too.

Now they stood looking across the seventy koner of open ground between the edge of the forest where King Roland had once slain a dragon and the walls of the castle where he had been slain himself. A few more snowflakes skirled down from the sky . . . and a few more . . . and suddenly, magically, the air was filled with snow.

In spite of his weariness, Ben felt a moment of peace and joy. He looked at Naomi and smiled. She tried a scowl but it wouldn't fit her face and so she smiled, too. A moment later, she ran her tongue out and tried to catch a flake of snow. Ben laughed quietly.

'How did he get inside, if he did?' Naomi asked.

'I don't know,' Ben said. He had grown up on a farm, and knew nothing of the castle's sewer system. Probably every bit as well for him, you might say, and you would be right. 'Perhaps your champion dog can show us how he did it.'

'You really think he did, don't you, Ben?'

'Oh, aye,' Ben said. 'What do you think, Frisky?'

At the sound of her name, Frisky got up, ranged along the scent for a few feet, and looked back at them.

Naomi looked at Ben. Ben shook his head.

'Not yet,' he said.

Naomi called Frisky softly, and she came back, whining.

'If she could talk, she'd tell you she's afraid of losing the scent. The snow will cover it.'

'We'll not wait long. Dennis had the snowshoes, but we're going to have something he didn't, Naomi.'

'What's that?'

'Cover.'

In spite of Frisky's growing restlessness at being checked on the scent, Ben made them wait fifteen minutes. By then the air had become a shifting cloud of white. Snow frosted Naomi's brown hair and his own blond hair; Frisky wore a cold ermine stole. They could no longer see the castle walls ahead of them.

'All right,' Ben said softly, 'let's go.'

They crossed the open ground behind Frisky. The big husky moved slowly now, her nose constantly at the snow, puffing it up every now and again in cold little bursts. The bright-blue runner of scent was dimming, being covered by the white no-smell stuff from the sky.

'We may have waited too long,' Naomi said quietly beside him.

Ben said nothing. He knew it, and the knowledge gnawed at his heart like a rat.

Now a dark bulk loomed out of the whiteness – the castle wall. Naomi had moved slightly ahead. Ben reached out and grabbed her arm. 'The moat,' he said. Don't forget that. It's up here somewhere. You'll go over the side and land on the ice and break your ne–'

He got just so far and then Naomi's eyes blazed with alarm. She pulled out of his grip. '*Frisky!*' she hissed. '*Hai!* Frisky! Danger! Drop-off!' She darted after the dog.

That girl is absolutely giddy bonkers, Ben thought with a certain admiration. Then *he* darted after *her.*

Naomi needn't have worried. Frisky had stopped at the edge of the moat. Her nose was buried in the snow and her tail was wagging happily. Now she bit down on something and dragged it out of the loose powder. She turned to Naomi, eyes asking:- *Now am I a good dog, or what? What do you think?*

Naomi laughed and hugged her dog.

Ben glanced towards the castle wall. 'Hush!' he whispered at her. 'If the guards hear you, we're in the slate-cracker for sure! Where do you think we are? Your back garden?'

'Pooh! If they heard anything, they'd think it was snow sprites and run for their mommies.' But she whispered, too. Then she buried her face in Frisky's fur and told her again what a good dog she was.

Ben scratched Frisky's head. Because of the snow, neither of them had the horribly exposed sense Dennis had had when he had sat in the same place, taking off the snowshoes Frisky had now found.

'Nose of the gods, all right,' Ben said. 'But what happened after he took off the snowshoes, Frisky? Did he grow wings and fly over the West'rd Redan? Where did he go from here?'

As if in answer, Frisky broke away from both of them and went floundering and slipping down the steep bank to the frozen moat.

'Frisky!' Naomi called, her voice low but alarmed.

Frisky only stood on the ice looking up at them, hock-deep in new snow. Her tail was wagging slightly, and her eyes begged them to come. She did not bark; somehow she knew better, even though Naomi had not thought to warn her to silence. But she barked in her *mind*. The scent was still here, and she wanted to follow it before it disappeared completely, as it now would within minutes.

Naomi looked questioningly at Ben.

'Yes,' he said. 'Of course. We have to. Come on. But keep her to heel – don't let her range ahead. There's danger here. I feel it.'

He held out his hand. Naomi grasped it, and they slid down to the moat together.

Frisky led them slowly across the ice towards the castle wall. She was now actually *digging* for the scent, her nose furrowing the snow. It had begun to be overlaid with a thick, unpleasant smell – dirty, warm water, garbage, ordure.

Dennis had known that the ice would begin to grow dangerously rotten as he got closer to the outflow pipe. Even if he hadn't known, he was able to see the three feet or so of open water next to the wall.

Things weren't so easy for Ben, Naomi, and Frisky. They had simply assumed that if the ice was thick along the moat's outer bank, it must be thick all the way across. And their eyes were of little use to them in the thickly falling snow.

Frisky's eyes were the weakest of the three, and she was in the lead. Her ears were sharp enough, and she had heard the ice groaning beneath the new snow . . . but the scent was too much on her mind for her to take much notice of the faint creaks . . . until the ice gave way beneath her and she plunged into the moat with a splash.

'*Frisky! Fr–*'

Ben clapped a hand over her mouth. She struggled to get away from him. Ben had now seen the danger, however, and held her fast.

Naomi needn't have worried. Of course all dogs can swim, and with her thick, oily coat, Frisky was safer in the water than either of the humans would have been. She paddled almost to the castle wall amid chunks of rotted ice and whipped-cream globs of snow that quickly turned into dark slush and disappeared. She raised her head, smelling, searching for the scent . . . and when she knew where it went, she

turned and paddled back towards Ben and Naomi.
She found the edge of the ice. Her paws broke it off,
and she tried again. Naomi cried out.

'Be still, Naomi, or you'll have us in the dungeons by dawn,' Ben said. 'Hold my ankles.' He
let her go and then sprawled on his belly. Naomi
crouched behind him and seized his boots. This close
to the ice, Ben could hear it groaning and muttering.
It could have been one of us, he thought, *and that would
have been trouble indeed.*

He spread his legs out a bit to distribute his
weight better, and then grabbed Frisky by the fore-
paws just below her wide, strong chest. 'Here you
come, girl,' Ben grunted. 'I hope.' Then he pulled.

For a moment, Ben thought that the ice would
just go on breaking under Frisky's weight as he
dragged her forward – first he and then Naomi
would follow Frisky into the moat. Crossing that
moat on his way into the castle to play with his friend
Peter on a summer's day, with blue sky and white
clouds reflecting off its surface, Ben had always
thought it beautiful, like a painting. He had never
once suspected that he might die in it one black night
during a snowstorm. And it smelled very bad.

'Pull me backward!' he grunted. 'Your damn
dog weighs a ton!'

'Don't you say mean things about my dog, Ben
Staad!'

Ben's eyes were slitted shut with strain, his lips
split open over clenched teeth. 'A million pardons.
And if you don't start pulling me, I'm going to be
taking a bath, I think.'

Somehow she managed to do it, although Ben

and Frisky together must have been three times her own weight. Ben's prone, splayed body dug a channel in the new powder; a snow pyramid built up in his crotch, the way it will build up in the angle of a wooden plough.

At last – it seemed like 'at last' to Ben and Naomi, although in truth it was probably only a matter of seconds – Frisky's chest stopped breaking the ice and slid on to it. A moment later, her rear paws were digging for purchase. Then she was up and shaking herself vigorously. Dirty moat water sprayed into Ben's face.

'Pah!' he grimaced, wiping it off. 'Thanks a lot, Frisky!'

But Frisky paid no attention. She was looking towards the wall of the castle again. Although the ice was already freezing to her pelt in dirty spicules, the scent was what interested her. She had smelled it clearly, above her but not *far* above her. There was a darkness there. No cold white no-smell stuff there.

Ben was getting to his feet, brushing the snow off.

'I'm sorry I yelled like that,' Naomi whispered. 'If it had been any other dog but Frisky . . . do you think I was heard?'

'If you'd been heard, we'd have been challenged,' Ben whispered back. 'Gods, that was close.' Now they could see the open water just in front of the ancient stone wall of Castle Delain's outer redan, because they were looking for it.

'What do we do?'

'We can't go on,' Ben whispered, 'that's obvious. But what did he *do*, Naomi? Where did he *go* from here? Maybe he *did* fly.'

'If we –'

But Naomi never finished the thought, because that was when Frisky took matters into her own paws. All of her ancestors had been famous hunters, and it was in her blood. She had been set upon this exciting, enticing electric-blue scent, and she found she could not leave it. So she screwed her haunches down to the ice, tensed her sled-toughened muscles, and leaped into the dark. Her eyes, as I've said, were the least of her sensory equipment, and her leap really *was* blind; she could not see the dark hole of the sewer pipe from the edge of the ice.

But she had seen it from the water, and even if she hadn't, she had her nose, and she *knew* it was there.

'**I**t's *Flagg*, Dennis's sleep-fuddled mind thought as that dark shape with the burning eyes swept down on him. *It's Flagg, he's found me, and now he'll rip my throat out with his teeth –*

He tried to scream, but no sound came out.

The mouth of the intruder *did* open; Dennis saw huge white teeth . . . and then a big warm tongue was lapping his face.

'Ulf!' Dennis said, trying to push the thing

away. Paws came up on either shoulder, and Dennis fell back on his mattress of napkins like a pinned wrestler. Lap-lap, lick-lick. '*Ulf!*' Dennis said again, and the dark, shaggy shape uttered a low, companionable woof, as if to say *I know it, I'm glad to see you, too.*

'Frisky!' a low voice called from the darkness. 'Stand down, Frisky! No sounds!'

The dark shape was not Flagg at all; it was an extremely large dog – a dog which looked too much like a wolf for comfort, Dennis thought. When the girl spoke, it drew away and sat down. It looked happily at Dennis; its tail thumped mutedly on Dennis's bed of napkins.

Two more shapes in the darkness, one taller than the other. Not Flagg, that much was clear. Castle guards, then. Dennis grabbed his dagger. If the gods were good, he might be able to get rid of both of them. If not, then he would try to die well in the service of his King.

The two figures had stopped a little short of him.

'Come on,' Dennis said, and raised his dagger (it was really not much more than a pocketknife, and was rather rusty and quite dull) in a brave gesture. 'First you two and then your devil-dog!'

'Dennis?' The voice was eerily familiar. 'Dennis, have we really found you?'

Dennis started to lower his dagger, then brought it up again. It had to be a trick. *Had* to be. But the voice sounded so much like –

'Ben?' he whispered. 'Is it Ben Staad?'

'It's Ben,' the taller shape confirmed, and gladness filled Dennis's heart. The shape began to come forward. Alarmed, Dennis raised his dagger again.

'Wait! Do you have a light?'

'Flint and steel, yes.'

'Strike it.'

'Aye.'

A moment later, a big yellow spark, surely dangerous in that room filled with dry cotton napkins, flared in the gloom.

'Come forward, Ben,' Dennis said, reseating his poor excuse for a dagger in its sheath. He got to his feet, trembling with gladness and relief. Ben was here. By what magic Dennis did not know – only that he had somehow happened. His feet caught in the napkins and he stumbled forward, but there was no danger that he might fall, because Ben's arms swept him up in a strong embrace. Ben was here and all would be well, Dennis thought, and it was all he could do to keep from bursting into unmanly tears.

107

There followed a great exchange of stories – I think you have heard most of them, and the parts you haven't can be told quickly enough.

Frisky's leap was a bull's-eye. She carried straight into the pipe and then turned around to see if Naomi and Ben would follow her.

If they hadn't done so, Frisky would have

eventually leaped back to the ice – she should have been greatly disappointed to do it, but she would not have left her mistress for the most exciting scent in the world. *Frisky* knew that; Naomi was less sure. She didn't even dare call Frisky back, for fear of a guard's overhearing. She therefore intended to go after the dog. She would not leave Frisky, and if Ben tried to make her, she would deck him with a right hook.

She needn't have worried. The minute he spotted the pipe, Ben understood where Dennis had gone.

'Noble nose, Frisky,' he said again. He turned to Naomi 'Can you make it?'

'If I draw back and run, I can make it.'

'Don't misjudge where the ice goes rotten or you'll take a dunking. And your heavy clothes will drag you down very quickly.'

'I won't misjudge.'

'Let me go first,' Ben said. 'If I have to, maybe I can catch you.'

He drew back a few paces and jumped so strongly that he almost took off the top of his head on the upper curve of the pipe. Frisky barked once, excitedly. 'Shut up, dog!' Ben said.

Naomi drew back to the edge of the moat, stood there for a moment (the snow had by then been coming down so heavily that Ben couldn't see her), and then ran forward. Ben held his breath, hoping she wouldn't misjudge the edge of the good ice. If she ran too far before trying to make her leap, the longest arms in the world wouldn't catch her.

But she timed it perfectly. Ben didn't need to

catch her; all he had to do was to get out of her way as she carried into the pipe. She didn't even bump her head, as Ben had done.

'The worst part of it was the smell,' Naomi said as they told their story to a wondering Dennis. 'How did you stand it?'

'Well, I just kept reminding myself of what would happen to me if I got caught,' Dennis said. 'Every time I did that, the air seemed to smell a little better.'

Ben laughed at this and nodded, and Dennis looked at him with shining eyes for a moment. Then he looked back at Naomi. 'It *did* smell awfully bad, though,' he agreed. 'I remember that it smelled bad when I was a kid, but not *that* bad. Maybe a kid doesn't really know how bad a smell is. Or something.'

'I guess that could be,' Naomi said.

Frisky was lying on a pile of royal napkins with her muzzle on her paws, her eyes moving from one person to the next as each spoke. She knew very little of what they were saying, but if she had, and if she could have spoken, she would have told Dennis that his perceptions of what made a really bad smell hadn't changed at all since he was a boy. It had been the last dying remainder of the Dragon Sand they had smelled, of course. The odour had been much stronger to Frisky than to THE GIRL and THE TALL-BOY. Dennis's scent had still been there, now mostly in splashes and blobs on the curved walls (these were the places Dennis had touched with his hands; the floor of the pipes was covered with a foul warm water that had washed away all scent). It was the same bright electric blue. The other scent was a dull leathery green – Frisky was afraid of it. She knew that some scents could kill, and she knew that, not so long ago, this had been just such a scent. But it was losing its potency now, and in any case, Dennis's scent led away from the greater concentrations of it. Not too long before they reached the grating Dennis had used to get out of the sewer system, she began to lose the green smell altogether – and Frisky was never in her whole life so happy to lose a smell.

'You met no one? No one at all?' Dennis asked anxiously.

'No one,' Ben said. 'I ranged a little bit ahead to keep an eye out. I saw guards several times, but we always had plenty of time to get to some cover before they could see us. In truth, I think we could have come directly here and passed twenty guards and only have been challenged once or twice. Most of them were drunk.'

Naomi nodded. 'Guards o' the Watch,' she said. 'Drunk. And not drunk out on picket along the northern borders of some pissy little barony no one ever heard of; drunk in the castle. *Right in the castle!*'

Dennis, remembering the toneless, nose-blowing singer, nodded gloomily. 'I suppose we should be glad. If the Guard o' the Watch was now what it was in Roland's day, we'd all be in the Needle along wi' Peter. But I can't be glad, somehow.'

'I'll tell you this,' Ben said in a soft voice, 'if I were Thomas, I'd quake in my boots every time I looked north, if such as we saw tonight are all he has around him.'

Naomi looked very troubled at this. 'Pray the gods it never comes to that,' she said.

Ben nodded.

Dennis reached out and stroked Frisky's head. 'Followed me all the way from Peyna's, did you? What a smart dog you are, aye!'

Frisky thumped her tail happily.

Naomi said: 'I would hear this story of the sleep-walking King, Dennis, if you would tell it again.'

So Dennis told his story, much as he told it to Peyna and as I have told it to you, and they listened as spellbound as children hearing the tale of the talking wolf in the gammer's nightcap.

108

By the time he had finished, it was seven o'clock. Outside, a dim glow had come over Delain – that clotted storm-light was as bright at seven as it would be at noon, for the greatest storm of that winter – and perhaps the greatest in history – had come to Delain. The wind howled around the eaves of the castle like a tribe of banshees. Even down here, the fugtives could hear it. Frisky raised her head and whined uneasily.

'What do we do now?' Dennis asked.

Ben, who had gone over Peter's brief note again and again, said: 'Until tonight, nothing. The castle's awake by now, and there's no way we could get out

of here without being seen under any circumstances.
We sleep. Get our strength back. And tonight, before
midnight –'

Ben spoke briefly. Naomi grinned; Dennis's
eyes grew bright with excitement. 'Yes!' Dennis
said. 'By the gods! You're a genius, Ben!'

'Please, I wouldn't go *that* far,' Naomi said, but
by then her grin was so broad it seemed in danger of
splitting her head in two. She reached over, put her
arms around Ben, and kissed him soundly.

Ben turned an absolutely alarming shade of red
(he looked as if he might be on the verge of 'bursting
his brains,' as they said in Delain in those long-ago
days) – I must tell you, though, that he also looked
delighted.

'Will Frisky help us?' Ben asked when he got his
breath back.

At the sound of her name, Frisky looked up
again.

'Of course she will. But we'll need . . .'

They discussed this new plan for some time
longer, and then Ben's lower face seemed to almost
disappear in a great yawn. Naomi also looked tired
out. They had been awake for over twenty-four
hours by then, you will remember, and had come a
great distance.

'Enough,' Ben said. 'It's time for sleep.'

'Hooray!' Naomi said, beginning to arrange
more napkins in a mattress for herself beside Frisky.
'My legs feel as if –'

Dennis cleared his throat politely.

'What is it?' Ben asked.

Dennis looked at their packs – Ben's big one,

Naomi's slightly smaller one. 'I don't suppose you've got . . . um, anything to eat in there, do you?'

Impatiently, Naomi said: 'Of course we do! What do you think –' Then she remembered that Dennis had left Peyna's farmhouse six days ago, and that the butler had been skulking and hiding ever since. He had a pallid, undernourished look, and his face was too narrow and too bony. 'Oh, Dennis, I'm sorry, we're idiots! When did you eat last?'

Dennis thought about this. 'I can't remember exactly,' he said. 'But the last sit-down meal I had was my lunch, a week ago.'

'Why didn't you say so first thing, you dolt?' Ben exclaimed.

'I guess because I was so excited to see you,' Dennis said, and grinned. As he watched the two of them open their packs and begin rooting through the remainder of their supplies, his stomach gurgled noisily. Saliva squirted into his mouth. Then a thought struck him.

'You didn't bring any turnips, did you?'

Naomi turned to look at him, puzzled. 'Turnips? *I* don't have any. Do you, Ben?'

'No.'

A gentle and supremely happy smile spread across Dennis's face. 'Good,' he said.

109

•**T**•hat was a mighty storm indeed, and it's still told of in Delain today. Five feet of new snow had fallen by the time an early, howling dark came down on the castle keep. Five feet of new snow in one day is mighty enough, but the wind made drifts that were much, much bigger. By the time dark fell, the wind was no longer blowing a force-gale; it was blowing a hurricane. In places along the castle walls, snow was piled twenty-five feet deep, and covered the windows of not just first and second floors, but the third-floor windows as well.

You might think this would have been good for Peter's escape plans, and it might have been if the Needle hadn't stood all alone in the Plaza. But it did, and here the wind blew its hardest. A strong man couldn't have stood against that wind; he would have been sent rolling, head over heels, until he crashed against the first stone wall on the far side of the Plaza. And the wind had another effect, as well – it was like a giant broom. As fast as the snow fell, the wind blew it out of the Plaza. By dark there were huge drifts piled against the castle and clogging most of the alleys on the west side of the castle keep, but the Plaza itself was clean as a whistle. There were only the frozen cobbles, waiting to break Peter's bones if his rope should break.

And I must tell you now that Peter's rope was *bound* to break. When he tested it, it had held his weight . . . but there was one fact about that mystic thing called 'breaking strain' that Peter didn't know. Yosef hadn't known, either. The ox drivers knew it, though, and if Peter had asked them, they would have told him an old axiom, one known to sailors, loggers, seamstresses, and anyone else who works with thread or rope: *The longer the cord, the sooner the break.*

Peter's short test rope had held him.

The rope to which he meant to entrust his life – the very *thin* rope – was about two hundred and sixty-five feet long.

It was bound to break, I tell you, and the cobbles below waited to catch him, and break his bones, and bleed away his life.

110

There were many disasters and near-disasters on that long, stormy day, just as there were many acts of heroism, some successful and some doomed to failure. Some farmhouses in the Inner Baronies blew over, as the houses of the indolent pigs were blown over by the wolf's hungry breath in the old story. Some of those who were thus rendered homeless managed to work their way across the white wastes to the castle keep, roped together for safety; others wandered off the Delain Great Road and into the whiteness, where they were lost – their frozen, wolf-gnawed bodies wouldn't be found until the spring.

But by seven that evening, the snow had finally begun to abate a little, and the wind to fall The excitement was ending, and the castle went to bed early. There was little else to do. Fires were banked, children tucked in, last cups of field-tea drunk, prayers said.

One by one, the lights went out. The Crier called in his loudest voice, but the wind still tore his voice out of his mouth at eight o' the clock and again at nine; it was not until ten that he could be heard again, and by then, most people were asleep.

Thomas was also asleep – but his sleep was not easy. There was no Dennis to stay with him and comfort him this night; Dennis was still home ill. Thomas had thought several times of sending a page to check on him (or even to go himself; he liked Dennis very much), but something always seemed to come up – papers to sign . . . petitions to hear . . . and, of course, bottles of wine to be drunk. Thomas hoped Flagg would come and give him a powder to help him sleep . . . but ever since Flagg's useless trip into the north, the magician had been strange and distant. It was as if Flagg knew there was something wrong, but could not quite tell what it was. Thomas hoped the magician would come, but hadn't dared to summon him.

As always, the shrieking wind reminded Thomas of the night his father died, and he feared he would have a hard time getting to sleep . . . and that, once he was asleep, horrible nightmares might come, dreams in which his father would scream and rant and finally burst into flames. So Thomas did what he had grown accustomed to doing; he spent the day with a glass of wine always in his hand, and if I told

you how many bottles of wine this mere boy consumed before he finally went to bed at ten o' the
clock, you probably wouldn't believe me – so I won't
say. But it was a lot.

Lying there miserably on his sofa, wishing that
Dennis was in his accustomed place on the hearth,
Thomas thought: *my head aches and my stomach feels
sick . . . Is being King worth all this? I wonder.* You
might wonder, too . . . but before Thomas himself
could wonder anymore, he fell heavily asleep.

He slept for almost an hour . . . and then he rose
and walked. Out the door he went and down the
halls, ghostly in his long white nightshirt. This night
a late-going maid with an armload of sheets saw him,
and he looked so much like old King Roland that the
maid dropped her sheets and fled, screaming.

Thomas's darkly dreaming mind heard her
screams and thought they were his father's.

He walked on, turning into the less used corridor. He paused halfway down and pushed the
secret stone. He went into the passageway, closed
the door behind him, and walked to the end of the
corridor. He pushed aside the panels which were
behind Niner's glass eyes, and though he was still
asleep, he pushed his face up to the holes, as if looking
into his dead father's sitting room. And here we will
leave the unfortunate boy for a while, with the smell
of wine surrounding him and tears of regret running
from his sleeping eyes and down his cheeks.

He was sometimes a cruel boy, often a sad boy,
this pretend King, and he had almost always been a
weak boy . . . but even now I must tell you that I do
not believe he was ever really a *bad* boy. If you hate

him because of the things he did – and the things he *allowed* to be done – I will understand; but if you do not pity him a little as well, I will be surprised.

At quarter past eleven on that momentous night, the storm breathed its last gasp. A tremendous cold gust of wind swept down on the castle. It ran in excess of a hundred miles an hour. It tore the thinning clouds overhead apart like the swipe of a great hand. Cold, watery moonlight shone through.

In the Third East'ard Alley was a squat stone tower called the Church of the Great Gods; it had stood there since time out of mind. Many people worshipped there, but it was empty now. A good thing, too. The tower was not very tall – nowhere near the height of the Needle – but it nevertheless stood high above the neighbouring buildings in the Third East'ard Alley, and all day long it had been punished by the unbroken force of the storm wind. This final gust was too much for it. The top thirty feet – all stone – simply blew off, as a hat might fly off a scarecrow in a high gale. Part landed in the alley; part hit the neighbouring buildings. There was a tremendous crash.

Most of the populace of the castle keep, wearied

by the excitement of the storm and already sleeping deeply, took no mind of the fall of the Church of the Great Gods (although they would wonder greatly over the snow-covered wreckage in the morning). Most simply muttered, turned over, and went back to sleep.

Some Guards of the Watch – those not too drunk to care – heard it, of course, and ran to see what had happened. Other than by these few, the fall of the tower went mostly unremarked when it happened . . . but there were a few others who heard it, and by now you know them all.

Ben, Dennis, and Naomi, who were getting ready for their attempt to rescue the rightful King, heard it in the napkin storeroom, and looked around at each other with wide eyes. 'Never mind,' Ben said, after a moment. 'I don't know what it was, but it doesn't matter. Let's get on with it.'

Beson and the Lesser Warders, all of them drunk, didn't hear the Church of the Great Gods fall down, but Peter did. He was sitting on the floor of his bedroom, carefully pulling his woven rope through his fingers, looking anxiously for weak points. He raised his head at the snow-muted thunder of falling stones, and went rapidly to the window. He could see nothing; whatever had fallen was on the Needle's far side. After considering for several moments, he went back to his rope. Midnight was close now, and he had come to much the same conclusion as his friend Ben. It didn't matter. The dice had been thrown. Now he must go on.

Deep in the darkness of the secret passage, Thomas heard the muffled thunder-thud of the falling tower and woke up. He heard the muffled barking of dogs below him and realized in horror where he was.

And one other who had been sleeping lightly and dreaming troubled dreams awoke at the fall of the tower. He woke even though he was deep in the bowels of the castle.

'*Disaster!*' one of the parrot's two heads screamed.

'*Fire, flood, and escape!*' the other screamed.

Flagg had awakened. I have told you that evil is sometimes strangely blind, and so it is. Sometimes evil is lulled with no reason, and sleeps.

But now Flagg had awakened.

112

Flagg had come back from his trip into the north with a bit of a fever, a heavy cold, and a troubled mind.

Something wrong, something wrong. The very stones of the castle seemed to whisper it to him . . . but Flagg was damned if he knew what it was. All he knew for sure was that unknown 'something wrong' had sharp teeth. It felt like a ferret running around in his brain, taking a bite here and a bite there. He knew exactly when that animal had begun to run and gnaw: while he was coming back from the fruitless expedition in search of the rebels. Because . . . because . . .

Because the rebels should have been there!

They hadn't been, and Flagg hated to be fooled.
Worse, he hated feeling that he might have made a
mistake. If he had made a mistake about where the
rebels were to be found, then perhaps he had made
mistakes about other things. What other things? He
didn't know. But his dreams were bad. That small,
bad-tempered animal ran around in his head, worrying him, insisting that he had forgotten things, that
other things were going on behind his back. It raced,
it gnawed, it ruined his sleep. Flagg had medicines
that would rid him of his cold, but none that would
touch that growing ferret in his brain.

What could possibly be wrong?

He asked himself this question over and over
again, and in truth it seemed – on the surface, at least
– that *nothing* could be. For many centuries, the old
dark chaos inside him had hated the love and light
and order of Delain, and he had worked hard to
destroy all that – to knock it down as that last cold
gust of storm had knocked down the Church of the
Great Gods. Always, something had interfered with
his plans – a Kyla the Good, a Sasha, some*one*, some-
thing. But now he saw no possible interference, no
matter where he looked. Thomas was totally his
creature; if Flagg told him to step off the highest
parapet of the castle, the fool would want to know
only at which o'clock he should do it. The farmers
were groaning under the weight of the killing taxes
Flagg had persuaded Thomas to impose.

Yosef had told Peter there was a breaking strain
on people as well as on ropes and chains, and so there
is – the farmers and the merchants of Delain had nearly

reached theirs. The rope by which the great blocks of taxes are attached to any citizenry is simple loyalty – loyalty to King, to country, to government. Flagg knew that if he made the tax-blocks big enough, all the ropes would snap, and the stupid oxen – for that was really how he saw the people of Delain – would stampede, knocking down everything in their path. The first of the oxen had already broken free and had gathered in the north. They called themselves exiles now, but Flagg knew they would call themselves rebels soon enough. Peyna had been driven away and Peter was locked in the Needle.

So what could be wrong?

Nothing! Damn it, *nothing!*

But the ferret ran and squirmed and gnawed and twisted. Many times over the last three or four weeks he had awakened in a cold sweat, not because of his recurring fever but because he had had some horrible dream. What was the substance of this dream? He could never remember. He only knew that he woke from it and with his left hand pressed to his left eye, as if he had been wounded there – and that eye would burn, although he could find nothing wrong with it.

113

On this night, Flagg awoke with his dream fresh in his mind, because he was awakened before it was over. It was, of course, the fall of the Church of the Great Gods which woke him.

'*Huh!*' Flagg cried, sitting bolt upright in his chair. His eyes were wide and staring, his white cheeks damp and shiny with sweat.

'*Disaster!*' one of the parrot's heads screamed.

'*Fire, flood, and escape!*' the other screamed.

Escape, Flagg thought. *Yes – that's what's been on my mind all this time, that's what's been gnawing at me.*

He looked down at his hands and saw that they were trembling. This infuriated him, and he sprang out of his chair.

'He means to escape,' he muttered, running his hands through his hair. 'He means to *try*, anyway. But how? *How?* What's his plan? Who helped him? They'll pay with their heads, I promise that . . . and they won't come off all in a chop, no! They'll come off an inch . . . a half-inch . . . a *quarter*-inch . . . at a time. They'll be driven insane with the agony long before they die . . .'

'*Insane!*' one of the parrot heads shrieked.

'*Agony!*' the other shrieked back.

'*Will you shut up and let me think!*' Flagg howled. He seized a jar filled with murky brown fluid from a nearby table and threw it at the parrot's cage. It struck and shattered; there was a flash of bright, heatless light. The parrot's two heads squawked in terror; it fell off its perch and lay stunned at the bottom of its cage until morning.

Flagg began to pace rapidly back and forth. His teeth were bared. His hands worked together restlessly, the fingers of one warring with the fingers of the other. His boots struck up greenish sparks from the nitre-caked stones of his laboratory floor; these sparks smelled like summer lightning.

How? When? Who helped?

He could not remember. Already the dream was fading. But . . .

'I *have* to know!' he whispered. 'I *have* to know!'

Because it would be soon; he sensed that much. It would be very, very soon.

He found his key ring and opened the bottom drawer of his desk. He took out a box made of finely carved ironwood, opened it, and drew out a leather bag. He opened the bag's drawstring top and carefully took out a chunk of rock that seemed to glow with its own inner light. This rock was as milky as an old man's blind eye. It looked like a piece of soapstone, but was in fact a crystal – Flagg's magic crystal.

He circled his room, turning down the lamps and capping the candles. Soon his apartment was in absolute darkness. Dark or not, Flagg returned to his desk with quick confidence, passing easily around objects that you or I would have barked our shins on or fallen over. The dark was nothing to the King's magician; he liked the dark, and he could see in it like a cat.

He sat down and touched the stone. He slipped his palms down its sides, feeling its ragged edges and angles.

'Show me,' he murmured. 'This is my command.'

At first, nothing. Then, little by little, the crystal began to glow from within. There was only a tiny light at first, diffuse and pallid. Flagg touched the crystal again, this time with the tips of his fingers. It had grown warm.

'Show me Peter. This is my command. Show me the whelp that dares put himself in my way, and show me what he plans to do.'

The light grew brighter . . . brighter . . . brighter. Eyes glittering, cruel thin lips parted to show his teeth, Flagg bent over his crystal. Now Peter, Ben, Dennis, and Naomi would have recognized their dream – and they would have recognized the glow which lit the magician's face, the glow which was not a candle.

The crystal's milky cast suddenly disappeared, drawing into the brightening glow. Now Flagg could see into its heart. His eyes widened . . . then narrowed in bewilderment.

It was Sasha, very pregnant, sitting at a little boy's bed. The little boy was holding a slate. On it were written two words: GOD and DOG.

Impatiently, Flagg passed his hands over the crystal, which now gave off waves of heat

'Show me what I need to know! This is my command!'

The crystal cleared again.

It was Peter, playing with his dead mother's doll's house, pretending the house and the family inside were being attacked by Indians . . . or dragons . . . or some foolish thing. The old King stood in the corner, watching his son, wanting to join in . . .

'Bah!' Flagg cried, waving his hands over the crystal again. 'Why do you show me these old, meaningless stories? I need to know how he plans to escape . . . and when! Now show me! *This is my command!*'

The crystal had grown hotter and hotter. If he

did not allow it to go dark soon, it would split apart
forever, Flagg knew, and magic crystals were not
easy to come by – it had taken thirty years of searching to find this one. But he would see it broken into
a billion pieces before he gave up.

'This is my command!' he repeated again, and for
the third time, the milkiness of the crystal drew inward.
Flagg bent over it until its heat made his eyes water and
gush tears. He slitted them . . . and then, in spite of the
heat, they flew open wide in shock and fury.

It was Peter. Peter was slowly descending the
side of the Needle. Surely this was some treacherous
magic, because, although he was making hand-over-
hand motions, there was no rope to be seen –

Or . . . *was* there?

Flagg waved a hand in front of his face, dissipating the heat for a moment. A rope? Not exactly. But
there was something . . . something as gossamer as
a strand of spiderweb . . . and yet it bore his weight.

'*Peter*,' Flagg breathed, and at the sound of his
voice, the tiny figure looked around.

Flagg blew on the crystal and its bright, wavering light went out. He saw its afterglow in front of
his eyes as he sat in the dark.

Peter. Escaping. When? It had been night in the
crystal, and Flagg had seen errant, gritty sheaves of
snow blowing past the tiny figure working its way
down the rounded wall. Was it to be later tonight?
Tomorrow night? Sometime next week? Or –

Flagg pushed back from his desk and stood up
with a lurch. His eyes filled with fire as he looked
around his dark and stinking basement rooms.

– *or had it happened already?*

'Enough,' he breathed. 'By all the gods that ever were and ever will be, this is *enough*.'

He strode across the darkened room and seized a huge weapon that hung on the wall. It was clumsy, but he held it with ease and familiarity. Familiar with it? Yes, of course he was! He had swung it many times when he had lived here and done business as Bill Hinch, the most feared executioner Delain had ever known. This terrible blade had bitten through hundreds of necks. Above the blades, which were of twice-forged Anduan steel, was Flagg's own modification – a spiked iron ball. Each spike had been tipped with poison.

'*ENOUGH!*' Flagg screamed again in a fury of rage and frustration and fear. The two-headed parrot even in the depths of its unconsciousness, moaned at that sound.

Flagg pulled his cloak from the hook by the door, swept it over his shoulders, and fastened the clasp – a hammered-silver scarab beetle – at his throat.

It was enough. This time his plans would not be thwarted, certainly not by one hateful boy. Roland was dead, Peyna unbenched, the nobles driven into exile. There was no one to raise an outcry over one dead prince . . . especially one who had murdered his own father.

If you have not escaped, my fine prince, you never will – and something tells me you're still in the coop. But part of you WILL leave tonight, I promise you that – that part I intend to carry out by the hair.

As he strode down the corridor toward the Dungeon Gate, Flagg began to laugh . . . a sound which would have given a stone statue bad dreams.

*F*lagg's intuition was right. Peter had finished going over his rope of twisted linen fibres, but he was still in his tower room, awaiting the Crier's announcement of midnight, when Flagg burst out of the Dungeon Gate and began to cross the Plaza of the Needle. The Church of the Great Gods had fallen at quarter past eleven; it was quarter of twelve when the crystal showed Flagg what he wanted to know (and perhaps you'll agree with my idea that it tried to show him the truth in two other ways at first), and when Flagg started across the Plaza, it was still lacking ten minutes of midnight.

The Dungeon Gate was on the northeast side of the Needle. On the southwest side was a little castle entrance known as the Peddlers' Gate. A straight diagonal line could have been drawn between the Dungeon Gate and the Peddlers' Gate. At the exact midpoint of that line was the Needle itself, of course.

At almost the same time that Flagg came out of the Dungeon Gate, Ben, Naomi, Dennis, and Frisky came out of the Peddlers' Gate. They approached each other without knowing it. The Needle was between them, but the wind had dropped, and Ben's party should have heard the clang-rasp of Flagg's boot heels against the cobbles; Flagg should have heard the faint squeak of an ungreased wheel. But all of them, including Frisky (who was back to her old job of pulling again), were lost in their own thoughts.

Ben and his party reached the Needle first.

'Now –' Ben began, and at that moment, from the *other* side, less than forty paces around the outside perimeter from where they now stood, Flagg began to hammer on the triple-bolted Warders' Door.

'*Open!*' Flagg screamed. '*Open in the name of the King!*'

'What –' Dennis began, and then Naomi clamped a hand like steel over his mouth and looked at Ben with frightened eyes.

115

The voice came spiralling up to Peter on the cold post-storm air. It was faint, that voice, but perfectly clear.

'*Open in the name of the King!*'

Open in the name of hell, you mean, Peter thought.

The good brave boy had become a good brave man, but when he heard that hoarse voice and remembered that narrow white face and those reddish eyes, always shadowed by the hood of his robe, Peter's bones turned to ice and his stomach to fire. His mouth went as dry as a wood chip. His tongue stuck to the roof of his mouth. His hair stood on end. If someone has ever told you that being good and being brave means you will never be afraid, what that someone told you is not so. At that moment, Peter had never been so afraid in his whole life.

It's Flagg, and he's come for me.

Peter got up and, for a moment, he thought he was going to simply fall over as his legs buckled under him. Doom was down there, hammering at the Warders' Door to be let in.

'*Open up! On your feet, you licey drunken buggers! Beson, you son of a sot!*'

Don't hurry, Peter told himself. *If you hurry you'll make a mistake and do his work for him. No one's come to let him in yet. Beson's drunk – he was tiddly at supper and probably paralyzed by the time he got to bed. Flagg hasn't a key or he wouldn't be wasting time knocking. So . . . one step at a time. Just as you planned it. He's got to get in, and then climb those stairs – all three hundred of them. You may beat him yet.*

He went into his bedroom and pulled out the rough iron cotter pins that held the crude bedframe together. The bed collapsed. Peter grabbed one of the iron side-bars and carried it back into the sitting room. He had measured this bar carefully and knew it was wider than his window, and while its outer surface was rusted, he thought it was strong yet through the middle. *It had better be*, he thought. *It would be a bitter joke indeed if my rope held but my anchor broke.*

He looked out briefly. He could see no one now, but he had observed three figures crossing the Plaza toward the Needle shortly before Flagg's wild pounding had begun. Dennis had recruited friends, then. Had one of them been Ben? Peter hoped so, but did not dare to really believe it. Who was the third? And why the wagon? They were questions he had no time for now.

'*Oh, you dogs! Open this door! Open it in the King's name! Open it in the name of FLAGG! Open the door! Open* –'

In the stillness of almost midnight, Peter heard the rattle-thud of the wrist-thick iron bolts far below being drawn back. He supposed the door opened, but he didn't hear that. Silence . . .

. . . and then a gurgling, choked scream.

The unfortunate Lesser Warder who finally answered Flagg's summons lived less than four seconds after drawing the third bolt on the Warders' Door. He caught a nightmare glimpse of a white face, glaring red eyes, and a black cloak that blew backward in the dying breeze like the wings of a raven. he screamed. Then the air was filled with a dry whooshing sound. The Lesser Warder, who was still half drunk, looked up just as Flagg's battle-axe split his head in two.

'Next time someone knocks in the name of the King, bestir yourselves and you won't have a mess to clean up in the morning!' Flagg bellowed. Then, laughing wildly, he kicked aside the body and strode up the corridor toward the stairs. Things were still all right. He had awakened to the danger in time. He knew it.

He *felt* it.

He opened a door on the right and stepped into the main corridor leading away from the courtroom where Anders Peyna had once dispensed justice. At the end of that corridor, the stairs began. He looked up, grinning his dreadful, sharklike grin.

'*Here I come, Peter!*' he cried happily, his voice echoing and rebounding, spiralling up and up and up to where Peter stood preparing to tie his thin rope to the bar he had taken from the bed. '*Here I come, dear Peter, to do what I should have done a long, long time ago!*'

Flagg's grin broadened and now he looked terrible indeed – he looked like a demon which might have climbed lately from some reeking pit in the earth. He raised the executioner's axe; drops of the slain warder's blood fell onto his face and ran down his cheeks like tears.

'*Here I come, dear Peter, to chop off your head!*' Flagg screamed and began to run up the stairs.

One. Three. Six. Ten.

117

Peter's shaking hands went wrong somehow. A knot he had made easily a thousand times before now fell apart and he had to start over again.

Don't let him scare you.

That was idiotic. He was scared, all right: scared green. Thomas would have been astounded to know that Peter had *always* been frightened of Flagg; Peter had just hid it better.

If he's going to kill you, make HIM *do it! Don't do it for him!*

The thought came from inside his own head . . . but it sounded like his mother's voice. Peter's hands steadied a bit, and he began to knot the end of his rope to his anchor again.

118

'**I**'*ll carry your head on my saddle horn for a thousand years!*' Flagg screamed. Up and up, around and around. '*Oh, what a pretty trophy you'll make!*'

Twenty. Thirty. Forty.

His boot heels struck green fire from the stones. His eyes glared. His grin was poison.

'*HERE I COME, PETER!*'

Seventy – two hundred and thirty steps to go.

119

'**I**f you have ever awakened in a strange place in the middle of the night, you'll know that just to be alone in the dark can be frightening enough;

now try to imagine waking in a secret passage, looking through concealed eyeholes into the room where you saw your own father murdered!

Thomas shrieked. No one heard him (unless the dogs below did, and I doubt that – they were old, deaf, and making too much noise themselves).

Now, there was an idea about sleepwalking in Delain – one that has also been commonly held as the truth in our world. This idea is that if a sleepwalker wakes up before returning to his or her bed, he or she will go mad.

Thomas might have heard this tale. If so, he could attest that it wasn't true at all. He'd had a bad scare, and he had screamed, but he did not come even *close* to going mad.

In fact, his initial fright passed rather quickly – more quickly than some of you might think – and he looked back into the peepholes again. This may strike some of you as strange, but you have to remember that, before the terrible night when Flagg had come with his own glass of wine after Peter left, Thomas had spent some pleasant times in this dark passageway. The pleasantness had a sour undertone of guilt, but he had also felt close to his father. Now, being back here, he felt a queer sense of nostalgia.

He saw that the room had hardly changed at all. The stuffed heads were still there – Bonsey the elk, Craker the lynx, Snapper the great white bear from the north. And, of course, Niner the dragon, which he now looked through, with Roland's bow and the arrow Foe-Hammer mounted above it.

Bonsey . . . Craker . . . Snapper . . . Niner.

I remember all their names, Thomas thought with

some wonder. *And I remember you. Dad. I wish you were alive now and that Peter was free, even if it meant no one even knew I was alive. At least I could sleep at night.*

Some of the furniture had been covered with white dust-sheets, but most had not. The fireplace was cold and dark, but a fire had been laid. Thomas saw with mounting wonder that even his father's old robe was still there, hung in its accustomed place on the hook by the bathroom door. The fireplace was cold, but it wanted only a match struck and held to the kindling to bring it alive, roaring and warm; the room wanted only his father to do the same for *it.*

Suddenly Thomas became aware of a strange, almost eerie desire in himself; he wanted to go into that room. He wanted to light the fire. He wanted to put on his father's robe. He wanted to drink a glass of his father's mead. He would drink it even if it had gone bad and bitter. He thought . . . he thought he might be able to sleep in there.

A wan, tired smile dawned on the boy's face, and he decided to do it. He wasn't even afraid of his father's ghost. He almost hoped it would come. If it did, he could tell his father something.

He could tell his father he was sorry.

'C<small>OMING, PETER!</small>' Flagg shrieked, grinning. He smelled like blood and doom; his eyes were deadly fire. The headsman's axe swished and whickered, and a last few drops of blood flew from the blade and splashed on the walls. 'COMING NOW! COMING FOR YOUR HEAD!'

Up and around, up and around, higher and higher. He was a devil with murder on his mind.

A hundred. A hundred and twenty-five.

'**E**aster,' Ben Staad panted to Dennis and Naomi. The temperature had begun to fall again, but all three of them were sweating. Some of the sweat came from exertion – they were working very hard. But much of their sweat had been caused by fear. They could hear Flagg shrieking. Even Frisky, with her brave heart, felt afraid. She had withdrawn a little and huddled on her haunches, whimpering.

'**C**OMING, YOU LITTLE WHELP!'

Closer now – his voice was flatter, with less echo.

*'COMING TO DO WHAT I SHOULD HAVE DONE A
LONG TIME AGO!'*
The twin blades swished and whickered.

123

•**T**•his time the knot held.

Gods help me, Peter thought, and looked back
once more toward the sound of Flagg's rising, shrieking voice. *Gods help me now.*

Peter threw one leg out the window. Now he
sat astride the sill as if it were Peony's saddle, one
leg on the stone floor of his sitting room, the other
dangling over the drop. He held the heap of his rope
and the iron bar from his bed in his lap. He tossed
the rope out the window, watching as it fell. It tangled and bound up halfway down, and he had to
spend more time shaking the rope like a fishline
before it would drop free again.

Then, uttering one final prayer, he grasped the
iron bar and pulled it against the window. His rope
hung down from the middle. Peter slipped the leg
that was inside over the sill, twisted around at the
waist, holding on to the bar for dear life. Now only
his bottom was on the sill. He made a half-turn so
that the cold outer edge of the sill was pressed against
his belly instead of his butt. His legs hung down.
The iron bar was seated firmly across the window.

Peter let go of it with his left hand and caught

hold of his narrow napkin rope. For a moment he paused, battling his fear.

Then he closed his eyes and let go of the bar with his right hand. His whole weight was on the rope now. He was committed. For better or worse, his life now depended on the napkins. Peter began to lower himself.

COMING –'
Two hundred.
'FOR YOUR HEAD —'
Two hundred and fifty.
'MY DEAR PRINCE!'
Two hundred and seventy-five.

Ben, Dennis, and Naomi could see Peter, a dark man-shape against the curved wall of the Needle, high above their heads – higher than even the bravest acrobat would dare to go.

'Faster,' Ben panted – almost moaned. 'For your lives . . . for *his* life!'

They went about emptying the cart even faster . . . but in truth, all they could do was almost done.

Flagg raced up the stairs, his hood falling back, his lank dark hair flying off his waxy brow.
Almost there now – almost there.

The wind was light now, but very cold. It blew against Peter's bare cheeks and bare hands, numbing them. Slowly, slowly, he descended, moving with careful deliberation. He knew that if he let his descent get out of hand, he would fall. In front of him, the great mortared stone blocks rolled steadily upward – very soon he came to feel that he was remaining still and it was the Needle itself which was moving. His breath came in tight gasps. Cold dry snow rattled on his face. The rope was thin – if his hands grew much number, he wouldn't be able to feel it at all.

How far had he come?

He didn't dare look down and see.

Above him, individual strands of thread, cunningly woven together as a woman might braid a rug, had begun to pop threads. Peter did not know this, which was probably just as well. The breaking strain had nearly been reached.

'Easter, King Peter?' Dennis whispered. The three of them had finished emptying the cart; now they could only watch. Peter had descended perhaps half of the distance.

'He's so high,' Naomi moaned. 'If he falls –'

'If he falls, he'll be killed,' Ben said with a flat and toneless finality that silenced them all.

'Flagg reached the top of the stairs and ran down the corridor, his chest heaving as he gasped for breath. Sweat stood out all over his face. His grin was huge, horrible.

He put his great axe down and pulled the first of the three bolts on the door to Peter's quarters. He pulled the second . . . and paused. It would not be smart to simply go rushing in, oh no, not smart at all. The caged bird might be trying to fly the coop right this moment, but he might also be standing to one side of the door, ready to brain Flagg with something the moment he rushed in.

When he opened the spyhole in the middle of the door and saw the bar from Peter's bed placed across the window, he understood everything and roared with rage.

'*Not so easy as that, my young bird!*' howled Flagg. '*Let's see how you fly with your rope cut, shall we?*'

Flagg yanked the third bolt and charged into Peter's room with his axe held high over his head. After one quick look out the window, his grin resurfaced. He decided not to cut the rope after all.

130

Down and down Peter went. His arm muscles trembled with exhaustion. His mouth was dry; he couldn't remember ever wanting a drink as badly as he did right now. It seemed that he had been on this rope for a very, very long time, and a queer certainty had stolen into his heart – he would never get the drink of water he wanted. He was meant to die after all, and that wasn't even the worst of it. He was going to die thirsty. Right now *that* seemed the worst of it.

He still did not dare look *down,* but he felt a queer compulsion – every bit as strong as his brother's compulsion to go into their father's sitting room – to look *up.* He obeyed it – and some two hundred feet above, he saw Flagg's white, murderous face grinning down at him.

'Hello, my little bird,' Flagg called down cheerfully. 'I've an axe, but I really don't think I'll need to use it after all. I've put it aside, see?' And the magician held out his bare hands.

All the strength was trying to run out of Peter's arms and hands – just the sight of Flagg's hateful face had done that. He concentrated on holding on. He couldn't feel the thin rope at all anymore – he knew he still had it because he could see it coming out of his fists, but that was all. His breath rasped in and out of his throat in hot gasps.

Now he looked down . . . and saw the white, upturned circles of three faces. Those circles were very, very small – he was not twenty feet above the frozen cobbles, or even forty feet; he was still a *hundred* feet up, as high as the fourth floor of one of our buildings.

He tried to move and found he could not – if he moved, he would fall. So he hung there against the side of the building. Cold, gritty snow blew in his face, and from the prison above, Flagg began to laugh.

131

Why doesn't he *move*?' Naomi cried, digging one mittened hand into Ben's shoulder. Her eyes were fixed on Peter's twisting form. The way it hung there, slowly turning, made it look dreadfully like the body of a man who had been hanged. 'What's *wrong* with him?'

'I don't –'

Above them, Flagg's chilly laughter abruptly stopped.

'Who goes there?' he called. His voice was like thunder, like doom. 'Answer me, if you want to keep your heads! *Who goes there?*'

Frisky whined and shrank against Naomi's side.

'Oh gods, now you've done it,' Dennis said. 'What do we do, Ben?'

'Wait,' Ben said grimly. 'And if the magician comes down, fight. We wait for what happens next. We –'

But that was all the waiting any of them had to do, for in the next few seconds, much – not all, but a great deal – was resolved.

132

Flagg had seen the thinness of Peter's rope, its whiteness — and in a trice he understood everything, from beginning to end — the napkins and the doll's house as well. Peter's means of escape had been under his nose the whole time, and he had very nearly missed it. But . . . he saw something else as well. Little pops of fibre where the strands were giving way, some fifteen feet down the taut length of rope.

Flagg could have turned the iron bar he was resting his hand on and sent Peter plummeting that way, with the anchor trailing after to perhaps bash his head in when he struck bottom. He could have swung the battle-axe and parted the fragile rope.

But he preferred to let matters take their course, and a moment after he had challenged the voices, matters *did* take their course.

The rope's breaking strain was reached. It parted with a twang like a lute string that has been wound too far on its peg.

'Goodbye, birdie,' Flagg cried happily, leaning far out to watch Peter's fall. He was laughing. 'Goodb—'

Then his voice ceased and his eyes widened as they had when he looked into the crystal and saw the tiny figure descending the side of the Needle. He opened his mouth and screamed with rage. That awful cry woke up more people in Delain than the fall of the Tower.

Peter heard that twanging sound, felt the rope part.

Cold wind rushed up past his face. He tried to steel himself for the crash, knowing it would come in less than a second. The pain if he didn't die instantly would be the worst.

And that was when Peter struck the thick, deep drift of royal napkins which Frisky had hauled out of the castle and across the Plaza in a stolen cart – the royal napkins which Ben, Dennis, and Naomi had worked so feverishly to pile up. The size of that pile – it looked like a whitewashed haystack – was never really known, because Ben, Dennis, and Naomi all had different estimates on the subject. Perhaps Peter's own idea was the best, since he was the one who fell squarely into the middle of it – he believed that messy, lovely, lifesaving pile of napkins must have been at least twenty feet high, and for all I know, he may have been right.

He fell squarely into the middle, as I have said, making a crater. Then he fell over on his back and lay still. Far above, Ben heard Flagg howl with rage and he thought: *You don't need to do that, everything's going to be just fine for you, magician. He has died anyway, in spite of all we could do.*

Then Peter sat up. He looked dazed but very much alive. In spite of Flagg, in spite of the fact that there might be Guards of the Watch racing toward them at that moment, Ben Staad whooped. It was a sound of pure triumph. He grabbed Naomi and kissed her.

'*Hoorah!*' Dennis cried, grinning dizzily. '*Hoorah for the King!*'

Then Flagg screeched again far above them – the sound of a devil-bird cheated of its prey. The whooping, the kissing and the hoorahing all stopped right then.

'*You'll pay with your heads!*' Flagg shrieked. He was insane with rage. '*You'll pay with your heads, all of you! Guards of the Watch, to the Needle! To the Needle! The regicide has escaped! To the Needle! Kill the murdering prince! Kill his gang! Kill them all!*'

And in the castle that surrounded the Plaza of the Needle on all four sides, windows began to be lit . . . and from two sides came the sound of running feet and the clash of metal as swords were drawn.

'*Kill the prince!*' Flagg shrieked hellishly from the top of the Needle. '*Kill his gang! KILL THEM ALL!*'

Peter tried to get up, floundered, and fell over again. Part of his mind was crying out urgently that he *must* get on his feet, that they *must* be away or they would be killed . . . but another part insisted that he was already dead, or severely wounded, and all of this was only a dream of his perishing mind. He seemed to have landed in a bed of the very napkins which had occupied so much of his mind over the last five years . . . and how could that be anything *but* a dream?

Ben's strong hand gripped his upper arm, and he knew it was all real, all happening.

'Peter, are you all right? Are you really all right?'

'Not hurt a bit,' Peter said. 'We have to get away from here.'

'*My King!*' Dennis cried, falling on his knees before the dazed Peter and grinning the same dizzy, foolish grin. '*My oath of fealty forever! I swear my –*'

'Swear later!' Peter cried, laughing in spite of himself. As Ben had pulled him to his feet, so Peter now pulled Dennis to his. 'Let's get out of here!'

'Which gate?' Ben asked. He knew – as Peter did himself – that Flagg would already be on his way back down. 'They come from all sides, by the sound.'

In truth, Ben thought any direction would do for the battle which would surely come, and result in their eventual slaughter. But dazed or not, Peter knew perfectly well where he wanted to go.

'The West Gate,' he said, 'and quickly! *Run!*'

The four of them ran, Frisky at their heels.

135

Still fifty yards from the West Gate, Peter's band met a party of seven sleepy, confused guards. Most of them had sheltered from the storm in one of the warm Lower Kitchens of the castle, drinking mead and exclaiming to one another that they would have something to tell their grandchildren about. They did not know the half of what they would have to tell their grandchildren about, as it happened. Their 'leader' was a man-boy of just twenty, and only a goshawk . . . what we would call a corporal, I suppose. Still, he hadn't had anything to drink and was reasonably alert. And he was determined to do his duty.

'Halt in the name of the King!' he called out as Peter's group closed with his slightly larger one. He tried to thunder this command, but a storyteller should tell as much of the truth as he can, and I must tell you that the goshawk's voice was more squeak than thunder.

Peter was unarmed, of course, but Ben and Naomi both carried shortswords, and Dennis had his rusty dagger. All three of them at once pushed in front of Peter. Ben's and Naomi's hands went to their hilts. Dennis had already pulled his dagger.

'*Stop!*' Peter cried; his voice *was* thunder. 'You must not draw!'

Surprised – shocked, even – Ben threw a glance at Peter.

Peter stepped to the fore. He stood with his eyes flashing moonlight and his beard riffling in the light, chill-edged wind. He was dressed in the rough clothes of a prisoner, but his face was commanding and regal.

'Halt in the name of the King, you say,' Peter said. He stepped calmly toward the terrified goshawk until the two of them were almost chest to

chest – less than six inches separated them. The guard
fell back a step in spite of his own drawn sword and
the fact that Peter's hands were empty. 'And yet I tell
you, goshawk: *I am the King.*'

The guard licked his lips. He looked around at
his men.

'But . . .' he began. 'You . . .'

'What is your name?' Peter asked quietly.

The goshawk gaped. He could have run Peter
through in a second, but he only gaped helplessly,
like a fish drawn from water.

'Your name, goshawk?'

'My Lord . . . I mean . . . prisoner . . .
you . . . I . . .' The young soldier fumbled once
more and then said helplessly, 'My name is Galen.'

'And do you know who I am?'

'Yes,' one of the others growled. 'We know
you, *murderer.*'

'I did not murder my father,' Peter said quietly.
'It was the King's magician who did that. He is hot
behind us now, and I advise you – very strongly, I
advise you – to 'ware of him. Soon he will trouble
Delain no more; I promise this on my father's name.
But for now you must let me pass.'

There was a long moment of silence. Galen held
his sword up again as if to run Peter through. Peter did
not flinch. He owed the gods a death; it was a debt he
had owed ever since he had come a shrieking, naked
baby from his mother's belly. It was a debt every man
and woman in creation owed. If he was to pay that
debt now, let it be so . . . but he was the rightful King,
not a rebel, not a usurper, and he would not run, or
stand aside, or let his friends hurt this lad.

The sword wavered. Then Galen let it fall until the tip of the blade touched the frozen cobbles.

'Let 'em pass,' he muttered. 'Mayhap he murdered, mayhap he didn't – all I know is that it's royal muck and I'll not step into it, lest I drown in a quicksand of Kings and princes.'

'You had a wise mother, goshawk,' Ben Staad said grimly.

'Yes, let 'im pass,' a second voice said unexpectedly. 'By gods, I'll not strike my blade at such – from the look of 'im, it would burn off my hand when it went in.'

'You will be remembered,' Peter said. He looked around at his friends. 'Follow me now,' he said 'and be quick. I know what I must have, and I know where to get it.'

At that moment Flagg burst from the base of the Needle, and such a howl of rage and fury rose in the night that the young guards quailed before it. They backed up, turned, and ran, scattering to the four pegs of the compass.

'Come on,' Peter said. 'Follow me. The West Gate!'

Flagg ran as he had never run before. He sensed the oncoming ruin of all his plans now, at what was practically the last moment. It must not happen! And he knew as well as Peter where all of this must end.

He passed the cowering guards without looking around. They sighed with relief, thinking he must not have seen them . . . but Flagg did. He saw them all, and marked each; after Peter died, their heads would decorate the tower walls for a year and a day, he thought. As for the brat in charge of their patrol – he would die a thousand deaths in the dungeon first.

He ran under the arch of the West Gate, and down the Main Western Gallery into the castle itself. Sleepy folk, who had come out in their nightclothes to see what all this row was about, cowered before his whitely burning face and fell aside, forking their first and last fingers at him to ward off evil . . . for now Flagg looked like what Flagg really was; a demon. He vaulted over the banister of the first staircase he came to, landed on his feet (the iron on his heels flashed green fire like the eyes of lynxes), and ran on.

On toward Roland's apartments.

137

'The locket,' Peter panted to Dennis as they ran. 'Do you still have the locket I threw down?'

Dennis clutched at his throat, and found the golden heart – Peter's own blood dried on the tip – and nodded.

'Give it to me.'

Dennis passed it to him as they ran. Peter did not put the chain over his neck, but looped it in his fist so that the heart bounced and spun as he ran, flashing red-gold in the light of the wall sconces.

'Soon, my friends,' Peter panted.

They turned a corner. Ahead Peter saw the door to his father's apartments. It was here that he had last seen Roland. He had been a King, responsible for the lives and welfare of thousands; he had also been an old man grateful for a warming glass of wine and a few minutes of talk with his son. It was here that it would end.

Once upon a time, his father had slain a dragon with an arrow called Foe-Hammer.

Now, Peter thought, as blood pounded in his temples and his heart raced hotly in his chest, *I must try to slay another dragon – a much greater one – with that same arrow.*

Thomas lit the fire, donned his dead father's robe, and drew Roland's chair close to the hearth. He felt that he would soon fall soundly asleep, and that was very good. But as he sat there, owlishly nodding, looking around at the trophies mounted on the walls with their glassy eyes sparkling eerily in the flames, it occurred to him that he wanted two more things – things that were almost sacred, things he would certainly never have dared touch when his father was alive. But Roland was dead, so Thomas had taken another chair to stand on, and from the wall he had taken down his father's bow and his father's great arrow, Foe-Hammer, from their places on the wall above Niner's head. For a moment he stared directly into one of the dragon's green-amber eyes. He had seen much through those eyes, but now, looking into them, he saw nothing but his own pallid face, like the face of a prisoner looking out of a cell.

Although everything in the room had been numbingly cold (the fire would warm things up, at least around the fireplace, but it would take a while), he thought that the arrow was strangely warm. He vaguely remembered an old tale he had heard as a small child – according to this tale, a weapon used to slay a dragon never lost the dragon's heat. *It seems that tale was true*, Thomas thought sleepily. But there was nothing scary about the arrow's heat; in fact, it seemed comforting. Thomas sat down with the bow clutched loosely in one hand and Foe-Hammer with its strange, sleeping warmth clutched in the other, never realizing that his brother was now coming in search of this very weapon, and that Flagg – the author of his birth and the Chief Warder of his life – was hot on Peter's heels.

Thomas hadn't stopped to consider what he would do if the door to his father's rooms had been locked, and Peter never did, either – in the old days it never had been, and as things turned out, the door wasn't locked now.

Peter had to do no more than lift the latch. He burst in, the others hot on his heels. Frisky was barking wildly, all of her fur standing on end. Frisky understood the true nature of things better, I'll warrant. Something was coming, something with a black scent like the poison fumes that sometimes killed the coal miners of the Eastern Barony when their tunnels went too deep. Frisky would fight the owner of that scent if she had to; fight and even die. But if she could have spoken, Frisky would have told them that the black scent approaching them from behind did not belong to a man; it was a monster chasing them, some horrible It.

'Peter, what –' Ben began, but Peter ignored him. He knew what he must have. He rushed across the room on his exhausted, trembling legs, looked up at the head of Niner, and reached for the bow and the arrow that had always hung above that head. Then his hand faltered.

Both were gone.

Dennis, the last one in, had closed the door behind him and shot the bolt. Now a single great blow fell on that door. The stout hardwood panels, reinforced with bands of iron, boomed.

Peter looked over his shoulder, eyes widening. Dennis and Naomi cringed backward. Frisky stood before her mistress snarling. Her grey-green eyes showed the whites all around.

'*Let me pass!*' Flagg roared. '*Let me pass the door!*'

'Peter!' Ben shouted, and drew his sword.

'*Stand away!*' Peter shouted back. '*If you value your lives stand away! All of you, stand away!*'

They scattered back just as Flagg's fist, now glowing with blue fire, slammed down against the door again. Hinges, bolt, and iron bands all burst at the same time with the noise of an exploding cannon. Blue fire spoked through the cracks between the boards in narrow rays. Then the stout planks burst apart. Shattered chunks of wood flew in a spray. The ragged remains of the door stood for a moment longer and then fell inward with a handclap sound.

Flagg stood in the corridor, his hood fallen back. His face was waxen white. His lips were strips of liver drawn back to show his teeth. His eyes flared with furnace fire.

In his hand he grasped his heavy executioner's axe.

He stood there a moment longer and then stepped inside. He looked left and saw Dennis. He looked right, and saw Ben and Naomi, with Frisky hunched, snarling, at her feet. His eyes marked them . . . catalogued them for future reference . . . and dismissed them. He strode through the remains of the door, now looking only at Peter.

'You fell but you did not die,' he said. 'You may think your God was kind. But I tell you, my own gods were saving you for me. Pray to your God now

that your heart should burst apart in your chest. Fall
on your knees and pray for that, because I tell you
that *my* death will be much worse than any you can
imagine.'

Peter stood where he was, between Flagg and his
father's chair, where Thomas sat, as yet unseen by all
the others. Peter met Flagg's infernal gaze, unafraid.
For a moment Flagg seemed to flinch under that firm
gaze, and then his unhuman grin blazed forth.

'You and your friends have cause me great
trouble, my prince,' Flagg whispered. '*Great* trouble.
I should have ended your miserable life long ago. But
now all troubles will end.'

'I know you,' Peter replied. Although he was
unarmed, his voice was steady and unafraid. 'I think my
father knew you, too, although he was weak. Now I
assume my kingship, *and I command you, demon!*'

Peter drew himself up to his full height. The
flames in the fireplace reflected from his eyes, making
them blaze. In that moment, Peter was every inch
Delain's King.

'*Get you gone from here. Leave Delain behind, now
and forever. You are cast out. GET YOU GONE!*'

Peter thundered this last in a voice which was
greater than his own; he thundered in a voice that
was *many* voices – all the Kings and Queens there had
ever been in Delain, stretching back to the time when
the castle had been little more than a collection of
mud huts and people had drawn together in terror
around their fires during the darks of winter as the
wolves howled and the trolls gobbled and screamed
in the Great Forests of Yestertime.

Flagg seemed to flinch again . . . almost to

cringe. Then he came forward – slowly, very slowly. His huge axe swung in his left hand.

'You may command in the next world,' he whispered. 'By escaping, you've played into my hands. If I'd thought of it – and in time I should have – I would have engineered a trumped-up escape myself! Oh, Peter, your head will roll into the fire and you'll smell your hair burning before your brain knows you're dead. You'll burn as your father burned . . . and they'll give me a *medal* for it in the Plaza! For did you not murder your own father for the crown?'

'*You* murdered him,' Peter said.

Flagg laughed. 'I? *I?* You've gone insane in the Needle, my boy.' Flagg sobered. His eyes glittered. 'But suppose – just for an instant – suppose I did? Who would believe it?'

Peter still held the chain of the locket looped over his right hand. Now he held that hand out and the locket hung below it, swinging hypnotically, raying flashes of ruddy light on the wall. At the sight of it, Flagg's eyes widened and Peter thought: *He recognizes it! By all the Gods, he recognizes it!*

'You killed my father, and it wasn't the first time you'd arranged things in the same way. You had forgotten, hadn't you? I see it in your eyes. When Leven Valera stood in your way during the evil days of Alan II, his wife was found poisoned. Circumstances made Valera's guilt seem without question . . . as they made *my* guilt seem without question.'

'Where did you find that, you little *bastard?*' Flagg whispered, and Naomi gasped.

'Yes, you forgot,' Peter repeated. 'I think that, sooner or later, things like you always begin to repeat themselves, because things like you know only a very few simple tricks. After a while, someone always sees through them. I think that is all that saves us, ever.'

The locket hung and swung in the firelight.

'Who would care now?' Peter asked. 'Who would believe? Many. If they believed nothing else, they would believe you are as old as their hearts tell them you are, monster.'

'Give it to me!'

'You killed Eleanor Valera, and you killed my father.'

'Yes, I brought him the wine,' Flagg said, his eyes blazing, 'and I *laughed* when his guts burned, and I laughed harder when you were taken up the stairs to the top of the Needle. But those who hear me say so in this room will all soon be dead, and no one saw me bring wine to these rooms! They only saw you?'

And then, from behind Peter, a new voice spoke. It was not strong, that voice; it was so low it could scarcely be heard, and it trembled. But it struck all of them – Flagg included – dumb with wonder.

'There was one other who saw,' Peter's brother, Thomas, said from the shadowed depths of his father's chair. '*I* saw you, magician.'

140

Peter drew aside and made a half-turn, the hand with the locket hanging from it still outstretched.

Thomas! he tried to say, but he could not speak, so struck was he by wonder and horror at the changes in his brother. He had grown fat and somehow old. He had always looked more like Roland than Peter had, and now the resemblance was so great it was eerie.

Thomas! he tried to say again, and realized why the bow and arrow were no longer in their places above the head of Niner. The bow was in Thomas's lap, and the arrow was nocked in the gut string.

It was then that Flagg shrieked and threw himself forward, raising the great executioner's axe over his head.

141

It was not a shriek of rage but of terror. Flagg's white face was drawn; his hair stood on end. His mouth trembled loosely. Peter had been surprised by the resemblance but knew his brother; Flagg was fooled completely by the flickering fire and the deep shadows cast by the wings of the chair in which Thomas sat.

He forgot Peter. It was the figure in the chair he charged with the axe. He had killed the old man once by poison, and yet here he was again, sitting in his smelly mead-soaked robe, sitting with his bow and arrow in his hands, looking at Flagg with haggard, accusing eyes.

'*Ghost!*' Flagg shrieked. '*Ghost or demon from hell, I care not! I killed you once! I can kill you again! Aiiiiyyyyyyyyeeeeee –!*'

Thomas had always excelled at archery. Although he rarely hunted, he had gone often to the archery ranges during the years of Peter's imprisonment, and, drunk or sober, he had his father's eye. He had a fine yew bow, but he had never drawn one like this. It was light and limber, and yet he felt an amazing strength in its lancewood bolt. It was a huge but graceful weapon, eight feet from end to end, and he did not have room to draw fully while sitting down; yet he pulled its ninety-pound draw with no strain at all.

Foe-Hammer was perhaps the greatest arrow ever made, its bolt of sandalwood, its three feathers honed from the wing of an Anduan peregrine, its tip of flashed steel. It grew hot at the draw; he felt its heat bake his face like an open furnace.

'You told me only lies, magician,' Thomas said softly. He released.

The arrow flew from the bow. As it crossed the room, it passed directly through the centre of Leven Valera's locket, which still dangled from the stunned

Peter's outstretched fist. The gold chain parted with a tiny *chink!* sound.

As I have told you, ever since that night in the north forests when he and the troop he had commanded had camped following their fruitless expedition in search of the exiles, Flagg had been plagued by a dream he couldn't remember. He always awoke from it with his hand pressed to his left eye, as if he had been wounded there. The eye would burn for minutes after he awoke, although he could find nothing wrong with it.

Now the arrow of Roland, bearing the heart-shaped locket of Valera on its tip, flew across Roland's sitting room and plunged into that eye.

Flagg screamed. The two-bladed axe dropped from his hands, and the haft of that blood-soaked weapon shattered apart once and for all when it struck the floor. He staggered backward, one eye glaring at Thomas. The other had been replaced by a golden heart with Peter's blood drying at the tip. From around the edges of that heart, some stinking black fluid – it was most assuredly not blood – dribbled out.

Flagg shrieked again, dropped to his knees –

– and suddenly he was gone.

Peter's eyes widened. Ben Staad cried out. For a moment Flagg's clothes held his shape; for a moment the arrow hung in empty air with the pierced heart dangling from it. Then the clothes crumpled and Foe-Hammer clattered to the cobbles. Its steel tip was smoking. So it had smoked, long ago, when Roland pulled it from the dragon's throat. The heart glowed a dull red for a moment, and forever after its shape was branded into the stones where it fell when the magician disappeared.

Peter turned to his brother.

Thomas's unearthly calm broke apart. No longer did he look like Roland: he looked like a scared and horribly tired little boy.

'Peter, I'm sorry,' he said, and he began to cry. 'I am sorrier than you will ever know. You'll kill me now, I guess, and I deserve to be killed – yes, I know I do – but before you do, I'll tell you something: I've paid. Yes, I have. Paid and paid and paid. Now kill me, if such is your pleasure.'

Thomas raised his throat and closed his eyes. Peter walked toward him. The others held their breaths, their eyes wide and round.

Gently, then, Peter pulled his brother from his father's chair and embraced him.

Peter held his brother until the storm of his weeping had passed, and told him that he loved him and would always love him; then both wept, there below the dragon's head with their father's bow at their feet; and at some point, the others stole from the room and left the two brothers alone.

142

Did they all live happily ever after?

They did not. No one ever does, in spite of what the stories may say. They had their good days, as you do, and they had their bad days, and you know about those. They had their victories, as you do, and they had their defeats, and you know about those, too. There were times when they felt ashamed of themselves, knowing that they had not done their best, and there were times when they knew they had stood where God had meant them to stand. All I'm trying to say is that they lived as well as they could, each and every one of them; some lived longer than others, but all lived well, and bravely, and I love them all, and am not ashamed of my love.

Thomas and Peter went to Delain's new Judge-General together, and Peter was taken back into custody. His second stint as a prisoner of the Kingdom was much shorter than the first – only two hours. It took Thomas fifteen minutes to tell his tale, and the Judge-General, who had been appointed with Flagg's approval and who was a timid little creature, took another hour and three-quarters to verify that the terrible magician was really gone.

Then all charges were overturned.

That evening all of them – Peter, Thomas, Ben, Naomi, Dennis, and even Frisky – met in Peter's old rooms. Peter poured wine all around, even giving Frisky some in a little dish. Only Thomas declined the vintage.

Peter wanted Thomas to stay with him, but Thomas insisted – rightly, I think – that if he stayed, the citizens would tear him apart for what he had allowed to happen.

'You were only a child,' Peter said, 'controlled by a powerful creature who terrified you.'

With a sad grin, Thomas replied: 'That is partly

true, but people would not remember that, Pete. They'd remember Tommy Tax-Bringer, and come for me. They'd tear through stone to get to me, I think. Flagg's gone, but I'm here. My head is a silly thing, but I've decided I'd like to keep it on my shoulders a while longer.' He paused, seemed to debate, and then went on. 'And I'm best away. My hate and jealousy were like a fever. It's now gone, but after a few years of being in your shadow as you ruled, I might relapse. I've come to know myself a little bit, you see. Yes – a little bit. No; I must leave, Peter, and tonight. The sooner the better.'

'But . . . where will you go?'

'On a quest,' Thomas said simply. 'To the south, I think. You may see me again, but you may not. I'll go south on a quest . . . I have many things on my conscience, and much to atone for.'

'What quest?' Ben asked.

'To find Flagg,' Thomas replied. 'He's out there, somewhere. In this world or in some other, he's out there. I know it; I feel his poison in the wind. He got away from us at the last second. You all know it, and I do, too. I would find him and kill him. I would avenge our father and make up for my own great sin. And I would go into the south first, for I sense him there.'

Peter said, 'But who'll go with you? I can't – there's too much to do here. But I won't just allow you to go alone!' He looked very concerned, and if you had seen a map of those days, you would have understood his expression, for the south was nothing but a great white space on the maps.

Surprising all of them, Dennis said: 'I would go, my Lord King.'

Both brothers looked toward him, surprised. Ben and Naomi also turned, and Frisky looked up from her wine, which she was lapping with cheerful enthusiasm (she liked the smell, which was a cool, velvety purple; not as good as the taste, but almost).

Dennis blushed mightily, but he didn't sit down.

'You were always a good master, Thomas, and – beggin' your pardon, King Peter – something inside me says you're my master still. And since I was the one to find that mouse and send you to the Needle, my King –'

'Bosh!' Peter said. 'That's all forgotten.'

'Not by me, it ain't,' Dennis said stubbornly. 'You could say I was too young, too, and didn't know no better, but maybe I've my own mistakes to atone for.'

He looked at Thomas, shyly.

'I would come with you, Lord Thomas, if you would have me; I would be at your side in your quest.'

On the verge of tears, Thomas said: 'I will have you and welcome, good old Dennis. I only hope you can cook better than I can.'

They left that very night, under cover of darkness – two figures on foot, their packs heavy with supplies, wending their way into the night. They looked back once and waved.

All three of them waved back. Peter was weeping as if his heart would break; indeed, he thought it might.

I'll never see him again, Peter thought.

Ah, well – perhaps he did, and perhaps he didn't; but I rather think he did, you know. All I can tell you is that Ben and Naomi were eventually married, that Peter ruled long and well, and that Thomas and Dennis had many strange adventures, and that they did see Flagg again, and confronted him.

But now the hour is late, and all of that is another tale, for another day.

Firestarter

New York/Albany

1

'Daddy, I'm tired,' the little girl in the red pants and the green blouse said fretfully. 'Can't we stop?'

'Not yet, honey.'

He was a big, broad-shouldered man in a worn and scuffed corduroy jacket and plain brown twill slacks. He and the little girl were holding hands and walking up Third Avenue in New York City, walking fast, almost running. He looked back over his shoulder and the green car was still there, crawling along slowly in the curbside lane.

'Please, Daddy. *Please.*'

He looked at her and saw how pale her face was. There were dark circles under her eyes. He picked her up and sat her in the crook of his arm, but he didn't know how long he could go on like that. He was tired, too, and Charlie was no lightweight anymore.

It was five-thirty in the afternoon and Third Avenue was clogged. They were crossing streets in the upper Sixties now, and these cross streets were both darker and less populated. . . . But that was what he was afraid of.

They bumped into a lady pushing a walker full of groceries. 'Look where you're goin, whyn't ya?' she said, and was gone, swallowed in the hurrying crowds.

His arm was getting tired, and he switched Charlie to the other one. He snatched another look behind, and the green car was still there, still pacing them, about half a block behind. There were two men in the front seat and, he thought, a third in the back.

7

What do I do now?

He didn't know the answer to that. He was tired and scared and it was hard to think. They had caught him at a bad time, and the bastards probably knew it. What he wanted to do was just sit down on the dirty curbing and cry out his frustration and fear. But that was no answer. He was the grownup. He would have to think for both of them.

What do we *do now?*

No money. That was maybe the biggest problem, after the fact of the men in the green car. You couldn't do anything with no money in New York. People with no money disappeared in New York; they dropped into the sidewalks, never to be seen again.

He looked back over his shoulder, saw the green car was a little closer, and the sweat began to run down his back and his arms a little faster. If they knew as much as he suspected they did – if they knew how little of the push he actually had left – they might try to take him right here and now. Never mind all the people, either. In New York, if it's not happening to you, you develop this funny blindness. Have they been charting me? Andy wondered desperately. If they have, they know, and it's all over but the shouting. If they had, they knew the pattern. After Andy got some money, the strange things stopped happening for a while. The things they were interested in.

Keep walking.

Sho, boss. Yassuh, boss. Where?

He had gone into the bank at noon because his radar had been alerted – that funny hunch that they were getting close again. There was money in the bank, and he and Charlie could run on it if they had to. And wasn't that funny? Andrew McGee no longer had an account at the Chemical Allied Bank of New York, not personal checking, not business checking, not savings. They had all disappeared into thin air, and that was when he knew they really meant to bring the hammer down this time. Had all of that really been only five and a half hours ago?

But maybe there was a tickle left. Just one little tickle. It had been nearly a week since the last time – that presuicidal man at Confidence Associates who had come to the regular Thursday-night counseling session and then begun to talk with an eerie calmness about how Hemingway had committed suicide. And on the way out, his arm casually around the presuicidal man's shoulders, Andy had given him a push. Now, bitterly, he hoped it had been worth it. Because it looked very much as if he and Charlie were going to be the ones to pay. He almost hoped an echo—

But no. He pushed that away, horrified and disgusted with himself. That was nothing to wish on *anybody*.

One little tickle, he prayed. That's all, God, just one little tickle. Enough to get me and Charlie out of this jam.

And oh God, how you'll pay . . . plus the fact that you'll be dead for a month afterward, just like a radio with a blown tube. Maybe six weeks. Or maybe really dead, with your worthless brains leaking out your ears. What would happen to Charlie then?

They were coming up on Seventieth Street and the light was against them. Traffic was pouring across and pedestrians were building up at the corner in a bottleneck. And suddenly he knew this was where the men in the green car would take them. Alive if they could, of course, but if it looked like trouble . . . well, they had probably been briefed on Charlie, too.

Maybe they don't even want us alive anymore. Maybe they've decided just to maintain the status quo. What do you do with a faulty equation? Erase it from the board.

A knife in the back, a silenced pistol, quite possibly something more arcane – a drop of rare poison on the end

9

of a needle. Convulsions at the corner of Third and Seventieth. Officer, this man appears to have suffered a heart attack.

He would have to try for that tickle. There was just nothing else.

They reached the waiting pedestrians at the corner. Across the way, DON'T WALK held steady and seemingly eternal. He looked back. The green car had stopped. The curbside doors opened and two men in business suits got out. They were young and smooth-cheeked. They looked considerably fresher than Andy McGee felt.

He began elbowing his way through the clog of pedestrians, eyes searching frantically for a vacant cab.

'Hey, man—'

'For Christ' sake, fella!'

'Please, mister, you're stepping on my *dog*—'

'Excuse me . . . excuse me . . .' Andy said desperately. He searched for a cab. There were none. At any other time the street would have been stuffed with them. He could feel the men from the green car coming for them, wanting to lay hands on him and Charlie, to take them with them God knew where, the Shop, some damn place, or do something even worse—

Charlie laid her head on his shoulder and yawned.

Andy saw a vacant cab.

'Taxi! Taxi!' he yelled, flagging madly with his free hand.

Behind him, the two men dropped all pretense and ran.

The taxi pulled over.

'Hold it!' one of the men yelled. 'Police! Police!'

A woman near the back of the crowd at the corner screamed, and then they all began to scatter.

Andy opened the cab's back door and handed Charlie in. He dived in after her. 'La Guardia, step on it,' he said.

'Hold it, cabby. Police!'

The cab driver turned his head toward the voice and

Andy pushed – very gently. A dagger of pain was planted squarely in the center of Andy's forehead and then quickly withdrawn, leaving a vague locus of pain, like a morning headache – the kind you get from sleeping on your neck.

'They're after that black guy in the checkered cap, I think,' he said to the cabby.

'Right,' the driver said, and pulled serenely away from the curb. They moved down East Seventieth.

Andy looked back. The two men were standing alone at the curb. The rest of the pedestrians wanted nothing to do with them. One of the men took a walkie-talkie from his belt and began to speak into it. Then they were gone.

'That black guy,' the driver said, 'whadde do? Rob a liquor store or somethin, you think?'

'I don't know,' Andy said, trying to think how to go on with this, how to get the most out of this cab driver for the least push. Had they got the cab's plate number? He would have to assume they had. But they wouldn't want to go to the city or state cops, and they would be surprised and scrambling, for a while at least.

'They're all a bunch of junkies, the blacks in this city,' the driver said. 'Don't tell me, I'll tell you.'

Charlie was going to sleep. Andy took off his corduroy jacket, folded it, and slipped it under her head. He had begun to feel a thin hope. If he could play this right, it might work. Lady Luck had sent him what Andy thought of (with no prejudice at all) as a pushover. He was the sort that seemed the easiest to push, right down the line: he was white (Orientals were the toughest, for some reason); he was quite young (old people were nearly impossible) and of medium intelligence (bright people were the easiest pushes, stupid ones harder, and with the mentally retarded it was impossible).

'I've changed my mind,' Andy said. 'Take us to Albany, please.'

11

'*Where?*' The driver stared at him in the rearview mirror. 'Man, I can't take a fare to Albany, you out of your mind?'

Andy pulled his wallet, which contained a single dollar bill. He thanked God that this was not one of those cabs with a bulletproof partition and no way to contact the driver except through a money slot. Open contact always made it easier to push. He had been unable to figure out if that was a psychological thing or not, and right now it was immaterial.

'I'm going to give you a five-hundred-dollar bill,' Andy said quietly, 'to take me and my daughter to Albany. Okay?'

'Jeee-*sus*, mister—'

Andy stuck the bill into the cabby's hand, and as the cabby looked down at it, Andy pushed . . . and pushed hard. For a terrible second he was afraid it wasn't going to work, that there was simply nothing left, that he had scraped the bottom of the barrel when he had made the driver see the nonexistent black man in the checkered cap.

Then the feeling came – as always accompanied by that steel dagger of pain. At the same moment, his stomach seemed to take on weight and his bowels locked in sick, griping agony. He put an unsteady hand to his face and wondered if he was going to throw up . . . or die. For that one moment he *wanted* to die, as he always did when he overused it – *use it, don't abuse it*, the sign-off slogan of some long-ago disc jockey echoing sickly in his mind – whatever 'it' was. If at that very moment someone had slipped a gun into his hand—

Then he looked sideways at Charlie, Charlie sleeping, Charlie trusting him to get them out of this mess as he had all the others, Charlie confident he would be there when she woke up. Yes, all the messes, except it was all the same mess, the same fucking mess, and all they were doing was running again. Black despair pressed behind his eyes.

The feeling passed . . . but not the headache. The headache would get worse and worse until it was a smashing weight, sending red pain through his head and neck with every pulsebeat. Bright lights would make his eyes water helplessly and send darts of agony into the flesh just behind his eyes. His sinuses would close and he would have to breathe through his mouth. Drill bits in his temples. Small noises magnified, ordinary noises as loud as jackhammers, loud noises insupportable. The headache would worsen until it felt as if his head were being crushed inside an inquisitor's lovecap. Then it would even off at that level for six hours, or eight, or maybe ten. This time he didn't know. He had never pushed it so far when he was so close to drained. For whatever length of time he was in the grip of the headache, he would be next to helpless. Charlie would have to take care of him. God knew she had done it before . . . but they had been lucky. How many times could you be lucky?

'Gee, mister, I don't know—'

Which meant he thought it was law trouble.

'The deal only goes as long as you don't mention it to my little girl,' Andy said. 'The last two weeks she's been with me. Has to be back with her mother tomorrow morning.'

'Visitation rights,' the cabby said. 'I know all about it.'

'You see, I was supposed to fly her up.'

'To Albany? Probably Ozark, am I right?'

'Right. Now, the thing is, I'm scared to death of flying. I know how crazy that sounds, but it's true. Usually I drive her back up, but this time my ex-wife started in on me, and . . . I don't know.' In truth, Andy didn't. He had made up the story on the spur of the moment and now it seemed to be headed straight down a blind alley. Most of it was pure exhaustion.

'So I drop you at the old Albany airport, and as far as Moms knows, you flew, right?'

13

'Sure.' His head was thudding.

'Also, as far as Moms knows, you're no plucka-plucka-plucka, am I four-oh?'

'Yes.' Plucka-plucka-plucka? What was that supposed to mean? The pain was getting bad.

'Five hundred bucks to skip a plane ride,' the driver mused.

'It's worth it to me,' Andy said, and gave one last little shove. In a very quiet voice, speaking almost into the cabby's ear, he added, 'And it ought to be worth it to you.'

'Listen,' the driver said in a dreamy voice. 'I ain't turning down no five hundred dollars. Don't tell me, I'll tell you.'

'Okay,' Andy said, and settled back. The cab driver was satisfied. He wasn't wondering about Andy's half-baked story. He wasn't wondering what a seven-year-old girl was doing visiting her father for two weeks in October with school in. He wasn't wondering about the fact that neither of them had so much as an overnight bag. He wasn't worried about anything. He had been pushed.

Now Andy would go ahead and pay the price.

He put a hand on Charlie's leg. She was fast asleep. They had been on the go all afternoon – ever since Andy got to her school and pulled her out of her second-grade class with some half-remembered excuse . . . grandmother's very ill . . . called home . . . sorry to have to take her in the middle of the day. And beneath all that a great, swelling relief. How he had dreaded looking into Mrs Mishkin's room and seeing Charlie's seat empty, her books stacked neatly inside her desk: *No, Mr McGee . . . she went with your friends about two hours ago . . . they had a note from you . . . wasn't that all right?* Memories of Vicky coming back, the sudden terror of the empty house that day. His crazy chase after Charlie. Because they had had her once before, oh yes.

14

But Charlie had been there. How close had it been? Had he beaten them by half an hour? Fifteen minutes? Less? He didn't like to think about it. He had got them a late lunch at Nathan's and they had spent the rest of the afternoon just *going* – Andy could admit to himself now that he had been in a state of blind panic – riding subways, buses, but mostly just walking. And now she was worn out.

He spared her a long, loving look. Her hair was shoulder length, perfect blond, and in her sleep she had a calm beauty. She looked so much like Vicky that it hurt. He closed his own eyes.

In the front seat, the cab driver looked wonderingly at the five-hundred-dollar bill the guy had handed him. He tucked it away in the special belt pocket where he kept all of his tips. He didn't think it was strange that this fellow in the back had been walking around New York with a little girl and a five-hundred-dollar bill in his pocket. He didn't wonder how he was going to square this with his dispatcher. All he thought of was how excited his girlfriend, Glyn, was going to be. Glynis kept telling him that driving a taxi was a dismal, unexciting job. Well, wait until she saw his dismal, unexciting five-hundred-dollar bill.

In the back seat, Andy sat with his head back and his eyes closed. The headache was coming, coming, as inexorable as a riderless black horse in a funeral cortege. He could hear the hoofbeats of that horse in his temples: *thud . . . thud . . . thud.*

On the run. He and Charlie. He was thirty-four years old and until last year he had been an instructor of English at Harrison State College in Ohio. Harrison was a sleepy little college town. Good old Harrison, the very heart of mid-America. Good old Andrew McGee, fine, upstanding young man. Remember the riddle? Why is a farmer the

15

pillar of his community? Because he's always outstanding in his field.

Thud, thud, thud, riderless black horse with red eyes coming down the halls of his mind, ironshod hooves digging up soft gray clods of brain tissue, leaving hoofprints to fill up with mystic crescents of blood.

The cabby had been a pushover. Sure. An outstanding cab driver.

He dozed and saw Charlie's face. And Charlie's face became Vicky's face.

Andy McGee and his wife, pretty Vicky. They had pulled her fingernails out, one by one. They had pulled out four of them and then she had talked. That, at least, was his deduction. Thumb, index, second, ring. Then: Stop. I'll talk. I'll tell you anything you want to know. Just stop the hurting. Please. So she had told. And then . . . perhaps it had been an accident . . . then his wife had died. Well, some things are bigger than both of us, and other things are bigger than all of us.

Things like the Shop, for instance.

Thud, thud, thud, riderless black horse coming on, coming on, and coming on: behold, a black horse.

Andy slept.

And remembered.

2

The man in charge of the experiment was Dr Wanless. He was fat and balding and had at least one rather bizarre habit.

'We're going to give each of you twelve young ladies and gentlemen an injection,' he said, shredding a cigarette into the ashtray in front of him. His small pink fingers plucked at the thin cigarette paper, spilling out neat little cones of golden-brown tobacco. 'Six of these injections will be

16

water. Six of them will be water mixed with a tiny amount of a chemical compound which we call Lot Six. The exact nature of this compound is classified, but it is essentially an hypnotic and mild hallucinogenic. Thus you understand that the compound will be administered by the double-blind method . . . which is to say, neither you nor we will know who has gotten a clear dose and who has not until later. The dozen of you will be under close supervision for forty-eight hours following the injection. Questions?'

There were several, most having to do with the exact composition of Lot Six – that word *classified* was like putting bloodhounds on a convict's trail. Wanless slipped these questions quite adroitly. No one had asked the question twenty-two-year-old Andy McGee was most interested in. He considered raising his hand in the hiatus that fell upon the nearly deserted lecture hall in Harrison's combined Psychology/Sociology building and asking, Say, why are you ripping up perfectly good cigarettes like that? Better not to. Better to let the imagination run on a free rein while this boredom went on. He was trying to give up smoking. The oral retentive smokes them; the anal retentive shreds them. (This brought a slight grin to Andy's lips, which he covered with a hand.) Wanless's brother had died of lung cancer and the doctor was symbolically venting his aggressions on the cigarette industry. Or maybe it was just one of those flamboyant tics that college professors felt compelled to flaunt rather than suppress. Andy had one English teacher his sophomore year at Harrison (the man was now mercifully retired) who sniffed his tie constantly while lecturing on William Dean Howells and the rise of realism.

'If there are no more questions, I'll ask you to fill out these forms and will expect to see you promptly at nine next Tuesday.'

Two grad assistants passed out photocopies with twenty-five ridiculous questions to answer yes or no. *Have you ever undergone psychiatric counselling? – #8. Do you believe you have ever had an authentic psychic experience? – #14. Have you ever used hallucinogenic drugs? – #18.* After a slight pause, Andy checked 'no' to that one, thinking, *In this brave year 1969, who* hasn't *used them?*

He had been put on to this by Quincey Tremont, the fellow he had roomed with in college. Quincey knew that Andy's financial situation wasn't so hot. It was May of Andy's senior year; he was graduating fortieth in a class of five hundred and six, third in the English program. But that didn't buy no potatoes, as he had told Quincey, who was a psych major. Andy had a GA lined up for himself starting in the fall semester, along with a scholarship-loan package that would be just about enough to buy groceries and keep him in the Harrison grad program. But all of that was fall, and in the meantime there was the summer hiatus. The best he had been able to line up so far was a responsible, challenging position as an Arco gas jockey on the night shift.

'How would you feel about a quick two hundred?' Quincey had asked.

Andy brushed long, dark hair away from his green eyes and grinned. 'Which men's room do I set up my concession in?'

'No, it's a psych experiment,' Quincey said. 'Being run by the Mad Doctor, though. Be warned.'

'Who he?'

'Him Wanless, Tonto. Heap big medicine man in-um Psych Department.'

'Why do they call him the Mad Doctor?'

'Well,' Quincey said, 'he's a rat man and a Skinner man both. A behaviorist. The behaviorists are not exactly being overwhelmed with love these days.'

'Oh,' Andy said, mystified.

'Also, he wears very thick little rimless glasses, which makes him look quite a bit like the guy that shrank the people in *Dr Cyclops*. You ever see that show?'

Andy, who was a late-show addict, had seen it, and felt on safer ground. But he wasn't sure he wanted to participate in any experiments run by a prof who was classified as a.) a rat man and b.) a Mad Doctor.

'They're not trying to shrink people, are they?' he asked.

Quincey had laughed heartily. 'No, that's strictly for the special-effects people who work on the B horror pictures,' he said. 'The Psych Department has been testing a series of low-grade hallucinogens. They're working with the U.S. Intelligence Service.'

'CIA?' Andy asked.

'Not CIA, DIA, or NSA,' Quincey said. 'Lower profile than any of them. Have you ever heard of an outfit called the Shop?'

'Maybe in a Sunday supplement or something. I'm not sure.'

Quincey lit his pipe. 'These things work in about the same way all across the board,' he said. 'Psychology, chemistry, physics, biology . . . even the sociology boys get some of the folding green. Certain programs are subsidized by the government. Anything from the mating ritual of the tsetse fly to the possible disposal of used plutonium slugs. An outfit like the Shop has to spend all of its yearly budget to justify a like amount the following year.'

'That shit troubles me mightily,' Andy said.

'It troubles almost any thinking person,' Quincey said with a calm, untroubled smile. 'But the train just keeps rolling. What does our intelligence branch want with low-grade hallucinogens? Who knows? Not me. Not you. Probably they don't either. But the reports look good in closed committees come budget-renewal time. They have their pets in every department. At Harrison, Wanless is their pet in the Psych Department.'

'The administration doesn't mind?'

'Don't be naïve, my boy.' He had his pipe going to his satisfaction and was puffing great stinking clouds of smoke out into the ratty apartment living room. His voice accordingly became more rolling, more orotund, more Buckleyesque. 'What's good for Wanless is good for the Harrison Psychology Department, which next year will have its very own building – no more slumming with those sociology types. And what's good for Psych is good for Harrison State College. And for Ohio. And all that blah-blah.'

'Do you think it's safe?'

'They don't test it on student volunteers if it isn't safe,' Quincey said. 'If they have even the slightest question, they test it on rats and then on convicts. You can be sure that what they're putting into you has been put into roughly three hundred people before you, whose reactions have been carefully monitored.'

'I don't like this business about the CIA—'

'The Shop.'

'What's the difference?' Andy asked morosely. He looked at Quincey's poster of Richard Nixon standing in front of a crunched-up used car. Nixon was grinning, and a stubby V-for-victory poked up out of each clenched fist. Andy could still hardly believe the man had been elected president less than a year ago.

'Well, I thought maybe you could use the two hundred dollars, that's all.'

'Why are they paying so much?' Andy asked suspiciously.

Quincey threw up his hands. 'Andy, it is the government's treat! Can't you follow that? Two years ago the Shop paid something like three hundred thousand dollars for a

feasibility study on a mass-produced exploding bicycle –
and *that* was in the Sunday *Times*. Just another Vietnam
thing, I guess, although probably nobody knows for sure.
Like Fibber McGee used to say, "It seemed like a good
idea at the time." ' Quincey knocked out his pipe with
quick, jittery movements. 'To guys like that, every college
campus in America is like one big Macy's. They buy a
little here, do a little window-shopping there. Now if you
don't want it—'

'Well, maybe I do. Are you going in on it?'

Quincey had smiled. His father ran a chain of extremely
successful menswear stores in Ohio and Indiana. 'Don't
need two hundred that bad,' he said. 'Besides, I hate.
needles.'

'Oh.'

'Look, I'm not trying to sell it, for Chrissakes; you just
looked sort of hungry. The chances are fifty-fifty you'll be
in the control group, anyway. Two hundred bucks for
taking on water. Not even tapwater, mind you. *Distilled*
water.'

'You can fix it?'

'I date one of Wanless's grad assistants,' Quincey said.
'They'll have maybe fifty applications, many of them
brownnosers who want to make points with the Mad
Doctor—'

'I wish you'd stop calling him that.'

'Wanless, then,' Quincey said, and laughed. 'He'll see
that the apple polishers are weeded out personally. My girl
will see that your application goes into his "in" basket.
After that, dear man, you are on your own.'

So he had made out the application when the notice for
volunteers went up on the Psych Department bulletin
board. A week after turning it in, a young female GA
(Quincey's girlfriend, for all Andy knew) had called on the
phone to ask him some questions. He told her that his

parents were dead; that his blood type was O; that he had never participated in a Psychology Department experiment before; that he was indeed currently enrolled in Harrison as an undergraduate, class of '69, in fact, and carrying more than the twelve credits needed to classify him as a full-time student. And yes, he was past the age of twenty-one and legally able to enter into any and all covenants, public and private.

A week later he had received a letter via campus mail telling him he had been accepted and asking for his signature on a release form. Please bring the signed form to Room 100, Jason Gearneigh Hall, on May the 6th.

And here he was, release form passed in, the cigarette-shredding Wanless departed (and he did indeed look a bit like the mad doctor in that Cyclops movie), answering questions about his religious experiences along with eleven other undergrads. Did he have epilepsy? No. His father had died suddenly of a heart attack when Andy was eleven. His mother had been killed in a car accident when Andy was seventeen – a nasty, traumatic thing. His only close family connection was his mother's sister, Aunt Cora, and she was getting well along in years.

He went down the column of questions, checking *no, no, no*. He checked only one YES question: *Have you ever suffered a fracture or serious sprain? If yes, specify.* In the space provided, he scribbled the fact that he had broken his left ankle sliding into second base during a Little League game twelve years ago.

He went back over his answers, trailing lightly upward with the tip of his Bic. That was when someone tapped him on the shoulder and a girl's voice, sweet and slightly husky, asked, 'Could I borrow that if you're done with it? Mine went dry.'

'Sure,' he said, turning to hand it to her. Pretty girl. Tall. Light-auburn hair, marvelously clear complexion.

Wearing a powder-blue sweater and a short skirt. Good legs. No stockings. Casual appraisal of the future wife.

He handed her his pen and she smiled her thanks. The overhead lights made copper glints in her hair, which had been casually tied back with a wide white ribbon, as she bent over her form again.

He took his form up to the GA at the front of the room. 'Thank you,' the GA said, as programmed as Robbie the Robot. 'Room Seventy, Saturday morning, nine A.M. Please be on time.'

'What's the countersign?' Andy whispered hoarsely.

The grad assistant laughed politely.

Andy left the lecture hall, started across the lobby toward the big double doors (outside, the quad was green with approaching summer, students passing desultorily back and forth), and then remembered his pen. He almost let it go; it was only a nineteen-cent Bic, and he still had his final round of prelims to study for. But the girl had been pretty, maybe worth chatting up, as the British said. He had no illusions about his looks or his line, which were both pretty nondescript, or about the girl's probable status (pinned or engaged), but it was a nice day and he was feeling good. He decided to wait. At the very least, he would get another look at those legs.

She came out three or four minutes later, a few notebooks and a text under her arm. She was very pretty indeed, and Andy decided her legs had been worth waiting for. They were more than good; they were spectacular.

'Oh, there you are,' she said, smiling.

'Here I am,' said Andy McGee. 'What did you think of that?'

'I don't know,' she said. 'My friend said these experiments go on all the time – she was in one last semester with those J. B. Rhine ESP cards and got fifty dollars for it even though she missed almost all of them. So I just thought –'

23

She finished the thought with a shrug and flipped her coppery hair neatly back over her shoulders.

'Yeah, me too,' he said, taking his pen back. 'Your friend in the Psych Department?'

'Yes,' she said, 'and my boyfriend, too. He's in one of Dr Wanless's classes, so he couldn't get in. Conflict of interest or something.'

Boyfriend. It stood to reason that a tall, auburn-haired beauty like this had one. That was the way the world turned.

'What about you?' she asked.

'Same story. Friend in the Psych Department. I'm Andy, by the way. Andy McGee.'

'I'm Vicky Tomlinson. And a little nervous about this, Andy McGee. What if I go on a bad trip or something?'

'This sounds like pretty mild stuff to me. And even if it is acid, well . . . lab acid is different from the stuff you can pick up on the street, or so I've heard. Very smooth, very mellow, and administered under very calm circumstances. They'll probably pipe in Cream or Jefferson Airplane.' Andy grinned.

'Do you know much about LSD?' she asked with a little cornerwise grin that he liked very much.

'Very little,' he admitted. 'I tried it twice – once two years ago, once last year. In some ways it made me feel better. It cleaned out my head . . . at least, that's what it felt like. Afterward, a lot of the old crud just seemed to be gone. But I wouldn't want to make a steady habit of it. I don't like feeling so out of control of myself. Can I buy you a Coke?'

'All right,' she agreed, and they walked over to the Union building together.

He ended up buying her two Cokes, and they spent the afternoon together. That evening they had a few beers at the local hangout. It turned out that she and the boyfriend

24

had come to a parting of the ways, and she wasn't sure exactly how to handle it. He was beginning to think they were married, she told Andy; had absolutely forbidden her to take part in the Wanless experiment. For that precise reason she had gone ahead and signed the release form and was now determined to go through with it even though she was a little scared.

'That Wanless really does look like a mad doctor,' she said, making rings on the table with her beer glass.

'How did you like that trick with the cigarettes?'

Vicky giggled. 'Weird way to quit smoking, huh?'

He asked her if he could pick her up on the morning of the experiment, and she had agreed gratefully.

'It would be good to go into this with a friend,' she said, and looked at him with her direct blue eyes. 'I really am a little scared, you know. George was so – I don't know, *adamant.*'

'Why? What did he say?'

'That's just it,' Vicky said. 'He wouldn't tell me anything, except that he didn't trust Wanless. He said hardly anyone in the department does, but a lot of them sign up for his tests because he's in charge of the graduate program. Besides, they know it's safe, because he just weeds them out again.'

He reached across the table and touched her hand. 'We'll both probably get the distilled water, anyway,' he said. 'Take it easy, kiddo. Everything's fine.'

But as it turned out, nothing was fine. Nothing.

3

albany
albany airport mister
hey mister, this is it we're here
Hand, shaking him. Making his head roll on his neck. Terrible headache – Jesus! Thudding, shooting pains.

25

'Hey mister, this is the airport.'

Andy opened his eyes, then shut them against the white light of an overhead sodium lamp. There was a terrible, shrieking whine, building up and up and up, and he winced against it. It felt as if steel darning needles were being jammed into his ears. Plane. Taking off. It began to come to him through the red fog of pain. Ah yes, Doc, it all comes back to me now.

'Mister?' The cabby sounded worried. 'Mister, you okay?'

'Headache.' His voice seemed to come from far away, buried in the jet-engine sound that was, mercifully, beginning to fade off. 'What time is it?'

'Nearly midnight. Slow haul getting up here. Don't tell me, I'll tell you. Buses won't be running, if that was your plan. Sure I can't take you home?'

Andy groped in his mind for the story he had told the cabby. It was important that he remember, monster headache or not. Because of the echo. If he contradicted the earlier story in any way, it could set up a ricochet effect in the cabby's mind. It might die out – in fact, probably would – but it might not. The cabby might seize on one point of it, develop a fixation on it; shortly it would be out of control, it would be all the cabby could think about; shortly after that, it would simply tear his mind apart. It had happened before.

'My car's in the lot,' he said. 'Everything is under control.'

'Oh.' The cabby smiled, relieved. 'Glyn isn't gonna believe this, you know. Hey! Don't tell me, I'll t—'

'Sure she'll believe it. You do, don't you?'

The driver grinned widely. 'I got the big bill to prove it, mister. Thanks.'

'Thank *you*,' Andy said. Struggle to be polite. Struggle to go on. For Charlie. If he had been alone, he would have

26

killed himself long ago. A man wasn't meant to bear pain like this.

'You sure you're okay, mister? You look awful white.'

'I'm fine, thanks.' He began to shake Charlie. 'Hey, kid.' He was careful not to use her name. It probably didn't matter, but the caution came as naturally as breathing. 'Wake up, we're here.'

Charlie muttered and tried to roll away from him.

'Come on, doll. Wake up, hon.'

Charlie's eyes fluttered open – the direct blue eyes she had got from her mother – and she sat up, rubbing her face. 'Daddy? Where are we?'

'Albany, hon. The airport.' And leaning closer, he muttered, 'Don't say anything yet.'

'Okay.' She smiled at the cab driver, and the cabby smiled back. She slipped out of the cab and Andy followed her, trying not to stagger.

'Thanks again, man,' the cabby said. 'Listen, hey. Great fare. Don't tell me, I'll tell you.'

Andy shook the outstretched hand. 'Take care.'

'I will. Glyn's just not gonna believe this action.'

The cabby got back in and pulled away from the yellow-painted curb. Another jet was taking off, the engine revving and revving until Andy felt as though his head would split in two pieces and fall to the pavement like a hollow gourd. He staggered a little, and Charlie put her hands on his arm.

'Oh, Daddy,' she said, and her voice was far away.

'Inside. I have to sit down.'

They went in, the little girl in the red pants and the green blouse, the big man with the shaggy black hair and the slumped shoulders. A skycap watched them go and thought it was a pure sin, a big man like that out after midnight, drunk as a lord by the look of him, with his little girl who should have been in bed hours ago leading

27

him around like a Seeing Eye dog. Parents like that ought to be sterilized, the skycap thought.

Then they went in through the electric-eye-controlled doors and the skycap forgot all about them until some forty minutes later, when the green car pulled up to the curb and the two men got out to talk to him.

4

It was ten past midnight. The lobby of the terminal had been given over to the early-morning people: servicemen at the end of their leaves, harried-looking women riding herd on scratchy, up-too-late children, businessmen with pouches of weariness under their eyes, cruising kids in big boots and long hair, some of them with packs on their backs, a couple with cased tennis rackets. The loudspeaker system announced arrivals and departures and paged people like some omnipotent voice in a dream.

Andy and Charlie sat side by side at desks with TVs bolted to them. The TVs were scratched and dented and painted dead black. To Andy they looked like sinister, futuristic cobras. He plugged his last two quarters into them so they wouldn't be asked to leave the seats. Charlie's was showing a rerun of *The Rookies* and Johnny Carson was yucking it up with Sonny Bono and Buddy Hackett on Andy's.

'Daddy, do I have to?' Charlie asked for the second time. She was on the verge of tears.

'Honey, I'm used up,' he said. 'We have no money. We can't stay here.'

'Those bad men are coming?' she asked, and her voice dropped to a whisper.

'I don't know.' Thud, thud, thud in his brain. Not a riderless black horse anymore; now it was mailsacks filled

28

with sharp scraps of iron being dropped on him from a fifth-story window. 'We have to assume they are.'

'How could I get money?'

He hesitated and then said, 'You know.'

The tears began to come and trickled down her cheeks. 'It's not right. It's not right to steal.'

'I know it,' he said. 'But it's not right for them to keep coming at us, either. I explained it to you, Charlie. Or at least I tried.'

'About little bad and big bad?'

'Yes. Lesser and greater evil.'

'Does your head really hurt?'

'It's pretty bad,' Andy said. There was no use telling her that in an hour, or possibly two, it would be so bad he would no longer be able to think coherently. No use frightening her worse than she already was. No use telling her that he didn't think they were going to get away this time.

'I'll try,' she said, and got out of the chair. 'Poor Daddy,' she said, and kissed him.

He closed his eyes. The TV played on in front of him, a faraway babble of sound in the midst of the steadily growing ache in his head. When he opened his eyes again, she was just a distant figure, very small, dressed in red and green, like a Christmas ornament, bobbing away through the scattered people on the concourse.

Please God, let her be all right, he thought. *Don't let anyone mess with her, or scare her worse than she is already. Please and thank you, God. Okay?*

He closed his eyes again.

29

5

Little girl in red stretch pants and a green rayon blouse. Shoulder-length blond hair. Up too late, apparently by herself. She was in one of the few places where a little girl by herself could go unremarked after midnight. She passed people, but no one really saw her. If she had been crying, a security guard might have come over to ask her if she was lost, if she knew which airline her mommy and daddy were ticketed on, what their names were so they could be paged. But she wasn't crying, and she looked as if she knew where she was going.

She didn't exactly – but she had a pretty fair idea of what she was looking for. They needed money; that was what Daddy had said. The bad men were coming, and Daddy was hurt. When he got hurt like this, it got hard for him to think. He had to lie down and have as much quiet as he could. He had to sleep until the pain went away. And the bad men might be coming . . . the men from the Shop, the men who wanted to pick them apart and see what made them work – and to see if they could be used, made to do things.

She saw a paper shopping bag sticking out of the top of a trash basket and took it. A little way farther down the concourse she came to what she was looking for: a bank of pay phones.

Charlie stood looking at them, and she was afraid. She was afraid because Daddy had told her again and again that she shouldn't do it . . . since earliest childhood it had been the Bad Thing. She couldn't always control the Bad Thing. She might hurt herself, or someone else, or lots of people. The time

(oh mommy i'm sorry the hurt the bandages the screams she screamed i made my mommy scream and i never will again . . . never . . . because it is a Bad Thing)

in the kitchen when she was little . . . but it hurt too much to think of that. It was a Bad Thing because when you let it go, it went . . . everywhere. And that was scary.

There were other things. The push, for instance; that's what Daddy called it, the push. Only she could push a lot harder than Daddy, and she never got headaches afterward. But sometimes, afterward . . . there were fires.

The word for the Bad Thing clanged in her mind as she stood nervously looking at the telephone booths: *pyrokinesis*. 'Never mind that,' Daddy had told her when they were still in Port City and thinking like fools that they were safe. 'You're a firestarter, honey. Just one great big Zippo lighter.' And then it had seemed funny, she had giggled, but now it didn't seem funny at all.

The other reason she wasn't supposed to push was because *they* might find out. The bad men from the Shop. 'I don't know how much they know about you now,' Daddy had told her, 'but I don't want them to find out anymore. Your push isn't exactly like mine, honey. You can't make people . . . well, change their minds, can you?'

'No-ooo . . .'

'But you can make things move. And if they ever began to see a pattern, and connect that pattern to you, we'd be in even worse trouble than we are now.'

And it was stealing, and stealing was also a Bad Thing.

Never mind. Daddy's head was hurting him and they had to get to a quiet, warm place before it got too bad for him to think at all. Charlie moved forward.

There were about fifteen phonebooths in all, with circular sliding doors. When you were inside the booth, it was like being inside a great big Contac capsule with a phone inside it. Most of the booths were dark, Charlie saw as she drifted down past them. There was a fat lady in a pantsuit crammed into one of them, talking busily and smiling. And three booths from the end a young man in a service uniform was sitting on the little stool with the door open and his legs poking out. He was talking fast.

'Sally, look, I understand how you feel, but I can explain everything. Absolutely. I know . . . I know . . . but if you'll just let me—' He looked up, saw the little girl looking at him, and yanked his legs in and pulled the circular door closed, all in one motion, like a turtle pulling into its shell. Having a fight with his girlfriend, Charlie thought. Probably stood her up. I'd never let a guy stand me up.

Echoing loudspeaker. Rat of fear in the back of her mind, gnawing. All the faces were strange faces. She felt lonely and very small, grief-sick over her mother even now. This was stealing, but what did that matter? They had stolen her mother's life.

She slipped into the phonebooth on the end, shopping bag crackling. She took the phone off the hook and pretended she was talking – hello, Grampa, yes, Daddy and I just got in, we're fine – and looked out through the glass to see if anyone was being nosy. No one was. The only person nearby was a black woman getting flight insurance from a machine, and her back was to Charlie.

Charlie looked at the pay phone and suddenly *shoved* it.

A little grunt of effort escaped her, and she bit down on her lower lip, liking the way it squeezed under her teeth. No, there was no pain involved. It felt *good* to shove things, and that was another thing that scared her. Suppose she got to *like* this dangerous thing?

She shoved the pay phone again, very lightly, and suddenly a tide of silver poured out of the coin return. She tried to get her bag under it, but by the time she did, most of the quarters and nickels and dimes had spewed onto the floor. She bent over and swept as much as she could into the bag, glancing again and again out the window.

With the change picked up, she went on to the next

32

booth. The serviceman was still talking on the next phone up the line. He had opened the door again and was smoking. 'Sal, honest to Christ I did! Just ask your brother if you don't believe me! He'll—'

Charlie slipped the door shut, cutting off the slightly whining sound of his voice. She was only seven, but she knew a snowjob when she heard one. She looked at the phone, and a moment later it gave up its change. This time she had the bag positioned perfectly and the coins cascaded to the bottom with a musical little jingling sound.

The serviceman was gone when she came out, and Charlie went into his booth. The seat was still warm and the air smelled nastily of cigarette smoke in spite of the fan.

The money rattled into her bag and she went on.

6

Eddie Delgardo sat in a hard plastic contour chair, looking up at the ceiling and smoking. Bitch, he was thinking. She'll think twice about keeping her goddam legs closed next time. Eddie this and Eddie that and Eddie I never want to see you again and Eddie how could you be so *crew-ool*. But he had changed her mind about the old I-never-want-to-see-you-again bit. He was on thirty-day leave and now he was going to New York City, the Big Apple, to see the sights and tour the singles bars. And when he came back, Sally would be like a big ripe apple herself, ripe and ready to fall. None of that don't-you-have-any-respect-for-me stuff went down with Eddie Delgardo of Marathon, Florida. Sally Bradford was going to put out, and if she really believed that crap about him having had a vasectomy, it served her right. And then let her go running to her hick schoolteacher brother if she wanted to.

Eddie Delgardo would be driving an army supply truck in West Berlin. He would be—

Eddie's half-resentful, half-pleasant chain of daydreams was broken by a strange feeling of warmth coming from his feet; it was as if the floor had suddenly heated up ten degrees. And accompanying this was a strange but not completely unfamiliar smell . . . not something burning but . . . something *singeing*, maybe?

He opened his eyes and the first thing he saw was that little girl who had been cruising around by the phone-booths, little girl seven or eight years old, looking really ragged out. Now she was carrying a big paper bag, carrying it by the bottom as if it were full of groceries or something.

But his feet, that was the thing.

They were no longer warm. They were *hot*.

Eddie Delgardo looked down and screamed, '*Godamighty Jeesus!*'

His shoes were on fire.

Eddie leaped to his feet. Heads turned. Some woman saw what was happening and yelled in alarm. Two security guards who had been noodling with an Allegheny Airlines ticket clerk looked over to see what was going on.

None of which meant doodly-squat to Eddie Delgardo. Thoughts of Sally Bradford and his revenge of love upon her were the furthest things from his mind. His army-issue shoes were burning merrily. The cuffs of his dress greens were catching. He was sprinting across the concourse, trailing smoke, as if shot from a catapult. The women's room was closer, and Eddie, whose sense of self-preservation was exquisitely defined, hit the door straight-arm and ran inside without a moment's hesitation.

A young woman was coming out of one of the stalls, her skirt rucked up to her waist, adjusting her Underalls. She saw Eddie, the human torch, and let out a scream that the bathroom's tiled walls magnified enormously. There was a babble of 'What was that?' and 'What's going on?' from the few other occupied stalls. Eddie caught the pay-toilet door before it could swing back all the way and latch. He grabbed both sides of the stall at the top and hoisted himself feet first into the toilet. There was a hissing sound and a remarkable billow of steam.

The two security guards burst in.

'Hold it, you in there!' one of them cried. He had drawn his gun. 'Come out of there with your hands laced on top of your head!'

'You mind waiting until I put my feet out?' Eddie Delgardo snarled.

7.

Charlie was back. And she was crying again.

'What happened, babe?'

'I got the money but . . . it got away from me again, Daddy . . . there was a man . . . a soldier . . . I couldn't help it . . .'

Andy felt the fear creep up on him. It was muted by the pain in his head and down the back of his neck, but it was there. 'Was . . . was there a fire, Charlie?'

She couldn't speak, but nodded. Tears coursed down her cheeks.

'Oh my God,' Andy whispered, and made himself get to his feet.

That broke Charlie completely. She put her face in her hands and sobbed helplessly, rocking back and forth.

A knot of people had gathered around the door of the women's room. It had been propped open, but Andy couldn't see . . . and then he could. The two security guards who had gone running down there were leading a tough-looking young man in an army uniform out of the bathroom and toward the security office. The young man

35

was jawing at them loudly, and most of what he had to say was inventively profane. His uniform was mostly gone below the knees, and he was carrying two dripping, blackened things that might once have been shoes. Then they were gone into the office, the door slamming behind them. An excited babble of conversation swept the terminal.

Andy sat down again and put his arm around Charlie. It was very hard to think now; his thoughts were tiny silver fish swimming around in a great black sea of throbbing pain. But he had to do the best he could. He needed Charlie if they were going to get out of this.

'He's all right, Charlie. He's okay. They just took him down to the security office. Now, what happened?'

Through diminishing tears, Charlie told him. Overhearing the soldier on the phone. Having a few random thoughts about him, a feeling that he was trying to trick the girl he was talking to. 'And then, when I was coming back to you, I saw him . . . and before I could stop it . . . it happened. It just got away. I could have hurt him, Daddy. I could have hurt him bad. I set him on *fire!*'

'Keep your voice down,' he said. 'I want you to listen to me, Charlie. I think this is the most encouraging thing that's happened in some time.'

'Y-you do?' She looked at him in frank surprise.

'You say it got away from you,' Andy said, forcing the words. 'And it did. But not like before. It only got away a little bit. What happened was dangerous, honey, but . . . you might have set his hair on fire. Or his face.'

She winced away from that thought, horrified. Andy turned her face gently back to his.

'It's a subconscious thing, and it always goes out at someone you don't like,' he said. 'But . . . you didn't really hurt that guy, Charlie. You . . .' But the rest of it was gone

36

and only the pain was left. Was he still talking? For a moment he didn't even know.

Charlie could still feel that thing, that Bad Thing, racing around in her head, wanting to get away again, to do something else. It was like a small, vicious, and rather stupid animal. You had to let it out of its cage to do something like getting money from the phones . . . but it could do something else, something really bad

(like mommy in the kitchen oh mom i'm sorry)

before you could get it back in again. But now it didn't matter. She wouldn't think about it now, she wouldn't think about

(the bandages my mommy has to wear bandages because i hurt her)

any of it now. Her father was what mattered now. He was slumped over in his TV chair, his face stamped with pain. He was paper white. His eyes were bloodshot.

Oh, Daddy, she thought, *I'd trade even-Steven with you if I could. You've got something that hurts you but it never gets out of its cage. I've got something that doesn't hurt me at all but oh sometimes I get so scared—*

'I've got the money,' she said. 'I didn't go to all the telephones, because the bag was getting heavy and I was afraid it would break.' She looked at him anxiously. 'Where can we go, Daddy? You have to lie down.'

Andy reached into the bag and slowly began to transfer the change in handfuls to the pockets of his corduroy coat. He wondered if this night would ever end. He wanted to do nothing more than grab another cab and go into town and check them into the first hotel or motel in sight . . . but he was afraid. Cabs could be traced. And he had a strong feeling that the people from the green car were still close behind.

He tried to put together what he knew about the Albany airport. First of all, it was the Albany County Airport; it

37

really wasn't in Albany at all but in the town of Colonie. Shaker country – hadn't his grandfather told him once that this was Shaker country? Or had all of them died out now? What about highways? Turnpikes? The answer came slowly. There was a road . . . some sort of Way. Northway or Southway, he thought.

He opened his eyes and looked at Charlie. 'Can you walk aways, kiddo? Couple of miles, maybe?'

'Sure.' She had slept and felt relatively fresh. 'Can you?'

That was the question. He didn't know. 'I'm going to try,' he said. 'I think we ought to walk out to the main road and try to catch a ride, hon.'

'Hitchhike?' she asked.

He nodded. 'Tracing a hitchhiker is pretty hard, Charlie. If we're lucky, we'll get a ride with someone who'll be in Buffalo by morning.' And if we're not, we'll still be standing in the breakdown lane with our thumbs out when that green car comes rolling up.

'If you think it's okay,' Charlie said doubtfully.

'Come on,' he said, 'help me.'

Gigantic bolt of pain as he got to his feet. He swayed a little, closed his eyes, then opened them again. People looked surreal. Colors seemed too bright. A woman walked by on high heels, and every click on the airport tiles was the sound of a vault door being slammed.

'Daddy, are you sure you can?' Her voice was small and very scared.

Charlie. Only Charlie looked right.

'I think I can,' he said. 'Come on.'

They left by a different door from the one they had entered, and the skycap who had noticed them getting out of the cab was busy unloading suitcases from the trunk of a car. He didn't see them go out.

'Which way, Daddy?' Charlie asked.

He looked both ways and saw the Northway, curving

38

away below and to the right of the terminal building. How to get there, that was the question. There were roads everywhere – overpasses, underpasses, NO RIGHT TURN, STOP ON SIGNAL, KEEP LEFT, NO PARKING ANYTIME. Traffic signals flashing in the early-morning blackness like uneasy spirits.

'This way, I think,' he said, and they walked the length of the terminal beside the feeder road that was lined with LOADING AND UNLOADING ONLY signs. The sidewalk ended at the end of the terminal. A large silver Mercedes swept by them indifferently, and the reflected glow of the overhead sodium arcs on its surface made him wince.

Charlie was looking at him questioningly.

Andy nodded. 'Just keep as far over to the side as you can. Are you cold?'

'No, Daddy.'

'Thank goodness it's a warm night. Your mother would—'

His mouth snapped shut over that.

The two of them walked off into darkness, the big man with the broad shoulders and the little girl in the red pants and the green blouse, holding his hand, almost seeming to lead him.

8

The green car showed up about fifteen minutes later and parked at the yellow curb. Two men got out, the same two who had chased Andy and Charlie to the cab back in Manhattan. The driver sat behind the wheel.

An airport cop strolled up. 'You can't park here, sir,' he said. 'If you'll just pull up to—'

'Sure I can,' the driver said. He showed the cop his ID. The airport cop looked at it, looked at the driver, looked back at the picture on the ID.

'Oh,' he said. 'I'm sorry, sir. Is it something we should know about?'

'Nothing that affects airport security,' the driver said, 'but maybe you can help. Have you seen either of these two people tonight?' He handed the airport cop a picture of Andy, and then a fuzzy picture of Charlie. Her hair had been longer then. In the snap, it was braided into pigtails. Her mother had been alive then. 'The girl's a year or so older now,' the driver said. 'Her hair's a bit shorter. About to her shoulders.'

The cop examined the pictures carefully, shuffling them back and forth. 'You know, I believe I did see this little girl,' he said. 'Towhead, isn't she? Picture makes it a little hard to tell.'

'Towhead, right.'

'The man her father?'

'Ask me no questions, I'll tell you no lies.'

The airport cop felt a wave of dislike for the bland-faced young man behind the wheel of the nondescript green car. He had had peripheral doings with the FBI, the CIA, and the outfit they called the Shop before. Their agents were all the same, blankly arrogant and patronizing. They regarded anyone in a bluesuit as a kiddy cop. But when they'd had the hijacking here five years ago, it had been the kiddy cops who got the guy, loaded down with grenades, off the plane, and he had been in custody of the 'real' cops when he committed suicide by opening up his carotid artery with his own fingernails. Nice going, guys.

'Look . . . sir. I asked if the man was her father to try and find out if there's a family resemblance. Those pictures make it a little hard to tell.'

'They look a bit alike. Different hair colors.'

That much I can see for myself, you asshole, the airport cop thought. 'I saw them both,' the cop told the driver of

40

the green car. 'He's a big guy, bigger than he looks in that picture. He looked sick or something.'

'Did he?' The driver seemed pleased.

'We've had a big night here, all told. Some fool also managed to light his own shoes on fire.'

The driver sat bolt upright behind the wheel. 'Say *what?*'

The airport cop nodded, happy to have got through the driver's bored façade. He would not have been so happy if the driver had told him he had just earned himself a debriefing in the Shop's Manhattan offices. And Eddie Delgardo probably would have beaten the crap out of him, because instead of touring the singles bars (and the massage parlors, and the Times Square porno shops) during the Big Apple segment of his leave, he was going to spend most of it in a drug-induced state of total recall, describing over and over again what had happened before and just after his shoes got hot.

9

The other two men from the green sedan were talking to airport personnel. One of them discovered the skycap who had noticed Andy and Charlie getting out of the cab and going into the terminal.

'Sure I saw them. I thought it was a pure-d shame, a man as drunk as that having a little girl out that late.'

'Maybe they took a plane,' one of the men suggested.

'Maybe so,' the skycap agreed. 'I wonder what that child's mother can be thinking of. I wonder if she knows what's going on.'

'I doubt if she does,' the man in the dark-blue Botany 500 suit said. He spoke with great sincerity. 'You didn't see them leave?'

'No, sir. Far as I know, they're still round here somewhere . . . unless their flight's been called, of course.'

10

The two men made a quick sweep through the main terminal and then through the boarding gates, holding their IDs up in their cupped hands for the security cops to see. They met near the United Airlines ticket desk.

'Dry,' the first said.

'Think they took a plane?' the second asked. He was the fellow in the nice blue Botany 500.

'I don't think that bastard had more than fifty bucks to his name . . . maybe a whole lot less than that.'

'We better check it.'

'Yeah. But quick.'

United Airlines. Allegheny. American. Braniff. The commuter airlines. No broad-shouldered man who looked sick had bought tickets. The baggage handler at Albany Airlines thought he had seen a little girl in red pants and a green shirt, though. Pretty blond hair, shoulder-length.

The two of them met again near the TV chairs where Andy and Charlie had been sitting not long ago. 'What do you think?' the first asked.

The agent in the Botany 500 looked excited. 'I think we ought to blanket the area,' he said. 'I think they're on foot.'

They headed back to the green car, almost trotting.

11

Andy and Charlie walked on through the dark along the soft shoulder of the airport feeder road. An occasional car swept by them. It was almost one o'clock. A mile behind them, in the terminal, the two men had rejoined their third partner at the green car. Andy and Charlie were now walking parallel to the Northway, which was to their right and below them, lit by the depthless glare of sodium lights. It might be possible to scramble down the embankment

42

and try to thumb a ride in the breakdown lane, but if a cop came along, that would end whatever poor chance they still had to get away. Andy was wondering how far they would have to walk before they came to a ramp. Each time his foot came down, it generated a thud that resounded sickly in his head.

'Daddy? Are you still okay?'

'So far, so good,' he said, but he was not so very okay. He wasn't fooling himself, and he doubted if he was fooling Charlie.

'How much further is it?'

'Are you getting tired?'

'Not yet . . . but Daddy . . .'

He stopped and looked solemnly down at her. 'What is it, Charlie?'

'I feel like those bad men are around again,' she whispered.

'All right,' he said. 'I think we better just take a shortcut, honey. Can you get down that hill without falling?'

She looked at the grade, which was covered with dead October grass.

'I guess so,' she said doubtfully.

He stepped over the guardrail cables and then helped Charlie over. As it sometimes did in moments of extreme pain and stress, his mind attempted to flee into the past, to get away from the stress. There had been some good years, some good times, before the shadow began to steal gradually over their lives – first just over him and Vicky, then over all three, blotting out their happiness a little at a time, as inexorably as a lunar eclipse. It had been—

'*Daddy!*' Charlie called in sudden alarm. She had lost her footing. The dry grass was slippery, treacherous. Andy grabbed for her flailing arm, missed, and overbalanced himself. The thud as he hit the ground caused such pain in his head that he cried out loud. Then they were both

43

rolling and sliding down the embankment toward the Northway where the cars rushed past, much too fast to stop if one of them – he or Charlie – should tumble out onto the pavement.

12

The GA looped a piece of rubber flex around Andy's arm just above the elbow and said, 'Make a fist, please.' Andy did. The vein popped up obligingly. He looked away, feeling a little ill. Two hundred dollars or not, he had no urge to watch the IV set in place.

Vicky Tomlinson was on the next cot, dressed in a sleeveless white blouse and dove-gray slacks. She offered him a strained smile. He thought again what beautiful auburn hair she had, how well it went with her direct blue eyes . . . then the prick of pain, followed by dull heat, in his arm.

'There,' the grad assistant said comfortingly.

'There yourself,' Andy said. He was not comforted.

They were in Room 70 of Jason Gearneigh Hall, upstairs. A dozen cots had been trucked in, courtesy of the college infirmary, and the twelve volunteers were lying propped up on hypoallergenic foam pillows, earning their money. Dr Wanless started none of the IVs himself, but he was walking up and down between the cots with a word for everyone, and a little frosty smile. *We'll start to shrink anytime now*, Andy thought morbidly.

Wanless had made a brief speech when they were all assembled, and what he had said, when boiled down, amounted to: *Do not fear. You are wrapped snugly in the arms of Modern Science*. Andy had no great faith in Modern Science, which had given the world the H-bomb, napalm and the laser rifle, along with the Salk vaccine and Clearasil.

44

The grad assistant was doing something else now. Crimping the IV line.

The IV drip was five percent dextrose in water, Wanless had said . . . what he called a D5W solution. Below the crimp, a small tip poked out of the IV line. If Andy got Lot Six, it would be administered by syringe through the tip. If he was in the control group, it would be normal saline. Heads or tails.

He glanced over at Vicky again. 'How you doin, kid?'

'Okay.'

Wanless had arrived. He stood between them, looking first at Vicky and then at Andy.

'You feel some slight pain, yes?' He had no accent of any kind, least of all a regional-American one, but he constructed his sentences in a way Andy associated with English learned as a second language.

'Pressure,' Vicky said. 'Slight pressure.'

'Yes? It will pass.' He smiled benevolently down at Andy. In his white lab coat he seemed very tall. His glasses seemed very small. The small and the tall.

Andy said, 'When do we start to shrink?'

Wanless continued to smile. 'Do you feel you will shrink?'

'Shhhhrrrrrink,' Andy said, and grinned foolishly. Something was happening to him. By God, he was getting high. He was getting off.

'Everything will be fine,' Wanless said, and smiled more widely. He passed on. Horseman, pass by, Andy thought bemusedly. He looked over at Vicky again. How bright her hair was! For some crazy reason it reminded him of the copper wire on the armature of a new motor . . . generator . . . alternator . . . flibbertigibbet . . .

He laughed aloud.

Smiling slightly, as if sharing the joke, the grad assistant crimped the line and injected a little more of the hypo's

45

contents into Andy's arm and strolled away again. Andy could look at the IV line now. It didn't bother him now. *I'm a pine tree*, he thought. *See my beautiful needles.* He laughed again.

Vicky was smiling at him. God, she was beautiful. He wanted to tell her how beautiful she was, how her hair was like copper set aflame.

'Thank you,' she said. 'What a nice compliment.' Had she said that? Or had he imagined it?

Grasping the last shreds of his mind, he said, 'I think I crapped out on the distilled water, Vicky.'

She said placidly, 'Me too.'

'Nice, isn't it?'

'Nice,' she agreed dreamily.

Somewhere someone was crying. Babbling hysterically. The sound rose and fell in interesting cycles. After what seemed like eons of contemplation, Andy turned his head to see what was going on. It was interesting. Everything had become interesting. Everything seemed to be in slow motion. Slomo, as the avant-garde campus film critic always put it in his columns. *In this film, as in others, Antonioni achieves some of his most spectacular effects with his use of slomo footage.* What an interesting, really clever word; it had the sound of a snake slipping out of a refrigerator: slomo.

Several of the grad assistants were running in slomo toward one of the cots that had been placed near Room 70's blackboard. The young fellow on the cot appeared to be doing something to his eyes. Yes, he was definitely doing something to his eyes, because his fingers were hooked into them and he seemed to be clawing his eyeballs out of his head. His hands were hooked into claws, and blood was gushing from his eyes. It was gushing in slomo. The needle flapped from his arm in slomo. Wanless was running in slomo. The eyes of the kid on the cot now

46

looked like deflated poached eggs, Andy noted clinically. Yes indeedy.

Then the white coats were all gathered around the cot, and you couldn't see the kid anymore. Directly behind him, a chart hung down. It showed the quadrants of the human brain. Andy looked at this with great interest for a while. *Verrry in-der-rresting*, as Arte Johnson said on *Laugh-In*.

A bloody hand rose out of the huddle of white coats, like the hand of a drowning man. The fingers were streaked with gore and shreds of tissue hung from them. The hand smacked the chart, leaving a bloodstain in the shape of a large comma. The chart rattled up on its roller with a smacking sound.

Then the cot was lifted (it was still impossible to see the boy who had clawed his eyes out) and carried briskly from the room.

A few minutes (hours? days? years?) later, one of the grad assistants came over to Andy's cot, examined his drip, and then injected some more Lot Six into Andy's mind.

'How you feeling, guy?' the GA asked, but of course he wasn't a GA, he wasn't a student, none of them were. For one thing, this guy looked about thirty-five, and that was a little long in the tooth for a graduate student. For another, this guy worked for the Shop. Andy suddenly knew it. It was absurd, but he knew it. And the man's name was . . .

Andy groped for it, and he got it. The man's name was Ralph Baxter.

He smiled. Ralph Baxter. Good deal.

'I feel okay,' he said. 'How's that other fella?'

'What other fella's that, Andy?'

'The one who clawed his eyes out,' Andy said serenely.

Ralph Baxter smiled and patted Andy's hand. 'Pretty visual stuff, huh, guy?'

'No, really,' Vicky said. 'I saw it, too.'

47

'You think you did,' the GA who was not a GA said. 'You just shared the same illusion. There was guy over there by the board who had a muscular reaction . . . something like a charley horse. No clawed eyes. No blood.'

He started away again.

Andy said, 'My man, it is impossible to share the same illusion without some prior consultation.' He felt immensely clever. The logic was impeccable, inarguable. He had old Ralph Baxter by the shorts.

Ralph smiled back, undaunted. 'With this drug, it's very possible,' he said. 'I'll be back in a bit, okay?'

'Okay, Ralph,' Andy said.

Ralph paused and came back toward where Andy lay on his cot. He came back in slomo. He looked thoughtfully down at Andy. Andy grinned back, a wide, foolish, drugged-out grin. Got you there, Ralph old son. Got you right by the proverbial shorts. Suddenly a wealth of information about Ralph Baxter flooded in on him, tons of stuff: he was thirty-five, he had been with the Shop for six years, before that he'd been with the FBI for two years, he had—

He had killed four people during his career, three men and one woman. And he had raped the woman after she was dead. She had been an AP stringer and she had known about—

That part wasn't clear. And it didn't matter. Suddenly Andy didn't want to know. The grin faded from his lips. Ralph Baxter was still looking down at him, and Andy was swept by a black paranoia that he remembered from his two previous LSD trips . . . but this was deeper and much more frightening. He had no idea how he could know such things about Ralph Baxter – or how he had known his name at all – but if he told Ralph that he knew, he was terribly afraid that he might disappear from Room 70 of Jason Gearneigh with the same swiftness as the boy who had clawed his eyes out. Or maybe all of that really had been a hallucination; it didn't seem real at all now.

Ralph was still looking at him. Little by little he began to smile. 'See?' he said softly. 'With Lot Six, all kinds of funky things happen.'

He left. Andy let out a slow sigh of relief. He looked over at Vicky and she was looking back at him, her eyes wide and frightened. *She's getting your emotions*, he thought. *Like a radio. Take it easy on her! Remember she's tripping, whatever else this weird shit is!*

He smiled at her, and after a moment, Vicky smiled uncertainly back. She asked him what was wrong. He told her he didn't know, probably nothing.

(but we're not talking – her mouth's not moving)

(it's not?)

(vicky? is that you)

(is it telepathy, andy? is it?)

He didn't know. It was something. He let his eyes slip closed.

Are those really grad assistants? she asked him, troubled. They don't look the same. Is it the drug, Andy? I don't know, he said, eyes still closed. I don't know who they are. What happened to that boy? The one they took away? He opened his eyes again and looked at her, but Vicky was shaking her head. She didn't remember. Andy was surprised and dismayed to find that he hardly remembered himself. It seemed to have happened years ago. Got a charley horse, hadn't he, that guy? A muscular twitch, that's all. He—

Clawed his eyes out.

But what did it matter, really?

Hand rising out of the huddle of white coats like the hand of a drowning man.

But it happened a long time ago. Like in the twelfth century.

Bloody hand. Striking the chart. The chart rattling up on its roller with a smacking sound.

Better to drift. Vicky was looking troubled again.

Suddenly music began to flood down from the speakers in the ceiling, and that was nice . . . much nicer than thinking about charley horses and leaking eyeballs. The music was soft and yet majestic. Much later, Andy decided (in consultation with Vicky) that it had been Rachmaninoff. And ever after when he heard Rachmaninoff, it brought back drifting, dreamy memories of that endless, timeless time in Room 70 of Jason Gearneigh Hall.

How much of it had been real, how much hallucination? Twelve years of off-and-on thought had not answered that question for Andy McGee. At one point, objects had seemed to fly through the room as if an invisible wind were blowing – paper cups, towels, a blood-pressure cuff, a deadly hail of pens and pencils. At another point, sometime later (or had it really been earlier? there was just no linear sequence), one of the test subjects had gone into a muscular seizure followed by cardiac arrest – or so it had seemed. There had been frantic efforts to restore him using mouth-to-mouth resuscitation, followed by a shot of something directly into the chest cavity, and finally a machine that made a high whine and had two black cups attached to thick wires. Andy seemed to remember one of the 'grad assistants' roaring, 'Zap him! Zap him! Oh, give them to me, you fuckhead!'

At another point he had slept, dozing in and out of a twilight consciousness. He spoke to Vicky and they told each other about themselves. Andy told her about the car accident that had taken his mother's life and how he had spent the next year with his aunt in a semi-nervous breakdown of grief. She told him that when she was seven, a teenage baby-sitter had assaulted her and now she was terribly afraid of sex, even more afraid that she might be

50

frigid, it was that more than anything else that had forced her and her boyfriend to the breakup. He kept . . . pressing her.

They told each other things that a man and a woman don't tell each other until they've known each other for years . . . things a man and a woman often never tell, not even in the dark marriage bed after decades of being together.

But did they *speak?*

That Andy never knew.

Time had stopped, but somehow it passed anyway.

13

He came out of the doze a little at a time. The Rachmaninoff was gone . . . if it had ever been there at all. Vicky was sleeping peacefully on the cot beside him, her hands folded between her breasts, the simple hands of a child who has fallen asleep while offering her bedtime prayers. Andy looked at her and was simply aware that at some point he had fallen in love with her. It was a deep and complete feeling, above (and below) question.

After a while he looked around. Several of the cots were empty. There were maybe five test subjects left in the room. Some were sleeping. One was sitting up on his cot and a grad assistant – a perfectly normal grad assistant of perhaps twenty-five – was questioning him and writing notes on a clipboard. The test subject apparently said something funny, because both of them laughed – in the low, considerate way you do when others around you are sleeping.

Andy sat up and took inventory of himself. He felt fine. He tried a smile and found that it fit perfectly. His muscles lay peacefully against one another. He felt eager and fresh, every perception sharply honed and somehow innocent. He

51

could remember feeling this way as a kid, waking up on Saturday morning, knowing his bike was heeled over on its kickstand in the garage, and feeling that the whole weekend stretched ahead of him like a carnival of dreams where every ride was free.

One of the grad assistants came over and said, 'How you feeling, Andy?'

Andy looked at him. This was the same guy that had injected him – when? A year ago? He rubbed a palm over his cheek and heard the rasp of beard stubble. 'I feel like Rip van Winkle,' he said.

The GA smiled. 'It's only been forty-eight hours, not twenty years. How do you feel, really?'

'Fine.'

'Normal?'

'Whatever that word means, yes. Normal. Where's Ralph?'

'Ralph?' The GA raised his eyebrows.

'Yes, Ralph Baxter. About thirty-five. Big guy. Sandy hair.'

The grad assistant smiled. 'You dreamed him up,' he said.

Andy looked at the GA uncertainly. 'I did what?'

'Dreamed him up. Hallucinated him. The only Ralph I know who's involved in all the Lot Six tests in any way is a Dartan Pharmaceutical rep named Ralph Steinham. And he's fifty-five or so.'

Andy looked at the GA for a long time without saying anything. Ralph an illusion? Well, maybe so. It had all the paranoid elements of a dope dream, certainly; Andy seemed to remember thinking Ralph was some sort of secret agent who had wasted all sorts of people. He smiled a little. The GA smiled back . . . a little too readily, Andy thought. Or was that paranoia, too? Surely it was.

The guy who had been sitting up and talking when Andy

woke up was now being escorted from the room, drinking from a paper cup of orange juice.

Cautiously, Andy said: 'No one got hurt, did they?'

'Hurt?'

'Well – no one had a convulsion, did they? Or—'

The grad assistant leaned forward, looking concerned. 'Say, Andy, I hope you won't go spreading anything like that around campus. It would play bloody hell with Dr Wanless's research program. We have Lots Seven and Eight coming up next semester, and—'

'Was there anything?'

'There was one boy who had a muscular reaction, minor but quite painful,' the GA said. 'It passed in less than fifteen minutes with no harm done. But there's a witch-hunt atmosphere around here now. End the draft, ban ROTC, ban Dow Chemical job recruiters because they make napalm . . . Things get out of proportion, and I happen to think this is pretty important research.'

'Who was the guy?'

'Now you know I can't tell you that. All I am saying is please remember you were under the influence of a mild hallucinogenic. Don't go mixing up your drug-induced fantasies with reality and then start spreading the combination around.'

'Would I be allowed to do that?' Andy asked.

The GA looked puzzled. 'I don't see how we could stop you. Any college experimental program is pretty much at the mercy of its volunteers. For a lousy two hundred bucks we can hardly expect you to sign an oath of allegiance, can we?'

Andy felt relief. If this guy was lying, he was doing a really superlative job of it. It had all been a series of hallucinations. And on the cot beside his, Vicky was beginning to stir.

53

'Now what about it?' the GA asked, smiling. 'I think I'm supposed to be asking the questions.'

And he did ask questions. By the time Andy finished answering them, Vicky was fully awake, looking rested and calm and radiant, and smiling at him. The questions were detailed. Many of them were the questions Andy himself would have asked.

So why did he have the feeling they were all window dressing?

14

Sitting on a couch in one of the smaller Union lounges that evening, Andy and Vicky compared hallucinations.

She had no memory of the thing that troubled him the most: that bloody hand waving limply above the knot of white tunics, striking the chart, and then disappearing. Andy had no recollection of the thing that was most vivid to her: a man with long blond hair had set up a folding table by her cot, so that it was just at her eye level. He had put a row of great big dominoes on the table and said, 'Knock them down, Vicky. Knock them all down.' And she had raised her hands to push them over, wanting to oblige, and the man had gently but firmly pressed her hands back down on her chest. 'You don't need your hands, Vicky,' he had said. 'Just knock them down.' So she had looked at the dominoes and they had all fallen over, one after the other. A dozen or so in all.

'It made me feel very tired,' she told Andy, smiling that small, slantwise smile of hers. 'And I had gotten this idea somehow that we were discussing Vietnam, you know. So I said something like, "Yes, that proves it, if South Vietnam goes, they all go." And he smiled and patted my hands and said, "Why don't you sleep for a while, Vicky? You must be tired." So I did.' She shook her head. 'But now it doesn't seem real at all. I think I must have made it up entirely or built a hallucination around some perfectly normal test. You don't remember seeing him, do you? Tall guy with shoulder-length blond hair and a little scar on his chin?'

Andy shook his head.

'But I still don't understand how we could share *any* of the same fantasies,' Andy said, 'unless they've developed a drug over there that's telepathic as well as an hallucinogenic. I know there's been some talk about that in the last few years . . . the idea seems to be that if hallucinogens can heighten perception . . .' He shrugged, then grinned. 'Carlos Castaneda, where are you when we need you?'

'Isn't it more likely that we just discussed the same fantasy and then forgot we did?' Vicky asked.

He agreed it was a strong possibility, but he still felt disquieted by the whole experience. It had been, as they say, a bummer.

Taking his courage in his hands, he said, 'The only thing I really am sure of is that I seem to be falling in love with you, Vicky.'

She smiled nervously and kissed the corner of his mouth. 'That's sweet, Andy, but—'

'But you're a little afraid of me. Of men in general, maybe.'

'Maybe I am,' she said.

'All I'm asking for is a chance.'

'You'll have your chance,' she said. 'I like you, Andy. A lot. But please remember that I get scared. Sometimes I just . . . get scared.' She tried to shrug lightly, but it turned into something like a shudder.

'I'll remember,' he said, and drew her into his arms and kissed her. There was a moment's hesitation, and then she kissed back, holding his hands firmly in hers.

15

'*Daddy!*' Charlie screamed.

The world revolved sickly in front of Andy's eyes. The sodium arc lamps lining the Northway were below him, the ground was above him and shaking him loose. Then he was on his butt, sliding down the lower half of the embankment like a kid on a slide. Charlie was below him rolling helplessly over and over.

Oh no, she's going to shoot right out into the traffic—

'Charlie!' he yelled hoarsely, hurting his throat, his head. 'Watch it!'

Then she was down, squatting in the breakdown lane, washed by the harsh lights of a passing car, sobbing. A moment later he landed beside her with a solid *whap!* that rocketed all the way up his spine to his head. Things doubled in front of his eyes, tripled, and then gradually settled down.

Charlie was sitting on her haunches, her head cradled in her arms.

'Charlie,' he said, touching her arm. 'It's all right, honey.'

'I wish I did go in front of the cars!' she cried out, her voice bright and vicious with a self-loathing that made Andy's heart ache in his chest. 'I deserve to for setting that man on fire!'

'Shhh,' he said. 'Charlie, you don't have to think of that anymore.'

He held her. The cars swashed by them. Any one of them could be a cop, and that would end it. At this point it would almost be a relief.

Her sobs faded off little by little. Part of it, he realized, was simple tiredness. The same thing that was aggravating his headache past the screaming point and bringing this unwelcome flood of memories. If they could only get somewhere and lie down. . . .

'Can you get up, Charlie?'

She got to her feet slowly, brushing the last of the tears away. Her face was a pallid moonlet in the dark. Looking at her, he felt a sharp lance of guilt. She should be snugly tucked into a bed somewhere in a house with a shrinking mortgage, a teddy bear crooked under one arm, ready to go back to school the next morning and do battle for God, country, and the second grade. Instead, she was standing in the breakdown lane of a turnpike spur in upstate New York at one-fifteen in the morning, on the run, consumed with guilt because she had inherited something from her mother and father – something she herself had had no more part in determining than the direct blue of her eyes. How do you explain to a seven-year-old girl that Daddy and Mommy had once needed two hundred dollars and the people they had talked to said it was all right, but they had lied?

'We're going to hook us a ride,' Andy said, and he couldn't tell if he had slung his arm around her shoulders to comfort her or to support himself. 'We'll get to a hotel or a motel and we'll sleep. Then we'll think about what to do next. That sound all right?'

Charlie nodded listlessly.

'Okay,' he said, and cocked this thumb. The cars rushed by it, unheeding, and less than two miles away the green car was on its way again. Andy knew nothing of this; his harried mind had turned back to that night with Vicky in the Union. She was staying at one of the dorms and he had dropped her off there, relishing her lips again on the step just outside the big double doors, and she had put her arms hesitantly around his neck, this girl who had still been a virgin. They had been young, Jesus they had been young.

57

The cars rushed by, Charlie's hair lifted and dropped in each backwash of air, and he remembered the rest of what had happened that night twelve years ago.

16

Andy started across campus after seeing Vicky into her dorm, headed for the highway where he would hitch a ride into town. Although he could feel it only faintly against his face, the May wind beat strongly through the elms lining the mall, as if an invisible river ran through the air just above him, a river from which he could detect only the faintest, farthest ripples.

Jason Gearneigh Hall was on his way and he stopped in front of its dark bulk. Around it, the trees with their new foliage danced sinuously in the unseen current of that river of wind. A cool chill wormed its way down his spine and then settled in his stomach, freezing him lightly. He shivered even though the evening was warm. A big silver-dollar moon rode between the growing rafts of clouds – gilded keelboats running before the wind, running on that dark river of air. The moonlight reflected on the building's windows, making them glare like blankly unpleasant eyes.

Something happened in there, he thought. *Something more than what we were told or led to expect. What was it?*

In his mind's eye he saw that drowning, bloody hand again – only this time he saw it striking the chart, leaving a bloodstain in the shape of a comma . . . and then the chart rolling up with a rattling, smacking sound.

He walked toward the building. Crazy. They're not going to let you into a lecture hall at past ten o'clock. And—

And I'm scared.

Yes. That was it. Too many disquieting half-memories. Too easy to persuade himself they had only been fantasies;

58

Vicky was already on her way to accomplishing that. A test subject clawing his eyes out. Someone screaming that she wished she were dead, that being dead would be better than this, even if it meant going to hell and burning there for eternity. Someone else going into cardiac arrest and then being bundled out of sight with chilling professionalism. Because, let's face it, Andy old kid, thinking about telepathy doesn't scare you. What scares you is the thought that one of those things might have happened.

Heels clicking, he walked up to the big double doors and tried them. Locked. Behind them he could see the empty lobby. Andy knocked, and when he saw someone coming out of the shadows, he almost ran. He almost ran because the face that was going to appear out of those swimming shadows would be the face of Ralph Baxter, or of a tall man with shoulder-length blond hair and a scar on his chin.

But it was neither; the man who came over to the lobby doors and unlocked them and stuck his querulous face out was a typical college security guard: about sixty-two, lined cheeks and forehead, wary blue eyes that were rheumy from too much bottle time. A big time clock was clipped to his belt.

'Building's closed!' he said.

'I know,' Andy said, 'but I was part of an experiment in Room Seventy that finished up this morning and—'

'That don't matter! Building closes at nine on week-nights! Come back tomorrow!'

'—and I think I left my watch in there,' Andy said. He didn't own a watch. 'Hey, what do you say? Just one quick look around.'

'I can't do that,' the night man said, but all at once he sounded strangely unsure.

With no thought at all about it one way or another, Andy said in a low voice: 'Sure you can. I'll just take a look and

59

then I'll be out of your way. You won't even remember I was here, right?'

A sudden weird feeling in his head: it was as if he had reached out and *pushed* this elderly night security man, only with his head instead of his hands. And the guard did take two or three uncertain steps backward, letting go of the door.

Andy stepped in, a little concerned. There was a sudden sharp pain in his head, but it subsided to a low throb that was gone half an hour later.

'Say, are you all right?' he asked the security man.

'Huh? Sure, I'm okay.' The security man's suspicion was gone; he gave Andy a smile that was entirely friendly. 'Go on up and look for your watch, if you want to. Take your time. I probably won't even remember that you're here.'

And he strolled off.

Andy looked after him disbelievingly and then rubbed his forehead absently, as if to soothe the mild ache there. What in God's name had he done to that old duck? *Something*, that was for sure.

He turned, went to the stairs, and began climbing them. The upper hall was deeply shadowed and narrow; a nagging feeling of claustrophobia slipped around him and seemed to tighten his breathing, like an invisible dogcollar. Up here, the building had poked into that river of wind, and the air went skating under the eaves, screaming thinly. Room 70 had two double doors, the top halves two squares of frosted, pebbled glass. Andy stood outside them, listening to the wind move through the old gutters and downspouts, rattling the rusty leaves of dead years. His heart was thudding heavily in his chest.

He almost walked away from it then; it seemed suddenly easier not to know, just to forget it. Then he reached out and grasped one of the doorknobs, telling himself there

60

was nothing to worry about anyway because the damn room would be locked and good riddance to it.

Except that it wasn't. The knob turned freely. The door opened.

The room was empty, lit only by stuttering moonlight through the moving branches of the old elms outside. There was enough light for him to see that the cots had been removed. The blackboard had been erased and washed. The chart was rolled up like a windowshade, only the pull ring dangling. Andy stepped toward it, and after a moment he reached up with a hand that trembled slightly and pulled it down.

Quadrants of the brain; the human mind served up and marked like a butcher's diagram. Just seeing it made him get that trippy feeling again, like an acid flash. Nothing fun about it; it was sickening, and a moan escaped his throat, as delicate as a silver strand of spiderweb.

The bloodstain was there, comma-black in the moon's uneasy light. A printed legend that had undoubtedly read *CORPUS CALLOSUM* before this weekend's experiment now read *COR   OSUM*, the comma-shaped stain intervening.

Such a small thing.

Such a huge thing.

He stood in the dark, looking at it, starting to shake for real. How much of it did this make true? Some? Most? All? None of the above?

From behind him he heard a sound, or thought he did: the stealthy squeak of a shoe.

His hands jerked and one of them struck the chart with that same awful smacking sound. It rattled back up on its roller, the sound dreadfully loud in this black pit of a room.

A sudden knocking on the moonlight-dusted far window; a branch, or perhaps dead fingers streaked with gore and tissue: *let me in I left my eyes in there oh let me in let me in—*

He whirled in a slow-motion dream, a *slomo* dream, sinkingly sure that it would be that boy, a spirit in a white robe, dripping black holes where his eyes had been. His heart was a live thing in his throat.

No one there.

No *thing* there.

But his nerve was broken and then the branch began its implacable knocking again, he fled, not bothering to close the classroom door behind him. He sprinted down the narrow corridor and suddenly footfalls *were* pursuing him, echoes of his own running feet. He went down the stairs two at a time and so came back into the lobby, breathing hard, the blood hammering at his temples. The air in his throat prickled like cut hay.

He didn't see the security man anywhere about. He left, shutting one of the big glass lobby doors behind him and slinking down the walk to the quad like the fugitive he would later become.

17

Five days later, and much against her will, Andy dragged Vicky Tomlinson down to Jason Gearneigh Hall. She had already decided she never wanted to think about the experiment again. She had drawn her two-hundred-dollar check from the Psychology Department, banked it, and wanted to forget where it had come from.

He persuaded her to come, using eloquence he hadn't been aware he possessed. They went at the two-fifty change of classes; the bells of Harrison Chapel played a carillon in the dozing May air. 'Nothing can happen to us in broad daylight,' he said, uneasily refusing to clarify, even in his own mind, exactly what he might be afraid of. 'Not with dozens of people all around.'

'I just don't want to go, Andy,' she had said, but she had gone.

There were two or three kids leaving the lecture room with books under their arms. Sunshine painted the windows a prosier hue than the diamond-dust of moonlight Andy remembered. As Andy and Vicky entered, a few others trickled in for their three-o'clock biology seminar. One of them began to talk softly and earnestly to a pair of the others about an end-ROTC march that was coming off that weekend. No one took the slightest notion of Andy and Vicky.

'All right,' Andy said, and his voice was thick and nervous. 'See what you think.'

He pulled the chart down by the dangling ring. They were looking at a naked man with his skin flayed away and his organs labeled. His muscles looked like interwoven skeins of red yarn. Some wit had labeled him Oscar the Grouch.

'Jesus!' Andy said.

She gripped his arm and her hand was warm with nervous perspiration. 'Andy,' she said. 'Please, let's go. Before someone recognizes us.'

Yes, he was ready to go. The fact that the chart had been changed somehow scared him more than anything else. He jerked the pull ring down sharply and let it go. It made that same smacking sound as it went up.

Different chart. Same sound. Twelve years later he could still hear the sound it made – when his aching head would let him. He never stepped into Room 70 of Jason Gearneigh Hall after that day, but he was acquainted with that sound.

He heard it frequently in his dreams . . . and saw that questing, drowning, bloodstained hand.

18

The green car whispered along the airport feeder road toward the Northway entrance ramp. Behind the wheel, Norville Bates sat with his hands firmly at ten and two o'clock. Classical music came from the FM receiver in a muted, smooth flow. His hair was now short and combed back, but the small, semicircular scar on his chin hadn't changed – the place where he had cut himself on a jagged piece of Coke bottle as a kid. Vicky, had she still been alive, would have recognized him.

'We have one unit on the way,' the man in the Botany 500 suit said. His name was John Mayo. 'The guy's a stringer. He works for DIA as well as us.'

'Just an ordinary whore,' the third man said, and all three of them laughed in a nervous, keyed-up way. They knew they were close; they could almost smell blood. The name of the third man was Orville Jamieson, but he preferred to be called OJ, or even better, The Juice. He signed all his office memos OJ. He had signed one The Juice and that bastard Cap had given him a reprimand. Not just an oral one; a written one that had gone in his record.

'You think it's the Northway, huh?' OJ asked.

Norville Bates shrugged. 'Either the Northway or they headed into Albany,' he said. 'I gave the local yokel the hotels in town because it's his town, right?'

'Right,' John Mayo said. He and Norville got along well together. They went back a long way. All the way back to Room 70 of Jason Gearneigh Hall, and *that*, my friend, should anyone ever ask you had been *hairy*. John never wanted to go through anything that hairy again. He had been the man who zapped the kid who went into cardiac arrest. He had been a medic during the early days in Nam and he knew what to do with the defibrillator – in theory, at least. In practice, it hadn't gone so well, and the kid had got away from them. Twelve kids got Lot Six that day. Two of them had died – the kid who had gone into cardiac arrest and a girl who died six days later in her dorm, apparently of a sudden brain embolism. Two others had gone hopelessly insane – one of them the boy who had blinded himself, the other a girl who later developed a total paralysis from the neck down. Wanless had said that was psychological, but who the fuck knew? It had been a nice day's work, all right.

'The local yokel is taking his wife along,' Norville was saying. 'She's looking for her granddaughter. Her son ran away with the little girl. Nasty divorce case, all of that. She doesn't want to notify the police unless she has to, but she's afraid the son might be going mental. If she plays it right, there isn't a night clerk in town that won't tell her if the two of them have checked in.'

'If she plays it right,' OJ said. 'With these stringers you can never tell.'

John said, 'We're going to the closest on-ramp, right?'

'Right,' Norville said. 'Just three, four minutes now.'

'Have they had enough time to get down there?'

'They have if they were busting ass. Maybe we'll be able to pick them up trying to thumb a ride right there on the ramp. Or maybe they took a shortcut and went over the side into the breakdown lane. Either way, all we have to do is cruise along until we come to them.'

'Where you headed, buddy, hop in,' The Juice said, and laughed. There was a .357 Magnum in a shoulder holster under his left arm. He called it The Windsucker.

'If they already hooked them a ride, we're shit out of luck, Norv,' John said.

Norville shrugged. 'Percentage play. It's quarter past one in the morning. With the rationing, traffic's thinner

65

than ever. What's Mr Businessman going to think if he sees a big guy and a little girl trying to hitch a ride?'

'He's gonna think it's bad news,' John said.

'That's a big ten-four.'

The Juice laughed again. Up ahead the stop-and-go light that marked the Northway ramp gleamed in the dark. OJ put his hand on the walnut stock of The Windsucker. Just in case.

19

The van passed them by, backwashing cool air . . . and then its brakelights flashed brighter and it swerved over into the breakdown lane about fifty yards farther up.

'Thank God,' Andy said softly. 'You let me do the talking, Charlie.'

'All right, Daddy.' She sounded apathetic. The dark circles were back under her eyes. The van was backing up as they walked toward it. Andy's head felt like a slowly swelling lead balloon.

There was a vision from the Thousand and One Nights painted on the side – caliphs, maidens hiding under gauzy masks, a carpet floating mystically in the air. The carpet was undoubtedly meant to be red, but in the light of the turnpike sodiums it was the dark maroon of drying blood.

Andy opened the passenger door and boosted Charlie up and in. He followed her. 'Thanks, mister,' he said. 'Saved our lives.'

'My pleasure,' the driver said. 'Hi, little stranger.'

'Hi,' Charlie said in a small voice.

The driver checked the outside mirror, drove down the breakdown lane at a steadily increasing pace, and then crossed into the travel lane. Glancing past Charlie's slightly bowed head, Andy felt a touch of guilt: the driver was exactly the sort of young man Andy himself always passed by when he saw him standing on the shoulder with his thumb out. Big but lean, he wore a heavy black beard that curled down to his chest and a big felt hat that looked like a prop in a movie about feudin Kentucky hillbillies. A cigarette that looked home-rolled was cocked in the corner of his mouth, curling up smoke. Just a cigarette, by the smell; no sweet odor of cannabis.

'Where you headed, my man?' the driver asked.

'Two towns up the line,' Andy said.

'Hastings Glen?'

'That's right.'

The driver nodded. 'On the run from someone, I guess.'

Charlie tensed and Andy put a soothing hand on her back and rubbed gently until she loosened up again. He had detected no menace in the driver's voice.

'There was a process server at the airport,' he said.

The driver grinned – it was almost hidden beneath his fierce beard – plucked the cigarette from his mouth, and offered it delicately to the wind sucking just outside his half-open vent window. The slipstream gulped it down.

'Something to do with the little stranger here is my guess,' he said.

'Not far wrong,' Andy said.

The driver fell silent. Andy settled back and tried to cope with his headache. It seemed to have leveled off at a final screaming pitch. Had it ever been this bad before? Impossible to tell. Each time he overdid it, it seemed like the worst ever. It would be a month before he dared use the push again. He knew that two towns up the line was not nearly far enough, but it was all he could manage tonight. He was tipped over. Hastings Glen would have to do.

'Who do you pick, man?' the driver asked him.

'Huh?'

'The Series. The San Diego Padres in the World Series – how do you figure that?'

'Pretty far out,' Andy agreed. His voice came from far away, a tolling undersea bell.

'You okay, man? You look pale.'

'Headache,' Andy said. 'Migraine.'

'Too much pressure,' the driver said. 'I can dig it. You staying at a hotel? You need some cash? I could let you have five. Wish it was more, but I'm on my way to California, and I got to watch it careful. Just like the Joads in *The Grapes of Wrath*.'

Andy smiled gratefully. 'I think we're okay.'

'Fine.' He glanced at Charlie, who had dozed off. 'Pretty little girl, my man. Are you watching out for her?'

'As best I can,' Andy said.

'All right,' the driver said. 'That's the name of that tune.'

20

Hastings Glen was little more than a wide place in the road; at this hour all the traffic lights in town had turned to blinkers. The bearded driver in the hillbilly hat took them up the exit ramp, through the sleeping town, and down Route 40 to the Slumberland Motel, a redwood place with the skeletal remains of a harvested cornfield in back and a pinkish-red neon sign out front that stuttered the nonword VA A CY into the dark. As her sleep deepened, Charlie had tilted farther and farther to the left, until her head was resting on the driver's blue-jeaned thigh. Andy had offered to shift her, and the driver shook his head.

'She's fine, man. Let her sleep.'

'Would you mind dropping us off a little bit past?' Andy asked. It was hard to think, but this caution came almost intuitively.

68

'Don't want the night man to know you don't have a car?' The driver smiled. 'Sure, man. But a place like that, they wouldn't give a squirt if you pedaled in on a unicycle.' The van's tires crunched the gravel shoulder. 'You positive you couldn't use five?'

'I guess I could,' Andy said reluctantly. 'Would you write down your address for me? I'll mail it back to you.'

The driver's grin reappeared. 'My address is "in transit," ' he said, getting out his wallet. 'But you may see my happy smiling face again, right? Who knows. Grab onto Abe, man.' He handed the five to Andy and suddenly Andy was crying – not a lot, but crying.

'No, man,' the driver said kindly. He touched the back of Andy's neck lightly. 'Life is short and pain is long and we were all put on this earth to help each other. The comic-book philosophy of Jim Paulson in a nutshell. Take good care of the little stranger.'

'Sure,' Andy said, brushing his eyes. He put the five-dollar bill in the pocket of his corduroy coat. 'Charlie? Hon? Wake up. Just a little bit longer now.'

21

Three minutes later Charlie was leaning sleepily against him while he watched Jim Paulson go up the road to a closed restaurant, turn around, and then head back past them toward the Interstate. Andy raised his hand. Paulson raised his in return. Old Ford van with the Arabian Nights on the side, jinns and grand viziers and a mystic, floating carpet. Hope California's good to you, guy, Andy thought, and then the two of them walked back toward the Slumberland Motel.

'I want you to wait for me outside and out of sight,' Andy said. 'Okay?'

'Okay, Daddy.' Very sleepy.

He left her by an evergreen shrub and walked over to the office and rang the night bell. After about two minutes, a middle-aged man in a bathrobe appeared, polishing his glasses. He opened the door and let Andy in without a word.

'I wonder if I could have the unit down on the end of the left wing,' Andy said. 'I parked there.'

'This time of year, you could have *all* of the west wing if you wanted it,' the night man said, and smiled around a mouthful of yellow dentures. He gave Andy a printed index card and a pen advertising business supplies. A car passed by outside, silent headlights that waxed and waned.

Andy signed the card Bruce Rozelle. Bruce was driving a 1978 Vega, New York license LMS 240. He looked at the blank marked ORGANIZATION/COMPANY for a moment, and then, in a flash of inspiration (as much as his aching head would allow), he wrote United Vending Company of America. And checked CASH under form of payment.

Another car went by out front.

The clerk initialed the card and tucked it away. 'That's seventeen dollars and fifty cents.'

'Do you mind change?' Andy asked. 'I never did get a chance to cash up, and I'm dragging around twenty pounds of silver. I hate these country milk runs.'

'Spends just as easy. I don't mind.'

'Thanks.' Andy reached into his coat pocket, pushed aside the five-dollar bill with his fingers, and brought out a fistful of quarters, nickels, and dimes. He counted out fourteen dollars, brought out some more change, and made up the rest. The clerk had been separating the coins into neat piles and now he swept them into the correct compartments of the cash drawer.

'You know,' he said, closing the drawer and looking at Andy hopefully, 'I'd knock five bucks off your room bill if you could fix my cigarette machine. It's been out of order for a week.'

Andy walked over to the machine, which stood in the corner, pretended to look at it, and then walked back. 'Not our brand,' he said.

'Oh. Shit. Okay. Goodnight, buddy. You'll find an extra blanket on the closet shelf if you should want it.'

'Fine.'

He went out. The gravel crunched beneath his feet, hideously amplified in his ears, sounding like stone cereal. He walked over to the evergreen shrub where he had left Charlie and Charlie wasn't there.

'Charlie?'

No answer. He switched the room key on its long green plastic tab from one hand to the other. Both hands were suddenly sweaty.

'Charlie?'

Still no answer. He thought back and now it seemed to him that the car that had gone past when he had been filling out the registration card had been slowing down. Maybe it had been a green car.

His heartbeat began to pick up, sending jolts of pain up to his skull. He tried to think what he should do if Charlie was gone, but he couldn't think. His head hurt too badly. He—

There was a low, snorting, snoring sound from deeper back in the bushes. A sound he knew very well. He leaped toward it, gravel spurting out from under his shoes. Stiff evergreen branches scraped his legs and raked back the tails of his corduroy jacket.

Charlie was lying on her side on the verge of the motel lawn, knees drawn up nearly to her chin, hands between them. Fast asleep. Andy stood with his eyes closed for a moment and then shook her awake for what he hoped would be the last time that night. That long, long night.

71

Her eyelids fluttered, and then she was looking up at him. 'Daddy?' she asked, her voice was blurred, still half in her dreams. 'I got out of sight like you said.'

'I know, honey,' he said. 'I know you did. Come on. We're going to bed.'

22

Twenty minutes later they were both in the double bed of Unit 16, Charlie fast asleep and breathing evenly, Andy still awake but drifting toward sleep, only the steady thump in his head still holding him up. And the questions.

They had been on the run for about a year. It was almost impossible to believe, maybe because it hadn't *seemed* so much like running, not when they had been in Port City, Pennsylvania, running the Weight-Off program. Charlie had gone to school in Port City, and how could you be on the run if you were holding a job and your daughter was going to first grade? They had almost been caught in Port City, not because they had been particularly good (although they were terribly dogged, and that frightened Andy a lot) but because Andy had made that crucial lapse – he had allowed himself temporarily to forget they were fugitives.

No chance of that now.

How close were they? Still back in New York? If only he could believe that – they hadn't got the cabby's number; they were still tracking him down. More likely they were in Albany, crawling over the airport like maggots over a pile of meat scraps. Hastings Glen? Maybe by morning. But maybe not. Hastings Glen was fifteen miles from the airport. No need to let paranoia sweep away good sense.

I deserve it! I deserve to go in front of the cars for setting that man on fire!

His own voice replying: *It could have been worse. It could have been his face.*

72

Voices in a haunted room.

Something else came to him. He was supposed to be driving a Vega. When morning came and the night man didn't see a Vega parked in front of Unit 16, would he just assume his United Vending Company man had pushed on? Or would he investigate? Nothing he could do about it now. He was totally wasted.

I thought there was something funny about him. He looked pale, sick. And he paid with change. He said he worked for a vending-machine company, but he couldn't fix the cigarette machine in the lobby.

Voices in a haunted room.

He shifted onto his side, listening to Charlie's slow, even breathing. He thought they had taken her, but she'd only gone farther back in the bushes. Out of sight. Charlene Norma McGee, Charlie since . . . well, since forever. *If they took you, Charlie, I don't know what I'd do.*

23

One last voice, his roommate Quincey's voice, from six years ago.

Charlie had been a year old then, and of course they knew she wasn't normal. They had known that since she was a week old and Vicky had brought her into their bed with them because when she was left in the little crib, the pillow began to . . . well, began to smolder. The night they had put the crib away forever, not speaking in their fright, a fright too big and too strange to be articulated, it had got hot enough to blister her cheek and she had screamed most of the night, in spite of the Solarcaine Andy had found in the medicine chest. What a crazyhouse that first year had been, no sleep, endless fear. Fires in the wastebaskets when her bottles were late; once the curtains had burst into flame, and if Vicky hadn't been in the room—

It was her fall down the stairs that had finally prompted him to call Quincey. She had been crawling then, and was quite good at going up the stairs on her hands and knees and then backing down again the same way. Andy had been sitting with her that day; Vicky was out at Senter's with one of her friends, shopping. She had been hesitant about going, and Andy nearly had to throw her out the door. She was looking too used lately, too tired. There was something starey in her eyes that made him think about those combat-fatigue stories you heard during wartime.

He had been reading in the living room, near the foot of the stairs. Charlie was going up and down. Sitting on the stairs was a teddy bear. He should have moved it, of course, but each time she went up, Charlie went around it, and he had become lulled – much as he had become lulled by what appeared to be their normal life in Port City.

As she came down the third time, her feet got tangled around the bear and she came all the way to the bottom, thump, bump, and tumble, wailing with rage and fear. The stairs were carpeted and she didn't even have a bruise – God watches over drunks and small children, that had been Quincey's saying, and that was his first conscious thought of Quincey that day – but Andy rushed to her, picked her up, held her, cooed a lot of nonsense to her while he gave her the quick once-over, looking for blood, or a limb hanging wrong, signs of concussion. And—

And he *felt* it pass him – the invisible, incredible bolt of death from his daughter's mind. It felt like the backwash of warm air from a highballing subway train, when it's summertime and you're standing maybe a little too close on the platform. A soft, soundless passage of warm air . . . and then the teddy bear was on fire. Teddy had hurt Charlie; Charlie would hurt Teddy. The flames roared up, and for a moment, as it charred, Andy was looking at its black shoebutton eyes through a sheet of flame, and the

74

flames were spreading to the carpeting on the stair where the bear had tumbled.

Andy put his daughter down and ran for the fire extinguisher on the wall near the TV. He and Vicky didn't talk about the thing their daughter could do – there were times when Andy wanted to, but Vicky wouldn't hear of it; she avoided the subject with hysterical stubbornness, saying there was nothing wrong with Charlie, *nothing wrong* – but fire extinguishers had appeared silently, undiscussed, with almost the same stealth as dandelions appear during that period when spring and summer overlap. They didn't talk about what Charlie could do, but there were fire extinguishers all over the house.

He grabbed this one, smelling the heavy aroma of frying carpet, and dashed for the stairs . . . and still there was time to think about that story, the one he had read as a kid, 'It's a *Good* Life,' by some guy named Jerome Bixby, and that had been about a little kid who had enslaved his parents with psychic terror, a nightmare of a thousand possible deaths, and you never knew . . . you never knew when the little kid was going to get mad . . .

Charlie was wailing, sitting on her butt at the foot of the stairs.

Andy twisted the knob on the fire extinguisher savagely and sprayed foam on the spreading fire, dousing it. He picked up Teddy, his fur stippled with dots and puffs and dollops of foam, and carried him back downstairs.

Hating himself, yet knowing in some primitive way that it had to be done, the line had to be drawn, the lesson learned, he jammed the bear almost into Charlie's screaming, frightened, tear-streaked face. *Oh you dirty bastard*, he had thought desperately, *why don't you just go out to the kitchen and get a paring knife and cut a line up each cheek? Mark her that way?* And his mind had seized on that. Scars.

Yes. That's what he had to do. Scar his child. Burn a scar on her soul.

'Do you like the way Teddy looks?' he roared. The bear was scalded, the bear was blackened, and in his hand it was still as warm as a cooling lump of charcoal. 'Do you like Teddy to be all burned so you can't play with him anymore, Charlie?'

Charlie was crying in great, braying whoops, her skin all red fever and pale death, her eyes swimming with tears. *'Daaaaa! Ted! Ted!'*

'Yes, Teddy,' he said grimly. 'Teddy's all burned, Charlie. You burned Teddy. And if you burn Teddy, you might burn Mommy. Daddy. Now . . . *don't you do it anymore!'* He leaned closer to her, not picking her up yet, not touching her. 'Don't you do it anymore because *it is a Bad Thing!'*

'Daaaaaaaaaa—'

And that was all the heartbreak he could stand to inflict, all the horror, all the fear. He picked her up, held her, walked her back and forth until – a very long time later – her sobs tapered off to irregular hitchings of her chest, and sniffles. When he looked at her, she was asleep with her cheek on his shoulder.

He put her on the couch and went to the phone in the kitchen and called Quincey.

Quincey didn't want to talk. He was working for a large aircraft corporation in that year of 1975, and in the notes that accompanied each of his yearly Christmas cards to the McGees he described his job as Vice-President in Charge of Stroking. When the men who made the airplanes had problems, they were supposed to go see Quincey. Quincey would help them with their problems – feelings of aliena-tion, identity crises, maybe just a feeling that their jobs were dehumanizing them – and they wouldn't go back to the line and put the widget where the wadget was supposed

76

to go and therefore the planes wouldn't crash and the world would continue to be safe for democracy. For this Quincey made thirty-two thousand dollars a year, seventeen thousand more than Andy made. 'And I don't feel a bit guilty,' he had written. 'I consider it a small salary to extract for keeping America afloat almost single-handed.'

That was Quincey, as sardonically funny as ever. Except he hadn't been sardonic and he hadn't been funny that day when Andy called from Ohio with his daughter sleeping on the couch and the smell of burned bear and singed carpeting in his nostrils.

'I've heard things,' Quincey said finally, when he saw that Andy wasn't going to let him off without *something*. 'But sometimes people listen in on phones, old buddy. It's the era of Watergate.'

'I'm scared,' Andy said. 'Vicky's scared. And Charlie's scared too. What have you heard, Quincey?'

'Once upon a time there was an experiment in which twelve people participated,' Quincey said. 'About six years ago. Do you remember that?'

'I remember it,' Andy said grimly.

'There aren't many of those twelve people left. There were four, the last I heard. And two of them married each other.'

'Yes,' Andy said, but inside he felt growing horror. Only four left? What was Quincey talking about?

'I understand one of them can bend keys and shut doors without even touching them.' Quincey's voice, thin, coming across two thousand miles of telephone cable, coming through switching stations, through the open-relay points, through junction boxes in Nevada, Idaho, Colorado, Iowa. A million places to tap into Quincey's voice.

'Yes?' he said, straining to keep his voice level. And he thought of Vicky, who could sometimes turn on the radio or turn off the TV without going anywhere near it – and

77

Vicky was apparently not even aware she was doing those things.

'Oh yes, he's for real,' Quincey was saying. 'He's – what would you say? – a documented case. It hurts his head if he does those things too often, but he can do them. They keep him in a little room with a door he can't open and a lock he can't bend. They do tests on him. He bends keys. He shuts doors. And I understand he's nearly crazy.'

'Oh . . . my . . . God,' Andy said faintly.

'He's part of the peace effort, so it's all right if he goes crazy,' Quincey went on. 'He's going crazy so two hundred and twenty million Americans can stay safe and free. Do you understand?'

'Yes,' Andy had whispered.

'What about the two people who got married? Nothing. So far as they know. They live quietly, in some quiet middle-American state like Ohio. There's maybe a yearly check on them. Just to see if they're doing anything like bending keys or closing doors without touching them or doing funny little mentalist routines at the local Backyard Carnival for Muscular Dystrophy. Good thing those people can't do anything like that, isn't it, Andy?'

Andy closed his eyes and smelled burned cloth. Sometimes Charlie would pull open the fridge door, look in, and then crawl off again. And if Vicky was ironing, she would glance at the fridge door and it would swing shut again – all without her being aware that she was doing anything strange. That was sometimes. At other times it didn't seem to work, and she would leave her ironing and close the refrigerator door herself (or turn off the radio, or turn on the TV). Vicky couldn't bend keys or read thoughts or fly or start fires or predict the future. She could sometimes shut a door from across the room and that was about the extent of it. Sometimes, after she had done several of these things, Andy had noticed that she would complain of a

78

headache or an upset stomach, and whether that was a physical reaction or some sort of muttered warning from her subconscious, Andy didn't know. Her ability to do these things got maybe a little stronger around the time of her period. Such small things, and so infrequently, that Andy had come to think of them as normal. As for himself . . . well he could push people. There was no real name for it; perhaps autohypnosis came closest. And he couldn't do it often, because it gave him headaches. Most days he could forget completely that he wasn't utterly normal and never really had been since that day in Room 70 of Jason Gearneigh.

He closed his eyes and on the dark field inside his eyelids he saw that comma-shaped bloodstain and the nonwords COR OSUM.

'Yes, it's a good thing,' Quincey went on, as if Andy had agreed. 'Or they might put them in two little rooms where they could work full-time to keep two hundred and twenty million Americans safe and free.'

'A good thing,' Andy agreed.

'Those twelve people,' Quincey said, 'maybe they gave those twelve people a drug they didn't fully understand. It might have been that someone – a certain Mad Doctor – might have deliberately misled them. Or maybe he thought he was misleading them and they were deliberately leading him on. It doesn't matter.'

'No.'

'So this drug was given to them and maybe it changed their chromosomes a little bit. Or a lot. Or who knows. And maybe two of them got married and decided to have a baby and maybe the baby got something more than her eyes and his mouth. Wouldn't they be interested in that child?'

'I bet they would,' Andy said, now so frightened he was

79

having trouble talking at all. He had already decided that he would not tell Vicky about calling Quincey.

'It's like you got lemon, and that's nice, and you got meringue, and *that's* nice, too, but when you put them together, you've got . . . a whole new taste treat. I bet they'd want to see just what that child could do. They might just want to take it and put it in a little room and see if it could help make the world safe for democracy. And I think that's all I want to say, old buddy, except . . . keep your head down.'

24

Voices in a haunted room.
Keep your head down.
He turned his head on the motel pillow and looked at Charlie, who was sleeping deeply. *Charlie kid, what are we going to do? Where can we go and be left alone? How is this going to end?*
No answer to any of these questions.
And at last he slept, while not so far away a green car cruised through the dark, still hoping to come upon a big man with broad shoulders in a corduroy jacket and a little girl with blond hair in red pants and a green blouse.

Longmont, Virginia:
The Shop

1

Two handsome Southern plantation homes faced each
other across a long and rolling grass lawn that was
crisscrossed by a few gracefully looping bike paths and a
two-lane crushed-gravel drive that came over the hill from
the main road. Off to one side of one of these houses was
a large barn, painted a bright red and trimmed a spotless
white. Near the other was a long stable, done in the same
handsome red with white trim. Some of the best horseflesh
in the South was quartered here. Between the barn and the
stable was a wide, shallow duckpond, calmly reflecting the
sky.

In the 1860s, the original owners of these two homes had
gone off and got themselves killed in the war, and all
survivors of both families were dead now. The two estates
had been consolidated into one piece of government
property in 1954. It was Shop headquarters.

At ten minutes past nine on a sunny October day – the
day after Andy and Charlie left New York for Albany in a
taxicab – an elderly man with kindly, sparkling eyes and
wearing a woolen British driving cap on his head biked
toward one of the houses. Behind him, over the second
knoll, was the checkpoint he had come through after a
computer ID system had okayed his thumbprint. The
checkpoint was inside a double run of barbed wire. The
outer run, seven feet high, was marked every sixty feet by

signs that read CAUTION! GOVERNMENT PROPERTY   LOW
ELECTRIC CHARGE RUNS THROUGH THIS FENCE! During the
day, the charge was indeed low. At night, the on-property
generator boosted it to a lethal voltage, and each morning
a squad of five groundskeepers circled it in little electric
golf carts, picking up the bodies of crisped rabbits, moles,
birds, groundhogs, an occasional skunk lying in a pool of
smell, sometimes a deer. And twice, human beings, equally
cooked. The space between the outer and inner runs of
barbed wire was ten feet. Day and night, guard dogs
circled the installation in this run. The guard dogs were
Dobermans, and they had been trained to stay away from
the electrified wire. At each corner of the installation there
were guard towers, also built of spanking-red barnboard
and trimmed in white. They were manned by personnel
who were expert in the use of various items of death-
dealing hardware. The whole place was monitored by TV
cameras, and the views these various cameras presented
were constantly scanned by computer. The Longmont
facility was secure.

The elderly man biked on, with a smile for the people he
passed. An old, baldheaded man in a baseball cap was
walking a thin-ankled filly. He raised his hand and called,
'Hi, Cap! Ain't this some kind of a day!'

'Knock your eye out,' the man on the bike agreed. 'Have
a good one, Henry.'

He reached the front of the northernmost of the two
homes, dismounted his bike, and put down its kickstand.
He breathed deeply of the mild morning air, then trotted
spryly up the wide porch steps and between the broad
Doric columns.

He opened the door and stepped into the wide receiving
hall. A young woman with red hair sat behind a desk, a
statistics-analysis book open in front of her. One hand was

82

holding her place in the book. The other was in her desk drawer, lightly touching a .38 Smith & Wesson.

'Good morning, Josie,' the elderly gent said.

'Hi, Cap. You're running a little behind, aren't you?' Pretty girls could get away with this; if it had been Duane's day on the front desk, he could not have done. Cap was not a supporter of women's liberation.

'My top gear's sticking, darlin'.' He put his thumb in the proper slot. Something in the console thudded heavily, and a green light fluttered and then remained steady on Josie's board. 'You be good, now.'

'Well, I'll be careful,' she said archly, and crossed her legs.

Cap roared laughter and walked down the hall. She watched him go, wondering for a moment if she should have told him that that creepy old man Wanless had come in some twenty minutes ago. He'd know soon enough, she supposed, and sighed. What a way to screw up the start of a perfectly fine day, having to talk to an old spook like that. But she supposed that a person like Cap, who held a position of great responsibility, had to take the sour with the sweet.

2

Cap's office was at the back of the house. A large bay window gave a magnificent view of the back lawn, the barn, and the duckpond, which was partially screened with alders. Rich McKeon was halfway down the lawn, sitting astride a miniature tractor-lawnmower. Cap stood looking at him with his arms crossed behind his back for a moment and then went over to the Mr Coffee in the corner. He poured some coffee in his U.S.N. cup, added Cremora and then sat down and thumbed the intercom.

'Hi, Rachel,' he said.

'Hello, Cap. Dr Wanless is—'

'I knew it,' Cap said. 'I *knew* it. I could smell that old whore the minute I came in.'

'Shall I tell him you're just too busy today?'

'Don't tell him any such thing,' Cap said stoutly. 'Just let him sit out there in the yellow parlor the whole frigging morning. If he doesn't decide to go home, I suppose I can see him before lunch.'

'All right, sir.' Problem solved – for Rachel, anyway, Cap thought with a touch of resentment. Wanless wasn't really her problem at all. And the fact was, Wanless was getting to be an embarrassment. He had outlived both his usefulness and his influence. Well, there was always the Maui compound. And then there was Rainbird.

Cap felt a little inward shudder at that . . . and he wasn't a man who shuddered easily.

He held down the intercom toggle again. 'I'll want the entire McGee file again, Rachel. And at ten-thirty I want to see Al Steinowitz. If Wanless is still here when I finish with Al, you can send him in.'

'Very good, Cap.'

Cap sat back, steepled his fingers, and looked across the room at the picture of George Patton on the wall. Patton was standing astride the top hatch of a tank as if he thought he were Duke Wayne or someone. 'It's a hard life if you don't weaken,' he told Patton's image, and sipped his coffee.

3

Rachel brought the file in on a whisper-wheeled library cart ten minutes later. There were six boxes of papers and reports, four boxes of photographs. There were telephone transcripts as well. The McGee phone had been bugged since 1978.

'Thanks, Rachel.'

'You're welcome. Mr Steinowitz will be here at ten-thirty.'

'Of course he will. Has Wanless died yet?'

'I'm afraid not,' she said, smiling. 'He's just sitting out there and watching Henry walk the horses.'

'Shredding his goddam cigarettes?'

Rachel covered her mouth like a schoolgirl, giggled, and nodded. 'He's gone through half a pack already.'

Cap grunted. Rachel left and he turned to the files. He had been through them how many times in the last eleven months? A dozen? Two dozen? He had the extracta nearly by heart. And if Al was right, he would have the two remaining McGees under detection by the end of the week. The thought caused a hot little trickle of excitement in his belly.

He began leafing through the McGee file at random, pulling a sheet here, reading a snatch there. It was his way of plugging back into the situation. His conscious mind was in neutral, his subconscious in high gear. What he wanted now was not detail but to put his hand to the whole thing. As baseball players say, he needed to find the handle.

Here was a memo from Wanless himself, a younger Wanless (ah, but they had all been younger then), dated September 12, 1968. Half a paragraph caught Cap's eye:

. . . of an enormous importance in the continuing study of controllable psychic phenomena. Further testing on animals would be counterproductive (see overleaf 1) and, as I emphasized at the group meeting this summer, testing on convicts or any deviant personality might lead to very real problems if Lot Six is even fractionally as powerful as we suspect (see overleaf 2). I therefore continue to recommend . . .

85

You continue to recommend that we feed it to controlled groups of college students under all outstanding contingency plans for failure, Cap thought. There had been no waffling on Wanless's part in those days. No indeed. His motto in those days had been full speed ahead and devil take the hindmost. Twelve people had been tested. Two of them had died, one during the test, one shortly afterward. Two had gone hopelessly insane, and both of them were maimed – one blind, one suffering from psychotic paralysis, both of them confined at the Maui compound, where they would remain until their miserable lives ended. So then there were eight. One of them had died in a car accident in 1972, a car accident that was almost certainly no accident at all but suicide. Another had leaped from the roof of the Cleveland Post Office in 1973, and there was no question at all about that one; he had left a note saying he 'couldn't stand the pictures in his head any longer.' The Cleveland police had diagnosed it as suicidal depression and paranoia. Cap and the Shop had diagnosed it as lethal Lot Six hangover. And that had left six.

Three others had committed suicide between 1974 and 1977, for a known total of four suicides and a probable total of five. Almost half the class, you might say. All four of the definite suicides had seemed perfectly normal right up to the time they had used the gun, or the rope, or jumped from the high place. But who knew what they might have been going through? Who really knew?

So then there were three. Since 1977, when the long-dormant Lot Six project had suddenly got red hot again, a fellow named James Richardson, who now lived in Los Angeles, had been under constant covert surveillance. In 1969 he had taken part in the Lot Six experiment, and during the course of the drug's influence, he had demonstrated the same startling range of talents as the rest of them: telekinesis, thought transference, and maybe the

86

most interesting manifestation of all, at least from the Shop's specialized point of view: mental domination.

But as had happened with the others, James Richardson's drug-induced powers seemed to have disappeared completely with the wearing off of the drug. Follow-up interviews in 1971, 1973, and 1975 had shown nothing. Even Wanless had had to admit that, and he was a fanatic on the subject of Lot Six. Steady computer readouts on a random basis (and they were a lot less random since the McGee thing had started to happen) had shown no indication at all that Richardson was using any sort of psi power, either consciously or unconsciously. He had graduated in 1971, drifted west through a series of lower-echelon managerial jobs – no mental domination there – and now worked for the Telemyne Corporation.

Also, he was a fucking faggot.

Cap sighed.

They were continuing to keep an eye on Richardson, but Cap had been personally convinced that the man was a washout. And that left two, Andy McGee and his wife. The serendipity of their marriage had not been lost on the Shop, or on Wanless, who had begun to bombard the office with memos, suggesting that any offspring of that marriage would bear close watching – counting his chickens before they had hatched, you could say – and on more than one occasion Cap had toyed with the idea of telling Wanless they had learned Andy McGee had had a vasectomy. That would have shut the old bastard up. By then Wanless had had his stroke and was effectively useless, really nothing but a nuisance.

There had been only the one Lot Six experiment. The results had been so disastrous that the coverup had been massive and complete . . . and expensive. The order came down from on high to impose an indefinite moratorium on further testing. Wanless had plenty to scream about that

87

day, Cap thought . . . and scream he had. But there had been no sign at all that the Russians or any other world power was interested in drug-induced psionics, and the top brass had concluded that in spite of some positive results, Lot Six was a blind alley. Looking at the long-term results, one of the scientists who had worked on the project compared it to dropping a jet engine into an old Ford. It went like hell, all right . . . until it hit the first obstacle. 'Give us another ten thousand years of evolution,' this fellow had said, 'and we'll try it again.'

Part of the problem had been that when the drug-induced psi powers were at their height, the test subjects had also been tripping out of their skulls. No control was possible. And coming out the other side, the top brass had been nearly shitting their pants. Covering up the death of an agent, or even of a bystander to an operation – that was one thing. Covering up the death of a student who had suffered a heart attack, the disappearance of two others, and lingering traces of hysteria and paranoia in yet others – that was a different matter altogether. All of them had friends and associates, even if one of the requirements by which the test subjects had been picked was a scarcity of close relatives. The costs and the risks had been enormous. They had involved nearly seven hundred thousand dollars in hush money and the sanction of at least one person – the godfather of the fellow who had clawed his eyes out. The godfather just would not quit. He was going to get to the root of the matter. As it turned out, the only place the godfather had got was to the bottom of the Baltimore Trench, where he presumably still was, with two cement blocks tied around whatever remained of his legs.

And still, a great deal of it – too damn much – had just been luck.

So the Lot Six project had been shelved with a continuing yearly budget allotment. The money was used to continue random surveillance on the survivors in case something turned up – some pattern.

Eventually, one had.

Cap hunted through a folder of photographs and came up with an eight-by-ten glossy black-and-white of the girl. It had been taken three years ago, when she was four and attending the Free Children's Nursery School in Harrison. The picture had been taken with a telephoto lens from the back of a bakery van and later blown up and cropped to turn a picture of a lot of boys and girls at playtime into a portrait of a smiling little girl with her pigtails flying and the pistol grip of a jumprope in each hand.

Cap looked at this picture sentimentally for some time. Wanless, in the aftermath of his stroke, had discovered fear. Wanless now thought the little girl would have to be sanctioned. And although Wanless was among the outs these days, there were those who concurred with his opinion – those who were among the ins. Cap hoped like hell that it wouldn't come to that. He had three grandchildren himself, two of them just about Charlene McGee's age.

Of course they would have to separate the girl from her father. Probably permanently. And he would almost certainly have to be sanctioned . . . after he had served his purpose, of course.

It was quarter past ten. He buzzed Rachel. 'Is Albert Steinowitz here yet?'

'Just this minute arrived, sir.'

'Very good. Send him in, please.'

4

'I want you to take personal charge of the endgame, Al.'

'Very good, Cap.'

Albert Steinowitz was a small man with a yellow-pale

89

complexion and very black hair; in earlier years he had sometimes been mistaken for the actor Victor Jory. Cap had worked with Steinowitz off and on for nearly eight years – in fact they had come over from the navy together – and to him Al had always looked like a man about to enter the hospital for a terminal stay. He smoked constantly, except in here, where it wasn't allowed. He walked with a slow, stately stride that invested him with a strange kind of dignity, and impenetrable dignity is a rare attribute in any man. Cap, who saw all the medical records of Section One agents, knew that Albert's dignified walk was bogus; he suffered badly from hemorrhoids and had been operated on for them twice. He had refused a third operation because it might mean a colostomy bag on his leg for the rest of his life. His dignified walk always made Cap think of the fairy tale about the mermaid who wanted to be a woman and the price she paid for legs and feet. Cap imagined that her walk had been rather dignified, too.

'How soon can you be in Albany?' he asked Al now.

'An hour after I leave here.'

'Good. I won't keep you long. What's the status up there?'

Albert folded his small, slightly yellow hands in his lap. 'The state police are cooperating nicely. All highways leading out of Albany have been roadblocked. The blocks are set up in concentric circles with Albany County Airport at their center. Radius of thirty-five miles.'

'You're assuming they didn't hitch a ride.'

'We have to,' Albert said. 'If they hooked a ride with someone who took them two hundred miles or so, of course we'll have to start all over again. But I'm betting they're inside that circle.'

'Oh? Why is that, Albert?' Cap leaned forward. Albert Steinowitz was, without a doubt, the best agent, except maybe for Rainbird, in the Shop's employ. He was bright, intuitive – and ruthless when the job demanded that.

'Partly hunch,' Albert said. 'Partly the stuff we got back from the computer when we fed in everything we knew about the last three years of Andrew McGee's life. We asked it to pull out any and all patterns that might apply to this ability he's supposed to have.'

'He does have it, Al,' Cap said gently. 'That's what makes this operation so damned delicate.'

'All right, he has it,' Al said. 'But the computer readouts suggest that his ability to use it is extremely limited. If he overuses it, it makes him sick.'

'Right. We're counting on that.'

'He was running a storefront operation in New York, a Dale Carnegie kind of thing.'

Cap nodded. Confidence Associates, an operation aimed mainly at timid executives. Enough to keep him and the girl in bread, milk, and meat, but not much more.

'We've debriefed his last group,' Albert Steinowitz said. 'There were sixteen of them, and each of them paid a split tuition fee – one hundred dollars at enrollment, a hundred more halfway through the course, if they felt the course was helping them. Of course they all did.'

Cap nodded. McGee's talent was admirably suited for investing people with confidence He literally *pushed* them into it.

'We fed their answers to several key questions into the computer. The questions were, did you feel better about yourself and the Confidence Associates course at specific times? Can you remember days at work following your Confidence Associates meetings when you felt like a tiger? Have you—'

'Felt like a tiger?' Cap asked. 'Jesus, you asked them if they felt like *tigers?*'

'The computer suggests the wording.'

'Okay, go on.'

'The third key question was, have you had any specific, measurable success at your job since taking the Confidence Associates course? That was the question they could all respond to with the most objectivity and reliability, because people tend to remember the day they got the raise or the pat on the back from the boss. They were eager to talk. I found it a little spooky, Cap. He sure did what he promised. Of the sixteen, eleven of them have had promotions – *eleven*. Of the other five, three are in jobs where promotions are made only at certain set times.'

'No one is arguing McGee's capability,' Cap said. 'Not anymore.'

'Okay. I'm getting back around to the point here. It was a six-week course. Using the answers to the key questions, the computer came up with four spike dates . . . that is, days when McGee probably supplemented all the usual hip-hip-hooray-you-can-do-it-if-you-try stuff with a good hard push. The dates we have are August seventeenth, September first, September nineteenth . . . and October fourth.'

'Proving?'

'Well, he pushed that cab driver last night. Pushed him hard. That dude is still rocking and reeling. We figure Andy McGee is tipped over. Sick. Maybe immobilized.' Albert looked at Cap steadily. 'Computer gave us a twenty-six-percent probability that he's dead.'

'*What?*'

'Well, he's overdone it before and wound up in bed. He's doing something to his brain . . . God knows what. Giving himself pinprick hemorrhages, maybe. It could be a progressive thing. The computer figures there's slightly better than a one-in-four chance he's dead, either of a heart attack or, more probably, a stroke.'

'He had to use it before he was recharged,' Cap said.

Albert nodded and took something out of his pocket. It was encased in limp plastic. He passed it to Cap, who looked at it and then passed it back.

'What's that supposed to mean?' he asked.

'Not that much,' Al said, looking at the bill in its plastic envelope meditatively. 'Just what McGee paid his cab fare with.'

'He went to Albany from New York City on a one-dollar bill, huh?' Cap took it back and looked at it with renewed interest. 'Cab fares sure must be . . . what the hell!' He dropped the plastic-encased bill on his desk as if it were hot and sat back, blinking.

'You too, huh?' Al said. 'Did you see it?'

'Christ, I don't know what I saw,' Cap said, and reached for the ceramic box where he kept his acid neutralizers. 'For just a second it didn't look like a one-dollar bill at all.'

'But now it does?'

Cap peered at the bill. 'It sure does. That's George, all – *Christ!*' He sat back so violently this time that he almost rapped the back of his head on the dark wood paneling behind his desk. He looked at Al. 'The face . . . seemed to change for a second there. Grew glasses, or something. Is it a trick?'

'Oh, it's a hell of a good trick,' Al said, taking the bill back. 'I saw it as well, although I don't anymore. I think I've adjusted to it now . . . although I'll be damned if I know how. It's not there, of course. It's just some kind of crazy hallucination. But I even made the face. It's Ben Franklin.'

'You got this from the cab driver?' Cap asked, looking at the bill, fascinated, waiting for the change again. But it was only George Washington.

Al laughed. 'Yeah,' he said. 'We took the bill and gave him a check for five hundred dollars. He's better off, really.'

93

'Why?'

'Ben Franklin isn't on the five hundred, he's on the hundred. Apparently McGee didn't know.'

'Let me see that again.'

Al handed the one-dollar bill back to Cap, and Cap stared fixedly at it for almost a full two minutes. Just as he was about to hand it back, it flickered again – unsettling. But at least this time he felt that the flicker was definitely in his mind, and not in the bill, or on it, or whatever.

'I'll tell you something else,' Cap said. 'I'm not sure, but I don't think Franklin's wearing glasses on his currency portrait, either. Otherwise, it's . . .' He trailed off, not sure how to complete the thought. Goddam *weird* came to mind, and he dismissed it.

'Yeah,' Al said. 'Whatever it is, the effect is dissipating. This morning I showed it to maybe six people. A couple of them thought they saw something, but not like that cab driver and the girl he lives with.'

'So you're figuring he pushed too hard?'

'Yes. I doubt if he could keep going. They may have slept in the woods, or in an outlying motel. They may have broken into a summer cabin in the area. But I think they're around and we'll be able to put the arm on them without too much trouble.'

'How many men do you need to do the job?'

'We've got what we need,' Al said. 'Counting the state police, there are better than seven hundred people in on this little houseparty. Priority A-one-A. They're going door to door and house to house. We've checked every hotel and motel in the immediate Albany area already – better than forty of them. We're spreading into the neighboring towns now. A man and a little girl . . . they stick out like a sore thumb. We'll get them. Or the girl, if he's dead.' Albert stood up. 'And I think I ought to get on it. I'd like to be there when it goes down.'

'Of course you would. Bring them to me, Al.'

'I will,' Albert said, and walked toward the door.

'Albert?'

He turned back, a small man with an unhealthy yellow complexion. 'Who *is* on the five hundred? Did you check that out?'

Albert Steinowitz smiled. 'McKinley,' he said. 'He was assassinated.'

He went out, closing the door gently behind him, leaving Cap to consider.

5

Ten minutes later, Cap thumbed the intercom again. 'Is Rainbird back from Venice yet, Rachel?'

'As of yesterday,' Rachel said, and Cap fancied he could hear the distaste even in Rachel's carefully cultivated Boss Secretary tones.

'Is he here or at Sanibel?' The Shop maintained an R-and-R facility on Sanibel Island, Florida.

There was a pause as Rachel checked with the computer.

'Longmont, Cap. As of eighteen hundred yesterday. Sleeping off the jet lag, perhaps.'

'Have someone wake him up,' Cap said. 'I'd like to see him when Wanless leaves . . . always assuming Wanless is still here?'

'As of fifteen minutes ago he was.'

'All right . . . let's say Rainbird at noon.'

'Yes, sir.'

'You're a good girl, Rachel.'

'Thank you, sir.' She sounded touched. Cap liked her, liked her very much.

'Send in Dr Wanless please, Rachel.'

He settled back, joined his hands in front of him, and thought, *For my sins*.

95

6

Dr Joseph Wanless had suffered his stroke on the same
day Richard Nixon announced his resignation of the
presidency – August 8, 1974. It had been a cerebral
accident of moderate severity, and he had never come all
the way back physically. Nor mentally, in Cap's opinion.
It was only following the stroke that Wanless's interest in
the Lot Six experiment and follow-up had become constant
and obsessive.

He came into the room leaning over a cane, the light
from the bay window catching his round, rimless glasses
and making them glare blankly. His left hand was a drawn-
up claw. The left side of his mouth drifted in a constant
glacial sneer.

Rachel looked at Cap sympathetically over Wanless's
shoulder and Cap nodded that she could go. She did,
closing the door quietly.

'The good doctor,' Cap said humorlessly.

'How does it progress?' Wanless asked, sitting down with
a grunt.

'Classified,' Cap said. 'You know that, Joe. What can I
do for you today?'

'I have seen the activity around this place,' Wanless said,
ignoring Cap's question. 'What else had I to do while I
cooled my heels all morning?'

'If you come without an appointment—'

'You think you nearly have them again,' Wanless said.
'Why else that hatchet man Steinowitz? Well, maybe you
do. Maybe so. But you have thought so before, haven't
you?'

'What do you want, Joe?' Cap didn't like to be reminded
of past failures. They had actually had the girl for a while.
The men who had been involved in that were still not
operational and maybe never would be.

'What do I always want?' Wanless asked, hunched over his cane. Oh Christ, Cap thought, the old fuck's going to wax rhetorical. 'Why do I stay alive? To persuade you to sanction them both. To sanction that James Richardson as well. To sanction the ones on Maui. Extreme sanction, Captain Hollister. Expunge them. Wipe them off the face of the earth.'

Cap sighed.

Wanless gestured toward the library cart with his claw-hand and said, 'You've been through the files again, I see.'

'I have them almost by heart,' Cap said, and then smiled a little. He had been eating and drinking Lot Six for the last year; it had been a constant item on the agenda at every meeting during the two years before that. So maybe Wanless wasn't the only obsessive character around here, at that.

The difference is, I get paid for it. With Wanless it's a hobby. A dangerous hobby.

'You read them but you don't learn,' Wanless said. 'Let me try once more to convert you to the way of truth, Captain Hollister.'

Cap began to protest, and then the thought of Rainbird and his noon appointment came to mind, and his face smoothed out. It became calm, even sympathetic. 'All right,' he said. 'Fire when ready, Gridley.'

'You still think I'm crazy, don't you? A lunatic.'

'You said that, not I.'

'It would be well for you to remember that I was the first one to suggest a testing program with di-lysergic triune acid.'

'I have days when I wish you hadn't,' Cap said. If he closed his eyes, he could still see Wanless's first report, a two-hundred-page prospectus on the drug that had first been known as DLT, then, among the technicians involved, as 'booster-acid,' and finally as Lot Six. Cap's predecessor

97

had okayed the original project; that gentleman had been buried in Arlington with full military honors six years ago.

'All I am saying is that my opinion should carry some weight,' Wanless said. He sounded tired this morning; his words were slow and furry. The twisted sneer on the left side of his mouth did not move as he spoke.

'I'm listening,' Cap said.

'So far as I am able to tell, I am the only psychologist or medical man who still has your ear at all. Your people have become blinded by one thing and one thing only: what this man and this girl can mean to the security of America . . . and possibly to the future balance of power. From what we've been able to tell by following this McGee's backtrail, he is a kind of benign Rasputin. He can make . . .'

Wanless droned on, but Cap lost him temporarily. *Benign Rasputin*, he thought. Purple as the phrase was, he rather liked it. He wondered what Wanless would say if told the computer had issued one-in-four odds that McGee had sanctioned himself getting out of New York City. Probably would have been overjoyed. And if he had showed Wanless that strange bill? Probably have another stroke, Cap thought, and covered his mouth to hide a smile.

'It is the girl I am primarily worried about,' Wanless told him for the twentieth? thirtieth? fiftieth? time. 'McGee and Tomlinson marrying . . . a thousand-to-one chance. It should have been prevented at all costs. Yet who could have foreseen—'

'You were all in favor of it at the time,' Cap said, and then added dryly, 'I do believe you would have given the bride away if they'd asked you.'

'None of us realized,' Wanless muttered. 'It took a stroke to make me see. Lot Six was nothing but a synthetic copy of a pituitary extract, after all . . . an incredibly powerful painkiller-hallucinogen that we did not understand then and that we don't understand now. We know – or at least we are ninety-nine-percent sure – that the natural counter-part of this substance is responsible in some way for the occasional flashes of psi ability that nearly all human beings demonstrate from time to time. A surprisingly wide range of phenomena: precognition, telekinesis, mental domina-tion, bursts of superhuman strength, temporary control over the sympathetic nervous system. Did you know that the pituitary gland becomes suddenly overactive in nearly all biofeedback experiments?'

Cap did. Wanless had told him this and all the rest times without number. But there was no need to answer; Wanless's rhetoric was in full fine flower this morning, the sermon well-launched. And Cap was disposed to listen . . . this one last time. Let the old man have his turn at bat. For Wanless, it was the bottom of the ninth.

'Yes, this is true,' Wanless answered himself. 'It's active in biofeedback, it's active in REM sleep, and people with damaged pituitaries rarely dream normally. People with damaged pituitaries have a tremendously high incidence of brain tumours and leukemia. The pituitary gland, Captain Hollister. It is, speaking in terms of evolution, the oldest endocrine gland in the human body. During early adoles-cence it dumps many times its own weight in glandular secretions into the bloodstream. It's a terribly important gland, a terribly mysterious gland. If I believed in the human soul, Captain Hollister, I would say it resides within the pituitary gland.'

Cap grunted.

'We know these things,' Wanless said, 'and we know that Lot Six somehow changed the physical composition of the pituitary glands of those who participated in the exper-iment. Even that of your so-called "quiet one," James Richardson. Most importantly, we can deduce from the girl that it also changes the chromosome structure in some way . . . and that the change in the pituitary gland may be a genuine mutation.'

'The X factor was passed on.'

'No,' Wanless said. 'That is one of the many things you fail to grasp, Captain Hollister. Andrew McGee became an X factor in his postexperiment life. Victoria Tomlinson became a Y factor – also affected, but not in the same way as her husband. The woman retained a low-threshold telekinetic power. The man retained a mid-level mental-dominance ability. The little girl, though . . . the little girl, Captain Hollister . . . what is she? We don't really know. She is the Z factor.'

'We intend to find out,' Cap said softly.

Now both sides of Wanless's mouth sneered. 'You intend to find out,' he echoed. 'Yes, if you persist, you certainly may . . . you blind, obsessive fools.' He closed his eyes for a moment and put one hand over them. Cap watched him calmly.

Wanless said: 'One thing you know already. She lights fires.'

'Yes.'

'You assume that she has inherited her mother's tele-kinetic ability. In fact, you strongly suspect it.'

'Yes.'

'As a very small child, she was totally unable to control these . . . these talents, for want of a better word . . .'

'A small child is unable to control its bowels,' Cap said, using one of the examples set forth in the extracta. 'But as the child grows older—'

'Yes, yes, I am familiar with the analogy. But an older child may still have accidents.'

Smiling, Cap answered, 'We're going to keep her in a fireproof room.'

'A cell.'

Still smiling, Cap said, 'If you prefer.'

'I offer you this deduction,' Wanless said. 'She does not like to use this ability she has. She has been frightened of it, and this fright has been instilled in her quite deliberately. I will give you a parallel example. My brother's child. There were matches in the house. Freddy wanted to play with them. Light them and then shake them out. "Pretty, pretty," he would say. And so my brother set out to make a complex. To frighten him so badly he would never play with the matches again. He told Freddy that the heads of the matches were sulfur and that they would make his teeth rot and fall out. That looking at struck matches would eventually blind him. And finally, he held Freddy's hand momentarily over a lit match and singed him with it.'

'Your brother,' Cap murmured, 'sounds like a true prince among men.'

'Better a small red place on the boy's hand than a child in the burn unit, wetpacked, with third-degree burns over sixty percent of his body,' Wanless said grimly.

'Better still to put the matches out of the child's reach.'

'Can you put Charlene McGee's matches out of her reach?' Wanless asked.

Cap nodded slowly. 'You have a point of a sort, but—'

'Ask yourself this, Captain Hollister: how must it have been for Andrew and Victoria McGee when this child was an infant? After they begin to make the necessary connection? The bottle is late. The baby cries. At the same time, one of the stuffed animals *right there in the crib with her* bursts into smoky flame. There is a mess in the diaper. The baby cries. A moment later the dirty clothes in the hamper begin to burn spontaneously. You have the records, Captain Hollister; you know how it was in that house. A fire extinguisher and a smoke detector in every single room. And once it was her *hair*, Captain Hollister; they came into her room and found her standing in her crib and screaming and her *hair* was on fire.'

'Yes,' Cap said, 'it must have made them goddam nervous.'

'So,' Wanless said, 'they toilet-trained her . . . and they fire-trained her.'

'Fire-training,' Cap mused.

'Which is only to say that, like my brother and his boy Freddy, they made a complex. You have quoted me that analogy, Captain Hollister, so let us examine it for a moment. What is toilet-training? It is making a complex, pure and simple.' And suddenly astonishingly, the old man's voice climbed to a high, wavering treble, the voice of a woman scolding a baby. Cap looked on with disgusted astonishment.

'You bad baby!' Wanless cried. 'Look what you've done! It's nasty, baby, see how nasty it is? It's nasty to do it in your pants! Do grown-ups do it in their pants? Do it on the pot, baby, on the *pot*.'

'Please,' Cap said, pained.

'It is the making of a complex,' Wanless said. 'Toilet-training is accomplished by focusing the child's attention on his own eliminatory processes in a way we would consider unhealthy if the object of fixation were something different. How strong is the complex inculcated in the child, you might ask? Richard Damon of the University of Washington asked himself this question and made an experiment to find out. He advertised for fifty student volunteers. He filled them up with water and soda and milk until they all badly needed to urinate. After a certain set time had passed, he told them they could go . . . if they went in their pants.'

'That's disgusting!' Cap said loudly. He was shocked and sickened. That wasn't an experiment; it was an exercise in degeneracy.

'See how well the complex has set in your own psyche,' Wanless said quietly. 'You did not think it was so disgusting when you were twenty months old. Then, when you had to go, you went. You would have gone sitting on the pope's lap if someone had set you there and you had to go. The point of the Damon experiment, Captain Hollister, is this: most of them *couldn't*. They understood that the ordinary rules of behavior had been set aside, at least for the course of the experiment; they were each alone in quarters at least as private as the ordinary bathroom . . . but fully eighty-eight percent of them just *couldn't*. No matter how strong the physical need was, the complex instilled by their parents was stronger.'

'This is nothing but pointless wandering,' Cap said curtly.

'No, it isn't. I want you to consider the parallels between toilet-training and fire-training . . . and the one significant difference, which is the quantum leap between the *urgency* of accomplishing the former and the latter. If the child toilet-trains slowly, what are the consequences? Minor unpleasantness. His room smells if not constantly aired. The mamma is chained to her washing machine. The cleaners may have to be called in to shampoo the carpet after the job is finally done. At the very worst, the baby may have a constant diaper rash, and that will only happen if the baby's skin is very sensitive or if the mamma is a sloven about keeping him clean. But the consequences to a child who can make *fire* . . .'

His eyes glittered. The left side of his mouth sneered.

'My estimation of the McGees as parents is very high,' Wanless said. 'Somehow they got her through it. I would imagine they began the job long before parents usually begin the toilet-training process; perhaps even before she was able to crawl. "Baby mustn't! Baby hurt herself! No, no, no! Bad girl! Bad girl! *Ba-ad* girl!" '

'But your own computer suggests by its readouts that she is overcoming her complex, Captain Hollister. She is in an enviable position to do it. She is young, and the complex has not had a chance to set in a bed of years until it becomes like cement. And she has her father with her! Do you realize the significance of that simple fact? No, you do not. The father is the authority figure. He holds the psychic reins of every fixation in the female child. Oral, anal, genital; behind each, like a shadowy figure standing behind a curtain, is the father-authority figure. To the girl-child he is Moses; the laws are his laws, handed down she knows not how, but his to enforce. He is perhaps the only person on earth who can remove this block. Our complexes, Captain Hollister, always give us the most agony and psychic distress when those who have inculcated them die and pass beyond argument . . . and mercy.'

Cap glanced at his watch and saw that Wanless had been in here almost forty minutes. It felt like hours. 'Are you almost done? I have another appointment—'

'When complexes go, they go like dams bursting after torrential rains,' Wanless said softly. 'We have a promiscuous girl who is nineteen years old. Already she has had three hundred lovers. Her body is as hot with sexual infection as that of a forty-year-old prostitute. But until she was seventeen she was a virgin. Her father was a minister who told her again and again as a little girl that sex inside marriage was a necessary evil, that sex outside marriage was hell and damnation, that sex was the apple of original sin. When a complex like that goes, it goes like a breaking dam. First there is a crack or two, little trickling rills of water so small as to escape notice. And according to your computer's information, that is where we are now with this little girl. Suggestions that she has used her ability to help her father, at her father's urging. And then it all goes at once, spewing out millions of gallons of water, destroying everything in its path, drowning everyone caught in its way, changing the landscape forever!'

Wanless's croaking voice had risen from its original soft pitch to a broken-voiced old man's shout – but it was more peevish than magnificent.

'Listen,' he said to Cap. 'For once, listen to me. Drop the blinders from your eyes. The man is not dangerous in and of himself. He has a little power, a toy, a plaything. He understands that. He has not been able to use it to make a million dollars. He does not rule men and nations. He has used his power to help fat women lose weight. He has used it to help timid executives gain confidence. He is unable to use the power often or well . . . some inner physiological factor limits him. But the girl is incredibly dangerous. She is on the run with her daddy, faced with a survival situation. She is badly frightened. And he is frightened as well, which is what makes him dangerous. Not in and of himself, but because you are forcing him to reeducate the little girl. You are forcing him to change her conceptions about the power inside her. You are forcing him to force her to *use* it.'

Wanless was breathing hard.

Playing out the scenario – the end was now in sight – Cap said calmly, 'What do you suggest?'

'The man must be killed. Quickly. Before he can do anymore pick-and-shovel work on the complex he and his wife built into the little girl. And the girl must also be killed, I believe. In case the damage has already been done.'

'She's only a little girl, Wanless, after all. She can light fires, yes. Pyrokinesis, we call it. But you're making it sound like armageddon.'

'Perhaps it will be,' Wanless said. 'You mustn't let her age and size fool you into forgetting the Z factor . . . which is exactly what you are doing, of course. Suppose lighting fires is only the tip of this iceberg? Suppose the talent grows? She is seven. When John Milton was seven, he was perhaps a small boy grasping a stick of charcoal and laboring to write his own name in letters his mamma and daddy could understand. He was a baby. John Milton grew up to write *Paradise Lost*.'

'I don't know what the hell you're talking about,' Cap said flatly.

'I am talking about the potential for destruction. I am talking about a talent which is linked to the pituitary gland, a gland which is nearly dormant in a child Charlene McGee's age. What happens when she becomes an adolescent and that gland awakes from its sleep and becomes for twenty months the most powerful force in the human body, ordering everything from the sudden maturation of the primary and secondary sex characteristics to an increased production of visual purple in the eye? Suppose you have a child capable of eventually creating a nuclear explosion *simply by the force of her will?*'

'That's the most insane thing I've ever heard.'

'Is it? Then let me progress from insanity to utter lunacy, Captain Hollister. Suppose there is a little girl out there someplace this morning who has within her, lying dormant only for the time being, the power to someday crack the very planet in two like a china plate in a shooting gallery?'

They looked at each other in silence. And suddenly the intercom buzzed.

After a moment, Cap leaned over and thumbed it. 'Yes, Rachel?' Goddamned if the old man hadn't had him there, for just a moment. He was like some awful gore-crow, and that was another reason Cap didn't like him. He was a go-getter himself, and if there was one thing he couldn't stand, it was a pessimist.

'You have a call on the scrambler,' Rachel said. 'From the service area.'

'All right, dear. Thanks. Hold it for a couple of minutes, okay?'

'Yes, sir.'

He sat back in his chair. 'I have to terminate this interview, Dr Wanless. You may be sure that I'll consider everything you've said very carefully.'

'Will you?' Wanless asked. The frozen side of his mouth seemed to sneer cynically.

'Yes.'

Wanless said: 'The girl . . . McGee . . . and this fellow Richardson . . . they are the last three marks of a dead equation, Captain Hollister. Erase them. Start over. The girl is very dangerous.'

'I'll consider everything you've said,' Cap repeated.

'Do so.' And Wanless finally began to struggle to his feet, propping himself on his cane. It took him a long time. At last he was up.

'Winter is coming,' he said to Cap. 'These old bones dread it.'

'Are you staying in Longmont tonight?'

'No, Washington.'

Cap hesitated and then said, 'Stay at the Mayflower. I may want to get in touch with you.'

Something in the old man's eyes – gratitude? Yes, almost certainly that. 'Very good, Captain Hollister,' he said, and worked his way back to the door on his cane – an old man who had once opened Pandora's box and now wanted to shoot all of the things that had flown out instead of putting them to work.

When the door had snicked closed behind him, Cap breathed a sigh of relief and picked up the scrambler phone.

'Who am I talking to?'

'Orv Jamieson, sir.'

'Have you got them, Jamieson?'

'Not yet, sir, but we found something interesting at the airport.'

'What's that?'

'All the pay phones are empty. We found a few quarters and dimes on the floors of some of them.'

'Jimmied?'

'No, sir. That's why I called you. They haven't been jimmied, they're just empty. Phone company's going crazy.'

'All right, Jamieson.'

'It speeds things up. We've been figuring that maybe the guy hid the girl outside and only checked himself in. But either way, we figure now that we're looking for a guy who paid with a lot of change.'

'If they are at a motel and not shacked up at a summer camp somewhere.'

'Yes, sir.'

'Carry on, OJ.'

'Yes, sir. Thank you.' He sounded absurdly pleased that his nickname had been remembered.

Cap hung up. He sat with his eyes half closed for five minutes, thinking. The mellow autumn light fell through the bay window and lit the office, warmed it. Then he leaned forward and got Rachel again.

'Is John Rainbird there?'

'Yes he is, Cap.'

'Give me another five minutes and then send him in. I want to talk to Norville Bates out in the service area. He's the head honcho until Al gets there.'

'Yes, sir,' Rachel said, a little doubtfully. 'It will have to be an open line. Walkie-talkie link-up. Not very—'

'Yes, that's fine,' he said impatiently.

It took two minutes. Bates's voice was thin and crackling. He was a good man – not very imaginative, but a plugger. The kind of man Cap wanted to have holding the fort until Albert Steinowitz could get there. At last Norville came on the line and told Cap they were beginning to spread out into the surrounding towns – Oakville, Tremont, Messalonsett, Hastings Glen, Looton.

'All right, Norville, that's good,' Cap said. He thought of Wanless saying *You are forcing him to reeducate the little girl.* He thought of Jamieson telling him all the phones were empty. McGee hadn't done that. The girl had done it. And then, because she was still up, she had burned that soldier's shoes off, probably by accident. Wanless would be pleased to know that Cap was going to take fifty percent of his advice after all – the old turd had been amazingly eloquent this morning.

'Things have changed,' Cap said. 'We've got to have the big boy sanctioned. Extreme sanction. You follow?'

'Extreme sanction,' Norville said flatly. 'Yes, sir.'

'Very good, Norville,' Cap said softly. He put the phone down and waited for John Rainbird to come in.

The door opened a moment later and there he stood, as big as life and twice as ugly. He was so naturally quiet, this half Cherokee, that if you had been looking down at your desk, reading or answering correspondence, you wouldn't have been aware that anyone was in the room with you at all. Cap knew how rare that was. Most people could sense another person in the room: Wanless had once called that ability not a sixth sense but a bottom-of-the-barrel sense, a knowledge born of infinitesimal input from the five normal senses. But with Rainbird, you didn't know. Not one of the whisker-thin sensory tripwires so much as vibrated. Al Steinowitz had said a strange thing about Rainbird once over glasses of port in Cap's living room: 'He's the one human being I ever met who doesn't push air in front of him when he walks.' And Cap was glad Rainbird was on their side, because he was the only human *he* had ever met who completely terrified him.

Rainbird was a troll, an orc, a balrog of a man. He stood two inches shy of seven feet tall, and he wore his glossy black hair drawn back and tied in a curt ponytail. Ten years before, a Claymore had blown up in his face during his second tour of Vietnam, and now his countenance was a horrorshow of scar tissue and runneled flesh. His left eye was gone. There was nothing where it had been but a ravine. He would not have plastic surgery or an artificial eye because, he said, when he got to the happy hunting ground beyond, he would be asked to show his battlescars. When he said such things, you did not know whether to believe him or not; you did not know if he was serious or leading you on for reasons of his own.

Over the years, Rainbird had been a surprisingly good agent – partially because the last thing on earth he looked like was an agent, mostly because there was an apt, ferociously bright mind behind that mask of flesh. He spoke four languages fluently and had an understanding of three others. He was taking a sleep course in Russian. When he spoke, his voice was low, musical, and civilized.

'Good afternoon, Cap.'

'Is it afternoon?' Cap asked, surprised.

Rainbird smiled, showing a big set of perfectly white teeth – shark's teeth, Cap thought. 'By fourteen minutes,' he said. 'I picked up a Seiko digital watch on the black market in Venice. It is fascinating. Little black numbers that change constantly. A feat of technology. I often think, Cap, that we fought the war in Vietnam not to win but to perform feats of technology. We fought it in order to create the cheap digital wristwatch, the home Ping-Pong game that hooks up to one's TV, the pocket calculator. I look at my new wristwatch in the dark of night. It tells me I am closer to my death, second by second. That is good news.'

'Sit down, old friend,' Cap said. As always when he talked to Rainbird, his mouth was dry and he had to restrain his hands, which wanted to twine and knot together on the polished surface of his desk. All of that, and he believed that Rainbird *liked* him – if Rainbird could be said to like anyone.

Rainbird sat down. He was wearing old bluejeans and a faded chambray shirt.

'How was Venice?' Cap asked.

'Sinking,' Rainbird said.

'I have a job for you, if you want it. It is a small one, but it may lead to an assignment you'll find considerably more interesting.'

'Tell me.'

'Strictly volunteer,' Cap persisted. 'You're still on R and R.'

'Tell me,' Rainbird repeated gently, and Cap told him. He was with Rainbird for only fifteen minutes, but it seemed an hour. When the big Indian left, Cap breathed a long sigh. Both Wanless and Rainbird in one morning – that would take the snap out of anyone's day. But the morning was over now, a lot had been accomplished, and who knew what might lie ahead this afternoon? He buzzed Rachel.

'Yes, Cap?'

'I'll be eating in, darling. Would you get me something from the cafeteria? It doesn't matter what. Anything. Thank you, Rachel.'

Alone at last. The scrambler phone lay silent on its thick base, filled with microcircuits and memory chips and God alone knew what else. When it buzzed again, it would probably be Albert or Norville to tell him that it was over in New York – the girl taken, her father dead. That would be good news.

Cap closed his eyes again. Thoughts and phrases floated through his mind like large, lazy kites. Mental domination. Their think-tank boys said the possibilities were enormous. Imagine someone like McGee close to Castro, or the Ayatollah Khomeini. Imagine him getting close enough to that pinko Ted Kennedy to suggest in a low voice of utter conviction that suicide was the best answer. Imagine a man like that sicced on the leaders of the various communist guerrilla groups. It was a shame they had to lose him. But . . . what could be made to happen once could be made to happen again.

The little girl. Wanless saying *The power to someday crack the very planet in two like a china plate in a shooting gallery* . . . ridiculous, of course. Wanless had gone as crazy as the little boy in the D. H. Lawrence story, the one who could pick the winners at the racetrack. Lot Six had turned into battery acid for Wanless; it had eaten a number of large, gaping holes in the man's good sense. She was a little *girl*, not a doomsday weapon. And they had to hang onto her at least long enough to document what she was and to chart what she could be. That alone would be enough to reactivate the Lot Six testing program. If she could be persuaded to use her powers for the good of the country, so much the better.

So much the better, Cap thought.

The scrambler phone suddenly uttered its long, hoarse cry.

His pulse suddenly leaping, Cap grabbed it.

The Incident at the
Manders Farm

1

While Cap discussed her future with Al Steinowitz in Longmont, Charlie McGee was sitting on the edge of the motel bed in Unit Sixteen of the Slumberland, yawning and stretching. Bright morning sunlight fell aslant through the window, out of a sky that was a deep and blameless autumn blue. Things seemed so much better in the good daylight.

She looked at her daddy, who was nothing but a motionless hump under the blankets. A fluff of black hair stuck out – that was all. She smiled. He always did his best. If he was hungry and she was hungry and there was only an apple, he would take one bite and make her eat the rest. When he was awake, he always did his best.

But when he was sleeping, he stole all the blankets.

She went into the bathroom, shucked off her underpants, and turned on the shower. She used the toilet while the water got warm and then stepped into the shower stall. The hot water hit her and she closed her eyes, smiling. Nothing in the world was any nicer than the first minute or two in a hot shower.

(you were bad last night)

A frown creased her brow.

(No. Daddy said not.)

(lit that man's shoes on fire, bad girl, very bad, do you like teddy all black?)

The frown deepened. Unease was now tinctured with fear and shame. The idea of her teddy bear never even fully surfaced; it was an underthought, and as so often happened, her guilt seemed to be summed up in a smell – a burned, charred smell. Smoldering cloth and stuffing. And this smell summoned hazy pictures of her mother and father leaning over her, and they were *big* people, giants; and they were scared; they were angry, their voices were big and crackling, like boulders jumping and thudding down a mountainside in a movie.

(*'bad girl! very bad! you mustn't, Charlie! never! never! never!'*)

How old had she been then? Three? Two? How far back could a person remember? She had asked Daddy that once and Daddy said he didn't know. He said he remembered getting a bee sting and his mother had told him that happened when he was only fifteen months old.

This was her earliest memory: the giant faces leaning over her; the big voices like boulders rolling downhill; and a smell like a burned waffle. That smell had been her hair. She had lit her own hair on fire and had burned nearly all of it off. It was after that that Daddy mentioned 'help' and Mommy got all funny, first laughing, then crying, then laughing again so high and strange that Daddy had slapped her face. She remembered that because it was the only time that she knew of that her daddy had done something like that to her mommy. Maybe we ought to think about getting 'help' for her, Daddy had said. They were in the bathroom and her head was wet because Daddy had put her in the shower. Oh, yes, her mommy had said, let's go see Dr Wanless, he'll give us plenty of 'help,' just like he did before . . . then the laughing, the crying, more laughter, and the slap.

(*you were so BAD last night*)

'No,' she murmured in the drumming shower. 'Daddy

said not. Daddy said it could have . . . been . . . his . . . face.'

(YOU WERE VERY *BAD LAST NIGHT)*

But they had needed the change from the telephones. Daddy had said so.

(VERY BAD!)

And then she began to think about Mommy again, about the time when she had been five, going on six. She didn't like to think about this but the memory was here now and she couldn't put it aside. It had happened just before the bad men had come and hurt Mommy

(killed her, you mean, they killed her)

yes, all right, before they *killed* her, and took Charlie away. Daddy had taken her on his lap for storytime, only he hadn't had the usual storybooks about Pooh and Tigger and Mr Toad and Willy Wonka's Great Glass Elevator. Instead he had a number of thick books with no pictures. She had wrinkled her nose in distaste and asked for Pooh instead.

'No, Charlie,' he had said. 'I want to read you some other stories, and I need you to listen. You're old enough now, I think, and your mother thinks so, too. The stories may scare you a little bit, but they're important. They're true stories.'

She remembered the names of the books Daddy had read the stories from, because the stories *had* scared her. There was a book called *Lo!* by a man named Charles Fort. A book called *Stanger Than Science* by a man named Frank Edwards. A book called *Night's Truth*. And there had been another book called *Pyrokinesis: A Case Book*, but Mommy would not let Daddy read anything from that one. 'Later,' Mommy had said, 'when she's much older, Andy.' And then that book had gone away. Charlie had been glad.

The stories were scary, all right. One was about a man who had burned to death in a park. One was about a lady who had burned up in the living room of her trailer home, and nothing in the whole room had been burned but the lady and a little bit of the chair she had been sitting in while she watched TV. Parts of it had been too complicated for her to understand, but she remembered one thing: a policeman saying: 'We have no explanation for this fatality. There was nothing left of the victim but teeth and a few charred pieces of bone. It would have taken a blowtorch to do that to a person, and nothing around her was even charred. We can't explain why the whole place didn't go up like a rocket.'

The third story had been about a big boy – he was eleven or twelve – who had burned up while he was at the beach. His daddy had put him in the water, burning himself badly in the process, but the boy had still gone on burning until he was all burned up. And a story about a teenage girl who had burned up while explaining all her sins to the priest in the confession room. Charlie knew all about the Catholic confession room because her friend Deenie had told her. Deenie said you had to tell the priest all the bad stuff you had done all week long. Deenie didn't go yet because she hadn't had first holy communion, but her brother Carl did. Carl was in the fourth grade, and he had to tell everything, even the time he sneaked into his mother's room and took some of her birthday chocolates. Because if you didn't tell the priest, you couldn't be washed in THE BLOOD OF CHRIST and you would go to THE HOT PLACE.

The point of all these stories had not been lost on Charlie. She had been so frightened after the one about the girl in the confession room that she burst into tears. 'Am I going to burn myself up?' She wept. 'Like when I was little and caught my hair on fire? Am I going to burn to pieces?'

And Daddy and Mommy had looked upset. Mommy was pale and kept chewing at her lips, but Daddy had put

116

an arm around her and said, 'No, honey. Not if you always remember to be careful and not think about that . . . thing. That thing you do sometimes when you're upset and scared.'

'What is it?' Charlie had cried. 'What is it, tell me what is it, I don't even know, I'll never do it, I *promise!*'

Mommy had said, 'As far as we can tell, honey, it's called pyrokinesis. It means being able to light fires sometimes just by thinking about fires. It usually happens when people are upset. Some people apparently have that . . . that power all their lives and never even know it. And some people . . . well, the power gets hold of them for a minute and they . . .' She couldn't finish.

'They burn themselves up,' Daddy had said. 'Like when you were little and caught your hair on fire, yes. But you can get control of that, Charlie. You *have* to. And God knows it isn't your fault.' His eyes and Mommy's had met for a moment when he said that, and something had seemed to pass between them.

Hugging her around the shoulders, he had said, 'Sometimes you can't help it, I know. It's an accident, like when you were smaller and you forget to go to the bathroom because you were playing and you wet your pants. We used to call that having an accident – do you remember?'

'I never do that anymore.'

'No, of course you don't. And in a little while, you'll have control of this other thing in just the same way. But for now, Charlie, you've got to promise us that you'll *never never never* get upset that way if you can help it. In that way that makes you start fires. And if you do, if you can't help it, push it *away* from yourself. At a wastebasket or an ashtray. Try to get outside. Try to push it at water, if there's any around.'

'But never at a person,' Mommy had said, and her face was still and pale and grave. 'That would be very danger-

117

ous, Charlie. That would be a very bad girl. Because you could' – she struggled, forced the words up and out – 'you could kill a person.'

And then Charlie had wept hysterically, tears of terror and remorse, because both of Mommy's hands were bandaged, and she knew why Daddy had read her all the scary stories. Because the day before, when Mommy told her she couldn't go over to Deenie's house because she hadn't picked up her room, Charlie had got *very* angry, and suddenly the firething had been there, popping out of nowhere as it always did, like some evil jack-in-the-box, nodding and grinning, and she had been so angry she had shoved it out of herself and at her mommy and then Mommy's hands had been on fire. And it hadn't been *too* bad

(*could have been worse could have been her face*)

because the sink had been full of soapy water for the dishes, it hadn't been *too* bad, but it had been *VERY BAD*, and she had promised them both that she would *never never never—*

The warm water drummed on her face, her chest, her shoulders, encasing her in a warm envelope, a cocoon, easing away memories and care. Daddy had *told* her it was all right. And if Daddy said a thing was so, it was. He was the smartest man in the world.

Her mind turned from the past to the present, and she thought about the men who were chasing them. They were from the government, Daddy said, but not a good part of the government. They worked for a part of the government called the Shop. The men chased them and chased them. Everywhere they went, after a little while, those Shop men showed up.

I wonder how they'd like it if I set them on fire? a part of her asked coolly, and she squeezed her eyes shut in guilty horror. It was nasty to think that way. It was bad.

Charlie reached out, grasped the HOT shower faucet, and shut it off with a sudden hard twist of her wrist. For the next two minutes she stood shivering and clutching her slight body under the ice-cold, needling spray, wanting to get out, not allowing herself to.

When you had bad thoughts, you had to pay for them.

Deenie had told her so.

2

Andy woke up a little at a time, vaguely aware of the drumming sound of the shower. At first it had been part of a dream: he was on Tashmore Pond with his grandfather and he was eight years old again, trying to get a squirming nightcrawler onto his hook without sticking the hook into his thumb. The dream had been incredibly vivid. He could see the splintery wicker creel in the bow of the boat, he could see the red tire patches on Granther McGee's old green boots, he could see his own old and wrinkled first baseman's mitt, and looking at it made him remember that he had Little League practice tomorrow at Roosevelt Field. But this was tonight, the last light and the drawing dark balanced perfectly on the cusp of twilight, the pond so still that you could see the small clouds of midges and noseeums skimming over its surface, which was the color of chrome. Heat lightning flashed intermittently . . . or maybe it was real lightning, because it was raining. The first drops darkened the wood of Granther's dory, weatherbeaten white, in penny-sized drops. Then you could hear it on the lake, a low and mysterious hissing sound, like—

—like the sound of a—

—*shower, Charlie must be in the shower.*

He opened his eyes and looked at an unfamiliar beamed ceiling. *Where are we?*

It fell back into place a piece at a time, but there was an

instant of frightened free-fall that came of having been in too many places over the last year, of having too many close shaves and being under too much pressure. He thought longingly of his dream and wished he could be back in it with Granther McGee, who had been dead for twenty years now.

Hastings Glen. He was in Hastings Glen. *They* were in Hastings Glen.

He wondered about his head. It hurt, but not like last night, when that bearded guy had let them off. The pain was down to a steady low throb. If this one followed previous history, the throb would be just a faint ache by this evening, and entirely gone by tomorrow.

The shower was turned off.

He sat up in bed and looked at his watch. It was quarter to eleven.

'Charlie?'

She came back into the bedroom, rubbing herself vigorously with a towel.

'Good morning, Daddy.'

'Good morning. How are you?'

'Hungry,' she said. She went over to the chair where she had put her clothes and picked up the green blouse. Sniffed it. Grimaced. 'I need to change my clothes.'

'You'll have to make do with those for a while, babe. We'll get you something later on today.'

'I hope we don't have to wait that long to eat.'

'We'll hitch a ride,' he said, 'and stop at the first café we come to.'

'Daddy, when I started school, you told me never to ride with strangers.' She was into her underpants and green blouse, and was looking at him curiously.

Andy got out of bed, walked over to her, and put his hands on her shoulders. 'The devil you don't know is

120

sometimes better than the one you do,' he said. 'Do you know what that means, keed?'

She thought about it carefully. The devil they knew was those men from the Shop, she guessed. The men that had chased them down the street in New York the day before. The devil they didn't know—

'I guess it means that most people driving cars don't work for that Shop,' she said.

He smiled back. 'You got it. And what I said before still holds, Charlie: when you get into a bad fix, you sometimes have to do things you'd never do if things were going good.'

Charlie's smile faded. Her face became serious, watchful. 'Like getting the money to come out of the phones?'

'Yes,' he said.

'And it wasn't bad?'

'No. Under the circumstances, it wasn't bad.'

'Because when you get into a bad fix, you do what you have to do to get out of it.'

'With some exceptions, yes.'

'What are exceptions, Daddy?'

He ruffled her hair. 'Never mind now, Charlie. Lighten up.'

But she wouldn't. 'And I didn't mean to set that man's shoes on fire. I didn't do it on purpose.'

'No, of course you didn't.'

Then she did lighten up; her smile, so much like Vicky's, came out radiantly. 'How does your head feel this morning, Daddy?'

'Much better, thanks.'

'Good.' She looked at him closely. 'Your eye looks funny.'

'Which eye?'

She pointed at his left. 'That one.'

'Yeah?' He went into the bathroom and wiped a clear place on the steamed mirror.

He looked at his eye for a long time, his good humor fading. His right eye looked just as it always had, a gray green – the color of the ocean on an overcast spring day. His left eye was also gray green, but the white was badly bloodshot, and the pupil looked smaller than the right pupil. And the eyelid had a peculiar droop that he had never noticed before.

Vicky's voice suddenly rang into his mind. It was so clear that she might have been standing beside him. *The headaches, they scare me, Andy. You're doing something to yourself as well as to other people when you use that push or whatever you want to call it.*

The thought was followed by the image of a balloon being blown up . . . and up . . . and up . . . and finally exploding with a loud bang.

He began to go over the left side of his face carefully, touching it everywhere with the tips of his right fingers. He looked like a man in a TV commercial marveling over the closeness of his shave. He found three spots – one below his left eye, one on his left cheekbone, and one just below the left temple – where there was no feeling at all. Fright drifted through the hollow places of his body like quiet early-evening mist. The fright was not so much for himself as it was for Charlie, for what would happen to her if she got left on her own.

As if he had called her, he could see her beyond him in the mirror.

'Daddy?' She sounded a little scared. 'You okay?'

'Fine,' he said. His voice sounded good. There was no tremor in it; nor was it too confident, falsely booming. 'Just thinking how much I need a shave.'

She put a hand over her mouth and giggled. 'Scratchy like a Brillo pad. Yuck. Gross.'

He chased her into the bedroom and rubbed his scratchy cheek against her smooth one. Charlie giggled and kicked.

3

As Andy was tickling his daughter with his stubbly beard, Orville Jamieson, aka OJ, aka The Juice, and another Shop agent named Bruce Cook were getting out of a light-blue Chevy outside the Hastings Diner.

OJ paused for a moment, looking down Main Street with its slant parking, its appliance store, its grocery store, its two gas stations, its one drugstore, its wooden municipal building with a plaque out front commemorating some historical event no one gave a shit about. Main Street was also Route 40, and the McGees were not four miles from where OJ and Bruce Cook now stood.

'Look at this burg,' OJ said, disgusted. 'I grew up close to here. Town called Lowville. You ever hear of Lowville, New York?'

Bruce Cook shook his head.

'It's near Utica, too. Where they make Utica Club beer. I was never so happy in my life as I was the day I got out of Lowville.' OJ reached under his jacket and readjusted The Windsucker in its holster.

'There's Tom and Steve,' Bruce said. Across the street, a light-brown Pacer had pulled into a parking slot just vacated by a farm truck. Two men in dark suits were getting out of the Pacer. They looked like bankers. Farther down the street, at the blinker light, two more Shop people were talking to the old cunt that crossed the school kids at lunchtime. They were showing her the picture and she was shaking her head. There were ten Shop agents here in Hastings Glen, all of them coordinating with Norville Bates, who was back in Albany waiting for Cap's personal ramrod, Al Steinowitz.

123

'Yeah, Lowville,' OJ sighed. 'I hope we get those two suckers by noon. And I hope my next assignment's Karachi. Or Iceland. Any place, as long as it's not upstate New York. This is too close to Lowville. Too close for comfort.'

'You think we will have them by noon?' Bruce asked.

OJ shrugged. 'We'll have them by the time the sun goes down. You can count on that.'

They went into the diner, sat at the counter, and ordered coffee. A young waitress with a fine figure brought it to them.

'How long you been on, sis?' OJ asked her.

'If you got a sis, I pity her,' the waitress said. 'If there's any fambly resemblance, that is.'

'Don't be that way, sis,' OJ said, and showed her his ID. She looked at it a long time. Behind her, an aging juvenile delinquent in a motorcycle jacket was pushing buttons on a Seeberg.

'I been on since seven,' she said. 'Same as any other morning. Prolly you want to talk to Mike. He's the owner.' She started to turn away and OJ caught her wrist in a tight grip. He didn't like women who made fun of his looks. Most women were sluts anyway, his mother had been right about that even if she hadn't been right about much else. And his mother surely would have known what to think about a high-tit bitch like this one.

'Did I say I wanted to talk to the owner, sis?'

She was starting to be frightened now, and that was okay with OJ. 'N-no.'

'That's right. Because I want to talk to you, not to some guy that's been out in the kitchen scrambling eggs and making Alpoburgers all morning.' He took the picture of Andy and Charlie out of his pocket and handed it to her, not letting go of her wrist. 'You recognize them, sis? Serve them their breakfast this morning, maybe?'

124

'Let go. You're *hurting* me.' All the color had gone out of her face except for the whore's rouge she had tricked herself up with. Probably she had been a cheerleader in high school. The kind of girl who laughed at Orville Jamieson when he asked them out because he had been president of the Chess Club instead of quarterback on the football team. Bunch of cheap Lowville whores. God, he hated New York. Even New York City was too fucking close.

'You tell me if you waited on them or if you didn't. Then I'll let go. *Sis*.'

She looked briefly at the picture. 'No! I didn't. Now let—'

'You didn't look long enough, *sis*. You better look again.'

She looked again. 'No! No!' she said loudly. 'I've never seen them! Let me go, can't you?'

The elderly jd in the cut-rate Mammoth Mart leather jacket sauntered over, zippers jingling, thumbs hooked in his pants pockets.

'You're bothering the lady,' he said.

Bruce Cook gazed at him with open, wide-eyed contempt. 'Be careful we don't decide to bother you next, pizza-face,' he said.

'Oh,' the old kid in the leather jacket said, and his voice was suddenly very small. He moved away quickly, apparently remembering that he had pressing business on the street.

Two old ladies in a booth were nervously watching the little scene at the counter. A big man in reasonably clean cook's whites – Mike, the owner, presumably – was standing in the kitchen doorway, also watching. He held a butcher knife in one hand, but he held it with no great authority.

'What do you guys want?' he asked.

'They're feds,' the waitress said nervously. 'They—'

125

'Didn't serve them? You're sure?' OJ asked. *'Sis?'*

'I'm sure,' she said. She was nearly crying now.

'You better be. A mistake can get you five years in jail, *sis.'*

'I'm sure,' she whispered. A tear spilled over the bottom curve of one eye and slipped down her cheek. 'Please let go. Don't hurt me anymore.'

OJ squeezed tighter for one brief moment, liking the feel of the small bones moving under his hand, liking the knowledge that he could squeeze harder yet and snap them . . . and then he let go. The diner was silent except for the voice of Stevie Wonder coming from the Seeberg, assuring the frightened patrons of the Hastings Diner that they could feel it all over. Then the two old ladies got up and left in a hurry.

OJ picked up his coffee cup, leaned over the counter, poured the coffee on the floor, and then dropped the cup, which shattered. Thick china shrapnel sprayed in a dozen different directions. The waitress was crying openly now.

'Shitty brew,' OJ said.

The owner made a halfhearted gesture with the knife, and OJ's face seemed to light up.

'Come on, man,' he said, half-laughing. 'Come on. Let's see you try.'

Mike put the knife down beside the toaster and suddenly cried out in shame and outrage: 'I fought in Vietnam! My brother fought in Vietnam! I'm gonna write my congressman about this! You wait and see if I don't!'

OJ looked at him. After a while Mike lowered his eyes, scared.

The two of them went out.

The waitress scooched and began to pick up broken pieces of coffee cup, sobbing.

Outside, Bruce said, 'How many motels?'

'Three motels, six sets of tourist cabins,' OJ said, looking down toward the blinker. It fascinated him. In the Lowville of his youth there had been a diner with a plaque over the double Silex hotplate and that plaque had read IF YOU DON'T LIKE OUR TOWN, LOOK FOR A TIMETABLE. How many times had he longed to pull that plaque off the wall and stuff it down someone's throat?

'There are people checking them out,' he said as they walked back toward their light-blue Chevrolet, part of a government motor pool paid for and maintained by tax dollars. 'We'll know soon now.'

4

John Mayo was with an agent named Ray Knowles. They were on their way out along Route 40 to the Slumberland Motel. They were driving a late-model tan Ford, and as they rode up the last hill separating them from an actual view of the motel, a tire blew.

'Shit-*fire*,' John said as the car began to pogo up and down and drag to the right. 'That's fucking government issue for you. Fucking retreads.' He pulled over onto the soft shoulder and put on the Ford's four-way flashers. 'You go on,' he said. 'I'll change the goddam tire.'

'I'll help,' Ray said. 'It won't take us five minutes.'

'No, go on. It's right over this hill, should be.'

'You sure?'

'Yeah. I'll pick you up. Unless the spare's flat, too. It wouldn't surprise me.'

A rattling farm truck passed them. It was the one OJ and Bruce Cook had seen leaving town as they stood outside the Hastings Diner.

Ray grinned. 'It better not be. You'd have to put in a requisition in quadruplicate for a new one.'

John didn't grin back. 'Don't I know it,' he said glumly.

127

They went around to the trunk and Ray unlocked it. The spare was in good shape.

'Okay,' John said. 'Go on.'

'It really wouldn't take but five minutes to change that sucker.'

'Sure, and those two aren't at that motel. But let's play it as if it were real. After all, they have to be somewhere.'

'Yeah, okay.'

John took the jack and spare out of the trunk. Ray Knowles watched him for a moment and then started walking along the shoulder toward the Slumberland Motel.

5

Just beyond the motel, Andy and Charlie McGee were standing on the soft shoulder of Highway 40. Andy's worries that someone might notice he didn't have a car had proved groundless; the woman in the office was interested in nothing but the small Hitachi TV on the counter. A miniature Phil Donahue had been captured inside, and the woman was watching him avidly. She swept the key Andy offered into the mail slot without even looking away from the picture.

'Hope y'enjoyed y'stay,' she said. She was working on a box of chocolate coconut doughnuts and had got to the halfway mark.

'Sure did,' Andy said, and left.

Charlie was waiting for him outside. The woman had given him a carbon copy of his bill, which he stuffed into the side pocket of his cord jacket as he went down the steps. Change from the Albany pay phones jingled mutedly.

'Okay, Daddy?' Charlie asked as they moved away toward the road.

'Lookin good,' he said, and put an arm around her

shoulders. To their right and back over the hill, Ray Knowles and John Mayo had just had their flat tire.

'Where are we going, Daddy?' Charlie asked.

'I don't know,' he said.

'I don't like it. I feel nervous.'

'I think we're well ahead of them,' he said. 'Don't worry. They're probably still looking for the cab driver who took us to Albany.'

But he was whistling past the graveyard; he knew it and probably Charlie did, too. Just standing here beside the road made him feel exposed, like a cartoon jailbird in a striped suit. Quit it, he told himself. Next thing you'll be thinking they're everywhere – one behind every tree and a bunch of them right over the next hill. Hadn't somebody said that perfect paranoia and perfect awareness were the same thing?

'Charlie—' he began.

'Let's go to Granther's,' she said.

He looked at her, startled. His dream rushed back at him, the dream of fishing in the rain, the rain that had turned into the sound of Charlie's shower. 'What made you think of that?' he asked. Granther had died long before Charlie was born. He had lived his whole life in Tashmore, Vermont, a town just west of the New Hampshire border. When Granther died, the place on the lake went to Andy's mother, and when she died, it came to Andy. The town would have taken it for back taxes long since, except that Granther had left a small sum in trust to cover them.

Andy and Vicky had gone up there once a year during the summer vacation until Charlie was born. It was twenty miles off the nearest two-lane road, in wooded, unpopulated country. In the summer there were all sorts of people on Tashmore Pond, which was really a lake with the small town of Bradford, New Hampshire, on the far side. But by this time of year all the summer camps would be empty. Andy doubted if the road in was even plowed in the winter.

'I don't know,' Charlie said. 'It just . . . came into my mind. This minute.' On the other side of the hill, John Mayo was opening the trunk of the Ford and making his inspection of the spare tire.

'I dreamed about Granther this morning,' Andy said slowly. 'First time I'd thought about him in a year or more, I guess. So I suppose you could say he just came into my head, too.'

'Was it a good dream, Daddy?'

'Yes,' he said, and smiled a little. 'Yes, it was.'

'Well, what do you think?'

'I think it's a great idea,' Andy said. 'We can go there and stay for a while and think about what we should do. How we should handle this. I was thinking if we could get to a newspaper and tell our story so that a lot of people knew about it, they'd have to lay off.'

An old farm truck was rattling toward them, and Andy stuck out his thumb. On the other side of the hill, Ray Knowles was walking up the soft shoulder of the road.

The farm truck pulled over, and a guy wearing biballs and a New York Mets baseball cap looked out.

'Well there's a purty little miss,' he said, smiling. 'What's your name, missy?'

'Roberta,' Charlie said promptly. Roberta was her middle name.

'Well, Bobbi, where you headed this morning?' the driver asked.

'We're on our way to Vermont,' Andy said. 'St Johnsbury. My wife was visiting her sister and she ran into a little problem.'

'Did she now,' the farmer said, and said no more, but gazed at Andy shrewdly from the corners of his eyes.

130

'Labor,' Andy said, and manufactured a wide smile. 'This one's got a new brother. One-forty-one this morning.'

'His name is Andy,' Charlie said. 'Isn't that a nice name?'

'I think it's a corker,' the farmer said. 'You hop on in here and I'll get you ten miles closer to St Johnsbury, anyhow.'

They got in and the farm truck rattled and rumbled back onto the road, headed into the bright morning sunlight. At the same time, Ray Knowles was breasting the hill. He saw an empty highway leading down to the Slumberland Motel. Beyond the Motel, he saw the farm truck that had passed their car a few minutes ago just disappearing from view.

He saw no need to hurry.

6

The farmer's name was Manders – Irv Manders. He had just taken a load of pumpkins into town, where he had a deal with the fellow who ran the A&P. He told them that he used to deal with the First National, but the fellow over there just had no understanding about pumpkins. A jumped-up meat cutter and no more, was the opinion of Irv Manders. The A&P manager, on the other hand, was a corker. He told them that his wife ran a touristy sort of shop in the summertime, and he kept a roadside produce stand, and between the two of them they got along right smart.

'You won't like me minding your beeswax,' Irv Manders told Andy, 'but you and your button here shouldn't be thumbin. Lord, no. Not with the sort of people you find ramming the roads these days. There's a Greyhound terminal in the drugstore back in Hastings Glen. That's what you want.'

'Well—' Andy said. He was nonplussed, but Charlie stepped neatly into the breach.

'Daddy's out of work,' she said brightly. 'That's why my mommy had to go and stay with Auntie Em to have the baby. Auntie Em doesn't like Daddy. So we stayed at home. But now we're going to see Mommy. Right, Daddy?'

'That's sort of private stuff, Bobbi,' Andy said, sounding uncomfortable. He *felt* uncomfortable. There were a thousand holes in Charlie's story.

'Don't you say another word,' Irv said. 'I know about trouble in families. It can get pretty bitter at times. And I know about being hard-up. It ain't no shame.'

Andy cleared his throat but said nothing. He could think of nothing to say. They rode in silence for a while.

'Say, why don't you two come home and take lunch with me and the wife?' Irv asked suddenly.

'Oh no, we couldn't do—'

'We'd be happy to,' Charlie said. 'Wouldn't we, Daddy?'

He knew that Charlie's intuitions were usually good ones, and he was too mentally and physically worn down to go against her now. She was a self-possessed and aggressive little girl, and more than once Andy had wondered to himself just who was running this show.

'If you're sure there's enough—' he said.

'Always enough,' Irv Manders said, finally shifting the farm truck into third gear. They were rattling between autumn-bright trees: maples, elms, poplars. 'Glad to have you.'

'Thank you very much,' Charlie said.

'My pleasure, button,' Irv said. 'Be my wife's, too, when she gets a look at you.'

Charlie smiled.

Andy rubbed his temples. Beneath the fingers of his left hand was one of those patches of skin where the nerves seemed to have died. He didn't feel good about this, somehow. That feeling that they were closing in was still very much with him.

7

The woman who had checked Andy out of the Slumberland Motel not twenty minutes ago was getting nervous. She had forgotten all about Phil Donahue.

'You're sure this was the man,' Ray Knowles was saying for the third time. She didn't like this small, trim, somehow tight man. Maybe he worked for the government, but that was no comfort to Lena Cunningham. She didn't like his narrow face, she didn't like the lines around his cool blue eyes, and most of all she didn't like the way he kept shoving that picture under her nose.

'Yes, that was him,' she said again. 'But there was no little girl with him. Honest, mister. My husband'll tell you the same. He works nights. It's got so we hardly ever see each other, except at supper. He'll tell—'

The other man came back in, and with ever-mounting alarm, Lena saw that he had a walkie-talkie in one hand and a great big pistol in the other.

'It was them,' John Mayo said. He was almost hysterical with anger and disappointment. 'Two people slept in that bed. Blond hairs on one pillow, black on the other. Goddam that flat tire! Goddam it all to hell! Damp towels hanging on the rod in the bathroom! Fucking shower's still dripping! We missed them by maybe five minutes, Ray!'

He jammed the pistol back into its shoulder holster.

'I'll get my husband,' Lena said faintly.

'Never mind,' Ray said. He took John's arm and led him outside. John was still swearing about the flat. 'Forget the tire, John. Did you talk to OJ back in town?'

'I talked to him and he talked to Norville. Norville's on

133

his way from Albany, and he's got Al Steinowitz with him. He landed not ten minutes ago.'

'Well, that's good. Listen, think a minute, Johnny. They must have been hitching.'

'Yeah, I guess so. Unless they boosted a car.'

'The guy's an English instructor. He wouldn't know how to boost a candy bar out of a concession stand in a home for the blind. They were hitching, all right. They hitched from Albany last night. They hitched this morning. I'd bet you this year's salary that they were standing there by the side of the road with their thumbs out while I was walking up that hill.'

'If it hadn't been for that flat—' John's eyes were miserable behind his wire-framed glasses. He saw a promotion flapping away on slow, lazy wings.

'Fuck the flat!' Ray said. 'What passed us? After we got the flat, what passed us?'

John thought about it as he hooked the walkie-talkie back on his belt. 'Farm truck,' he said.

'That's what I remember, too,' Ray said. He glanced around and saw Lena Cunningham's large moon face peering out the motel office window at them. She saw him seeing her and the curtain fell back into place.

'Pretty rickety truck,' Ray said. 'If they don't turn off the main road, we ought to be able to catch up to them.'

'Let's go, then,' John said. 'We can keep in touch with Al and Norville by way of OJ on the walkie-talkie.'

They trotted back to the car and got in. A moment later the tan Ford roared out of the parking lot, spewing white crushed gravel out from beneath its rear tires. Lena Cunningham watched them go with relief. Running a motel was not what it once had been.

She went back to wake up her husband.

8

As the Ford with Ray Knowles behind the wheel and
John Mayo riding shotgun was roaring down Route 40 at
better than seventy miles an hour (and as a caravan of ten
or eleven similar nondescript late-model cars were heading
toward Hastings Glen from the surrounding areas of
search), Irv Manders hand-signaled left and turned off the
highway onto an unmarked stretch of tar-and-patch that
headed roughly northeast. The truck rattled and banged
along. At his urging, Charlie had sung most of her nine-
song repertoire, including such golden hits as 'Happy
Birthday to You,' 'This Old Man,' 'Jesus Loves Me,' and
'Camptown Races.' Irv and Andy both sang along with
that one.

The road twisted and wound its way over a series of
increasingly wooded ridges and then began to descend
toward flatter country that had been cultivated and harvested. Once a partridge burst from a cover of goldenrod
and old hay at the left side of the road and Irv shouted,
'Get im, Bobbi!' and Charlie pointed her finger and chanted
Bam-ba-DAM!' and then giggled wildly.

A few minutes later Irv turned off on a dirt road, and a
mile farther along they came to a battered red, white, and
blue mailbox with MANDERS stenciled on the side. Irv
turned into a rutted driveway that was nearly half a mile
long.

'Must cost you an arm and a leg to keep it plowed in the
winter,' Andy said.

'Do it m'self,' Irv said.

They came to a big white frame farmhouse, three stories
tall and set off with mint-green trim. To Andy it looked
like the sort of house that might have started off fairly
ordinary and then grown eccentric as the years passed. Two
sheds were attached to the rear, one of them zigging

thisaway, the other zagging thataway. On the south side, a greenhouse wing had been added, and a big screened-in porch stood out from the north side like a stiff skirt.

Behind the house was a red barn that had seen better days, and between the house and the barn was what New Englanders call a dooryard – a flat dirt stretch of ground where a couple of dozen chickens clucked and strutted. When the truck rattled toward them they fled, squawking and fluttering their useless wings, past a chopping block with an ax buried in it.

Irv drove the truck into the barn, which had a sweet hay smell Andy remembered from his summers in Vermont. When Irv switched the truck off, they all heard a low, musical mooing from somewhere deeper in the barn's shadowy interior.

'You got a *cow*,' Charlie said, and something like rapture came over her face. 'I can *hear* it.'

'We've got three,' Irv said. 'That's Bossy you hear – a very original name, wouldn't you say, button? She thinks she's got to be milked three times a day. You can see her later, if your daddy says you can.'

'Can I, Daddy?'

'I guess so,' Andy said, mentally surrendering. Somehow they had gone out beside the road to thumb a ride and had got shanghaied instead.

'Come on in and meet the wife.'

They strolled across the dooryard, pausing for Charlie to examine as many of the chickens as she could get close to. The back door opened and a woman of about forty-five came out onto the back steps. She shaded her eyes and called, 'You there, Irv! Who you brought home?'

Irv smiled. 'Well, the button here is Roberta. This fellow is her daddy. I didn't catch his name yet, so I dunno if we're related.'

Andy stepped forward and said, 'I'm Frank Burton,

ma'am. Your husband invited Bobbi and me home for lunch, if that's all right. We're pleased to know you.'

'Me too,' Charlie said, still more interested in the chickens than in the woman – at least for the moment.

'I'm Norma Manders,' she said. 'Come in. You're welcome.' But Andy saw the puzzled look she threw at her husband.

They all went inside, through an entryway where stovelengths were stacked head high and into a huge kitchen that was dominated by a woodstove and a long table covered with red and white checked oilcloth. There was an elusive smell of fruit and paraffin in the air. The smell of canning, Andy thought.

'Frank here and his button are on their way to Vermont,' Irv said. 'I thought it wouldn't hurt em to get outside of a little hot food on their way.'

'Of course not,' she agreed. 'Where is your car, Mr Burton?'

'Well—' Andy began. He glanced at Charlie, but she was going to be no help; she was walking around the kitchen in small steps, looking at everything with a child's frank curiosity.

'Frank's had a little trouble,' Irv said, looking directly at his wife. 'But we don't have to talk about that. At least, not right now.'

'All right,' Norma said. She had a sweet and direct face – a handsome woman who was used to working hard. Her hands were red and chapped. 'I've got chicken and I could put together a nice salad. And there's lots of milk. Do you like milk, Roberta?'

Charlie didn't look around. She's lapsed on the name, Andy thought. Oh, Jesus, this just gets better and better.

'Bobbi!' he said loudly.

She looked around then, and smiled a little too widely. 'Oh, sure,' she said. 'I love milk.'

137

Andy saw a warning glance pass from Irv to his wife: *No questions, not now.* He felt a sinking despair. Whatever had been left of their story had just gone swirling away. But there was nothing to do except sit down to lunch and wait to see what Irv Manders had on his mind.

9

'How far from the motel are we?' John Mayo asked.

Ray glanced down at the odometer. 'Seventeen miles,' he said, and pulled over. 'That's far enough.'

'But maybe—'

'No, if we were going to catch them, we would have by now. We'll go on back and rendezvous with the others.'

John struck the heel of his hand against the dashboard. 'They turned off somewhere,' he said. 'That goddam flat shoe! This job's been bad luck from the start, Ray. An egghead and a little girl. And we keep missing them.'

'No, I think we've got them,' Ray said, and took out his walkie-talkie. He pulled the antenna and tipped it out the window. 'We'll have a cordon around the whole area in half an hour. And I bet we don't hit a dozen houses before someone around here recognizes that truck. Late-sixties dark-green International Harvester, snowplow attachment on the front, wooden stakes around the truck bed to hold on a high load. I still think we'll have them by dark.'

A moment later he was talking to Al Steinowitz, who was nearing the Slumberland Motel. Al briefed his agents in turn. Bruce Cook remembered the farm truck from town. OJ did, too. It had been parked in front of the A&P.

Al sent them back to town, and half an hour later they all knew that the truck that had almost certainly stopped to give the two fugitives a lift belonged to Irving Manders, RFD #5, Baillings Road, Hastings Glen, New York.

It was just past twelve-thirty P.M.

138

10

The lunch was very nice. Charlie ate like a horse – three helpings of chicken with gravy, two of Norma Manders's hot biscuits, a side dish of salad, and three of her home-canned dill pickles. They finished off with slices of apple pie garnished with wedges of cheddar – Irv offering his opinion that 'Apple pie without a piece of cheese is like a smooch without a squeeze.' This earned him an affectionate elbow in the side from his wife. Irv rolled his eyes, and Charlie laughed. Andy's appetite surprised him. Charlie belched and then covered her mouth guiltily.

Irv smiled at her. 'More room out than there is in, button.'

'If I eat any more, I think I'll split,' Charlie answered. 'That's what my mother always used to . . . I mean, that's what she always says.'

Andy smiled tiredly.

'Norma,' Irv said, getting up, 'why don't you and Bobbi go on out and feed those chickens?'

'Well, lunch is still spread over half an acre,' Norma said.

'I'll pick up lunch,' Irv said. 'Want to have a little talk with Frank, here.'

'Would you like to feed the chickens, honey?' Norma asked Charlie.

'I sure would.' Her eyes were sparkling.

'Well, come on then. Do you have a jacket? It's turned a bit chilly.'

'Uh . . .' Charlie looked at Andy.

'You can borrow a sweater of mine,' Norma said. That look passed between her and Irv again. 'Roll the sleeves up a little bit and it will be fine.'

'Okay.'

Norma got an old and faded warmup jacket from the

entryway and a frayed white sweater that Charlie floated in, even with the cuffs turned up three or four times.

'Do they peck?' Charlie asked a little nervously.

'Only their food, honey.'

They went out and the door closed behind them. Charlie was still chattering. Andy looked at Irv Manders, and Irv looked back calmly.

'You want a beer, Frank?'

'It isn't Frank,' Andy said. 'I guess you know that.'

'I guess I do. What is your handle?'

Andy said, 'The less you know, the better off you are.'

'Well, then,' Irv said, 'I'll just call you Frank.'

Faintly, they heard Charlie squeal with delight from outside. Norma said something, and Charlie agreed.

'I guess I could use a beer,' Andy said.

'Okay.'

Irv got two Utica Clubs from the refrigerator, opened them, set Andy's on the table and his on the counter. He got an apron from a hook by the sink and put it on. The apron was red and yellow and the hem was flounced, but somehow he managed to avoid looking silly.

'Can I help you?' Andy asked.

'No, I know where everything goes,' Irv said. 'Most everything, anyhow. She changes things from week to week. No woman wants a man to feel right at home in her kitchen. They like help, sure, but they feel better if you have to ask them where to put the casserole dish or where they put the Brillo.'

Andy, remembering his own days as Vicky's kitchen apprentice, smiled and nodded.

'Meddling around in other folk's business isn't my strong point,' Irv said, drawing water in the kitchen sink and adding detergent. 'I'm a farmer, and like I told you, my wife runs a little curio shop down where Baillings Road

140

crosses the Albany Highway. We've been here almost twenty years.'

He glanced back at Andy.

'But I knew there was somethin wrong from the minute I saw you two standing by the road back there. A grown man and a little girl just aren't the kind of pair you usually see hitching the roads. Know what I mean?'

Andy nodded and sipped his beer.

'Furthermore, it looked to me like you'd just come out of the Slumberland, but you had no traveling gear, not so much as an overnight case. So I just about decided to pass you by. Then I stopped. Because . . . well, there's a difference between not meddling in other folks' business and seeing something that looks damn bad and turning a blind eye to it.'

'Is that how we look to you? Damn bad?'

'Then,' Irv said, 'not now.' He was washing the old mismatched dishes carefully, stacking them in the drainer. 'Now I don't know just what to make of you two. My first thought was it must be you two the cops are looking for.' He saw the change come over Andy's face and the sudden way Andy set his beer can down. 'I guess it is you,' he said softly. 'I was hopin it wasn't.'

'What cops?' Andy asked harshly.

'They've got all the main roads blocked off coming in and out of Albany,' Irv said. 'If we'd gone another six miles up Route Forty, we would have run on one of those blocks right where Forty crosses Route Nine.'

'Well, why didn't you just go ahead?' Andy asked. 'That would have been the end of it for you. You would have been out of it.'

Irv was starting on the pots now, pausing to hunt through the cupboards over the sink. 'See what I was saying? I can't find the gloriosky Brillo . . . Wait, here it is . . . Why didn't I just take you up the road to the cops? Let's say I wanted to satisfy my own natural curiosity.'

'You have some questions, huh?'

'All kinds of them,' Irv said. 'A grown man and a little girl hitching rides, the little girl hasn't got any overnight case, and the cops are after them. So I have an idea. It isn't so farfetched. I think that maybe here's a daddy who wanted custody of his button and couldn't get it. So he snatched her.'

'It sounds pretty farfetched to me.'

'Happens all the time, Frank. And I think to myself, the mommy didn't like that so well and swore out a warrant on the daddy. That would explain all the roadblocks. You only get coverage like that for a big robbery . . . or a kidnapping.'

'She's my daughter, but her mother didn't put the police on us,' Andy said. 'Her mother has been dead for a year.'

'Well, I'd already kind of shitcanned the idea,' Irv said. 'It don't take a private eye to see the two of you are pretty close. Whatever else may be going on, it doesn't appear you've got her against her will.'

Andy said nothing.

'So here we are at my problem,' Irv said. 'I picked the two of you up because I thought the little girl might need help. Now I don't know where I'm at. You don't strike me as the desperado type. But all the same, you and your little girl are going under false names, you're telling a story that's just as thin as a piece of tissue paper, and you look sick, Frank. You look just about as sick as a man can get and still stay on his feet. So those are my questions. Any you could answer, it might be a good thing.'

'We came to Albany from New York and hitched a ride to Hastings Glen early this morning,' Andy said. 'It's bad to know they're here, but I think I knew it. I think Charlie

knew it, too.' He had mentioned Charlie's name, and that
was a mistake, but at this point it didn't seem to matter.

'What do they want you for, Frank?'

Andy thought for a long time, and then he met Irv's
frank gray eyes. He said: 'You came from town, didn't
you? See any strange people there? City types? Wearing
these neat, off-the-rack suits that you forget almost as soon
as the guys wearing them are out of sight? Driving late-
model cars that sort of just fade into the scenery?'

It was Irv's turn to think. 'There were two guys like that
in the A&P,' he said. 'Talking to Helga. She's one of the
checkers. Looked like they were showing her something.'

'Probably our picture,' Andy said. 'They're government
agents. They're working with the police, Irv. A more
accurate way of putting it would be that the police are
working for them. The cops don't know why we're wanted.'

'What sort of government agency we talking about?
FBI?'

'No. The Shop.'

'What? That CIA outfit?' Irv looked frankly disbeliev-
ing.

'They don't have anything at all to do with the CIA,'
Andy said. 'The Shop is really the DSI – Department of
Scientific Intelligence. I read in an article about three years
ago that some wiseacre nicknamed it the Shop in the early
sixties, after a science-fiction story called "The Weapon
Shops of Ishtar." By a guy named van Vogt, I think, but
that doesn't matter. What they're supposed to be involved
in are domestic scientific projects which may have present
or future application to matters bearing on national security. That definition is from their charter, and the thing
they're most associated with in the public mind is the
energy research they're funding and supervising – electro-
magnetic stuff and fusion power. They're actually involved
in a lot more. Charlie and I are part of an experiment that

143

happened a long time ago. It happened before Charlie was even born. Her mother was also involved. She was murdered. The Shop was responsible.'

Irv was silent for a while. He let the dishwater out of the sink, dried his hands, and then came over and began to wipe the oilcloth that covered the table. Andy picked up his beer can.

'I won't say flat out that I don't believe you,' Irv said finally. 'Not with some of the things that have gone on under cover in this country and then come out. CIA guys giving people drinks spiked with LSD and some FBI agent accused of killing people during the Civil Rights marches and money in brown bags and all of that. So I can't say right out that I don't believe you. Let's just say you haven't convinced me yet.'

'I don't think it's even me that they really want anymore,' Andy said. 'Maybe it was, once. But they've shifted targets. It's Charlie they're after now.'

'You mean the national government is after a first- or second-grader for reasons of national security?'

'Charlie's no ordinary second-grader,' Andy said. 'Her mother and I were injected with a drug which was coded Lot Six. To this day I don't know exactly what it was. Some sort of synthetic glandular secretion would be my best guess. It changed the chromosomes of myself and of the lady I later married. We passed those chromosomes on to Charlie, and they mixed in some entirely new way. If she could pass them on to her children, I guess she'd be called a mutant. If for some reason she can't, or if the change has caused her to be sterile, I guess she'd be called a sport or a mule. Either way, they want her. They want to study her, see if they can figure out what makes her able to do what she can do. And even more, I think they want her as an exhibit. They want to use her to reactivate the Lot Six program.'

144

'What is it she can do?' Irv asked.

Through the kitchen window they could see Norma and Charlie coming out of the barn. The white sweater flopped and swung around Charlie's body, the hem coming down to her calves. There was high color in her cheeks, and she was talking to Norma, who was smiling and nodding.

Andy said softly, 'She can light fires.'

'Well, so can I,' Irv said. He sat down again and was looking at Andy in a peculiar, cautious way. The way you look at people you suspect of madness.

'She can do it simply by thinking about it,' Andy said. 'The technical name for it is pyrokinesis. It's a psi talent, like telepathy, telekinesis, or precognition – Charlie has a dash of some of those as well, by the way – but pyrokinesis is much rarer . . . and much more dangerous. She's very much afraid of it, and she's right to be. She can't always control it. She could burn up your house, your barn, or your front yard if she set her mind to it. Or she could light your pipe.' Andy smiled wanly. 'Except that while she was lighting your pipe, she might also burn up your house, your barn, and your front yard.'

Irv finished his beer and said, 'I think you ought to call the police and turn yourself in, Frank. You need help.'

'I guess it sounds pretty nutty, doesn't it?'

'Yes,' Irv said gravely. 'It sounds nutty as anything I ever heard.' He was sitting lightly, slightly tense on his chair, and Andy thought, *He's expecting me to do something loony the first chance I get.*

'I suppose it doesn't matter much anyway,' Andy said. 'They'll be here soon enough. I think the police would actually be better. At least you don't turn into an unperson as soon as the police get their hands on you.'

Irv started to reply, and then the door opened. Norma and Charlie came in. Charlie's face was bright, her eyes sparkling. 'Daddy!' she said. 'Daddy, I fed the—'

She broke off. Some of the color left her cheeks, and she looked narrowly from Irv Manders to her father and back to Irv again. Pleasure faded from her face and was replaced with a look of harried misery. *The way she looked last night*, Andy thought. *The way she looked yesterday when I grabbed her out of school. It goes on and on, and where's the happy ending for her?*

'You told,' she said. 'Oh Daddy, why did you tell?'

Norma stepped forward and put a protective arm around Charlie's shoulders. 'Irv, what's going on here?'

'I don't know,' Irv said. 'What do you mean he told, Bobbi?'

'That's not my name,' she said. Tears had appeared in her eyes. 'You know that's not my name.'

'Charlie,' Andy said. 'Mr Manders knew something was wrong. I told him, but he didn't believe me. When you think about it, you'll understand why.'

'I don't understand anyth—' Charlie began, her voice rising stridently. Then she was quiet. Her head cocked sideways in a peculiar listening gesture, although as far as any of the others could tell there was nothing to listen to. As they watched, Charlie's face simply drained of color; it was like watching some rich liquid poured out of a pitcher.

'What's the matter, honey?' Norma asked, and cast a worried glance at Irv.

'They're coming, Daddy,' Charlie whispered. Her eyes were wide circles of fear. 'They're coming for us.'

11

They had rendezvoused at the corner of Highway 40 and the unnumbered blacktop road Irv had turned down – on the Hastings Glen town maps it was marked as the Old Baillings Road. Al Steinowitz had finally caught up with the rest of his men and had taken over quickly and decisively. There were sixteen of them in five cars. Heading up the road toward Irv Manders's place, they looked like a fast-moving funeral procession.

Norville Bates had handed over the reins – and the responsibility – of the operation to Al with genuine relief and with a question about the local and state police who had been rung in on the operation.

'We're keeping this one dark for now,' Al said. 'If we get them, we'll tell them they can fold their roadblocks. If we don't, we'll tell them to start moving in toward the center of the circle. But between you and me, if we can't handle them with sixteen men, we can't handle them, Norv.'

Norv sensed the mild rebuke and said no more. He knew it would be best to take the two of them with no outside interference, because Andrew McGee was going to have an unfortunate accident as soon as they got him. A fatal accident. With no bluesuits hanging around, it could happen that much sooner.

Ahead of him and Al, the brakelights of OJ's car flashed briefly, and then the car turned onto a dirt road. The others followed.

12

'I don't understand any of this,' Norma said. 'Bobbi . . . Charlie . . . can't you calm down?'

'You don't understand,' Charlie said. Her voice was high and strangled. Looking at her made Irv jumpy. Her face was like that of a rabbit caught in a snare. She pulled free of Norma's arm and ran to her father, who put his hands on her shoulders.

'I think they're going to kill you, Daddy,' she said.

'What?'

'Kill you,' she repeated. Her eyes were staring and

147

glazed with panic. Her mouth worked frantically. 'We have to run. We have to—'

Hot. Too hot in here.

He glanced to his left. Mounted on the wall between the stove and the sink was an indoor thermometer, the kind that can be purchased from any mail-order catalogue. At the bottom of this one, a plastic red devil with a pitchfork was grinning and mopping his brow. The motto beneath his cloven hooves read: HOT ENOUGH FOR YA?

The mercury in the thermometer was slowly rising, an accusing red finger.

'Yes, that's what they want to do,' she said. 'Kill you, kill you like they did Mommy, take me away, I won't, I won't let it happen, *I won't let it—*'

Her voice was rising. Rising like the column of mercury.

'*Charlie!* Watch what you're doing!'

Her eyes cleared a little. Irv and his wife had drawn together.

'Irv . . . what—?'

But Irv had seen Andy's glance at the thermometer, and suddenly he believed. It was hot in here now. Hot enough to sweat. The mercury in the thermometer stood just above ninety degrees.

'Holy Jesus Christ,' he said hoarsely. 'Did she do that, Frank?'

Andy ignored him. His hands were still on Charlie's shoulders. He looked into her eyes. 'Charlie – do you think it's too late? How does it feel to you?'

'Yes,' she said. All the color was gone from her face. 'They're coming up the dirt road now. Oh Daddy, I'm scared.'

'You can stop them, Charlie,' he said quietly.

She looked at him.

'Yes,' he said.

'But – Daddy – it's bad. I know it is. I could kill them.'

'Yes,' he said. 'Maybe now it's kill or be killed. Maybe it's come down to that.'

'It's not bad?' Her voice was almost inaudible.

'Yes,' Andy said. 'It is. Never kid yourself that it isn't. And don't do it if you can't handle it, Charlie. Not even for me.'

They looked at each other, eye to eye, Andy's eyes tired and bloodshot and frightened, Charlie's eyes wide, nearly hypnotized.

She said: 'If I do . . . something . . . will you still love me?'

The question hung between them, lazily revolving.

'Charlie,' he said, 'I'll always love you. No matter what.'

Irv had been at the window and now he crossed the room to them. 'I think I got some tall apologizing to do,' he said. 'There's a whole line of cars coming up the road. I'll stand with you, if you want. I got my deer gun.' But he looked suddenly frightened, almost sick.

Charlie said: 'You don't need your gun.'

She slipped out from under her father's hands and walked across to the screen door, in Norma Manders's knitted white sweater looking even smaller than she was. She let herself out.

After a moment, Andy found his feet and went after her. His stomach felt frozen, as if he'd just gobbled a huge Dairy Queen cone in three bites. The Manderses stayed behind. Andy caught one last look at the man's baffled, frightened face, and a random thought – *that'll teach you to pick up hitchhikers* – darted across his consciousness.

Then he and Charlie were on the porch, watching the first of the cars turn up the long driveway. The hens squawked and fluttered. In the barn, Bossy mooed again for someone to come and milk her. And thin October sunshine lay over the wooded ridges and autumn-brown fields of this small upstate–New York town. It had been

almost a year of running, and Andy was surprised to find
an odd sense of relief mixed in with his sharp terror. He
had heard that in its extremity, even a rabbit will sometimes
turn and face the dogs, driven back to some earlier, less
meek nature at the instant before it must be torn apart.

At any rate, it was good not to be running. He stood
with Charlie, the sunshine mellow on her blond hair.

'Oh Daddy,' she moaned. 'I can't hardly stand up.'

He put his arm around her shoulders and pulled her
more tightly against his side.

The first car stopped at the head of the dooryard and
two men got out.

13

'Hi, Andy,' Al Steinowitz said, and smiled. 'Hi, Charlie.'
His hands were empty, but his coat was open. Behind him
the other man stood alertly by the car, hands at his sides.
The second car stopped behind the first and four more
men spilled out. All the cars were stopping, all the men
getting out. Andy counted a dozen and then stopped
counting.

'Go away,' Charlie said. Her voice was thin and high in
the cool early afternoon.

'You've led us a merry chase,' Al said to Andy. He
looked at Charlie. 'Honey, you don't have to—'

'*Go away!*' she screamed.

Al shrugged and smiled disarmingly. 'Fraid I can't do
that, honey. I have my orders. No one wants to hurt you
or your daddy.'

'*You liar! You're s'posed to kill him! I know it!*'

Andy spoke and was a little surprised to find that his
voice was completely steady. 'I advise you to do as my
daughter says. You've surely been briefed enough to know

why she's wanted. You know about the soldier at the airport.'

OJ and Norville Bates exchanged a sudden uneasy look.

'If you'll just get in the car, we can discuss all of this,' Al said. 'Honest to gosh, there's nothing going on here except—'

'We know what's going on,' Andy said.

The men who had been in the last two or three cars were beginning to fan out and stroll, almost casually toward the porch.

'Please,' Charlie said to the man with the strangely yellow face. 'Don't make me do anything.'

'It's no good, Charlie,' Andy said.

Irv Manders came out onto the porch. 'You men are trespassing,' he said. 'I want you to get the hell off my property.'

Three of the Shop men had come up the front steps of the porch and were now standing less than ten yards away from Andy and Charlie, to their left. Charlie threw them a warning, desperate glance and they stopped – for the moment.

'We're government agents, sir,' Al Steinowitz said to Irv in a low, courteous voice. 'These two folks are wanted for questioning. Nothing more.'

'I don't care if they're wanted for assassinating the President,' Irv said. His voice was high, cracking. 'Show me your warrant or get the Christ off my property.'

'We don't need a warrant,' Al said. His voice was edged with steel now.

'You do unless I woke up in Russia this morning,' Irv said. 'I'm telling you to get off, and you better get high-steppin, mister. That's my last word on it.'

'Irv, come inside!' Norma cried.

Andy could feel something building in the air, building up around Charlie like an electric charge. The hair on his arms suddenly began to stir and move, like kelp in an invisible tide. He looked down at her and saw her face, so small, now so strange.

It's coming, he thought helplessly. *It's coming, oh my God it really is.*

'Get out!' he shouted at Al. 'Don't you understand what she's going to do? Can't you feel it? Don't be a fool, man!'

'Please,' Al said. He looked at the three men standing at the far end of the porch and nodded to them imperceptibly. He looked back at Andy. 'If we can only discuss this—'

'Watch it, Frank!' Irv Manders screamed.

The three men at the end of the porch suddenly charged at them, pulling their guns as they came. 'Hold it, hold it!' one of them yelled. 'Just stand still! Hands over your—'

Charlie turned toward them. As she did so, half a dozen other men, John Mayo and Ray Knowles among them, broke for the porch's back steps with their guns drawn.

Charlie's eyes widened a little, and Andy felt something hot pass by him in a warm puff of air.

The three men at the front end of the porch had got halfway toward them when their hair caught on fire.

A gun boomed, deafeningly loud, and a splinter of wood perhaps eight inches long jumped from one of the porch's supporting posts. Norma Manders screamed, and Andy flinched. But Charlie seemed not to notice. Her face was dreamy and thoughtful. A small Mona Lisa smile had touched the corners of her mouth.

She's enjoying this, Andy thought with something like horror. *Is that why she's so afraid of it? Because she* likes *it?*

Charlie was turning back toward Al Steinowitz again. The three men he had sent running down toward Andy and Charlie from the front end of the porch had forgotten their duty to God, country, and the Shop. They were beating at the flames on their heads and yelling. The pungent smell of fried hair suddenly filled the afternoon.

Another gun went off. A window shattered.

'Not the girl!' Al shouted. *'Not the girl!'*

Andy was seized roughly. The porch swirled with a confusion of men. He was dragged toward the railing through the chaos. Then someone tried to pull him a different way. He felt like a tug-of-war rope.

'Let him go!' Irv Manders shouted, bull-throated. 'Let him—'

Another gun went off and suddenly Norma was screaming again, screaming her husband's name over and over.

Charlie was looking down at Al Steinowitz, and suddenly the cold, confident look was gone from Al's face and he was in terror. His yellow complexion grew positively cheesy.

'No, don't,' he said in an almost conversational tone of voice. 'Don't—'

It was impossible to tell where the flames began. Suddenly his pants and his sportcoat were blazing. His hair was a burning bush. He backed up, screaming, bounced off the side of his car, and half-turned to Norville Bates, his arms stretched out.

Andy felt that soft rush of heat again, a displacement of air, as if a hot slug thrown at rocket-speed had just passed his nose.

Al Steinowitz's face caught on fire.

For a moment he was all there, screaming silently under a transparent caul of flame, and then his features were blending, merging, running like tallow. Norville shrank away from him. Al Steinowitz was a flaming scarecrow. He staggered blindly down the driveway, waving his arms, and then collapsed facedown beside the third car. He didn't look like a man at all; he looked like a burning bundle of rags.

The people on the porch had frozen, staring dumbly at this unexpected blazing development. The three men

153

whose hair Charlie had fired had all managed to put themselves out. They were all going to look decidedly strange in the future (however short that might be); their hair, short by regulation, now looked like blackened, tangled clots of ash on top of their heads.

'Get out,' Andy said hoarsely. 'Get out quickly. She's never done anything like this before *and I don't know if she can stop.*'

'I'm all right, Daddy,' Charlie said. Her voice was calm, collected, and strangely indifferent. 'Everything's okay.'

And that was when the cars began to explode.

They all went up from the rear; later, when Andy replayed the incident at the Manders farm in his mind, he was quite sure of that. They all went up from the rear, where the gas tanks were.

Al's light-green Plymouth went first, exploding with a muffled *whrrr-rump!* sound. A ball of flame rose from the back of the Plymouth, too bright to look at. The rear window blew in. The Ford John and Ray had come in went next, barely two seconds later. Hooks of metal whickered through the air and pattered on the roof.

'Charlie!' Andy shouted. *'Charlie, stop it!'*

She said in that same calm voice: 'I can't.'

The third car went up.

Someone ran. Someone else followed him. The men on the porch began to back away. Andy was tugged again, he resisted, and suddenly no one at all was holding him. And suddenly they were all running, their faces white, eyes stare-blind with panic. One of the men with the charred hair tried to vault over the railing, caught his foot, and fell headfirst into a small side garden where Norma had grown beans earlier in the year. The stakes for the beans to climb on were still there, and one of them rammed through this fellow's throat and came out the other side with a wet punching sound that Andy never forgot. He twitched in the garden like a landed trout, the bean-pole protruding from his neck like the shaft of an arrow, blood gushing down the front of his shirt as he made weak gargling sounds.

The rest of the cars went up then like an ear-shattering string of firecrackers. Two of the fleeing men were tossed aside like ragdolls by the concussion, one of them on fire from the waist down, the other peppered with bits of safety glass.

Dark, oily smoke rose in the air. Beyond the driveway, the far hills and fields twisted and writhed through the heat-shimmer as if recoiling in horror. Chickens ran madly everywhere, clucking crazily. Suddenly three of them exploded into flame and went rushing off, balls of fire with feet, to collapse on the far side of the dooryard.

'Charlie, stop it right now! Stop it!'

A trench of fire raced across the dooryard on a diagonal, the very dirt blazing in a single straight line, as if a train of gunpowder had been laid. The flame reached the chopping block with Irv's ax buried in it, made a fairy-ring around it, and suddenly collapsed inward. The chopping block whooshed into flame.

'CHARLIE FOR CHRIST'S SAKE!'

Some Shop agent's pistol was lying on the verge of grass between the porch and the blazing line of cars in the driveway. Suddenly the cartridges in it began to go off in a series of sharp, clapping explosions. The gun jigged and flipped bizarrely in the grass.

Andy slapped her as hard as he could.

Her head rocked back, her eyes blue and vacant. Then she was looking at him, surprised and hurt and dazed, and he suddenly felt enclosed in a capsule of swiftly building heat. He took in a breath of air that felt like heavy glass. The hairs in his nose felt as if they were crisping.

155

Spontaneous combustion, he thought. *I'm going up in a burst of spontaneous combustion—*

Then it was gone.

Charlie staggered on her feet and put her hands up to her face. And then, through her hands, came a shrill, building scream of such horror and dismay that Andy feared her mind had cracked.

'*DAAAAADEEEEEEEEE—*'

He swept her into his arms, hugged her.

'Shhh,' he said. 'Oh Charlie, honey, shhhh.'

The scream stopped, and she went limp in his arms. Charlie had fainted.

14

Andy picked her up in his arms and her head rolled limply against his chest. The air was hot and rich with the smell of burning gasoline. Flames had already crawled across the lawn to the ivy trellis; fingers of fire began to climb the ivy with the agility of a boy on midnight business. The house was going to go up.

Irv Manders was leaning against the kitchen screen door, his legs splayed. Norma knelt beside him. He had been shot above the elbow, and the sleeve of his blue workshirt was a bright red. Norma had torn a long strip of her dress off at the hem and was trying to get his shirtsleeve up so she could bind the wound. Irv's eyes were open. His face was an ashy gray, his lips were faintly blue, and he was breathing fast.

Andy took a step toward them and Norma Manders flinched backward, at the same time placing her body over her husband's. She looked up at Andy with shiny, hard eyes.

'Get away,' she hissed. 'Take your monster and get away.'

15

OJ ran.

The Windsucker bounced up and down under his arm as he ran. He ignored the road as he ran. He ran in the field. He fell down and got up and ran on. He twisted his ankle in what might have been a chuckhole and fell down again, a scream jerking out of his mouth as he sprawled. Then he got up and ran on. At times it seemed that he was running alone, and at times it seemed that someone was running with him. It didn't matter. All that mattered was getting away, away from that blazing bundle of rags that had been Al Steinowitz ten minutes before, away from that burning train of cars, away from Bruce Cook who lay in a small garden patch with a stake in his throat. Away, away, away. The Windsucker fell out of its holster, struck his knee painfully, and fell in a tangle of weeds, forgotten. Then OJ was in a patch of woods. He stumbled over a fallen tree and sprawled full length. He lay there, breathing raggedly, one hand pressed to his side, where a painful stitch had formed. He lay weeping tears of shock and fear. He thought: *No more assignments in New York. Never. That's it. Everybody out of the pool. I'm never setting foot in New York again even if I live to be two hundred.*

After a little while OJ got up and began to limp toward the road.

16

'Let's get him off the porch,' Andy said. He had laid Charlie on the grass beyond the dooryard. The side of the house was burning now, and sparks were drifting down on the porch like big, slow-moving fireflies.

'Get away,' she said harshly. 'Don't touch him.'

'The house is burning,' Andy said. 'Let me help you.'

'Get away! You've done enough!'

'Stop it, Norma.' Irv looked at her. 'None of what happened was this man's fault. So shut your mouth.'

She looked at him as if she had a great many things to say, and then shut her mouth with a snap.

'Get me up,' Irv said. 'Legs feel all rubber. Think maybe I pissed myself. Shouldn't be surprised. One of those bastards shot me. Don't know which one. Lend a hand, Frank.'

'It's Andy,' he said, and got an arm around Irv's back. Little by little Irv came up. 'I don't blame your missus. You should have passed us by this morning.'

'If I had it to do over again, I'd do it just the same way,' Irv said. 'Gosh-damn people coming on my land with guns. Gosh-damn bastards and fucking bunch of government whoremasters and . . . oooww-oooh, *Christ!*'

'Irv?' Norma cried.

'Hush, woman. I got it nocked now. Come on, Frank, or Andy, or whatever your name is. It's gettin hot.'

It was. A puff of wind blew a coil of sparks onto the porch as Andy half dragged Irv down the steps and into the dooryard. The chopping block was a blackened stump. There was nothing left of the chickens Charlie had set on fire but a few charred bones and a peculiar, dense ash that might have been feathers. They had not been roasted; they had been cremated.

'Set me down by the barn,' Irv gasped. 'I want to talk to you.'

'You need a doctor,' Andy said.

'Yeah, I'll get my doctor. What about your girl?'

'Fainted.' He set Irv down with his back against the barn door. Irv was looking up at him. A little color had come into his face, and that bluish cast was leaving his lips. He was sweating. Behind them, the big white farmhouse that had stood here on the Baillings Road since 1868 was going up in flames.

'There's no human being should be able to do what she can,' Irv said.

'That may well be,' Andy said, and then he looked from Irv and directly into Norma Manders's stony, unforgiving face. 'But then, no human being should have to have cerebral palsy or muscular dystrophy or leukemia. But it happens. And it happens to children.'

'She didn't get no say.' Irv nodded. 'All right.'

Still looking at Norma, Andy said, 'She's no more a monster than a kid in an iron lung or in a home for retarded children.'

'I'm sorry I said that,' Norma replied, and her glance wavered and fell from Andy's. 'I was out feeding the chickens with her. Watching her pet the cow. But mister, my house is burning down, and people are dead.'

'I'm sorry.'

'The house is insured, Norma,' Irv said, taking her hand with his good one.

'That doesn't do anything about my mother's dishes that her mother gave to her,' Norma said. 'Or my nice secretary, or the pictures we got at the Schenectady art show last July.' A tear slipped out of one eye and she wiped it away with her sleeve. 'And all the letters you wrote to me when you were in the army.'

'Is your button going to be all right?' Irv asked.

'I don't know.'

'Well, listen. Here's what you can do if you want to. There's an old Willys Jeep out behind the barn—'

'Irv, no! Don't get into this any deeper!'

He turned to look at her, his face gray and lined and sweaty. Behind them, their home burned. The sound of popping shingles was like that of horse chestnuts in a Christmas fire.

'Those men came with no warrants nor blueback paper of any kind and tried to take them off our land,' he said. 'People I'd invited in like it's done in a civilized country with decent laws. One of them shot me, and one of them tried to shoot Andy here. Missed his head by no more than a quarter of an inch.' Andy remembered the first deafening report and the splinter of wood that had jumped from the porch support post. He shivered. 'They came and did those things. What do you want me to do, Norma? Sit here and turn them over to the secret police if they get their peckers up enough to come back? Be a good German?'

'No,' she said huskily. 'No, I guess not.'

'You don't have to—' Andy began.

'I feel I do,' Irv said. 'And when they come back . . . they will be back, won't they, Andy?'

'Oh yes. They'll be back. You just bought stock in a growth industry, Irv.'

Irv laughed, a whistling, breathless sound. 'That's pretty good, all right. Well, when they show up here, all I know is that you took my Willys. I don't know more than that. And to wish you well.'

'Thank you,' Andy said quietly.

'We got to be quick,' Irv said. 'It's a long way back to town, but they'll have seen the smoke by now. Fire trucks'll be coming. You said you and the button were going to Vermont. Was that much the truth?'

'Yes,' Andy said.

There was a moaning sound to their left. 'Daddy—'

Charlie was sitting up. The red pants and green blouse were smeared with dirt. Her face was pale, her eyes were terribly confused. 'Daddy, what's burning? I smell something burning. Am I doing it? *What's burning?*'

Andy went to her and gathered her up. 'Everything is all right,' he said, and wondered why you had to say that to children even when they knew perfectly well, as you did,

160

that it wasn't true. 'Everything's fine. How do you feel, hon?'

Charlie was looking over his shoulder at the burning line of cars, the convulsed body in the garden, and the Manders house, which was crowned with fire. The porch was also wrapped in flames. The wind was carrying the smoke and heat away from them, but the smell of gas and hot shingles was strong.

'I did that,' Charlie said, almost too low to hear. Her face began to twist and crumple again.

'Button!' Irv said sternly.

She glanced over at him, through him. 'Me,' she moaned.

'Set her down,' Irv said. 'I want to talk to her.'

Andy carried Charlie over to where Irv sat propped up against the barn door and set her down.

'You listen to me, button,' Irv said. 'Those men meant to kill your daddy. You knew it before I did, maybe before he did, although I'll be damned if I know how. Am I right?'

'Yes,' Charlie said. Her eyes were still deep and miserable. 'But you don't get it. It was like the soldier, but worse. I couldn't . . . couldn't hold onto it anymore. It was going everyplace. I burned up some of your chickens . . . and I almost burned up my father.' The miserable eyes spilled over and she began to cry helplessly.

'Your daddy's fine,' Irv said. Andy said nothing. He remembered that sudden strangling sensation, being enclosed in that heat capsule.

'I'm never going to do it again,' she said. '*Never.*'

'All right,' Andy said, and put a hand on her shoulder. 'All right, Charlie.'

'*Never,*' she repeated with quiet emphasis.

'You don't want to say that, button,' Irv said, looking up at her. 'You don't want to block yourself off like that. You'll do what you have to do. You'll do the best you can.

And that's all you can do. I believe the one thing the God of this world likes best is to give the business to people who say "never." You understand me?'

'No,' Charlie whispered.

'But you will, I think,' Irv said, and looked at Charlie with such deep compassion that Andy felt his throat fill with sorrow and fear. Then Irv glanced at his wife. 'Bring me that there stick by your foot, Norma.'

Norma brought the stick and put it into his hand and told him again that he was overdoing it, that he had to rest. And so it was only Andy that heard Charlie say 'Never' again, almost inaudibly, under her breath, like a vow taken in secrecy.

17

'Look here, Andy,' Irv said, and drew a straight line in the dust. 'This is the dirt road we came up. The Baillings Road. If you go a quarter of a mile north, you'll come to a woods road on your right. A car can't make it up that road, but the Willys should do it if you keep her wound up and use an educated foot on the clutch. A couple of times it's gonna look like that road just up and died, but you keep going and you'll pick it up again. It's not on any map, you understand? Not on any map.'

Andy nodded, watching the stick draw the woods road.

'It'll take you twelve miles east, and if you don't get stuck or lost, you'll come out on Route One-fifty-two near Hoag Corners. You turn left – north – and about a mile up One-fifty-two you'll come to another woods road. It's low ground, swampy, mushy. The Willys might do it, might not. I ain't been on that road in five years, I guess. It's the only one I know that goes east toward Vermont and won't be road-blocked off. That second road is gonna bring you out on Highway Twenty-two, north of Cherry Plain and

162

south of the Vermont border. By then you should be out of the worst of it – although I s'pose they'll have your name and pictures on the wire. But we wish you the best. Don't we, Norma?'

'Yes,' Norma said, and the word was almost a sigh. She looked at Charlie. 'You saved your dad's life, little girl. That's the thing to remember.'

'Is it?' Charlie said, and her voice was so perfectly toneless that Norma Manders looked bewildered and a little afraid. Then Charlie tried a hesitant smile and Norma smiled back, relieved.

'Keys are in the Willys, and—' He cocked his head to one side. 'Hark!'

It was the sound of sirens, rising and falling in cycles, still faint but drawing closer.

'It's the FD,' Irv said. 'You better go, if you're goin.'

'Come on, Charlie,' Andy said. She came to him, her eyes red from her tears. The small smile had disappeared like hesitant sunlight behind the clouds, but Andy felt greatly encouraged that it had been there at all. The face she wore was a survivor's face, shocked and wounded. In that moment, Andy wished he had her power; he would use it, and he knew whom he would use it on.

He said, 'Thank you, Irv.'

'I'm sorry,' Charlie said in a small voice. 'About your house and your chickens and . . . and everything else.'

'It sure wasn't your fault, button,' Irv said. 'They brought it on themselves. You watch out for your daddy.'

'All right,' she said.

Andy took her hand and led her around the barn to where the Willys was parked under a shakepole leanto.

The fire sirens were very close by the time he had got it started and driven it across the lawn to the road. The house was an inferno now. Charlie would not look at it. The last Andy saw of the Manderses was in the rearview mirror of the canvas-topped Jeep: Irv leaning against the barn, the piece of white skirting knotted around his wounded arm stained red, Norma sitting beside him. His good arm was around her. Andy waved, and Irv gestured a bit in return with his bad arm. Norma didn't wave, thinking, perhaps, of her mother's china, her secretary, the love letters – all the things of which insurance money is ignorant and always has been.

18

They found the first woods road just where Irv Manders had said they would. Andy put the Jeep in four-wheel drive and turned onto it.

'Hold on, Charlie,' he said. 'We're gonna bounce.'

Charlie held on. Her face was white and listless, and looking at her made Andy nervous. *The cottage*, he thought. *Granther McGee's cottage on Tashmore Pond. If we can only get there and rest. She'll get herself back together and then we'll think about what we should do.*

We'll think about it tomorrow. Like Scarlett said, it's another day.

The Willys roared and pitched its way up the road, which was no more than a two-wheel track with bushes and even a few stunted pines growing along the crown. This land had been logged over maybe ten years ago, and Andy doubted if it had been used since then, except by an occasional hunter. Six miles up it did seem to 'up and die,' and Andy had to stop twice to move trees that had blown down. The second time he looked up from his exertions, heart and head pounding almost sickeningly, and saw a large doe looking at him thoughtfully. She held a moment longer and then was gone into the deeper woods with a flip of her white tail. Andy looked back at Charlie and saw she was watching the deer's progress with something like

164

wonder . . . and he felt encouraged again. A little farther on they found the wheel-ruts again, and around three o'clock they came out on the stretch of two-lane blacktop that was Route 152.

19

Orville Jamieson, scratched and muddy and barely able to walk on his bad ankle, sat by the side of the Baillings Road about a half a mile from the Manders farm and spoke into his walkie-talkie. His message was relayed back to a temporary command post in a van parked in the main street of Hastings Glen. The van had radio equipment with a built-in scrambler and a powerful transmitter. OJ's report was scrambled, boosted, and sent to New York City, where a relay station caught it and sent it on to Longmont, Virginia, where Cap sat in his office, listening.

Cap's face was no longer bright and jaunty, as it had been when he biked to work that morning. OJ's report was nearly unbelievable: they had known the girl had *something*, but this story of sudden carnage and reversal was (at least to Cap) like a bolt of lightning from a clear blue sky. Four to six men dead, the others driven helter-skelter into the woods, half a dozen cars in flames, a house burning to the ground, a civilian wounded and about to blab to anyone and everyone who cared to listen that a bunch of neo-Nazis had turned up on his doorstep with no warrant and had attempted to kidnap a man and a little girl whom he had invited home to lunch.

When OJ finished his report (and he never really did; he only began to repeat himself in a kind of semihysteria), Cap hung up and sat in his deep swivel chair and tried to think. He did not think a covert operation had gone so spectacularly wrong since the Bay of Pigs – and this was on American soil.

165

The office was gloomy and filled with thick shadows now that the sun had got around to the other side of the building, but he didn't turn on the lights. Rachel had buzzed him on the intercom and he had told her curtly he didn't want to talk to anyone, anyone at all.

He felt old.

He heard Wanless saying: *I am talking about the potential for destruction.* Well, it wasn't just a question of potential any longer, was it? *But we're going to have her,* he thought, looking blankly across the room. *Oh yes, we're going to have her.*

He thumbed for Rachel.

'I want to talk to Orville Jamieson as soon as he can be flown here,' he said. 'And I want to talk to General Brackman in Washington, A-one-A priority. We've got a potentially embarrassing situation in New York State, and I want you to tell him that right out.'

'Yes, sir,' Rachel said respectfully.

'I want a meeting with all six subdirectors at nineteen hundred hours. Also A-one-A. And I want to talk to the chief of state police up there in New York.' They had been part of the search sweep, and Cap wanted to point that out to them. If mud was going to be thrown, he would be sure to save back a good, big bucket of it for them. But he also wanted to point out that behind a united front, they might still all be able to come out of this looking fairly decent.

He hesitated and then said, 'And when John Rainbird calls in, tell him I want to talk to him. I have another job for him.'

'Yes, sir.'

Cap let go of the intercom toggle. He sat back in his chair and studied the shadows.

'Nothing has happened that can't be fixed,' he said to the shadows. That had been his motto all his life – not

166

printed in crewel and hung up, not embossed on a copper desk plaque, but it was printed on his heart as truth.

Nothing that can't be fixed. Until tonight, until OJ's report, he had believed that. It was a philosophy that had brought a poor Pennsylvania miner's kid a long way. And he believed it still, although in a momentarily shaken manner. Between Manders and his wife, they probably had relatives scattered from New England to California, and each one was a potential lever. There were enough top-secret files right here in Longmont to ensure that any congressional hearing on Shop methods would be . . . well, a little hard of hearing. The cars and even the agents were only hardware, although it would be a long time before he would really be able to get used to the idea that Al Steinowitz was gone. Who could there possibly be to replace Al? That little kid and her old man were going to pay for what they had done to Al, if for nothing else. He would see to it.

But the girl. Could the girl be fixed?

There were ways. There were methods of containment.

The McGee files were still on the library cart. He got up, went to them, and began thumbing through them restlessly. He wondered where John Rainbird was at this moment.

Washington, D.C.

1

At the moment Cap Hollister had his passing thought about him, John Rainbird was sitting in his room at the Mayflower Hotel watching a television game called *The Crosswits*. He was naked. He sat in the chair with his bare feet neatly together and watched the program. He was waiting for it to get dark. After it got dark, he would begin waiting for it to get late. When it was late, he would begin waiting for it to get early. When it got early and the pulse of the hotel was at its slowest, he would stop waiting and go upstairs to Room 1217 and kill Dr Wanless. Then he would come down here and think about whatever Wanless would have told him before he died, and sometime after the sun came up, he would sleep briefly.

John Rainbird was a man at peace. He was at peace with almost everything – Cap, the Shop, the United States. He was at peace with God, Satan, and the universe. If he was not yet at complete peace with himself, that was only because his pilgrimage was not yet over. He had many coups, many honorable scars. It did not matter that people turned away from him in fear and loathing. It did not matter that he had lost one eye in Vietnam. What they paid him did not matter. He took it and most of it went to buy shoes. He had a great love of shoes. He owned a home in Flagstaff, and although he rarely went there himself, he had all his shoes sent there. When he did get a chance to go to his house, he admired the shoes – Gucci, Bally, Bass, Adidas, Van Donen. Shoes. His house was a strange forest;

shoe trees grew in every room and he would go from room to room admiring the shoefruit that grew on them. But when he was alone, he went barefoot. His father, a full-blooded Cherokee, had been buried barefoot. Someone had stolen his burial moccasins.

Other than shoes, John Rainbird was interested in only two things. One of them was death. His own death, of course; he had been preparing for this inevitability for twenty years or more. Dealing death had always been his business and was the only trade he had ever excelled at. He became more and more interested in it as he grew older, as an artist will become more interested in the qualities and levels of light, as writers will feel for character and nuance like blindmen reading braille. What interested him most was the actual *leaving* . . . the actual exhalation of the soul . . . the exit from the body and what human beings knew as life and the passing into something else. What must it be like to feel yourself slipping away? Did you think it was a dream from which you would awake? Was the Christian devil there with his fork, ready to jam it through your shrieking soul and carry it down to hell like a piece of meat on a shish kebab? Was there joy? Did you know you were going? What is it that the eyes of the dying see?

Rainbird hoped he would have the opportunity to find out for himself. In his business, death was often quick and unexpected, something that happened in the flick of an eye. He hoped that when his own death came, he would have time to prepare and feel everything. More and more lately he had watched the faces of the people he killed, trying to see the secret in the eyes.

Death interested him.

What also interested him was the little girl they were all so concerned with. This Charlene McGee. As far as Cap knew, John Rainbird had only the vaguest knowledge of the McGees and none at all of Lot Six. Actually, Rainbird knew almost as much as Cap himself – something that surely would have marked him for extreme sanction if Cap had known. They suspected that the girl had some great or potentially great power – maybe a whole batch of them. He would like to meet this girl and see what her powers were. He also knew that Andy McGee was what Cap called 'a potential mental dominant,' but that did not concern John Rainbird. He had not yet met a man who could dominate him.

The Crosswits ended. The news came on. None of it was good. John Rainbird sat, not eating, not drinking, not smoking, clean and empty and husked out, and waited for the killing time to come around.

2

Earlier that day Cap had thought uneasily of how silent Rainbird was. Dr Wanless never heard him. He awoke from a sound sleep. He awoke because a finger was tickling him just below the nose. He awoke and saw what appeared to be a monster from a nightmare hulking over his bed. One eye glinted softly in the light from the bathroom, the light he always left on when he was in a strange place. Where the other eye should have been there was only an empty crater.

Wanless opened his mouth to scream, and John Rainbird pinched his nostrils shut with the fingers of one hand and covered his mouth with the other. Wanless began to thrash.

'Shhh,' Rainbird said. He spoke with the pleased indulgence of a mother to her baby at fresh-diaper time.

Wanless struggled harder.

'If you want to live, be still and be quiet,' Rainbird said.

Wanless looked up at him, heaved once, and then lay still.

'Will you be quiet?' Rainbird asked.

Wanless nodded. His face was growing very red.

Rainbird removed his hands and Wanless began to gasp hoarsely. A small rivulet of blood trickled from one nostril.

'Who . . . are you . . . Cap . . . send you?'

'Rainbird,' he said gravely. 'Cap sent me, yes.'

Wanless's eyes were huge in the dark. His tongue snaked out and licked his lips. Lying in his bed with the sheets kicked down around his knuckly ankles, he looked like the world's oldest child.

'I have money,' he whispered very fast. 'Swiss bank account. Lots of money. All yours. Never open my mouth again. Swear before God.'

'It's not your money that I want, Dr Wanless,' Rainbird said.

Wanless gazed up at him, the left side of his mouth sneering madly, his left eyelid drooping and quivering.

'If you would like to be alive when the sun comes up,' Rainbird said, 'you will talk to me, Dr Wanless. You will lecture me. I will be a seminar of one. I will be attentive; a good pupil. And I will reward you with your life, which you will live far away from the view of Cap and the Shop. Do you understand?'

'Yes,' Wanless said hoarsely.

'Do you agree?'

'Yes . . . but what—?'

Rainbird held two fingers to his lips and Dr Wanless hushed immediately. His scrawny chest rose and fell rapidly.

'I am going to say two words,' Rainbird said, 'and then your lecture will begin. It will include everything that you know, everything you suspect, everything you theorize. Are you ready for those two words, Dr Wanless?'

'Yes,' Dr Wanless said.

'Charlene McGee,' Rainbird said, and Dr Wanless began

172

to speak. His words came slowly at first, and then he began to speed up. He talked. He gave Rainbird the complete history of the Lot Six tests and the climactic experiment. Much of what he said Rainbird already knew, but Wanless also filled in a number of blank spots. The professor went through the entire sermon he had given Cap that morning, and here it did not fall on deaf ears. Rainbird listened carefully, frowning sometimes, clapping softly and chuckling at Wanless's toilet-training metaphor. This encouraged Wanless to speak even faster, and when he began to repeat himself, as old men will, Rainbird reached down again, pinched Wanless's nose shut with one hand again, and covered his mouth with the other again.

'Sorry,' Rainbird said.

Wanless bucked and sunfished under Rainbird's weight. Rainbird applied more pressure, and when Wanless's struggles began to lessen, Rainbird abruptly removed the hand he had been using to pinch Wanless's nose shut. The sound of the good doctor's hissing breath was like air escaping from a tire with a big nail in it. His eyes were rolling wildly in their sockets, rolling like the eyes of a fear-maddened horse . . . but they were still too hard to see.

Rainbird seized the collar of Dr Wanless's pajama jacket and yanked him sideways on the bed so that the cold white light from the bathroom shone directly across his face.

Then he pinched the doctor's nostrils closed again.

A man can sometimes survive for upward of nine minutes without permanent brain damage if his air is cut off and he remains completely quiet; a woman, with slightly greater lung capacity and a slightly more efficient carbon-dioxide-disposal system, may last ten or twelve. Of course, struggling and terror cuts that survival time a great deal.

Dr Wanless struggled briskly for forty seconds, and then his efforts to save himself began to flag. His hands beat

173

lightly at the twisted granite that was John Rainbird's face. His heels drummed a muffled retreat tattoo on the carpeting. He began to drool against Rainbird's callused palm.

This was the moment.

Rainbird leaned forward and studied Wanless's eyes with a childlike eagerness.

But it was the same, always the same. The eyes seemed to lose their fear and fill instead with a great puzzlement. Not wonder, not dawning comprehension or realization or awe, just puzzlement. For a moment those two puzzled eyes fixed on John Rainbird's one, and Rainbird knew he was being seen. Fuzzily, perhaps, fading back and back as the doctor went out and out, but he was being *seen*. Then there was nothing but glaze. Dr Joseph Wanless was no longer staying at the Mayflower Hotel; Rainbird was sitting on this bed with a life-size doll.

He sat still, one hand still over the doll's mouth, the other pinching the doll's nostrils tightly together. It was best to be sure. He would remain so for another ten minutes.

He thought about what Wanless had told him concerning Charlene McGee. Was it possible that a small child could have such a power? He supposed it might be. In Calcutta he had seen a man put knives into his body – his legs, his belly, his chest, his neck – and then pull them out, leaving no wounds. It might be possible. And it was certainly . . . interesting.

He thought about these things, and then found himself wondering what it would be like to kill a child. He had never knowingly done such a thing (although once he had placed a bomb on an airliner and the bomb had exploded, killing all sixty-seven aboard, and perhaps one or more of them had been children, but that was not the same thing; it was impersonal). It was not a business in which the death of children was often required. They were not, after all, some terrorist organization like the IRA or the PLO, no matter how much some people – some of the yellowbellies in the Congress, for instance – would like to believe they were.

They were, after all, a scientific organization.

Perhaps with a child the result would be different. There might be another expression in the eyes at the end, something besides the puzzlement that made him feel so empty and so – yes, it was true – so sad.

He might discover part of what he needed to know in the death of a child.

A child like this Charlene McGee.

'My life is like the straight roads in the desert,' John Rainbird said softly. He looked absorbedly into the dull blue marbles that had been the eyes of Dr Wanless. 'But your life is no road at all, my friend . . . my good friend.'

He kissed Wanless first on one cheek and then on the other. Then he pulled him back onto the bed and threw a sheet over him. It came down softly, like a parachute, and outlined Wanless's jutting and now tideless nose in white lawn.

Rainbird left the room.

That night he thought about the girl who could supposedly light fires. He thought about her a great deal. He wondered where she was, what she was thinking, what she was dreaming. He felt very tender about her, very protective.

By the time he drifted off to sleep, at just past six A.M., he was sure: the girl would be his.

Tashmore, Vermont

1

Andy and Charlie McGee arrived at the cottage on Tashmore Pond two days after the burning at the Manders farm. The Willys hadn't been in great shape to start with, and the muddy plunge over the woods roads that Irv had directed them onto had done little to improve it.

When dusk came on the endless day that had begun in Hastings Glen, they had been less then twenty yards from the end of the second – and worse – of the two woods roads. Below them, but screened off by a heavy growth of bushes, was Route 22. Although they couldn't see the road, they could hear the occasional swish and whine of passing cars and trucks. They slept that night in the Willys, bundled up for warmth. They set out again the next morning – yesterday morning – at just past five A.M., with daylight nothing but a faint white tone in the east.

Charlie looked pallid and listless and used up. She hadn't asked him what would happen to them if the roadblocks had been shifted east. It was just as well, because if the roadblocks had been shifted, they would be caught, and that was simply all there was to it. There was no question of ditching the Willys, either; Charlie was in no shape to walk, and for that matter, neither was he.

So Andy had pulled out onto the highway and all that day in October they had jigged and jogged along secondary roads under a white sky that promised rain but never quite delivered it. Charlie slept a great deal, and Andy worried about her – worried that she was using the sleep in an unhealthy way, using it to flee what had happened instead of trying to come to terms with it.

He stopped twice at roadside diners and picked up burgers and fries. The second time he used the five-dollar bill that the van driver, Jim Paulson, had laid on him. Most of the remaining phone change was gone. He must have lost some of it out of his pockets during that crazy time at the Manders place, but he didn't recall it. Something else was gone as well; those frightening numb places on his face had faded away sometime during the night. Those he didn't mind losing.

Most of Charlie's share of the burgers and fries went uneaten.

Last night they had driven into a highway rest area about an hour after dark. The rest area was deserted. It was autumn, and the season of the Winnebagos had passed for another year. A rustic woodburned sign read: NO CAMP-ING   NO FIRES   LEASH YOUR DOG $500 FINE FOR LITTER-ING.

'They're real sports around here,' Andy muttered, and drove the Willys down the slope beyond the far edge of the gravel parking lot and into a copse beside a small, chuckling stream. He and Charlie got out and went wordlessly down to the water. The overcast held, but it was mild; there were no stars visible and the night seemed extraordinarily dark. They sat down for a while and listened to the brook tell its tale. He took Charlie's hand and that was when she began to cry – great, tearing sobs that seemed to be trying to rip her apart.

He took her in his arms and rocked her. 'Charlie,' he murmured. 'Charlie, Charlie, don't. Don't cry.'

'Please don't make me do it again, Daddy,' she wept. 'Because if you said to I'd do it and then I guess I'd kill myself, so please . . . please . . . never . . .'

'I love you,' he said. 'Be quiet and stop talking about killing yourself. That's crazy-talk.'

'No,' she said. 'It isn't. Promise, Daddy.'

He thought for a long time and then said slowly: 'I don't know if I can, Charlie. But I promise to try. Will that be good enough?'

Her troubled silence was answer enough.

'I get scared, too,' he said softly. 'Daddies get scared, too. You better believe it.'

They spent that night, too, in the cab of the Willys. They were back on the road by six o'clock in the morning. The clouds had broken up, and by ten o'clock it had become a flawless, Indian-summery day. Not long after they crossed the Vermont state line they saw men riding ladders like masts in tossing apple trees and trucks in the orchards filled with bushel baskets of Macs.

At eleven-thirty they turned off Route 34 and onto a narrow, rutted dirt road marked PRIVATE PROPERTY, and something in Andy's chest loosened. They had made it to Granther McGee's place. They were here.

They drove slowly down toward the pond, a distance of perhaps a mile and a half. October leaves, red and gold, swirled across the road in front of the Jeep's blunt nose. Just as glints of water began to show through the trees, the road branched in two. A heavy steel chain hung across the smaller branch, and from the chain a rust-flecked yellow sign: NO TRESPASSING BY ORDER OF COUNTY SHERIFF. Most of the rust flecks had formed around six or eight dimples in the metal, and Andy guessed that some summer kid had spent a few minutes working off his boredom by plinking at the sign with his .22. But that had been years ago.

He got out of the Willys and took his keyring out of his pocket. There was a leather tab on the ring with his initials. A.McG., almost obliterated. Vicky had given him that piece of leather for Christmas one year – a Christmas before Charlie had been born.

He stood by the chain for a moment, looking at the leather tab, then at the keys themselves. There were almost two dozen of them. Keys were funny things; you could index a life by the keys that had a way of collecting on your keyring. He supposed that some people, undoubtedly people who had realized a higher degree of organization than he had, simply threw their old keys away, just as those same organizational types made a habit of cleaning their wallets out every six months or so. Andy had never done either.

Here was the key that opened the east-wing door of Prince Hall back in Harrison, where his office had been. His key to the office itself. To the English Department office. Here was the key to the house in Harrison that he had seen for the last time on the day the Shop killed his wife and kidnapped his daughter. Two or three more he couldn't even identify. Keys were funny things, all right.

His vision blurred. Suddenly he missed Vicky, and needed her as he hadn't needed her since those first black weeks on the road with Charlie. He was so tired, so scared, and so full of anger. In that moment, if he'd had every employee of the Shop lined up in front of him along Granther's road, and if someone had handed him a Thompson submachine gun . . .

'Daddy?' It was Charlie's voice, anxious. 'Can't you find the key?'

'Yes, I've got it,' he said. It was among the rest, a small Yale key on which he had scratched T.P. for Tashmore Pond with his jackknife. The last time they had been here was the year Charlie was born, and now Andy had to wiggle the key a little before the stiff tumblers would turn. Then the lock popped open and he laid the chain down on the carpet of fall leaves.

180

He drove the Willys through and then repadlocked the chain.

The road was in bad shape, Andy was glad to see. When they came up regularly every summer, they would stay three or four weeks and he would always find a couple of days to work on the road – get a load of gravel from Sam Moore's gravel pit and put it down in the worst of the ruts, cut back the brush, and get Sam himself to come down with his old dragger and even it out. The camp road's other, broader fork led down to almost two dozen camp homes and cottages strung along the shorefront, and those folks had their Road Association, annual dues. August business meeing and all (although the business meeting was really only an excuse to get really loaded before Labor Day came and put an end to another summer), but Granther's place was the only one down this way, because Granther himself had bought all the land for a song back in the depths of the Depression.

In the old days they'd had a family car, a Ford wagon. He doubted if the old wagon would have made it down here now, and even the Willys, with its high axles, bottomed out once or twice. Andy didn't mind at all. It meant that no one had been down here.

'Will there be electricity, Daddy?' Charlie asked.

'No,' he said, 'and no phone, either. We don't dare get the electricity turned on, kiddo. It'd be like holding up a sign saying HERE WE ARE. But there are kerosene lamps and two range-oil drums. If the stuff hasn't been ripped off, that is.' That worried him a little. Since the last time they'd been down here, the price of range oil had gone up enough to make the theft worthwhile, he supposed.

'Will there be—' Charlie began.

'Holy shit,' Andy said. He jammed on the brakes. A tree had fallen across the road up ahead, a big old birch pushed down by some winter storm. 'I guess we walk from here.

It's only a mile or so anyway. We'll hike it.' Later he would have to come back with Granther's one-handed buck and cut the tree up. He didn't want to leave Irv's Willys parked here. It was too open.

He ruffled her hair. 'Come on.'

They got out of the Willys, and Charlie scooted effortlessly under the birch while Andy clambered carefully over, trying not to skewer himself anywhere important. The leaves crunched agreeably under their feet as they walked on, and the woods were aromatic with fall. A squirrel looked down at them from a tree, watching their progress closely. And now they began to see bright slashes of blue again through the trees.

'What did you start to say back there when we came to the tree?' Andy asked her.

'If there would be enough oil for a long time. In case we stay the winter.'

'No, but there's enough to start with. And I'm going to cut a lot of wood. You'll haul plenty of it, too.'

'Ten minutes later the road widened into a clearing on the shore of Tashmore Pond and they were there. They both stood quietly for a moment. Andy didn't know what Charlie was feeling, but for him there was a rush of remembrance too total to be called anything so mild as nostalgia. Mixed up in the memories was his dream of three mornings ago – the boat, the squirming nightcrawler, even the tire patches on Granther's boots.

The cottage was five rooms, wood over fieldstone base. A deck jutted out toward the lake, and a stone pier poked out into the water itself. Except for the drifts of leaves and the blowdowns of three winters, the place hadn't changed a bit. He almost expected Granther himself to come strolling out, wearing one of those green and black checked shirts, waving and bellowing for him to come on up, asking

182

him if he'd got his fishing license yet, because the brown trout were still biting good around dusk.

It had been a good place, a safe place. Far across Tashmore Pond, the pines glimmered gray-green in the sunshine. *Stupid trees,* Granther had said once, *don't even know the difference between summer and winter.* The only sign of civilization on the far side was still the Bradford Town Landing. No one had put up a shopping center or an amusement park. The wind still talked in the trees here. The green shingles still had a mossy, woodsy look, and pine needles still drifted in the roof angles and in the cup of the wooden gutter. He had been a boy here, and Granther had shown him how to bait a hook. He had had his own bedroom here, paneled in good maple, and he had dreamed a boy's dreams in a narrow bed and had awakened to the sound of water lapping the pier. He had been a man here as well, making love to his wife in the double bed that had once belonged to Granther and his wife – that silent and somehow baleful woman who was a member of the American Society of Atheists and would explain to you, should you ask, the Thirty Greatest Inconsistencies in the King James Bible, or, should you prefer, the Laughable Fallacy of the Clockspring Theory of the Universe, all with the thudding, irrevocable logic of a dedicated preacher.

'You miss Mom, don't you?' Charlie said in a forlorn voice.

'Yeah,' he said. 'Yeah, I do.'

'Me too,' Charlie said. 'You had fun here, didn't you?'

'We did,' he agreed. 'Come on, Charlie.'

She held back, looking at him.

'Daddy, will things ever be all right for us again? Will I be able to go to school and things?'

He considered a lie, but a lie was a poor answer. 'I don't know,' he said. He tried to smile, but it wouldn't come; he found he could not even stretch his lips convincingly. 'I don't know, Charlie.'

2

Granther's tools were all still neatly racked in the toolshed portion of the boathouse, and Andy found a bonus he had hoped for but had told himself not to hope for too much: nearly two cords of wood, neatly split and time-seasoned in the bay beneath the boathouse. Most of it he had split himself, and it was still under the sheet of ragged, dirty canvas he had thrown over it. Two cords wouldn't take them through the winter, but by the time he finished carving up the blowdowns around the camp and the birch back on the road, they would be well set.

He took the bucksaw back up to the fallen tree and cut it up enough to get the Willys through. By then it was nearly dark, and he was tired and hungry. No one had bothered to rip off the well-stocked pantry, either; if there had been vandals or thieves on snowmobiles over the last six winters, they had stuck to the more populous southern end of the lake. There were five shelves packed with Campbell's soups and Wyman's sardines and Dinty Moore beef stew and all sorts of canned vegetables. There was also still half a case of Rival dog food on the floor – a legacy of Granther's good old dog Bimbo – but Andy didn't think it would come to that.

While Charlie looked at the books on the shelves in the big living room, Andy went into the small root cellar that was three steps down from the pantry, scratched a wooden match on one of the beams, stuck his finger into the knothole in one of the boards that lined the sides of the little dirt-floored room, and pulled. The board came out and Andy looked inside. After a moment he grinned. Inside the cobweb-festooned little bolt-hole were four mason jars filled with a clear, slightly oily-looking liquid that was one-hundred-percent-pure white lightning – what Granther called 'father's mule-kick.'

The match burned Andy's fingers. He shook it out and lit a second. Like the dour New England preachers of old (from whom she had been a direct descendant), Hulda McGee had no liking, understanding, or tolerance for the simple and slightly stupid male pleasures. She had been a Puritan atheist, and this had been Granther's little secret, which he had shared with Andy the year before he died.

Besides the white lightning, there was a caddy for poker chips. Andy pulled it out and felt in the slot at the top. There was a crackling sound, and he pulled out a thin sheaf of bills – a few tens and fives and some ones. Maybe eighty dollars all told. Granther's weakness had been seven-card stud, and this was what he called his 'struttin money.'

The second match burned his fingers, and Andy shook it out. Working in the dark, he put the poker chips back, money and all. It was good to know it was there. He replaced the board and went back through the pantry.

'Tomato soup do you?' he asked Charlie. Wonder of wonders, she had found all the Pooh books on one of the shelves and was currently somewhere in the Hundred Acre Wood with Pooh and Eeyore.

'Sure,' she said, not looking up.

He made a big pot of tomato soup and opened them each a tin of sardines. He lit one of the kerosene lamps after carefully drawing the drapes and put it in the middle of the dining table. They sat down and ate, neither of them talking much. Afterward he smoked a cigarette, lighting it over the chimney of the lamp. Charlie discovered the card drawer in Grandma's Welsh dresser; there were eight or nine decks in there, each of them missing a jack or a deuce or something, and she spent the rest of the evening sorting them and playing with them while Andy prowled through the camp.

Later, tucking her into bed, he asked her how she felt.

'Safe,' she said with no hesitation at all. 'Goodnight, Daddy.'

If it was good enough for Charlie, it was good enough for him. He sat with her awhile, but she dropped off to sleep quickly and with no trouble, and he left after propping her door open so he would hear her if she became restless in the night.

3

Before turning in, Andy went back down to the root cellar, got one of the jars of white lightning, poured himself a small knock in a juice glass, and went out through the sliding door and onto the deck. He sat in one of the canvas director's chairs (mildewy smell; he wondered briefly if something could be done about that) and looked out at the dark, moving bulk of the lake. It was a trifle chilly, but a couple of small sips at Granther's mule-kick took care of the chill quite nicely. For the first time since that terrible chase up Third Avenue, he too felt safe and at rest.

He smoked and looked out across Tashmore Pond.

Safe and at rest, but not for the first time since New York City. For the first time since the Shop had come back into their lives on that terrible August day fourteen months ago. Since then they had either been running or hunkering down, and either way there was no rest.

He remembered talking to Quincey on the telephone with the smell of burned carpeting in his nostrils. He in Ohio, Quincey out there in California, which in his few letters he always called the Magic Earthquake Kingdom. *Yes, it's a good thing,* Quincey had said. *Or they might put them in two little rooms where they could work full-time to keep*

two hundred and twenty million Americans safe and free. . . .
I bet they'd just want to take that child and put it in a little
room and see if it could help make the world safe for democracy.
And I think that's all I want to say, old buddy, except . . .
keep your head down.

He thought he had been scared then. He hadn't known
what scared was. Scared was coming home and finding
your wife dead with her fingernails pulled out. They had
pulled out her nails to find out where Charlie was. Charlie
had been spending two days and two nights at her friend
Terri Dugan's house. A month or so later they had been
planning to have Terri over to their house for a similar
length of time. Vicky had called it the Great Swap of 1980.

Now, sitting on the deck and smoking, Andy could
reconstruct what had happened, although then he had
existed in nothing but a blur of grief and panic and rage:
it had been the blindest good luck (or perhaps a little more
than luck) that had enabled him to catch up with them at
all.

They had been under surveillance, the whole family.
Must have been for some time. And when Charlie hadn't
come home from summer daycamp that Wednesday afternoon, and didn't show up on Thursday or Thursday
evening either, they must have decided that Andy and
Vicky had tumbled to the surveillance. Instead of discovering that Charlie was doing no more than staying at a
friend's house not two miles away, they must have decided
that they had taken their daughter and gone underground.

It was a crazy, stupid mistake, but it hadn't been the
first such on the Shop's part – according to an article Andy
had read in *Rolling Stone*, the Shop had been involved and
heavily influential in precipitating a bloodbath over an
airplane hijacking by Red Army terrorists (the hijack had
been aborted – at the cost of sixty lives), in selling heroin
to the Organization in return for information on mostly

187

harmless Cuban-American groups in Miami, and in the communist takeover of a Caribbean island that had once been known for its multimillion-dollar beachfront hotels and its voodoo-practicing population.

With such a series of colossal gaffes under the Shop's belt, it became less difficult to understand how the agents employed to keep watch on the McGee family could mistake a child's two nights at a friend's house as a run for the tall timber. As Quincey would have said (and maybe he had), if the most efficient of the Shop's thousand or more employees had to go to work in the private sector, they would have been drawing unemployment benefits before their probationary periods were up.

But there had been crazy mistakes on both sides, Andy reflected – and if the bitterness in that thought had become slightly vague and diffuse with the passage of time, it had once been sharp enough to draw blood, a many-tined bitterness, with each sharp point tipped with the curare of guilt. He had been scared by the things Quincey implied on the phone that day Charlie tripped and fell down the stairs, but apparently he hadn't been scared enough. If he had been, perhaps they *would* have gone underground.

He had discovered too late that the human mind can become hypnotized when a life, or the life of a family, begins to drift out of the normal range of things and into a fervid fantasy-land that you are usually asked to accept only in sixty-minute bursts on TV or maybe for one-hundred-ten-minute sittings in the local Cinema I.

In the wake of his conversation with Quincey, a peculiar feeling had gradually crept over him: it began to seem that he was constantly stoned. A tap on his phone? People watching them? A possibility that they might all be scooped up and dropped into the basement rooms of some government complex? There was such a tendency to smile a silly smile and just watch these things loom up, such a tendency to do the civilized thing and pooh-pooh your own instincts. . . .

Out on Tashmore Pond there was a sudden dark flurry and a number of ducks took off into the night, headed west. A half-moon was rising, casting a dull silver glow across their wings as they went. Andy lit another cigarette. He was smoking too much, but he would get a chance to go cold turkey soon enough; he had only four or five left.

Yes, he had suspected there was a tap on the phone. Sometimes there would be an odd double click after you picked it up and said hello. Once or twice, when he had been talking to a student who had called to ask about an assignment or to one of his colleagues, the connection had been mysteriously broken. He had suspected that there might be bugs in the house, but he had never torn the place apart looking for them (had he suspected he might find them?). And several times he had suspected – no, had been almost sure – that they were being watched.

They had lived in the Lakeland district of Harrison, and Lakeland was the sublime archetype of suburbia. On a drunk night you could circle six or eight blocks for hours, just looking for your own house. The people who were their neighbors worked for the IBM plant outside town, Ohio Semi-Conductor in town, or taught at the college. You could have drawn two ruler-straight lines across an average-family-income sheet, the lower line at eighteen and a half thousand and the upper one at maybe thirty thousand, and almost everyone in Lakeland would have fallen in the area between.

You got to know people. You nodded on the street to Mrs Bacon, who had lost her husband and had since been remarried to vodka – and she looked it; the honeymoon with that particular gentleman was playing hell with her face and figure. You tipped a V at the two girls with the white Jag who were renting the house on the corner of

Jasmine Street and Lakeland Avenue – and wondered what spending the night with the two of them would be like. You talked baseball with Mr Hammond on Laurel Lane as he everlastingly trimmed his hedges. Mr Hammond was with IBM ('Which stands for I've Been Moved,' he would tell you endlessly as the electric clippers hummed and buzzed), originally from Atlanta and a rabid Atlanta Braves fan. He loathed Cincinnati's Big Red Machine, which did not exactly endear him to the neighborhood. Not that Hammond gave a shit. He was just waiting for IBM to hand him a fresh set of walking papers.

But Mr Hammond was not the point. Mrs Bacon wasn't the point, nor were those two luscious peaches in their white Jag with the dull red primer paint around the headlights. The point was that after a while your brain formed its own subconscious subset: people who belong in Lakeland.

But in the months before Vicky was killed and Charlie snatched from the Dugans' house, there had been people around who didn't belong to that subset. Andy had dismissed them, telling himself it would be foolish to alarm Vicky just because talking to Quincey had made him paranoid.

The people in the light-gray van. The man with the red hair that he had seen slouched behind the wheel of an AMC Matador one night and then behind the wheel of a Plymouth Arrow one night about two weeks later and then in the shotgun seat of the gray van about ten days after that. Too many salesmen came to call. There had been evenings when they had come home from a day out or from taking Charlie to see the latest Disney epic when he had got the feeling that someone had been in the house, that things had been moved around the tiniest bit.

That feeling of being watched.

But he hadn't believed it would go any further than

watching. That had been *his* crazy mistake. He was still not entirely convinced that it had been a case of panic on their part. They might have been planning to snatch Charlie and himself, killing Vicky because she was relatively useless – who really needed a low-grade psychic whose big trick for the week was closing the refrigerator door from across the room?

Nevertheless, the job had a reckless, hurry-up quality to it that made him think that Charlie's surprise disappearance had made them move more quickly than they had intended. They might have waited if it had been Andy who dropped out of sight, but it hadn't been. It had been Charlie, and she was the one they were really interested in. Andy was sure of that now.

He got up and stretched, listening to the bones in his spine crackle. Time he went to bed, time he stopped hashing over these old, hurtful memories. He was not going to spend the rest of his life blaming himself for Vicky's death. He had only been an accessory before the fact, after all. And the rest of his life might not be that long, either. The action on Irv Manders's porch hadn't been lost on Andy McGee. They had meant to waste him. It was only Charlie they wanted now.

He went to bed, and after a while he slept. His dreams were not easy ones. Over and over he saw that trench of fire running across the beaten dirt of the dooryard, saw it divide to make a fairy-ring around the chopping block, saw the chickens going up like living incendiaries. In the dream, he felt the heat capsule around him, building and building.

She said she wasn't going to make fires anymore.

And maybe that was best.

Outside, the cold October moon shone down on Tashmore Pond on Bradford, New Hampshire, across the

water, and on the rest of New England. To the south, it
shone down on Longmont, Virginia.

4

Sometimes Andy McGee had feelings – hunches of
extraordinary vividness. Ever since the experiment in Jason
Gearneigh Hall. He didn't know if the hunches were a low-
grade sort of precognition or not, but he had learned to
trust them when he got them.

Around noon on that August day in 1980, he got a bad
one.

It began during lunch in the Buckeye Room, the faculty
lounge on the top floor of the Union building. He could
even pinpoint the exact moment. He had been having
creamed chicken on rice with Ev O'Brian, Bill Wallace,
and Don Grabowski, all in the English Department. Good
friends, all of them. And as usual, someone had brought
along a Polish joke for Don, who collected them. It had
been Ev's joke, something about being able to tell a Polish
ladder from a regular one because the Polish ladder had
the word STOP lettered on the top rung. All of them were
laughing when a small, very calm voice spoke up in Andy's
mind.

(*something's wrong at home*)

That was all. That was enough. It began to build up
almost the same way that his headaches built up when he
overused the push and tipped himself over. Only this
wasn't a head thing; all his emotions seemed to be tangling
themselves up, almost lazily, as if they were yarn and some
bad-tempered cat had been let loose along the runs of his
nervous system to play with them and snarl them up.

He stopped feeling good. The creamed chicken lost
whatever marginal appeal it had had to begin with. His
stomach began to flutter, and his heart was beating rapidly,

as if he had just had a bad scare. And then the fingers of his right hand began abruptly to throb, as if he had got them jammed in a door.

Abruptly he stood up. Cold sweat was breaking on his forehead.

'Look, I don't feel so good,' he said. 'Can you take my one o'clock, Bill?'

'Those aspiring poets? Sure. No problem. What's wrong?'

'I don't know. Something I ate, maybe.'

'You look sort of pale,' Don Grabowski said. 'You ought to cruise over to the infirmary, Andy.'

'I may do that,' Andy said.

He left, but with no intention whatever of going to the infirmary. It was quarter past twelve, the late-summer campus drowsing through the last week of the final summer session. He raised a hand to Ev, Bill, and Don as he hurried out. He had not seen any of them since that day.

He stopped on the Union's lower level, let himself into a telephone booth, and called home. There was no answer. No real reason why there should have been; with Charlie at the Dugans, Vicky could have been out shopping, having her hair done, she could have been over at Tammy Upmore's house or even having lunch with Eileen Bacon. Nevertheless, his nerves cranked up another notch. They were nearly screaming now.

He left the Union building and half walked, half ran to the station wagon, which was in the Prince Hall parking lot. He drove across town to Lakeland. His driving was jerky and poor. He jumped lights, tailgated, and came close to knocking a hippie off his ten-speed Olympia. The hippie gave him the finger. Andy barely noticed. His heart was triphammering now. He felt as if he had taken a hit of speed.

They lived on Conifer Place – in Lakeland, as in so many

suburban developments built in the fifties, most of the streets seemed named for trees or shrubs. In the midday August heat, the street seemed queerly deserted. It only added to his feeling that something bad had happened. The street looked wider with so few cars parked along the curbs. Even the few kids playing here and there could not dispel that strange feeling of desertion; most of them were eating lunch or over at the playground. Mrs Flynn from Laurel Lane walked past with a bag of groceries in a wheeled caddy, her paunch as round and tight as a soccer ball under her avocado-colored stretch pants. All up and down the street, lawn sprinklers twirled lazily, fanning water onto the grass and rainbows into the air.

Andy drove the offside wheels of the wagon up over the curb and then slammed on the brakes hard enough to lock his seatbelt momentarily and to make the wagon's nose dip toward the pavement. He turned off the engine with the gearshift still in Drive, something he never did, and went up the cracked cement walk that he kept meaning to patch and somehow never seemed to get around to. His heels clacked meaninglessly. He noticed that the venetian blind over the big living-room picture window (*mural window*, the realtor who had sold them the house called it, *here ya gotcha basic mural window*) was drawn, giving the house a closed, secretive aspect he didn't like. Did she usually pull the blind? To keep as much of the summer heat out as possible, maybe? He didn't know. He realized there were a great many things he didn't know about her life when he was away.

He reached for the doorknob, but it didn't turn; it only slipped through his fingers. Did she lock the door when he was gone? He didn't believe it. That wasn't Vicky. His worry – no, it was terror now – increased. And yet there was one moment (which he would never admit to himself later), one small moment when he felt nothing but an urge

194

to turn away from that locked door. Just hightail it. Never mind Vicky, or Charlie, or the weak justifications that would come later.

Just run.

Instead, he groped in his pocket for his keys.

In his nervousness he dropped them and had to bend to pick them up – car keys, the key to the east wing of Prince Hall, the blackish key that unlocked the chain he put across Granther's road at the end of each summer visit. Keys had a funny way of accumulating.

He plucked his housekey from the bunch and unlocked the door. He went in and shut it behind him. The light in the living room was a low, sick yellow. It was hot. And still. Oh God it was so still.

'Vicky?'

No answer. And all that no answer meant was that she wasn't here. She had put on her boogie shoes, as she liked to say, and had gone marketing or visiting. Except that she wasn't doing either of those things. He felt sure of it. And his hand, his right hand . . . why were the fingers throbbing so?

'Vicky!'

He went into the kitchen. There was a small Formica table out there with three chairs. He and Vicky and Charlie usually ate their breakfast in the kitchen. One of the chairs now lay on its side like a dead dog. The salt shaker had overturned and salt was spilled across the table's surface. Without thinking about what he was doing, Andy pinched some of it between the thumb and first finger of his left hand and tossed it back over his shoulder, muttering under his breath, as both his father and his Granther had done before him, 'Salt salt malt malt bad luck stay away.'

There was a pot of soup on the Hotpoint. It was cold. The empty soup can stood on the counter. Lunch for one. But where was she?

195

'Vicky!' he hollered down the stairs. Dark down there. The laundry room and the family room, which ran the length of the house.

No answer.

He looked around the kitchen again. Neat and tidy. Two of Charlie's drawings, made at the Vacation Bible School she had attended in July, held on the refrigerator with small plastic vegetables that had magnetic bases. An electric bill and a phone bill stuck on the spike with the motto PAY THESE LAST written across the base. Everything in its place and a place for everything.

Except the chair was overturned. Except the salt was spilled.

There was no spit in his mouth, none at all. His mouth was as dry and slick as chrome on a summer day.

Andy went upstairs, looked through Charlie's room, their room, the guest room. Nothing. He went back through the kitchen, flicked on the stairway light, and went downstairs. Their Maytag washer gaped open. The dryer fixed him with one glassy porthole eye. Between them, on the wall, hung a sampler Vicky had bought somewhere; it read HONEY, WE'RE ALL WASHED UP. He went into the family room and fumbled for the light switch, fingers brushing at the wall, crazily sure that at any moment unknown cold fingers would close over his and guide them to the switch. Then he found the plate at last, and the fluorescent bars set into the Armstrong ceiling glowed alive.

This was a good room. He had spent a lot of time down here, fixing things up, smiling at himself all the time because, in the end, he had become all those things that as undergraduates they had sworn they would not become. All three of them had spent a lot of time down here. There was a TV built into the wall, a Ping-Pong table, an oversized backgammon board. More board games were cased against one wall, there were some coffee-table-sized books ranged along a low table that Vicky had made from barnboard. One wall had been dressed in paperbacks. Hung on the walls were several framed and matted afghan squares that Vicky had knitted; she joked that she was great at individual squares but simply didn't have the stamina to knit a whole damn blanket. There were Charlie's books in a special kid-sized bookcase, all of them carefully arranged in alphabetical order, which Andy had taught her one boring snowy night two winters before and which still fascinated her.

A good room.

An empty room.

He tried to feel relief. The premonition, hunch, whatever you wanted to call it, had been wrong. She just wasn't here. He snapped off the light and went back into the laundry room.

The washing machine, a front-loader they had picked up at a yard sale for sixty bucks, still gaped open. He shut it without thinking, much as he had tossed a pinch of the spilled salt over his shoulder. There was blood on the washer's glass window. Not much. Only three or four drops. But it was blood.

Andy stood staring at it. It was cooler down here, too cool, it was like a morgue down here. He looked at the floor. There was more blood on the floor. It wasn't even dry. A little sound, a soft, squealing whisper, came from his throat.

He began to walk around the laundry room, which was nothing but a small alcove with white plaster walls. He opened the clothes hamper. It was empty but for one sock. He looked in the cubbyhole under the sink. Nothing but Lestoil and Tide and Biz and Spic 'n Span. He looked under the stairs. Nothing there but cobwebs and the plastic leg of one of Charlie's older dolls – that dismembered limb lying patiently down here and waiting for rediscovery for God knew how long.

He opened the door between the washer and the dryer and the ironing board whistled down with a ratchet and a crash and there beneath it, her legs tied up so that her knees were just below her chin, her eyes open and glazed and dead, was Vicky Tomlinson McGee with a cleaning rag stuffed in her mouth. There was a thick and sickening smell of Pledge furniture polish in the air.

He made a low gagging noise and stumbled backward. His hands flailed, as if to drive this terrible vision away, and one of them struck the control panel of the dryer and it whirred into life. Clothes began to tumble and click inside. Andy screamed. And then he ran. He ran up the stairs and stumbled going around the corner into the kitchen and sprawled flat and bumped his forehead on the linoleum. He sat up, breathing hard.

It came back. It came back in slow motion, like a football instant replay where you see the quarterback sacked or the winning pass caught. It haunted his dreams in the days that came later. The door swinging open, the ironing board falling down to the horizontal with a ratcheting sound, reminding him somehow of a guillotine, his wife crammed into the space beneath and in her mouth a rag that had been used to polish the furniture. It came back in a kind of total recall and he knew he was going to scream again and so he slammed his forearm into his mouth and he bit it and the sound that came out was a fuzzy, blocked howl. He did that twice, and something came out of him and he was calm. It was the false calm of shock, but it could be used. The amorphous fear and the unfocused terror fell away. The throbbing in his right hand was gone. And the thought that stole into his mind now was as cold as the calmness that had settled over him, as cold as the shock, and that thought was *CHARLIE*.

He got up, started for the telephone, and then turned back to the stairs. He stood at the top for a moment, biting at his lips, steeling himself, and then he went back down. The dryer turned and turned. There was nothing in there but a pair of his jeans, and it was the big brass button at the waist that made that clicking, clinking sound as they turned and fell, turned and fell. Andy shut the dryer off and looked into the ironing-board closet.

'Vicky,' he said softly.

She stared at him with her dead eyes, his wife. He had walked with her, held her hand, entered her body in the dark of night. He found himself remembering the night she had drunk too much at a faculty party and he had held her head while she threw up. And that memory became the day he had been washing the station wagon and he had gone into the garage for a moment to get the can of Turtle Wax and she had picked up the hose and had run up behind him and stuffed the hose down the back of his pants. He remembered getting married and kissing her in front of everyone, relishing that kiss, her mouth, her ripe, soft mouth.

'Vicky,' he said again, and uttered a long, trembling sigh.

He pulled her out and worked the rag from her mouth. Her head lolled limp on her shoulders. He saw that the blood had come from her right hand, where some of her fingernails had been pulled. There was a small trickle of blood from one of her nostrils, but none anywhere else. Her neck had been broken by a single hard blow.

'Vicky,' he whispered.

Charlie, his mind whispered back.

In the still calm that now filled his head, he understood that Charlie had become the important thing, the only important thing. Recriminations were for the future.

He went back into the family room, not bothering to

turn on the light this time. Across the room, by the Ping-Pong table, was a couch with a drop cloth over it. He took the drop cloth and went back into the laundry room and covered Vicky with it. Somehow, the immobile shape of her under the sofa's drop cloth was worse. It held him nearly hypnotized. Would she never move again? Could that be?

He uncovered her face and kissed her lips. They were cold.

They pulled her nails, his mind marveled. *Jesus Christ, they pulled her nails*.

And he knew why. They wanted to know where Charlie was. Somehow they had lost track of her when she went to Terri Dugan's house instead of coming home after day-camp. They had panicked, and now the watching phase was over. Vicky was dead – either on purpose or because some Shop operative had got overzealous. He knelt beside Vicky and thought it was possible that, prodded by her fear, she had done something rather more spectacular than shutting the fridge door from across the room. She might have shoved one of them away or knocked the feet out from beneath one of them. Too bad she hadn't had enough to throw them into the wall at about fifty miles an hour, he thought.

It could have been that they knew just enough to make them nervous, he supposed. Maybe they had even been given specific orders: *The woman may be extremely danger-ous. If she does something – anything – to jeopardize the operation, get rid of her. Quick.*

Or maybe they just didn't like leaving witnesses. Something more than their share of the taxpayer's dollar was at stake, after all.

But the blood. He should be thinking about the blood, which hadn't even been dry when he discovered it, only tacky. They hadn't been gone long when he arrived.

More insistently his mind said: *Charlie!*

He kissed his wife again and said, 'Vicky, I'll be back.'

But he had never seen Vicky again, either.

He had gone upstairs to the telephone and looked up the Dugans' number in Vicky's Phone-Mate. He dialed the number and Joan Dugan answered.

'Hi, Joan,' he said, and now the shock was aiding hi.... his voice was perfectly calm, an everyday voice. 'Could I speak to Charlie for a second?'

'Charlie?' Mrs Dugan sounded doubtful. 'Well, she went with those two friends of yours. Those teachers. Is . . . wasn't that all right?'

Something inside of him went skyrocketing up and then came plunging down. His heart, maybe. But it would do no good to panic this nice woman whom he had only met socially four or five times. It wouldn't help him, and it wouldn't help Charlie.

'Damn,' he said. 'I was hoping to catch her still there. When did they go?'

Mrs Dugan's voice faded a little. 'Terri, when did Charlie go?'

A child's voice piped something. He couldn't tell what. There was sweat between his knuckles.

'She says about fifteen minutes ago.' She was apologetic. 'I was doing the laundry and I don't have a watch. One of them came down and spoke to me. It *was* all right, wasn't it, Mr McGee? He looked all right . . .'

A lunatic impulse came to him, to just laugh lightly and say *Doing the laundry, were you? So was my wife. I found her crammed in under the ironing board. You got off lucky today, Joan.*

He said, 'That's fine. Were they coming right here, I wonder?'

The question was relayed to Terri, who said she didn't

know. Wonderful, Andy thought. My daughter's life is in the hands of another six-year-old girl.

He grasped at a straw.

'I have to go down to the market on the corner,' he said to Mrs Dugan. 'Will you ask Terri if they had the car or the van? In case I see them.'

This time he heard Terri. 'It was the van. They went away in a gray van, like the one David Pasioco's father has.'

'Thanks,' he said. Mrs Dugan said not to mention it. The impulse came again, this time just to scream *My wife is dead!* down the line at her. *My wife is dead and why were you doing your laundry while my daughter was getting into a gray van with a couple of strange men?*

Instead of screaming that or anything, he hung up and went outside. The heat whacked him over the head and he staggered a little. Had it been this hot when he came? It seemed much hotter now. The mailman had come. There was a Woolco advertising circular sticking out of the mailbox that hadn't been there before. The mailman had come while he was downstairs cradling his dead wife in his arms. His poor dead Vicky: they had pulled out her nails, and it was funny – much funnier than the way the keys had of accumulating, really – how the fact of death kept coming at you from different sides and different angles. You tried to jig and jog, you tried to protect yourself on one side, and the truth of it bored right in on another side. Death is a football player, he thought, one big mother. Death is Franco Harris or Sam Cunningham or Mean Joe Green. And it keeps throwing you down on your ass right there at the line of scrimmage.

Get your feet moving, he thought. Fifteen minutes' lead time – that's not so much. It's not a cold trail yet. Not unless Terri Dugan doesn't know fifteen minutes from half an hour to two hours. Never mind that, anyway. Get going.

He got going. He went back to the station wagon, which was parked half on and half off the sidewalk. He opened the driver's-side door and then spared a glance back at his neat suburban house on which the mortgage was half paid. The bank let you take a 'payment vacation' two months a year if you needed it. Andy had never needed it. He looked at the house dozing in the sun, and again his shocked eyes were caught by the red flare of the Woolco circular sticking out of the mailbox, and *whap!* death hit him again, making his eyes blur and his teeth clamp down.

He got in the car and drove away toward Terri Dugan's street, not going on any real, logical belief that he could pick up their trail but only on blind hope. He had not seen his house on Conifer Place in Lakeland since then.

His driving was better now. Now that he knew the worst, his driving was a lot better. He turned on the radio and there was Bob Seger singing 'Still the Same.'

He drove across Lakeland, moving as fast as he dared. For one terrible moment he came up blank on the name of the street, and then it came to him. The Dugans lived on Blassmore Place. He and Vicky had joked about that: Blassmore Place, with houses designed by Bill Blass. He started to smile a little at the memory, and *whap!* the fact of her death hit him again, rocking him.

He was there in ten minutes. Blassmore Place was a short dead end. No way out for a gray van at the far end, just a cyclone fence that marked the edge of the John Glenn Junior High School.

Andy parked the wagon at the intersection of Blassmore Place and Ridge Street. There was a green-over-white house on the corner. A lawn sprinkler twirled. Out front were two kids, a girl and a boy of about ten. They were

203

taking turns on a skateboard. The girl was wearing shorts, and she had a good set of scabs on each knee.

He got out of the wagon and walked toward them. They looked him up and down carefully.

'Hi,' he said. 'I'm looking for my daughter. She passed by here about half an hour ago in a gray van. She was with . . . well, some friends of mine. Did you see a gray van go by?'

The boy shrugged vaguely.

The girl said, 'You worried about her, mister?'

'You saw the van, didn't you?' Andy asked pleasantly, and gave her a very slight push. Too much would be counterproductive. She would see the van going in any direction he wanted, including skyward.

'Yeah, I saw a van,' she said. She got on the skateboard and glided toward the hydrant on the corner and then jumped off. 'It went right up there.' She pointed farther up Blassmore Place. Two or three intersections up was Carlisle Avenue, one of Harrison's main thoroughfares. Andy had surmised that would be the way they would go, but it was good to be sure.

'Thanks,' he said, and got back into the wagon.

'You worried about her?' the girl repeated.

'Yes, I am, a little,' Andy said.

He turned the wagon around and drove three blocks up Blassmore Place to the junction with Carlisle Avenue. This was hopeless, utterly hopeless. He felt a touch of panic, just a small hot spot, but it would spread. He made it go away, made himself concentrate on getting as far down their trail as possible. If he had to use the push, he would. He could give a lot of small helping pushes without making himself feel ill. He thanked God that he hadn't used the talent – or the curse, if you wanted to look at it that way – all summer long. He was up and fully charged, for whatever that was worth.

Carlisle Avenue was four lanes wide and regulated here by a stop-and-go light. There was a car wash on his right and an abandoned diner on his left. Across the street was an Exxon station and Mike's Camera Store. If they had turned left, they had headed downtown. Right, and they would be headed out toward the airport and Interstate 80.

Andy turned into the car wash. A young guy with an incredible shock of wiry red hair spilling over the collar of his dull green coverall jived over. He was eating a Popsicle.

'No can do, man,' he said before Andy could even open his mouth. 'The rinse attachment busted about an hour ago. We're closed.'

'I don't want a wash,' Andy said. 'I'm looking for a gray van that went through the intersection maybe half an hour ago. My daughter was in it, and I'm a little worried about her.'

'You think somebody might have snatched her?' He went right on eating his Popsicle.

'No, nothing like that,' Andy said. 'Did you see the van?'

'Gray van? Hey, goodbuddy, you have any idea how many cars go by here in just one hour? Or half an hour? Busy street, man. Carlisle is a very busy street.'

Andy cocked his thumb over his shoulder. 'It came from Blassmore Place. That's not so busy.' He got ready to add a little push, but he didn't have to. The young guy's eyes suddenly brightened. He broke his Popsicle in two like a wishbone and sucked all the purple ice off one of the sticks in a single improbable slurp.

'Yeah, okay, right,' he said. 'I did see it. I'll tell you why I noticed. It cut across our tarmac to beat the light. I don't care myself, but it irritates the *shit* out of the boss when they do that. Not that it matters today with the rinser on the fritz. He's got something else to be irritated about.'

'So the van headed toward the airport.'

205

The guy nodded, flipped one of the Popsicle sticks back over his shoulder, and started on the remaining chunk. 'Hope you find your girl, goodbuddy. If you don't mind a little, like, gray-tuitous advice, you ought to call the cops if you're really worried.'

'I don't think that would do much good,' Andy said. 'Under the circumstances.'

He got back in the wagon again, crossed the tarmac himself, and turned onto Carlisle Avenue. He was now headed west. The area was cluttered with gas stations, car washes, fast-food franchises, used-car lots. A drive-in advertised a double bill consisting of THE CORPSE GRINDERS and BLOODY MERCHANTS OF DEATH. He looked at the marquee and heard the ironing board ratcheting out of its closet like a guillotine. His stomach rolled over.

He passed under a sign announcing that you could get on I-80 a mile and a half farther west, if that was your pleasure. Beyond that was a smaller sign with an airplane on it. Okay, he had got this far. Now what?

Suddenly he pulled into the parking lot of a Shakey's Pizza. It was no good stopping and asking along here. As the car-wash guy had said, Carlisle was a busy street. He could push people until his brains were leaking out his ears and only succeed in confusing himself. It was the turnpike or the airport, anyway. He was sure of it. The lady or the tiger.

He had never in his life *tried* to make one of the hunches come. He simply took them as gifts when they did come, and usually acted on them. Now he slouched farther down in the driver's seat of the wagon, touching his temples lightly with the tips of his fingers, and tried to make something come. The motor was idling, the radio was still on. The Rolling Stones. Dance, little sister, dance.

Charlie, he thought. She had gone off to Terri's with her clothes stuffed in the knapsack she wore just about everywhere. That had probably helped to fool them. The last time he had seen her, she was wearing jeans and a salmon-colored shell top. Her hair was in pigtails, as it almost always was. A nonchalant good-bye, Daddy, and a kiss and holy Jesus, Charlie, where are you now?

Nothing came.

Never mind. Sit a little longer. Listen to the Stones. Shakey's Pizza. You get your choice, thin crust or crunchy. You pays your money and you takes your choice, as Granther McGee used to say. The Stones exhorting little sister to dance, dance, dance. Quincey saying they'd probably put her in a room so two hundred and twenty million Americans could be safe and free. Vicky. He and Vicky had had a hard time with the sex part of it at first. She had been scared to death. Just call me the Ice Maiden, she had said through her tears after that first miserable botched time. No sex, please, we're British. But somehow the Lot Six experiment had helped with that – the totality they had shared was, in its own way, like mating. Still it had been difficult. A little at a time. Gentleness. Tears. Vicky beginning to respond, then stiffening, crying out *Don't, it'll hurt, don't, Andy, stop it!* And somehow it was the Lot Six experiment, that common experience, that had enabled him to go on trying, like a safecracker who knows that there is a way, always a way. And there had come a night when they got through it. Later there came a night when it was all right. Then, suddenly, a night when it was glorious. Dance, little sister, dance. He had been with her when Charlie was born. A quick, easy delivery. Quick to fix, easy to please. . . .

Nothing was coming. The trail was getting colder and he had nothing. The airport or the turnpike? The lady or the tiger?

The Stones finished. The Doobie Brothers came on, wanting to know without love, where would you be right now. Andy didn't know. The sun beat down. The lines in the Shakey's parking lot had been freshly painted. They were very white and firm against the black-top. The lot was more than three quarters full. It was lunchtime. Had Charlie got her lunch? Would they feed her? Maybe

(maybe they'll stop make a service stop you know at one of those HoJos along the pike – after all they can't drive can't drive can't drive)

Where? Can't drive where?

(can't drive all the way to Virginia without making a rest stop can they? I mean a little girl has got to stop and take a tinkle sometime, doesn't she?)

He straightened up, feeling an immense but numb feeling of gratitude. It had come, just like that. Not the airport, which would have been his first guess, if he had only been guessing. Not the airport but the turnpike. He wasn't completely sure the hunch was bona fide, but he was pretty sure. And it was better than not having any idea at all.

He rolled the station wagon over the freshly painted arrow pointing the way out and turned right on Carlisle again. Ten minutes later he was on the turnpike, headed east with a toll ticket tucked into the battered, annotated copy of *Paradise Lost* on the seat beside him. Ten minutes after that, Harrison, Ohio, was behind him. He had started on the trip east that would bring him to Tashmore, Vermont, fourteen months later.

The calm held. He played the radio loud and that helped. Song followed song and he only recognized the older ones because he had pretty much stopped listening to pop music three or four years ago. No particular reason; it had just happened. They still had the jump on him, but the calm insisted with its own cold logic that it wasn't a very good jump – and that he would be asking for trouble if he just started roaring along the passing lane at seventy.

He pegged the speedometer at just over sixty, reasoning that the men who had taken Charlie would not want to exceed the fifty-five speed limit. They could flash their credentials at any Smokey who pulled them down for speeding, that was true, but they might have a certain amount of difficulty explaining a screaming six-year-old child just the same. It might slow them down, and it would surely get them in dutch with whoever was pulling the strings on this show.

They could have drugged her and hidden her, his mind whispered. *Then if they got stopped for busting along at seventy, even eighty, they'd only have to show their paper and keep right on going. Is an Ohio state cop going to toss a van that belongs to the Shop?*

Andy struggled with that as eastern Ohio flowed by. First, they might be scared to drug Charlie. Sedating a child can be a tricky business unless you're an expert . . . and they might not be sure what sedation would do to the powers they were supposed to be investigating. Second, a state cop might just go ahead and toss the van anyway, or at least hold them in the breakdown lane while he checked the validity of their ID. Third, why should they be busting their asses? They had no idea anyone was onto them. It was still not one o'clock. Andy was supposed to be at the college until two o'clock. The Shop people would not expect him to arrive back home until two-twenty or so at the earliest and probably felt they could count on anywhere from twenty minutes to two hours after that before the alarm was raised. Why shouldn't they just be loafing along?

Andy went a little faster.

Forty minutes passed, then fifty. It seemed longer. He was beginning to sweat a little; worry was nibbling through the artificial ice of calm and shock. Was the van really someplace up ahead, or had the whole thing been so much wishful thinking?'

The traffic patterns formed and re-formed. He saw two gray vans. Neither of them looked like the one he had seen cruising around Lakeland. One was driven by an elderly man with flying white hair. The other was full of freaks smoking dope. The driver saw Andy's close scrutiny and waved a roach clip at him. The girl beside him popped up her middle finger, kissed it gently, and tipped it Andy's way. Then they were behind him.

His head was beginning to ache. The traffic was heavy, the sun was bright. Each car was loaded with chrome, and each piece of chrome had its own arrow of sun to flick into his eyes. He passed a sign that said REST AREA I MILE AHEAD.

He had been in the passing lane. Now he signaled right and slipped into the travel lane again. He let his speed drop to forty-five, then to forty. A small sports car passed him and the driver blipped his horn at Andy in irritated fashion as he went by.

REST AREA, the sign announced. It wasn't a service stop, simply a turn-out with slant parking, a water fountain, and bathrooms. There were four or five cars parked in there and one gray van. *The* gray van. He was almost sure of it. His heart began to slam against the walls of his chest. He turned in with a quick twist of the station wagon's wheel, and the tires made a low wailing sound.

He drove slowly down the entranceway toward the van, looking around, trying to take in everything at once. There were two picnic tables with a family at each one. One group was just clearing up and getting ready to go, the mother putting leftovers into a bright orange carrier bag, the father and the two kids policing up the junk and taking it over to the trash barrel. At the other table a young man and woman were eating sandwiches and potato salad. There was a sleeping baby in a carrier seat between them. The baby was wearing a corduroy jumper with a lot of dancing elephants on it. On the grass, between two big and beautiful old elms, were two girls of about twenty, also having lunch. There was no sign of Charlie or of any men who looked both young enough and tough enough to belong to the Shop.

Andy killed the station wagon's engine. He could feel his heartbeat in his eyeballs now. The van looked empty. He got out.

An old woman using a cane came out of the ladies' comfort station and walked slowly toward an old burgundy Biscayne. A gent of about her age got out from behind the wheel, walked around the hood, opened her door, and handed her in. He went back, started up the Biscayne, a big jet of oily blue smoke coming from the exhaust pipe, and backed out.

The men's-room door opened and Charlie came out. Flanking her on the left and right were men of about thirty in sport coats, open-throated shirts, and dark double-knit pants. Charlie's face looked blank and shocked. She looked from one of the men to the other and then back at the first. Andy's guts began to roll helplessly. She was wearing her packsack. They were walking toward the van. Charlie said something to one of them and he shook his head. She turned to the other. He shrugged, then said something to his partner over Charlie's head. The other one nodded. They turned around and walked toward the drinking fountain.

Andy's heart was beating faster than ever. Adrenaline spilled into his body in a sour, jittery flood. He was scared, scared plenty, but something else was pumping up inside him and it was anger, it was total fury. The fury was even better than the calm. It felt almost sweet. Those were the two men out there that had killed his wife and stolen his daughter, and if they weren't right with Jesus, he pitied them.

As they went to the drinking fountain with Charlie, their backs were to him. Andy got out of the wagon and stepped behind the van.

The family of four who had just finished their lunch walked over to a new midsized Ford, got in, and backed out. The mother glanced over at Andy with no curiosity at all, the way people look at each other when they are on long trips, moving slowly through the digestive tract of the U.S. turnpike system. They drove off, showing a Michigan plate. There were now three cars and the gray van and Andy's station wagon parked in the rest area. One of the cars belonged to the girls. Two more people were strolling across the grounds, and there was one man inside the little information booth, looking at the I-80 map, his hands tucked into the back pockets of his jeans.

Andy had no idea of exactly what he was going to do.

Charlie finished her drink. One of the two men bent over and took a sip. Then they started back toward their van. Andy was looking at them from around the van's back-left corner. Charlie looked scared, really scared. She had been crying. Andy tried the back door of the van, not knowing why, but it was no good anyway; it was locked.

Abruptly he stepped out into full view.

They were very quick. Andy saw the recognition come into their eyes immediately, even before the gladness flooded Charlie's face, driving away that look of blank, frightened shock.

'*Daddy!*' she cried shrilly, causing the young couple with the baby to look around. One of the girls under the elms shaded her eyes to see what was happening.

Charlie tried to run to him and one of the men grabbed her by the shoulder and hauled her back against him, half-twisting her packsack from her shoulders. An instant later there was a gun in his hand. He had produced it from

212

somewhere under his sport coat like a magician doing an evil trick. He put the barrel against Charlie's temple.

The other man began to stroll unhurriedly away from Charlie and his partner, then began to move in on Andy. His hand was in his coat, but his conjuring was not as good as his partner's had been; he was having a little trouble producing his gun.

'Move away from the van if you don't want anything to happen to your daughter,' the one with the gun said.

'*Daddy!*' Charlie cried again.

Andy moved slowly away from the van. The other fellow, who was prematurely bald, had his gun out now. He pointed it at Andy. He was less than five feet away. 'I advise you very sincerely not to move,' he said in a low voice. 'This is a Colt forty-five and it makes a *giant* hole.'

The young guy with his wife and baby at the picnic table got up. He was wearing rimless glasses and he looked severe. 'What exactly is going on here?' he asked in the carrying, enunciated tones of a college instructor.

The man with Charlie turned toward him. The muzzle of his gun floated slightly away from her so that the young man could see it. 'Government business,' he said. 'Stay right where you are; everything is fine.'

The young man's wife grabbed his arm and pulled him down.

Andy looked at the balding agent and said in a low, pleasant voice, 'That gun is much too hot to hold.'

Baldy looked at him, puzzled. Then, suddenly, he screamed and dropped his revolver. It struck the pavement and went off. One of the girls under the elms let out a puzzled, surprised shout. Baldy was holding his hand and dancing around. Fresh white blisters appeared on his palm, rising like bread dough.

The man with Charlie stared at his partner, and for a

213

moment the gun was totally distracted from her small head.

'You're blind,' Andy told him, and pushed just as hard as he could. A sickening wrench of pain twisted through his head.

The man screamed suddenly. He let go of Charlie and his hands went to his eyes.

'Charlie,' Andy said in a low voice, and his daughter ran to him and clutched his legs in a trembling bear hug. The man inside the information booth ran out to see what was going on.

Baldy, still clutching his burned hand, ran toward Andy and Charlie. His face worked horribly.

'Go to sleep,' Andy said curtly, and pushed again. Baldy dropped sprawling as if pole-axed. His forehead bonked on the pavement. The young wife of the stern young man moaned.

Andy's head hurt badly now, and he was remotely glad that it was summer and that he hadn't used the push, even to prod a student who was letting his grades slip for no good reason, since perhaps May. He was charged up – but charged up or not, God knew he was going to pay for what he was doing this hot summer afternoon.

The blind man was staggering around on the grass, holding his hands up to his face and screaming. He walked into a green barrel with PUT LITTER IN ITS PLACE stenciled on its side and fell down in an overturned jumble of sandwich bags, beer cans, cigarette butts, and empty soda bottles.

'Oh Daddy, jeez I was so scared,' Charlie said, and began to cry.

'The wagon's right over there. See it?' Andy heard himself say. 'Get in and I'll be with you in a minute.'

'Is Mommy here?'

'No. Just get in, Charlie.' He couldn't deal with that now. Now, somehow, he had to deal with these witnesses.

'What the hell is this?' the man from the information booth asked, bewildered.

'My eyes,' the man who had had his gun up to Charlie's head screamed 'My *eyes*, my *eyes*. What did you do to my eyes, you son of a bitch?' He got up. There was a sandwich bag sticking to one of his hands. He began to totter off toward the information booth, and the man in the bluejeans darted back inside.

'Go, Charlie.'

'Will you come, Daddy?'

'Yes, in just a second. Now go.'

Charlie went, blond pigtails bouncing. Her packsack was still hanging askew.

Andy walked past the sleeping Shop agent, thought about his gun, and decided he didn't want it. He walked over to the young people at the picnic table. Keep it small, he told himself. Easy. Little taps. Don't go starting any echoes. The object is not to hurt these people.

The young woman grabbed her baby from its carrier seat rudely, waking it. It began to cry. 'Don't you come near me, you crazy person!' she said.

Andy looked at the man and his wife.

'None of this is very important,' he said, and pushed. Fresh pain settled over the back of his head like a spider . . . and sank in.

The young man looked relieved. 'Well, thank God.'

His wife offered a tentative smile. The push hadn't taken so well with her; her maternity had been aroused.

'Lovely baby you have there,' Andy said. 'Little boy, isn't it?'

The blind man stepped off the curbing, pitched forward, and struck his head on the doorpost of the red Pinto that

215

probably belonged to the two girls. He howled. Blood flowed from his temple. *'I'm blind!'* he screamed again.

The young woman's tentative smile became radiant. 'Yes, a boy,' she said. 'His name is Michael.'

'Hi, Mike,' Andy said. He ruffled the baby's mostly bald head.

'I can't think why he's crying,' the young woman said. 'He was sleeping so well until just now. He must be hungry.'

'Sure, that's it,' her husband said.

'Excuse me.' Andy walked toward the information booth. There was no time to lose now. Someone else could turn into this roadside bedlam at any time.

'What is it, man?' the fellow in the bluejeans asked. 'Is it a bust?'

'Nah, nothing happened,' Andy said, and gave another light push. It was starting to make him feel sick now. His head thudded and pounded.

'Oh,' the fellow said. 'Well, I was just trying to figure out how to get to Chagrin Falls from here. Excuse me.' And he sauntered back inside the information booth.

The two girls had retreated to the security fence that separated the turn-out from the private farmland beyond it. They stared at him with wide eyes. The blind man was now shuffling around on the pavement in a circle with his arms held stiffly out in front of him. He was cursing and weeping.

Andy advanced slowly toward the girls, holding his hands out to show them there was nothing in them. He spoke to them. One of them asked him a question and he spoke again. Shortly they both began to smile relieved smiles and to nod. Andy waved to them and they both waved in return. Then he walked rapidly across the grass toward the station wagon. His forehead was beaded with cold sweat and his stomach was rolling greasily. He could only pray that no one would drive in before he and Charlie got away, because there was nothing left. He was completely tipped over. He slid in behind the wheel and keyed the engine.

'Daddy,' Charlie said, and threw herself at him, buried her face against his chest. He hugged her briefly and then backed out of the parking slot. Turning his head was agony. The black horse. In the aftermath, that was the thought that always came to him. He had let the black horse out of its stall somewhere in the dark barn of his subconscious and now it would again batter its way up and down through his brain. He would have to get them someplace and lay up. Quick. He wasn't going to be capable of driving for long.

'The black horse,' he said thickly. It was coming. No . . . no. It wasn't coming; it was here. *Thud* . . . *thud* . . . *thud*. Yes, it was here. It was free.

'*Daddy, look out!*' Charlie screamed.

The blind man had staggered directly across their path. Andy braked. The blind man began to pound on the hood of the wagon and scream for help. To their right, the young mother had begun to breast-feed her baby. Her husband was reading a paperback. The man from the information booth had gone over to talk to the two girls from the red Pinto – perhaps hoping for some quickie experience kinky enough to write up for the Penthouse *Forum*. Sprawled out on the pavement, Baldy slept on.

The other operative pounded on the hood of the wagon again and again. 'Help me!' he screamed. 'I'm blind! Dirty bastard did something to my eyes! *I'm blind!*'

'Daddy,' Charlie moaned.

For a crazy instant, he almost floored the accelerator. Inside his aching head he could hear the sound the tires would make, could feel the dull thudding of the wheels as they passed over the body. He had kidnapped Charlie and

217

held a gun to her head. Perhaps he had been the one who had stuffed the rag into Vicky's mouth so she wouldn't scream when they pulled out her fingernails. It would be so very good to kill him . . . except then what would separate him from them?

He laid on the horn instead. It sent another bright spear of agony through his head. The blind man leaped away from the car as if stung. Andy hauled the wheel around and drove past him. The last thing he saw in the rearview mirror as he drove down the reentry lane was the blind man sitting on the pavement, his face twisted in anger and terror . . . and the young woman placidly raising baby Michael to her shoulder to burp him.

He entered the flow of turnpike traffic without looking. A horn blared; tires squalled. A big Lincoln swerved around the wagon and the driver shook his fist at them.

'Daddy, are you okay?'

'I will be,' he said. His voice seemed to come from far away. 'Charlie, look at the toll ticket and see what the next exit is.'

The traffic blurred in front of his eyes. It doubled, trebled, came back together, then drifted into prismatic fragments again. Sun reflecting off bright chrome everywhere.

'And fasten your seatbelt, Charlie.'

The next exit was Hammersmith, twenty miles farther up. Somehow he made it. He thought later that it was only the consciousness of Charlie sitting next to him, depending on him, that kept him on the road. Just as Charlie had got him through all the things that came after – the knowledge of Charlie, needing him. Charlie McGee, whose parents had once needed two hundred dollars.

There was a Best Western at the foot of the Hammersmith ramp, and Andy managed to get them checked in, specifying a room away from the turnpike. He used a bogus name.

'They'll be after us, Charlie,' he said. 'I need to sleep. But only until dark, that's all the time we can take . . . all we dare to take. Wake me up when it's dark.'

She said something else, but then he was falling on the bed. The world was blurring down to a gray point, and then even the point was gone and everything was darkness, where the pain couldn't reach. There was no pain and there were no dreams. When Charlie shook him awake again on that hot August evening at quarter past seven, the room was stifling hot and his clothes were soaked with sweat. She had tried to make the air conditioner work but hadn't been able to figure out the controls.

'It's okay,' he said. He swung his feet onto the floor and put his hands on his temples, squeezing his head so it wouldn't blow up.

'Is it any better, Daddy?' she asked anxiously.

'A little,' he said. And it was . . . but only a little. 'We'll stop in a little while and get some chow. That'll help some more.'

'Where are we going?'

He shook his head slowly back and forth. He had only the money he had left the house with that morning – about seventeen dollars. He had his Master Charge and his Visa, but he had paid for their room with the two twenties he always kept in the back of his wallet (*my run-out money, he sometimes told Vicky, joking, but how hellishly true* that had turned out to be) rather than use either one of them. Using either of those cards would be like painting a sign: THIS WAY TO THE FUGITIVE COLLEGE INSTRUCTOR AND HIS DAUGHTER. The seventeen dollars would buy them some burgers and top off the wagon's gas tank once. Then they would be stone broke.

'I don't know, Charlie,' he said. 'Just away.'

219

'When are we going to get Mommy?'

Andy looked up at her and his headache started to get worse again. He thought of the drops of blood on the floor and on the washing-machine porthole. He thought of the smell of Pledge.

'Charlie—' he said, and could say no more. There was no need, anyway.

She looked at him with slowly widening eyes. Her hand drifted up to her trembling mouth.

'Oh no, Daddy . . . please say it's no.'

'Charlie—'

She screamed, *'Oh please say it's no!'*

'Charlie, those people who—'

'Please say she's all *right*, say she's all *right*, say she's all *right!'*

The room, the room was so hot, the air conditioning was off, that was all it was, but it was so *hot*, his head aching, the sweat rolling down his face, not cold sweat now but hot, like oil, *hot—*

'No,' Charlie was saying, 'No, no, no, no, no.' She shook her head. Her pigtails flew back and forth, making him think absurdly of the first time he and Vicky had taken her to the amusement park, the carousel—

It wasn't the lack of air conditioning.

'Charlie!' He yelled. 'Charlie, the bathtub! *The water!'*

She screamed. She turned her head toward the open bathroom door and there was a sudden blue flash in there like a lightbulb burning out. The showerhead fell off the wall and clattered into the tub, twisted and black. Several of the blue tiles shattered to fragments.

He barely caught her when she fell, sobbing.

'Daddy, I'm sorry, I'm sorry—'

'It's all right,' he said shakily, and enfolded her. From the bathroom, thin smoke drifted out of the fused tub. All the porcelain surfaces had crack-glazed instantly. It was as

220

if the entire bathroom had been run through some powerful but defective firing kiln. The towels were smoldering.

'It's all right,' he said, holding her, rocking her. 'Charlie, it's all right, it's gonna be all right, somehow it'll come right, I promise.'

'I want Mommy,' she sobbed.

He nodded. He wanted her, too. He held Charlie tightly to him and smelled ozone and porcelain and cooked Best Western towels. She had almost flash-fried them both.

'It's gonna be all right,' he told her, and rocked her, not really believing it, but it was the litany, it was the Psalter, the voice of the adult calling down the black well of years into the miserable pit of terrorized childhood; it was what you said when things went wrong; it was the nightlight that could not banish the monster from the closet but perhaps only keep it at bay for a little while; it was the voice without power that must speak nevertheless.

'It's gonna be all right,' he told her, not really believing it, knowing as every adult knows in his secret heart that nothing is really all right, ever. 'It's gonna be all right.'

He was crying. He couldn't help it now. His tears came in a flood and he held her to his chest as tightly as he could.

'Charlie, I swear to you, somehow, it's gonna be all right.'

5

The one thing they had not been able to hang around his neck – as much as they might have liked to – was the murder of Vicky. Instead, they had elected to simply erase what had happened in the laundry room. Less trouble for them. Sometimes – not often – Andy wondered what their neighbors back in Lakeland might have speculated. Bill collectors? Marital problems? Maybe a drug habit or an incident of child abuse? They hadn't known anyone on Conifer Place well enough for it to have been any more than idle dinnertable chat, a nine days' wonder soon forgotten when the bank that held the mortgage released their house.

Sitting on the deck now and looking out into darkness, Andy thought he might have had more luck that day than he had known (or been able to appreciate). He had arrived too late to save Vicky, but he had left before the Removal People arrived.

There had never been a thing about it in the paper, not even a squib about how – funny thing! – an English instructor named Andrew McGee and his family had just up and disappeared. Perhaps the Shop had got that quashed, too. Surely he had been reported missing; one or all of the guys he had been eating lunch with that day would have done that much. But it hadn't made the papers, and of course, bill collectors don't advertise.

They would have hung it on me if they could,' he said, unaware that he had spoken aloud.

But they couldn't have. The medical examiner could have fixed the time of death, and Andy, who had been in plain sight of some disinterested third party (and in the case of Eh-116, Style and the Short Story, from ten to eleven-thirty, twenty-five disinterested third parties) all that day, could not have been set up to take the fall. Even if he'd been unable to provide substantiation for his movements during the critical time, there was no motive.

So the two of them had killed Vicky and then gone haring off after Charlie – but not without notifying what Andy thought of as the Removal People (and in his mind's eye he even saw them that way, smooth-faced young men dressed in white coveralls). And sometime after *he* had gone haring off after Charlie, maybe as short a time as five minutes, but almost surely no longer than an hour, the

Removal People would have rolled up to his door. While Conifer Place dozed the afternoon away, Vicky had been Removed.

They might even have reasoned – correctly – that a missing wife would have been more of a problem for Andy than a provably dead one. No body, no estimated time of death. No estimated time of death, no alibi. He would be watched, cosseted, politely tied down. Of course they would have put Charlie's description out on the wire – Vicky's too, for that matter – but Andy would not have been free to simply go tearing off on his own. So she had been Removed, and now he didn't even know where she was buried. Or maybe she had been cremated. Or—

Oh shit why are you doing this to yourself?

He stood up abruptly and poured the remainder of Granther's mule-kick over the deck railing. It was all in the past; none of it could be changed; it was time to stop thinking about it.

A neat trick if you could do it.

He looked up at the dark shapes of the trees and squeezed the glass tightly in his right hand, and the thought crossed his mind again.

Charlie I swear to you, somehow it's gonna be all right.

6

That winter in Tashmore, so long after his miserable awakening in that Ohio motel, it seemed his desperate prediction had finally come true.

It was not an idyllic winter for them. Not long after Christmas, Charlie caught a cold and snuffled and coughed her way through to early April, when it finally cleared up for good. For a while she ran a fever. Andy fed her aspirin halves and told himself that if the fever did not go down in three days' time, he would have to take her to the doctor across the lake in Bradford, no matter what the consequences. But her fever did go down, and for the rest of the winter Charlie's cold was only a constant annoyance to her. Andy managed to get himself a minor case of frostbite on one memorable occasion in March and nearly managed to burn them both up one screaming, subzero night in February by overloading the woodstove. Ironically, it was Charlie who woke up in the middle of the night and discovered the cottage was much too hot.

On December 14 they celebrated his birthday and on March 24 they celebrated Charlie's. She was eight, and sometimes Andy looked at her with a kind of wonder, as if catching sight of her for the first time. She was not a little girl anymore; she stood to past his elbow. Her hair had got long again, and she had taken to braiding it to keep it out of her eyes. She was going to be beautiful. She already was, red nose and all.

They were without a car. Irv Manders's Willys had frozen solid in January, and Andy thought the block was cracked. He had started it every day, more from a sense of responsibility than anything else, because not even four-wheel drive would have pulled them out of Granther's camp after the New Year. The snow, undisturbed except for the tracks of squirrels, chipmunks, a few deer, and a persistent raccoon that came around to sniff hopefully at the garbage hold, was almost two feet deep by then.

There were old-fashioned cross-country skis in the small shed behind the cottage – three pairs of them, but none that would fit Charlie. It was just as well. Andy kept her indoors as much as possible. They could live with her cold, but he did not want to risk a return of the fever.

He found an old pair of Granther's ski boots, dusty and cracked with age, tucked away in a cardboard toilet-tissue box under the table where the old man had once planed shutters and made doors. Andy oiled them, flexed them, and then found he still could not fill Granther's shoes without stuffing the toes full of newspaper. There was something funny about that, but he also found it a touch ominous. He thought about Granther a lot that long winter and wondered what he would have made of their predicament.

Half a dozen times that winter he hooked up the cross-country skis (no modern snap-bindings here, only a confusing and irritating tangle of straps, buckles, and rings) and worked his way across the wide, frozen expanse of Tashmore Pond to the Bradford Town Landing. From there, a small, winding road led into the village, tucked neatly away in the hills two miles east of the lake.

He always left before first light, with Granther's knapsack on his back, and never arrived back before three in the afternoon. On one occasion he barely beat a howling snowstorm that would have left him blinded and directionless and wandering on the ice. Charlie cried with relief when he came in – and then went into a long, alarming coughing fit.

The trips to Bradford were for supplies and clothes for him and Charlie. He had Granther's struttin money, and later on, he broke into three of the larger camps at the far end of Tashmore Pond and stole money. He was not proud of this, but it seemed to him a matter of survival. The camps he chose might have sold on the real-estate market for eighty thousand dollars apiece, and he supposed the owners could afford to lose their thirty or forty dollars' worth of cookie-jar money – which was exactly where most of them kept it. The only other thing he touched that winter was the large range-oil drum behind the large, modern cottage quaintly named CAMP CONFUSION. From this drum he took about forty gallons of oil.

He didn't like going to Bradford. He didn't like the certain knowledge that the oldsters who sat around the big potbellied stove down by the cash register were talking about the stranger who was staying across the lake in one of the camps. Stories had a way of getting around, and sometimes they got into the wrong ears. It wouldn't take much – only a whisper – for the Shop to make an inevitable connection between Andy, his grandfather, and his grandfather's cottage in Tashmore, Vermont. But he simply didn't know what else to do. They had to eat, and they couldn't spend the entire winter living on canned sardines. He wanted fresh fruit for Charlie, and vitamin pills, and clothes. Charlie had arrived with nothing to her name but a dirty blouse, a pair of red pants, and a single pair of underdrawers. There was no cough medicine that he trusted, there were no fresh vegetables, and, crazily enough, hardly any matches. Every camp he broke into had a fireplace, but he found only a single box of Diamond wooden matches.

He could have gone farther afield – there were other camps and cottages – but many of the other areas were plowed out and patrolled by the Tashmore constabulary. And on many of the roads there were at least one or two year-round residents.

In the Bradford general store he was able to buy all the things he needed, including three pairs of heavy pants and three woolen shirts that were approximately Charlie's size. There was no girls' underwear, and she had to make do with size-eight Jockey shorts. This disgusted and amused Charlie by turns.

Making the six-mile round trip across to Bradford on Granther's skis was both a burden and a pleasure to Andy. He didn't like leaving Charlie alone, not because he didn't trust her but because he always lived with the fear of coming back and finding her gone . . . or dead. The old boots gave him blisters no matter how many pairs of socks he put on. If he tried to move too fast, he gave himself headaches, and then he would remember the small numb places on his face and envision his brain as an old bald tire, a tire that had been used so long and hard that it was down to the canvas in places. If he had a stroke in the middle of this damned lake and froze to death, what would happen to Charlie then?

But he did his best thinking on these trips. The silence had a way of clearing the head. Tashmore Pond itself was not wide – Andy's path across it from the west bank to the east was less than a mile – but it was very long. With the snow lying four feet deep over the ice by February, he sometimes paused halfway across and looked slowly to his right and left. The lake then appeared to be a long corridor floored with dazzling white tile – clean, unbroken, stretching out of sight in either direction. Sugar-dusted pines bordered it all around. Above was the hard, dazzling, and merciless blue sky of winter, or the low and featureless white of coming snow. There might be the far-off call of a crow, or the low, rippling thud of the ice stretching, but that was all. The exercise toned up his body. He grew a warm singlet of sweat between his skin and his clothes, and it felt good to work up a sweat and then wipe it off your brow. He had somehow forgotten that feeling while teaching Yeats and Williams and correcting bluebooks.

In this silence, and through the exertion of working his body hard, his thoughts came clear and he worked the problem over in his mind. Something had to be done – should have been done long since, but that was in the past. They had come to Granther's place for the winter, but they were still running. The uneasy way he felt about the old-timers sitting around the stove with their pipes and their inquisitive eyes was enough to ram that fact home. He and Charlie were in a corner, and there had to be some way out of it.

And he was still angry, because *it wasn't right*. They *had*

227

no right. His family were American citizens, living in a supposedly open society, and his wife had been murdered, his daughter kidnapped, the two of them hunted like rabbits in a hedgerow.

He thought again that if he could get the story across to someone – or to several someones – the whole thing could be blown out of the water. He hadn't done it before because that odd hypnosis – the same sort of hypnosis that had resulted in Vicky's death – had continued, at least to some degree. He hadn't wanted his daughter growing up like a freak in a sideshow. He hadn't wanted her institutionalized – not for the good of the country and not for her own good. And worst of all, he had continued to lie to himself. Even after he had seen his wife crammed into the ironing closet in the laundry with that rag in her mouth, he had continued to lie to himself and tell himself that sooner or later they would be left alone. *Just playing for funzies*, they had said as kids. *Everybody has to give back the money at the end.*

Except they weren't kids, they weren't playing for funzies, and nobody was going to give him and Charlie anything back when the game was over. This game was for keeps.

In silence he began to understand certain hard truths. In a way, Charlie *was* a freak, not much different from the thalidomide babies of the sixties or those girl children of mothers who had taken DES; the doctors just hadn't known that those girl children were going to develop vaginal tumors in abnormal numbers fourteen or sixteen years down the road. It was not Charlie's fault, but that did not change the fact. Her strangeness, her freakishness, was simply on the inside. What she had done at the Manders farm had been terrifying, totally terrifying, and since then Andy had found himself wondering just how far her ability reached, how far it *could* reach. He had read a lot of the literature of parapsychology during their year on the dodge,

228

enough to know that both pyrokinesis and telekinesis were suspected to be tied in with certain poorly understood ductless glands. His reading had also told him that the two talents were closely related, and that most documented cases centered around girls not a whole lot older than Charlie was right now.

She had been able to initiate that destruction at the Manders farm at the age of seven. Now she was nearly eight. What might happen when she turned twelve and entered adolescence? Maybe nothing. Maybe a great deal. She said she wasn't going to use the power anymore, but if she was forced to use it? What if it began to come out spontaneously? What if she began to light fires in her sleep as a part of her own strange puberty, a fiery counterpart of the nocturnal seminal emissions most teenage boys experienced? What if the Shop finally decided to call off its dogs. . . and Charlie was kidnapped by some foreign power?

Questions, questions.

On his trips across the pond, Andy tried to grapple with them and came reluctantly to believe that Charlie might have to submit to some sort of custody for the rest of her life, if only for her own protection. It might be as necessary for her as the cruel leg braces were for the victims of muscular dystrophy or the strange prosthetics for the thalidomide babies.

And then there was the question of his own future. He remembered the numb places, the bloodshot eye. No man wants to believe that his own death-warrant has been signed and dated, and Andy did not completely believe that, but he was aware that two or three more hard pushes might kill him, and he realized that his normal life expectancy might already have been considerably shortened. Some provision had to be made for Charlie in case that happened.

But not the Shop's way.

Not the small room. He would not allow that to happen.

So he thought it over, and at last he came to a painful decision.

7

Andy wrote six letters. They were almost identical. Two were to Ohio's United States senators. One was to the woman who represented the district of which Harrison was a part in the U.S. House of Representatives. One was to the New York *Times*. One was to the Chicago *Tribune*. And one was to the Toledo *Blade*. All six letters told the story of what had happened, beginning with the experiment in Jason Gearneigh Hall and ending with his and Charlie's enforced isolation on Tashmore Pond.

When he had finished, he gave one of the letters to Charlie to read. She went through it slowly and carefully, taking almost an hour. It was the first time she had got the entire story, from beginning to end.

'You're going to mail these?' she asked when she finished.

'Yes,' he said. 'Tomorrow. I think tomorrow will be the last time I dare go across the pond.' It had at last begun to warm up a little. The ice was still solid, but it creaked constantly now, and he didn't know how much longer it would be safe.

'What will happen, Daddy?'

He shook his head. 'I don't know for sure. All I can do is hope that once the story is out, those people who have been chasing us will have to give it up.'

Charlie nodded soberly. 'You should have done it before.'

'Yes,' he said, knowing that she was thinking of the near cataclysm at the Manders farm last October. 'Maybe I should have. But I never had a chance to think much,

230

Charlie. Keeping us going was all I had time to think about. And what thinking you do get a chance to do when you're on the run . . . well, mostly it's stupid thinking. I kept hoping they'd give up and leave us alone. That was a terrible mistake.'

'They won't make me go away, will they?' Charlie asked. 'From you, I mean. We can stay together, can't we, Daddy?'

'Yes,' he said, not wanting to tell her that his conception of what might happen after the letters were mailed and received was probably as vague as hers. It was just 'after.'

'Then that's all I care about. And I'm not going to make anymore fires.'

'All right,' he said, and touched her hair. His throat was suddenly thick with a premonitory dread, and something that had happened near here suddenly occurred to him, something that he hadn't thought of for years. He had been out with his father and Granther, and Granther had given Andy his .22, which he called his varmint rifle, when Andy clamored for it. Andy had seen a squirrel and wanted to shoot it. His dad had started to protest, and Granther had hushed him with an odd little smile.

Andy had aimed the way Granther taught him; he squeezed the trigger rather than just jerking back on it (as Granther had also taught him), and he shot the squirrel. It tumbled off its limb like a stuffed toy, and Andy ran excitedly for it after handing the gun back to Granther. Up close, he had been struck dumb by what he saw. Up close, the squirrel was no stuffed toy. It wasn't dead. He had got it in the hindquarters and it lay there dying in its own bright dapples of blood, its black eyes awake and alive and full of a horrible suffering. Its fleas, knowing the truth already, were trundling off the body in three busy little lines.

His throat had closed with a snap, and at the age of nine,

231

Andy tasted for the first time that bright, painty flavor of self-loathing. He stared numbly at his messy kill, aware that his father and grandfather were standing behind him, their shadows lying over him – three generations of McGees standing over a murdered squirrel in the Vermont woods. And behind him, Granther said softly, *Well, you done it, Andy. How do you like it?* And the tears had come suddenly, overwhelming him, the hot tears of horror and realization – the realization that once it's done, it's done. He swore suddenly that he would never kill anything with a gun again. He swore it before God.

I'm not going to make anymore fires, Charlie had said, and in his mind Andy heard Granther's reply to him on the day he had shot the squirrel, the day he had sworn to God he would never do anything like that again. *Never say that, Andy. God loves to make a man break a vow. It keeps him properly humble about his place in the world and his sense of self-control*. About what Irv Manders had said to Charlie.

Charlie had found a complete set of Bomba the Jungle Boy books in the attic and was working her way slowly but surely through them. Now Andy looked at her, sitting in a dusty shaft of sunlight in the old black rocker, sitting just where his grandmother had always sat, usually with a basket of mending between her feet, and he struggled with an urge to tell her to take it back, to take it back while she still could, to tell her that she didn't understand the terrible temptation: if the gun was left there long enough, sooner or later you would pick it up again.

God loves to make a man break a vow.

8

No one saw Andy mail his letters except Charles Payson, the fellow who had moved into Bradford in November and had since been trying to make a go of the old Bradford

Notions 'n' Novelties shop. Payson was a small, sad-faced man who had tried to buy Andy a drink on one of his visits to town. In the town itself, the expectation was that if Payson didn't make it work during the coming summer, Notions 'n' Novelties would have a FOR SALE OR LEASE sign back in the window by September 15. He was a nice enough fellow, but he was having a hard scrabble. Bradford wasn't the town it used to be.

Andy walked up the street – he had left his skis stuck in the snow at the head of the road leading down to the Bradford Town Landing – and approached the general store. Inside, the oldsters watched him with mild interest. There had been a fair amount of talk about Andy that winter. The consensus about yonder man there was that he was on the run from something – a bankruptcy, maybe, or a divorce settlement. Maybe an angry wife who had been cheated out of custody of the kid: the small clothes Andy had bought hadn't been lost on them. The consensus was also that he and the kid had maybe broken into one of the camps across the Pond and were spending the winter there. Nobody brought this possibility up to Bradford's constable, a johnny-come-lately who had lived in town for only twelve years and thought he owned the place. Yonder man came from across the lake, from Tashmore, from Vermont. None of the old-timers who sat around Jake Rowley's stove in the Bradford general store had much liking for Vermont ways, them with their income tax and their snooty bottle law and that fucking Russian laid up in his house like a Czar, writing books no one could understand. Let Vermonters handle their own problems, was the unanimous, if unstated, view.

'He won't be crossin the pond much longer,' one of them said. He took another bite from his Milky Way bar and began to gum it.

'Not less he's got him a pair of water wings,' another answered, and they all chuckled.

'We won't be seein him much longer,' Jake said complacently as Andy approached the store. Andy was wearing Granther's old coat and had a blue wool band pulled over his ears, and some memory – perhaps a family resemblance going back to Granther himself – danced fleetingly in Jake's mind and then blew away. 'When the ice starts to go out, he'll just dry up and blow away. Him and whoever he's keepin over there.'

Andy stopped outside, unslung his pack, and took out several letters. Then he came inside. The men forgathered there examined their nails, their watches, the old Pearl Kineo stove itself. One of them took out a gigantic blue railroad bandanna and hawked mightily into it.

Andy glanced around. 'Morning, gentlemen.'

'Mawnin to you,' Jake Rowley said. 'Get you anything?'

'You sell stamps, don't you?'

'Oh yes, Gov'ment trusts me that far.'

'I'd like six fifteens, please.'

Jake produced them, tearing them carefully from one of the sheets in his old black postage book. 'Something else for you today.'

Andy thought, then smiled. It was the tenth of March. Without answering Jake, he went to the card rack beside the coffe grinder and picked out a large, ornate birthday card. TO YOU, DAUGHTER, ON YOUR SPECIAL DAY, it said. He brought it back and paid for it.

'Thanks,' Jake said, and rang it up.

'Very welcome,' Andy replied, and went out. They watched him adjust his headband, then stamp his letters one by one. The breath smoked out of his nostrils. They watched him go around the building to where the postbox stood, but none of them sitting around the stove could

234

have testified in court as to whether or not he mailed those letters. He came back into view shouldering into his pack.

'Off he goes,' one of the old-timers remarked.

'Civil enough fella,' Jake said, and that closed the subject. Talk turned to other matters.

Charles Payson stood in the doorway of his store, which hadn't done three hundred dollars' worth of custom all winter long, and watched Andy go. Payson could have testified that the letters had been mailed; he had stood right here and watched him drop them into the slot in a bunch.

When Andy disappeared from sight, Payson went back inside and through the doorway behind the counter where he sold penny candy and Bang caps and bubble gum and into the living quarters behind. His telephone had a scrambler device attached to it. Payson called Virginia for instructions.

9

There was and is no post office in Bradford, New Hampshire (or in Tashmore, Vermont, for that matter); both towns were too small. The nearest post office to Bradford was in Teller, New Hampshire. At one-fifteen P.M. on that March 10, the small postal truck from Teller pulled up in front of the general store and the postman emptied the mail from the standing box around to the side where Jake had pumped Jenny gas until 1970. The deposited mail consisted of Andy's six letters and a postcard from Miss Shirley Devine, a fifty-year-old maiden lady, to her sister in Tampa, Florida. Across the lake, Andy McGee was taking a nap and Charlie McGee was building a snowman.

The postman, Robert Everett, put the mail in a bag, swung the bag into the back of his blue and white truck, and then drove on to Williams, another small New Hampshire town in Teller's zip-code area. Then he U-turned in the middle of what the Williams residents laughingly called Main Street and started back to Teller, where all the mail would be sorted and sent on at about three o'clock that afternoon. Five miles outside of town, a beige Chevrolet Caprice was parked across the road, blocking both of the narrow lanes. Everett parked by the snowbank and got out of his truck to see if he could help.

Two men approached him from the car. They showed him their credentials and explained what they wanted.

'No!' Everett said. He tried on a laugh and it came out sounding incredulous, as if someone had just told him they were going to open Tashmore Beach for swimming this very afternoon.

'If you doubt we are who we say we are—' one of them began. This was Orville Jamieson, sometimes known as OJ, sometimes known as The Juice. He didn't mind dealing with this hick postman; he didn't mind anything as long as his orders didn't take him any closer than three miles to that hellish little girl.

'No, it ain't that; it ain't that at all,' Robert Everett said. He was scared, as scared as any man is when suddenly confronted with the force of the government, when gray enforcement bureaucracy suddenly takes on a real face, like something grim and solid swimming up out of a crystal ball. He was determined nonetheless. 'But what I got here is the mail. The *U.S.* mail. You guys must understand that.'

'This is a matter of national security,' OJ said. After the fiasco in Hastings Glen, a protective cordon had been thrown around the Manders place. The grounds and the remains of the house had got the fine-tooth-comb treatment. As a result, OJ had recovered The Windsucker, which now rested comfortably against the left side of his chest.

236

'You say so, but that ain't good enough,' Everett said.

OJ unbuttoned his Carroll Reed parka so that Robert Everett could see The Windsucker. Everett's eyes widened, and OJ smiled a little. 'Now, you don't want me to pull this, do you?'

Everett couldn't believe this was happening. He tried one last time. 'Do you guys know the penalty for robbing the U.S. mail? They put you in Leavenworth, Kansas, for that.'

'You can clear it with your postmaster when you get back to Teller,' the other man said, speaking for the first time. 'Now let's quit this fucking around, okay? Give us the bag of out-of-town mail.'

Everett gave him the small sack of mail from Bradford and Williams. They opened it right there on the road and sorted through it impersonally. Robert Everett felt anger and a kind of sick shame. What they were doing wasn't right, not even if it was the secrets of the nuclear bomb in there. Opening the U.S. mail by the side of the road wasn't right. Ludicrously, he found himself feeling about the same way he would have felt if a strange man had come barging into his house and pulled off his wife's clothes.

'You guys are going to hear about this,' he said in a choked, scared voice. 'You'll see.'

'Here they are,' the other fellow said to OJ. He handed him six letters, all addressed in the same careful hand. Robert Everett recognized them well enough. They had come from the box at the Bradford general store. OJ put the letters in his pocket and the two of them walked back to their Caprice, leaving the opened bag of mail on the road.

'You guys are going to hear about this!' Everett cried in a shaking voice.

Without looking back, OJ said, 'Speak to your postmas-

237

ter before you speak to anyone else. If you want to keep your Postal Service pension, that is.'

They drove away. Everett watched them go, raging, scared, sick to his stomach. At last he picked up the mailbag and tossed it back into the truck.

'Robbed,' he said, surprised to find he was near tears. 'Robbed, I been robbed, oh goddammit, I been robbed.'

He drove back to Teller as fast as the slushy roads would allow. He spoke to his postmaster, as the men had suggested. The Teller postmaster was Bill Cobham, and Everett was in Cobham's office for better than an hour. At times their voices came through the office door, loud and angry.

Cobham was fifty-six. He had been with the Postal Service for thirty-five years, and he was badly scared. At last he succeeded in communicating his fright to Robert Everett as well. And Everett never said a word, not even to his wife, about the day he had been robbed on the Teller Road between Bradford and Williams. But he never forgot it, and he never completely lost that sense of anger and shame . . . and disillusion.

10

By two-thirty Charlie had finished her snowman, and Andy, a little rested from his nap, had got up. Orville Jamieson and his new partner, George Sedaka, were on an airplane. Four hours later, as Andy and Charlie were sitting down to a game of five hundred rummy, the supper dishes washed and drying in the drainer, the letters were on Cap Hollister's desk.

Cap and Rainbird

1

On March 24, Charlie McGee's birthday, Cap Hollister sat behind his desk filled with a great and ill-defined unease. The *reason* for the unease was not ill-defined; he expected John Rainbird in not quite an hour, and that was too much like expecting the devil to turn up on the dime. So to speak. And at least the devil stuck to a bargain once it was struck, if you believed his press releases, but Cap had always felt there was something in John Rainbird's personality that was fundamentally ungovernable. When all was said and done, he was nothing more than a hit man, and hit men always self-destruct sooner or later. Cap felt that when Rainbird went, it would be with a spectacular bang. Exactly how much did he know about the McGee operation? No more than he had to, surely, but . . . it nagged at him. Not for the first time he wondered if after this McGee affair was over it might not be wise to arrange an accident for the big Indian. In the memorable words of Cap's father, Rainbird was as crazy as a man eating rat-turds and calling it caviar.

He sighed. Outside, a cold rain flew against the windows, driven by a strong wind. His study, so bright and pleasant in summer, was now filled with shifting gray shadows. They were not kind to him as he sat here with the McGee file on its library trolley at his left hand. The winter had aged him; he was not the same jaunty man who had biked up to the front door on that day in October when the McGees had escaped again, leaving a firestorm behind.

Lines on his face that had been barely noticeable then had now deepened into fissures. He had been forced into the humiliation of bifocals – old man's glasses, he thought them – and adjusting to them had left him feeling nauseated for the first six weeks he wore them. These were the small things, the outward symbols of the way things had gone so crazily, maddeningly wrong. These were the things he bitched about to himself because all of his training and upbringing had schooled him against bitching about the grave matters that lay so closely below the surface.

As if that damned little girl were a personal jinx, the only two women he had cared deeply about since the death of his mother had both died of cancer this winter – his wife, Georgia, three days after Christmas, and his personal secretary, Rachel, only a little over a month ago.

He had known Georgia was gravely ill, of course; a mastectomy fourteen months before her death had slowed but not stopped the progress of the disease. Rachel's death had been a cruel surprise. Near the end he could remember (how unforgivable we sometimes seem in retrospect) joking that she needed fattening up, and Rachel throwing the jokes right back at him.

Now all he had left was the Shop – and he might not have that much longer. An insidious sort of cancer had invaded Cap himself. What would you call it? Cancer of the confidence? Something like that. And in the upper echelons, that sort of disease was nearly always fatal. Nixon, Lance, Helms . . . all victims of cancer of the credibility.

He opened the McGee file and took out the latest additions – the six letters Andy had mailed less than two weeks ago. He shuffled through them without reading them. They were all essentially the same letter and he had the contents almost by heart. Below them were glossy photographs, some taken by Charles Payson, some taken

240

by other agents on the Tashmore side of the Pond. There were photos showing Andy walking up Bradford's main street. Photos of Andy shopping in the general store and paying for his purchases. Photos of Andy and Charlie standing by the boathouse at the camp, Irv Manders's Willys a snow-covered hump in the background. A photo showing Charlie sliding down a hard and sparkling incline of snow-crust on a flattened cardboard box, her hair flying out from beneath a knitted cap that was too large for her. In this photo her father was standing behind her, mittened hands on hips, head thrown back, bellowing laughter. Cap had looked at this photo often and long and soberly and was sometimes surprised by a trembling in his hands when he put it aside. He wanted them that badly.

He got up and went to the window for a moment. No Rich McKeon cutting grass today. The alders were bare and skeletal, the duckpond between the two houses a slatelike, bare expanse. There were dozens of important items on the Shop's plate this early spring, a veritable smorgasbord, but for Cap there was really only one, and that was the matter of Andy McGee and his daughter Charlene.

The Manders fiasco had done a lot of damage. The Shop had ridden that out, and so had he, but it had begun a critical groundswell that would break soon enough. The critical center of that groundswell was the way the McGees had been handled from the day Victoria McGee had been killed and the daughter lifted – lifted however briefly. A lot of the criticism had to do with the fact that a college instructor who had never even been in the army had been able to take his daughter away from two trained Shop agents, leaving one of them mad and one in a coma that had lasted for six months. The latter agent was never going to be any good for anything again; if anyone spoke the word 'sleep' within his earshot, he keeled over bonelessly

241

and might stay out from four hours to an entire day. In a bizarre sort of way it was funny.

The other major criticism had to do with the fact that the McGees had managed to stay one step ahead for so long. It made the Shop look bad. It made them all look dumb.

But most of the criticism was reserved for the incident at the Manders farm itself, because that had damned near blown the entire agency out of the water. Cap knew that the whispering had begun. The whispering, the memos, maybe even the testimony at the ultrasecret congressional hearings. *We don't want him hanging on like Hoover. This Cuban business went entirely by the boards because he couldn't get his head out of that damned McGee file. Wife died very recently, you know. Great shame. Hit him hard. Whole McGee business nothing but a catalogue of ineptitude. Perhaps a younger man . . .*

But none of them understood what they were up against. They thought they did, but they didn't. Again and again he had seen the rejection of the simple fact that the little girl was a pyrokinetic – a firestarter. Literally dozens of reports suggested that the fire at the Manders farm had been started by a gasoline spill, by the woman's breaking a kerosene lamp, by spontaneous-fucking-combustion, and God only knew what other nonsense. Some of those reports came from people who had been there.

Standing at the window, Cap found himself perversely wishing that Wanless were here. Wanless had understood. He could have talked to Wanless about this . . . this dangerous blindness.

He went back to the desk. There was no sense kidding himself; once the undermining process began, there was no way to stop it. It really was like a cancer. You could retard its growth by calling in favors (and Cap had called in ten years' worth just to keep himself in the saddle this

242

last winter); you might even be able to force it into remission. But sooner or later, you were gone. He felt he had from now until July if he played the game by the rules, from now until maybe November if he decided to really dig in and get tough. That, however, might mean ripping the agency apart at the seams, and he did not want to do that. He had no wish to destroy something he had invested half his life in. But he would if he had to: he was going to see this through to the end.

The major factor that had allowed him to stay in control was the speed with which they had located the McGees again. Cap was glad to take credit for that since it helped to prop up his position, but all it had really taken was computer time.

They had been living with this business long enough to have time to plow the McGee field both wide and deep. Filed away in the computer were facts on more than two hundred relatives and four hundred friends all the way around the McGee-Tomlinson family tree. These friendships stretched all the way back to Vicky's best friend in the first grade, a girl named Kathy Smith, who was now Mrs Frank Worthy, of Cabral, California, and who had probably not spared a thought for Vicky Tomlinson in twenty years or more.

The computer was given the 'last-seen' data and promptly spit out a list of probabilities. Heading the list was the name of Andy's deceased grandfather, who had owned a camp on Tashmore Pond in Vermont; ownership had since passed to Andy. The McGees had vacationed there, and it was within reasonable striking distance of the Manders farm by way of the back roads. The computer felt that if Andy and Charlie were to make for any 'known place,' it would be this place.

Less than a week after they had moved into Granther's, Cap knew they were there. A loose cordon of agents was set up around the camp. Arrangements had been made for the purchase of Notions 'n' Novelties in Bradford on the probability that whatever shopping they needed to do would be done in Bradford.

Passive surveillance, nothing more. All the photographs had been taken with telephoto lenses under optimum conditions for concealment. Cap had no intention of risking another firestorm.

They could have take Andy quietly on any of his trips across the lake. They could have shot them both as easily as they had got the picture of Charlie sledding on the cardboard carton. But Cap wanted the girl, and he had now come to believe that if they were going to have any real control over her, they would need her father as well.

After locating them again, the most important objective had been to make sure they kept quiet. Cap didn't need a computer to tell him that as Andy grew more frightened, the chances that he would seek outside help went up and up. Before the Manders affair, a press leak could have been handled or lived with. Afterward, press interference became a different ballgame altogether. Cap had nightmares just thinking about what would happen if the New York *Times* got hold of such a thing.

For a brief period, during the confusion that had followed the firestorm, Andy could have got his letters out. But apparently the McGees had been living with their own confusion. Their golden chance to mail the letters or make some phone calls had passed unused . . . and very well mightn't have come to anything, anyway. The woods were full of crackpots these days, and newspeople were as cynical as anyone else. Theirs had become a glamour occupation. They were more interested in what Margaux and Bo and Suzanne and Cheryl were doing. It was safer.

Now the two of them were in a box. Cap had had the entire winter to consider options. Even at his wife's funeral he had been running through his options. Gradually he had settled upon a plan of action and now he was prepared to tip that plan into motion. Payson, their man in Bradford, said that the ice was getting ready to go out on Tashmore Pond. And McGee had finally mailed his letters. Already he would be getting impatient for a response – and perhaps beginning to suspect his letters had never arrived at their intended sources. They might be getting ready to move, and Cap liked them right where they were.

Beneath the photos was a thick typed report – better than three hundred pages – bound in a blue TOP SECRET cover. Eleven doctors and psychologists had put the combination report and prospectus together under the overall direction of Dr Patrick Hockstetter, a clinical psychologist and psychotherapist. He was, in Cap's opinion, one of the ten or twelve most astute minds at the Shop's disposal. At the eight hundred thousand dollars it had cost the taxpayer to put the report together, he ought to have been. Thumbing through the report now, Cap wondered what Wanless, that old doomsayer, would have made of it.

His own intuition that they needed Andy alive was confirmed in here. The postulate Hockstetter's crew had based their own chain of logic on was the idea that all the powers they were interested in were exercised voluntarily, having their first cause in the willingness of the possessor to use them . . . and the key word was *will*.

The girl's powers, of which pyrokinesis was only the cornerstone, had a way of getting out of control, of jumping nimbly over the barriers of her will, but this study, which incorporated all the available information, indicated that it was the girl herself who elected whether or not to set things in motion – as she had done at the Manders farm when she realized that the Shop agents were trying to kill her father.

He rifled through the recap of the original Lot Six

245

experiment. All the graphs and computer readouts boiled down to the same thing: will as the first cause.

Using will as the basis for everything. Hockstetter and his colleagues had gone through an amazing catalogue of drugs before deciding on Thorazine for Andy and a new drug called Orasin for the girl. Seventy pages of gobbledygook in the report came down to the fact that the drugs would make them feel high, dreamy, floaty. Neither of them would be able to exercise enough will to choose between chocolate milk and white, let alone enough to start fires or convince people they were blind, or whatever.

They could keep Andy McGee drugged constantly. They had no real use for him; both the report and Cap's own intuition suggested that he was a dead end, a burned-out case. It was the girl who interested them. Give me six months, Cap thought, and we'll have enough. Just long enough to map the terrain inside that amazing little head. No House or Senate subcommittee would be able to resist the promise of chemically induced psi powers and the enormous implications it would have on the arms race if that little girl was even half of what Wanless suspected.

And there were other possibilities. They were not in the blue-backed report, because they were too explosive for even a TOP SECRET heading. Hockstetter, who had become progressively more excited as the picture took shape before him and his committee of experts, had mentioned one of these possibilities to Cap only a week ago.

'This Z factor,' Hockstetter said. 'Have you considered any of the ramifications if it turns out that the child isn't a mule but a genuine mutation?'

Cap had, although he did not tell Hockstetter that. It raised the interesting question of eugenics . . . the potentially explosive question of eugenics, with its lingering connotations of Nazism and superraces – all the things Americans had fought World War II to put an end to. But it was one thing to sink a philosophical well and produce a gusher of bullshit about usurping the power of God and quite another to produce laboratory evidence that the offspring of Lot Six parents might be human torches, levitators, tele- or telempaths, or God only knew what else. Ideals were cheap things to hold as long as there were no solid arguments for their overthrow. If there were, what then? Human breeding farms? As crazy as it sounded, Cap could visualize it. It could be the key to everything. World peace, or world domination, and when you got rid of the trick mirrors of rhetoric and bombast, weren't they really the same thing?

It was a whole can of worms. The possibilities stretched a dozen years into the future. Cap knew the best he himself could realistically hope for was six months, but it might be enough to set policy – to survey the land on which the tracks would be laid and the railroad would run. It would be his legacy to the country and to the world. Measured against this, the lives of a runaway college instructor and his ragamuffin daughter were less than dust in the wind.

The girl could not be tested and observed with any degree of validity if she was constantly drugged, but her father would be their hostage to fortune. And on the few occasions they wanted to run tests on him, the reverse would hold. It was a simple system of levers. And as Archimedes had observed, a lever long enough would move the world.

The intercom buzzed.

'John Rainbird is here,' the new girl said. Her usual bland receptionist's tone was threadbare enough to show the fear beneath.

On that one I don't blame you, babe, Cap thought.

'Send him in, please.'

Same old Rainbird.

He came in slowly, dressed in a brown and balding leather jacket over a faded plaid shirt. Old and scuffed Dingos peeked out from beneath the cuffs of his faded straight-leg jeans. The top of his huge head seemed almost to brush the ceiling. The gored ruin of his empty eye-socket made Cap shudder inwardly.

'Cap,' he said, and sat down. 'I have been in the desert too long.'

'I've heard about your Flagstaff house,' Cap said. 'And your shoe collection.'

John Rainbird only stared at him unblinkingly with his good eye.

'How come I never see you in anything but those old shitkickers?' Cap asked.

Rainbird smiled thinly and said nothing. The old unease filled Cap and he found himself wondering again how much Rainbird knew, and why it bothered him so much.

'I have a job for you,' he said.

'Good. Is it the one I want?'

Cap looked at him, surprised, considering, and then said, 'I think it is.'

'Then tell me, Cap.'

Cap outlined the plan that would bring Andy and Charlie McGee to Longmont. It didn't take long.

'Can you use the gun?' he asked when he was finished.

'I can use any gun. And your plan is a good one. It will succeed.'

'How nice of you to give it your stamp of approval,' Cap said. He tried for light irony and only succeeded in sounding petulant. God damn the man anyway.

'And I will fire the gun,' Rainbird said. 'On one condition.'

Cap stood up, planted his hands on his desk, which was littered with components from the McGee file, and leaned toward Rainbird.

'No,' he said. 'You don't make conditions with me.'

'I do this time,' Rainbird said. 'But you will find it an easy one to fulfill, I think.'

'No,' Cap repeated. Suddenly his heart was hammering in his chest, although with fear or anger he was not sure. 'You misunderstand. I am in charge of this agency and this facility. I am your superior. I believe you spent enough time in the army to understand the concept of a superior officer.'

'Yes,' Rainbird said, smiling, 'I scragged one or two in my time. Once directly on Shop orders. *Your* orders, Cap.'

'Is that a threat?' Cap cried. Some part of him was aware that he was overreacting, but he seemed unable to help himself. 'God damn you, is that a threat? If it is, I think you've lost your senses completely! If I decide I don't want you to leave this building, all I have to do is press a button! There are thirty men who can fire that rifle—'

'But none can fire it with such assurance as this one-eyed red nigger,' Rainbird said. His gentle tone had not changed. 'You think you have them now, Cap, but they are will-o'-the-wisps. Whatever gods there are may not want you to have them. They may not want you to set them down in your rooms of deviltry and emptiness. You have thought you had them before.' He pointed to the file material heaped on the library trolley and then to the blue-backed folder. 'I've read the material. And I've read your Dr Hockstetter's report.'

'The devil you have!' Cap exclaimed, but he could see the truth in Rainbird's face. He had. Somehow he had. Who gave it to him? he raged. Who?

'Oh yes,' Rainbird said. 'I have what I want, when I want it. People give it to me. I think . . . it must be my

249

pretty face.' His smile widened and became suddenly, horribly predatory. His good eye rolled in its socket.

'What are you saying to me?' Cap asked. He wanted a glass of water.

'Just that I have had a long time in Arizona to walk and smell the winds that blow . . . and for you, Cap, it smells bitter, like the wind off an alkali flat. I had time to do a lot of reading and a lot of thinking. And what I think is that I may be the only man in all the world who can surely bring those two here. And it may be that I am the only man in all the world who can do something with the little girl once she's here. Your fat report, your Thorazine and your Orasin – there may be more here than drugs can cope with. More dangers than you can understand.'

Hearing Rainbird was like hearing the ghost of Wanless, and Cap was now in the grip of such fear and such fury that he couldn't speak.

'I will do all this,' Rainbird said kindly. 'I will bring them here and you will do all your tests.' He was like a father giving a child permission to play with some new toy. 'On the condition that you give the girl to me for disposal when you are finished with her.'

'You're mad,' Cap whispered.

'How right you are,' Rainbird said, and laughed. 'So are you. Mad as a hatter. You sit here and make your plans for controlling a force beyond your comprehension. A force that belongs only to the gods themselves . . . and to this one little girl.'

'And what's to stop me from having you erased? Right here and now?'

'My word,' Rainbird said, 'that if I disappear, such a shockwave of revulsion and indignation will run through this country within the month that Watergate will look like the filching of penny candy in comparison. My word that if I disappear, the Shop will cease to exist within six weeks, and that within six months you will stand before a judge for sentencing on crimes serious enough to keep you behind bars for the rest of your life.' He smiled again, showing crooked tombstone teeth. 'Do not doubt me, Cap. My days in this reeking, putrescent vineyard have been long, and the vintage would be a bitter one indeed.'

Cap tried to laugh. What came out was a choked snarl.

'For over ten years I have been putting my nuts and forage by,' Rainbird said serenely, 'like any animal that has known winter and remembers it. I have such a potpourri, Cap – photos, tapes, Xerox copies of documents that would make the blood of our good friend John Q. Public run cold.'

'None of that is possible,' Cap said, but he knew Rainbird was not bluffing, and he felt as if a cold, invisible hand were pressing down on his chest.

'Oh, very possible,' Rainbird said. 'For the last three years I've been in a state of information passing-gear, because for the last three years I've been able to tap into your computer whenever I liked. On a time-sharing basis, of course, which makes it expensive, but I have been able to pay. My wages have been very fine, and with investment they have grown. I stand before you, Cap – or sit, which is the truth, but less poetic – as a triumphant example of American free enterprise in action.'

'No,' Cap said.

'Yes,' Rainbird replied. 'I am John Rainbird, but I am also the U.S. Bureau for Geological Understudies. Check, if you like. My computer code is AXON. Check the time-sharing codes in your main terminal. Take the elevator. I'll wait.' Rainbird crossed his legs and the cuff of his right pantsleg pulled up, revealing a rip and a bulge in a seam of one of his boots. He looked like a man who could wait out the age, if that were necessary.

Cap's mind was whirling. 'Access to the computer on a

time-sharing basis, perhaps. That still doesn't tap you into—'

'Go see Dr Noftzieger,' Rainbird said kindly. 'Ask him how many ways there are to tap into a computer once you have access on a time-sharing basis. Two years ago, a bright twelve-year-old tapped into the USC computer. And by the way, I know *your* access code, Cap. It's BROW this year. Last year it was RASP. I thought that was much more appropriate.'

Cap sat and looked at Rainbird. His mind had divided, it seemed, had become a three-ring circus. Part of it was marveling that he had never heard John Rainbird say so much at one time. Part of it was trying to grapple with the idea that this maniac knew all of the Shop's business. A third part was remembering a Chinese curse, a curse that sounded deceptively pleasant until you sat down and really thought about it. *May you live in interesting times.* For the last year and a half he had lived in extremely interesting times. He felt that just one more interesting thing would drive him totally insane.

And then he thought of Wanless again – with dragging, dawning, horror. He felt almost as if . . . as if . . . he were turning into Wanless. Beset with demons on every side but helpless to fight them off or even to enlist help.

'What do you want, Rainbird?'

'I've told you already, Cap. I want nothing but your word that my involvement with this girl Charlene McGee will not end with the rifle but begin there. I want to' – Rainbird's eye darkened and became thoughtful, moody, introspective – 'I want to know her intimately.'

Cap looked at him, horror-struck.

Rainbird understood suddenly, and he shook his head at Cap contemptuously. 'Not *that* intimately. Not in the biblical sense. But I'll know her. She and I are going to be

252

friends, Cap. If she is as powerful as all things indicate, she and I are going to be great friends.'

Cap made a sound of humor: not a laugh, exactly; more of a shrill giggle.

The expression of contempt on Rainbird's face did not change. 'No, of course you don't think that is possible. You look at my face and you see a monster. You look at my hands and see them covered with the blood you ordered me to spill. But I tell you, Cap, it will happen. The girl has had no friend for going on two years. She has had her father and that is all. You see her as you see me, Cap. It is your great failing. You look, you see a monster. Only in the girl's case, you see a useful monster. Perhaps this is because you are a white man. White men see monsters everywhere. White men look at their own pricks and see monsters.' Rainbird laughed again.

Cap had at last begun to calm down and to think reasonably. 'Why should I allow it, even if all you say is true? Your days are numbered and we both know it. You've been hunting your own death for twenty years. Anything else has been incidental, only a hobby. You'll find it soon enough. And then it ends for all of us. So why should I give you the pleasure of having what you want?'

'Perhaps it's as you say. Perhaps I have been hunting my own death – a more colorful phrase than I would have expected from you, Cap. Maybe you should have the fear of God put into you more often.'

'You're not my idea of God,' Cap said.

Rainbird grinned. 'More like the Christian devil, sure. But I tell you this – if I had really been hunting my own death, I believe I would have found it long before this. Perhaps I've been stalking it for play. But I have no desire to bring you down, Cap, or the Shop, or U.S. domestic intelligence. I am no idealist. I only want this little girl. And you may find you need me. You may find that I am able to accomplish things that all the drugs in Dr Hock-stetter's cabinet will not.'

'And in return?'

· 'When the affair of the McGees ends, the U.S. Bureau for Geological Understudies will cease to exist. Your computer chief, Noftzieger, can change all his codings. And you, Cap, will fly to Arizona with me on a public airline. We will enjoy a good dinner at my favorite Flagstaff restaurant and then we will go back to my house, and behind it, in the desert, we will start a fire of our own and barbecue a great many papers and tapes and films. I will even show you my shoe collection, if you like.'

Cap thought it over. Rainbird gave him time, sitting calmly.

At last Cap said, 'Hockstetter and his colleagues suggest it may take two years to open the girl up completely. It depends on how deeply her protective inhibitions go.'

'And you will be gone in four to six months.'

Cap shrugged.

Rainbird touched the side of his nose with one index finger and cocked his head – a grotesque fairy-tale gesture. 'I think we can keep you in the saddle much longer than that, Cap. Between the two of us, we know where hundreds of bodies are buried – literally as well as figuratively. And I doubt if it will take years. We'll both get what we want, in the end. What do you say?'

Cap thought about it. He felt old and tired and at a complete loss. 'I guess,' he said, 'that you have made yourself a deal.'

'Fine,' Rainbird said briskly. 'I will be the girl's orderly, I think. No one at all in the established scheme of things. That will be important to her. And of course she will never know I was the one who fired the rifle. That would be dangerous knowledge, wouldn't it? Very dangerous.'

'Why?' Cap said finally. 'Why have you gone to these insane lengths?'

'Do they seem insane?' Rainbird asked lightly. He got up and took one of the pictures from Cap's desk. It was the photo of Charlie sliding down the slope of crusted snow on her flattened cardboard box, laughing. 'We all put our nuts and forage by for winter in this business, Cap. Hoover did it. So did CIA directors beyond counting. So have you, or you would be drawing a pension right now. When I began, Charlene McGee wasn't even born, and I was only covering my own ass.'

'But why the girl?'

Rainbird didn't answer for a long time. He was looking at the photograph carefully, almost tenderly. He touched it.

'She is very beautiful,' he said. 'And very young. Yet inside her is your Z factor. The power of the gods. She and I will be close.' His eye grew dreamy. 'Yes, we will be very close.'

In the Box

1

On March 27, Andy McGee decided abruptly that they could stay in Tashmore no longer. It had been more than two weeks since he had mailed his letters, and if anything was going to come of them, it already would have. The very fact of the continuing silence around Granther's camp made him uneasy. He supposed he could simply have been dismissed out of hand as a crackpot in every case, but . . . he didn't believe it.

What he believed, what his deepest intuition whispered, was that his letters had been somehow diverted.

And that would mean they knew where he and Charlie were.

'We're going,' he told Charlie. 'Let's get our stuff together.'

She only looked at him with her careful eyes, a little scared, and said nothing. She didn't ask him where they were going or what they were going to do, and that made him nervous, too. In one of the closets he had found two old suitcases, plastered with ancient vacation decals – Grand Rapids, Niagara Falls, Miami Beach – and the two of them began to sort what they would take and what they would leave.

Blinding bright sunlight streamed in through the windows on the east side of the cottage. Water dripped and gurgled in the downspouts. The night before, he had got little sleep; the ice had gone out and he had lain awake listening to it – the high, ethereal, and somehow uncanny sound of the old yellow ice splitting and moving slowly down toward the neck of the pond, where the Great Hancock River spilled eastward across New Hampshire and all of Maine, growing progressively more smelly and polluted until it vomited, noisome and dead, into the Atlantic. The sound was like a prolonged crystal note or perhaps that of a bow drawn endlessly across a high violin string – a constant, fluted *zzziiiiiinnnggg* that settled over the nerve endings and seemed to make them vibrate in sympathy. He had never been here at ice-out before and was not sure he would ever want to be again. There was something terrible and otherworldly about that sound as it vibrated between the silent evergreen walls of this low and eroded bowl of hills.

He felt that they were very near again, like the barely seen monster in a recurring nightmare. The day after Charlie's birthday, he had been on one of his tramps, the cross-country skis buckled uncomfortably onto his feet, and he had come across a line of snowshoe tracks leading up to a tall spruce tree. There were indents in the crust like periods where the snowshoes had been taken off and jammed into the snow on their tails. There was a flurried confusion where the wearer had later refastened his snowshoes ('slushboats,' Granther had always called them, holding them in contempt for some obscure reason of his own). At the base of the tree, Andy had found six Vantage cigarette butts and a crumpled yellow package that had once contained Kodak Tri-X film. More uneasy than ever, he had taken off the skis and climbed up into the tree. Halfway up he had found himself on a direct line-of-sight with Granther's cottage a mile away. It was small and apparently empty. But with a telephoto lens . . .

He hadn't mentioned his find to Charlie.

The suitcases were packed. Her continued silence forced

him into nervous speech, as if by not talking she was accusing him.

'We're going to hitch a ride into Berlin,' he said, 'and then we'll get a Greyhound back to New York City. We're going to the offices of the New York *Times*—'

'But, Daddy, you sent them a letter.'

'Honey, they might not have gotten it.'

She looked at him in silence for a moment and then said, 'Do you think *they* took it?'

'Of course n—' He shook his head and started again. 'Charlie, I just don't know.'

Charlie didn't reply. She knelt, closed one of the suitcases, and began fumbling ineffectually with the clasps.

'Let me help you, hon.'

'*I can do it!*' She screamed at him, and then began to cry.

'Charlie, don't,' he said. 'Please, hon. It's almost over.'

'No, it's not,' she said, crying harder. 'It's never going to be over.'

2

There were an even dozen agents around Granther McGee's cabin. They had taken up their positions the night before. They all wore mottled white and green clothing. None of them had been at the Manders farm, and none of them was armed except for John Rainbird, who had the rifle, and Don Jules, who carried a .22 pistol.

'I am taking no chances of having someone panic because of what happened back in New York,' Rainbird had told Cap. 'That Jamieson still looks as if his balls are hanging around his knees.'

Similarly, he would not hear of the agents going armed. Things had a way of happening, and he didn't want to come out of the operation with two corpses. He had handpicked all of the agents, and the one he had chosen to take Andy McGee was Don Jules. Jules was small, thirty-ish, silent, morose. He was good at his job. Rainbird knew, because Jules was the only man he had chosen to work with more than once. He was quick and practical. He did not get in the way at critical moments.

'McGee will be out at some point during the day,' Rainbird had told them at the briefing. 'The girl usually comes out, but McGee always does. If the man comes out alone, I'll take him and Jules will get him out of sight quickly and quietly. If the girl should come out alone, same thing. If they come out together, I'll take the girl and Jules will take McGee. The rest of you are just spear carriers – do you understand that?' Rainbird's eye glared over them. 'You're there in case something goes drastically wrong, and that is all. Of course, if something *does* go drastically wrong, most of you will be running for the lake with your pants on fire. You're along in case that one chance in a hundred turns up where you can do something. Of course, it's understood that you're also along as observers and witnesses in case I fuck up.'

This had earned a thin and nervous chuckle.

Rainbird raised one finger. 'If any one of you miscues and puts their wind up somehow, I'll personally see that you end up in the lousiest jungle valley of South America I can find – with a cored asshole. Believe that, gentlemen. You are spear carriers in my show. Remember it.'

Later, at their 'staging area' – an abandoned motel in St Johnsbury – Rainbird had taken Don Jules aside.

'You have read the file on this man,' Rainbird said.

Jules was smoking a Camel. 'Yeah.'

'You understand the concept of mental domination?'

'Yeah.'

'You understand what happened to the two men in Ohio? The men that tried to take his daughter away?'

260

'I worked with George Waring,' Jules said evenly. 'That guy could burn water making tea.'

'In this man's outfit, that is not so unusual. I only need us to be clear. You'll need to be very quick.'

'Yeah, okay.'

'He's had a whole winter to rest, this guy. If he gets time to give you a shot, you're a good candidate to spend the next three years of your life in a padded room, thinking you're a bird or a turnip or something.'

'All right.'

'All right what?'

'I'll be quick. Give it a rest, John.'

'There's a good chance that they will come out together,' Rainbird said, ignoring him. 'You'll be around the corner of the porch, out of sight of the door where they'll come out. You wait for me to take the girl. Her father will go to her. You'll be behind him. Get him in the neck.'

'Sure.'

'Don't screw this up, Don.'

Jules smiled briefly and smoked. 'No,' he said.

3

The suitcases were packed. Charlie had put on her coat and her snowpants. Andy shrugged into his own jacket, zipped it, and picked up the suitcases. He didn't feel good, not at all good. He had the jumps. One of his hunches.

'You feel it, too, don't you?' Charlie asked. Her small face was pale and expressionless.

Andy nodded reluctantly.

'What do we do?'

'We hope the feeling's a little early,' he said, although in his heart he didn't think it was so. 'What else can we do?'

'What else can we do?' she echoed.

She came to him then and lifted her arms to be picked

up, something he could not remember her doing for a long time – maybe two years. It was amazing how time got by, how quickly a child could change, change in front of your eyes with an unobtrusiveness that was nearly terrible.

He put the suitcases down and picked her up and hugged her. She kissed his cheek and then hugged him again, very tightly.

'Are you ready?' he asked, setting her down.

'I guess so,' Charlie said. She was close to tears again. 'Daddy . . . I won't make fires. Not even if they come before we can get away.'

'Yes,' he said. 'That's all right, Charlie. I understand that.'

'I love you, Dad.'

He nodded. 'I love you too, kiddo.'

Andy went to the door and opened it. For a moment the sunlight was so bright that he could see nothing at all. Then his pupils contracted and the day cleared before him, bright with melting snow. To his right was Tashmore Pond, dazzling, jaggedly irregular patches of blue water showing between the floating chunks of ice. Straight ahead were pine woods. Through them he could barely see the green shingled roof of the next camp, free of snow at last.

The woods were still, and Andy's feeling of disquiet intensified. Where was the birdsong that had greeted their mornings ever since the winter temperatures had begun to moderate? There was none today . . . only the drip of snow melting from the branches. He found himself wishing desperately that Granther had put in a phone out here. He had to restrain an urge to shout *Who's there?* at the top of his lungs. But that would only frighten Charlie more.

'Looks fine,' he said. 'I think we're still ahead of them . . . if they're coming at all.'

'That's good,' she said colorlessly.

'Let's hit the road, kid,' Andy said, and thought for the

262

hundredth time, *What else is there to do?* and thought again how much he hated them.

Charlie came across the room to him, past the drainer full of dishes they had washed that morning after breakfast. The entire cottage was the way they had found it, spick-and-span. Granther would have been pleased.

Andy slipped an arm around Charlie's shoulders and gave her one more brief hug. Then he picked up the suitcases and they stepped out into the early spring sunshine together.

4

John Rainbird was halfway up a tall spruce one hundred and fifty yards away. He was wearing lineman's spikes on his feet and a lineman's belt held him firmly against the trunk of the tree. When the cabin door opened, he threw the rifle to his shoulder and seated it firmly. Total calm fell over him in a reassuring cloak. Everything became startlingly clear in front of his one good eye. When he lost his other eye, he had suffered a blurring of his depth of perception, but at moments of extreme concentration, like this one, his old, clear seeing came back to him; it was as if the ruined eye could regenerate itself for brief periods.

It was not a long shot, and he would not have wasted a moment's worry if it had been a bullet he was planning to put through the girl's neck – but he was dealing with something far more clumsy, something that jumped the risk element by a factor of ten. Fixed inside the barrel of this specially modified rifle was a dart tipped with an ampul of Orasin, and at this distance there was always a chance it might tumble or veer. Luckily, the day was almost without wind.

If it is the will of the Great Spirit and of my ancestors,

263

Rainbird prayed silently, *guide my hands and my eye that the shot may be true.*

The girl came out with her father by her side – Jules was in it, then. Through the telescopic sight the girl looked as big as a barn door. The parka was a bright blue blaze against the weathered boards of the cabin. Rainbird had a moment to note the suitcases in McGee's hands, to realize they were just in time after all.

The girl's hood was down, the tab of her zipper pulled up only to her breastbone, so that the coat spread open slightly at the throat. The day was warm, and that was in his favor, too.

He tightened down on the trigger and sighted the crosshairs on the base of her throat.

If it is the will—

He squeezed the trigger. There was no explosion, only a hollow *phut!* and a small curl of smoke from the rifle's breech.

5

They were on the edge of the steps when Charlie suddenly stopped and made a strangled swallowing noise. Andy dropped the suitcases immediately. He had heard nothing, but something was terribly wrong. Something about Charlie had changed.

'Charlie? *Charlie?*'

He stared at her. She stood as still as a statue, incredibly beautiful against the bright snowfield. Incredibly small. And suddenly he realized what the change was. It was so fundamental, so awful, that he had not been able to grasp it at first.

What appeared to be a long needle was sticking out of Charlie's throat just below the Adam's apple. Her mittened hand groped for it, found it, twisted it to a new and grotesque, upward-jutting angle. A thin trickle of blood began to flow from the wound and down the side of her throat. A flower of blood, small and delicate, stained the collar of her shirt and just touched the edging of fake fur that bordered the zipper of her parka.

'Charlie!' he screamed. He leaped forward and grabbed her arm just as her eyes rolled up and she pitched outward. He let her down to the porch, crying her name over and over. The dart in her throat twinkled brightly in the sun. Her body had the loose, boneless feel of a dead thing. He held her, cradled her, and looked out at the sunshiny woods that seemed so empty – and where no birds sang.

'Who did it?' he screamed? *'Who did it? Come out where I can see you!'*

Don Jules stepped around the corner of the porch. He was wearing Adidas tennis sneakers. He held the .22 in one hand.

'Who shot my daughter?' Andy screamed. Something in his throat vibrated painfully with the force of his scream. He held her to him, so terribly loose and boneless inside her warm blue parka. His fingers went to the dart and pulled it out, starting a fresh trickle of blood.

Get her inside, he thought. *Got to get her inside*.

Jules approached him and shot him in the back of the neck, much as the actor Booth had once shot a President. For a moment Andy jerked upward on his knees, holding Charlie even more tightly against him. Then he collapsed forward over her.

Jules looked at him closely, then waved the men out of the woods.

'Nothing to it,' he said to himself as Rainbird came toward the cabin, wading through the sticky, melting snow of late March. 'Nothing to it. What was all the fuss about?'

The Blackout

1

The chain of events that ended in such destruction and loss of life began with a summer storm and the failure of two generators.

The storm came on August 19, almost five months after Andy and Charlie were taken at Granther's camp in Vermont. For ten days the weather had been sticky and still. That August day, the thunderheads began to pile up shortly after noon, but nobody who worked on the grounds of the two handsome antebellum homes which faced each other across the rolling expanse of green lawn and manicured flowerbeds believed that the thunderheads were telling the truth – not the groundsmen astride their Lawnboys, not the woman who was in charge of computer subsections A–E (as well as the computer-room coffee-maker), who took one of the horses and cantered it lovingly along the well-kept bridle paths during her lunch hour, certainly not Cap, who ate a hero sandwich in his air-conditioned office and went right on working on next year's budget, oblivious of the heat and humidity outside.

Perhaps the only person in the Shop compound at Longmont that day who thought it really would rain was the man who had been named for the rain. The big Indian drove in at twelve-thirty, prefatory to clocking in at one. His bones, and the shredded hollow where his left eye had been, ached when rain was on the way.

He was driving a very old and rusty Thunderbird with a *D* parking sticker on the windshield. He was dressed in orderly's whites. Before he got out of the car, he put on an embroidered eyepatch. He wore it when he was on the job, because of the girl, but only then. It bothered him. It was only the patch that made him think about the lost eye.

There were four parking lots inside the Shop enclave. Rainbird's personal car, a new yellow Cadillac that ran on diesel fuel, bore an *A* sticker. *A* was the VIP parking lot, located beneath the southernmost of the two plantation houses. An underground tunnel-and-elevator system connected the VIP lot directly with the computer room, the situation rooms, the extensive Shop library and newsrooms, and, of course, the Visitors' Quarters – a nondescript name for the complex of laboratories and nearby apartments where Charlie McGee and her father were being kept.

The *B* lot was for second-echelon employees; it was farther away. *C* parking lot was for secretaries, mechanics, electricians, and the like; it was farther away still. *D* lot was for unskilled employees – spear carriers, in Rainbird's own terms. It was almost half a mile from anything, and always filled with a sad and motley collection of Detroit rolling iron only a step and a half away from the weekly demo derby at Jackson Plains, the nearby stock-car track.

The bureaucratic pecking order, Rainbird thought, locking his wreck of a T-bird and tilting his head up to look at the thunderheads. The storm was coming. It would arrive around four o'clock, he reckoned.

He began to walk toward the small Quonset hut set tastefully back in a grove of sugarpines where low-level employees, Class Vs and VIs, punched in. His whites flapped around him. A gardener putted by him on one of the Groundskeeping Department's dozen or so riding lawnmowers. A gaily colored sun parasol floated above the seat. The gardener took no notice of Rainbird; that was also part of the bureaucratic pecking order. If you were a Class IV, a Class V became invisible. Not even Rainbird's half-destroyed face caused much comment; like every other government agency, the Shop hired enough vets to look good. Max Factor had little to teach the U.S. government about good cosmetics. And it went without saying that a vet with some visible disability – a prosthetic arm, a motorized wheelchair, a scrambled face – was worth any three vets who looked 'normal.' Rainbird knew men who had had their minds and spirits mauled as badly as his own face had been in the Vietnam traveling house party, men who would have been happy to find a job clerking in a Piggly Wiggly. But they just didn't look right. Not that Rainbird had any sympathy for them. In fact, he found the whole thing rather funny.

Nor was he recognized by any of the people he now worked with as a former Shop agent and hatchet man; he would have sworn to that. Until seventeen weeks ago, he had been only a shadow shape behind his yellow Cadillac's polarized windshield, just someone else with an *A* clearance.

'Don't you think you're going overboard with this a bit?' Cap had asked. 'The girl has no connection with the gardeners or the steno pool. You're only onstage with her.'

Rainbird shook his head. 'All it would take is a single slip. One person to mention, just casually, that the friendly orderly with the messed-up face parks his car in the VIP lot and changes to his whites in the executive washroom. What I am trying to build here is a sense of trust, that trust to be based on the idea that we're both outsiders – both freaks, if you will – buried in the bowels of the KGB's American branch.'

Cap hadn't liked that; he didn't like anyone taking cheap shots at the Shop's methods, particularly in this case, where the methods were admittedly extreme.

'Well, you're sure doing one hell of a job,' Cap had answered.

And to that there was no satisfactory answer, because in fact, he *wasn't* doing a hell of a job. The girl had not done so much as light a match in all the time she had been here. And the same could be said for her father, who had demonstrated not the slightest sign of any mental-domination ability, if the ability still existed within him. More and more they were coming to doubt that it did.

The girl fascinated Rainbird. The first year he had been with the Shop, he had taken a series of courses not to be found in any college curriculum – wiretapping, car theft, unobtrusive search, a dozen others. The only one that had engaged Rainbird's attention fully was the course in safecracking, taught by an aging burglar named G. M. Rammaden. Rammaden had been sprung from an institution in Atlanta for the specific purpose of teaching this craft to new Shop agents. He was supposed to be the best in the business, and Rainbird would not have doubted that, although he believed that by now he was almost Rammaden's equal.

Rammaden, who had died three years ago (Rainbird had sent flowers to his funeral – what a comedy life could sometimes be!), had taught them about Skidmore locks, about square-door boxes, about secondary locking devices that can permanently freeze a safe's tumblers if the combination dial is knocked off with a hammer and chisel; he had taught them about barrel boxes, and niggerheads, and cutting keys; the many uses of graphite; how you could take a key impression with a Brillo pad and how to make bathtub nitroglycerine and how to peel a box from the back, one layer at a time.

Rainbird had responded to G. M. Rammaden with a cold and cynical enthusiasm. Rammaden had said once that safes were like women: given the tools and the time, any box could be opened. There were, he said, tough cracks and easy cracks, but no impossible cracks.

270

This girl was tough.

At first they had had to feed Charlie intravenously just to keep her from starving herself to death. After a while she began to understand that not eating was gaining her nothing but a lot of bruises on the insides of her elbows, and she began to eat, not with any enthusiasm but simply because using her mouth was less painful.

She read some of the books that were given her – leafed through them, at any rate – and would sometimes turn on the color TV in her room only to turn it off again a few minutes later. She had watched a local movie presentation of *Black Beauty* all the way through in June, and she had sat through *The Wonderful World of Disney* once or twice. That was all. On her weekly reports the phrase 'sporadic aphasia' had begun to crop up more and more often.

Rainbird had looked the term up in a medical dictionary and understood it at once – because of his own experiences as Indian and warrior, he understood it perhaps better than the doctors themselves. Sometimes the girl ran out of words. She would simply stand there, not a bit upset, her mouth working soundlessly. And sometimes she would use a totally out-of-context word, apparently without realizing it at all. 'I don't like this dress, I'd rather have the hay one.' Sometimes she would correct herself absently – 'I mean the *green* one' – but more often it would simply pass unnoticed.

According to the dictionary, aphasia was forgetfulness caused by some cerebral disorder. The doctors had immediately begun monkeying with her medication. Orasin was changed to Valium with no appreciable change for the better. Valium and Orasin were tried together, but an unforeseen interaction between the two had caused her to cry steadily and monotonously until the dose wore off. A brand-new drug, a combination of tranquilizer and light hallucinogenic, was tried and seemed to help for a while.

Then she had begun to stutter and broke out in a light rash. Currently she was back on Orasin, but she was being monitored closely in case the aphasia got worse.

Reams had been written about the girl's delicate psychological condition and about what the shrinks called her 'basic fire conflict,' a fancy way of saying that her father had told her not to and the Shop people were telling her to go ahead . . . all of it complicated by her guilt over the incident at the Manders farm.

Rainbird bought none of it. It wasn't the drugs, it wasn't being locked up and watched constantly, it wasn't being separated from her father.

She was just tough, that was all.

She had made up her mind somewhere along the line that she wasn't going to cooperate, no matter what. The end. Toot finnee. The psychiatrists could run around showing her inkblots until the moon was blue, the doctors could play with her medication and mutter in their beards about the difficulty of successfully drugging an eight-year-old girl. The papers could pile up and Cap could rave on.

And Charlie McGee would simply go on toughing it out.

Rainbird sensed it as surely as he sensed the coming of rain this afternoon. And he admired her for it. She had the whole bunch of them chasing their tails, and if it was left up to them they would still be chasing their tails when Thanksgiving and then Christmas rolled around. But they wouldn't chase their tails forever, and this more than anything worried John Rainbird.

Rammaden, the safecracker, had told an amusing story about two thieves who had broken into a supermarket one Friday night when they knew a snowstorm had kept the Wells Fargo truck from arriving and taking the heavy end-of-the-week receipts to the bank. The safe was a barrel box. They tried to drill out the combination dial with no success. They had tried to peel it but had been totally

272

unable to bend back a corner and get a start. Finally they had blown it. That was a total success. They blew that barrel wide open, so wide open in fact that all the money inside had been totally destroyed. What was left had looked like the shredded money you sometimes see in those novelty pens.

'The point is,' Rammaden had said in his dry and wheezing voice, 'those two thieves didn't beat the safe. The whole game is beating the safe. You don't beat the safe unless you can take away what was in it in usable condition, you get my point? They overloaded it with soup. They killed the money. They were assholes and the safe beat them.'

Rainbird had got the point.

There were better than sixty college degrees in on this, but it still came down to safecracking. They had tried to drill the girl's combination with their drugs; they had enough shrinks to field a softball team, and these shrinks were all doing their best to resolve the 'basic fire conflict'; and all that particular pile of horseapples boiled down to was that they were trying to peel her from the back.

Rainbird entered the small Quonset hut, took his time card from the rack, and punched in. T. B. Norton, the shift supervisor, looked up from the paperback he was reading.

'No overtime for punching in early, Injun.'

'Yeah?' Rainbird said.

'Yeah.' Norton stared at him challengingly, full of the grim, almost holy assurance that so often goes with petty authority.

Rainbird dropped his eyes and went over to look at the bulletin board. The orderlies' bowling team had won last night. Someone wanted to sell '2 good used washing machine's.' An official notice proclaimed that ALL W-1

273

THROUGH W-6 WORKERS MUST WASH HANDS BEFORE LEAVING
THIS OFFICE.

'Looks like rain,' he said over his shoulder to Norton.

'Never happen, Injun,' Norton said. 'Why don't you blow? You're stinking the place up.'

'Sure, boss,' Rainbird said. 'Just clockin in.'

'Well next time clock in when you're spozed to.'

'Sure, boss,' Rainbird said again, going out, sparing one glance at the side of Norton's pink neck, the soft spot just below the jawbone. Would you have time to scream, boss? Would you have time to scream if I stuck my forefinger through your throat at that spot? Just like a skewer through a piece of steak . . . boss.

He went back out into the muggy heat. The thunder-heads were closer now, moving slowly, bowed down with their weight of rain. It was going to be a hard storm. Thunder muttered, still distant.

The house was close now. Rainbird would go around to the side entrance, what had once been the pantry, and take C elevator down four levels. Today he was supposed to wash and wax all the floors in the girl's quarters; it would give him a good shot. And it wasn't that she was unwilling to talk with him; it wasn't that. It was just that she was always so damned distant. He was trying to peel the box in his own way, and if he could get her to *laugh*, just once get her to laugh, to share a joke with him at the Shop's expense, it would be like prying up that one vital corner. It would give him a place to set his chisel. Just that one laugh. It would make them insiders together, it would make them a committee in secret session. Two against the house.

But so far he hadn't been able to get that one laugh, and Rainbird admired her for that more than he could have said.

274

Rainbird put his ID card in the proper slot and then went down to the orderlies' station to grab a cup of coffee before going on. He didn't want coffee, but it was still early. He couldn't afford to let his eagerness show; it was bad enough that Norton had noticed and commented on it.

He poured himself a slug of mud from the hotplate and sat down with it. At least none of the other nerds had arrived yet. He sat down on the cracked and sprung gray sofa and drank his coffee. His blasted face (and Charlie had shown nothing but the most passing interest in that) was calm and impassive. His thoughts ran on, analyzing the situation as it now stood.

The staff on this were like Rammaden's green safecrackers in the supermarket office. They were handling the girl with kid gloves now, but they weren't doing it out of any love for the girl. Sooner or later they would decide that the kid gloves were getting them nowhere, and when they ran out of 'soft' options, they would decide to blow the safe. When they did, Rainbird was almost sure that they would 'kill the money,' in Rammaden's pungent phrase.

Already he had seen the phrase 'light shock treatments' in two of the doctors' reports – and one of the doctors had been Pynchot, who had Hockstetter's ear. He had seen a contingency report that had been couched in such stulti-fying jargon that it was nearly another language. Trans-lated, what it boiled down to was a lot of strongarm stuff: if the kid sees her dad in enough pain, she'll break. What Rainbird thought the kid might do if she saw her dad hooked up to a Delco battery and doing a fast polka with his hair on end was to go calmly back to her room, break a waterglass, and eat the pieces.

But you couldn't tell them that. The Shop, like the FBI and CIA, had a long history of killing the money. If you can't get what you want with foreign aid, go in there with some Thompsons and gelignite and assassinate the bastard. Put some cyanide gas in Castro's cigars. It was crazy, but you couldn't tell them that. All they could see were RESULTS, glittering and blinking like some mythical Vegas jackpot. So they killed the money and stood there with a bunch of useless green scraps sifting through their fingers and wondered what the hell had happened.

Now other orderlies began to drift in, joking, smacking each other on the fat part of the arm, talking about the strikes they made and the spares they converted the night before, talking about women, talking about cars, talking about getting shitfaced. The same old stuff that went on even unto the end of the world, hallelujah, amen. They steered clear of Rainbird. None of them liked Rainbird. He didn't bowl and he didn't want to talk about his car and he looked like a refugee from a Frankenstein movie. He made them nervous. If one of them had smacked him on the heavy part of the arm, Rainbird would have put him in traction.

He took out a sack of Red Man, a Zig-Zag paper, and made a quick cigarette. He sat and smoked and waited for it to be time to go down to the girl's quarters.

All things taken together, he felt better, more alive, than he had in years. He realized this and was grateful to the girl. In a way she would never know of, she had given him back his life for a while – the life of a man who feels things keenly and hopes for things mightily; which is to say, a man with vital concerns. It was good that she was tough. He would get to her eventually (tough cracks and easy cracks, but no impossible cracks); he would make her do her dance for them, for whatever that was worth; when the dance was done he would kill her and look into her eyes, hoping to catch that spark of understanding, that message, as she crossed over into whatever there was.

In the meantime, he would live.

He crushed his cigarette out and got up, ready to go to work.

3

The thunderheads built up and up. By three o'clock, the skies over the Longmont complex were low and black. Thunder rolled more and more heavily, gaining assurance, making believers out of the people below. The grounds-keepers put away their mowers. The tables on the patios of the two homes were taken in. In the stables, two hostlers tried to soothe nervous horses that shifted uneasily at each ominous thud from the skies.

The storm came around three-thirty; it came as suddenly as a gunslinger's draw and with all-out fury. It started as rain, then quickly turned to hail. The wind blew from west to east and then suddenly shifted around to exactly the opposite direction. Lightning flashed in great blue-white strokes that left the air smelling like weak gasoline. The winds began to swirl counterclockwise, and on the evening weathercasts there was film of a small tornado that had just skirted Longmont Center and had torn the roof off a shopping-center Fotomat in passing.

The Shop weathered most of the storm well. Two windows were driven in by hail, and the windstorm picked up a low picket fence surrounding a quaint little gazebo on the far side of the duckpond and threw it sixty yards, but that was the extent of the damage (except for flying branches and some ruined flowerbeds – more work for the groundskeeping force). The guard dogs ran between the inner and outer fences crazily at the height of the storm, but they calmed down quickly as it began to slack off.

The damage was done by the electrical storm that came after the hail, rain, and wind. Parts of eastern Virginia were without power until midnight as a result of lightning strikes on the Rowantree and Briska power stations. The area served by the Briska station included Shop headquarters.

In his office, Cap Hollister looked up in annoyance as the lights went off and the solid, unobtrusive hum of the air conditioner wound down to nothing. There were perhaps five seconds of shadowy semi-darkness caused by the power outage and the heavy stormclouds – long enough for Cap to whisper 'Goddam!' under his breath and wonder what the hell had happened to their backup electrical system.

He glanced out the window and saw lightning flickering almost continuously. That evening one of the guardhouse sentries would tell his wife that he had seen an electrical fireball that looked as big as two serving platters bouncing from the weakly charged outer fence to the more heavily charged inner fence and back again.

Cap reached for the phone to find out about the power – and then the lights came on again. The air conditioner took up its hum, and instead of reaching for the phone, Cap reached for his pencil.

Then the lights went out again.

'Shit!' Cap said. He threw the pencil down and picked up the phone after all, daring the lights to come on again before he had the chance to chew someone's ass. The lights declined the dare.

The two graceful homes facing each other across the rolling lawns – and all of the Shop complex underneath – were served by the Eastern Virginia Power Authority, but there were two backup systems powered by diesel generators. One system served the 'vital functions' – the electrical fence, the computer terminals (a power failure can cost unbelievable amounts of money in terms of computer time), and the small infirmary. A second system served the lesser functions of the complex – lights, air conditioning, elevators, and all of that. The secondary system was built to 'cross' – that is, to come in if the primary system showed signs of overloading – but the primary system would not cross if the secondary system began to overload. On August 19, both systems overloaded. The secondary system crossed when the primary system began to overload, just as the power-system architects had planned (although in truth, they had never planned for the primary system to overload in the first place), and as a result, the primary system operated for a full seventy seconds longer than the secondary system. Then the generators for both systems blew, one after the other, like a series of firecrackers. Only these firecrackers had cost about eighty thousand dollars each.

Later, a routine inquiry had brought back the smiling and benign verdict of 'mechanical failure,' although a more accurate conclusion would have been 'greed and venality.' When the backup generators had been installed in 1971, a senator privy to the acceptable-low-bid figures on that little operation (as well as sixteen million dollars' worth of other Shop construction) had tipped his brother-in-law, who was an electrical-engineering consultant. The consultant had decided he could quite handily come in under the lowest bid by cutting a corner here and there.

It was only one favor in an area that lives on favors and under-the-table information, and it was notable only because it was the first link in the chain that led to the final destruction and loss of life. The backup system had been used only piecemeal in all the years since it had been constructed. In its first major test, during the storm that knocked out the Briska power station, it failed completely. By then, of course, the electrical-engineering consultant had gone onward and upward; he was helping to build a multimillion-dollar beach resort at Coki Beach, on St Thomas.

The Shop didn't get its power back until the Briska station came on line again . . . which is to say, at the same time the rest of eastern Virginia got its juice back – around midnight.

By then, the next links had already been forged. As a result of the storm and the blackout, something tremendous had happened to both Andy and Charlie McGee, although neither of them had the slightest idea of what had happened to the other.

After five months of stasis, things had begun to roll onward again.

4

When the power went off, Andy McGee was watching *The PTL Club* on TV. The PTL stood for 'Praise the Lord.' On one of the Virginia stations, *The PTL Club* seemed to run continuously, twenty-four hours a day. This was probably not the case, but Andy's perceptions of time had become so screwed up it was hard to tell.

He had put on weight. Sometimes – more often when he was straight – he would catch a glimpse of himself in the mirror and think of Elvis Presley and the way the man had softly ballooned near the end of his life. At other times, he would think of the way a tomcat that had been 'fixed' would sometimes get fat and lazy.

He wasn't fat yet, but he was getting there. In Hastings Glen, he had weighed himself on the bathroom scale in the Slumberland Motel and had come in at one-sixty-two. These days he was tipping the scales at about one-ninety. His cheeks were fuller, and he had the suggestion of a double chin and what his old high-school gym teacher used to call (with utter contempt) 'man-tits.' And more than a suggestion of a gut. There was not much exercise – or much urge to exercise while in the grip of a solid Thorazine high – and the food was very good.

He did not worry about his weight when he was high, and that was most of the time. When they were ready to make some more of their fruitless tests, they would iron him out over an eighteen-hour period, a doctor would test his physical reactions, an EEG would be taken to make sure his brainwaves were nice and sharp, and then he would be taken into a testing cubicle, which was a small white room with drilled-cork paneling.

They had began, back in April, with human volunteers. They told him what to do and told him that if he did anything overenthusiastic – like striking someone blind, for instance – that he would be made to suffer. An undertone to this threat was that he might not suffer alone. This threat struck Andy as an empty one; he didn't believe that they would really harm Charlie. She was their prize pupil. He was very much the B feature on the program.

The doctor in charge of testing him was a man named Herman Pynchot. He was in his late thirties and perfectly ordinary except for the fact that he grinned too much. Sometimes all that grinning made Andy nervous. Occasionally an older doctor named Hockstetter would drop by, but mostly it was Pynchot.

Pynchot told him as they approached the first test that there was a table in the small testing room. On this table was a bottle of grape Kool-Aid, labeled INK, a fountain pen in a stand, a pad of notepaper, a pitcher of water, and two glasses. Pynchot told him that the volunteer would have no idea that there was anything other than ink in the ink bottle. Pynchot further told Andy that they would be grateful if he would 'push' the volunteer into pouring himself a glass of water, then dumping a goodish quantity of the 'ink' into it, and then quaffing the whole mess.

'Neat,' Andy said. He himself had not been feeling so

neat. He missed his Thorazine and the peace that it brought.

'Very neat,' Pynchot said. 'Will you do it?'

'Why should I?'

'You'll get something in return. Something nice.'

'Be a good rat and you get the cheese,' Andy said. 'Right?'

Pynchot shrugged and grinned. His smock was screamingly neat; it looked as if it might have been tailored by Brooks Brothers.

'All right,' Andy said. 'I give up. What's my prize for making this poor sucker drink ink?'

'Well, you can go back to taking your pills, for one thing.'

Suddenly it was a little hard to swallow, and he wondered if Thorazine was addicting, and if it was, if the addiction was psychological or physiological. 'Tell me, Pynchot,' he said. 'How does it feel to be a pusher? Is that in the Hippocratic oath?'

Pynchot shrugged and grinned. 'You also get to go outdoors for a while,' he said. 'I believe you've expressed an interest in that?'

Andy had. His quarters were nice – so nice you could sometimes almost forget they were nothing but a padded jail cell. There were three rooms plus a bath; there was a color TV equipped with Home Box Office, where a new choice of three recent films appeared each week. One of the munchkins – possibly it had been Pynchot – must have pointed out that there was no use taking away his belt and giving him only Crayolas to write with and plastic spoons to eat with. If he wanted to commit suicide, there was just no way they could stop him. If he pushed hard enough and long enough, he would simply blow his brain like an old tire.

So the place had all the amenities, even extending to a

microwave oven in the kitchenette. It was all done in decorator colors, there was a thick shag rug on the living-room floor, the pictures were all good prints. But for all of that, a dog turd covered with frosting is not a wedding cake; it is simply a frosted dog turd, and none of the doors leading out of this tasteful little apartment had doorknobs on the inside. There were small glass loopholes scattered here and there around the apartment – the sort of loopholes you see in the doors of hotel rooms. There was even one in the bathroom, and Andy had calculated that they provided sightlines to just about anyplace in the apartment. TV monitoring devices was Andy's guess, and probably equipped with infrared as well, so you couldn't even jerk off in relative privacy.

He wasn't claustrophobic, but he didn't like being closed up for long periods of time. It made him nervous, even with the drugs. It was a low nervousness, usually evidenced by long sighs and periods of apathy. He had indeed asked to go out. He wanted to see the sun again, and green grass.

'Yes,' he said softly to Pynchot. 'I have expressed an interest in going out.'

But he didn't get to go out.

The volunteer was nervous at first, undoubtedly expecting Andy to make him stand on his head and cluck like a chicken or something equally ridiculous. He was a football fan. Andy got the man, whose name was Dick Albright, to bring him up to date on the previous season – who had made it to the playoffs and how they went, who had won the Super Bowl.

Albright kindled. He spent the next twenty minutes reliving the entire season, gradually losing his nervousness. He was up to the lousy reffing that had allowed the Pats to triumph over the Dolphins in the AFC championship game when Andy said, 'Have a glass of water, if you want. You must be thirsty.'

283

Albright glanced up at him. 'Yeah, I am kinda thirsty. Say . . . am I talkin too much? Is it screwin up their tests, do you think?'

'No, I don't think so,' Andy said. He watched Dick Albright pour himself a glass of water from the pitcher.

'You want some?' Albright asked.

'No, I'll pass,' Andy said, and suddenly gave a hard push. 'Have some ink in it, why don't you?'

Albright looked up at him, then reached for the bottle of 'ink.' He picked it up, looked at it, and put it back down again. 'Put *ink* in it? You must be crazy.'

Pynchot grinned as much after the test as before it, but he was not pleased. Not pleased at all. Andy was not pleased either. When he had pushed out at Albright there had been none of that sideslipping sensation . . . that curious feeling of *doubling* that usually accompanied the push. And no headache. He had concentrated all of his will toward suggesting to Albright that putting ink in his water would be a perfectly reasonable thing to do, and Albright had made a perfectly reasonable reply: that Andy was nuts. In spite of all the pain it had caused him, he had felt a touch of panic at the thought the talent might have deserted him.

'Why do you want to keep it under wraps?' Pynchot asked him. He lit a Chesterfield and grinned. 'I don't understand you, Andy. What *good* does it do you?'

'For the tenth time,' Andy had replied, 'I wasn't holding back. I wasn't faking. I pushed him as hard as I could. Nothing happened, that's all.' He wanted his pill. He felt depressed and nervous. All the colors seemed too bright, the light too strong, voices too loud. It was better with the pills. With the pills, his useless outrage over what had happened and his loneliness for Charlie and his worry over what might be happening to her – these things faded back and became manageable.

284

'I'm afraid I don't believe that,' Pynchot said, and grinned. 'Think it over, Andy. We're not asking you to make someone walk off a cliff or shoot himself in the head. I guess you didn't want that walk as badly as you thought you did.'

He stood up as if to go.

'Listen,' Andy said, unable to keep the desperation entirely out of his voice, 'I'd like one of those pills.'

'Would you?' Pynchot said. 'Well, it might interest you to know that I'm lightening your dosage . . . just in case it's the Thorazine that's interfering with your ability.' His grin bloomed anew. 'Of course, if your ability suddenly came back . . .'

'There are a couple of things you should know,' Andy told him. 'First, the guy was nervous, expecting something. Second, he wasn't all that bright. It's a lot harder to push old people and people with low or low-normal IQs. Bright people go easier.'

'Is that so?' Pynchot said.

'Yes.'

'Then why don't you push me into giving you a pill right now? My tested IQ is one-fifty-five.'

Andy had tried – with no results at all.

Eventually he had got his walk outside, and eventually they had increased the dosage of his medication again as well – after they became convinced that he really wasn't faking, that he was, in fact, trying desperately hard to use the push, with no success at all. Quite independently of each other, both Andy and Dr Pynchot began to wonder if he hadn't tipped himself over permanently in the run that had taken him and Charlie from New York to Albany County Airport to Hastings Glen, if he hadn't simply used the talent up. And both of them wondered if it wasn't some kind of psychological block. Andy himself came to believe that either the talent was really gone or it was simply a defense mechanism: his mind refusing to use the talent because it knew it might kill him to do so. He hadn't forgotten the numb places on his cheek and neck, and the bloodshot eye.

Either way, it amounted to the same thing – a big goose-egg. Pynchot, his dreams of covering himself with glory as the first man to get provable, empirical data on psychic mental domination now flying away, came around less and less often.

The tests had continued through May and June – first more volunteers and then totally unsuspecting test subjects. Using the latter was not precisely ethical, as Pynchot was the first to admit, but some of the first tests with LSD hadn't been precisely ethical, either. Andy marveled that by equating these two wrongs in his mind, Pynchot seemed to come out the other side feeling that everything was okay. It didn't matter, because Andy had no success pushing any of them.

A month ago, just after the Fourth of July, they had begun testing him with animals. Andy protested that pushing an animal was even more impossible than trying to push a stupid person, but his protests cut zero ice with Pynchot and his team, who were really only going through the motions of a scientific investigation at this point. And so once a week Andy found himself sitting in a room with a dog or a cat or a monkey, feeling like a character from an absurdist novel. He remembered the cab driver who had looked at a dollar bill and had seen a five hundred. He remembered the timid executives he had managed to tip gently in the direction of more confidence and assertiveness. Before them, in Port City, Pennsylvania, there had been the Weight-Off program, the classes attended mostly by lonely fat housewives with an addiction to Snackin' Cakes, Pepsi-Cola, and anything between two slices of bread. These were things that filled up the emptiness of their lives a little. That had simply been a matter of pushing a little bit, because most of them had really wanted to lose weight. He had helped them do that. He thought also of what had happened to the two Shop ramrods who had taken Charlie.

He *had* been able to do it, but no more. It was hard even to remember exactly what it had felt like. So he sat in the room with dogs that lapped his hand and cats that purred and monkeys that moodily scratched their asses and sometimes showed their teeth in apocalyptic, fang-filled grins that were obscenely like Pynchot's grins, and of course none of the animals did anything unusual at all. And later on he would be taken back to his apartment with no doorknobs on the doors and there would be a blue pill in a white dish on the counter in the kitchenette and in a little while he would stop feeling nervous and depressed. He would start feeling pretty much okay again. And he would watch one of the Home Box Office movies – something with Clint Eastwood, if he could get it – or perhaps *The PTL Club*. It didn't bother him so much that he had lost his talent and become a superfluous person.

5

On the afternoon of the big storm, he sat watching *The PTL Club*. A woman with a beehive hairdo was telling the host how the power of God had cured her of Bright's disease. Andy was quite fascinated with her. Her hair gleamed under the studio lighting like a varnished table-leg. She looked like a time traveler from the year 1963. That was one of the fascinations *The PTL Club* held for him, along with the shameless carny pitches for money in the name of God. Andy would listen to these pitches delivered by hard-faced young men in expensive suits and think, bemused, of how Christ had driven the money-

287

changers from the temple. And *all* the people on *PTL* looked like time travelers from 1963.

The woman finished her story of how God had saved her from shaking herself to pieces. Earlier in the program an actor who had been famous in the early 1950s had told how God had saved him from the bottle. Now the woman with the beehive hairdo began to cry and the once-famous actor embraced her. The camera dollied in for a close-up. In the background, the PTL Singers began to hum. Andy shifted in his seat a little. It was almost time for his pill.

In a dim sort of way he realized that the medication was only partially responsible for the peculiar changes that had come over him in the last five months, changes of which his soft weight gain was only an outward sign. When the Shop had taken Charlie away from him, they had knocked the one solid remaining prop out from under his life. With Charlie gone – oh, she was undoubtedly somewhere near, but she might as well have been on the moon – there seemed to be no reason for holding himself together.

On top of that, all the running had induced a nervous kind of shellshock. He had lived on the tightrope for so long that when he had finally fallen off, total lethargy had been the result. In fact, he believed he had suffered a very quiet sort of nervous breakdown. If he *did* see Charlie, he wasn't even sure she would recognize him as the same person, and that made him sad.

He had never made any effort to deceive Pynchot or cheat on the tests. He did not really think that doing so would rebound on Charlie, but he would not have taken even the most remote chance of that happening. And it was easier to do what they wanted. He had become passive. He had screamed the last of his rage on Granther's porch, as he cradled his daughter with the dart sticking out of her neck. There was no more rage left in him. He had shot his wad.

288

That was Andy McGee's mental state as he sat watching TV that August 19 while the storm walked the hills outside. The *PTL* host made a donations pitch and then introduced a gospel trio. The trio began to sing, and suddenly the lights went out.

The TV also went, the picture dwindling down to a bright speck. Andy sat in his chair, unmoving, not sure just what had happened. His mind had just enough time to register the scary totality of the dark, and then the lights went on again. The gospel trio reappeared, singing 'I Got a Telephone Call from Heaven and Jesus Was on the Line.' Andy heaved a sigh of relief, and then the lights went out again.

He sat there, gripping the arms of the chair as if he would fly away if he let go. He kept his eyes desperately fixed on the bright speck of light from the TV even after he knew it was gone and he was only seeing a lingering after-image . . . or wishful thinking.

It'll be back on in a second or two, he told himself. *Secondary generators somewhere. You don't trust to house current to run a place like this.*

Still, he was scared. He suddenly found himself recalling the boys'-adventure stories of his childhood. In more than one of them, there had been an incident in some cave with the lights or candles blown out. And it seemed that the author would always go to great lengths to describe the dark as 'palpable' or 'utter' or 'total.' There was even that tried-and-true old standby 'the living dark,' as in 'The living dark engulfed Tom and his friends.' If all of this had been meant to impress the nine-year-old Andy McGee, it hadn't done. As far as he was concerned, if he wanted to be 'engulfed by the living dark,' all he had to do was go into his closet and put a blanket along the crack at the bottom of the door. Dark was, after all, dark.

Now he realized that he had been wrong about that; it

wasn't the only thing he'd been wrong about as a kid, but it was maybe the last one to be discovered. He would just as soon have forgone the discovery, because dark *wasn't* dark. He had never been in a dark like this one in his life. Except for the sensation of the chair beneath his butt and under his hands, he could have been floating in some lightless Lovecraftian gulf between the stars. He raised one hand and floated it in front of his eyes. And although he could feel the palm lightly touching his nose, he couldn't see it.

He took the hand away from his face and gripped the arm of the chair with it again. His heart had taken on a rapid and thready beat in his chest. Outside, someone called out hoarsely, 'Richie! Where the fuck areya?' and Andy cringed back in his chair as if he had been threatened. He licked his lips.

It'll be back on in just a second or two now, he thought, but a scared part of his mind that refused to be comforted by mere rationalities asked: *How long is a second or two, or a minute or two, in total darkness? How do you measure time in total darkness?*

Outside, beyond his 'apartment,' something fell over and someone screamed in pain and surprise. Andy cringed back again and moaned shakily. He didn't like this. This was no good.

Well, if it takes them longer than a few minutes to fix it – to reset the breakers or whatever – they'll come and let me out. They'll have to.

Even the scared part of his mind – the part that was only a short distance away from gibbering – recognized the logic of this, and he relaxed a little. After all, it was just the *dark*; that's all it was – just the absence of light. It wasn't as if there were *monsters* in the dark, or anything like that.

He was very thirsty. He wondered if he dared get up and go get a bottle of ginger ale out of the fridge. He decided he could do it if he was careful. He got up, took two shuffling steps forward, and promptly barked his shin on the edge of the coffee table. He bent and rubbed it, eyes watering with pain.

This was like childhood, too. They had played a game called 'blind man'; he supposed all kids did. You had to try to get from one end of the house to the other with a bandanna or something over your eyes. And everyone else thought it was simply the height of humor when you fell over a hassock or tripped over the riser between the dining room and the kitchen. The game could teach you a painful lesson about how little you actually remembered about the layout of your supposedly familiar house and how much more you relied upon your eyes than your memory. And the game could make you wonder how the hell you'd live if you went blind.

But I'll be all right, Andy thought. *I'll be all right if I just take it slow and easy.*

He moved around the coffee table and then began to shuffle his way slowly across the open space of the living room with his hands out in front of him. It was funny how threatening open space could feel in the dark. *Probably the lights'll come on right now and I can have a good laugh at myself. Just have a good l—*

'*Ow!*'

His outstretched fingers struck the wall and bent back painfully. Something fell – the picture of the barn and hayfield after the style of Wyeth that hung near the kitchen door, he guessed. It swished by him, sounding ominously like a whickering sword blade in the dark, and clattered to the floor. The sound was shockingly loud.

He stood still, holding his aching fingers, feeling the throb of his barked shin. He was cotton-mouthed with fear.

'Hey!' he shouted. 'Hey, don't forget about me, you guys!'

He waited and listened. There was no answer. There were still sounds and voices, but they were farther away now. If they got much farther away, he would be in total silence.

Forgotten all about me, he thought, and his fright deepened.

His heart was racing. He could feel cold sweat on his arms and brow, and he found himself remembering the time at Tashmore Pond when he had gone out too deep, got tired and begun to thrash and scream, sure he was going to die . . . but when he put his feet down the bottom was there, the water only nipple high. Where was the bottom now? He licked at his dry lips, but his tongue was dry, too.

'*HEY!*' he shouted at the top of his lungs, and the sound of terror in his voice terrified him even more. He had to get hold of himself. He was within arm's length of total panic now, just bulling around mindlessly in here and screaming at the top of his lungs. All because someone had blown a fuse.

Oh goddammit all anyway, why'd it have to happen when it was time for my pill? If I had my pill I'd be all right. I'd be okay then. Christ it feels like my head's full of broken glass—

He stood there, breathing heavily. He had aimed for the kitchen door, had gone off course and run into the wall. Now he felt totally disoriented and couldn't even remember if that stupid barn picture had been hung to the right or left of the doorway. He wished miserably that he had stayed in his chair.

'Get hold,' he muttered aloud. 'Get hold.'

It was not *just* panic, he recognized that. It was the pill that was now overdue, the pill on which he had come to

292

depend. It just wasn't fair that this had happened when his pill was due.

'Get hold,' he muttered again.

Ginger ale. He had got up to get ginger ale and he was going to by-God get it. He had to fix on something. That's all it came down to, and ginger ale would do as well as anything else.

He began to move again, toward the left, and promptly fell over the picture that had come off the wall.

Andy screamed and went down, pinwheeling his arms wildly and fruitlessly for balance. He struck his head hard and screamed again.

Now he was very frightened. Help me, he thought. Somebody help me, bring me a candle, for Christ's sake, something, I'm scared—

He began to cry. His fumbling fingers felt thick wetness on the side of his head – blood – and he wondered with numb terror how bad it was.

'*Where are you people?*' he screamed. There was no answer. He heard – or thought he heard – a single faraway shout, and then there was silence. His fingers found the picture he had tripped over and he threw it across the room, furious at it for hurting him. It struck the end table beside the couch, and the now-useless lamp that stood there fell over. The lightbulb exploded with a hollow sound, and Andy cried out again. He felt the side of his head. More blood there now. It was crawling over his cheek in little rivulets.

Panting, he began to crawl, one hand out to feel the wall. When its solidity abruptly ended in blankness, he drew in both his breath and his hand, as if he expected something nasty to snake out of the blackness and grab him. A little *whhh!* sound sucked in past his lips. For just one second the totality of childhood came back and he could hear the whisper of trolls as they crowded eagerly toward him.

'Just the kitchen door, for fuck's sake,' he muttered raggedly. 'That's all.'

He crawled through it. The fridge was to the right and he began to bear that way, crawling slowly and breathing fast, his hands cold on the tile.

Somewhere overhead, on the next level, something fell over with a tremendous clang. Andy jerked up on his knees. His nerve broke and he lost himself. He began to scream *Help! Help! Help!* over and over until he was hoarse. He had no idea how long he might have screamed there, on his hands and knees in the black kitchen.

At last he stopped and tried to get hold of himself. His hands and arms were shaking helplessly. His head ached from the thump he had given it, but the flow of blood seemed to have stopped. That was a little reassuring. His throat felt hot and flayed from all his screaming, and that made him think of the ginger ale again.

He began to crawl once more, and he found the refrigerator with no further incident. He opened it (ridiculously expecting the interior light to come on with its familiar frosty-white glow) and fumbled around in the cool dark box until he found a can with a ringtab on top. Andy shut the fridge door and leaned against it. He opened the can and swilled half the ginger ale at a draft. His throat blessed him for it.

Then a thought came and his throat froze.

The place is on fire, his mind told him with spurious calmness. *That's why no one's come to get you out. They're evacuating. You, now . . . you're expendable.*

This thought brought on an extremity of claustrophobic terror that was beyond panic. He simply cringed back against the refrigerator, his lips pulled back from his teeth in a grimace. The strength went out of his legs. For a

294

moment, he even imagined he could smell smoke, and heat seemed to rush over him. The soda can slipped from his fingers and gurgled its contents out onto the floor, wetting his pants.

Andy sat in the wetness, moaning.

6

John Rainbird thought later that things could not have worked better if they had planned it . . . and if those fancy psychologists had been worth a tin whistle in a high wind, they *would* have planned it. But as it happened, it was only the lucky happenstance of the blackout's occurring when it did that allowed him to finally get his chisel under one corner of the psychological steel that armored Charlie McGee. Luck, and his own inspired intuition.

He let himself into Charlie's quarters at three-thirty, just as the storm was beginning to break outside. He pushed a cart before him that was no different from the ones most hotel and motel maids push as they go from room to room. It contained clean sheets and pillow slips, furniture polish, a rug-shampoo preparation for spot stains. There was a floor bucket and a mop. A vacuum cleaner was clipped to one end of the cart.

Charlie was sitting on the floor in front of the couch, wearing a bright blue Danskin leotard and nothing else. Her long legs were crossed in a lotuslike position. She sat that way a great deal. An outsider might have thought she was stoned, but Rainbird knew better. She was still being lightly medicated, but now the dosage was little more than a placebo. All of the psychologists were in disappointed agreement that she meant what she said about never lighting fires again. The drugs had originally been meant to keep her from burning her way out, but now it seemed sure that she wasn't going to do that . . . or anything else.

'Hi, kid,' Rainbird said. He unclipped the vacuum cleaner.

She glanced over at him but didn't respond. He plugged the vacuum in, and when he started it, she got up gracefully and went into the bathroom. She shut the door.

Rainbird went on vacuuming the rug. He had no plan in mind. It was a case of looking for small signs and signals, picking up on them, and following them. His admiration for the girl was unalloyed. Her father was turning into a fat, apathetic pudding, the psychologists had their own terms for it – 'dependency shock,' and 'loss of identity,' and 'mental fugue,' and 'mild reality dysfunction' – but what it all came down to was he had given up and could now be canceled out of the equation. The girl hadn't done that. She had simply hidden herself. And Rainbird never felt so much like an Indian as he did when he was with Charlie McGee.

He vacuumed and waited for her to come out – maybe. He thought she was coming out of the bathroom a little more frequently now. At first she had always hidden there until he was gone. Now sometimes she came out and watched him. Perhaps she would today. Perhaps not. He would wait. And watch for signs.

7

Charlie sat in the bathroom with the door shut. She would have locked it if she could. Before the orderly came to clean the place, she had been doing some simple exercises she had found in a book. The orderly came to keep it orderly. Now the toilet seat felt cold under her. The white light from the fluorescents that ringed the bathroom mirror made everything seem cold, and too bright.

At first there had been a live-in 'companion,' a woman

of about forty-five. She was supposed to be 'motherly,' but the 'motherly companion' had hard green eyes with small flecks in them. The flecks were like ice. These were the people who had killed her real mother; now they wanted her to live here with the 'motherly companion.' Charlie told them she didn't want the 'motherly companion.' They smiled. Then Charlie stopped talking, and she didn't say another word until the 'motherly companion' left, taking her green ice-chip eyes with her. She had made a deal with that man Hockstetter: she would answer his questions, and his alone, if he would get that 'motherly companion' out. The only companion she wanted was her father, and if she couldn't have him, she would be alone.

In many ways she felt that the last five months (they told her it was five months; it didn't feel like anything) had been a dream. There was no way to mark time, faces came and went with no memories attached to them, disembodied as balloons, and food had no particular taste. She felt like a balloon herself sometimes. She felt as if she were floating. But in a way, her mind told her with perfect certitude, it was fair. She was a murderer. She had broken the worst of the Ten Commandments and was surely damned to hell.

She thought about this at night, with the lights turned down low so that the apartment itself seemed like a dream. She saw it all. The men on the porch wearing their crowns of flame. The cars exploding. The chickens catching fire. The smell of burning that was always the smell of smoldering stuffing, the smell of her teddy bear.

(*and she had liked it*)

That was it; that was the trouble. The more she had done it the more she had liked it; the more she had done it the more she had been able to feel the power, a living thing, getting stronger and stronger. It was like a pyramid standing upside down, standing on its tip, and the more you did it the harder it got to stop it. It *hurt* to stop it

297

(and it was fun)

and so she was never going to do it again. She would die in here before she did it again. Maybe she even wanted to die in here. The idea of dying in a dream wasn't scary at all.

The only two faces that weren't totally dissociated were Hockstetter's and that of the orderly who came to clean her apartment every day. Charlie had asked him once why he had to come every day, since she wasn't messy.

John – that was his name – had taken a scrungy old pad from his back pocket and a cheap ballpoint pen from his breast pocket. He said 'That's just my job, kid.' And on the paper he wrote *Because they're full of shit, why else?*

She had almost giggled but had stopped herself in time by thinking of men with crowns of fire, men who smelled like smoldering teddy bears. Giggling would have been dangerous. So she simply pretended that she hadn't seen the note or didn't understand it. The orderly's face was a mess. He wore an eyepatch. She felt sorry for him and once she had almost asked him what happened – if he had been in a car accident or something – but that would have been even more dangerous than giggling at his note. She didn't know why, but she felt that in every fiber.

His face was very horrible to look at, but he seemed pleasant enough, and his face was no worse than the face of little Chuckie Eberhardt back in Harrison. Chuckie's mother had been frying potatoes when Chuckie was three and Chuckie had pulled the pan of hot fat off the stove all over himself and had almost died. Afterward the other kids sometimes called him Chuckie Hamburger and Chuckie Frankenstein, and Chuckie would cry. It was mean. The other kids didn't seem to understand that a thing like that could happen to any kid. When you were three you didn't have much in the smarts department.

John's face was all ripped up, but that didn't scare her.

It was Hockstetter's face that scared her, and his face – except for the eyes – was as ordinary as anyone else's. His eyes were even worse than the eyes of the 'motherly companion.' He was always using them to pry at you. Hockstetter wanted her to make fires. He asked her again and again. He took her to a room, and sometimes there would be crumpled-up pieces of newspaper and sometimes there would be little glass dishes filled with oil and sometimes there would be other things. But for all the questions, and all the fake sympathy, it always came down to the same thing: Charlie, set this on fire.

Hockstetter scared her. She sensed that he had all sorts of . . . of

(*things*)

that he could use on her to make her light fires. But she wouldn't. Except she was scared that she would. Hockstetter would use anything. He didn't play fair, and one night she had had a dream, and in this dream she had set Hockstetter on fire and she had awakened with her hands stuffed into her mouth to keep back a scream.

One day, in order to postpone the inevitable request, she had asked when she could see her father. It had been much on her mind, but she hadn't asked, because she knew what the answer would be. But on this day she was feeling specially tired and low-spirited, and it had just slipped out.

'Charlie, I think you know the answer to that,' Hockstetter had said. He pointed to the table in the little room. There was a steel tray on the table and it was filled with heaps of curly woodshavings. 'If you'll light that, I'll take you to your father right away. You can be with him in two minutes.' Beneath his cold, watching eyes, Hockstetter's mouth spread wide in a just-pals sort of grin. 'Now, what say?'

'Give me a match,' Charlie had answered, feeling the tears threaten. 'I'll light it.'

'You can light it just by thinking about it. You know that.'

'No. I can't. And even if I could, I wouldn't. It's wrong.'

Hockstetter looked at her sadly, the just-pals smile fading. 'Charlie, why do you hurt yourself like this? Don't you want to see your dad? He wants to see you. He told me to tell you it was all right.'

And then she *did* cry, she cried hard and long, because she did want to see him, not a minute of any day went by without her thoughts turning to him, without missing him, without wanting to feel his solid arms around her. Hockstetter watched her cry and there was no sympathy in his face, no sorrow or kindness. There was, however, careful calculation. Oh, she hated him.

That had been three weeks ago. Since then she had stubbornly not mentioned her father, although Hockstetter had dangled him before her constantly, telling her that her father was sad, that her father said it was okay to make fires, and worst of all, that her father had told Hockstetter that he guessed Charlie didn't love him anymore.

She looked at her pale face in the bathroom mirror and listened to the steady whine of John's vacuum cleaner. When he finished that, he would change her bed. Then he would dust. Then he would be gone. Suddenly she didn't want him to be gone, she wanted to listen to him talk.

At first she had always gone into the bathroom and stayed in there until he was gone, and once he had turned off the vacuum cleaner and knocked on the bathroom door, calling worriedly: 'Kid? You all right? You ain't sick, are you?'

His voice was so kind – and kindness, simple kindness, was so hard to come by in here – that she had had to

300

struggle to keep her voice calm and cool because the tears were threatening again. 'Yes . . . I'm okay.'

She waited, wondering if he would try to take it further, try to get inside her like the others did, but he had simply gone away and started his vacuum up again. In a way she had been disappointed.

Another time he had been washing the floor and when she came out of the bathroom, he had said, without looking up, 'Watch out for that wet floor, kid, you don't want to break your arm.' That was all, but again she had been nearly surprised into tears – it was concern, so simple and direct it was unconscious.

Just lately she had been coming out of the bathroom to watch him more and more. To watch him . . . and to listen to him. He would ask her questions sometimes, but they were never threatening ones. Still, most times she wouldn't answer, just on general principles. It didn't stop John. He would talk to her anyway. He would talk about his bowling scores, about his dog, about how his TV got broken and it would be a couple of weeks before he could get it fixed because they wanted so much for those little tiny tubes.

She supposed he was lonely. With a face like his, he probably didn't have a wife or anything. She liked to listen to him because it was like a secret tunnel to the outside. His voice was low, musical, sometimes wandering. It was never sharp and interrogative, like Hockstetter's. He required no reply, seemingly.

She got off the toilet seat and went to the door, and that was when the lights went out. She stood there, puzzled, one hand on the doorknob, her head cocked to one side. It immediately came to her that this was some sort of trick. She could hear the dying whine of John's vacuum cleaner and then he said, 'Well, what the *Christ?*'

Then the lights came back on. Still Charlie didn't come out. The vacuum cleaner cycled back up again. Footsteps approached the door and John said, 'Did the lights go out in there for a second?'

'Yes.'

'It's the storm, I guess.'

'What storm?'

'Looked like it was going to storm when I came to work. Big thunderheads.'

Looked like it was going to storm. Outside. She wished she could go outside and see the big thunderheads. Smell that funny way the air got before a summer storm. It got a rainy, wet smell. Everything looked gr—

The lights went out again.

The vacuum died. The darkness was total. Her only connection with the world was her hand on the brushed-chrome doorknob. She began to tap her tongue thoughtfully against her upper lip.

'Kid?'

She didn't answer. A trick? A storm, he had said. And she believed that. She believed John. It was surprising and scary to find that she believed what someone had told her, after all this time.

'*Kid?*' It was him again. And this time he sounded . . . frightened.

Her own fear of the dark, which had only begun to creep up on her, was sublimated in his.

'John, what's the matter?' She opened the door and groped in front of her. She didn't go out, not yet. She was afraid of tripping over the vacuum cleaner.

'What happened?' Now there was a beat of panic in his voice. It scared her. 'Where's the lights?'

'They went out,' she said. 'You said . . . the storm . . .'

'I can't stand the dark,' he said. There was terror in his voice and a kind of grotesque apology. 'You don't understand. I can't . . . I got to get out. . . .' She heard him make a sudden blundering rush across the living room,

302

and then there was a loud and frightening crash as he fell over something – the coffee table, most likely. He cried out miserably and that frightened her even more.

'John? John! Are you all right?'

'I got to get out!' he screamed. 'Make them let me out, kid!'

'What's wrong?'

There was no answer, not for a long time. Then she heard a low, choked sound and understood that he was crying.

'Help me,' he said then, and Charlie stood in the bathroom doorway, trying to decide. Part of her fear had already dissolved into sympathy, but part of it remained questioning, hard and bright.

'Help me, oh somebody help me,' he said in a low voice, so low it was as if he expected no one to hear or heed. And that decided her. Slowly she began to feel her way across the room toward him, her hands held out in front of her.

8

Rainbird heard her coming and could not forbear a grin in the dark – a hard, humorless grin that he covered with the palm of his hand, in case the power should come back on at that precise instant.

'John?'

He made a voice of strained agony through his grin. 'I'm sorry, kid. I just . . . it's the dark. I can't stand the dark. It's like the place where they put me after I was captured.'

'Who put you?'

'The Cong.'

She was closer now. The grin left his face and he began to put himself into the part. *Scared. You're scared because the Cong put you in a hole in the ground after one of their mines*

blew most of your face off . . . and they kept you there . . . and
now you need a friend.

In a way, the part was a natural. All he had to do was make her believe that his extreme excitement at this unexpected chance was extreme fear. And of course he *was* afraid – afraid of blowing it. This made the shot from the tree with the ampul of Orasin look like child's play. Her intuitions were deadly sharp. Nervous perspiration was flowing off him in rivers.

'Who are the Cong?' she asked, very close now. Her hand brushed lightly past his face and he clutched it. She gasped nervously.

'Hey, don't be scared,' he said. 'It's just that—'

'You . . . that hurts. You're hurting me.'

It was exactly the right tone. She was scared too, scared of the dark and scared of him . . . but worried about him, too. He wanted her to feel she had been clutched by a drowning man.

'I'm sorry, kid.' He loosened his grip but didn't let go. 'Just . . . can you sit beside me?'

'Sure.' She sat down, and he jumped at the mild thud of her body coming down on the floor. Outside, far away, someone hollered something to someone else.

'Let us out!' Rainbird screamed immediately. 'Let us out! Hey, let us out! People in here!'

'Stop it,' Charlie said, alarmed. 'We're okay . . . I mean, aren't we?'

His mind, that overtuned machine, was clicking along at high speed, writing the script, always three or four lines ahead, enough to be safe, not enough to destroy hot spontaneity. Most of all he wondered just how long he had, how long before the lights went back on. He cautioned himself not to expect or hope for too much. He had got his chisel under the edge of the box. Anything else would be gravy.

'Yeah, I guess we are,' he said. 'It's just the dark, that's all. I don't even have a fucking match or— Aw, hey, kid, I'm sorry. That just slipped out.'

'That's okay,' Charlie said. 'Sometimes my dad says that word. Once when he was fixing my wagon out in the garage he hit his hand with the hammer and said it five or six times. Other ones, too.' This was by far the longest speech she had ever made in Rainbird's presence. 'Will they come and let us out pretty soon?'

'They can't until they get the power back on,' he said, miserable on the outside, gleeful on the inside. 'These doors, kid, they've all got electric locks. They're built to lock solid if the power goes off. They've got you in a fuh— they've got you in a cell, kid. It looks like a nice little apartment, but you might as well be in jail.'

'I know,' she said quietly. He was still holding her hand tightly but she didn't seem to mind as much now. 'You shouldn't say it, though. I think they listen.'

They! Rainbird thought, and a hot triumphant joy flashed through him. He was faintly aware that he had not felt such intensity of emotion in ten years. *They! She's talking about they!*

He felt his chisel slip farther under the corner of the box that was Charlie McGee, and he involuntarily squeezed her hand again.

'Ow!'

'Sorry, kid,' he said, letting off. 'I know damn well they listen. But they ain't listening now, with the power off. Oh kid, I don't like this, I gotta get out of here!' He began to tremble.

'Who are the Cong?'

'You don't know? . . . No, you're too young, I guess. It was the war, kid. The war in Vietnam. The Cong were the bad guys. They wore black pajamas. In the jungle. You know about the Vietnam war, don't you?'

She knew about it . . . vaguely.

'We were on patrol and we walked into an ambush,' he said. That much was the truth, but this was where John Rainbird and the truth parted company. There was no need to confuse her by pointing out that they had all been stoned, most of the grunts smoked up well on Cambodian red, and their West Point lieutenant, who was only one step away from the checkpoint between the lands of sanity and madness, on the peyote buttons that he chewed whenever they were out on patrol. Rainbird had once seen this looey shoot a pregnant woman with a semiautomatic rifle, had seen the woman's six-month fetus ripped from her body in disintegrating pieces; that, the looey told them later, was known as a West Point Abortion. So there they were, on their way back to base, and they had indeed walked into an ambush, only it had been laid by their own guys, even more stoned than they were, and four guys had been blown away. Rainbird saw no need to tell Charlie all of this, or that the Claymore that had pulverized half his face had been made in a Maryland munitions plant.

'There were only six of us that got out. We ran. We ran through the jungle and I guess I went the wrong way. Wrong way? Right way? In that crazy war you didn't know which way was the right way because there weren't any real lines. I got separated from the rest of my guys. I was still trying to find something familiar when I walked over a land mine. That's what happened to my face.'

'I'm very sorry,' Charlie said.

'When I woke up, *they* had me,' Rainbird said, now off into the never-never land of total fiction. He had actually come to in a Saigon army hospital with an IV drip in his arm. 'They wouldn't give me any medical treatment, nothing like that, unless I answered their questions.'

Now carefully. If he did it carefully it would come right; he could feel it.

306

His voice rose, bewildered and bitter. 'Questions, all the time questions. They wanted to know about troop movements . . . supplies . . . light-infantry deployment . . . everything. They never let up. They were always at me.'

'Yes,' Charlie said fervently, and his heart gladdened.

'I kept telling them I didn't know anything, couldn't tell them anything, that I was nothing but a lousy grunt, just a number with a pack on its back. They didn't believe me. My face . . . the pain . . . I got down on my knees and begged for morphine . . . they said after . . . after I told them I could have the morphine. I could be treated in a good hospital . . . after I told them.'

Now Charlie's grip was the one that was tightening. She thought about Hockstetter's cool gray eyes, of Hockstetter pointing at the steel tray filled with curly woodshavings. *I think you know the answer . . . if you light that, I'll take you to see your father right away. You can be with him in two minutes.* Her heart went out to this man with the badly wounded face, this grown man who was afraid of the dark. She thought she could understand what he had been through. She knew his pain. And in the dark she began to cry silently for him, and in a way the tears were also for herself . . . all the unshed tears of the last five months. They were tears of pain and rage for John Rainbird, her father, her mother, herself. They burned and scourged.

The tears were not silent enough to go unheard by Rainbird's radar ears. He had to struggle to suppress another smile. Oh yes, the chisel was well-planted. Tough cracks and easy cracks, but no impossible cracks.

'They just never believed me. Finally they threw me into a hole in the ground, and it was always dark. There was a little . . . a room, I guess you'd say, with roots sticking out of the earth walls . . . and sometimes I could see a little sunlight about nine feet up. They'd come – their commandant, I guess he was – and he'd ask me if I was

307

ready to talk yet. He said I was turning white down there, like a fish. That my face was getting infected, that I'd get gangrene in my face and then it would get into my brain and rot it and make me crazy and then I'd die. He'd ask me if I'd like to get out of the dark and see the sun again. And I'd plead with him . . . I'd beg . . . I'd swear on my mother's name that I didn't know anything. And then they'd laugh and put the boards back and cover them up with dirt. It was like being buried alive. The dark . . . like this . . .'

He made a choked sound in his throat and Charlie squeezed his hand tighter to show him that she was there.

'There was the room and there was a little tunnel about seven feet long. I had to go down to the end of the tunnel to . . . you know. And the air was bad and I kept thinking I'm going to smother down here in the dark, I'm going to choke on the smell of my own sh—' He groaned. 'I'm sorry. This is nothing to tell a kid.'

'That's all right. If it makes you feel better, it's all right.'

He debated, and then decided to go just a little further.

'I was down there for five months before they exchanged me.'

'What did you eat?'

'They threw down rotted rice. And sometimes spiders. Live spiders. Great big ones – tree spiders, I guess. I'd chase after them in the dark, you know, and kill them and eat them.

'Oh, *gross!*'

'They turned me into an animal,' he said, and was quiet for a moment, breathing loudly. 'You got it better than me, kid, but it comes down to pretty much the same thing. A rat in a trap. You think they'll get the lights on pretty soon?'

She didn't say anything for a long time, and he was

coldly afraid that he had gone too far. Then Charlie said, 'It doesn't matter. We're together.'

'All right,' he said, and then in a rush: 'You won't tell, will you? They'd fire me for the way I been talking. I need this job. When you look the way I do, you need a good job.'

'No, I won't tell.'

He felt the chisel slip smoothly in another notch. They had a secret between them now.

He was holding her in his hands.

In the dark, he thought how it would be to slip his hands around her neck. That was the final object in view, of course – not their stupid tests, their playground games. Her . . . and then perhaps himself. He liked her, he really did. He might even be falling in love with her. The time would come when he would send her over, looking carefully into her eyes all the time. And then, if her eyes gave him the signal he had looked for so long, perhaps he would follow her. Yes. Perhaps they would go into the real darkness together.

Outside, beyond the locked door, eddies of confusion passed back and forth, sometimes near, sometimes far away.

Rainbird mentally spat on his hands and then went back to work on her.

9

Andy had no idea that they hadn't come to get him out because the power failure had automatically locked the doors. He sat in a half-swoon of panic for some unknown time, sure the place was burning down, imagining the smell of smoke. Outside, the storm had cleared and late afternoon sunshine was slanting down toward dusk.

Quite suddenly Charlie's face came into his mind, as clearly as if she had been standing there in front of him.

(*she's in danger charlie's in danger*)

It was one of his hunches, the first he'd had since that last day in Tashmore. He thought he had lost that along with the push, but apparently that was not so, because he had never had a hunch clearer than this one – not even on the day Vicky was killed.

Did that mean the push was still there, too? Not gone at all, but only hiding?

(*charlie's in danger!*)

What sort of danger?

He didn't know. But the thought, the fear, had brought her face clearly in front of him, outlined on this darkness in every detail. And the image of her face, her wide-set blue eyes and fine-spun blond hair, brought guilt like a twin . . . except that guilt was too mild a word for what he felt; it was something like horror that he felt. He had been in a craze of panic ever since the lights went out, and the panic had been completely for himself. It had never even occurred to him that Charlie must be in the dark, too.

No, they'll come and get her out, they probably came and got her out long ago. Charlie's the one they want. Charlie's their meal ticket.

That made sense, but he still felt that suffocating surety that she was in some terrible danger.

His fear for her had the effect of sweeping the panic for himself away, or at least of making it more manageable. His awareness turned outward again and became more objective. The first thing he became aware of was that he was sitting in a puddle of ginger ale. His pants were wet and tacky with it, and he made a small sound of disgust.

Movement. Movement was the cure for fear.

He got on his knees, felt for the overturned Canada Dry can, and batted it away. It went clink-rolling across the

310

tiled floor. He got another can out of the fridge; his mouth was still dry. He pulled the tab and dropped it down into the can and then drank. The ringtab tried to escape into his mouth and he spat it back absently, not pausing to reflect that only a little while ago, that alone would have been excuse enough for another fifteen minutes of fear and trembling.

He began to feel his way out of the kitchen, trailing his free hand along the wall. This level was entirely quiet now, and although he heard an occasional faraway call, there seemed to be nothing upset or panicky about the sound. The smell of smoke had been a hallucination. The air was a bit stale because all the convectors had stopped when the power went off, but that was all.

Instead of crossing the living room, Andy turned left and crawled into his bedroom. He felt his way carefully to the bed, set his can of ginger ale on the bedtable, and then undressed. Ten minutes later he was dressed in fresh clothes and feeling much better. It occurred to him that he had done all of this with no particular trouble, whereas after the lights went out, crossing the living room had been like crossing a live minefield.

(*charlie – what's wrong with charlie?*)

But it wasn't really a feeling that something was *wrong* with her, just a feeling that she was in danger of something happening. If he could see her, he could ask her what—

He laughed bitterly in the dark. Yes, right. And pigs will whistle, beggars will ride. Might as well wish for the moon in a mason jar. Might as well—

For a moment his thoughts stopped entirely, and then moved on – but more slowly, and with no bitterness.

Might as well wish to think businessmen into having more self-confidence.

Might as well wish to think fat ladies thin.

Might as well wish to blind one of the goons who had kidnapped Charlie.

Might as well wish for the push to come back.

His hands were busy on the bedspread, pulling it, kneading it, feeling it – the mind's need, nearly unconscious, for some sort of constant sensory input. There was no sense in hoping for the push to come back. The push was gone. He could no more push his way to Charlie than he could pitch for the Reds. It was gone.

(*is it!*)

Quite suddenly he wasn't sure. Part of him – some very deep part – had maybe just decided it didn't buy his conscious decision to follow the path of least resistance and give them whatever they wanted. Perhaps some deep part of him had decided not to give up.

He sat feeling the bedspread, running his hands over and over it.

Was that true, or only wishful thinking brought on by one sudden and unprovable hunch? The hunch itself might have been as false as the smoke he'd thought he smelled, brought on by simple anxiety. There was no way to check the hunch, and there was certainly no one here to push.

He drank his ginger ale.

Suppose the push *had* come back. That was no universal cure-all; he of all people knew that. He could give a lot of little pushes or three or four wallopers before he tipped himself over. He might get to Charlie, but he didn't have a snowflake's chance in hell of getting them out of here. All he would succeed in doing was pushing himself into the grave via a brain hemorrhage (and as he thought of this, his fingers went automatically to his face, where the numb spots had been).

Then there was the matter of the Thorazine they had been feeding him. The lack of it – the lateness of the dose due when the lights had gone out – had played a large part in his panic, he knew. Even now, feeling more in control of himself, he *wanted* that Thorazine and the tranquil, coasting feeling it brought. At the beginning, they had kept him off the Thorazine for as long as two days before testing him. The result had been constant nervousness and a low depression like thick clouds that never seemed to let up . . . and back then he hadn't built up a heavy thing, as he had now.

'Face it, you're a junky,' he whispered.

He didn't know if that was true or not. He knew that there were physical addictions like the one to nicotine, and to heroin, which caused physical changes in the central nervous system. And then there were psychological addictions. He had taught with a fellow named Bill Wallace who got very, very nervous without his three or four Cokes a day, and his old college buddy Quincey had been a potato-chip freak – but he had to have an obscure New England brand, Humpty Dumpty; he claimed no other kind satisfied. Andy supposed those qualified as psychological addictions. He didn't know if his craving for his pill was physical or psychological; he only knew that he needed it, he really *needed* it. Just sitting here and thinking about the blue pill in the white dish had him cotton-mouthed all over again. They no longer kept him without the drug for forty-eight hours before testing him, although whether that was because they felt he couldn't go that long without getting the screaming meemies or because they were just going through the motions of testing, he didn't know.

The result was a cruelly neat, insoluble problem; he couldn't push if he was full of Thorazine, and yet he simply didn't have the will to refuse it (and, of course, if they *caught* him refusing it, that would open a whole new can of worms for them, wouldn't it? – real night-crawlers). When they brought him the blue pill in the white dish after this was over, he would take it. And little by little, he would work his way back to the calmly apathetic steady state he had been in when the power went off. All of this was just a spooky little side-trip. He would be back to watching *PTL Club* and Clint Eastwood on Home Box Office soon enough, and snacking too much out of the always-well-stocked fridge. Back to putting on weight.

(*charlie, charlie's in danger, charlie's in all sorts of trouble, she's in a world of hurt*)

If so, there was nothing he could do about it.

And even if there was, even if he could somehow conquer the monkey on his back and get them out of here – pigs will whistle and beggars will ride, why the hell not? – any ultimate solution concerning Charlie's future would be as far away as ever.

He lay back on his bed, spread-eagled. The small department of his mind that now dealt exclusively with Thorazine continued to clamor restlessly.

There were no solutions in the present, and so he drifted into the past. He saw himself and Charlie fleeing up Third Avenue in a kind of slow-motion nightmare, a big man in a scuffed cord jacket and a little girl in red and green. He saw Charlie, her face strained and pale, tears running down her cheeks after she had got all the change from the pay phones at the airport . . . she got the change and set some serviceman's shoes on fire.

His mind drifted back even further to the storefront in Port City, Pennsylvania, and Mrs Gurney. Sad, fat Mrs Gurney, who had come into the Weight-Off office in a green pantsuit, clutching at the carefully lettered slogan that had actually been Charlie's idea. *You Will Lose Weight or We Will Buy Your Groceries for the Next Six Months*.

Mrs Gurney, who had borne her truck-dispatcher husband four children between 1950 and 1957, and now the children were grown and they were disgusted with her, and her husband was disgusted with her, and he was seeing another woman, and she could understand that because Stan Gurney was still a good-looking, vital, virile man at fifty-five, and she had slowly gained one hundred and sixty pounds over the years since the second-to-last child had left for college, going from the one-forty she had weighed at marriage to an even three hundred pounds. She had come in, smooth and monstrous and desperate in her green pantsuit, and her ass was nearly as wide as a bank president's desk. When she looked down into her purse to find her checkbook, her three chins became six.

He had put her in a class with three other fat women. There were exercises and a mild diet, both of which Andy had researched at the Public Library; there were mild pep talks, which he billed as 'counseling' – and every now and then there was a medium-hard push.

Mrs Gurney had gone from three hundred to two-eighty to two-seventy, confessing with mixed fear and delight that she didn't seem to want second helpings anymore. The second helping just didn't seem to taste good. Before, she had always kept bowls and bowls of snacks in the refriger-ator (and doughnuts in the breadbox, and two or three Sara Lee cheesecakes in the freezer) for watching TV at night, but now she somehow . . . well, it sounded almost crazy, but . . . she kept *forgetting* they were there. And she had always heard that when you were dieting, snacks were all you *could* think of. It certainly hadn't been this way, she said, when she tried Weight Watchers.

The other three women in the group had responded eagerly in kind. Andy merely stood back and watched them, feeling absurdly paternal. All four of them were astounded and delighted by the commonality of their experience. The toning-up exercises, which had always seemed so boring and painful before, now seemed almost pleasant. And then there was this weird compulsion to *walk*. They all agreed that if they hadn't walked a good bit

315

by the end of the day, they felt somehow ill at ease and restless. Mrs Gurney confessed that she had got into the habit of walking downtown and back every day, even though the round trip was more than two miles. Before, she had always taken the bus, which was surely the sensible thing to do, since the stop was right in front of her house.

But the one day she had taken it – because her thigh muscles did ache *that* much – she had got to feeling so uneasy and restless that she had got off at the second stop. The others agreed. And they all blessed Andy McGee for it, sore muscles and all.

Mrs Gurney had dropped to two-fifty at her third weigh-in, and when her six-week course ended, she was down to two hundred and twenty-five pounds. She said her husband was stunned at what had happened, especially after her failure with countless dieting programs and fads. He wanted her to go see a doctor; he was afraid she might have cancer. He didn't believe it was possible to lose seventy-five pounds in six weeks by natural means. She showed him her fingers, which were red and callused from taking in her clothes with needle and thread. And then she threw her arms around him (nearly breaking his back) and wept against his neck.

His alumni usually came back, just as his more successful college students usually came back at least once, some to say thanks, some merely to parade their success before him – to say, in effect, Look here, the student has outraced the teacher . . . something that was hardly as uncommon as they seemed to think, Andy sometimes thought.

But Mrs Gurney had been one of the former. She had come back to say hello and thanks a lot only ten days or so before Andy had begun to feel nervous and watched in Port City. And before the end of that month, they had gone on to New York City.

Mrs Gurney was still a big woman; you noticed the

startling difference only if you had seen her before – like one of those before-and-after ads in the magazines. When she dropped in that last time, she was down to a hundred and ninety-five pounds. But it wasn't her exact weight that mattered, of course. What mattered was that she was losing weight at the same measured rate of six pounds a week, plus or minus two pounds, and she would go on losing at a decreasing rate until she was down to one hundred and thirty pounds, plus or minus ten pounds. There would be no explosive decompression, and no lingering hangover of food horror, the sort of thing that sometimes led to *anorexia nervosa*. Andy wanted to make some money, but he didn't want to kill anyone doing it.

'You ought to be declared a national resource for what you're doing,' Mrs Gurney had declared, after telling Andy that she had effected a rapprochement with her children and that her relations with her husband were improving. Andy had smiled and thanked her, but now, lying on his bed in the darkness, growing drowsy, he reflected that that was pretty close to what had happened to him and Charlie: they had been declared national resources.

Still, the talent was not all bad. Not when it could help a Mrs Gurney.

He smiled a little.

And smiling, slept.

10

He could never remember the details of the dream afterward. He had been looking for something. He had been in some labyrinthine maze of corridors, lit only by dull red trouble lights. He opened doors on empty rooms and then closed them again. Some of the rooms were littered with balls of crumpled paper and in one there was an overturned table lamp and a fallen picture done in the style of Wyeth. He felt that he was in some sort of installation that had been shut down and cleared out in one hell of a tearing hurry.

And yet he had at last found what he was looking for. It was . . . what? A box? A chest? It was terribly heavy, whatever it was, and it had been marked with a white-stenciled skull and crossbones, like a jar of rat poison kept on a high cellar shelf. Somehow, in spite of its weight (it had to weigh at least as much as Mrs Gurney), he managed to pick it up. He could feel all his muscles and tendons pulling taut and hard, yet there was no pain.

Of course there isn't, he told himself. *There's no pain because it's a dream. You'll pay for it later. You'll have the pain later.*

He carried the box out of the room where he had found it. There was a place he had to take it, but he didn't know what or where it was—

You'll know it when you see it, his mind whispered.

So he carried the box or chest up and down endless corridors, its weight tugging painlessly at his muscles, stiffening the back of his neck; and although his muscles didn't hurt, he was getting the beginnings of a headache.

'*The brain is a muscle,* his mind lectured, and the lecture became a chant like a child's song, a little girl's skipping rhyme: *The brain is a muscle that can move the world. The brain is a muscle that can move—*

Now all the doors were like subway doors, bulging outward in a slight curve, fitted with large windows; all these windows had rounded corners. Through these doors (if they were doors) he saw a confusion of sights. In one room Dr Wanless was playing a huge accordion. He looked like some crazed Lawrence Welk with a tin cup full of pencils in front of him and a sign around his neck that read THERE ARE NONE SO BLIND AS THOSE WHO WILL NOT SEE. Through another window he could see a girl in a white caftan flying through the air, screaming, careering off the walls, and Andy hurried past that one quickly.

Through another he saw Charlie and he became convinced again that this was some sort of pirate dream – buried treasure, yo-ho-ho and all of that – because Charlie appeared to be talking with Long John Silver. This man had a parrot on his shoulder and an eyepatch over one eye. He was grinning at Charlie with a kind of smarmy false friendship that made Andy nervous. As if in confirmation of this, the one-eyed pirate slipped an arm around Charlie's shoulders and cried hoarsely, 'We'll do 'em yet, kid!'

Andy wanted to stop there and knock on the window until he attracted Charlie's attention – she was staring at the pirate as if hypnotized. He wanted to make sure she saw through this strange man, to make sure she understood that he wasn't what he seemed.

But he couldn't stop. He had this damned

(*box? chest?*)

to

(*???*)

to what? Just what the hell was he supposed to do with it?

But he would know when it was time.

He went past dozens of other rooms – he couldn't remember all of the things he saw – and then he was in a long blank corridor that ended in a blank wall. But not entirely blank; there was something in the exact center of it, a big steel rectangle like a mail slot.

Then he saw the word that had been stamped on it in raised letters, and understood.

DISPOSAL, it read.

And suddenly Mrs Gurney was beside him, a slim and pretty Mrs Gurney with a shapely body and trim legs that looked made for dancing all night long, dancing on a terrace until the stars went pale in the sky and dawn rose

319

in the east like sweet music. You'd never guess, he thought, bemused, that her clothes were once made by Omar the Tentmaker.

He tried to lift the box, but couldn't. Suddenly it was just too heavy. His headache was worse. It was like the black horse, the riderless horse with the red eyes, and with dawning horror he realized it was loose, it was somewhere in this abandoned installation, and it was coming for him, thudding, thudding—

'I'll help you,' Mrs Gurney said. 'You helped me; now I'll help you. After all, you are the national resource, not me.'

'You look so pretty,' he said. His voice seemed to come from far away, through the thickening headache.

'I feel like I've been let out of prison,' Mrs Gurney responded. 'Let me help you.'

'It's just that my head aches—'

'Of course it does. After all, the brain is a muscle.'

Did she help him, or did he do it himself? He couldn't remember. But he could remember thinking that he understood the dream now, it was the push he was getting rid of, once and for all, the push. He remembered tipping the box against the slot marked DISPOSAL, tipping it up, wondering what it would look like when it came out, this thing that had sat inside his brain since his college days. But it wasn't the push that came out; he felt both surprise and fear as the top opened. What spilled into the chute was a flood of blue pills, *his* pills, and he was scared, all right; he was, in the words of Granther McGee, suddenly scared enough to shit nickels.

'No!' he shouted.

'Yes,' Mrs Gurney answered firmly. 'The brain is a muscle that can move the world.'

Then he saw it her way.

It seemed that the more he poured the more his head

320

ached, and the more his head ached the darker it got, until there was no light, the dark was total, it was a living dark, someone had blown all the fuses somewhere and there was no light, no box, no dream, only his headache and the riderless horse with the red eyes coming on and coming on.

Thud, thud, thud . . .

11

He must have been awake a long time before he actually realized he was awake. The total lack of light made the exact dividing line hard to find. A few years before, he had read of an experiment in which a number of monkeys had been put into environments designed to muffle all their senses. The monkeys had all gone crazy. He could understand why. He had no idea how long he had been sleeping, no concrete input except—

'Oww, Jesus!'

Sitting up drove two monstrous bolts of chromium pain into his head. He clapped his hands to his skull and rocked it back and forth, and little by little the pain subsided to a more manageable level.

No concrete sensory input except this rotten headache. I must have slept on my neck or something, he thought. I must have—

No. Oh, no. He knew this headache, knew it well. It was the sort of headache he got from a medium-to-hard push . . . harder than the ones he had given the fat ladies and shy businessmen, not quite as hard as the ones he had given the fellows at the turnpike rest stop that time.

Andy's hands flew to his face and felt it all over, from brow to chin. There were no spots where the feeling trailed away to numbness. When he smiled, both corners of his mouth went up just as they always had. He wished to God for a light so he could look into his own eyes in the bathroom mirror to see if either of them showed that tell-tale blood sheen. . . .

Push? Pushing?

That was ridiculous. Who was there to push?

Who, except—

His breath slowed to a stop in his throat and then resumed slowly.

He had thought of it before but had never tried it. He thought it would be like overloading a circuit by cycling a charge through it endlessly. He had been scared to try it.

My pill, he thought. *My pill is overdue and I want it, I really want it, I really need it. My pill will make everything all right.*

It was just a thought. It brought on no craving at all. The idea of taking a Thorazine had all the emotional gradient of *please pass the butter*. The fact was, except for the rotten headache, he felt pretty much all right. And the fact also was he had had headaches a lot worse than this – the one at the Albany airport, for instance. This one was a baby compared to that.

I've pushed myself, he thought, amazed.

For the first time he could really understand how Charlie felt, because for the first time he was a little frightened by his own psi talent. For the first time he really understood how little he understood about what it was and what it could do. Why had it gone? He didn't know. Why had it come back? He didn't know that either. Did it have something to do with his intense fear in the dark? His sudden feeling that Charlie was being threatened (he had a ghostly memory of the piratical one-eyed man and then it floated away, gone) and his own dismal self-loathing at the way he had forgotten her? Possibly even the rap on the head he had taken when he fell down?

He didn't know; he knew only that he had pushed himself.

The brain is a muscle that can move the world.

It suddenly occurred to him that while he was giving little nudges to businessmen and fat ladies, he could have become a one-man drug-rehabilitation center, and he was seized in a shivery ecstasy of dawning supposition. He had gone to sleep thinking that a talent that could help poor fat Mrs Gurney couldn't be all bad. What about a talent that could knock the monkey off the back of every poor junkie in New York City? What about *that*, sports fans?

'Jesus,' he whispered. 'Am I really clean?'

There was no craving. Thorazine, the image of the blue pill on the white plate – that thought had become unmistakably neutral.

'I am clean,' he answered himself.

Next question: could he stay clean?

But he had no more than asked himself that one when other questions flooded in. Could he find out exactly what was happening to Charlie? He had used the push on himself in his sleep, like a kind of autohypnosis. Could he use it on others while awake? The endlessly, repulsively grinning Pynchot, for instance? Pynchot would know what was happening to Charlie. Could he be made to tell? Could he maybe even get her out of here after all? Was there a way to do that? And if they did get out, what then? No more running, for one thing. That was no solution. There had to be a place to go.

For the first time in months he felt excited, hopeful. He began to try scraps of plan, accepting, rejecting, questioning. For the first time in months he felt at home in his own head, alive and vital, capable of action. And above all else, there was this: if he could fool them into believing two things – that he was still drugged and that he was still incapable of using his mental-domination talent, he might – he just might have a chance of doing – doing *something*.

He was still turning it all over restlessly in his mind when the lights came back on. In the other room, the TV began spouting that same old Jesus-will-take-care-of-your-soul-and-we'll-take-care-of-your-bank-book jive.

The eyes, the electric eyes! They're watching you again, or soon will be. . . . Don't forget that!

For one moment, everything came home to him – the days and weeks of subterfuge that would surely lie ahead if he was to have any chance at all, and the near certainty that he would be caught at some point. Depression waved in . . . but it brought no craving for the pill with it, and that helped him to catch hold of himself.

He thought of Charlie, and that helped more.

He got up slowly from the bed and walked into the living room. 'What happened?' he cried loudly. 'I was scared! Where's my medication? Somebody bring me my medication!'

He sat down in front of the TV, his face slack and dull and heavy.

And behind that vapid face, his brain – that muscle that could move the world – ticked away faster and faster.

12

Like the dream her father had had at the same time, Charlie McGee could never remember the details of her long conversation with John Rainbird, only the high spots. She was never quite sure how she came to pour out the story of how she came to be here, or to speak of her intense loneliness for her father and her terror that they would find some way to trick her into using her pyrokinetic ability again.

Part of it was the blackout, of course, and the knowledge

324

that *they* weren't listening. Part of it was John himself, he had been through so much, and he was so pathetically afraid of the dark and of the memories it brought of the terrible hole those 'Congs' had put him in. He had asked her, almost apathetically, why they had locked her up, and she had begun talking just to distract his mind. But it had quickly become more than that. It began to come out faster and faster, everything she had kept bottled up, until the words were tumbling out all over one another, helter-skelter. Once or twice she had cried, and he held her clumsily. He was a sweet man . . . in many ways he reminded her of her father.

'Now if they find out you know all of that,' she said, 'they'll probably lock you up, too. I shouldn't have told.'

'They'd lock me up, all right,' John said cheerfully. 'I got a D clearance, kid. That gives me clearance to open bottles of Johnson's Wax and that's about all.' He laughed. 'We'll be all right if you don't let on that you told me, I guess.'

'I won't,' Charlie said eagerly. She had been a little uneasy herself, thinking if John told, they might use him on her like a lever. 'I'm awful thirsty. There's icewater in the refrigerator. You want some?'

'Don't leave me,' he said immediately.

'Well, let's go together. We'll hold hands.'

He appeared to think about this. 'All right,' he said.

They shuffled across to the kitchen together, hands gripped tightly.

'You'd better not let on, kid. Especially about this. Heap-big Indian afraid of the dark. The guys'd laugh me right out of this place.'

'They wouldn't laugh if they knew—'

'Maybe not. Maybe so.' He chuckled a little. 'But I'd just as soon they never found out. I just thank God you was here, kid.'

She was so touched that her eyes filled again and she had to struggle for control of herself. They reached the fridge, and she located the jug of icewater by feel. It wasn't icy cold anymore, but it soothed her throat. She wondered with fresh unease just how long she had talked, and didn't know. But she had told . . . everything. Even the parts she had meant to hold back, like what had happened at the Manders farm. Of course, the people like Hockstetter knew, but she didn't care about them. She did care about John . . . and his opinion of her.

But she had told. He would ask a question that somehow pierced right to the heart of the matter, and . . . she had told, often with tears. And instead of more questions and cross-examination and mistrust, there had been only acceptance and calm sympathy. He seemed to understand the hell she had been through, maybe because he had been through hell himself.

'Here's the water,' she said.

'Thanks.' She heard him drink, and then it was placed back in her hands. 'Thanks a lot.'

She put it away.

'Let's go back in the other room,' he said. 'I wonder if they'll ever get the lights back on.' He was impatient for them to come on now. They had been off more than seven hours, he guessed. He wanted to get out of here and think about all of this. Not what she had told him – he knew all of that – but how to use it.

'I'm sure they'll be on soon,' Charlie said.

They shuffled their way back to the sofa and sat down.

'They haven't told you anything about your old man?'

'Just that he's all right,' she said.

'I'll bet I could get in to see him,' Rainbird said, as if this idea had just occurred to him.

'You could? You really think you could?'

'I could change with Herbie someday. See him. Tell him

326

you're okay. Well, not tell him but pass him a note or something.'

'Oh, wouldn't that be dangerous?'

'It would be dangerous to make a business of it, kid. But I owe you one. I'll see how he is.'

She threw her arms around him in the dark and kissed him. Rainbird gave her an affectionate hug. In his own way, he loved her, now more than ever. She was his now, and he supposed he was hers. For a while.

They sat together, not talking much, and Charlie dozed. Then he said something that woke her up as suddenly as completely as a dash of cold water in the face.

'Shit, you ought to light their damn fires, if you can do it.'

Charlie sucked her breath in, shocked, as if he had suddenly hit her.

'I *told* you,' she said. 'It's like letting a . . . a wild animal out of a cage. I promised myself I'd never do it again. That soldier at the airport . . . and those men at that farm . . . I killed them . . . burned them *up*!' Her face was hot, burning, and she was on the verge of tears again.

'The way you told it, it sounded like self-defense.'

'Yes, but that's no excuse to—'

'It also sounded like maybe you saved your old man's life.'

Silence from Charlie. But he could feel trouble and confusion and misery coming off her in waves. He hastened on, not wanting her to remember right now that she had come very close to killing her father as well.

'As for that guy Hockstetter, I've seen him around. I saw guys like him in the war. Every one of them a ninety-day wonder, King Shit of Turd Mountain. If he can't get what he wants from you one way, he'll try some other way.'

'That's what scares me the most,' she admitted in a low voice.

327

'Besides, there's one guy who could use a hotfoot.'

Charlie was shocked, but giggled hard – the way a dirty joke could sometimes make her laugh harder just because it was so bad to tell them. When she was over her giggles, she said: 'No, I won't light fires. I promised myself. It's bad and I won't.

It was enough. It was time to stop. He felt that he could keep going on pure intuition, but he recognized that it might be a false feeling. He was tired now. Working on the girl had been every bit as exhausting as working on one of Rammaden's safes. It would be too easy to go on and make a mistake that could never be undone.

'Yeah, okay. I guess you're right.'

'You really will see my dad?'

'I'll try, kid.'

'I'm sorry you got stuck in here with me, John. But I'm awful glad, too.'

'Yeah.'

They talked of inconsequential things, and she put her head on his arm. He felt that she was dozing off again – it was very late now – and when the lights went on about forty minutes later, she was fast asleep. The light in her face made her stir and turn her head into his darkness. He looked down thoughtfully at the slender willow stem of her neck, the tender curve of her skull. So much power in that small, delicate cradle of bone. Could it be true? His mind still rejected it, but his heart felt it was so. It was a strange and somehow wonderful feeling to find himself so divided. His heart felt it was true to an extent they wouldn't believe, true perhaps to the extent of that mad Wanless's ravings.

He picked her up, carried her to her bed, and slipped her between the sheets. As he pulled them up to her chin, she stirred half awake.

He leaned over impulsively and kissed her. 'Goodnight, kid.'

'Goodnight, Daddy,' she said in a thick, sleeping voice. Then she rolled over and became still.

He looked down at her for several minutes longer, then went back into the living room. Hockstetter himself came bustling in ten minutes later.

'Power failure,' he said. 'Storm. Damn electronic locks, all jammed. Is she—'

'She'll be fine if you keep your goddam voice down,' Rainbird said in a low voice. His huge hands pistoned out, caught Hockstetter by the lapels of his white lab coat, and jerked him forward, so that Hockstetter's suddenly terrified face was less than an inch from his own. 'And if you ever behave as if you know me in here again, if you ever behave toward me as if I am anything but a D-clearance orderly, I'll kill you, and then I'll cut you into pieces, and Cuisinart you, and turn you into catmeat.'

Hockstetter spluttered impotently. Spit bubbled at the corners of his lips.

'Do you understand? I'll kill you.' He shook Hockstetter twice.

'I-I-I un-un-understand.'

'Then let's get out of here,' Rainbird said, and shoved Hockstetter, pale and wide-eyed, out into the corridor.

He took one last look around and then wheeled his cart out and closed the self-locking door behind him. In the bedroom, Charlie slept on, more peacefully than she had in months. Perhaps years.

Small Fires,
Big Brother

1

The violent storm passed. Time passed – three weeks of it. Summer, humid and overbearing, still held sway over eastern Virginia, but school was back in session and lumbering yellow school buses trundled up and down the well-kept rural roads in the Longmont area. In not-too-distant Washington, D.C., another year of legislation, rumor, and innuendo was beginning, marked with the usual freak-show atmosphere engendered by national television, planned information leaks, and overmastering clouds of bourbon fumes.

None of that made much of an impression in the cool, environmentally controlled rooms of the two antebellum houses and the corridors and levels honeycombed beneath. The only correlative might have been that Charlie McGee was also going to school. It was Hockstetter's idea that she be tutored, and Charlie had balked, but John Rainbird had talked her into it.

'What hurt's it gonna do?' he asked. 'There's no sense in a smart girl like you getting way behind. Shit – excuse me, Charlie – but I wish to God sometimes that I had more than an eighth-grade education. I wouldn't be moppin floors now – you can bet your boots on that. Besides, it'll pass the time.'

So she had done it – for John. The tutors came: the young man who taught English, the older woman who taught mathematics, the younger woman with the thick glasses who began to teach her French, the man in the wheelchair who taught science. She listened to them, and she supposed she learned, but she had done it for John.

On three occasions John had risked his job to pass her father notes, and she felt guilty about that and hence was more willing to do what she thought would please John. And he had brought her news of her dad – that he was well, that he was relieved to know Charlie was well too, and that he was cooperating with their tests. This had distressed her a little, but she was now old enough to understand – a little bit, anyway – that what was best for her might not always be best for her father. And lately she had begun to wonder more and more if John might know best about what was right for her. In his earnest, funny way (he was always swearing and then apologizing for it, which made her giggle), he was very persuasive.

He had not said anything about making fires for almost ten days after the blackout. Whenever they talked of these things, they did it in the kitchen, where he said there were no 'bugs,' and they always talked in low voices.

On that day he had said, 'You thought any more about that fire business, Charlie?' He always called her Charlie now instead of 'kid.' She had asked him to.

She began to tremble. Just thinking about making fires had this effect on her since the Manders farm. She got cold and tense and trembly; on Hockstetter's reports this was called a 'mild phobic reaction.'

'I told you,' she said. 'I can't do that. I won't do that.'

'Now, can't and won't aren't the same thing,' John said. He was washing the floor – but very slowly, so he could talk to her. His mop swished. He talked the way cons talk in prison, barely moving his lips.

Charlie didn't reply.

'I just had a couple of thoughts on this,' he said. 'But if

332

you don't want to hear them – if your head's really set – I'll just shut up.'

'No, that's okay,' Charlie said politely, but she did really wish he would shut up, not talk about it, not even think about it, because it made her feel bad. But John had done so much for her . . . and she desperately didn't want to offend him or hurt his feelings. She needed a friend.

'Well, I was just thinking that they must know how it got out of control at that farm,' he said. 'They'd probably be really careful. I don't think they'd be apt to test you in a room full of paper and oily rags, do you?'

'No, but—'

He raised one hand a little way off his mop. 'Hear me out, hear me out.'

'Okay.'

'And they sure know that was the only time you caused a real – what's it? – a conflagration. Small fires, Charlie. That's the ticket. Small fires. And if something did happen – which I doubt, cause I think you got better control over yourself than you think you do – but say something *did* happen. Who they gonna blame, huh? They gonna blame you? After the fuckheads spent half a year twisting your arm to do it? Oh hell, I'm sorry.'

The things he was saying scared her, but still she had to put her hands to her mouth and giggle at the woebegone expression on his face.

John smiled a little too, then shrugged. 'The other thing I was thinkin is that you can't learn to control something unless you practice it and practice it.'

'I don't care if I ever control it or not, because I'm just not going to do it.'

'Maybe or maybe not,' John said stubbornly, wringing out his mop. He stood it in the corner, then dumped his soapy water down the sink. He began to run a bucket of fresh to rinse with. 'You might get *surprised* into using it.'

333

'No, I don't think so.'

'Or suppose you got a bad fever sometime. From the flu or the croup or, hell, I dunno, some kind of infection.' This was one of the few profitable lines Hockstetter had given him to pursue. 'You ever have your appendix out, Charlie?'

'No-ooo . . .'

John began to rinse the floor.

'My brother had his out, but it went bust first and he almost died. That was cause we were reservation Indians and nobody gave a – nobody cared much if we lived or died. He got a high fever, a hundred and five, I guess, and he went ravin right off his head, sayin horrible curses and talkin to people who weren't there. Do you know he thought our father was the Angel of Death or somethin, come to carry him off, and he tried to stick im with a knife that was on his bedside table there? I told you this story, didn't I?'

'No,' Charlie said, whispering now not to keep from being overheard but out of horrified fascination. 'Really?'

'Really,' John affirmed. He squeezed the mop out again. 'It wasn't his fault. It was the fever that did it. People are apt to say or do anything when they're delirious. *Anything.*'

Charlie understood what he was saying and felt a sinking fear. Here was something she had never even considered.

'But if you had control of this pyro-whatsis . . .'

'How could I have control of it if I was delirious?'

'Just because you *do.*' Rainbird went back to Wanless's original metaphor, the one that had so disgusted Cap almost a year ago now. 'It's like toilet-training, Charlie. Once you get hold of your bowels and bladder, you're in control for good. Delirious people sometimes get their beds all wet from sweat, but they rarely piss the bed.'

Hockstetter had pointed out that this was not invariably true, but Charlie wouldn't know that.

'Well, anyway, all I mean is that if you got *control*, don't you see, you wouldn't have to worry about this anymore. You'd have it licked. But to get control you have to practice and practice. The same way you learned to tie your shoes, or to make your letters in kinnygarden.'

'I . . . I just don't want to make fires! And I won't! I *won't!*'

'There, I went and upset you,' John said, distressed. 'I sure didn't mean to do that. I'm sorry, Charlie. I won't say no more. Me and my big fat mouth.'

But the next time she brought it up herself.

It was three or four days later, and she had thought over the things he had said very carefully . . . and she believed that she had put her finger on the one flaw. 'It would just never end,' she said. 'They'd always want more and more and more. If you only knew the way they *chased* us, they *never* give up. Once I started they'd want bigger fires and then even bigger ones and then bonfires and then . . . I don't know . . . but I'm afraid.'

He admired her again. She had an intuition and a native wit that was incredibly sharp. He wondered what Hockstetter would think when he, Rainbird, told him that Charlie McGee had an extremely good idea what their top-secret master plan was. All of their reports on Charlie theorized that pyrokinesis was only the centerpiece of many related psionic talents, and Rainbird believed that her intuition was one of them. Her father had told them again and again that Charlie had *known* Al Steinowitz and the others were coming up to the Manders farm even before they had arrived. That was a scary thought. If she should ever get one of her funny intuitions about *his* authenticity . . . well, they said hell had no fury like a woman scorned, and if half of what he believed about Charlie was true, then she was perfectly capable of manufacturing hell, or a reasonable facsimile. He might suddenly

335

find himself getting very hot. It added a certain spice to the proceedings . . . a spice that had been missing for too long.

'Charlie,' he said, 'I'm not sayin you should do any of these things for *free*.'

She looked at him, puzzled.

John sighed. 'I don't hardly know how to put it to you,' he said. 'I guess I love you a little. You're like the daughter I never had. And the way they're keeping you cooped up here, not letting you see your daddy and all, never getting to go out, missing all the things other little girls have . . . it just about makes me *sick*.'

Now he allowed his good eye to blaze out at her, scaring her a little.

'You could get all kinds of things just by going along with them . . . and attaching a few strings.'

'Strings,' Charlie said, utterly mystified.

'Yeah! You could get them to let you go outside in the sun, I bet. Maybe even into Longmont to shop for things. You could get out of this goddam box and into a regular house. See other kids. And—'

'And see my father?'

'Sure, that, too.' But that was one thing that was never going to happen, because if the two of them put their information together they would realize that John the Friendly Orderly was just too good to be true. Rainbird had never passed along a single message to Andy McGee. Hockstetter thought it would be running a risk for no gain, and Rainbird, who thought Hockstetter a total bleeding asshole about most things, agreed.

It was one thing to fool an eight-year-old kid with fairy stories about there being no bugs in the kitchen and about how they could talk in low voices and not be overheard, but it would be quite another thing to fool the girl's father with the same fairy story, even though he was hooked

336

through the bag and back. McGee might not be hooked enough to miss the fact that they were now doing little more than playing Nice Guy and Mean Guy with Charlie, a technique police departments have used to crack criminals for hundreds of years.

So he maintained the fiction that he was taking her messages to Andy just as he was maintaining so many other fictions. It was true that he saw Andy quite often, but he saw him only on the TV monitors. It was true that Andy was cooperating with their tests, but it was also true that he was tipped over, unable to push a kid into eating a Popsicle. He had turned into a big fat zero, concerned only with what was on the tube and when his next pill was going to arrive, and he never asked to see his daughter anymore. Meeting her father face to face and seeing what they had done to him might stiffen her resistance all over again, and he was very close to breaking her now; she *wanted* to be convinced now. No, all things were negotiable except that. Charlie McGee was never going to see her father again. Before too long, Rainbird surmised, Cap would have McGee on a Shop plane to the Maui compound. But the girl didn't need to know that, either.

'You really think they'd let me see him?'

'No question about it,' he responded easily. 'Not at first, of course; he's their ace with you, and they know it. But if you went to a certain point and then said you were going to cut them off unless they let you see him—' He let it dangle there. The bait was out, a big sparkling lure dragged through the water. It was full of hooks and not good to eat anyway, but that was something else this tough little chick didn't know.

She looked at him thoughtfully. No more was said about it. That day.

Now, about a week later, Rainbird abruptly reversed his field. He did this for no concrete reason, but his own intuition told him he could get no further by advocacy. It was time to beg, as Br'er Rabbit had begged Br'er Fox not to be thrown into that briar patch.

'You remember what we was talkin about?' He opened the conversation. He was waxing the kitchen floor. She was pretending to linger over her selection of a snack from the fridge. One clean, pink foot was cocked behind the other so he could see the sole – a pose that he found curiously evocative of mid-childhood. It was somehow pre-erotic, almost mystic. His heart went out to her again. Now she looked back over her shoulder at him doubtfully. Her hair, done up in a ponytail, lay over one shoulder.

'Yes,' she said. 'I remember.'

'Well, I been thinkin, and I started to ask myself what makes me an expert on givin advice,' he said. 'I can't even float a thousand-dollar bank loan for a car.'

'Oh, John, that doesn't mean anything—'

'Yes it does. If I knew something, I'd be one of those guys like that Hockstetter. College-educated.'

With great disdain she replied, 'My daddy says any fool can buy a college education somewhere.'

In his heart, he rejoiced.

2

Three days after that, the fish swallowed the lure.

Charlie told him that she had decided to let them make their tests. She would be careful, she said. And she would make *them* be careful, if they didn't know how. Her face was thin and pinched and pale.

'Don't you do it,' John said, 'unless you've thought it all out.'

'I've tried,' she whispered.

'Are you doing it for them?'

'*No!*'

338

'Good! Are you doing it for you?'

'Yes. For me. And for my father.'

'All right,' he said. 'And Charlie – make them play it your way. Understand me? You've shown them how tough you can be. Don't let them see a weak streak now. If they see it, they'll use it. Play tough. You know what I mean?'

'I . . . think so.'

'They get something, you get something. Every time. No freebies.' His shoulders slumped a bit. The fire went out of his eye. She hated to see him this way, looking depressed and defeated. 'Don't let them treat you like they treated me. I gave my country four years of my life and one eye. One of those years I spent in a hole in the ground eating bugs and running a fever and smelling my own shit all the time and picking lice out of my hair. And when I got out they said thanks a lot, John, and put a mop in my hand. They stole from me, Charlie. Get it? Don't let them do that to you.'

'I get it,' she said solemnly.

He brightened a little, then smiled. 'So when's the big day?'

'I'm seeing Dr Hockstetter tomorrow. I'll tell him I've decided to cooperate . . . a little. And I'll . . . I'll tell him what *I* want.'

'Well, just don't ask for too much at first. It's just like the carny at the midway, Charlie. You got to show em some flash before you take their cash.'

She nodded.

'But you show them who's in the saddle, right? Show them who's boss.'

'Right.'

He smiled more broadly. 'Good kid!' he said.

Hockstetter was furious.

'What the *hell* sort of game are you playing?' he shouted at Rainbird. They were in Cap's office. He dared to shout, Rainbird thought, because Cap was here to play referee. Then he took a second look at Hockstetter's hot blue eyes, his flushed cheeks, his white knuckles, and admitted that he was probably wrong. He had dared to make his way through the gates and into Hockstetter's sacred garden of privilege. The shaking-out Rainbird had administered after the blackout ended was one thing; Hockstetter had lapsed dangerously and had known it. This was something else altogether. He thought.

Rainbird only stared at Hockstetter.

'You've carefully set it up around an impossibility! You know damned well she isn't going to see her father! "They get something, you get something," ' Hockstetter mimicked furiously. 'You fool!'

Rainbird continued to stare at Hockstetter. 'Don't call me a fool again,' he said in a perfectly neutral voice. Hockstetter flinched . . . but only a little.

'Please, gentlemen,' Cap said wearily. 'Please.'

There was a tape recorder on his desk. They had just finished listening to the conversation Rainbird had had with Charlie that morning.

'Apparently Dr Hockstetter had missed the point that he and his team are finally going to get *something*,' Rainbird said. 'Which will improve their store of practical knowledge by one hundred percent, if my mathematics are correct.'

'As the result of a totally unforeseen accident,' Hockstetter said sullenly.

'An accident you people were too shortsighted to manufacture for yourselves,' Rainbird countered. 'Too busy playing with your rats, maybe.'

'Gentlemen, that's enough!' Cap said. 'We're not here to indulge in a lot of recriminations; that is not the purpose of this meeting.' He looked at Hockstetter. 'You're going to get to play ball,' he said. 'I must say you show remarkably little gratitude.'

Hockstetter muttered.

Cap looked at Rainbird. 'All the same, I also think you took your role of *amicus curiae* a little bit too far in the end.'

'Do you think so? Then you still don't understand.' He looked from Cap to Hockstetter and then back to Cap again. 'I think both of you have shown an almost paralyzing lack of understanding. You've got two child psychiatrists at your disposal, and if they are an accurate representation of the caliber of that field, there are a lot of disturbed kids out there who have got big-time trouble.'

'Easy to say,' Hockstetter said. 'This—'

'You just don't understand how *smart* she is,' Rainbird cut him off. 'You don't understand how . . . how adept she is at seeing the causes and effects of things. Working with her is like picking your way through a minefield. I pointed out the carrot-and-stick idea to her because she would have thought of it herself. By thinking of it for her, I've shored up the trust she has in me . . . in effect, turned a disadvantage into an advantage.'

Hockstetter opened his mouth. Cap held up one hand and then turned to Rainbird. He spoke in a soft, placatory tone that he used with no one else . . . but then, no one else was John Rainbird. 'That doesn't alter the fact that you seem to have limited how far Hockstetter and his people can go. Sooner or later she's going to understand that her ultimate request – to see her father – is not going to be granted. We're all in agreement that to allow that might close off her usefulness to us forever.'

'Right on,' Hockstetter said.

341

'And if she's as sharp as you say,' Cap said, 'she's apt to make the ungrantable request sooner rather than later.'

'She'll make it,' Rainbird agreed, 'and that will end it. For one thing, she'd realize as soon as she saw him that I was lying all along about his condition. That would lead her to the conclusion that I had been shilling for you guys all along. So it becomes entirely a question of how long you can keep her going.'

Rainbird leaned forward.

'A couple of points. First, you've both got to get used to the idea that she's simply not going to light fires for you *ad infinitum*. She's a human being, a little girl who wants to see her father. She's not a lab rat.'

'We've already—' Hockstetter began impatiently.

'No. No, you haven't. It goes back to the very basis of the reward system in experimentation. The carrot and the stick. By lighting fires, Charlie thinks she's holding the carrot out to you and that she will eventually lead you – and herself – to her father. But we know differently. In truth, her father is the carrot, and we are leading her. Now a mule will plow the whole south forty trying to get that carrot dangling in front of his eyes, because a mule is stupid. *But this little girl isn't.*'

He looked at Cap and Hockstetter.

'I keep saying that. It is like pounding a nail into oak – oak of the first cutting. Hard going, don't you know; you both seem to keep forgetting. Sooner or later she's going to wise up and tell you to stick it. Because she isn't a mule. Or a white lab rat.'

And you want her to quit, Cap thought with slow loathing. You want her to quit so you can kill her.

'So you start with that one basic fact,' Rainbird continued. 'That's Go. Then you start thinking of ways to prolong her cooperation as long as possible. Then, when it's over, you write your report. If you got enough data, you get

342

rewarded with a big cash appropriation. You get to eat the carrot. Then you can start injecting a bunch of poor, ignorant slobs with your witch's brew all over again.'

'You're being insulting,' Hockstetter said in a shaking voice.

'It beats the terminal stupids,' Rainbird answered.

'How do you propose to prolong her cooperation?'

'You'll get some mileage out of her just by granting small privileges,' Rainbird said. 'A walk on the lawn. Or . . . every little girl loves horses. I'll bet you could get half a dozen fires out of her just by having a groom lead her around the bridle paths on one of those stable nags. That ought to be enough to keep a dozen paper pushers like Hockstetter dancing on the head of a pin for five years.'

Hockstetter pushed back from the table. 'I don't have to sit here and listen to this.'

'Sit down and shut up,' Cap said.

Hot blood slammed into Hockstetter's face and he looked ready to fight; it left as suddenly as it had come and he looked ready to cry. Then he sat down again.

'You let her go into town and shop,' Rainbird said. 'Maybe you arrange for her to go to Seven Flags over Georgia and ride the roller-coaster. Maybe even with her good friend John the orderly.'

'You seriously think just those things—' Cap began.

'No, I don't. Not for long. Sooner or later it will get back to her father. But she's only human. She wants things for herself as well. She'll go quite aways down the road you want her to go down just by rationalizing it to herself, telling herself she's showing you the flash before grabbing the cash. But eventually it's going to get back to dear old Dads, yes. She's no sellout, that one. She's tough.'

'And that's the end of the trolley-car ride,' Cap said thoughtfully. 'Everybody out. The project ends. This

343

phase of it, anyway.' In many ways, the prospect of an end in sight relieved him tremendously.

'Not right there, no,' Rainbird said, smiling his mirthless smile. 'We have one more card up our sleeve. One more very large carrot when the smaller ones play out. Not her father – not the grand prize – but something that will keep her going yet a while longer.'

'And what would that be?' Hockstetter asked.

'You figure it out,' Rainbird said, still smiling, and said no more. Cap might, in spite of how far he had come unraveled over the last half year or so. He had more smarts on half power than most of his employees (and all the pretenders to his throne) had on full power. As for Hockstetter, he would never see it. Hockstetter had risen several floors past his level of incompetency, a feat more possible in the federal bureaucracy than elsewhere. Hockstetter would have trouble following his nose to a shit-and-cream-cheese sandwich.

Not that it mattered if any of them figured out what the final carrot (the Game Carrot, one might say) in this little contest was; the results would still be the same. It was going to put him comfortably in the driver's seat one way or the other. He might have asked them: *Who do you think her father is now that her father isn't there?*

Let them figure it out for themselves. If they could.

John Rainbird went on smiling.

4

Andy McGee sat in front of his television set. The little amber Home Box Office pilot light glowed in the square gadget on top of the TV. On the screen, Richard Dreyfuss was trying to build the Devil's Butte in his living room. Andy watched with a calm and vapid expression of pleasure. Inside he was boiling with nervousness. Today was the day.

For Andy, the three weeks since the blackout had been a period of almost unbearable tension and strain interwoven with bright threads of guilty exhilaration. He could understand simultaneously how the Russian KGB could inspire such terror and how George Orwell's Winston Smith must have enjoyed his brief period of crazy, furtive rebellion. He had a secret again. It gnawed and worked in him, as all grave secrets do within the minds of their keepers, but it also made him feel whole and potent again. He was putting one over on them. God knew how long he would be able to continue or if it would come to anything, but right now he was *doing* it.

It was almost ten in the morning and Pynchot, that eternally grinning man, was coming at ten. They would be going for a walk in the garden to 'discuss his progress.' Andy intended to push him . . . or to at least try. He might have made the effort before this, except for the TV monitors and the endless bugging devices. And the wait had given him time to think out his line of attack and probe it again and again for weak spots. He had, in fact, rewritten parts of the scenario in his mind many times.

At night, lying in bed in the dark, he had thought over and over again: *Big Brother is watching. Just keep telling yourself that, keep it foremost in your mind. They've got you locked up right in the forebrain of Big Brother, and if you really expect to help Charlie, you've got to keep on fooling them.*

He was sleeping less than he ever had in his life, mostly because he was terrified of talking in his sleep. Some nights he lay wakeful for hours, afraid even to toss and turn in case they should wonder why a drugged man should be so restless. And when he did sleep it was thin, shot with strange dreams (often the Long John Silver figure, the one-

345

eyed pirate with the pegleg, recurred in these) and easily broken.

Slipping the pills was the easiest part, because they believed he wanted them. The pills came four times a day now, and there had been no more tests since the blackout. He believed they had given up, and that was what Pynchot wanted to tell him today on his walk.

Sometimes he would cough the pills out of his mouth into his cupped hand and put them in food scraps he would later scrape down the garbage disposal. More went down the toilet. Still others he had pretended to take with ginger ale. He spat the pills into the half-empty cans to dissolve and then let them stand, as if forgotten. Later he would turn them down the sink.

God knew he was no professional at this, and presumably the people who were monitoring him were. But he didn't think they were monitoring him very closely anymore. If they were, he would be caught. That was all.

Dreyfuss and the woman whose son had been taken for a ride by the saucer people were scaling the side of Devil's Butte when the buzzer that marked the breaking of the door circuit went off briefly. Andy didn't let himself jump.

This is it, he told himself again.

Herman Pynchot came into the living room. He was shorter than Andy but very slender; there was something about him that had always struck Andy as slightly effeminate, although it was nothing you could put your finger on. Today he was looking extremely reet and compleat in a thin gray turtleneck sweater and a summerweight jacket. And of course he was grinning.

'Good morning, Andy,' he said.

'Oh,' Andy said, and then paused, as if to think. 'Hello, Dr Pynchot.'

'Do you mind if I turn this off? We ought to go for our walk, you know.'

'Oh.' Andy's brow furrowed, then cleared. 'Sure. I've seen it three or four times already. But I like the ending. It's pretty. The UFOs take him away, you know. To the stars.'

'Really,' Pynchot said, and turned off the TV. 'Shall we go?'

'Where?' Andy asked.

'Our walk,' Herman Pynchot said patiently. 'Remember?'

'Oh,' Andy said. 'Sure.' He got up.

5

The hall outside Andy's room was wide and tile-floored. The lighting was muted and indirect. Somewhere not far away was a communications or computer center; people strolled in with keypunch cards, out with swatches of printouts, and there was the hum of light machinery.

A young man in an off-the-rack sport coat – the essence of government agent – lounged outside the door of Andy's apartment. There was a bulge under his arm. The agent was a part of the standard operating procedure, but as he and Pynchot strolled, he would fall behind them, watching but out of earshot. Andy thought he would be no problem.

The agent fell in behind them now as he and Pynchot strolled to the elevator. Andy's heartbeat was now so heavy it felt as if it were shaking his entire ribcage. But without seeming to, he was watching everything closely. There were perhaps a dozen unmarked doors. Some of them he had seen standing open on other walks up this corridor – a small, specialized library of some kind, a photocopying room in another – but about many of them he simply had no idea. Charlie might be behind any one of them right now . . . or in some other part of the installation entirely.

They got into the elevator, which was big enough to

347

accommodate a hospital gurney. Pynchot produced his keys, twisted one of them in the keyway, and pushed one of the unmarked buttons. The doors closed and the elevator rose smoothly. The Shop agent lounged at the back of the car. Andy stood with his hands in the pockets of his Lee Riders, a slight, vapid smile on his face.

The elevator door opened on what had once been a ballroom. The floor was polished oak, pegged together. Across the wide expanse of the room, a spiral staircase made a graceful double twist on its way to the upper levels. To the left, French doors gave on to a sunny terrace and the rock garden beyond it. From the right, where heavy oak doors stood half open, came the clacking sound of a typing pool, putting out that day's two bales of paperwork.

And from everywhere came the smell of fresh flowers.

Pynchot led the way across the sunny ballroom, and as always Andy commented on the pegged-together floor as if he had never noticed it before. They went through the French doors with their Shop-shadow behind them. It was very warm, very humid. Bees buzzed lazily through the air. Beyond the rock garden were hydrangea, forsythia, and rhododendron bushes. There was the sound of riding lawnmowers making their eternal rounds. Andy turned his face up to the sun with a gratitude that wasn't feigned.

'How are you feeling, Andy?' Pynchot asked.

'Good. Good.'

'You know, you've been here almost half a year now,' Pynchot said in an isn't-it-amazing-how-the-time-flies-when-you're-having-a-good-time tone of mild surprise. They turned right, onto one of the graveled paths. The smell of honeysuckle and sweet sassafras hung in the still air. On the other side of the duckpond, near the other house, two horses cantered lazily along.

'That long,' Andy said.

'Yes, it is a long time,' Pynchot said, grinning. 'And

we've decided that your power has . . . diminished, Andy. In fact, you know we've had no appreciable results at all.'

'Well, you keep me drugged all the time,' Andy said reproachfully. 'You can't expect me to do my best if I'm stoned.'

Pynchot cleared his throat but did not point out that Andy had been totally clean for the first three series of tests and all three had been fruitless.

'I mean, I've done my best, Dr Pynchot. I've *tried*.'

'Yes, yes. Of course you have. And we think – that is, *I* think – that you deserve a rest. Now, the Shop has a small compound on Maui, in the Hawaii chain, Andy. And I have a six-month report to write very soon. How would you like it' – Pynchot's grin broadened into a game-show host's leer and his voice took on the tones of a man about to offer a child an incredible treat – 'how would you like it if I recommended that you be sent there for the immediate future?'

And the immediate future might be two years, Andy thought. Maybe five. They would want to keep an eye on him in case the mental-domination ability recurred, and maybe as an ace in the hole in case some unforeseen difficulty with Charlie cropped up. But in the end, he had no doubt that there would be an accident or an overdose or a 'suicide.' In Orwell's parlance, he would become an unperson.

'Would I still get my medication?' Andy asked.

'Oh, of course,' Pynchot said.

'Hawaii . . .' Andy said dreamily. Then he looked around at Pynchot with what he hoped was an expression of rather stupid cunning. 'Probably Dr Hockstetter won't let me go. Dr Hockstetter doesn't like me. I can tell.'

'Oh, he does,' Pynchot assured him. 'He does like you, Andy. And in any case, you're my baby, not Dr Hockstetter's. I assure you, he'll go along with what I advise.'

349

'But you haven't written your memorandum on the subject yet,' Andy said.

'No, I thought I'd talk to you first. But, really, Hockstetter's approval is just a formality.'

'One more series of tests might be wise,' Andy said, and pushed out lightly at Pynchot. 'Just for safety's sake.'

Pynchot's eyes suddenly fluttered in a strange way. His grin faltered, became puzzled, and then faded altogether. Now Pynchot was the one who looked drugged, and the thought gave Andy a vicious kind of satisfaction. Bees droned in the flowers. The scent of new-cut grass, heavy and cloying, hung in the air.

'When you write your report, suggest one more series of tests,' Andy repeated.

Pynchot's eyes cleared. His grin came splendidly back. 'Of course, this Hawaii thing is just between us for the time being,' he said. 'When I write my report, I will be suggesting one more series of tests. I think it might be wise. Just for safety's sake, you know.'

'But after that I might go to Hawaii?'

'Yes,' Pynchot said. 'After that.'

'And another series of tests might take three months or so?'

'Yes, about three months.' Pynchot beamed on Andy as if he were a prize pupil.

They were nearing the pond now. Ducks sailed lazily across its mirror surface. The two men paused by it. Behind them, the young man in the sport coat was watching a middle-aged man and woman cantering along side by side on the far side of the pond. Their reflections were broken only by the long, smooth glide of one of the white ducks. Andy thought the couple looked eerily like an ad for mail-order insurance, the kind of ad that's always falling out of your Sunday paper and into your lap – or your coffee.

There was a small pulse of pain in his head. Not bad at all. But in his nervousness he had come very close to pushing Pynchot much harder than he had to, and the young man might have noticed the results of that. He didn't seem to be watching them, but Andy wasn't fooled.

'Tell me a little about the roads and the countryside around here,' he said quietly to Pynchot, and pushed out lightly again. He knew from various snatches of conversation that they were not terribly far from Washington, D.C., but nowhere as close as the CIA's base of operations in Langley. Beyond that he knew nothing.

'Very pretty here,' Pynchot said dreamily, 'since they've filled the holes.'

'Yes, it is nice,' Andy said, and lapsed into silence. Sometimes a push triggered an almost hypnotic trace memory in the person being pushed – usually through some obscure association – and it was unwise to interrupt whatever was going on. It could set up an echo effect, and the echo could become a ricochet, and the ricochet could lead to . . . well, to almost anything. It had happened to one of his Walter Mitty businessmen, and it had scared the bejesus out of Andy. It had turned out okay, but if friend Pynchot suddenly got a case of the screaming horrors, it would be anything but okay.

'My wife loves that thing,' Pynchot said in that same dreamy voice.

'What's that?' Andy asked. 'That she loves?'

'Her new garbage disposer. It's very . . .'

He trailed off.

'Very pretty,' Andy suggested. The guy in the sport coat had drifted a little closer and Andy felt a fine sweat break on his upper lip.

'Very pretty,' Pynchot agreed, and looked vaguely out at the pond.

The Shop agent came closer still, and Andy decided he might have to risk another push . . . a very small one. Pynchot was standing beside him like a TV set with a blown tube.

351

The shadow picked up a small chunk of wood and tossed it in the water. It struck lightly and ripples spread, shimmering. Pynchot's eyes fluttered.

'The country is very pretty around here,' Pynchot said. 'Quite hilly, you know. Good riding country. My wife and I ride here once a week, if we can get away. I guess Dawn's the closest town going west . . . southwest, actually. Pretty small. Dawn's on Highway Three-oh-one. Gether's the closest town going east.'

'Is Gether on a highway?'

'Nope. Just on a little road.'

'Where does Highway Three-oh-one go? Besides Dawn?'

'Why, all the way up to D.C., if you go north. Most of the way to Richmond, if you go south.'

Andy wanted to ask about Charlie now, had planned to ask about Charlie, but Pynchot's reaction had scared him a little. His association of *wife*, *holes*, *pretty*, and – very strange! – *garbage disposer* had been peculiar and somehow disquieting. It might be that Pynchot, although accessible, was nevertheless not a good subject. It might be that Pynchot was a disturbed personality of some sort, tightly corseted into an appearance of normality while God knew what forces might be delicately counterbalanced underneath. Pushing people who were mentally unstable could lead to all sorts of unforeseen results. If it hadn't been for the shadow he might have tried anyway (after all that had happened to him, he had damn few compunctions about messing with Herman Pynchot's head), but now he was afraid to. A psychiatrist with the push might be a great boon to mankind . . . but Andy McGee was no shrink.

Maybe it was foolish to assume so much from a single trace-memory reaction; he had got them before from a good many people and very few of them had freaked out. But he didn't trust Pynchot. Pynchot smiled too much.

A sudden cold and murderous voice spoke from deep inside

him, from some well sunk far into his subconscious: *Tell him to go home and commit suicide. Then push him. Push him hard.*

He thrust the thought away, horrified and a little sickened.

'Well,' Pynchot said, looking around, grinning. 'Shall we returnez-vous?'

'Sure,' Andy said.

And so he had begun. But he was still in the dark about Charlie.

6

INTERDEPARTMENTAL MEMO

From   Herman Pynchot
To   Patrick Hockstetter
Date   September 12
Re   Andy McGee

I've been over all of my notes and most of the tapes in the last three days, and have spoken to McGee. There is no essential change in the situation since we last discussed it 9/5, but for the time being I'd like to put the Hawaii idea on hold if there is no big objection (as Captain Hollister himself says, 'it's only money'!).

The fact is, Pat, I believe that a final series of tests might be wise – just for safety's sake. After that we might go ahead and send him to the Maui compound. I believe that a final series might take three months or so.

Please advise before I start the necessary paperwork.

Herm

7

INTERDEPARTMENTAL MEMO

From   P. H.
To   Herm Pynchot
Date   September 13
Re   Andy McGee

I don't get it! The last time we all got together we agreed – you as much as any of us – that McGee was as dead as a used fuse. You can only hesitate so long at the bridge, you know!

If you want to schedule another series of tests – an *abbreviated* series, then be my guest. We're starting with the girl next week, but thanks to a good deal of inept interference from a certain source, I think it likely that her cooperation may not last long. While it does, it might not be a bad idea to have her father around . . . as a 'fire-extinguisher'???

Oh yes – it may be 'only money,' but it is the taxpayer's money, and levity on that subject is rarely encouraged, Herm. *Especially* by Captain Hollister. Keep it in mind.

Plan on having him for 6 to 8 weeks at most, unless you get results . . . and if you do, I'll personally eat your Hush Puppies.

                                                                    Pat

8

'Son-of-a-fucking-bitch,' Herm Pynchot said aloud as he finished reading this memorandum. He reread the third paragraph: here was Hockstetter, Hockstetter who owned a completely restored 1958 Thunderbird, spanking *him* about money. He crumpled up the memo and threw it at the wastebasket and leaned back in his swivel chair. Two months at most! He didn't like that. Three would have been more like it. He really felt that—

Unbidden and mysterious, a vision of the garbage-disposal unit he had installed at home rose in his mind. He didn't like that, either. The disposal unit had somehow got into his mind lately, and he didn't seem to be able to get it out. It came to the fore particularly when he tried to deal with the question of Andy McGee. The dark hole in the center of the sink was guarded by a rubber diaphragm . . . vaginal, that . . .

He leaned farther back in his chair, dreaming. When he came out of it with a start, he was disturbed to see that almost twenty minutes had gone by. He drew a memo form toward him and scratched out a note to that dirty bird Hockstetter, eating the obligatory helping of crow about his ill-advised 'it's only money' comment. He had to restrain himself from repeating his request for three months (and in his mind, the image of the disposer's smooth dark hole rose again). If Hockstetter said two, it was two. But if he did get results with McGee, Hockstetter was going to find two size-nine Hush Puppies sitting on his desk blotter fifteen minutes later, along with a knife, a fork, and a bottle of Adolph's Meat Tenderizer.

He finished the note, scrawled *Herm* across the bottom, and sat back, massaging his temples. He had a headache.

In high school and in college, Herm Pynchot had been a closet transvestite. He liked to dress up in women's clothes because he thought they made him look . . . well, very pretty. His junior year in college, as a member of Delta Tau Delta, he had been discovered by two of his fraternity brothers. The price of their silence had been a ritual humiliation, not much different from the pledge hazing that Pynchot himself had participated in with high good humor.

At two o'clock in the morning, his discoverers had spread trash and garbage from one end of the fraternity kitchen to the other and had forced Pynchot, dressed only in ladies' panties, stockings and garter belt, and a bra stuffed with toilet paper, to clean it all up and then wash the floor, under constant threat of discovery: all it would have taken was another frat 'brother' wandering down for an early-morning snack.

The incident had ended in mutual masturbation, which, Pynchot supposed, he should have been grateful for – it was probably the only thing that caused them to really keep their promise. But he had dropped out of the frat, terrified and disgusted with himself – most of all because he had found the entire incident somehow exciting. He had never 'cross-dressed' since that time. He was not gay. He had a lovely wife and two fine children and that proved he was not gay. He hadn't even thought of that humiliating, disgusting incident in years. And yet—

The image of the garbage disposal, that smooth black hole faced with rubber, remained. And his headache was worse.

The echo set off by Andy's push had begun. It was lazy and slow-moving now; the image of the disposal, coupled with the idea of being very pretty, was still an intermittent thing.

But it would speed up. Begin to ricochet.

Until it became unbearable.

9

'No,' Charlie said. 'It's wrong.' And she turned around to march right out of the small room again. Her face was white and strained. There were dark, purplish dashes under her eyes.

'Hey, whoa, wait a minute,' Hockstetter said, putting out his hands. He laughed a little. 'What's wrong, Charlie?'

'Everything,' she said. 'Everything's wrong.'

Hockstetter looked at the room. In one corner, a Sony TV camera had been set up. Its cords led through the pressed-cork wall to a VCR in the observation room next door. On the table in the middle of the room was a steel tray loaded with woodchips. To the left of this was an electroencephalograph dripping wires. A young man in a white coat presided over this.

'That's not much help,' Hockstetter said. He was still smiling paternally, but he was mad. You didn't have to be a mind reader to know that; you had only to look in his eyes.

'You don't listen,' she said shrilly. 'None of you listen except—'

(*except John but you can't say that*)

'Tell us how to fix it,' Hockstetter said.

She would not be placated. 'If you *listened*, you'd know. That steel tray with the little pieces of wood, *that's* all right, but that's the only thing that is. The table's wood, that wall stuff, that's fluh-flammable . . . and so's that guy's clothes.' She pointed to the technician, who flinched a little.

'Charlie—'

'That camera is, too.'

'Charlie, that camera's—'

'It's plastic and if it gets hot enough it will explode and little pieces will go everywhere. And there's no water! I told you, I have to push it at water once it gets started. My father and my mother told me so. I have to push it at water to put it out. Or . . . or . . .'

She burst into tears. She wanted John. She wanted her father. More than anything, oh, more than *anything*, she didn't want to be here. She had not slept at all last night.

357

For his part, Hockstetter looked at her thoughtfully. The tears, the emotional upset . . . he thought those things made it as clear as anything that she was really prepared to go through with it.

'All right,' he said. 'All right, Charlie. You tell us what to do and we'll do it.'

'You're right,' she said. 'Or you don't get nothing.'

Hockstetter thought: *We'll get plenty, you snotty little bitch.*

As it turned out, he was absolutely right.

10

Late that afternoon they brought her into a different room. She had fallen asleep in front of the TV when they brought her back to her apartment – her body was still young enough to enforce its need on her worried, confused mind – and she'd slept for nearly six hours. As a result of that and a hamburger and fries for lunch, she felt much better, more in control of herself.

She looked carefully at the room for a long time.

The tray of woodchips was on a metal table. The walls were gray industrial sheet steel, unadorned.

Hockstetter said, 'The technician there is wearing an asbestos uniform and asbestos slippers.' He spoke down to her, still smiling his paternal smile. The EEG operator looked hot and uncomfortable. He was wearing a white cloth mask to avoid aspirating any asbestos fiber. Hockstetter pointed to a long, square pane of mirror glass set into the far wall. 'That's one-way glass. Our camera is behind it. And you see the tub.'

Charlie went over to it. It was an old-fashioned clawfoot tub and it looked decidedly out of place in these stark surroundings. It was full of water. She thought it would do.

358

'All right,' she said.

Hockstetter's smile widened. 'Fine.'

'Only you go in the other room there. I don't want to have to look at you while I do it.' Charlie stared at Hockstetter inscrutably. 'Something might happen.'

Hockstetter's paternal smile faltered a little.

11

'She was right, you know,' Rainbird said. 'If you'd listened to her, you could have got it right the first time.'

Hockstetter looked at him and grunted.

'But you still don't believe it, do you?'

Hockstetter, Rainbird, and Cap were standing in front of the one-way glass. Behind them the camera peered into the room and the Sony VCR hummed almost inaudibly. The glass was lightly polarized, making everything in the testing room look faintly blue, like scenery seen through the window of a Greyhound bus. The technician was hooking Charlie up to the EEG. A TV monitor in the observation room reproduced her brainwaves.

'Look at those alphas,' one of the technicians murmured. 'She's really jacked up.'

'Scared,' Rainbird said. 'She's really scared.'

'You believe it, don't you?' Cap asked suddenly. 'You didn't at first, but now you do.'

'Yes,' Rainbird said. 'I believe it.'

In the other room, the technician stepped away from Charlie. 'Ready in here.'

Hockstetter flipped a toggle switch. 'Go ahead, Charlie. When you're ready.'

Charlie glanced toward the one-way glass, and for an eerie moment she seemed to be looking right into Rainbird's one eye.

He looked back, smiling faintly.

359

12

Charlie McGee looked at the one-way glass and saw nothing save her own reflection . . . but the sense of eyes watching her was very strong. She wished John could be back there; that would have made her feel more at ease. But she had no feeling that he was.

She looked back at the tray of woodchips.

It wasn't a push; it was a *shove*. She thought about doing it and was again disgusted and frightened to find herself *wanting* to do it. She thought about doing it the way a hot and hungry person might sit in front of a chocolate ice-cream soda and think about gobbling and slurping it down. That was okay, but first you wanted just a moment to . . . to savor it.

That wanting made her feel ashamed of herself, and then she shook her head almost angrily. *Why shouldn't I want to do it? If people are good at things, they always want to do them. Like Mommy with her double-crostics and Mr Douray down the street in Port City, always making bread. When they had enough at his house, he'd make some for other people. If you're good at something, you want to do it . . .*

Woodchips, she thought a little contemptuously. *They should have given me something* hard.

13

The technician felt it first. He was hot and uncomfortable and sweaty in the asbestos clothing, and at first he thought that was all it was. Then he saw that the kid's alpha waves had taken on the high spike rhythm that is the hallmark of extreme concentration, and also the brain's signature of imagination.

The sense of heat grew – and suddenly he was scared.

14

'Something happening in there,' one of the technicians in the observation room said in a high, excited voice. 'Temperature just jumped ten degrees. Her alpha pattern looks like the fucking Andes—'

'There it goes!' Cap exclaimed. '*There it goes!*' His voice vibrated with the shrill triumph of a man who has waited years for the one moment now at hand.

She *shoved* as hard as she could at the tray of woodchips. They did not so much burst into flames as explode. A moment later the tray itself flipped over twice, spraying chunks of burning wood, and clanged off the wall hard enough to leave a dimple in the sheet steel.

The technician who had been monitoring at the EEG cried out in fear and made a sudden, crazy dash for the door. The sound of his cry hurled Charlie suddenly back in time to the Albany airport. It was the cry of Eddie Delgardo, running for the ladies' bathroom with his army-issue shoes in flames.

She thought in sudden terror and exaltation, *Oh God it's gotten so much* stronger!

The steel wall had developed a strange, dark ripple. The room had become explosively hot. In the other room, the digital thermometer, which had gone from seventy degrees to eighty and then paused, now climbed rapidly past ninety to ninety-four before slowing down.

Charlie threw the firething at the tub; she was nearly panicked now. The water swirled, then broke into a fury of bubbles. In a space of five seconds, the contents of the tub went from cool to a rolling, steaming boil.

The technician had exited, leaving the testing-room door

heedlessly ajar. In the observation room there was a sudden, startled turmoil. Hockstetter was bellowing. Cap was standing gape-jawed at the window, watching the tubful of water boil. Clouds of steam rose from it and the one-way glass began to fog over. Only Rainbird was calm, smiling slightly, hands clasped behind his back. He looked like a teacher whose star pupil has used difficult postulates to solve a particularly aggravating problem.

(*back off!*)

Screaming in her mind.

(*back off! back off! BACK OFF!*)

And suddenly it was gone. Something disengaged, spun free for a second or two, and then simply stopped. Her concentration broke up and let the fire go. She could see the room again and feel the heat she had created bringing sweat to her skin. In the observation room, the thermometer crested at ninety-six and then dropped a degree. The wildly bubbling caldron began to simmer down – but at least half of its contents had boiled away. In spite of the open door, the little room was as hot and moist as a steam room.

16

Hockstetter was checking his instruments feverishly. His hair, usually combed back so neatly and tightly that it almost seemed to scream, had now come awry, sticking up in the back. He looked a bit like Alfalfa of *The Little Rascals*.

'Got it!' he panted. 'Got it, we got it all . . . it's on tape . . . the temperature gradient . . . did you see the water in that tub boil? . . . Jesus! . . . did we get the audio? . . . we did? . . . my *God*, did you see what she did?'

He passed one of his technicians, whirled back, and

grabbed him roughly by the front of his smock. 'Would you say there was any doubt that she *made* that happen?' he shouted.

The technician, nearly as excited as Hockstetter, shook his head. 'No doubt at all, Chief. None.'

'Holy God,' Hockstetter said, whirling away, distracted again. 'I would have thought . . . something . . . yes, something . . . but that tray . . . *flew* . . .'

He caught sight of Rainbird, who was still standing at the one-way glass with his hands crossed behind his back, that mild, bemused smile on his face. For Hockstetter, old animosities were forgotten. He rushed over to the big Indian, grabbed his hand, pumped it.

'We got it,' he told Rainbird with savage satisfaction. 'We got it all, it would be good enough to stand up in court! *Right up in the fucking Supreme Court!*'

'Yes, you got it,' Rainbird agreed mildly. 'Now you better send somebody along to get *her*.'

'Huh?' Hockstetter looked at him blankly.

'Well,' Rainbird said, still in his mildest tone, 'the guy that was in there maybe had an appointment he forgot about, because he left in one hell of an ass-busting rush. He left the door open, and your firestarter just walked out.'

Hockstetter gaped at the glass. The steaming effect had got worse, but there was no doubt that the room was empty except for the tub, the EEG, the overturned steel tray, and the flaming scatter of woodchips.

'One of you men go get her!' Hockstetter cried, turning around. The five or six men stood by their instruments and didn't move. Apparently no one but Rainbird had noticed that Cap had left as soon as the girl had.

Rainbird grinned at Hockstetter and then raised his eye to include the others, these men whose faces had suddenly gone almost as pale as their lab smocks.

363

'Sure,' he said softly. 'Which of you wants to go get the little girl?'

No one moved. It was amusing, really; it occurred to Rainbird that this was the way the politicians were going to look when they found out it was finally done, that the missiles were really in the air, the bombs raining down, the woods and cities on fire. It was so amusing he had to laugh . . . and laugh . . . and laugh.

17

'They're so beautiful,' Charlie said softly. 'It's all so beautiful.'

They were standing near the duckpond, not far from where her father and Pynchot had stood only a few days previously. This day was much cooler than that one had been, and a few leaves had begun to show color. A light wind, just a little too stiff to be called a breeze, ruffled the surface of the pond.

Charlie turned her face up to the sun and closed her eyes, smiling. John Rainbird, standing beside her, had spent six months on stockade duty at Camp Stewart in Arizona before going overseas, and he had seen the same expression on the faces of men coming out after a long hard bang inside.

'Would you like to walk over to the stables and look at the horses?'

'Oh yes, sure,' she said immediately, and then glanced shyly at him. 'That is, if you don't mind.'

'Mind? I'm glad to be outside, too. This is recess for me.'

'Did they assign you?'

'Naw,' he said. They began to walk along the edge of the pond toward the stables on the far side. 'They asked for volunteers. I don't think they got many, after what happened yesterday.'

'It scared them?' Charlie asked, just a little too sweetly.

'I guess it did,' Rainbird said, and he was speaking nothing but the truth. Cap had caught up with Charlie as she wandered down the hall and escorted her back to her apartment. The young man who had bolted his position at the EEG was now being processed for duty in Panama City. The staff meeting following the test had been a nutty affair, with the scientists at both their best and worst, blue-skying a hundred new ideas on one hand and worrying tiresomely – and considerably after the fact – about how to control her on the other hand.

It was suggested that her quarters be fireproofed, that a full-time guard be installed, that the drug series be started on her again. Rainbird had listened to as much of this as he could bear and then rapped hard on the edge of the conference table with the band of the heavy turquoise ring he wore. He rapped until he had the attention of everyone there. Because Hockstetter disliked him (and perhaps 'hated' would not have been too strong a word), his cadre of scientists also disliked him, but Rainbird's star had risen in spite of that. He had, after all, been spending a good part of each day with this human blowtorch.

'I suggest,' he had said, rising to his feet and glaring around at them benignly from the shattered lens of his face, 'that we continue exactly as we have been. Up until today you have been proceeding on the premise that the girl probably didn't have the ability which you all knew had been documented two dozen times over, and that if she did have it, it was a small ability, and if it wasn't a small ability, she would probably never use it again anyway. Now you know differently, and you'd like to upset her all over again.'

365

'That's not true,' Hockstetter said, annoyed. 'That is simply—'

'*It is true!*' Rainbird thundered at him, and Hockstetter shrank back in his chair. Rainbird smiled again at the faces around the table. 'Now. The girl is eating again. She has put on ten pounds and is no longer a scrawny shadow of what she should be. She is reading, talking, doing paint-by-the-numbers kits; she has asked for a dollhouse, which her friend the orderly has promised to try and get for her. In short, her frame of mind is better than it has been since she came here. Gentlemen, we are not going to start monkeying around with a fruitful status quo, are we?'

The man who had been monitoring the videotape equipment earlier had said hesitantly, 'But what if she sets that little suite of hers on fire?'

'If she was going to,' Rainbird said quietly, 'she would have done it already.' To that there had been no response.

Now, as he and Charlie left the edge of the pond and crossed toward the dark-red stables with their fresh piping of white paint, Rainbird laughed out loud. 'I guess you did scare them, Charlie.'

'But you're not scared?'

'Why should I be scared?' Rainbird said, and ruffled her hair. 'I only turn into a baby when it's dark and I can't get out.'

'Oh John, you don't have to be ashamed of that.'

'If you were going to light me up,' he said, rephrasing his comment of the night before, 'I guess you would've by now.'

She stiffened immediately. 'I wish you wouldn't . . . wouldn't even say things like that.'

'Charlie, I'm sorry. Sometimes my mouth gets ahead of my brains.'

They went into the stables, which were dim and fragrant.

366

Dusky sunlight slanted in, making mellow bars and stripes in which motes of haychaff danced with dreamy slowness.

A groom was currying the mane of a black gelding with a white blaze on its forehead. Charlie stopped, looking at the horse with delighted wonder. The groom looked around at her and grinned. 'You must be the young miss. They told me to be on the watch-out for you.'

'She's so *beautiful*,' Charlie whispered. Her hands trembled to touch that silky coat. One look in the horse's dark, calm, mellow eyes and she was in love.

'Well, it's a boy, actually,' the groom said, and tipped a wink at Rainbird, whom he had never seen before and didn't know from Adam. 'After a fashion, that is.'

'What's his name?'

'Necromancer,' the groom said. 'Want to pet him?'

Charlie drew hesitantly near. The horse lowered his head and she stroked him; after a few moments she spoke to him. It did not occur to her that she would light another half-dozen fires just to ride on him with John beside her . . . but Rainbird saw it in her eyes, and he smiled.

She looked around at him suddenly and saw the smile, and for a moment the hand she had been stroking the horse's muzzle with paused. There was something in that smile she didn't like, and she had thought she liked everything about John. She got feelings about most people and did not consider this much; it was part of her, like her blue eyes and her double-jointed thumb. She usually dealt with people on the basis of these feelings. She didn't like Hockstetter, because she felt that he didn't care for her anymore than he would care for a test tube. She was just an object to him.

But with John, her liking was based only on what he did, his kindness to her, and perhaps part of it was his disfigured face: she could identify and sympathize with him on that account. After all, why was she here if not because she was also a freak? Yet beyond that, he was one of those rare people – like Mr Raucher, the delicatessen owner in New York who often played chess with her daddy – who were for some reason completely closed to her. Mr Raucher was old and wore a hearing aid and had a faded blue number tattooed on his forearm. Once Charlie had asked her father if that blue number meant anything, and her daddy had told her – after cautioning her never to mention it to Mr Raucher – that he would explain it later. But he never had. Sometimes Mr Raucher would bring her slices of kielbasa which she would eat while watching TV.

And now, looking at John's smile, which seemed so strange and somehow disquieting, she wondered for the first time, *What are you thinking?*

Then such trifling thoughts were swept away by the wonder of the horse.

'John,' she said, 'what does "Necromancer" mean?'

'Well,' he said, 'so far as I know, it means something like "wizard," or "sorcerer." '

'Wizard. Sorcerer.' She spoke the words softly, tasting them as she stroked the dark silk of Necromancer's muzzle.

18

Walking back with her, Rainbird said: 'You ought to ask that Hockstetter to let you ride that horse, if you like him so much.'

'No . . . I couldn't . . .' she said, looking at him wide-eyed and startled.

'Oh, sure you could,' he said, purposely misunderstanding. 'I don't know much about geldings, but I know they're supposed to be gentle. He looks awful big, but I don't think he'd run away with you, Charlie.'

'No – I don't mean that. They just wouldn't let me.'

He stopped her by putting his hands on her shoulders.

368

'Charlie McGee, sometimes you're really dumb,' he said. 'You done me a good turn that time the lights went out, Charlie, and you kept it to yourself. So now you listen to me and I'll do you one. You want to see your father again?'

She nodded quickly.

'Then you want to show them that you mean business. It's like poker, Charlie. If you ain't dealin from strength . . . why, you just ain't dealin. Every time you light a fire for them, for one of their tests, you get something from them.' He gave her shoulders a soft shake. 'This is your uncle John talking to you. Do you hear what I'm sayin?'

'Do you really think they'd let me? If I asked?'

'If you *asked*? Maybe not. But if you *told* them, yeah. I hear them sometimes. You go in to empty their wastebaskets and ashtrays, they think you're just another piece of the furniture. That Hockstetter's just about wettin his pants.'

'Really?' She smiled a little.

'Really.' They began to walk again. 'What about you, Charlie? I know how scared of it you were before. How do you feel about it now?'

She was a long time answering. And when she did, it was in a more thoughtful and somehow adult tone than Rainbird had ever heard from her. 'It's different now,' she said. 'It's a lot stronger. But . . . I was more in control of it than I ever was before. That day at the farm' – she shivered a little and her voice dropped a little – 'it just . . . just got away for a little while. It . . . it went everywhere.' Her eyes darkened. She looked inside memory and saw chickens exploding like horrible living fireworks. 'But yesterday, when I told it to back off, it did. I said to myself, it's just going to be a small fire. And it was. It was like I let it out in a single straight line.'

'And then you pulled it back into yourself?'

369

'God, no,' she said, looking at him. 'I put it into the water. If I pulled it back into myself . . . I guess *I'd* burn up.'

They walked in silence for a while.

'Next time there has to be more water.'

'But you're not scared now?'

'Not as scared as I was,' she said, making the careful distinction. 'When do you think they'll let me see my dad?'

He put an arm around her shoulders in rough good comradeship.

'Give them enough rope, Charlie,' he said.

19

It began to cloud up that afternoon and by evening a cold autumn rain had begun to fall. In one house of a small and very exclusive suburb near the Shop complex – a suburb called Longmont Hills – Patrick Hockstetter was in his workshop, building a model boat (the boats and his restored T-bird were his only hobbies, and there were dozens of his whalers and frigates and packets about the house) and thinking about Charlie McGee. He was in an extremely good mood. He felt that if they could get another dozen tests out of her – even another ten – his future would be assured. He could spend the rest of his life investigating the properties of Lot Six . . . and at a substantial raise in pay. He carefully glued a mizzenmast in place and began to whistle.

In another house in Longmont Hills, Herman Pynchot was pulling a pair of his wife's panties over a gigantic erection. His eyes were dark and trancelike. His wife was at a Tupperware party. One of his two fine children was at a Cub Scout meeting and the other fine child was at an intramural chess tourney at the junior high school. Pynchot carefully hooked one of his wife's bras behind his back. It hung limply on his narrow chest. He looked at himself in the mirror and thought he looked . . . well, very pretty. He walked out into the kitchen, heedless of the unshaded windows. He walked like a man in a dream. He stood by the sink and looked down into the maw of the newly installed Waste-King disposer. After a long, thoughtful time, he turned it on. And to the sound of its whirling, gnashing steel teeth, he took himself in hand and masturbated. When his orgasm had come and gone, he started and looked around. His eyes were full of blank terror, the eyes of a man waking from a nightmare. He shut off the garbage disposal and ran for the bedroom, crouching low as he passed the windows. His head ached and buzzed. What in the name of God was happening to him?

In yet a third Longmont Hills house – a house with a hillside view that the likes of Hockstetter and Pynchot could not hope to afford – Cap Hollister and John Rainbird sat drinking brandy from snifters in the living room. Vivaldi issued from Cap's stereo system. Vivaldi had been one of his wife's favorites. Poor Georgia.

'I agree with you,' Cap said slowly, wondering again why he had invited this man whom he hated and feared into his home. The girl's power was extraordinary, and he supposed extraordinary power made for strange bedfellows. 'The fact that she mentioned a "next time" in such an offhand way is extremely significant.'

'Yes,' Rainbird said. 'It appears we do indeed have a string to play out.'

'But it won't last forever.' Cap swirled his brandy, then forced himself to meet Rainbird's one glittering eye. 'I believe I understand how you intend to lengthen that string, even if Hockstetter does not.'

'Do you?'

'Yes,' Cap said, paused a moment, then added. 'It's dangerous to you.'

Rainbird smiled.

'If she finds out what side you're really on,' Cap said, 'you stand a good chance of finding out what a steak feels like in a microwave oven.'

Rainbird's smile lengthened into an unfunny shark's grin. 'And would you shed a bitter tear, Captain Hollister?'

'No,' Cap said. 'No sense lying to you about that. But for some time now – since before she actually went and did it – I've felt the ghost of Dr Wanless drifting around in here. Sometimes as close as my own shoulder.' He looked at Rainbird over the rim of his glass. 'Do you believe in ghosts, Rainbird?'

'Yes. I do.'

'Then you know what I mean. During the last meeting I had with him, he tried to warn me. He made a metaphor – let me see – John Milton at seven, struggling to write his name in letters that were legible, and that same human being growing up to write *Paradise Lost*. He talked about her . . . her potential for destruction.'

'Yes,' Rainbird said, and his eye gleamed.

'He asked me what we'd do if we found we had a little girl who could progress from starting fires to causing nuclear explosions to cracking the very planet open. I thought he was funny, irritating, and almost certainly mad.'

'But now you think he may have been right.'

'Let us say that I find myself wondering sometimes at three in the morning. Don't you?'

'Cap, when the Manhattan Project group exploded their first atomic device, no one was quite sure what would happen. There was a school of thought which felt that the chain reaction would never end – that we would have a miniature sun glowing in the desert out there even unto the end of the world.'

Cap nodded slowly.

372

'The Nazis were also horrible,' Rainbird said. 'The Japs were horrible. Now the Germans and the Japanese are nice and the Russians are horrible. The Muslims are horrible. Who knows who may become horrible in the future?'

'She's dangerous,' Cap said, rising restlessly. 'Wanless was right about that. She's a dead end.'

'Maybe.'

'Hockstetter says that the place where that tray hit the wall was rippled. It was sheet steel, but it rippled with the heat. The tray itself was twisted entirely out of shape. She smelted it. That little girl might have put out three thousand degrees of heat for a split second there.' He looked at Rainbird, but Rainbird was looking vaguely around the living room, as if he had lost interest. 'What I'm saying is that what you plan to do is dangerous for all of us, not just for you.'

'Oh yes,' Rainbird agreed complacently. 'There's a risk. Maybe we won't have to do it. Maybe Hockstetter will have what he needs before it becomes necessary to implement . . . uh, plan B.'

'Hockstetter's a type,' Cap said curtly. 'He's an information junkie. He'll never have enough. He could test her for two years and still scream we were too hasty when we . . . when we took her away. You know it and I know it, so let's not play games.'

'We'll know when it's time,' Rainbird said. '*I'll* know.'

'And then what will happen?'

'John the friendly orderly will come in,' Rainbird said, smiling a little. 'He will greet her, and talk to her, and make her smile. John the friendly orderly will make her feel happy because he's the only one who can. And when John feels she is at the moment of greatest happiness, he will strike her across the bridge of the nose, breaking it explosively and driving bone fragments into her brain. It

373

will be quick . . . and I will be looking into her face when it happens.'

He smiled – nothing sharklike about it this time. The smile was gentle, kind . . . and *fatherly*. Cap drained his brandy. He needed it. He only hoped that Rainbird would indeed know the right time when it came, or they might all find out what a steak felt like in a microwave oven.

'You're crazy,' Cap said. The words escaped before he could hold them back, but Rainbird did not seem offended.

'Oh yes,' he agreed, and drained his own brandy. He went on smiling.

20

Big Brother. Big Brother was the problem.

Andy moved from the living room of his apartment to the kitchen, forcing himself to walk slowly, to hold a slight smile on his face – the walk and expression of a man who is pleasantly stoned out of his gourd.

So far he had succeeded only in keeping himself here, near Charlie, and finding out that the nearest road was Highway 301 and that the countryside was fairly rural. All of that had been a week ago. It had been a month since the blackout, and he still knew nothing more about the layout of this installation than he had been able to observe when he and Pynchot went for their walks.

He didn't want to push anyone down here in his quarters, because Big Brother was always watching and listening. And he didn't want to push Pynchot anymore, because Pynchot was cracking up – Andy was sure of it. Since their little walk by the duckpond, Pynchot had lost weight. There were dark circles under his eyes, as if he were sleeping poorly. He sometimes would begin speaking and then trail off, as if he had lost his train of thought . . . or as if it had been interrupted.

374

All of which made Andy's own position that much more precarious.

How long before Pynchot's colleagues noticed what was happening to him? They might think it nothing but nervous strain, but suppose they connected it with him? That would be the end of whatever slim chance Andy had of getting out of here with Charlie. And his feeling that Charlie was in big trouble had got stronger and stronger.

What in the name of Jesus Christ was he going to do about Big Brother?

He got a Welch's Grape from the fridge, went back to the living room, and sat down in front of the TV without seeing it, his mind working restlessly, looking for some way out. But when that way out came, it was (like the power blackout) a complete surprise. In a way, it was Herman Pynchot who opened the door for him: he did it by killing himself.

21

Two men came and got him. He recognized one of them from Manders's farm.

'Come on, big boy,' this one said. 'Little walk.'

Andy smiled foolishly, but inside, the terror had begun. Something had happened. Something bad had happened; they didn't send guys like this if it was something good. Perhaps he had been found out. In fact, that was the most likely thing. 'Where to?'

'Just come on.'

He was taken to the elevator, but when they got off in the ballroom, they went farther into the house instead of outside. They passed the secretarial pool, entered a smaller room where a secretary ran off correspondence on an IBM typewriter.

'Go right in,' she said.

They passed her on the right and went through a door into a small study with a bay window that gave a view of the duckpond through a screen of low alders. Behind an old-fashioned roll-top desk sat an elderly man with a sharp, intelligent face; his cheeks were ruddy, but from sun and wind rather than liquor, Andy thought.

He looked up at Andy, then nodded at the two men who had brought him in. 'Thank you. You can wait outside.'

They left.

The man behind the desk looked keenly at Andy, who looked back blandly, still smiling a bit. He hoped to God he wasn't overdoing it. 'Hello, who are you?' he asked.

'My name is Captain Hollister, Andy. You can call me Cap. They tell me I am in charge of this here rodeo.'

'Pleased to meet you,' Andy said. He let his smile widen a little. Inside, the tension screwed itself up another notch.

'I've some sad news for you, Andy.'

(*oh God no it's Charlie something's happened to Charlie*)

Cap was watching him steadily with those small, shrewd eyes, eyes caught so deeply in their pleasant nets of small wrinkles that you almost didn't notice how cold and studious they were.

'Oh?'

'Yes,' Cap said, and fell silent for a moment. And the silence spun out agonizingly.

Cap had fallen into a study of his hands, which were neatly folded on the blotter in front of him. It was all Andy could do to keep from leaping across the desk and throttling him. Then Cap looked up.

'Dr Pynchot is dead, Andy. He killed himself last night.'

Andy's jaw dropped in unfeigned surprise. Alternating waves of relief and horror raced through him. And over it all, like a boiling sky over a confused sea, was the realization that this changed everything . . . but how? *How?*

Cap was watching him. *He suspects. He suspects something. But are his suspicions serious or only a part of his job?*

A hundred questions. He needed time to think and he had no time. He would have to do his thinking on his feet.

'That surprises you?' Cap asked.

'He was my friend,' Andy said simply, and had to close his mouth to keep from saying more. This man would listen to him patiently; he would pause long after Andy's every remark (as he was pausing now) to see if Andy would plunge on, the mouth outracing the mind. Standard interrogation technique. And there were man-pits in these woods; Andy felt it strongly. It had been an echo, of course. An echo that had turned into a ricochet. He had pushed Pynchot and started a ricochet and it had torn the man apart. And for all of that, Andy could not find it in his heart to be sorry. There was horror . . . and there was a caveman who capered and rejoiced.

'Are you sure it was . . . I mean, sometimes an accident can look like—'

'I'm afraid it was no accident.'

'He left a note?'

(*naming me?*)

'He dressed up in his wife's underwear, went out into the kitchen, started up the garbage disposal, and stuck his arm into it.'

'Oh . . . my . . . *God.*' Andy sat down heavily. If there hadn't been a chair handy he would have sat on the floor. All the strength had left his legs. He stared at Cap Hollister with sick horror.

'You didn't have anything to do with that, did you, Andy?' Cap asked. 'You didn't maybe push him into it?'

'No,' Andy said. 'Even if I could still do it, why would I do a thing like that?'

'Maybe because he wanted to send you to the Hawaiians,' Cap said. 'Maybe you didn't want to go to Maui, because your daughter's here. Maybe you've been fooling us all along, Andy.'

And although this Cap Hollister was crawling around on top of the truth, Andy felt a small loosening in his chest. If Cap really thought he had pushed Pynchot into doing that, this interview wouldn't be going on between just the two of them. No, it was just doing things by the book; that was all. They probably had all they needed to justify suicide in Pynchot's own file without looking for arcane methods of murder. Didn't they say that psychiatrists had the highest suicide rate of any profession?

'No, that's not true at all,' Andy said. He sounded afraid, confused, close to blubbering. 'I *wanted* to go to Hawaii. I told him that. I think that's why he wanted to make more tests, because I wanted to go. I don't think he liked me in some ways. But I sure didn't have anything to do with . . . with what happened to him.'

Cap looked at him thoughtfully. Their eyes met for a moment and then Andy dropped his gaze.

'Well, I believe you, Andy,' Cap said. 'Herm Pynchot had been under a lot of pressure lately. It's a part of this life we live, I suppose. Regrettable. Add this secret transvestism on top of that, and, well, it's going to be hard on his wife. Very hard. But we take care of our own, Andy.' Andy could feel the man's eyes boring into him. 'Yes, we always take care of our own. That's the most important thing.'

'Sure,' Andy said dully.

There was a lengthening moment of silence. After a little bit Andy looked up, expecting to see Cap looking at him. But Cap was staring out at the back lawn and the alders and his face looked saggy and confused and old, the face of a man who has been seduced into thinking of other, perhaps happier, times. He saw Andy looking at him and a small wrinkle of disgust passed over his face and was

378

gone. Sudden sour hate flared inside Andy. Why shouldn't this Hollister look disgusted? He saw a fat drug addict sitting in front of him – or that was what he thought he saw. But who gave the orders? *And what are you doing to my daughter, you old monster?*

'Well,' Cap said. 'I'm happy to tell you you'll be going to Maui anyway, Andy – it's an ill wind that doesn't blow somebody good, or something like that, hmmm? I've started the paperwork already.'

'But . . . listen, you don't really think I had anything to do with what happened to Dr Pynchot, do you?'

'No, of course not.' That small and involuntary ripple of disgust again. And this time Andy felt the sick satisfaction that he imagined a black guy who has successfully tommed an unpleasant white must feel. But over this was the alarm brought on by that phrase *I've started the paperwork already*.

'Well, that's good. Poor Dr Pynchot.' He looked downcast for only a token instant and then said eagerly, 'When am I going?'

'As soon as possible. By the end of next week at the latest.'

Nine days at the outside! It was like a battering ram in his stomach.

'I've enjoyed our talk, Andy. I'm sorry we had to meet under such sad and unpleasant circumstances.'

He was reaching for the intercom switch, and Andy suddenly realized he couldn't let him do that. There was nothing he could do in his apartment with its cameras and listening devices. But if this guy really was the big cheese, this office would be as dead as a doornail: he would have the place washed regularly for bugs. Of course, he might have his own listening devices, but—

'Put your hand down,' Andy said, and pushed.

Cap hesitated. His hand drew back and joined its mate

379

on the blotter. He glanced out at the back lawn with that drifting, remembering expression on his face.

'Do you tape meetings in here?'

'No,' Cap said evenly. 'For a long time I had a voice-activated Uher-Five thousand – like the one that got Nixon in trouble – but I had it taken out fourteen weeks ago.'

'Why?'

'Because it looked like I was going to lose my job.'

'Why did you think you were going to lose your job?'

Very rapidly, in a kind of litany, Cap said: 'No production. No production. No production. Funds must be justified with results. Replace the man at the top. No tapes. No scandal.'

Andy tried to think it through. Was this taking him in a direction he wanted to go? He couldn't tell, and time was short. He felt like the stupidest, slowest kid at the Easter-egg hunt. He decided he would go a bit further down this trail.

'Why weren't you producing?'

'No mental-domination ability left in McGee. Permanently tipped over. Everyone in agreement on that. The girl wouldn't light fires. Said she wouldn't no matter what. People saying I was fixated on Lot Six. Shot my bolt.' He grinned. 'Now it's okay. Even Rainbird says so.'

Andy renewed the push, and a small pulse of pain began to beat in his forehead. 'Why is it okay?'

'Three tests so far. Hockstetter's ecstatic. Yesterday she flamed a piece of sheet steel. Spot temp over twenty thousand degrees for four seconds, Hockstetter says.'

Shock made the headache worse, made it harder to get a handle on his whirling thoughts. Charlie was lighting fires? What had they done to her? What, in the name of God?

He opened his mouth to ask and the intercom buzzed, jolting him into pushing much harder than he had to. For a moment, he gave Cap almost everything there was. Cap shuddered all over as if he had been whipped with an electric cattle prod. He made a low gagging sound and his ruddy face lost most of its color. Andy's headache took a quantum leap and he cautioned himself uselessly to take it easy; having a stroke in this man's office wouldn't help Charlie.

'Don't do that,' Cap whined. 'Hurts—'

'Tell them no calls for the next ten minutes,' Andy said. Somewhere the black horse was kicking at its stable door, wanting to get out, wanting to run free. He could feel oily sweat running down his cheeks.

The intercom buzzed again. Cap leaned forward and pushed the toggle switch down. His face had aged fifteen years.

'Cap, Senator Thompson's aide is here with those figures you asked for on Project Leap.'

'No calls for the next ten minutes,' Cap said, and clicked off.

Andy sat drenched in sweat. Would that hold them? Or would they smell a rat? It didn't matter. As Willy Loman had been so wont to cry, the woods were burning. Christ, what was he thinking of Willy Loman for? He was going crazy. The black horse would be out soon and he could ride there. He almost giggled.

'Charlie's been lighting fires?'

'Yes.'

'How did you get her to do that?'

'Carrot and stick. Rainbird's idea. She got to take walks outside for the first two. Now she gets to ride the horse. Rainbird thinks that will hold her for the next couple of weeks.' And he repeated, 'Hockstetter's ecstatic.'

'Who is this Rainbird?' Andy asked, totally unaware that he had just asked the jackpot question.

Cap talked in short bursts for the next five minutes. He

told Andy that Rainbird was a Shop hitter who had been horribly wounded in Vietnam, had lost an eye there (the one-eyed pirate in my dream, Andy thought numbly). He told Andy that it was Rainbird who had been in charge of the Shop operation that had finally netted Andy and Charlie at Tashmore Pond. He told him about the blackout and Rainbird's inspired first step on the road to getting Charlie to start lighting fires under test conditions. Finally, he told Andy that Rainbird's personal interest in all of this was Charlie's life when the string of deception had finally run itself out. He spoke of these matters in a voice that was emotionless yet somehow urgent. Then he fell silent.

Andy listened in growing fury and horror. He was trembling all over when Cap's recitation had concluded. Charlie, he thought. Oh, Charlie, Charlie.

His ten minutes were almost up, and there was still so much he needed to know. The two of them sat silent for perhaps forty seconds; an observer might have decided they were companionable older friends who no longer needed to speak to communicate. Andy's mind raced.

'Captain Hollister,' he said.

'Yes?'

'When is Pynchot's funeral?'

'The day after tomorrow,' Cap said calmly.

'We're going. You and I. You understand?'

'Yes, I understand. We're going to Pynchot's funeral.'

'I asked to go. I broke down and cried when I heard he was dead.'

'Yes, you broke down and cried.'

'I was very upset.'

'Yes, you were.'

'We're going to go in your private car, just the two of us. There can be Shop people in cars ahead and behind us, motorcycles on either side if that's standard operating procedure, *but we're going alone*. Do you understand?'

382

'Oh, yes. That's perfectly clear. Just the two of us.'

'And we're going to have a good talk. Do you also understand that?'

'Yes, a good talk.'

'Is your car bugged?'

'Not at all.'

Andy began to push again, a series of light taps. Each time he pushed, Cap flinched a little, and Andy knew there was an excellent chance that he might be starting an echo in there, but it had to be done.

'We're going to talk about where Charlie is being kept. We're going to talk about ways of throwing this whole place into confusion without locking all the doors the way the power blackout did. And we're going to talk about ways that Charlie and I can get out of here. Do you understand?'

'You're not supposed to escape,' Cap said in a hateful, childish voice. 'That's not in the scenario.'

'*It is now*,' Andy said, and pushed again.

'*Owwwww!*' Cap whined.

'Do you understand that?'

'Yes, I understand, don't, don't do that anymore, it hurts!'

'This Hockstetter – will he question my going to the funeral?'

'No, Hockstetter is all wrapped up in the little girl. He thinks of little else these days.'

'Good.' It wasn't good at all. It was desperation. 'Last thing, Captain Hollister. You're going to forget that we had this little talk.'

'Yes, I'm going to forget all about it.'

The black horse was loose. It was starting its run. *Take me out of here*, Andy thought dimly. *Take me out of here; the horse is loose and the woods are burning.* The headache came in a sickish cycle of thudding pain.

'Everything I've told you will occur naturally to you as your own idea.'

'Yes.'

Andy looked at Cap's desk and saw a box of Kleenex there. He took one of them and began dabbing at his eyes with it. He was not crying, but the headache had caused his eyes to water and that was just as good.

'I'm ready to go now,' he said to Cap.

He let go. Cap looked out at the alders again, thoughtfully blank. Little by little, animation came back into his face, and he turned toward Andy, who was wiping at his eyes a bit and sniffing. There was no need to overact.

'How are you feeling now, Andy?'

'A little better,' Andy said. 'But . . . you know . . . to hear it like that . . .'

'Yes, you were very upset,' Cap said. 'Would you like to have a coffee or something?'

'No, thanks. I'd like to go back to my apartment, please.'

'Of course. I'll see you out.'

'Thank you.'

22

The two men who had seen him up to the office looked at Andy with doubtful suspicion – the Kleenex, the red and watering eyes, the paternal arm that Cap had put around his shoulders. Much the same expression came into the eyes of Cap's secretary.

'He broke down and cried when he heard Pynchot was dead,' Cap said quietly. 'He was very upset. I believe I'll see if I can arrange for him to attend Herman's funeral with me. Would you like to do that, Andy?'

'Yes,' Andy said. 'Yes, please. If it can be arranged. Poor Dr Pynchot.' And suddenly he burst into real tears. The two men led him past Senator Thompson's bewildered,

384

embarrassed aide, who had several blue-bound folders in his hands. They took Andy out, still weeping, each with a hand clasped lightly at his elbow. Each of them wore an expression of disgust that was very similar to Cap's – disgust for this fat drug addict who had totally lost control of his emotions and any sense of perspective and gushed tears for the man who had been his captor.

Andy's tears were real . . . but it was Charlie he wept for.

23

John always rode with her, but in her dreams Charlie rode alone. The head groom, Peter Drabble, had fitted her out with a small, neat English saddle, but in her dreams she rode bareback. She and John rode on the bridle paths that wove their way across the Shop grounds, moving in and out of the toy forest of sugarpines and skirting the duckpond, never doing more than an easy canter, but in her dreams she and Necromancer galloped together, faster and faster, through a real forest; they plunged at speed down a wild trail and the light was green through the interlaced branches overhead, and her hair streamed out behind her.

She could feel the ripple of Necromancer's muscles under his silky hide, and she rode with her hands twisted in his mane and whispered in his ear that she wanted to go faster . . . faster . . . faster.

Necromancer responded. His hooves were thunder. The path through these tangled, green woods was a tunnel, and from somewhere behind her there came a faint crackling and

(*the woods are burning*)

a whiff of smoke. It was a fire, a fire she had started, but there was no guilt – only exhilaration. They could outrace it. Necromancer could go anywhere, do anything. They would escape the forest-tunnel. She could sense brightness ahead.

'Faster. Faster.'

The exhilaration. The freedom. She could no longer tell where her thighs ended and Necromancer's sides began. They were one, fused, as fused as the metals she welded with her power when she did their tests. Ahead of them was a huge deadfall, a blowdown of white wood like a tangled cairn of bones. Wild with lunatic joy, she kicked at Necromancer lightly with her bare heels and felt his hindquarters bunch.

They leaped it, for a moment floating in the air. Her head was back; her hands held horsehair and she screamed – not in fear but simply because not to scream, to hold in, might cause her to explode. *Free, free, free . . . Necromancer, I love you.*

They cleared the deadfall easily but now the smell of smoke was sharper, clearer – there was a popping sound from behind them and it was only when a spark spiraled down and briefly stung her flesh like a nettle before going out that she realized she was naked. Naked and

(*but the woods are burning*)

free, unfettered, loose – she and Necromancer, running for the light.

'Faster,' she whispered. 'Faster, oh please.'

Somehow the big black gelding produced even more speed. The wind in Charlie's ears was rushing thunder. She did not have to breathe; air was scooped into her throat through her half-open mouth. Sun shone through these old trees in dusty bars like old copper.

And up ahead was the light – the end of the forest, open land, where she and Necromancer would run forever. The fire was behind them, the hateful smell of smoke, the feel of fear. The sun was ahead, and she would ride Necromancer all the way to the sea, where she would perhaps find her father and the two of them would live by pulling in nets full of shining, slippery fish.

'Faster!' she cried triumphantly. 'Oh, Necromancer, go *faster*, go *faster*, go—'

And that was when the silhouette stepped into the widening funnel of light where the woods ended, blocking the light in its own shape, blocking the way out. At first, as always in this dream, she thought it was her father, was *sure* it was her father, and her joy became almost hurtful . . . before suddenly transforming into utter terror.

She just had time to register the fact that the man was too big, too tall – and yet somehow familiar, dreadfully familiar, even in silhouette – before Necromancer reared, screaming.

Can horses scream? I didn't know they could scream—

Struggling to stay on, her thighs slipping as his hooves pawed at the air, and he wasn't screaming, he was whinnying, but it was a *scream* and there were other screaming whinnies somewhere behind her, *oh dear God*, she thought, *horses back there, horses back there and the woods are burning—*

Up ahead, blocking the light, that silhouette, that dreadful shape. Now it began to come toward her; she had fallen onto the path and Necromancer touched her bare stomach gently with his muzzle.

'Don't you hurt my horse!' she screamed at the advancing silhouette, the dream-father who was not her father. 'Don't you hurt the horses. Oh, please don't hurt the horses!'

But the figure came on and it was drawing a gun and that was when she awoke, sometimes with a scream, sometimes only in a shuddery cold sweat, knowing that she had dreamed badly but unable to remember anything save the mad, exhilarating plunge down the wooded trail and the smell of fire . . . these things, and an almost sick feeling of betrayal. . . .

And in the stable that day, she would touch Necromancer or perhaps put the side of her face against his warm shoulder and feel a dread for which she had no name.

Endgame

1

It was a bigger room.

Until last week, in fact, it had been the Shop's non-denominational chapel. The speed with which things were picking up could have been symbolized by the speed and ease with which Cap had rammed through Hockstetter's requests. A new chapel – not an odd spare room but a real chapel – was to be built at the eastern end of the grounds. Meanwhile, the remainder of the tests on Charlie McGee would be held here.

The fake wood paneling and the pews had been ripped out. Both flooring and walls had been insulated with asbestos batting that looked like steel wool and then covered over with heavy-guage tempered sheet steel. The area that had been the altar and the nave had been partitioned off. Hockstetter's monitoring instruments and a computer terminal had been installed. All of this had been done in a single week; work had begun just four days before Herman Pynchot ended his life in such grisly fashion.

Now, at two in the afternoon on an early October day, a cinderblock wall stood in the middle of the long room. To the left of it was a huge, low tank of water. Into this tank, which was six feet deep, had been dumped more than two thousand pounds of ice. In front of it stood Charlie McGee, looking small and neat in a blue denim jumper and red and black striped rugby socks. Blond pigtails tied off with small black velvet bows hung down to her shoulder blades.

'All right, Charlie,' Hockstetter's voice said over the intercom. Like everything else, the intercom had been hastily installed, and its reproduction was tinny and poor. 'We're ready when you are.'

The cameras filmed it all in living color. In these films, the small girl's head dips slightly, and for a few seconds nothing happens at all. Inset at the left of the film frame is a digital temperature readout. All at once it begins to move upward, from seventy to eighty to ninety. After that the figures jump up so rapidly that they are just a shifting reddish blur; the electronic temperature probe has been placed in the center of the cinderblock wall.

Now the film switches to slow motion; it is the only way that the entire action can be caught. To the men who watched it through the observation room's leaded-glass viewing ports, it happened with the speed of a gunshot.

In extreme slow motion, the cinderblock wall begins to smoke; small particles of mortar and concrete begin to jump lazily upward like popping corn. Then the mortar holding the blocks together can be observed to be *running*, like warm molasses. Then the bricks begin to crumble, from the center outward. Showers of particles, then clouds of them, blow back as the blocks explode with the heat. Now the digital heat sensor implanted in the center of this wall freezes at a reading of over seven thousand degrees. It freezes not because the temperature has stopped climbing but because the sensor itself has been destroyed.

Set around this testing room that used to be a chapel are eight huge Kelvinator air conditioners, all running at high speed, all pumping freezing air into the testing room. All eight kicked into operation as soon as the room's *overall* temperature passed ninety-five. Charlie had got very good at directing the stream of heat that somehow came from her at a single point, but as anyone who has ever burned his or her hand on a hot skillet handle knows, even so-called nonconductable surfaces will conduct heat – if there is enough heat to conduct.

With all eight of the industrial Kelvinators running, the temperature in the testing room should have been minus fifteen degrees Fahrenheit, plus or minus five degrees. Instead, the records show a continued climb, up over a hundred degrees, then a hundred and five, then a hundred and seven. But all of the sweat running down the faces of the observers cannot be accounted for by the heat alone.

Now not even extreme slow motion will give a clear picture of what is happening, but one thing is clear: as the cinderblocks continue to explode outward and backward, there can be no doubt that they are burning; these blocks are burning as briskly as newspapers in a fireplace. Of course, an eighth-grade science book teaches that *anything* will burn if it gets hot enough. But it is one thing to read such information and quite another to see cinderblock blazing with blue and yellow flame.

Then everything is obscured by a furious blowback of disintegrating particles as the whole wall vaporizes. The little girl makes a slow-motion half turn and a moment later the calm surface of the icy water in the tank is convulsed and boiling. And the heat in the room, which has crested at a hundred twelve, (even with all eight air conditioners, it is as hot as a summer noontime in Death Valley), begins to go back.

There's one for the sweeper.

2

INTERDEPARTMENTAL
MEMO

From   Bradford Hyuck
To   Patrick Hockstetter

391

Date   October 2
Re   Telemetry, latest C. McGee Test (#4)

Pat – I've watched the films four times now and still can't believe it isn't some sort of special effects trick. Some unsolicited advice: When you get before the Senate subcommittee that's going to deal with the Lot Six appropriations and renewal plans, have your ducks in a row and do more than cover your ass – armor-plate it! Human nature being what it is, those guys are going to look at those films and have a hard job believing it isn't a flat-out shuck-and-jive.

To business: The readouts are being delivered by special messenger, and this memo should beat them by no more than two or three hours. You can read them over for yourself, but I'll briefly sum up our findings. Our conclusions can be summed up in two words: We're stumped. She was wired up this time like an astronaut going into space. You will note:

1.) Blood pressure within normal parameters for a child of eight, and there's hardly a jog when that wall goes up like the Hiroshima bomb.
2.) Abnormally high alpha wave readings; what we'd call her 'imagination circuitry' is well-engaged. You may or may not agree with Clapper and me that the waves are rather more even, suggesting a certain 'controlled imaginative dexterity' (Clapper's rather fulsome phrase, not mine). Could indicate she's getting in control of it and can manipulate the ability with greater precision. Practice, as they say, makes perfect. Or it may mean nothing at all.
3.) All metabolic telemetry is within normal parameters – nothing strange or out of place. It's as if she was reading a good book or writing a class theme instead of creating what you say must have been upwards of 30,000 degrees of spot heat. To my mind the most fascinating (and frustrating!) information of all is the Beal-Searles CAT test. *Next to no caloric burn!* In case you've forgotten your physics – occupational hazard with you shrinks – a calorie is nothing but a unit of heat; the amount of heat necessary to raise

a gram of water one degree centigrade, to be exact. She burned maybe 25 calories during that little exhibition, what we would burn doing half a dozen sit-ups or walking twice around the building. But calories measure heat, damn it, *heat*, and what she's producing is heat . . . or is she? Is it coming *from* her or *through* her? And if it's the latter, where is it coming from? Figure that one out and you've got the Nobel Prize in your hip pocket! I'll tell you this: if our test series is as limited as you say it is, I'm positive we'll never find out.

Last word: Are you sure you *want* to continue these tests? Lately I just have to think about that kid and I start to get very antsy. I start thinking about things like pulsars and neutrinos and black holes and Christ knows what else. There are forces loose in this universe that we don't even know about yet, and some we can observe only at a remove of millions of light-years . . . and breathe a sigh of relief because of it. The last time I looked at that film I began to think of the girl as a crack – a chink, if you like – in the very smelter of creation. I know how that sounds, but I feel I would be remiss not to say it. God forgive me for saying this, with three lovely girls of my own, but I personally will breathe a sigh of relief when she's been neutralized.

If she can produce 30,000 degrees of spot heat without even trying, have you ever thought what might happen if she really set her mind to it?

Brad

3

'I want to see my father,' Charlie said when Hockstetter came in. She looked pale and wan. She had changed from her jumper into an old nightgown, and her hair was loose on her shoulders.

'Charlie—' he began, but anything he had been meaning to follow with was suddenly gone. He was deeply troubled by Brad Hyuck's memo and by the supporting telemetry readouts. The fact that Brad had trusted those final two paragraphs to print said much, and suggested more.

Hockstetter himself was scared. In authorizing the changeover of chapel to testing room, Cap had also authorized the installation of more Kelvinator air conditioners around Charlie's apartment – not eight but twenty. Only six had been installed so far, but after Test #4, Hockstetter didn't care if they were installed or not. He thought they could set up two hundred of the damned things and not impede her power. It was no longer a question of whether or not she could kill herself; it was a question of whether or not she could destroy the entire Shop installation if she wanted to – and maybe all of eastern Virginia in the bargain. Hockstetter now thought that if she wanted to do those things, she could. And the last stop on that line of reasoning was even scarier: only John Rainbird had an effective checkrein on her now. And Rainbird was nuts.

'I want to see my father,' she repeated.

Her father was at the funeral of poor Herman Pynchot. He attended with Cap, at the latter's request. Even Pynchot's death, as unrelated to anything going on here as it was, seemed to have cast its own evil pall over Hockstetter's mind.

'Well, I think that can be arranged,' Hockstetter said cautiously, 'if you can show us a little more—'

'I've shown you enough,' she said. 'I want to see my daddy.' Her lower lip trembled; her eyes had taken on a sheen of tears.

'Your orderly,' Hockstetter said, 'that Indian fellow, said you didn't want to go for a ride on your horse this morning after the test. He seemed worried about you.'

'It's not my horse,' Charlie said. Her voice was husky. 'Nothing here is mine. Nothing except my daddy and I . . .

want . . . to . . . *see him!*' Her voice rose to an angry, tearful shout.

'Don't get excited, Charlie,' Hockstetter said, suddenly frightened. Was it suddenly getting hotter in here, or was it just his imagination? 'Just . . . just don't get excited.'

Rainbird. This should have been Rainbird's job, goddammit.

'Listen to me, Charlie.' He smiled a wide, friendly smile. 'How would you like to go to Six Flags over Georgia? It's just about the neatest amusement park in the whole South, except maybe for Disney World. We'd rent the whole park for a day, just for you. You could ride the Ferris wheel, go in the haunted mansion, the merry-go-round—'

'I don't want to go to any amusement park, I just want to see my daddy. And I'm going to. I hope you hear me, because I'm going to!'

It *was* hotter.

'You're sweating,' Charlie said.

He thought of the cinderblock wall, exploding so fast you could see the flames only in slow motion. He thought of the steel tray flipping over twice as it flew across the room, spraying burning chunks of wood. If she flicked that power out at him, he would be a pile of ashes and fused bone almost before he knew what was happening to him.

Oh God please—

'Charlie, getting mad at me won't accomplish anyth—'

'Yes,' she said with perfect truth. 'Yes it will. And I'm mad at you, Dr Hockstetter. I'm really mad at you.'

'Charlie, please—'

'I want to see him,' she said again. 'Now go away. You tell them I want to see my father and then they can test me some more if they want. I don't mind. But if I don't see him, I'll make something happen. Tell them that.'

He left. He felt that he should say something more –

something that would redeem his dignity a little, make up a little for the fear

(*'you're sweating'*)

she had seen scrawled on his face – but nothing occurred. He left, and not even the steel door between him and her could completely ease his fear . . . or his anger at John Rainbird. Because Rainbird had foreseen this, and Rainbird had said nothing. And if he accused Rainbird of that, the Indian would only smile his chilling smile and ask who was the psychiatrist around here, anyway?

The tests had diminished her complex about starting fires until it was like an earthen dam that had sprung leaks in a dozen places. The tests had afforded her the practice necessary to refine a crude sledgehammer of power into something she could flick out with deadly precision, like a circus performer throwing a weighted knife.

And the tests had been the perfect object lesson. They had shown her, beyond a shadow of a doubt, who was in charge here.

She was.

4

When Hockstetter was gone, Charlie fell on the couch, her hands to her face, sobbing. Waves of conflicting emotion swept her – guilt and horror, indignation, even a kind of angry pleasure. But fear was the greatest of them all. Things had changed when she agreed to their tests; she feared things had changed forever. And now she didn't just *want* to see her father; she *needed* him. She needed him to tell her what to do next.

At first there had been rewards – walks outside with John, currying Necromancer, then riding him. She loved John and she loved Necromancer . . . if that stupid man could only have known how badly he had hurt her by saying Necromancer was hers when Charlie knew he never could be. The big gelding was only hers in her uneasy half-remembered dreams. But now . . . now . . . the tests themselves, the chance to use her power and feel it grow . . . *that* was starting to become the reward. It had become a terrible but compelling game. And she sensed she had barely scratched the surface. She was like a baby who has just learned how to walk.

She needed her father, she needed him to tell her what was right, what was wrong, whether to go on or to stop forever. If—

'If I *can* stop,' she whispered through her fingers.

That was the most frightening thing of all – no longer being sure that she *could* stop. And if she could not, what would that mean? Oh, what would that mean?

She began to cry again. She had never felt so dreadfully alone.

5

The funeral was a bad scene.

Andy had thought he would be okay; his headache was gone, and, after all, the funeral was only an excuse to be alone with Cap. He hadn't liked Pynchot, although in the end Pynchot had proved to be just a little too small to hate. His barely concealed arrogance and his unconcealed pleasure at being on top of a fellow human being – because of those things and because of his overriding concern for Charlie, Andy had felt little guilt about the ricochet that he had inadvertently set up in Pynchot's mind. The ricochet that had finally torn the man apart.

The echo effect had happened before, but he had always had a chance to put things right again. It was something he had got pretty good at by the time he and Charlie had to run from New York City. There seemed to be land mines

397

planted deep in almost every human brain, deep-seated fears and guilts, suicidal, schizophrenic, paranoid impulses – even murderous ones. A push caused a state of extreme suggestibility, and if a suggestion tended down one of those dark paths, it could destroy. One of his housewives in the Weight-Off program had begun to suffer frightening catatonic lapses. One of his businessmen had confessed a morbid urge to take his service pistol down from the closet and play Russian roulette with it, an urge that was somehow connected in his mind with a story by Edgar Allan Poe, 'William Wilson,' that he had read way back in high school. In both cases, Andy had been able to stop the echo before it sped up and turned into that lethal ricochet. In the case of the businessman, a quiet, sandy-haired, third-echelon bank officer, all it had taken was another push and the quiet suggestion that he had never read the Poe story at all. The connection – whatever it had been – was broken. The chance to break the echo had never come with Pynchot.

Cap talked restlessly of the man's suicide as they drove to the funeral through a cold, swishing autumn rain; he seemed to be trying to come to terms with it. He said he wouldn't have thought it possible for a man just to . . . to keep his arm in there once those blades had begun to chop and grind. But Pynchot had. Somehow Pynchot had. That was when the funeral started being bad for Andy.

The two of them attended only the graveside services, standing well back from the small group of friends and family, clustered under a bloom of black umbrellas. Andy discovered it was one thing to remember Pynchot's arrogance, the little-Caesar power-tripping of a small man who had no real power; to remember his endless and irritating nervous tic of a smile. It was quite another to look at his pallid, washed-out wife in her black suit and veiled hat, holding the hands of her two boys (the younger was about Charlie's age, and they both looked utterly stunned and out of it, as if drugged), knowing – as she must – that the friends and relatives must all know how her husband was found, dressed in her underwear, his right arm vaporized nearly to the elbow, sharpened like a living pencil, his blood splattered in the sink and on the Wood-Mode cabinets, chunks of his flesh—

Andy's gorge rose helplessly. He bent forward in the cold rain, struggling with it. The minister's voice rose and fell senselessly.

'I want to go,' Andy said. 'Can we go?'

'Yes, of course,' Cap said. He looked pale himself, old and not particularly well. 'I've been to quite enough funerals this year to hold me.'

They slipped away from the group standing around the fake grass, the flowers already drooping and spilling petals in this hard rain, the coffin on its runners over the hole in the ground. They walked side by side back toward the winding, graveled drive where Cap's economy-sized Chevy was parked near the rear of the funeral cortege. They walked under willows that dripped and rustled mysteriously. Three or four other men, barely seen, moved around them. Andy thought that he must know now how the President of the United States feels.

'Very bad for the widow and the little boys,' Cap said. 'The scandal, you know.'

'Will she . . . uh, will she be taken care of?'

'Very handsomely, in terms of money,' Cap said almost tonelessly. They were nearing the lane now. Andy could see Cap's orange Vega, parked on the verge. Two men were getting quietly into a Biscayne in front of it. Two more got into a gray Plymouth behind it. 'But nobody's going to be able to buy off those two little boys. Did you see their faces?'

Andy said nothing. Now he felt guilt; it was like a sharp sawblade working in his guts. Not even telling himself that

399

his own position had been desperate would help. All he could do now was hold Charlie's face in front of him . . . Charlie and a darkly ominous figure behind her, a one-eyed pirate named John Rainbird who had wormed his way into her confidence so he could hasten the day when—

They got into the Vega and Cap started the engine. The Biscayne ahead pulled out and Cap followed. The Plymouth fell into place behind them.

Andy felt a sudden, almost eerie certainty that the push had deserted him again – that when he tried there would be nothing. As if to pay for the expression on the faces of the two boys.

But what else was there to do but try?

'We're going to have a little talk,' he said to Cap, and pushed. The push was there, and the headache settled in almost at once – the price he was going to have to pay for using it so soon after the last time. 'It won't interfere with your driving.'

Cap seemed to settle in his seat. His left hand, which had been moving toward his turnsignal, hesitated a moment and then went on. The Vega followed the lead car sedately between the big stone pillars and onto the main road.

'No, I don't think our little talk will interfere with my driving at all,' Cap said.

They were twenty miles from the compound; Andy had checked the odometer upon leaving and again upon arriving at the cemetery. A lot of it was over the highway Pynchot had told him about, 301. It was a fast road. He guessed he had no more than twenty-five minutes to arrange everything. He had thought of little else over the last two days and thought he had everything pretty well mapped out . . . but there was one thing he badly needed to know.

'How long can you and Rainbird ensure Charlie's co-operation, Captain Hollister?'

400

'Not much longer,' Cap said. 'Rainbird arranged things very cleverly so that in your absence, he's the only one really in control of her. The father surrogate.' In a low, almost chanting voice, he said, 'He's her father when her father isn't there.'

'And when she stops, she's to be killed?'

'Not immediately. Rainbird can keep her at it awhile longer.' Cap signaled his turn onto 301. 'He'll pretend we found out. Found out that they were talking. Found out that he was giving her advice on how to handle her . . . her problem. Found out he had passed notes to you.'

He fell silent, but Andy didn't need any more. He felt sick. He wondered if they had congratulated each other on how easy it was to fool a little kid, to win her affections in a lonely place and then twist her to their own purposes once they had earned her trust. When nothing else would work, just tell her that her only friend, John the orderly, was going to lose his job and maybe be prosecuted under the Official Secrets Act for presuming to be her friend. Charlie would do the rest on her own. Charlie would deal with them. She would continue to cooperate.

I hope I meet this guy soon. I really do.

But there was no time to think about that now . . . and if things went right, he would never have to meet Rainbird at all.

'I'm slated to go to Hawaii a week from today,' Andy said.

'Yes, that's right.'

'How?'

'By army transport plane.'

'Who did you contact to arrange that?'

'Puck,' Cap said immediately.

'Who's Puck, Captain Hollister?'

'Major Victor Puckeridge,' Cap said. 'At Andrews.'

'Andrews Air Force Base?'

'Yes, of course.'

'He's a friend?'

'We play golf.' Cap smiled vaguely. 'He slices.'

Wonderful news, Andy thought. His head was throbbing like a rotted tooth.

'Suppose you called him this afternoon and said you wanted to move that flight up by three days?'

'Yes?' Cap said doubtfully.

'Would that present a problem? A lot of paperwork?'

'Oh, no. Puck would slice right through the paperwork.' The smile reappeared, slightly odd and not really happy. 'He slices. Did I tell you that?'

'Yes. Yes, you did.'

'Oh. Good.'

The car hummed along at a perfectly legal fifty-five. The rain had mellowed to a steady mist. The windshield wipers clicked back and forth.

'Call him this afternoon, Cap. As soon as you get back.'

'Call Puck, yes. I was just thinking I ought to do that.'

'Tell him I've got to be moved on Wednesday instead of Saturday.'

Four days was not much time to recuperate – three weeks would have been more like it – but things were moving rapidly to a climax now. The endgame had begun. The fact was there, and Andy, out of necessity, recognized it. He wouldn't – couldn't – leave Charlie in the path of this Rainbird creature any longer than he had to.

'Wednesday instead of Saturday.'

'Yes. And then you tell Puck that you'll be coming along.'

'Coming along? I can't—'

Andy renewed the push. It hurt him, but he pushed hard. Cap jerked in his seat. The car swerved minutely on the road, and Andy thought again that he was practically begging to start up an echo in this guy's head.

'Coming along, yes. I'm coming along.'

'That's right,' Andy said grimly. 'Now – what sort of arrangements have you made about security?'

'No particular security arrangements,' Cap said. 'You're pretty much incapacitated by Thorazine. Also, you're tipped over and unable to use your mental-domination ability. It has become dormant.'

'Ah, yes,' Andy said, and put a slightly shaky hand to his forehead. 'Do you mean I'll be riding the plane alone?'

'No,' Cap said immediately, 'I believe I'll come along myself.'

'Yes, but other than the two of us?'

'There will be two Shop men along, partly to act as stewards and partly to keep an eye on you. SOP, you know. Protect the investment.'

'Only two operatives are scheduled to go with us? You're sure?'

'Yes.'

'And the flight crew, of course.'

'Yes.'

Andy looked out the window. They were halfway back now. This was the crucial part, and his head was already aching so badly that he was afraid he might forget something. If he did, the whole cardhouse would come tumbling down.

Charlie, he thought, and tried to hold on.

'Hawaii's a long way from Virginia, Captain Hollister. Will the plane make a refueling stop?'

'Yes.'

'Do you know where?'

'No.' Cap said serenely, and Andy could have punched him in the eye.

'When you speak to . . .' What was his name? He groped frantically in his tired, hurt mind and retrieved it. 'When

403

you speak to Puck, find out where the plane will set down for refueling.'

'Yes, all right.'

'Just work it naturally into your conversation with him.'

'Yes, I'll find out where it's going to refuel by working it naturally into our conversation.' He glanced at Andy with thoughtful, dreamy eyes, and Andy found himself wondering if this man had given the order that Vicky be killed. There was a sudden urge to tell him to floor the accelerator pedal and drive into that oncoming bridge abutment. Except for Charlie. Charlie! his mind said. Hold on for Charlie. 'Did I tell you that Puck slices?' Cap said fondly.

'Yes. You did.' Think! Think, dammit! Somewhere near Chicago or Los Angeles seemed the most likely. But not at a civilian airport like O'Hare or L. A. International. The plane would refuel at an airbase. That in itself presented no problem to his rag of a plan – it was one of the few things that did not – as long as he could find out where in advance.

'We'd like to leave at three in the afternoon,' he told Cap.

'Three.'

'You'll see that this John Rainbird is somewhere else.'

'Send him away?' Cap said hopefully, and it gave Andy a chill to realize that Cap was afraid of Rainbird – quite badly afraid.

'Yes. It doesn't matter where.'

'San Diego?'

'All right.'

Now. Last lap. He was just going to make it; up ahead a green reflectorized sign pointed the way to the Longmont exit. Andy reached into the front pocket of his pants and pulled out a folded slip of paper. For the moment, he only held it in his lap, between first and second fingers.

404

'You're going to tell the two Shop guys who are going to Hawaii with us to meet us at the airbase,' he said. 'They're to meet us at Andrews. You and I will go to Andrews just as we are now.'

'Yes.'

Andy drew in a deep breath. 'But my daughter will be with us.'

'Her?' Cap showed real agitation for the first time. '*Her?* She's dangerous! She can't – we can't—'

'She wasn't dangerous until you people started playing with her,' Andy said harshly. 'Now she is coming with us and you are not to contradict me again, *do you understand that?*'

This time the car's swerve was more pronounced, and Cap moaned. 'She'll be coming with us,' he agreed. 'I won't contradict you anymore. That hurts. That hurts.'

But not as much as it hurts me.

Now his voice seemed to be coming from far away, through the blood-soaked net of pain that was pulling tighter and tighter around his brain. 'You're going to give her this,' Andy said, and passed the folded note to Cap. 'Give it to her today, but do it carefully, so that no one suspects.'

Cap tucked the note into his breast pocket. Now they were approaching the Shop; on their left were the double runs of electrified fence. Warning signs flashed past every fifty yards or so.

'Repeat back the salient points,' Andy said.

Cap spoke quickly and concisely – the voice of a man who had been trained in the act of recall since the days of his military-academy boyhood.

'I will arrange for you to leave for Hawaii on an army transport plane on Wednesday instead of Saturday. I will be coming with you; your daughter will also accompany us. The two Shop agents who will also be coming will meet

405

us at Andrews. I will find out from Puck where the plane will be refueling. I'll do that when I call him to change the flight date. I have a note to give your daughter. I'll give it to her after I finish talking to Puck, and I will do it in a way which will arouse no undue suspicion. And I will arrange to have John Rainbird in San Diego next Wednesday. I believe that covers the waterfront.'

'Yes,' Andy said, 'I believe it does.' He leaned back against the seat and closed his eyes. Jumbled fragments of past and present flew through his mind, aimlessly, jackstraws blown in the high wind. Did this really have a chance to work, or was he only buying death for both of them? They knew what Charlie could do now; they'd had firsthand experience. If it went wrong, they would finish their trip in the cargo bay of that army transport plane. In two boxes.

Cap paused at the guardbooth, rolled down his window, and handed over a plastic card, which the man on duty slipped into a computer terminal.

'Go ahead, sir,' he said.

Cap drove on.

'One last thing, Captain Hollister. You're going to forget all about this. You'll do each of the things we've discussed perfectly spontaneously. You'll discuss them with no one.'

'All right.'

Andy nodded. It wasn't all right, but it would have to do. The chances of setting up an echo here were extraordinarily high because he had been forced to push the man terribly hard and also because the instructions he had given Cap would go completely against the grain. Cap might be able to bring everything off simply by virtue of his position here. He might not. Right now Andy was too tired and in too much pain to care much.

He was barely able to get out of the car; Cap had to take

406

his arm to steady him. He was dimly aware that the cold autumn drizzle felt good against his face.

The two men from the Biscayne looked at him with a kind of cold disgust. One of them was Don Jules. Jules was wearing a blue sweatshirt that read U.S. OLYMPIC DRINKING TEAM.

Get a good look at the stoned fat man, Andy thought groggily. He was close to tears again, and his breath began to catch and hitch in his throat. You get a good look now, because if the fat guy gets away this time, he's going to blow this whole rotten cesspool right out of the swamp.

'There, there,' Cap said, and patted him on the shoulder with patronizing and perfunctory sympathy.

Just do your job, Andy thought, holding on grimly against the tears; he would not cry in front of them again, none of them. Just do your job, you son of a bitch.

6

Back in his apartment, Andy stumbled to his bed, hardly aware of what he was doing, and fell asleep. He lay like a dead thing for the next six hours, while blood seeped from a minute rupture in his brain and a number of brain cells grew white and died.

When he woke up, it was ten o'clock in the evening. The headache was still raging. His hands went to his face. The numb spots – one below his left eye, one on his left cheekbone, and one just below the jawbone – were back. This time they were bigger.

I can't push it much further without killing myself, he thought, and knew it was true. But he would hold on long enough to see this through, to give Charlie her chance, if he possibly could. Somehow he would hold on that long.

He went to the bathroom and got a glass of water. Then he lay down again, and after a long time, sleep returned.

His last waking thought was that Charlie must have read his note by now.

7

Cap Hollister had had an extremely busy day since getting back from Herm Pynchot's funeral. He had no more than got settled into his office when his secretary brought him an interdepartmental memo marked URGENT. It was from Pat Hockstetter. Cap told her to get him Vic Puckeridge on the phone and settled back to read the memo. I should get out more often, he thought; it aerates the brain cells or something. It had occurred to him on the ride back that there was really no sense waiting a whole week to ship McGee off to Maui; this Wednesday would be plenty late enough.

Then the memo captured his whole attention.

It was miles from Hockstetter's usual cool and rather baroque style; in fact, it was couched in nearly hysterical purple prose, and Cap thought with some amusement that the kid must have really hit Hockstetter with the chicken-stick. Hit him hard.

What it came down to was that Charlie had dug in her heels. It had come sooner than they had expected, that was all. Maybe – no, probably – even sooner than Rainbird had expected. Well, they would let it lie for a few days and then . . . then . . .

His train of thought broke up. His eyes took on a faraway, slightly puzzled cast. In his mind he saw a golf club, a five iron, whistling down and connecting solidly with a Spalding ball. He could hear that low, whistling *whhoooop* sound. Then the ball was gone, high and white against the blue sky. But it was slicing . . . slicing . . .

His brow cleared. What had he been thinking of? It wasn't like him to wander off the subject like that. Charlie

408

had dug in her heels; that was what he had been thinking. Well, that was all right. Nothing to get bent out of shape about. They would let her alone for a while, until the weekend maybe, and then they could use Rainbird on her. She would light a lot of fires to keep Rainbird out of dutch.

His hand stole to his breast pocket and felt the small paper folded in there. In his mind he heard the soft swinging sound of a golf club again; it seemed to reverberate in the office. But now it was not a *whhoooop* sound. It was a quiet *sssssss*, almost the sound of a . . . a snake. That was unpleasant. He had always found snakes unpleasant, ever since earliest childhood.

With an effort, he swept all this foolishness about snakes and golf clubs from his mind. Perhaps the funeral had upset him more than he had thought.

The intercom buzzed and his secretary told him Puck was on line one. Cap picked up the phone and after some small talk asked Puck if there would be a problem if they decided to move the Maui shipment up from Saturday to Wednesday. Puck checked and said he saw no problem there at all.

'Say, around three in the afternoon?'

'No problem,' Puck repeated. 'Just don't move it up anymore, or we'll be in the bucket. This place is getting worse than the freeway at rush hour.'

'No, this is solid,' Cap said. 'And here's something else: I'm going along. But you keep that under your hat, okay?'

Puck burst into hearty baritone laughter. 'A little sun, fun, and grass skirts?'

'Why not?' Cap agreed. 'I'm escorting a valuable piece of cargo. I could justify myself in front of a Senate committee if I had to, I think. And I haven't had a real vacation since 1973. The goddamned Arabs and their oil bitched up the last week of that one.'

'I'll keep it to myself,' Puck agreed. 'You going to play

some golf while you're out there? I know of at least two great courses on Maui.'

Cap fell silent. He looked thoughtfully at the top of his desk, through it. The phone sagged away from his ear slightly.

'Cap? You there?'

Low and definite and ominous in this small, cozy study: *Sssssssssss*—

'Shit, I think we been cut off,' Puck muttered. 'Cap? Ca—'

'You still slicing the ball, old buddy?' Cap asked.

Puck laughed. 'You kidding? When I die, they're going to bury me in the fucking rough. Thought I lost you for a minute there.'

'I'm right here,' Cap said. 'Puck, are there snakes in Hawaii?'

Now it was Puck's turn to pause. 'Say again?'

'Snakes. Poisonous snakes.'

'I . . . gee, damn if I know. I can check it for you if it's important . . .' Puck's dubious tone seemed to imply that Cap employed about five thousand spooks to check just such things.

'No, that's okay,' Cap said. He held the telephone firmly against his ear again. 'Just thinking out loud, I guess. Maybe I'm getting old.'

'Not you, Cap. There's too much vampire in you.'

'Yeah, maybe. Thanks, goodbuddy.'

'No trouble at all. Glad you're getting away for a bit. Nobody deserves it more than you, after the last year you've put in.' He meant Georgia, of course; he didn't know about the McGees. Which meant, Cap thought wearily, that he didn't know the half of it.

He started to say good-bye and then added, 'By the way, Puck, where will that plane be stopping to refuel? Any idea?'

'Durban, Illinois,' Puck said promptly. 'Outside Chicago.'

Cap thanked him, said good-bye, hung up. His fingers went to the note in his pocket again and touched it. His eye fell on Hockstetter's memo. It sounded as if the girl had been pretty upset, too. Perhaps it wouldn't hurt if he went down and spoke to her, stroked her a little.

He leaned forward and thumbed the intercom.

'Yes, Cap?'

'I'll be going downstairs for a while,' he said. 'I should be back in thirty minutes or so.'

'Very good.'

He got up and left the study. As he did so, his hand stole to his breast pocket and felt the note there again.

8

Charlie lay on her bed fifteen minutes after Cap left, her mind in a total whirl of dismay, fear, and confused speculation. She literally didn't know what to think.

He had come at quarter of five, half an hour ago, and had introduced himself as Captain Hollister ('but please just call me Cap; everyone does'). He had a kindly, shrewd face that reminded her a little of the illustrations in *The Wind in the Willows*. It was a face she had seen somewhere recently, but she hadn't been able to place it until Cap jogged her memory. It had been he who had taken her back to her rooms after the first test, when the man in the white suit had bolted, leaving the door open. She had been so much in a fog of shock, guilt, and – yes – exhilarated triumph that it was really no wonder she hadn't been able to place his face. Probably she could have been escorted back to her apartment by Gene Simmons of Kiss without noticing it.

He talked in a smooth, convincing way that she immediately mistrusted.

He told her Hockstetter was concerned because she had declared the testing at an end until she saw her father. Charlie agreed that was so and would say no more, maintaining a stubborn silence . . . mostly out of fear. If you discussed your reasons for things with a smooth talker like this Cap, he would strip those reasons away one by one until it seemed that black was white and white black. The bare demand was better. Safer.

But he had surprised her.

'If that's the way you feel, okay,' he had said. The expression of surprise on her face must have been slightly comical, because he chuckled. 'It will take a bit of arranging, but—'

At the words 'a bit of arranging,' her face closed up again. 'No more fires,' she said. 'No more tests. Even if it takes you ten years to "arrange" it.'

'Oh, I don't think it will take that long,' he had said, not offended. 'It's just that I have people to answer to, Charlie. And a place like this runs on paperwork. But you don't have to light so much as a candle while I'm setting it up.'

'Good,' she said stonily, not believing him, not believing he was going to set anything up. 'Because I won't.'

'I think I ought to be able to arrange it . . . by Wednesday. Yes, by Wednesday, for sure.'

He had fallen suddenly silent. His head cocked slightly, as if he were listening to something just a bit too high-pitched for her to hear. Charlie looked at him, puzzled, was about to ask if he was all right, and then closed her mouth with a snap. There was something . . . something almost familiar about the way he was sitting.

'Do you really think I could see him on Wednesday?' she asked timidly.

'Yes, I think so,' Cap said. He shifted in his chair and

sighed heavily. His eye caught hers and he smiled a puzzled little smile . . . also familiar. Apropos of nothing at all, he said: 'Your dad plays a mean game of golf, I hear.'

Charlie blinked. So far as she knew, her father had never touched a golf club in his life. She got ready to say so . . . and then it came together in her mind and a dizzying burst of bewildered excitement ran through her.

(*Mr Merle! He's like Mr Merle!*)

Mr Merle had been one of Daddy's executives when they were in New York. Just a little man with light-blond hair and pink-rimmed glasses and a sweet, shy smile. He had come to get more confidence, like the rest of them. He worked in an insurance company or a bank or something. And Daddy had been very worried about Mr Merle for a while. It was a 'rick-o-shay.' It came from using the push. It had something to do with a story Mr Merle had read once. The push Daddy used to give Mr Merle more confidence made him remember that story in a bad way, a way that was making him sick. Daddy said the 'rick-o-shay' came from that story and it was bouncing around in Mr Merle's head like a tennis ball, only instead of finally stopping the way a bouncing tennis ball would, the memory of that story would get stronger and stronger until it made Mr Merle very sick. Only Charlie had got the idea that Daddy was afraid it might do more than make Mr Merle sick; he was afraid it might kill him. So he had kept Mr Merle after the others left one night and pushed him into believing he had never read that story at all. And after that, Mr Merle was all right. Daddy told her once that he hoped Mr Merle would never go to see a movie called *The Deer Hunter*, but he didn't explain why.

But before Daddy fixed him up, Mr Merle had looked like Cap did now.

She was suddenly positive that her father had pushed this man, and the excitement in her was like a tornado.

After hearing nothing about him except for the sort of general reports John sometimes brought her, after not seeing him or knowing where he was, it was in a strange way as if her father were suddenly in this room with her, telling her it was all right and that he was near.

Cap suddenly stood up. 'Well, I'll be going now. But I'll be seeing you, Charlie. And don't worry.'

She wanted to tell him not to go, to tell her about her dad, where he was, if he was okay . . . but her tongue was rooted to the bottom of her mouth.

Cap went to the door, then paused. 'Oh, almost forgot.' He crossed the room to her, took a folded piece of paper from his breast pocket, and handed it to her. She took it numbly, looked at it, and put it in her robe pocket. 'And when you're out riding that horse, you watch out for snakes,' he said confidentially. 'If a horse sees a snake, he is going to bolt. Every time. He'll—'

He broke off, raised a hand to his temple, and rubbed it. For a moment, he looked old and distracted. Then he shook his head a little, as if dismissing the thought. He bid her good-bye and left.

Charlie stood there for a long moment after he was gone. Then she took out the note, unfolded it, read what was written there and everything changed.

9

Charlie, love—

First thing: When you finish reading this, flush it down the toilet, okay?

Second thing: If everything goes the way I'm planning – the way I hope – we'll be out of here next Wednesday. The man who gave you this note is on our team, although he doesn't know he is . . . get it?

Third thing: I want you to be in the stables on Wednesday afternoon at one o'clock. I don't care how you do it – make another fire for them if that's what it takes. But be there.

Fourth, most important thing: *Don't trust this man John Rainbird.* This may upset you. I know you have trusted him. But he is a very dangerous man, Charlie. No way anyone's going to blame you for your trust in him – Hollister says he has been convincing enough to win an Academy Award. But know this: he was in charge of the men who took us prisoner at Granther's place. I hope this doesn't upset you too much, but knowing how you are, it probably will. It's no fun to find out that someone has been using you for his own purposes. Listen, Charlie: if Rainbird comes around – and he probably will – it is *very important* for him to think your feelings toward him haven't changed. He will be out of our way on Wednesday afternoon.

We are going to Los Angeles or Chicago, Charlie, and I think I know a way to arrange a press conference for us. I have an old friend named Quincey I'm counting on to help us, and I believe – I must believe – that he will come through for us if I can get in touch with him. A press conference would mean that the whole country would know about us. They may still want to keep us someplace, but we can be together. I hope you still want that as much as I do.

This wouldn't be so bad except that they want you to make fires for all the wrong reasons. If you have any doubts at all about running again, remember it is for the last time . . . and that it is what your mother would have wanted.

I miss you, Charlie, and love you lots.

Dad

10

John?

John in charge of the men that shot her and her father with tranquilizer darts?

John?

She rolled her head from side to side. The feeling of desolation in her, the heartbreak, seemed too great to be contained. There was no answer to this cruel dilemma. If she believed her father, she had to believe that John had been tricking her all along only to get her to agree to their tests. If she continued to believe in John, then the note she had crumpled and flushed down the toilet was a lie with her father's name signed to it. Either way, the hurt, the *cost*, was enormous. Was this what being grownup was about? Dealing with that hurt? That cost? If it was, she hoped she would die young.

She remembered looking up from Necromancer that first time and seeing John's smile . . . something in that smile that she didn't like. She remembered that she had never got any real feeling from him, as if he were closed off, or . . . or . . .

She tried to shunt the thought aside

(*or dead inside*)

but it would not be shunted.

But he wasn't *like* that. He *wasn't*. His terror in the blackout. His story about what those Cong had done to him. Could that be a lie? Could it, with the ruined map of his face to back up the tale?

Her head went back and forth on the pillow, back and forth, back and forth, in an endless gesture of negation. She did not want to think about it, did not, did not.

But couldn't help it.

Suppose . . . suppose they had made the blackout happen? Or suppose it had just happened . . . *and he had used it?*

(*NO! NO! NO! NO!*)

And yet her mind was now out of her conscious control, and it circled this maddening, horrifying patch of nettles with a kind of inexorable, cold determination. She was a bright girl, and she handled her chain of logic carefully,

416

one bead at a time, telling it as a bitter penitent must tell the terrible beads of utter confession and surrender.

She remembered a TV show she had seen once, it had been on *Starsky and Hutch*. They put this cop into jail in the same cell with this bad guy who knew all about a robbery. They had called the cop pretending to be a jailbird a 'ringer.'

Was John Rainbird a ringer?

Her father said he was. And why would her father lie to her?

Who do you believe in? John or Daddy? Daddy or John?

No, no, no, her mind repeated steadily, monotonously . . . and to no effect. She was caught in a torture of doubt that no eight-year-old girl should have to stand, and when sleep came, the dream came with it. Only this time she saw the face of the silhouette, which stood to block the light.

11

'All right, what is it?' Hockstetter asked grumpily.

His tone indicated that it had better be pretty goddam good. He had been home watching James Bond on the Sunday Night Movie when the phone rang and a voice told him that they had a potential problem with the little girl. Over an open line, Hockstetter didn't dare ask what the problem was. He just went as he was, in a pair of paint-splattered jeans and a tennis shirt.

He had come frightened, chewing a Rolaid to combat the boil of sour acid in his stomach. He had kissed his wife good-bye, answering her raised eyebrows by saying it was a slight problem with some of the equipment and he would be right back. He wondered what she would say if she knew the 'slight problem' could kill him at any moment.

Standing here now, looking into the ghostly infrared

417

monitor they used to watch Charlie when the lights were out, he wished again that this was over and the little girl out of the way. He had never bargained for this when the whole thing was just an academic problem outlined in a series of blue folders. The truth was the burning cinder-block wall; the truth was spot temperatures of thirty thousand degrees or more; the truth was Brad Hyuck talking about whatever forces fired the engine of the universe; and the truth was that he was very scared. He felt as if he were sitting on top of an unstable nuclear reactor.

The man on duty, Neary, swung around when Hock-stetter came in. 'Cap came down to visit her around five,' he said. 'She turned her nose up at supper. Went to bed early.'

Hockstetter looked into the monitor. Charlie was tossing restlessly on top of her bed, fully dressed. 'She looks like maybe she's having a nightmare.'

'One, or a whole series of them,' Neary said grimly. 'I called because the temperature in there has gone up three degrees in the last hour.'

'That's not much.'

'It is when a room's temperature-controlled the way that one is. Not much doubt that she's doing it.'

Hockstetter considered this, biting on a knuckle.

'I think someone should go in there and wake her up,' Neary said, finally drifting down to the bottom line.

'Is that what you got me down here for?' Hockstetter cried. 'To wake up a kid and give her a glass of warm milk?'

'I didn't want to exceed my authority,' Neary said stonily.

'No.' Hockstetter said, and had to bite down on the rest of the words. The little girl would have to be wakened if the temperature went much higher, and there was always a chance that if she was frightened enough, she might strike out at the first person she saw upon waking. After all, they had been busy removing the checks and balances on her pyrokinetic ability and had been quite successful.

'Where's Rainbird?' he asked.

Neary shrugged. 'Whipping his weasel in Winnipeg, for all I know. But as far as she's concerned, he's off duty. I think she'd be pretty suspicious if he showed up n—'

The digital thermometer inset on Neary's control board flicked over another degree, hesitated, and then flicked over two more in quick succession.

'Somebody's *got* to go in there,' Neary said, and now his voice was a bit unsteady. 'It's seventy-four in there now. What if she blows sky-high?'

Hockstetter tried to think what to do, but his brain seemed frozen. He was sweating freely now, but his mouth had gone as dry as a woolly sock. He wanted to be back home, tipped back in his La-Z-Boy, watching James Bond go after SMERSH or whatever the hell it was. He didn't want to be here. He didn't want to be looking at the red numbers under the little square of glass, waiting for them to suddenly blur upward in tens, thirties, hundreds, as they had when the cinderblock wall—

Think! he screamed at himself. *What do you do? What do you—*

'She just woke up,' Neary said softly.

They both stared intently at the monitor. Charlie had swung her legs over onto the floor and was sitting with her head down, her palms on her cheeks, her hair obscuring her face. After a moment she got up and went into the bathroom, face blank, eyes mostly closed – more asleep than awake, Hockstetter guessed.

Neary flicked a switch and the bathroom monitor came on. Now the picture was clear and sharp in the light of the fluorescent bar. Hockstetter expected her to urinate, but Charlie just stood inside the door, looking at the toilet.

'Oh Mother of Mary, look at that,' Neary murmured.

The water in the toilet bowl had begun to steam slightly. This went on for more than a minute (one-twenty-one in Neary's log), and then Charlie went to the toilet, flushed it, urinated, flushed it again, drank two glasses of water, and went back to bed. This time her sleep seemed easier, deeper. Hockstetter glanced at the thermometer and saw it had dropped four degrees. As he watched, it dropped another degree, to sixty-nine – just one degree above the suite's normal temperature.

He remained with Neary until after midnight. 'I'm going home to bed. You'll get this written up, won't you?'

'That's what I get paid for,' Neary said stolidly.

Hockstetter went home. The next day he wrote a memo suggesting that any further gains in knowledge that further testing might provide ought to be balanced against the potential hazards, which in his opinion were growing too fast for comfort.

12

Charlie remembered little of the night. She remembered being hot, getting up, getting rid of the heat. She remembered the dream but only vaguely – a sense of freedom

(*up ahead was the light – the end of the forest, open land where she and Necromancer would ride forever*)

mingled with a sense of fear and a sense of loss. It had been his face, it had been John's face, all along. And perhaps she had known it. Perhaps she had known that

(*the woods are burning don't hurt the horses o please don't hurt the horses*)

all along.

When she woke up the next morning, her fear, confusion, and desolation had begun their perhaps inevitable change into a bright, hard gem of anger.

He better be out of the way on Wednesday, she thought. *He just better. If it's true about what he did, he better not come near me or Daddy on Wednesday.*

13

Late that morning Rainbird came in, rolling his wagon of cleaning products, mops, sponges, and rags. His white orderly's uniform flapped softly around him.

'Hi, Charlie,' he said.

Charlie was on the sofa, looking at a picture book. She glanced up, her face pale and unsmiling in that first moment . . . cautious. The skin seemed stretched too tightly over her cheekbones. Then she smiled. But it was not, Rainbird thought, her usual smile.

'Hello, John.'

'You don't look so great this morning, Charlie, you should forgive me for sayin.'

'I didn't sleep very well.'

'Oh yeah?' He knew she hadn't. That fool Hockstetter was almost foaming at the mouth because she'd popped the temperature five or six degrees in her sleep. 'I'm sorry to hear that. Is it your dad?'

'I guess so.' She closed her book and stood up. 'I think I'll go and lie down for a while. I just don't feel like talking or anything.'

'Sure. Gotcha.'

He watched her go, and when the bedroom door had clicked shut, he went into the kitchen to fill his floorbucket. Something about the way she had looked at him. The smile. He didn't like it. She'd had a bad night, yes, okay. Everyone has them from time to time, and the next morning you snap at your wife or stare right through the paper or whatever. Sure. But . . . something inside had begun to jangle an alarm. It had been weeks since she had looked at him that way. She hadn't come to him this morning, eager and glad to see him, and he didn't like that, either. She had kept her own space today. It disturbed him. Maybe it was just the aftermath of a bad night, and maybe the bad dreams of the night before had just been caused by something she ate, but it disturbed him all the same.

And there was something else nibbling at him: Cap had been down to see her late yesterday afternoon. He had never done that before.

Rainbird set down his bucket and hooked the mop squeegee over its rim. He dunked the mop, wrung it out, and began to mop the floor in long, slow strokes. His mauled face was calm and at rest.

Have you been putting a knife in my back, Cap? Figure you've got enough? Or maybe you just went chickenshit on me.

If that last was true, then he had badly misjudged Cap. Hockstetter was one thing. Hockstetter's experience with Senate committees and subcommittees was almost zilch; a piddle here and a piddle there. Corroborative stuff. He could allow himself the luxury of indulging his fear. Cap couldn't. Cap would know there was no such thing as sufficient evidence, especially when you were dealing with something as potentially explosive (pun *certainly* intended) as Charlie McGee. And it wasn't just funding Cap would be asking for; when he got before that closed session, the most dread and mystic of all bureaucratic phrases would fall from his lips: *long-term funding.* And in the background, lurking unspoken but potent, the implication of eugenics. Rainbird guessed that in the end, Cap would find it impossible to avoid having a group of senators down here to watch Charlie perform. Maybe they should be allowed

422

to bring their kids, Rainbird thought, mopping and rinsing. Better than the trained dolphins at Sea World.

Cap would know he needed all the help he could get.

So why had he come to see her last night? Why was he rocking the boat?

Rainbird squeezed his mop and watched dirty gray water run back into the bucket. He looked through the open kitchen door at the closed door of Charlie's bedroom. She had shut him out and he didn't like that.

It made him very, very nervous.

14

On that early October Monday night, a moderate windstorm came up from the Deep South, sending black clouds flying raggedly across a full moon that lolled pregnantly just above the horizon. The first leaves fell, rattling across the neatly manicured lawns and grounds for the indefatigable corps of groundskeepers to remove in the morning. Some of them swirled into the duckpond, where they floated like small boats. Autumn had come to Virginia again.

In his quarters, Andy was watching TV and still getting over his headache. The numb spots on his face had diminished in size but had not disappeared. He could only hope he would be ready by Wednesday afternoon. If things worked as he had planned, he could keep the number of times he would have to actively push to a bare minimum. If Charlie had got his note, and if she was able to meet him at the stables across the way . . . then *she* would become his push, his lever, his weapon. Who was going to argue with him when he had the equivalent of a nuclear rifle in his possession?

Cap was at home in Longmont Hills. As on the night Rainbird had visited him, he had a snifter of brandy, and music was coming from the stereo at low volume. Chopin tonight. Cap was sitting on the couch. Across the room, leaning below a pair of van Gogh prints, was his old and scuffed golf bag. He had fetched it from the basement, where a rickrack of sports equipment had built up over the twelve years he had lived here with Georgia, while not on assignment somewhere else in the world. He had brought the golf bag into the living room because he couldn't seem to get golf off his mind lately. Golf, or snakes.

He had brought the golf bag up meaning to take out each of the irons and his two putters and look them over, touch them, see if that wouldn't ease his mind. And then one of the irons had seemed to . . . well, it was funny (ridiculous, in fact), but one of the irons had seemed to *move*. As if it wasn't a golf club at all but a snake, a poison snake that had crawled in there—

Cap dropped the bag against the wall and scuttled away. Half a glass of brandy had stopped the minute shakes in his hands. By the time he finished the glass, he might be able to tell himself they had never trembled at all.

He started the glass on its way to his mouth and then halted. There it was again! Movement . . . or just a trick of his eyes?

Trick of his eyes, most definitely. There were no snakes in his damned golf bag. Just clubs he hadn't been using enough lately. Too busy. And he was a pretty good golfer, too. No Nicklaus or Tom Watson, hell no, but he could keep it on the course. Not always slicing, like Puck. Cap didn't like to slice the ball, because then you were in the rough, the tall grass, and sometimes there were—

Get hold of yourself. Just get hold of yourself. Is you still the Captain or is you ain't?

The trembling was back in his fingers again. What had done this. What in God's name had done this? Sometimes it seemed that there was an explanation, a perfectly

424

reasonable one – something, perhaps, that someone had said and he just . . . couldn't remember. But at other times

(*like now Jesus Christ like now*)

it felt as if he were on the verge of a nervous breakdown. It felt as if his brain was being pulled apart like warm taffy by these alien thoughts he couldn't get rid of.

(*is you the Captain or is you ain't?*)

Cap suddenly threw his brandy glass into the fireplace, where it shattered like a bomb. A strangled sound – a sob – escaped his tight throat like something rotten that had to be sicked up whatever the miserable cost. Then he made himself cross the room (and he went at a drunken, stiltlike lurch), grab the strap of his golf bag (again something seemed to move and shift in there . . . to *shifffft* . . . and *hisssss*) and slip it over his shoulder. He hauled it back into the shadow-draped cavern of the cellar, going on nothing but guts, drops of sweat perched huge and clear on his forehead. His face was frozen in a grimace of fear and determination.

Nothing there but golf clubs, nothing there but golf clubs, his mind chanted over and over again, and at every step of the way he expected something long and brown, something with beady black eyes and small sharp fangs dripping poison, to slither out of the bag and jab twin hypos of death into his neck.

Back in his own living room he felt much better. Except for a nagging headache, he felt much better.

He could think coherently again.

Almost.

He got drunk.

And in the morning he felt better again.

For a while.

425

15

Rainbird spent that windy Monday night gathering information. Disturbing information. First he went in and talked to Neary, the man who had been watching the monitors when Cap paid his visit to Charlie the night before.

'I want to see the videotapes,' Rainbird said.

Neary didn't argue. He set Rainbird up in a small room down the hall with the Sunday tapes and a Sony deck complete with close-up and freeze-frame features. Neary was glad to be rid of him and only hoped that Rainbird wouldn't be coming back and wanting something else. The girl was bad enough. Rainbird, in his own reptilian way, was somehow worse.

The tapes were three-hour Scotch jobs, marked from 0000 to 0300 and so on. Rainbird found the one with Cap on it and watched it four times, not moving except to rewind the tape at the point where Cap said, 'Well, I'll be going now. But I'll be seeing you, Charlie. And don't worry.'

But there was plenty in that tape that worried John Rainbird.

He didn't like the way Cap looked. He seemed to have got older; at times while he was talking to Charlie he seemed to lose the thread of what he was saying, like a man on the edge of senility. His eyes had a vague, bemused look that was uncannily similar to the look Rainbird associated with the onset of combat fatigue, which a comrade-in-arms had once aptly dubbed The Brain Squitters and Trots.

I think I ought to be able to arrange it . . . by Wednesday. Yes, by Wednesday, for sure.

Now why in the name of God had he said that?

Setting up an expectation like that in the kid's mind was

the surest way Rainbird could think of to blow further testing right out of the water. The obvious conclusion was that Cap was playing his own little game – intriguing in the best Shop tradition.

But Rainbird didn't believe it. Cap didn't look like a man engaged in an intrigue. He looked like a man who was profoundly fucked up. That remark about Charlie's father playing golf, for instance. That had come right out of left field. It bore on nothing they had said before and nothing they said afterward. Rainbird toyed briefly with the idea that it was some sort of code phrase, but that was patently ridiculous. Cap knew that everything that went on in Charlie's rooms was monitored and recorded, subject to almost constant review. He was capable of disguising a trip phrase better than that. A remark about golf. It just hung there, irrelevant and puzzling.

And then there was the last thing.

Rainbird played it over and over. Cap pauses. *Oh, almost forgot.* And then he hands her something that she looks at curiously and then puts away in the pocket of her robe.

With Rainbird's finger on the buttons of the Sony VCR, Cap said *Oh, almost forgot* half a dozen times. He passed the thing to her half a dozen times. At first Rainbird thought it was a stick of gum, and then he used the freeze-frame and zoom gadgets. That convinced him that it was, very likely, a note.

Cap, what the fuck are you up to?

16

He spent the rest of that night and the early hours of Tuesday morning at a computer console, calling up every scrap of information he could think of on Charlie McGee, trying to make out some kind of pattern. And there was nothing. His head began to ache from eyestrain.

427

He was getting up to shut off the lights when a sudden thought, a totally off-the-wall connection, occurred to him. It had to do not with Charlie but with the portly, drugged-out cipher that was her father.

Pynchot. Pynchot had been in charge of Andy McGee, and last week Herman Pynchot had killed himself in one of the most grisly ways Rainbird could imagine. Obviously unbalanced. Crackers. Toys in the attic. Cap takes Andy to the funeral – maybe a little strange when you really stopped to think about it, but in no way remarkable.

The Cap starts to act a little weird – talking about golf and passing notes.

That's ridiculous. He's tipped over.

Rainbird stood with his hand on the light switches. The computer-console screen glowed a dull green, the color of a freshly dug emerald.

Who says he's tipped over? Him?

There was another strange thing here as well, Rainbird suddenly realized. Pynchot had given up on Andy, had decided to send him to the Maui compound. If there was nothing Andy could do that would demonstrate what Lot Six was capable of, there was no reason to keep him around at all . . . and it would be safer to separate him from Charlie. Fine. But then Pynchot abruptly changes his mind and decides to schedule another run of tests.

Then Pynchot decides to clean out the garbage disposal . . . while it's still running.

Rainbird walked back to the computer console. He paused, thinking, than tapped HELLO COMPUTER/ QUERY STATUS ANDREW MCGEE 14112/ FURTHER TESTING/MAUI INSTALLATION/Q4

PROCESS, the computer flashed. And a moment later: HELLO RAINBIRD/ANDREW MCGEE 14112 NO FURTHER TESTING/AUTHORIZATION/'STARLING'/ SCHEDULED DEPARTURE FOR MAUI 1500 HOURS

OCTOBER 9/AUTHORIZATION "STARLING"/
ANDREWS AFB-DURBAN (ILL) AFB-KALAMI
AIRFIELD (HI)/BREAK

Rainbird glanced at his watch. October 9 was Wednesday. Andy was leaving Longmont for Hawaii tomorrow afternoon. Who said so? Authorization Starling said so, and that was Cap himself. But this was the first Rainbird knew of it.

His fingers danced over the keys again.

QUERY PROBABILITY ANDREW MCGEE 14112/
SUPPOSED MENTAL DOMINATION ABILITY/
CROSS-REF HERMON PYNCHOT

He had to pause to look up Pynchot's code number in the battered and sweat-stained code book he had folded into his back pocket before coming down here.

14409 Q4

PROCESS, the computer replied, and then remained blank so long that Rainbird began to think that he had misprogrammed and would end up with nothing but a '609' for his trouble.

Then the computer flashed ANDREW MCGEE 14112/MENTAL DOMINATION PROBABILITY 35%/ CROSS-REF HERMAN PYNCHOT/BREAK

Thirty-five percent?

How was that possible?

All right, Rainbird thought. Let's leave Pynchot out of the goddam equation and see what happens.

He tapped out QUERY PROBABILITY ANDREW MCGEE 14112/SUPPOSED MENTAL DOMINATION ABILITY Q4

PROCESS, the computer flashed, and this time its response came within a space of fifteen seconds. ANDREW MCGEE 14112/MENTAL DOMINATION PROBABILITY 2%/BREAK

Rainbird leaned back and closed his good eye and felt a

429

kind of triumph through the sour thud in his head. He had asked the important questions backward, but that was the price humans paid for their intuitive leaps, leaps a computer knew nothing about, even though it had been programmed to say 'Hello,' 'Good-bye,' 'I am sorry [programmer's name],' 'That is too bad,' and 'Oh shit.'

The computer didn't believe there was much of a probability Andy had retained his mental-domination ability . . . until you added in the Pynchot factor. Then the percent jumped halfway to the moon.

He tapped QUERY WHY SUPPOSED MENTAL DOM-INATION ABILITY ANDREW MCGEE 14112 (PROB-ABILITY) RISES FROM 2% to 35% WHEN CROSS-REFERENCED W/HERMAN PYNCHOT 14409 Q4

PROCESS, the computer answered, and then: HER-MAN PYNCHOT 14409 ADJUDGED SUICIDE/ PROBABILITY TAKES INTO ACCOUNT ANDREW MCGEE 14112 MAY HAVE CAUSED SUICIDE/ MENTAL DOMINATION/BREAK

There it was, right here in the banks of the biggest and most sophisticated computer in the Western Hemisphere. Only waiting for someone to ask it the right questions.

Suppose I feed it what I suspect about Cap as a certainty? Rainbird wondered, and decided to go ahead and do it. He dragged out his code book again and looked up Cap's number.

FILE, he tapped. CAPTAIN JAMES HOLLISTER 16040/ATTENDED FUNERAL OF HERMAN PYNCHOT 14409 W/ANDREW MCGEE 14112 F4

FILED, the computer returned.

FILE, Rainbird tapped back. CAPTAIN JAMES HOL-LISTER 16040/CURRENTLY SHOWING SIGNS OF GREAT MENTAL STRESS F4

609, the computer returned. It apparently didn't know 'mental stress' from 'Shinola.'

'Bite my bag,' Rainbird muttered, and tried again.

FILE/CAPTAIN JAMES HOLLISTER 16040/ CURRENTLY BEHAVING COUNTER TO DIRECTIVES REF CHARLENE MCGEE 14111 F4

FILED

'File it, you whore,' Rainbird said. 'Let's see about this.' His fingers went back to the keys.

QUERY PROBABILITY ANDREW MCGEE 14112/ SUPPOSED MENTAL DOMINATION ABILITY/ CROSS-REF HERMAN PYNCHOT 14409/CROSS-REF CAPTAIN JAMES HOLLISTER 16040 Q4

PROCESS, the computer showed, and Rainbird sat back to wait, watching the screen. Two percent was too low. Thirty-five percent was still not betting odds. But—

The computer now flashed this: ANDREW MCGEE 14112/MENTAL DOMINATION PROBABILITY 90%/CROSS-REF HERMAN PYNCHOT 14409/ CROSS-REF CAPTAIN JAMES HOLLISTER 16040 BREAK

Now it was up to ninety percent. And those *were* betting odds.

And two other things that John Rainbird would have bet on were, one, that what Cap handed to the girl was indeed a note to Charlie from her father and, two, that it contained some sort of escape plan.

'You dirty old son of a bitch,' John Rainbird murmured – not without admiration.

Pulling himself to the computer again, Rainbird tapped

600 GOODBYE COMPUTER 600

604 GOODBYE RAINBIRD 604

Rainbird turned off the keyboard and began to chuckle.

17

Rainbird went back to the house where he was staying and fell asleep with his clothes on. He woke up just after noon on Tuesday and called Cap to tell him he wouldn't be in that afternoon. He had come down with a bad cold, possibly the onset of the grippe, and he didn't want to chance passing it on to Charlie.

'Hope that won't keep you from going to San Diego tomorrow,' Cap said briskly.

'San Diego?'

'Three files,' Cap said. 'Top secret. I need a courier. You're it. Your plane leaves from Andrews at oh-seven-hundred tomorrow.'

Rainbird thought fast. This was more of Andy McGee's work. McGee knew about him. Of course he did. That had been in the note to Charlie, along with whatever crazy escape plan McGee had concocted. And that explained why the girl had acted so strangely yesterday. Either going to Herman Pynchot's funeral or coming back, Andy had given Cap a good hard shove and Cap had spilled his guts about everything. McGee was scheduled to fly out of Andrews tomorrow afternoon; now Cap told him that he, Rainbird, was going tomorrow morning. McGee was using Cap to get him safely out of the way first. He was—

'Rainbird? Are you there?'

'I'm here,' he said. 'Can you send someone else? I feel pretty punky, Cap.'

'No one I trust as well as you,' Cap replied. 'This stuff is dynamite. We wouldn't want . . . any snake in the grass to . . . to get it.'

'Did you say "snakes"?' Rainbird asked.

'Yes! Snakes!' Cap fairly screamed.

McGee had pushed him, all right, and some sort of slow-motion avalanche was going on inside of Cap Hollister.

Rainbird suddenly had the feeling – no, the intuitive certainty– that if he refused Cap and just kept hammering away, Cap would blow up . . . the way Pynchot had blown up.

Did he want to do that?

He decided he did not.

'All right,' he said. 'I'll be on the plane. Oh-seven-hundred. And all the goddam antibiotics I can swallow. You're a bastard, Cap.'

'I can prove my parentage beyond a shadow of a doubt,' Cap said, but the badinage was forced and hollow. He sounded relieved and shaky.

'Yeah, I'll bet.'

'Maybe you'll get in a round of golf while you're out there.'

'I don't play—' Golf. He had mentioned golf to Charlie as well – golf and snakes. Somehow those two things were part of the weird merry-go-round McGee had set in motion in Cap's brain. 'Yeah, maybe I will,' he said.

'Get to Andrews by oh-six-thirty,' Cap said, 'and ask for Dick Folsom. He's Major Puckeridge's aide.'

'All right,' Rainbird said. He had no intention of being anywhere near Andrews Air Force Base tomorrow. 'Goodbye, Cap.'

He hung up, then sat on the bed. He pulled on his old desert boots and started planning.

18

HELLO COMPUTER/QUERY STATUS JOHN RAIN-BIRD 14222/ANDREW AFB (DC) TO SAN DIEGO (CA) FINAL DESTINATION/Q9
HELLO CAP/STATUS JOHN RAINBIRD14222/ ANDREWS (DC) TO SAN DIEGO (CA) FINAL DESTINATION/LEAVES ANDREWS AFB 0700 HRS EST/STATUS OK/BREAK

433

Computers are children, Rainbird thought, reading this message. He had simply punched in Cap's new code – which Cap would have been stunned to know he had – and as far as the computer was concerned, he was Cap. He began to whistle tunelessly. It was just after sunset, and the Shop moved somnolently along the channels of routine.

FILE TOP SECRET
CODE PLEASE
CODE 19180
CODE 19180, the computer returned. **READY TO FILE TOP SECRET**

Rainbird hesitated only briefly and then tapped **FILE/JOHN RAINBIRD 14222/ANDREWS (DC) TO SAN DIEGO (CA) FINAL DESTINATION/ CANCEL/CANCEL/CANCEL F9 (19180)**
FILED

Then, using the code book, Rainbird told the computer whom to inform of the cancellation: Victor Puckeridge and his aide, Richard Folsom. These new instructions would be in the midnight telex to Andrews, and the plane on which he was to hitch a ride would simply take off without him. No one would know a thing, including Cap.

600 GOODBYE COMPUTER 600
604 GOODBYE CAP 604

Rainbird pushed back from the keyboard. It would be perfectly possible to put a stop to the whole thing tonight, of course. But that would not be conclusive. The computer would back him up to a certain degree, but computer probabilities do not butter any bread. Better to stop them after the thing had begun, with everything hanging out. More amusing, too.

The whole thing was amusing. While they had been watching the girl, the man had regained his ability or had successfully hidden it from them all along. He was likely

434

ditching his medication. Now he was running Cap as well, which means that he was only one step away from running the organization that had taken him prisoner in the first place. It really was quite funny; Rainbird had learned that endgames often were.

He didn't know exactly what McGee had planned, but he could guess. They would go to Andrews, all right, only Charlie would be with them. Cap could get her off the Shop grounds without much trouble – Cap and probably no one else on earth. They would go to Andrews, but not to Hawaii. It might be that Andy had planned for them to disappear into Washington, D.C. Or maybe they would get off the plane at Durban and Cap would be programmed to ask for a staff car. In that case it would be Shytown they would disappear into – only to reappear in screaming Chicago *Tribune* headlines a few days later.

He had played briefly with the idea of not standing in their way at all. That would be amusing, too. He guessed that Cap would end up in a mental institution, raving about golf clubs and snakes in the grass, or dead by his own hand. As for the Shop: might as well imagine what would happen to an anthill with a quart jar of nitroglycerine planted beneath it. Rainbird guessed that no more than five months after the press got its first whiff of the Strange Ordeal of the Andrew McGee Family, the Shop would cease to exist. He felt no fealty to the Shop and never had. He was his own man, crippled soldier of fortune, copper-skinned angel of death, and the status quo here didn't mean bullrag in a pasture to him. It was not the Shop that owned his loyalty at this point.

It was Charlie.

The two of them had an appointment. He was going to look into her eyes, and she was going to look into his . . . and it might well be that they would step out together, in flames. The fact that he might be saving the world from some almost

435

unimaginable armageddon by killing her had not played a part in his calculations, either. He owed the world no more fealty than he did the Shop. It was the world as much as the Shop that had cast him rootless from a closed desert society that might have been his only salvation . . . or, lacking that, have turned him into a harmless Sterno-guzzling Injun Joe pumping gas at a 76 station or selling fake kachina dolls at a shitty little roadside stand somewhere along the highway between Flagstaff and Phoenix.

But Charlie, Charlie!

They had been locked in a long waltz of death since that endless night of darkness during the power blackout. What he had only suspected that early morning in Washington when he had done Wanless had developed into an irrefutable certainty: the girl was his. But it would be an act of love, not of destruction, because the converse was almost certainly true as well.

It was acceptable. In many ways he wanted to die. And to die at her hands, in her flames, would be an act of contrition . . . and possibly of absolution.

Once she and her father were together again, she would become a loaded gun . . . no, a loaded flamethrower.

He would watch her and he would let the two of them get together. What would happen then? Who knew?

And wouldn't knowing spoil the fun?

19

That night Rainbird went to Washington and found a hungry lawyer who worked late hours. To this lawyer he gave three hundred dollars in small bills. And in the lawyer's office, John Rainbird neatened his few affairs in order to be ready for the next day.

Firestarter

1

At six o'clock on Wednesday morning, Charlie McGee got up, took off her nightgown, and stepped into the shower. She washed her body and her hair, then turned the water to cold and stood shivering under the spray for a minute more. She toweled dry and then dressed carefully – cotton underpants, silk slip, dark-blue knee socks, her denim jumper. She finished by putting on her scuffed and comfortable loafers.

She hadn't thought she would be able to sleep at all last night; she had gone to bed full of fear and nervous excitement. But she had slept. And dreamed incessantly not of Necromancer and the run through the woods but of her mother. That was peculiar, because she didn't think of her mother as often as she used to; at times her face seemed misty and distant in her memory, like a faded photograph. But in her dreams of last night, her mother's face – her laughing eyes, her warm, generous mouth – had been so clear that Charlie might last have seen her just the day before.

Now, dressed and ready for the day, some of the unnatural lines of strain had gone out of her face and she seemed calm. On the wall beside the door leading into the kitchenette there was a call button and a speaker grille set into a brushed-chrome plate just below the light switch. She pressed the button now.

'Yes, Charlie?'

She knew the owner of the voice only as Mike. At seven

437

o'clock – about half an hour from now – Mike went off and Louis came on. 'I want to go out to the stables this afternoon,' she said, 'and see Necromancer. Will you tell someone?'

'I'll leave a note for Dr Hockstetter, Charlie.'

'Thank you.' She paused, just for a moment. You got to know their voices. Mike, Louis, Gary. You got pictures of how they must look in your mind, the way you got pictures of how the DJs you heard on the radio must look. You got to like them. She suddenly realized that she would almost certainly never talk to Mike again.

'Was there something else, Charlie?'

'No, Mike. Have . . . have a good day.'

'Why, thank you, Charlie.' Mike sounded both surprised and pleased. 'You too.'

She turned on the TV and tuned to a cartoon show that came on every morning over the cable. Popeye was inhaling spinach through his pipe and getting ready to beat the sauce out of Bluto. One o'clock seemed an age away.

What if Dr Hockstetter said, she couldn't go out?

On the TV screen, they were showing a cutaway view of Popeye's muscles. There were about sixteen turbine engines in each one.

He better not say that. He better not. Because I'm going. One way or the other, I'm going.

2

Andy's rest hadn't been as easy or as healing as his daughter's. He had tossed and turned, sometimes dozing, then starting out of the doze just as it began to deepen because the terrible leading edge of some nightmare touched his mind. The only one he could remember was Charlie staggering down the aisle between the stalls in the

438

stable, her head gone and red-blue flames spouting from her neck instead of blood.

He had meant to stay in bed until seven o'clock, but when the digital face of the clock beside the bed got to 6:15, he could wait no longer. He swung out and headed for the shower.

Last night at just past nine, Pynchot's former assistant, Dr Nutter, had come in with Andy's walking papers. Nutter, a tall, balding man in his late fifties, was bumbling and avuncular. Sorry to be losing you; hope you enjoy your stay in Hawaii; wish I was going with you, ha-ha; please sign this.

The paper Nutter wanted him to sign was a list of his few personal effects (including his keyring, Andy noticed with a nostalgic pang). He would be expected to inventory them once in Hawaii and initial another sheet that said that they had, indeed, been returned. They wanted him to sign a paper concerning his personal effects after they had murdered his wife, chased him and Charlie across half the country, and then kidnapped and held them prisoner: Andy found that darkly hilarious and Kafkaesque. *I sure wouldn't want to lose any of those keys*, he thought, scrawling his signature; *I might need one of them to open a bottle of soda with sometime, right, fellows?*

There was also a carbon of the Wednesday schedule, neatly initialed by Cap at the bottom of the page. They would be leaving at twelve-thirty, Cap picking Andy up at his quarters. He and Cap would proceed toward the eastern checkpoint, passing Parking Area C, where they would pick up an escort of two cars. They would then drive to Andrews and board the plane at approximately fifteen hundred hours. There would be one stop for refueling – at Durban Air Force Base, near Chicago.

All right, Andy thought. *Okay.*

He dressed and began to move about the apartment,

packing his clothes, shaving tackle, shoes, bedroom slippers. They had provided him with two Samsonite suitcases. He remembered to do it all slowly, moving with the careful concentration of a drugged man.

After he found out about Rainbird from Cap, his first thought had been a hope that he would meet him: it would be such a great pleasure to push the man who had shot Charlie with the tranquilizer dart and later betrayed her in even more terrible fashion, to put his gun to his temple and pull the trigger. But he no longer wanted to meet Rainbird. He wanted no surprises of any kind. The numb spots on his face had shrunk to pinpricks, but they were still there – a reminder that if he had to overuse the push, he would very likely kill himself.

He only wanted things to go off smoothly.

His few things were packed all too soon, leaving him with nothing to do but sit and wait. The thought that he would be seeing his daughter again soon was like a small coal of warmth in his brain.

To him too one o'clock seemed an age away.

3

Rainbird didn't sleep at all that night. He arrived back from Washington around five-thirty A.M., garaged his Cadillac, and sat at his kitchen table drinking cup after cup of coffee. He was waiting for a call from Andrews, and until that call came, he would not rest easy. It was still theoretically possible for Cap to have found out what he had done with the computer. McGee had messed up Cap Hollister pretty well, but it still did not pay to underestimate.

Around six-forty-five, the telephone rang. Rainbird set his coffee cup down, rose, went into the living room, and answered it. 'Rainbird here.'

'Rainbird? This is Dick Folsom at Andrews. Major Puckeridge's aide.'

'You woke me up, man,' Rainbird said. 'I hope you catch crabs as big as orange crates. That's an old Indian curse.'

'You've been scrubbed,' Folsom said. 'I guess you knew.'

'Yes, Cap called me himself last night.'

'I'm sorry,' Folsom said. 'It's standard operating procedure, that's all.'

'Well, you operated in standard fashion. Can I go back to sleep now?'

'Yeah. I envy you.'

Rainbird uttered the obligatory chuckle and hung up. He went back into the kitchen, picked up his coffee cup, went to the window, looked out, saw nothing.

Floating dreamily through his mind was the Prayer for the Dead.

4

Cap did not arrive in his office that morning until almost ten-thirty, an hour and a half later than usual. He had searched his small Vega from stem to stern before leaving the house. He had become sure during the night that the car was infested with snakes. The search had taken him twenty minutes – the need to make sure there were no rattlers or copperheads (or something even more sinister and exotic) nesting in the darkness of the trunk, dozing on the fugitive warmth of the engine block, curled up in the glove compartment. He had pushed the glove-compartment button with a broomhandle, not wanting to be too close in case some hissing horror should leap out at him, and when a map of Virginia tumbled out of the square hole in the dash, he had nearly screamed.

Then, halfway to the Shop, he had passed the Greenway

Golf Course and had pulled over onto the shoulder to watch with a dreamy sort of concentration as the golfers played through the eighth and ninth. Every time one of them sliced into the rough, he was barely able to restrain a compulsion to step out of the car and yell for them to beware of snakes in the tall grass.

At last the blare of a ten-wheeler's airhorn (he had parked with his lefthand wheels still on the pavement) had startled him out of his daze and he drove on.

His secretary greeted him with a pile of overnight telex cables, which Cap simply took without bothering to shuffle through them to see if there was anything hot enough to demand immediate attention. The girl at the desk was going over a number of requests and messages when she suddenly looked up at Cap curiously. Cap was paying no attention to her at all. He was gazing at the wide drawer near the top of her desk with a bemused expression on his face.

'Pardon me,' she said. She was still very much aware of being the new girl, even after all these months, of having replaced someone Cap had been close to. And perhaps had been sleeping with, she had sometimes speculated.

'Hmmmm?' He looked around at her at last. But the blankness did not leave his eyes. It was somehow shocking . . . like looking at the shuttered windows of a house reputed to be haunted.

She hesitated, then plunged. 'Cap, do you feel all right? You look . . . well, a little white.'

'I feel fine,' he said, and for a moment he was his old self, dispelling some of her doubts. His shoulders squared, his head came up, and the blankness left his eyes. 'Anybody who's going to Hawaii ought to feel fine, right?'

'Hawaii?' Gloria said doubtfully. It was news to her.

'Never mind these now,' Cap said, taking the message forms and interdepartmental memos and stuffing them all

442

together with the telex cables. 'I'll look at them later. Anything happening with either of the McGees?'

'One item,' she said. 'I was just getting to it. Mike Kellaher says she asked to go out to the stable this afternoon and see a horse—'

'Yes, that's fine,' Cap said.

'—and she buzzed back a little later to say she'd like to go out at quarter of one.'

'Fine, fine.'

'Will Mr Rainbird be taking her out?'

'Rainbird's on his way to San Diego,' Cap said with unmistakable satisfaction. 'I'll send a man to take her over.'

'All right. Will you want to see the . . .' She trailed off. Cap's eyes had wandered away from her and he appeared to be staring at the wide drawer again. It was partway open. It always was, per regulations. There was a gun in there. Gloria was a crack shot, just as Rachel before her had been.

'Cap, are you sure there's nothing wrong?'

'Ought to keep that shut,' Cap said. 'They like dark places. They like to crawl in and hide.'

'They?' she asked cautiously.

'Snakes,' Cap said, and marched into his office.

5

He sat behind his desk, the cables and messages in an untidy litter before him. They were forgotten. Everything was forgotten now except snakes, golf clubs, and what he was going to do at quarter of one. He would go down and see Andy McGee. He felt strongly that Andy would tell him what to do next. He felt strongly that Andy would make everything all right.

Beyond quarter of one this afternoon, everything in his life was a great funneling darkness.

He didn't mind. It was sort of a relief.

6

At quarter of ten, John Rainbird slipped into the small monitoring room near Charlie's quarters. Louis Tranter, a hugely fat man whose buttocks nearly overflowed the chair he sat in, was watching the monitors. The digital thermometer read a steady sixty-eight degrees. He looked over his shoulder when the door opened and his face tightened at the sight of Rainbird.

'I heard you were leaving town,' he said.

'Scrubbed,' Rainbird said. 'And you never saw me this morning at all, Louis.'

Louis looked at him doubtfully.

'You never saw me,' Rainbird repeated. 'After five this afternoon I don't give a shit. But until then, you never saw me. And if I hear you did, I'm going to come after you and cut me some blubber. Can you dig it?'

Louis Tranter paled noticeably. The Hostess Twinkie he had been eating dropped from his hand onto the slanted steel panel that housed the TV monitors and microphone pickup controls. It rolled down the slant and tumbled to the floor unheeded, leaving a trail of crumbs behind. Suddenly he wasn't a bit hungry. He had heard this guy was crazy, and now he was seeing that what he had heard was certainly true.

'I can dig it,' he said, whispering in the face of that weird grin and glittering one-eyed stare.

'Good,' Rainbird said, and advanced toward him. Louis shrank away from him, but Rainbird ignored him altogether for the moment and peered into one of the monitors. There was Charlie, looking pretty as a picture in her blue jumper. With a lover's eye, Rainbird noted that she had not braided her hair today; it lay loose and fine and lovely

444

over her neck and shoulders. She wasn't doing anything but sitting on the sofa. No book. No TV. She looked like a woman waiting for a bus.

Charlie, he thought admiringly, *I love you. I really do.*

'What's she got going for today?' Rainbird asked.

'Nothing much,' Louis said eagerly. He was, in fact, nearly babbling. 'Just going out at quarter of one to curry that horse she rides. We're getting another test out of her tomorrow.'

'Tomorrow, huh?'

'Yep.' Louis didn't give a tin shit about the tests one way or the other, but he thought it would please Rainbird, and maybe Rainbird would leave.

He seemed to be pleased. His grin reappeared.

'She's going out to the stables at quarter of one, huh?'

'Yeah.'

'Who's taking her? Since I'm on my way to San Diego?'

Louis uttered a highpitched, almost female giggle to show that this piece of wit was appreciated.

'Your buddy there. Don Jules.'

'He's no buddy of mine.'

'No, course he isn't,' Louis agreed quickly. 'He . . . he thought the orders were a little funny, but since they came right from Cap—'

'Funny? What did he think was funny about them?'

'Well, just to take her out and leave her there. Cap said the stable boys would keep an eye on her. But they don't know from nothing. Don seemed to think it would be taking a helluva—'

'Yeah, but he doesn't get paid to think. Does he, fatty?' He slapped Louis on the shoulder, hard. It made a sound like a minor thunderclap.

'No, course he doesn't,' Louis came back smartly. He was sweating now.

445

'See you later,' Rainbird said, and went to the door again.

'Leaving?' Louis was unable to disguise his relief.

Rainbird paused with his hand on the doorknob and looked back. 'What do you mean?' he said. 'I was never here.'

'No sir, never here,' Louis agreed hastily.

Rainbird nodded and slipped out. He closed the door behind him. Louis stared at the closed door for several seconds and then uttered a great and gusty sigh of relief. His armpits were humid and his white shirt was stuck to his back. A few moments later he picked up his fallen Twinkie, brushed it off, and began to eat it again. The girl was still sitting quietly, not doing anything. How Rainbird – *Rainbird* of all people – had got her to like him was a mystery to Louis Tranter.

7

At quarter to one, an eternity after Charlie had awakened, there was a brief buzz at her door, and Don Jules came in, wearing a baseball warmup jacket and old cord pants. He looked at her coldly and without much interest.

'C'mon,' he said.

Charlie went with him.

8

That day was cool and beautiful. At twelve-thirty Rainbird strolled slowly across the still-green lawn to the low, L-shaped stable with its dark-red paint – the color of drying blood – and its brisk white piping. Overhead, great fair-weather clouds marched slowly across the sky. A breeze tugged at his shirt.

If dying was required, this was a fine day for it.

446

Inside the stable, he located the head groom's office and went in. He showed his ID with its A-rating stamp.

'Yes, sir?' Drabble said.

'Clear this place,' Rainbird said. 'Everyone out. Five minutes.'

The groom did not argue or bumble, and if he paled a bit, his tan covered it. 'The horses too?'

'Just the people. Out the back.'

Rainbird had changed into fatigues – what they had sometimes called gook-shooters in Nam. The pants pockets were large, deep, and flapped. From one of these he now took a large handgun. The head groom looked at it with wise, unsurprised eyes. Rainbird held it loosely, pointed at the floor.

'Is there going to be trouble, sir?'

'There may be,' Rainbird said quietly. 'I don't really know. Go on, now, old man.'

'I hope no harm will come to the horses,' Drabble said.

Rainbird smiled then. He thought, *So will she.* He had seen her eyes when she was with the horses. And this place, with its bays of loose hay and its lofts of baled hay, with its dry wood all about, was a tinderbox with NO SMOKING signs posted everywhere.

It was a thin edge.

But, as the years had drawn on and he had become more and more careless of his life, he had walked thinner ones.

He walked back to the big double doors and looked out. No sign of anyone just yet. He turned away and began to walk between the stall doors, smelling the sweet, pungent, nostalgic aroma of horse.

He made sure all of the stalls were latched and locked.

He went back to the double doors again. Now someone was coming. Two figures. They were still on the far side of the duckpond, five minutes' walk away. Not Cap and Andy McGee. It was Don Jules and Charlie.

447

Come to me, Charlie, he thought tenderly. *Come to me now.*

He glanced around at the shadowed upper lofts for a moment and then went to the ladder – simple wooden rungs nailed to a support beam – and began to climb with lithe ease.

Three minutes later, Charlie and Don Jules stepped into the shadowed, empty coolness of the stable. They stood just inside the doors for a moment as their eyes adjusted to the dimness. The .357 Mag in Rainbird's hand had been modified to hold a silencer of Rainbird's own construction; it crouched over the muzzle like a strange black spider. It was not, as a matter of fact, a very silent silencer: it is nearly impossible to completely quiet a big handgun. When – if – he pulled the trigger, it would utter a husky bark the first time, a low report the second time, and then it would be mostly useless. Rainbird hoped not to have to use the gun at all, but now he brought it down with both hands and leveled it so that the silencer covered a small circle on Don Jules's chest.

Jules was looking around carefully.

'You can go now,' Charlie said.

'Hey!' Jules said, raising his voice and paying no attention to Charlie. Rainbird knew Jules. A book man. Follow each order to the letter and nobody could put you in hack. Keep your ass covered at all times. 'Hey, groom! Somebody! I got the kid here!'

'You can go now,' Charlie said again, and once more Jules ignored her.

'Come on,' he said, clamping a hand over Charlie's wrist. 'We got to find somebody.'

A bit regretfully, Rainbird prepared to shoot Don Jules. It could be worse; at least Jules would die by the book, and with his ass covered.

'I *said* you could go now,' Charlie said, and suddenly

448

Jules let go of her wrist. He didn't just let go; he pulled his hand away, the way you do when you've grabbed hold of something hot.

Rainbird watched this interesting development closely.

Jules had turned and was looking at Charlie. He was rubbing his wrist, but Rainbird was unable to see if there was a mark there or not.

'You get out of here,' Charlie said softly.

Jules reached under his coat and Rainbird once more prepared to shoot him. He wouldn't do it until the gun was clear of Jules's jacket and his intention to march her back to the house was obvious.

But the gun was only partway out when he dropped it to the barnboard floor with a cry. He took two steps backward, away from the girl, his eyes wide.

Charlie made a half turn away, as if Jules no longer interested her. There was a faucet protruding from the wall halfway up the long side of the *L*, and beneath it was a bucket half full of water.

Steam began to rise lazily from the bucket.

Rainbird didn't think Jules noticed that; his eyes were riveted on Charlie.

'Get out of here, you bastard,' she said, 'or I'll burn you up. I'll fry you.'

John Rainbird raised Charlie a silent cheer.

Jules stood looking at her, indecisive. At this moment, with his head down and slightly cocked, his eyes moving restlessly from side to side, he looked ratlike and dangerous. Rainbird was ready to back her play if she had to make one, but he hoped Jules would be sensible. The power had a way of getting out of control.

'Get out right now,' Charlie said. 'Go back where you came from. I'll be watching to see that you do. *Move! Get out of here!*'

The shrill anger in her voice decided him.

'Take it easy,' he said. 'Okay. But you got nowhere to go, girl. You got nothing but a hard way to go.'

As he spoke he was easing past her, then backing toward the door.

'I'll be watching,' Charlie said grimly. 'Don't you even turn around, you . . . you turd.'

Jules went out. He said something else, but Rainbird didn't catch it.

'Just *go!*' Charlie cried.

She stood in the double doorway, back to Rainbird, in a shower of drowsy afternoon sunlight, a small silhouette. Again his love for her came over him. This was the place of their appointment, then.

'Charlie,' he called down softly.

She stiffened and took a single step backward. She didn't turn around, but he could feel the sudden recognition and fury flooding through her, although it was visible only in the slow way that her shoulders came up.

'Charlie,' he called again. 'Hey, Charlie.'

'You!' she whispered. He barely caught it. Somewhere below him, a horse nickered softly.

'It's me,' he agreed. 'Charlie, it's been me all along.'

Now she did turn and swept the long side of the stable with her eyes. Rainbird saw her do this, but she didn't see him; he was behind a stack of bales, well out of sight in the shadowy second loft.

'Where are you?' she rasped. 'You tricked me! It was you! My daddy says it was you that time at Granther's!' Her hand had gone unconsciously to her throat, where he had laid in the dart. '*Where are you?*'

Ah, Charlie, wouldn't you like to know?

A horse whinnied; no quiet sound of contentment this, but one of sudden sharp fear. The cry was taken up by another horse. There was a heavy double thud as one of the thoroughbreds kicked at the latched door of his stall.

450

'*Where are you?*' she screamed again, and Rainbird felt the temperature suddenly begin to rise. Directly below him, one of the horses – Necromancer, perhaps – whinnied loudly, and it sounded like a woman screaming.

9

The door buzzer made its curt, rasping cry, and Cap Hollister stepped into Andy's apartment below the north plantation house. He was not the man he had been a year before. That man had been elderly but tough and hale and shrewd; that man had possessed a face you might expect to see crouching over the edge of a duck blind in November and holding a shotgun with easy authority. This man walked in a kind of distracted shamble. His hair, a strong iron gray a year ago, was now nearly white and baby-fine. His mouth twitched infirmly. But the greatest change was in his eyes, which seemed puzzled and somehow childlike; this expression would occasionally be broken by a shooting sideways glance that was suspicious and fearful and almost cringing. His hands hung loosely by his sides and the fingers twitched aimlessly. The echo had become a ricochet that was now bouncing around his brain with crazy, whistling, deadly velocity.

Andy McGee stood to meet him. He was dressed exactly as he had been on that day when he and Charlie had fled up Third Avenue in New York with the Shop sedan trailing behind them. The cord jacket was torn at the seam of the left shoulder now, and the brown twill pants were faded and seat-shiny.

The wait had been good for him. He felt that he had been able to make his peace with all of this. Not understanding, no. He felt he would never have that, even if he and Charlie somehow managed to beat the fantastic odds and get away and go on living. He could find no fatal flaw in his own character on which to blame this royal balls-up, no sin of the father that needed to be expiated upon his daughter. It wasn't wrong to need two hundred dollars or to participate in a controlled experiment, anymore than it was wrong to want to be free. *If I could get clear,* he thought, *I'd tell them this: teach your children, teach your babies, teach them well, they say they know what they are doing, and sometimes they do, but mostly they lie.*

But it was what it was, *n'est-ce pas?* One way or another they would at least have a run for their money. But that brought him no feeling of forgiveness or understanding for the people who had done this. In finding peace with himself, he had banked the fires of his hate for the faceless bureaucretins who had done this in the name of national security or whatever it was. Only they weren't faceless now: one of them stood before him, smiling and twitching and vacant. Andy felt no sympathy for Cap's state at all.

You brought it on yourself, chum.

'Hello, Andy,' Cap said. 'All ready?'

'Yes,' Andy said. 'Carry one of my bags, would you?'

Cap's vacuity was broken by one of those falsely shrewd glances. 'Have you checked them?' he barked. 'Checked them for snakes?'

Andy pushed – not hard. He wanted to save as much as he could for an emergency. 'Pick it up,' he said, gesturing at one of the two suitcases.

Cap walked over and picked it up. Andy grabbed the other one.

'Where's your car?'

'It's right outside,' Cap said. 'It's been brought around.'

'Will anyone check on us?' What he meant was *Will anyone try to stop us?*

'Why would they?' Cap asked, honestly surprised. 'I'm in charge.'

452

Andy had to be satisfied with that. 'We're going out,' he said, 'and we're going to put these bags in the trunk—'

'Trunk's okay,' Cap broke in. 'I checked it this morning.'

'—and then we're going to drive around to the stable and get my daughter. Any questions?'

'No,' Cap said.

'Fine. Let's go.'

They left the apartment and walked to the elevator. A few people moved up and down the hall on their own errands. They glanced cautiously at Cap and then looked away. The elevator took them up to the ballroom and Cap led the way down a long front hall.

Josie, the redhead who had been on the door the day Cap had ordered Al Steinowitz to Hastings Glen, had gone on to bigger and better things. Now a young, prematurely balding man sat there, frowning over a computer-programming text. He had a yellow felt-tip pen in one hand. He glanced up as they approached.

'Hello, Richard,' Cap said. 'Hitting the books?'

Richard laughed. 'They're hitting me is more like it.' He glanced at Andy curiously. Andy looked back noncommittally.

Cap slipped his thumb into a slot and something thumped. A green light shone on Richard's console.

'Destination?' Richard asked. He exchanged his felt-tip for a ball-point. It hovered over a small bound book.

'Stable,' Cap said briskly. 'We're going to pick up Andy's daughter and they are going to escape.'

'Andrews Air Force Base,' Andy countered, and pushed. Pain settled immediately into his head like a dull meat cleaver.

'Andrews AFB,' Richard agreed, and jotted it into the book, along with the time. 'Have a good day, gentlemen.'

They went out into breezy October sunshine. Cap's Vega was drawn up on the clean white crushed stone of the circular driveway. 'Give me your keys,' Andy said. Cap handed them over, Andy opened the trunk, and they stowed the luggage. Andy slammed the trunk and handed the keys back. 'Let's go.'

Cap drove them on a loop around the duckpond to the stables. As they went, Andy noticed a man in a baseball warmup jacket running across to the house they had just left, and he felt a tickle of unease. Cap parked in front of the open stable doors.

He reached for the keys and Andy slapped his hand lightly. 'No. Leave it running. Come on.' He got out of the car. His head was thudding, sending rhythmic pulses of pain deep into his brain, but it wasn't too bad yet. Not yet.

Cap got out, then stood, irresolute. 'I don't want to go in there,' he said. His eyes shifted back and forth wildly in their sockets. 'Too much dark. They like the dark. They hide. They bite.'

'There are no snakes,' Andy said, and pushed out lightly. It was enough to get Cap moving, but he didn't look very convinced. They walked into the stable.

For one wild, terrible moment Andy thought she wasn't there. The change from the light to shadow left his eyes momentarily helpless. It was hot and stuffy in here, and something had upset the horses; they were whinnying and kicking at their stalls. Andy could see nothing.

'Charlie?' he called, his voice cracked and urgent. *'Charlie?'*

'Daddy!' she called, and gladness shot through him – gladness that turned to dread when he heard the shrill fear in her voice. 'Daddy, don't come in! Don't come—'

'I think it's a little late for that,' a voice said from somewhere overhead.

10

'Charlie,' the voice had called down softly. It was somewhere overhead, but where? It seemed to come from everywhere.

The anger had gusted through her – anger that was fanned by the hideous unfairness of it, the way that it never ended, the way they had of being there at every turn, blocking every lunge for escape. Almost at once she felt *it* start to come up from inside her. *It* was always so much closer to the surface now . . . so much more eager to come bursting out. Like with the man who had brought her over. When he drew his gun, she had simply made it hot so he would drop it. He was lucky the bullets hadn't exploded right inside it.

Already she could feel the heat gathering inside her and beginning to radiate out as the weird battery or whatever it was turned on. She scanned the dark lofts overhead but couldn't spot him. There were too many stacks of bales. Too many shadows.

'I wouldn't, Charlie.' His voice was a little louder now, but still calm. It cut through the fog of rage and confusion.

'You ought to come down here?' Charlie cried loudly. She was trembling. 'You ought to come down before I decide to set everything on fire! I can do it!'

'I know you can,' the soft voice responded. It floated down from nowhere, everywhere. 'But if you do, you're going to burn up a lot of horses, Charlie. Can't you hear them?'

She could. Once he had called it to her attention, she could. They were nearly mad with fear, whinnying and battering at their latched doors. Necromancer was in one of those stalls.

Her breath caught in her throat. Again she saw the

trench of fire running across the Manders yard and the chickens exploding.

She turned toward the bucket of water again and was now badly frightened. The power was trembling on the edge of her ability to control it, and in another moment

(*back off!*)

it was going to blow loose

(*!BACK OFF!*)

and just go sky high.

(*!!BACK OFF, BACK OFF, DO YOU HEAR ME, BACK OFF!!*)

This time the half-full bucket did not just steam; it came to an instant, furious boil. A moment later the chrome faucet just over the bucket twisted twice, spun like a propeller, and then blew off the pipe jutting from the wall. The fixture flew the length of the stable like a rocket payload and caromed off the far wall. Water gushed from the pipe. Cold water; she could *feel* its coldness. But moments after the water spurted out it turned to steam and a hazy mist filled the corridor between the stalls. A coiled green hose that hung on a peg next to the pipe had fused its plastic loops.

(*BACK OFF!*)

She began to get control of it again and pull it down. A year ago she would have been incapable of that; the thing would have had to run its own destructive course. She was able to hold on better now . . . ah, but there was so much more to control!

She stood there, shivering.

'What more do you want?' she asked in a low voice. 'Why can't you just let us go?'

A horse whinnied, high and frightened. Charlie understood exactly how it felt.

'No one thinks you can just be let go,' Rainbird's quiet voice answered. 'I don't think even your father thinks so.

456

You're dangerous, Charlie. And you know it. We could let you go and the next men that grabbed you might be Russians, or North Koreans, maybe even the Heathen Chinese. You may think I'm kidding, but I'm not.'

'That's not my fault!' she cried.

'No,' Rainbird said meditatively. 'Of course it isn't. But it's all bullshit anyway. I don't care about the Z factor, Charlie. I never did. I only care about you.'

'*Oh, you liar!*' Charlie screamed shrilly. 'You tricked me, pretended to be something you weren't—'

She stopped. Rainbird climbed easily over a low pile of bales, then sat down on the edge of the loft with his feet dangling down. The pistol was in his lap. His face was like a ruined moon above her.

'Lied to you? No. I mixed up the truth, Charlie, that's all I ever did. And I did it to keep you alive.'

'Dirty liar,' she whispered, but was dismayed to find that she *wanted* to believe him; the sting of tears began behind her eyes. She was so tired and she wanted to believe him, wanted to believe he had liked her.

'You weren't testing,' Rainbird said. 'Your old man wasn't testing, either. What were they going to do? Say "Oh, sorry, we made a mistake" and put you back on the street? You've seen these guys at work, Charlie. You saw them shoot that guy Manders in Hastings Glen. They pulled out your own mother's fingernails and then k—'

'*Stop it!*' she screamed in agony, and the power stirred again, restlessly close to the surface.

'No, I won't,' he said. 'Time you had the truth, Charlie. I got you going. I made you important to them. You think I did it because it's my job? The fuck I did. They're assholes. Cap, Hockstetter, Pynchot, that guy Jules who brought you over here – they're all assholes.'

She stared up at him, as if hypnotized by his hovering face. He was not wearing his eyepatch, and the place where

457

his eye had been was a twisted, slitted hollow, like a memory of horror.

'I didn't lie to you about this,' he said, and touched his face. His fingers moved lightly, almost lovingly, up the scars gored in the side of his chin to his flayed cheek to the burned-out socket itself. 'I mixed up the truth, yeah. There was no Hanoi Rathole, no Cong. My own guys did it. Because they were assholes, like these guys.'

Charlie didn't understand, didn't know what he meant. Her mind was reeling. Didn't he know she could burn him to a crisp where he sat?

'None of this matters,' he said. 'Nothing except you and me. We've got to get straight with each other, Charlie. That's all I want. To be straight with you.'

And she sensed he was telling the truth – but that some darker truth lay just below his words. There was something he wasn't telling.

'Come on up,' he said, 'and let's talk this out.'

Yes, it was like hypnosis. And, in a way, it was like telepathy. Because even though she understood the shape of that dark truth, her feet began to move toward the loft ladder. It wasn't talking that he was talking about. It was ending. Ending the doubt, the misery, the fear . . . ending the temptation to make ever bigger fires until some awful end came of it. In his own twisted, mad way, he was talking about being her friend in a way no one else could be. And . . . yes, part of her wanted that. Part of her wanted an ending and a release.

So she began to move toward the ladder, and her hands were on the rungs when her father burst in.

'*Charlie?*' he called, and the spell broke.

Her hands left the rungs and terrible understanding spilled through her. She turned toward the door and saw him standing there. Her first thought

(*daddy you got fat!*)

passed through her mind and was gone so quickly she barely had a chance to recognize it. And fat or not, it was he; she would have known him anywhere, and her love for him spilled through her and swept away Rainbird's spell like mist. And the understanding was that whatever John Rainbird might mean to her, he meant only death for her father.

'Daddy!' she cried. 'Don't come in!'

A sudden wrinkle of irritation passed over Rainbird's face. The gun was no longer in his lap; it was pointed straight at the silhouette in the doorway.

'I think it's a little late for that,' he said.

There was a man standing beside her daddy. She thought it was that man they all called Cap. He was just standing there, his shoulders slumped as if they had been broken.

'Come in,' Rainbird said, and Andy came. 'Now stop.'

Andy stopped. Cap had followed him, a pace or two behind, as if the two of them were tied together. Cap's eyes shifted nervously back and forth in the stable's dimness.

'I know you can do it,' Rainbird said, and his voice became lighter, almost humorous. 'In fact, you can both do it. But, Mr McGee . . . Andy? May I call you Andy?'

'Anything you like,' her father said. His voice was calm.

'Andy, if you try using what you've got on me, I'm going to try to resist it just long enough to shoot your daughter. And, of course, Charlie, if you try using what you've got on me, who knows what will happen?'

Charlie ran to her father. She pressed her face against the rough wale of his corduroy jacket.

'Daddy, Daddy,' she whispered hoarsely.

'Hi, cookie,' he said, and stroked her hair. He held her, then looked up at Rainbird. Sitting there on the edge of the loft like a sailor on a mast, he was the one-eyed pirate of Andy's dream to the life. 'So what now?' he asked Rainbird. He was aware that Rainbird could probably hold them here until the fellow he had seen running across the lawn brought back help, but somehow he didn't think that was what this man wanted.

Rainbird ignored his question. 'Charlie?' he said.

Charlie shuddered beneath Andy's hands but did not turn around.

'Charlie,' he said again, softly, insistently. 'Look at me, Charlie.'

Slowly, reluctantly, she turned around and looked up at him.

'Come on up here,' he said, 'like you were going to do. Nothing has changed. We'll finish our business and all of this will end.'

'No, I can't allow that,' Andy said, almost pleasantly. 'We're leaving.'

'Come up, Charlie,' Rainbird said, 'or I'm going to put a bullet into your father's head right now. You can burn me, but I'm betting I can pull this trigger before it happens.'

Charlie moaned deep in her throat like a hurt animal.

'Don't move, Charlie,' Andy said.

'He'll be fine,' Rainbird said. His voice was low, rational, persuasive. 'They'll send him to Hawaii and he'll be fine. You choose, Charlie. A bullet in the head for him or the golden sands there on Kalami Beach. Which is it going to be? You choose.'

460

Her blue eyes never leaving Rainbird's one, Charlie took a trembling step away from her father.

'Charlie!' he said sharply. 'No!'

'It'll be over,' Rainbird said. The barrel of the pistol was unwavering; it never left Andy's head. 'And that's what you want, isn't it? I'll make it gentle and I'll make it clean. Trust me, Charlie. Do it for your father and do it for yourself. Trust me.'

She took another step. And another.

'No,' Andy said. 'Don't listen to him, Charlie.'

But it was as if he had given her a reason to go. She walked to the ladder again. She put her hands on the rung just above her head and then paused. She looked up at Rainbird, and locked her gaze with his.

'*Do you promise he'll be all right?*'

'Yes,' Rainbird said, but Andy felt it suddenly and completely: the force of the lie . . . all his lies.

I'll have to push her, he thought with dumb amazement. *Not him, but her.*

He gathered himself to do it. She was already standing on the first rung, her hands grasping the next one over her head.

And that was when Cap – they had all forgotten him – began to scream.

12

When Don Jules got back to the building Cap and Andy had left only minutes before, he was so wild-looking that Richard, on door duty, grasped the gun inside his drawer.

'What—' he began.

'The alarm, the alarm!' Jules yelled.

'Do you have auth—'

'I've got all the authorization I need, you fucking twit! The girl! The girl's making a break for it!'

On Richard's console there were two simple combination-type dials, numbered from one to ten. Flustered, Richard dropped his pen and set the lefthand dial to a little past seven. Jules came around and set the righthand dial just past one. A moment later a low burring began to come from the console, a sound that was being repeated all over the Shop compound.

Groundskeepers were turning off their mowers and running for sheds where rifles were kept. The doors to the rooms where the vulnerable computer terminals were slid closed and locked. Gloria, Cap's secretary, produced her own handgun. All available Shop agents ran toward loudspeakers to await instructions, unbuttoning coats to free weapons. The charge in the outer fence went from its usual mild daytime tickle to killing voltage. The Dobermans in the run between the two fences heard the buzzing, sensed the change as the Shop geared up to battle status, and began to bark and leap hysterically. Gates between the Shop and the outside world slid shut and locked automatically. A bakery truck that had been servicing the commissary had its rear bumper chewed off by one sliding gate, and the driver was lucky to escape electrocution.

The buzz seemed endless, subliminal.

Jules grabbed the mike from Richard's console and said, 'Condition Bright Yellow. I say again, Condition Bright Yellow. No drill. Converge on stables; use caution.' He searched his mind for the code term assigned to Charlie McGee and couldn't come up with it. They changed the fucking things by the day, it seemed. 'It's the girl, and she's using it! Repeat, she's using it!'

13

Orv Jamieson was standing underneath the loudspeaker in the third-floor lounge of the north house, holding The Windsucker in one hand. When he heard Jules's message, he sat down abruptly and holstered it.

'Uh-uh,' he said to himself as the three others he had been shooting eight ball with ran out. 'Uh-uh, not me, count me out.' The others could run over there like hounds on a hot scent if they wanted to. They had not been at the Manders farm. They had not seen this particular third-grader in action.

What OJ wanted more than anything at that point in time was to find a deep hole and pull it over him.

14

Cap Hollister had heard very little of the three-way conversation between Charlie, her father, and Rainbird. He was on hold, his old orders completed, no new ones yet issued. The sounds of the talk flowed meaninglessly over his head and he was free to think of his golf game, and snakes, and nine irons, and boa constrictors, and mashies, and timber rattlers, and niblicks, and pythons big enough to swallow a goat whole. He did not like this place. It was full of loose hay that reminded him of the way the rough on a golf course smelled. It had been in the hay that his brother had been bitten by a snake when Cap himself was only three, it wasn't a very dangerous snake, but his big brother had *screamed*, he had *screamed*, and there had been the smell of hay, the smell of clover, the smell of timothy, and his big brother was the strongest, bravest boy in the world but now he was *screaming*, big, tough, nine-year-old Leon Hollister was *screaming* 'Go get *Daddy!*' and tears were running down his cheeks as he held his puffing leg between his hands and as three-year-old

Cap Hollister turned to do what his brother said, terrified and blubbering, it had slithered over his *foot*, his own *foot*, like deadly green water – and later the doctor had said the bite wasn't dangerous, that the snake must have bitten something else only a little while before and exhausted its poison sac, but Lennie thought he was *dying* and everywhere had been the sweet summer smell of grass and the hoppers were jumping, making their eternal *rickety-rickety* sound and spitting tobacco juice ('Spit and I'll let you go' had been the cry in those long-ago Nebraska days); good smells, good sounds, golf-course smells and sounds, and the *screaming* of his brother and the dry, scaly feel of the snake, looking down and seeing its flat, triangular head, its black eyes . . . the snake had slithered across Cap's foot on its way back into the high grass . . . back into the rough, you might say . . . and the smell had been like this . . . and he didn't like this place.

Four irons and adders and putters and copperheads—

Faster and faster now the ricochet bounded back and forth, and Cap's eyes moved vacuously around the shadowy stable while John Rainbird confronted the McGees. Eventually his eyes fixed upon the partially fused green plastic hose by the burst waterpipe. It hung in coils on its peg, still partially obscured by the last of the drifting steam.

Terror flashed up in him suddenly, as explosive as flames in an old blowdown. For a moment the terror was so great that he could not even breathe, let alone cry a warning. His muscles were frozen, locked.

Then they let go. Cap drew in a great lungful of breath in a convulsive, heaving lurch and let out an earsplitting, sudden scream. '*Snake! SNAKE! SNAAAYYYKE!*'

He did not run away. Even reduced as he was, it wasn't in Cap Hollister to run. He lurched forward like a rusty automaton and seized a rake that was leaning against the wall. It was a snake and he would beat it and break it and crush it. He would . . . would . . .

464

He would save Lennie!

He rushed at the partially fused hose, brandishing the rake.

Then things happened very fast.

15

The agents, most of them armed with handguns, and the gardeners, most of them with rifles, were converging on the low L-shaped stable in a rough circle when the screaming began. A moment later there was a heavy thudding sound and what might have been a muffled cry of pain. Only a second later there was a low ripping sound, then a muted report that was surely a silenced revolver.

The circle around the stable paused and then began to move inward once more.

16

Cap's scream and sudden dash for the rake only broke Rainbird's concentration for a moment, but a moment was enough. The gun jerked away from Andy's head toward Cap; it was an instinctive movement, the quick and alert shift of a hunting tiger in the jungle. And so it was that his keen instincts betrayed him and caused him to tumble off the thin edge he had walked so long.

Andy used the push just as quickly and just as instinctively. When the gun jerked toward Cap, he called up to Rainbird, 'Jump!' and pushed harder than he ever had in his life. The pain that ripped through his head like splintering shards of shrapnel was sickening in its force, and he felt something *give*, finally and irrevocably.

Blowout, he thought. The thought was thick and sludgy. He staggered back. The entire left side of his body had gone numb. His left leg no longer wanted to hold him.

465

(*it finally came it's a blowout damn thing finally let go*)

Rainbird pushed himself away from the edge of the over-head loft with one hard thrust of his arms. His face was almost comically surprised. He held onto his gun; even when he hit the floor badly and sprawled forward with a broken leg, he held onto the gun. He could not stifle a cry of pain and bewilderment, but he held onto the gun.

Cap had reached the green hose and was beating it wildly with the rake. His mouth worked, but no sound came out – only a fine spray of spit.

Rainbird looked up. His hair had fallen over his face. He jerked his head to flip it out of his line of sight. His one eye glimmered. His mouth was drawn down in a bitter line. He raised the gun and pointed it at Andy.

'No!' Charlie screamed. 'No!'

Rainbird fired, and smoke belched from the vents of the silencer. The bullet dug bright, fresh splinters beside Andy's lolling head. Rainbird braced one arm on the floor and fired again. Andy's head snapped viciously to the right, and blood flew from the left side of his neck in a flood.

'*No!*' Charlie screamed again, and clapped her hands to her face. '*Daddy! Daddy!*'

Rainbird's hand slid out from under him; long splinters whispered into the palm of his hand.

'Charlie,' he murmured. 'Charlie, look at me.'

17

They ringed the outside of the stable now and paused, uncertain of just how to handle this.

'The girl,' Jules said. 'We rub her—'

'*No!*' the girl screamed from inside, as if she had heard what Jules had planned. Then '*Daddy! Daddy!*'

Then there was another report, this one much louder, and a sudden, vicious flash that made them shade their eyes. A wave of heat rolled out of the open stable doors, and the men standing in front reeled back from it.

Smoke came next, smoke and the red glimmer of fire.

Somewhere inside that infant hell, horses began to scream.

18

Charlie ran for her father, her mind in a horrified whirl, and when Rainbird spoke, she did turn toward him. He was sprawled on his belly, trying to steady the gun with both hands.

Incredibly, he was smiling.

'There,' he croaked. 'So I can see your eyes. I love you, Charlie.'

And he fired.

The power leaped crazily out of her, totally out of control. On its way to Rainbird, it vaporized the chunk of lead that otherwise would have buried itself in her brain. For a moment it seemed that a high wind was rippling Rainbird's clothes— and those of Cap behind him— and that nothing else was happening. But it was not just clothes that were rippling; it was the flesh itself, rippling, running like tallow, and then being hurled off bones that were already charring and blackening and flaming.

There was a soundless flashgun sizzle of light that momentarily blinded her; she saw no more but could hear the horses in their stalls, going mad with fear . . . and she could smell smoke.

The horses! The horses! she thought, groping in the dazzle before her eyes. It was her dream. It was changed, but it was here. And suddenly, momentarily, she was back in the Albany airport, a little girl who had been two inches shorter and ten pounds lighter and ever so much more innocent, a little girl with a shopping bag scavenged from a wastecan, going from phonebooth to phonebooth, shoving at them, the silver cascading out of the coin returns. . . .

She shoved now, almost blindly, groping with her mind for what she needed to do.

A ripple ran along the doors of the stalls that formed the L's long side. The latches fell, smoking, to the board floor one after another, twisted out of shape by the heat.

The back of the stable had blown out in a tangle of smoking timbers and boards as the power passed Cap and Rainbird and bellowed onward, like something shot from a psychic cannon. The splintered shrapnel whistled for sixty yards or more in a widening fan, and those Shop agents who had been standing in its path might as well have been hit with a broadside blast of hot grapeshot. A fellow by the name of Clayton Braddock was nearly decapitated by a whirling slice of barnboard siding. The man next to him was cut in two by a beam that came whirling through the air like a runaway propeller. A third had an ear clipped off by a smoking chunk of wood and was not aware of it for nearly ten minutes.

The skirmish line of Shop agents dissolved. Those who could not run crawled. Only one man kept his position even momentarily. This was George Sedaka, the man who, in the company of Orv Jamieson, had hijacked Andy's letters in New Hampshire. Sedaka had only been laying over at the Shop compound before going on to Panama City. The man who had been on Sedaka's left was now lying on the ground, groaning. The man on Sedaka's right had been the unfortunate Clayton Braddock.

Sedaka himself was miraculously untouched. Splinters and hot shrapnel had flown all around him. A baling hook, sharp-edged and lethal, had buried itself in the earth less than four inches from his feet. It glowed a dull red.

The back of the stable looked as if half a dozen sticks of dynamite had gone off there. Tumbled, burning beams framed a blackened hole that was perhaps twenty-five feet

468

across. A large compost heap had absorbed the bulk of Charlie's extraordinary force when it made its explosive exit; it was now in flames, and what remained of the rear of the stable was catching.

Sedaka could hear horses whinnying and screaming inside, could see the lurid red-orange gleam of fire as the flames raced into the lofts full of dry hay. It was like looking through a porthole into Sheol.

Sedaka suddenly decided he wanted no more of this.

It was a little heavier than sticking up unarmed mailmen on back-country roads.

George Sedaka reholstered his pistol and took to his heels.

19

She was still groping, unable to grasp all that had happened. '*Daddy!*' she screamed. '*Daddy! Daddy!*'

Everything was blurred, ghostly. The air was full of hot, choking smoke and red flashes. The horses were still battering at their stall doors, but now the doors, latchless, were swinging open. Some of the horses, at least, had been able to back out.

Charlie fell to her knees, feeling for her father, and the horses began to flash past her on their way out, little more than dim, dreamlike shapes. Overhead, a flaming rafter fell in a shower of sparks and ignited the loose hay in one of the lower bays. In the short side of the *L*, a thirty-gallon drum of tractor gas went up with a dull, coughing roar.

Flying hooves passed within scant inches of Charlie's head as she crawled with her hands out like a blind thing. Then one of the fleeing horses struck her a glancing blow and she fell backward. One of her hands found a shoe.

'Daddy?' she whimpered. 'Daddy?'

He was dead. She was sure he was dead. Everything was

dead; the world was flame; they had killed her mother and now they had killed her father.

Her sight was beginning to come back, but still everything was dim. Waves of heat pulsed over her. She felt her way up his leg, touched his belt, and then went lightly up his shirt until her fingers reached a damp, sticky patch. It was spreading. There she paused in horror, and she was unable to make her fingers go on.

'Daddy,' she whispered.

'Charlie?'

It was no more than a low, husky croak . . . but it was he. His hand found her face and tugged her weakly. 'Come here. Get . . . get close.'

She came to his side, and now his face swam out of the gray dazzle. The left side of it was pulled down in a grimace; his left eye was badly bloodshot, reminding her of that morning in Hastings Glen when they woke up in that motel.

'Daddy, look at this mess,' Charlie groaned, and began to cry.

'No time,' he said. 'Listen. Listen, Charlie!'

She bent over him, her tears wetting his face.

'This was coming, Charlie. . . . Don't waste your tears on me. But—'

'No! No!'

'Charlie, shut up!' he said roughly. 'They're going to want to kill you now. You understand? No . . . no more games. Gloves off.' He pronounced it 'glubs' from the corner of his cruelly twisted mouth. 'Don't let them, Charlie. And don't let them cover it up. Don't let them say . . . just a fire . . .'

He had raised his head slightly and now he lay back, panting. From outside, dim over the hungry crackle of the fire, came the faint and unimportant pop of guns . . . and once more the scream of horses.

'Daddy, don't talk . . . rest . . .'

'No. Time.' Using his right arm, he was able to get partway

470

up again to confront her. Blood trickled from both corners of his mouth. 'You have got to get away if you can, Charlie.' She wiped the blood away with the hem of her jumper. From behind, the fire baked into her. 'Get away if you can. If you have to kill the ones in your way, Charlie, do it. It's a war. Make them know they've been in a war.' His voice was failing now. 'You get away if you can, Charlie. Do it for me. Do you understand?'

She nodded.

Overhead, near the back, another rafter let go in a flaming Catherine wheel of orange-yellow sparks. Now the heat rushed out at them as if from an open furnace flue. Sparks lit on her skin and winked out like hungry, biting insects.

'Make it' – he coughed up thick blood and forced the words out – 'make it so they can never do anything like this again. Burn it down, Charlie. *Burn it all down.*'

'Daddy—'

'Go on, now. Before it all goes up.'

'I can't leave you,' she said in a shaking, helpless voice.

He smiled and pulled her even closer, as if to whisper in her ear. But instead he kissed her.

'—love you, Ch—' he said, and died.

20

Don Jules had found himself in charge by default. He held on as long as he could after the fire started, convinced that the little girl would run out into their field of fire. When it didn't happen – and when the men in front of the stables began to catch their first glimpse of what had happened to the men behind it – he decided he could wait no longer, not if he wanted to hold them. He began to move forward, and the others came with him . . . but their faces were tight and set. They no longer looked like men on a turkey shoot.

Then shadows moved rapidly inside the double doors. She

471

was coming out. Guns came up: two men fired before anything at all came out. Then—

But it wasn't the girl; it was the horses, half a dozen of them, eight, ten, their coats flecked with foam, their eyes rolling and white-rimmed, mad with fear.

Jules's men, on hair trigger, opened fire. Even those who had held back, seeing that horses rather than humans were leaving the stable, seemed unable to hold back once their colleagues had begun firing. It was a slaughter. Two of the horses pitched forward to their knees, one of them whinnying miserably. Blood flew in the bright October air and slicked the grass.

'*Stop!*' Jules bawled. '*Stop, dammit! Stop shooting the fucking horses!*'

He might as well have been King Canute giving orders to the tide. The men – afraid of something they could not see, hyped by the alarm buzzer, the Bright Yellow alert, the fire that was now pluming thick black smoke at the sky, and the heavy *ka-whummm!* of the exploding tractor-gas – finally had moving targets to shoot at . . . and they were shooting.

Two of the horses lay dead on the grass. Another lay half on and half off the crushed-stone driveway, sides heaving rapidly. Three more, crazed with fear, veered to the left and made at the four or five men spread there. They gave way, still shooting, but one of the men tripped over his own feet and was trampled, screaming.

'*Quit it!*' Jules screamed. '*Quit it! Cease – cease firing! Goddammit, cease firing, you assholes!*'

But the slaughter went on. Men were reloading with strange, blank expressions on their faces. Many of them, like Rainbird, were veterans of the Vietnam war, and their faces wore the dull, twisted-rag expressions of men reliving an old nightmare at lunatic intensity. A few others had quit firing, but they were a minority. Five horses lay wounded or dead on the grass and in the driveway. A few others had run away,

472

and Necromancer was among these, his tail waving like a battle flag.

'The girl!' someone screamed, pointing at the stable doors. '*The girl!*'

It was too late. The slaughter of the horses had barely ended and their attention was divided. By the time they swung back toward where Charlie stood with her head down, small and deadly in her denim jumper and dark-blue knee socks, the trenches of fire had already begun to radiate from her toward them, like strands of some deadly spider's web.

21

Charlie was submerged in the power again, and it was a relief.

The loss of her father, as keen and sharp as a stiletto, receded and became no more than a numb ache.

As always, the power drew her, like some fascinating and awful toy whose full range of possibilities still awaited discovery.

Trenches of fire raced across the grass toward the ragged line of men.

You killed the horses, you bastards, she thought, and her father's voice echoed, as if in agreement: *If you have to kill the ones in your way, Charlie, do it. It's a war. Make them know they've been in a war.*

Yes, she decided, she would make them know they had been in a war.

Some of the men were breaking and running now. She skewed one of the lines of fire to the right with a mild twist of her head and three of them were engulfed, their clothes becoming so many flaming rags. They fell to the ground, convulsed and screaming.

Something buzzed by her head, and something else

473

printed thin fire across her wrist. It was Jules, who had got another gun from Richard's station. He stood there, legs spread, gun out, shooting at her.

Charlie pushed out at him: one hard, pumping bolt of force.

Jules was thrown backward so suddenly and with such force that the wrecking ball of a great invisible crane might have struck him. He flew forty feet, not a man anymore but a boiling ball of fire.

Then they all broke and ran. They ran the way they had run at the Manders farm.

Good thing, she thought. *Good thing for you.*

She did not want to kill people. That had not changed. What had changed was that she'd kill them if she had to. If they stood in her way.

She began to walk toward the nearer of the two houses, which stood a little distance in front of a barn as perfect as the picture on a country calendar and facing its mate across the expanse of lawn.

Windows broke like gunshots. The ivy trellis climbing the east side of the house shuddered and then burst into arteries of fire. The paint smoked, then bubbled, then flamed. Fire ran up onto the roof like grasping hands.

One of the doors burst open, letting out the whooping, panicked bray of a fire alarm and two dozen secretaries, technicians, and analysts. They ran across the lawn toward the fence, veered away from the deaths of electricity and yapping, leaping dogs, and then milled like frightened sheep. The power wanted to go out toward them but she turned it away from them and onto the fence itself, making the neat chain-link diamonds droop and run and weep molten-metal tears. There was a low thrumming sound, a low-key *zapping* sound as the fence overloaded and then began to short out in segment after segment. Blinding purple sparks leaped up. Small fireballs began to jump from the top of the

474

fence, and white porcelain conductors exploded like clay ducks in a shooting gallery.

The dogs were going mad now. Their coats stood out in crazy spikes and they raced back and forth like banshees between the inner and outer fences. One of them caromed into the spitting high-voltage fence and went straight up in the air, its legs splayed stiffly. It came down in a smoking heap. Two of its mates attacked it with savage hysteria.

There was no barn behind the house where Charlie and her father had been held, but there was a long, low, perfectly maintained building that was also red barnboard trimmed with white. This building housed the Shop motor pool. Now the wide doors burst open and an armored Cadillac limousine with government plates raced out. The sunroof was open and a man's head and torso poked through it. Elbows braced on the roof, he began to fire a light submachine gun at Charlie. In front of her, firm turf spun away in ragged digs and divots.

Charlie turned toward the car and let the power loose in that direction. The power was still growing; it was turning into something that was lithe yet ponderous, an invisible something that now seemed to be feeding itself in a spiraling chain reaction of exponential force. The limo's gas tank exploded, enveloping the rear of the car and shooting the tailpipe into the sky like a javelin. But even before that happened the head and torso of the shooter were incinerated, the car's windshield had blown in, and the limousine's special self-sealing tires had begun to run like tallow.

The car continued on through its own ring of fire, plowing out of control, losing its original shape, melting into something that looked like a torpedo. It rolled over twice and a second explosion shook it.

Secretaries were fleeing from the other house now, running like ants. She could have swept them with fire – and a part of her *wanted* to – but with an effort of her waning

475

volition, she turned the power on the house itself, the house where the two of them had been kept against their will . . . the house where John had betrayed her.

She sent the force out, all of it. For just a moment it seemed that nothing at all was happening; there was a faint shimmer in the air, like the shimmer above a barbecue pit where the coals have been well banked . . . and then the entire house exploded.

The only clear image she was left with (and later, the testimony of the survivors repeated it several times) was that of the chimney of the house rising into the sky like a brick rocketship, seemingly intact, while beneath it the twenty-five-room house disintegrated like a little girl's cardboard playhouse in the flame of a blowtorch. Stone, lengths of board, planks, rose into the air and flew away on the hot dragon breath of Charlie's force. An IBM typewriter, melted and twisted into something that looked like a green steel dishrag tied in a knot, whirled up into the sky and crashed down between the two fences, digging a crater. A secretary's chair, the swivel seat whirling madly, was flung out of sight with the speed of a bolt shot from a crossbow.

Heat baked across the lawn at Charlie.

She looked around for something else to destroy. Smoke rose to the sky now from several sources – from the two graceful antebellum homes (only one of them still recognizable as a home now), from the stable, from what had been the limousine. Even out here in the open, the heat was becoming intense.

And still the power spun and spun, wanting to be sent out, *needing* to be sent out, lest it collapse back on its source and destroy it.

Charlie had no idea what unimaginable thing might eventually have happened. But when she turned back to the fence and the road leading out of the Shop compound, she saw people throwing themselves against the fence in a blind frenzy of panic. In some places the fence was shorted out and they had been able to climb over. The dogs had got one of them, a young woman in a yellow gaucho skirt who was screaming horribly. And as clearly as if he had still been alive and standing next to her, Charlie heard her father cry: *Enough, Charlie! It's enough! Stop while you still can!*

But could she?

Turning away from the fence, she searched desperately for what she needed, fending off the power at the same time, trying to hold it balanced and suspended. It began to scrawl directionless, crazy spirals across the grass in a widening pattern.

Nothing. Nothing except—

The duckpond.

22

OJ was getting out, and no dogs were going to stop him.

He had fled the house when the others began to converge on the stable. He was very frightened but not quite panicked enough to charge the electrified fence after the gates automatically slid shut on their tracks. He had watched the entire holocaust from behind the thick, gnarled trunk of an old elm. When the little girl shorted the fence, he waited until she had moved on a little way and turned her attention to the destruction of the house. Then he ran for the fence, The Windsucker in his right hand.

When one section of the fence was dead, he climbed over it and let himself down into the dog run. Two of them came for him. He grasped his right wrist with his left hand and shot them both. They were big bastards, but The Windsucker was bigger. They were all done eating Gravy Train, unless they served the stuff up in doggy heaven.

A third dog got him from behind, tore out the seat of his pants and a good chunk of his left buttock, knocked him to the ground. OJ turned over and grappled with it one-handed, holding The Windsucker with the other. He clubbed it with the butt of the gun, and then thrust forward with the muzzle when the dog came for his throat. The muzzle slid neatly between the Doberman's jaws and OJ pulled the trigger. The report was muffled.

'Cranberry sauce!' OJ cried, getting shakily to his feet. He began to laugh hysterically. The outer gate was not electrified any longer; even its weak keeper charge had shorted out. OJ tried to open it. Already other people were crowding and jouncing him. The dogs that were left had backed away, snarling. Some of the other surviving agents also had their guns out and were taking potshots at them. Enough discipline had returned so that those with guns stood in a rough perimeter around the unarmed secretaries, analysts and technicians.

OJ threw his whole weight against the gate. It would not open. It had locked shut along with everything else. OJ looked around, not sure what to do next. Sanity of a sort had returned; it was one thing to cut and run when you were by yourself and unobserved, but now there were too many witnesses around.

If that hellacious kid left any witnesses.

'You'll have to climb over it!' he shouted. His voice was lost in the general confusion. *'Climb over, goddammit!'* No response. They only crowded against the outer fence, their faces dumb and shiny with panic.

OJ grabbed a woman huddled against the gate next to him. *'Nooooo!'* she screamed.

'Climb, you cunt!' OJ roared, and goosed her to get her going. She began to climb.

Others saw her and began to get the idea. The inner fence was still smoking and spitting sparks in places; a fat man OJ recognized as one of the commissary cooks was holding onto roughly two thousand volts. He was jittering and jiving, his feet doing a fast boogaloo in the grass, his mouth open, his cheeks turning black.

Another one of the Dobermans lunged forward and tore a chunk from the leg of a skinny, bespectacled young man in a lab coat. One of the other agents snapped a shot at the dog, missed, and shattered the bespectacled young man's elbow. The young lab technician fell on the ground and began rolling around, clutching his elbow and screaming for the Blessed Virgin to help him. OJ shot the dog before it could tear the young man's throat out.

What a fuckup, he groaned inside. Oh dear God, what a fuckup.

Now there were maybe a dozen of them climbing the wide gate. The woman OJ had set in motion reached the top, tottered, and fell over on the outside with a strangled cry. She began to shriek immediately. The gate was high; it had been a nine-foot drop; she had landed wrong and broken her arm.

Oh Jesus Christ, what a fuckup.

Clawing their way up the gate, they looked like a lunatic's vision of training exercises at Marine bootcamp.

OJ craned back, trying to see the kid, trying to see if she was coming for them. If she was, the witnesses could take care of themselves; he was up over that gate and gone.

Then one of the analysts yelled, 'What in the name of *God*–'

The hissing sound rose immediately, drowning out his voice. OJ would say later that the first thing he thought of was his grandmother frying eggs, only this sound was a million times louder than that, as if a tribe of giants had all decided to fry eggs at once.

It swelled and grew, and suddenly the duckpond between the two houses was obscured in rising white steam. The whole pond, roughly fifty feet across and four feet deep at its center, was boiling.

479

For a moment OJ could see Charlie, standing about twenty yards from the pond, her back to those of them still struggling to get out, and then she was lost in the steam. The hissing sound went on and on. White fog drifted across the green lawn, and the bright autumn sun cast crazy arcs of rainbow in the cottony moisture. The cloud of steam billowed and drifted. Would-be escapees hung onto the fence in. flies, their heads craned back over their shoulders, wა hing.

What if there isn't enough water? OJ thought suddenly. What if there isn't enough to put out her match or torch or whatever the hell it is? What happens then?

Orville Jamieson decided he didn't want to stick around to find out. He'd had enough of the hero bit. He jammed The Windsucker back into its shoulder holster and went up the gate at what was nearly a run. At the top he vaulted over neatly and landed in a flexed crouch near the woman who was still holding her broken arm and screaming.

'I advise you to save your breath and get the hell out of here,' OJ told her, and promptly took his own advice.

23

Charlie stood in her own world of white, feeding her power into the duckpond, grappling with it, trying to bring it down, to make it have done. Its vitality seemed endless. She had it under control now, yes; it fed smoothly into the pond as if through an invisible length of pipe. But what would happen if all the water boiled away before she could disrupt its force and disperse it?

No more destruction. She would let it fall back in on herself and destroy her before she allowed it to range out and begin feeding itself again.

(*Back off! Back off!*)

Now, at last, she could feel it losing some of its urgency,

its . . . its ability to stick together. It was falling apart. Thick white steam everywhere, and the smell of laundries. The giant bubbling hiss of the pond she could no longer see.

(*!!BACK OFF!!*)

She thought dimly of her father again, and fresh grief sliced into her: dead; he was dead; the thought seemed to diffuse the power still more, and now, at last, the hissing noise began to fade. The steam rolled majestically past her. Overhead, the sun was a tarnished silver coin.

I changed the sun, she thought disjointedly, and then, *No – not really – it's the steam – the fog – it'll blow away—*

But with a sudden sureness that came from deep inside she knew that she *could* change the sun if she wanted to . . . in time.

The power was still growing.

This act of destruction, this apocalypse, had only approached its current limit.

The *potential* had hardly been tapped.

Charlie fell to her knees on the grass and began to cry, mourning her father, mourning the other people she had killed, even John. Perhaps what Rainbird had wanted for her would have been best, but even with her father dead and this rain of destruction on her head, she felt her response to life, a tough, mute grasping for survival.

And so, perhaps most of all, she mourned herself.

24

How long she sat on the grass with her head cradled in her arms she didn't know; as impossible as it seemed, she believed she might even have dozed. However long it was, when she came to herself she saw that the sun was brighter and a little more westerly in the sky. The steam of the boiling pond had been pulled to tatters by the light breeze and blown away.

481

Slowly, Charlie stood up and looked around.

The pond caught her eye first. She saw that it had been close . . . very close. Only puddles of water remained, flatly sheened with sunlight like bright glass gems set in the slick mud of the pond's bottom. Draggled lilypads and water-weeds lay here and there like corroded jewelry; already in places the mud was beginning to dry and crack. She saw a few coins in the mud, and a rusted thing that looked like a very long knife or perhaps a lawnmower blade. The grass all around the pond had been scorched black.

A deadly silence lay over the Shop compound, broken only by the brisk snap and crackle of the fire. Her father had told her to make them know they had been in a war, and what was left looked very much like an abandoned battleground. The stable, barn, and house on one side of the pond were burning furiously. All that remained of the house on the other side was smoky rubble; it was as if the place had been hit by a large incendiary bomb or a World War II V-rocket.

Blasted and blackened lines lay across the grass in all directions, making those idiot spiral patterns, still smoking. The armored limo had burned itself out at the end of a gouged trench of earth. It no longer resembled a car; it was only a meaningless hunk of junk.

The fence was the worst.

Bodies lay scattered along its inner perimeter, nearly half a dozen of them. In the space between there were two or three more bodies, plus a scattering of dead dogs.

As if in a dream, Charlie began walking in that direction.

Other people were moving on the lawn, but not many. Two of them saw her coming and shied away. The others seemed to have no conception of who she was and no knowledge that she had caused it all. They walked with the dreamy, portentous paces of shock-blasted survivors.

Charlie began to clamber up the inner fence.

'I wouldn't do that,' a man in orderly's whites called over conversationally. 'Dogs goan get you if you do that, girl.'

Charlie took no notice. The remaining dogs growled at her but did not come near; they, too, had had enough, it seemed. She climbed the outer gate, moving slowly and carefully, holding tight and poking the toes of her loafers into the diamond-shaped holes in the link. She reached the top, swung one leg over carefully, then the other. Then, moving with the same deliberation, she climbed down and, for the first time in half a year stepped onto ground that didn't belong to the Shop. For a moment she only stood there, as if in shock.

I'm free, she thought dully. *Free.*

In the distance, the sound of wailing sirens arose, drawing near.

The woman with the broken arm still sat on the grass, about twenty paces from the abandoned guardhouse. She looked like a fat child too weary to get up. There were white shock circles under her eyes. Her lips had a bluish tinge.

'Your arm,' Charlie said huskily.

The woman looked up at Charlie, and recognition came into her eyes. She began to scrabble away, whimpering with fear. 'Don't you come near me,' she hissed raggedly. 'All their tests! All their tests! I don't need no tests! You're a witch! A witch!'

Charlie stopped. 'Your arm,' she said. 'Please. Your arm. I'm sorry. Please?' Her lips were trembling again. It seemed to her now that the woman's panic, the way her eyes rolled, the way she unconsciously curled her lip up over her teeth – these were the worst things of all.

'Please!' she cried. 'I'm sorry! They killed my daddy!'

'Should have killed you as well,' the woman said, panting. 'Why don't you burn yourself up, if you're so sorry?'

Charlie took a step toward her and the woman moved away again, screaming as she fell over on her injured arm.

'Don't you come near me!'

483

And suddenly all of Charlie's hurt and grief and anger found its voice.

'*None of it was my fault!*' she screamed at the woman with the broken arm. '*None of it was my fault; they brought it on themselves, and I won't take the blame, and I won't kill myself! Do you hear me! Do you?*'

The woman cringed away, muttering.

The sirens were closer.

Charlie felt the power, surging up eagerly with her emotions.

She slammed it back down, made it gone.

(*and I won't do that either*)

She walked across the road, leaving the muttering, cringing woman behind. On the far side of the road was a field, thigh-high with hay and timothy, silver white with October, but still fragrant.

(*where am I going?*)

She didn't know yet.

But they were never going to catch her again.

Charlie Alone

1

The story appeared in fragments on the late television news that Wednesday night, but Americans were not greeted with the entire story until they rose the next morning. By then all the available data had been coordinated into what Americans really seem to mean when they say they want 'the news' – and what they really mean is 'Tell me a story' and make sure it has a beginning, a middle, and some kind of ending.

The story America got over its collective coffee cup, via *Today*, *Good Morning, America*, and *The CBS Morning News*, was this: There had been a terrorist firebomb attack at a top-secret scientific think tank in Longmont, Virginia. The terrorist group was not positively known yet, although three of them had already stepped forward to claim the credit – a group of Japanese Reds, the Khafadi splinter of Black September, and a domestic group who went by the rich and wonderful name of the Militant Midwest Weatherpeople.

Though no one was sure exactly who was behind the attack, the reports seemed quite clear on how it had been carried out. An agent named John Rainbird, an Indian and a Vietnam vet, had been a double agent who had planted the firebombs on behalf of the terrorist organization. He had either killed himself by accident or had committed suicide at the site of one of the firebombings, a stable. One source claimed that Rainbird had actually been overcome by heat and smoke while trying to drive the horses out of the burning stable; this occasioned the usual newscom irony about coldblooded terrorists who cared more for animals than they did for people. Twenty lives had been lost in the tragedy; forty-five people had been injured, ten of them seriously. The survivors had all been 'sequestered' by the government.

That was the story. The name of the Shop hardly surfaced at all. It was quite satisfactory.

Except for one dangling loose end.

2

'I don't care where she is,' the new head of the Shop said four weeks after the conflagration and Charlie's escape. Things had been in total confusion for the first ten days, when the girl might easily have been swept back into the Shop's net; they were still not back to normal. The new head sat behind a make-do desk; her own would not be delivered for another three days. 'And I don't care what she can do, either. She's an eight-year-old kid, not Superwoman. She can't stay out of sight long. I want her found and then I want her killed.'

She was speaking to a middle-aged man who looked like a small-town librarian. Needless to say, he was not.

He tapped a series of neat computer printouts on the head's desk. Cap's files had not survived the burning, but most of his information had been stored in the computer memory banks. 'What's the status of this?'

'The Lot Six proposals have been tabled indefinitely,' the head told him. 'It's all political, of course. Eleven old men, one young man, and three blue-haired old ladies who probably own stock in some Swiss goat-gland clinic . . . all of them with sweat under their balls about what would happen if the girl showed up. They—'

'I doubt very much if the senators from Idaho, Maine,

486

and Minnesota have any sweat under their balls,' the man who was not a librarian murmured.

The head shrugged it off. 'They're interested in Lot Six. Of course they are. I would describe the light as amber.' She began to play with her hair, which was long – a shaggy, handsome dark auburn. ' "Tabled indefinitely" means until we bring them the girl with a tag on her toe.'

'We must be Salome,' the man across the desk murmured. 'But the platter is yet empty.'

'What the fuck are you talking about?'

'Never mind,' he said. 'We seem to be back to square one.'

'Not exactly,' the head replied grimly. 'She doesn't have her father to watch out for her anymore. She's on her own. And I want her found. Quickly.'

'And if she spills her guts before we can find her?'

The head leaned back in Cap's chair and laced her hands behind her neck. The man who was not a librarian eyed appreciatively the way her sweater pulled taut across the rounds of her breasts. Cap had never been like this.

'If she were going to spill her guts, I think she would have by now.' She leaned forward again, and tapped the desk calendar. 'November fifth,' she said, 'and nothing. Meantime, I think we've taken all the reasonable precautions. The *Times*, the Washington *Post*, the Chicago *Tribune* . . . we're watching all the majors, but so far, nothing.'

'Suppose she decides to go to one of the minors? The Podunk *Times* instead of the New York *Times*? We can't watch every news organ in the country.'

'That is regrettably true,' the head agreed. 'But there has been nothing. Which means she has said nothing.'

'Would anyone really believe such a wild tale from an eight-year-old girl anyway?'

'If she lit a fire at the end of the story, I think that they might be disposed to,' the head answered. 'But shall I tell you what the computer says?' She smiled and tapped the sheets. 'The computer says there's an eighty-percent probability that we can bring the committee her dead body without lifting a finger . . . except to ID her.'

'Suicide?'

The head nodded. The prospect seemed to please her a great deal.

'That's nice,' the man who was not a librarian said, standing up. 'For my own part, I'll remember that the computer also said that Andrew McGee was almost certainly tipped over.'

The head's smile faltered a bit.

'Have a nice day, Chief,' the man who was not a librarian said, and strolled out.

3

On the same November day, a man in a flannel shirt, flannel pants, and high green boots stood chopping wood under a mellow white sky. On this mild day, the prospect of another winter still seemed distant; the temperature was an agreeable fifty degrees. The man's coat, which his wife had scolded him into wearing, hung over a fencepost. Behind him, stacked against the side of the old barn, was a spectacular drift of orange pumpkins – some of them starting to go punky now, sad to say.

The man put another log on the chopping block, slung the ax up, and brought it down. There was a satisfying thud, and two stove lengths fell to either side of the block. He was bending down to pick them up and toss them over with the others when a voice said from behind him: 'You got a new block, but the mark's still there, isn't it? It's still there.'

Startled, he turned around. What he saw caused him to step back involuntarily, knocking the ax to the ground,

488

where it lay across the deep, indelible mark in the earth. At first he thought it was a ghost he was looking at, some gruesome specter of a child risen from the Dartmouth Crossing graveyard three miles up the road. She stood, pallid and dirty and thin in the driveway, her eyes hollow and glistening in their sockets, her jumper ragged and torn. A scrape mark skidded up her right arm almost to the elbow. It looked infected. There were loafers on her feet, or what had once been loafers; now it was hard to tell.

And then, suddenly, he recognized her. It was the little girl from a year ago; she had called herself Roberta, and she had a flamethrower in her head.

'Bobbi?' he said. 'My sainted hat, is that Bobbi?'

'Yes, it's still right there,' she repeated as if she had not heard him, and he suddenly realized what the glisten in her eyes was: she was weeping.

'Bobbi,' he said, 'honey, what's the matter? Where's your dad?'

'Still there,' she said a third time, and then collapsed forward in a faint. Irv Manders was barely able to catch her. Cradling her, kneeling in the dirt of his dooryard, Irv Manders began to scream for his wife.

4

Dr Hofferitz arrived at dusk and was in the back bedroom with the girl for about twenty minutes. Irv and Norma Manders sat in the kitchen, doing more looking at their supper than eating. Every now and then, Norma would look at her husband, not accusingly but merely questioningly, and there was the drag of fear, not in her eyes but around them – the eyes of a woman fighting a tension headache or perhaps low-back pain.

The man named Tarkington had arrived the day after the great burning; he had come to the hospital where Irv

489

was being kept, and he had presented them with his card, which said only WHITNEY TARKINGTON   GOVERNMENT ADJUSTMENTS.

'You just want to get out of here,' Norma had said. Her lips were tight and white, and her eyes had that same look of pain they had now. She had pointed at her husband's arm, wrapped in bulky bandages; drains had been inserted, and they had been paining him considerably. Irv had told her he had gone through most of World War II with nothing much to show for it except a case of roaring hemorrhoids; it took being at home at his place in Hastings Glen to get shot up. 'You just want to get out,' Norma repeated.

But Irv, who had perhaps had more time to think, only said, 'Say what you have to, Tarkington.'

Tarkington had produced a check for thirty-five thousand dollars – not a government check but one drawn on the account of a large insurance company. Not one, however, that the Manderses did business with.

'We don't want your hush money,' Norma had said harshly, and reached for the call button over Irv's bed.

'I think you had better listen to me before you take any action you might regret later,' Whitney Tarkington had replied quietly and politely.

Norma looked at Irv, and Irv had nodded. Her hand fell away from the call button. Reluctantly.

Tarkington had a briefcase with him. Now he put it on his knees, opened it, and removed a file with the names MANDERS and BREEDLOVE written on the tab. Norma's eyes had widened, and her stomach began to twist and untwist. Breedlove was her maiden name. No one likes to see a government folder with his name on it; there is something terrible about the idea that tabs have been kept, perhaps secrets known.

Tarkington had talked for perhaps forty-five minutes in

490

a low, reasonable tone. He occasionally illustrated what he had to say with Xerox copies from the Manders/Breedlove file. Norma would scan these sheets with tight lips and then pass them on to Irv in his hospital bed.

We are in a national-security situation, Tarkington had said on that horrible evening. You must realize that. We don't enjoy doing this, but the simple fact is, you must be made to see reason. These are things you know very little about.

I know you tried to kill an unarmed man and his little girl, Irv had replied.

Tarkington had smiled coldly – a smile reserved for people who foolishly pretend to a knowledge of how the government works to protect its charges – and replied, You don't know what you saw or what it means. My job is not to convince you of that fact but only to try and convince you not to talk about it. Now, look here: this needn't be so painful. The check is tax-free. It will pay for repairs to your house and your hospital bills with a nice little sum left over. And a good deal of unpleasantness will be avoided.

Unpleasantness, Norma thought now, listening to Dr Hofferitz move around in the back bedroom and looking at her almost untouched supper. After Tarkington had gone, Irv had looked at her, and his mouth had been smiling, but his eyes had been sick and wounded. He told her: My daddy always said that when you was in a shit-throwing contest, it didn't matter how much you threw but how much stuck to you.

Both of them had come from large families. Irv had three brothers and three sisters; Norma had four sisters and one brother. There were uncles, nieces, nephews, and cousins galore. There were parents and grandparents, in-laws . . . and, as in every family, a few outlaws.

One of Irv's nephews, a boy named Fred Drew whom he

491

had met only three or four times, had a little pot garden growing in his backyard in Kansas, according to Tarkington's papers. One of Norma's uncles, a contractor, was up to his eyebrows in debt and shaky business ventures on the Gulf Coast of Texas; this fellow, whose name was Milo Breedlove, had a family of seven to support, and one whisper from the government would send Milo's whole desperate house of cards tumbling and put them all on the state, common bankrupts. A cousin of Irv's (twice removed; he thought he had met her once but couldn't recall what she had looked like) had apparently embezzled a small sum of money from the bank where she worked about six years ago. The bank had found out and had let her go, electing not to prosecute so as to avoid adverse publicity. She had made restitution over a period of two years and was now making a moderate success of her own beauty parlor in North Fork, Minnesota. But the statute of limitations had not run out and she could be federally prosecuted under some law or other having to do with banking practices. The FBI had a file on Norma's youngest brother, Don. Don had been involved with the SDS in the middle sixties and might have been briefly involved with a plot to firebomb a Dow Chemical Company office in Philadelphia. The evidence was not strong enough to stand up in court (and Don had told Norma himself that when he got wind of what was going on, he had dropped the group, horrified), but a copy of the file forwarded to the division of the corporation he worked for would undoubtedly lose him his job.

It had gone on and on, Tarkington's droning voice in the closed, tight little room. He had saved the best for last. Irv's family's last name had been Mandroski when his great-grandparents came to America from Poland in 1888. They were Jews, and Irv himself was part Jewish, although there had been no pretension to Judaism in the family since the time of his grandfather, who had married a Gentile; the two of them had lived in happy agnosticism ever after. The blood had been further thinned when Irv's father had gone and done him likewise (as Irv himself had done, marrying Norma Breedlove, a sometime Methodist). But there were still Mandroskis in Poland, and Poland was behind the Iron Curtain, and if the CIA wanted to, they could set in motion a short chain of events that would end up making life very, very difficult for these relatives whom Irv had never seen. Jews were not loved behind the Iron Curtain.

Tarkington's voice ceased. He replaced his file, snapped his briefcase shut, put it between his feet again, and looked at them brightly, like a good student who has just given a winning recitation.

Irv lay against his pillow, feeling very weary. He felt Tarkington's eyes on him, and that he didn't particularly mind, but Norma's eyes were on him as well, anxious and questioning.

You haff relatives in the old country, yesss? Irv thought. It was such a cliché that it was funny, but he didn't feel like laughing at all, somehow. *How many removes before they're not your relatives anymore? Fourth-cousin remove? Sixth? Eighth? Christ on a sidecar. And if we stand up to this sanctimonious bastard and they ship those people off to Siberia, what do I do? Send them a postcard saying they're working in the salt mines because I picked up a little button and her daddy hitching on the road in Hastings Glen? Christ on a sidecar.*

Dr Hofferitz, who was nearly eighty, came slowly out of the back bedroom, brushing his white hair back with one gnarled hand. Irv and Norma, both glad to be jerked out of their memories of the past, looked around at him.

'She's awake,' Dr Hofferitz said, and shrugged. 'She's not in very good shape, your little ragamuffin, but she is in no danger, either. She has an infected cut on her arm and

493

another on her back, which she says she got crawling under a barbed-wire fence to get away from "a pig that was mad at her." '

Hofferitz sat down at the kitchen table with a sigh, produced a pack of Camels, and lit one. He had smoked all his life, and, he had sometimes told colleagues, as far as he was concerned, the surgeon general could go fuck himself.

'Do you want something to eat, Karl?' Norma asked.

Hofferitz looked at their plates. 'No – but if I was to, it looks like you wouldn't have to dish up anything new,' he said dryly.

'Will she have to stay in bed for long?' Irv asked.

'Ought to have her down to Albany,' Hofferitz said. There was a dish of olives on the table and he took a handful. 'Observation. She's got a fever of a hundred and one. It's from the infection. I'll leave you some penicillin and some antibiotic ointment. Mostly what she needs to do is eat and drink and rest. Malnutrition. Dehydration.' He popped an olive into his mouth. 'You were right to give her that chicken broth, Norma. Anything else, she would have sicked it up, almost as sure as shooting. Nothing but clear liquids for her tomorrow. Beef broth, chicken broth, lots of water. And plenty of gin, of course; that's the best of those clear liquids.' He cackled at this old joke, which both Irv and Norma had heard a score of times before, and popped another olive into his mouth. 'I ought to notify the police about this, you know.'

'No,' Irv and Norma said together, and then they looked at each other, so obviously surprised that Dr Hofferitz cackled again.

'She's in trouble, ain't she?'

Irv looked uncomfortable. He opened his mouth, then closed it again.

'Got something to do with that trouble you had last year, maybe?'

494

This time Norma opened her mouth, but before she could speak, Irv said, 'I thought it was only gunshot wounds you had to report, Karl.'

'By law, by law,' Hofferitz said impatiently, and stubbed out his cigarette. 'But you know there's a spirit of the law as well as a letter, Irv. Here's a little girl and you say her name is Roberta McCauley and I don't believe that anymore than I believe a hog will shit dollar bills. She says she scraped her back open crawling under barbed wire, and I got to think that's a funny thing to have happen to you on the way to your relatives, even with gas as tight as it is. She says she don't remember much of the last week or so, and that I do believe. Who is she, Irv?'

Norma looked at her husband, frightened. Irv rocked back in his chair and looked at Dr Hofferitz.

'Yeah,' he said finally, 'she's part of that trouble from last year. That's why I called you, Karl. You've seen trouble, both here and back in the old country. You know what trouble is. And you know that sometimes the laws are only as good as the people in charge of them. I'm just saying that if you let out that little girl is here, it's going to mean trouble for a lot of people who haven't earned it. Norma and me, a lot of our kin . . . and her in there. And that's all I think I can tell you. We've known each other twenty-five years. You'll have to decide what you're going to do.'

'And if I keep my mouth shut,' Hofferitz said, lighting another cigarette, 'what are you going to do?'

Irv looked at Norma, and she looked back at him. After a moment she gave her head a bewildered little shake and dropped her eyes to her plate.

'I dunno,' Irv said quietly.

'You just gonna keep her like a parrot in a cage?' Hofferitz asked. 'This is a small town, Irv. I can keep my mouth shut, but I'm in the minority. Your wife and you belong to the church. To the Grange. People come and people go. Dairy inspectors gonna drop by to check your cows. Tax assessor's gonna drop by some fine day – that bald bastard – to reassess your buildings. What are you gonna do? Build her a room down cellar? Nice life for a kid, all right.'

Norma was looking more and more troubled.

'I dunno,' Irv repeated. 'I guess I have got to think on it some. I see what you're sayin . . . but if you knew the people that was after her . . .'

Hofferitz's eyes sharpened at this, but he said nothing.

'I got to think on it some. But will you keep quiet about her for the time being?'

Hofferitz popped the last of his olives into his mouth, sighed, stood up, holding onto the edge of the table. 'Yeah,' he said. 'She's stable. That V-Cillin will knock out the bugs. I'll keep my mouth shut, Irv. But you better think on it, all right. Long and hard. Because a kid ain't a parrot.'

'No,' Norma said softly. 'No, of course not.'

'Something strange about that kid,' Hofferitz said, picking up his black bag. 'Something damn funny about her. I couldn't see it and I couldn't put my finger on it . . . but I felt it.'

'Yeah,' Irv said. 'There's something strange about her, all right, Karl. That's why she's in trouble.'

He saw the doctor out into the warm and rainy November night.

5

After the doctor had finished probing and pressing with his old, gnarled, but wonderfully gentle hands, Charlie fell into a feverish but not unpleasant doze. She could hear their voices in the other room and understood that they

496

were talking about her, but she felt sure that they were only talking . . . not hatching plans.

The sheets were cool and clean; the weight of the crazy quilt was comforting on her chest. She drifted. She remembered the woman calling her a witch. She remembered walking away. She remembered hitching a ride with a vanful of hippies, all of them smoking dope and drinking wine, and she remembered that they had called her little sister and asked her where she was going.

'North,' she had replied, and that had caused a roar of approval.

After that she remembered very little until yesterday, and the hog that had charged her, apparently meaning to eat her. How she had got to the Manders farm, and why she had come here – whether it had been a conscious decision or something else – she could not remember.

She drifted. The doze deepened. She slept. And in her dream they were back in Harrison and she was starting up in her bed, her face wet with tears, screaming with terror, and her mother rushed in, auburn hair blinding and sweet in the morning light, and she had cried, 'Mommy, I dreamed you and Daddy were dead!' And her mother stroked her hot forehead with a cool hand and said, 'Shhh, Charlie, shhh. It's morning now, and wasn't that a silly dream?'

6

There was very little sleep for Irv and Norma Manders that night. They sat watching a succession of inane prime-time sitcoms, then the news, then the *Tonight* show. And every fifteen minutes or so Norma would get up, leave the living room quietly, and go to check on Charlie.

'How is she?' Irv asked around quarter of one.

'Fine. Sleeping.'

Irv grunted.

'Have you thought of it, Irv?'

'We've got to keep her until she's better,' Irv said. 'Then we'll talk to her. Find out about her dad. I can only see that far ahead.'

'If they come back—'

'Why should they?' Irv asked. 'They shut us up. They think they scared us—'

'They *did* scare me,' Norma said softly.

'But it wasn't right,' Irv replied, just as softly. 'You know that. That money . . . that "insurance money" . . . I never felt right about that, did you?'

'No,' she said, and shifted restlessly. 'But what Doc Hofferitz said is true, Irv. A little girl has got to have people . . . and she's got to go to school . . . and have friends . . . and . . . and—'

'You saw what she did that time,' Irv said flatly. 'That pyrowhatsis. You called her a monster.'

'I've regretted that unkind word ever since,' Norma said. 'Her father – he seemed like such a nice man. If only we knew where he was now.

'He's dead,' a voice said from behind them, and Norma actually cried out as she turned and saw Charlie standing in the doorway, clean now and looking all the more pallid for that. Her forehead shone like a lamp. She floated in one of Norma's flannel nightgowns. 'My daddy is dead. They killed him and now there's nowhere I can go. Won't you please help me? I'm sorry. It's not my fault. I told them it wasn't my fault . . . I told them . . . but the lady said I was a witch . . . she said . . .' The tears were coming now, streaming down her cheeks, and Charlie's voice dissolved into incoherent sobs.

'Oh, honey, come here,' Norma said, and Charlie ran to her.

Dr Hofferitz came the next day and pronounced Charlie improved. He came two days after that and pronounced her much improved. He came over the weekend and pronounced her well.

'Irv, you decided what you're going to do?'

Irv shook his head.

Norma went to church by herself that Sunday morning, telling people that Irv had 'a touch of the bug.' Irv sat home with Charlie, who was still weak but able to get around inside the house now. The day before, Norma had bought her a lot of clothes – not in Hastings Glen, where such a purchase would have caused comment, but in Albany.

Irv sat beside the stove whittling, and after a while Charlie came and sat with him. 'Don't you want to know?' she said. 'Don't you want to know what happened after we took your car and left here?'

He looked up from his whittling and smiled at her. 'Figure you'll tell when you're ready, button.'

Her face, white, tense, and unsmiling, didn't change. 'Aren't you afraid of me?'

'Should I be?'

'Aren't you afraid I'll burn you up?'

'No, button. I don't think so. Let me tell you something. You're no little girl anymore. Maybe you ain't a big girl – you're someplace in the middle – but you're big enough. A kid your age – any kid – could get hold of matches if she wanted to, burn up the house or whatever. But not many do. Why would they want to? Why should you want to? A kid your age should be able to be trusted with a jackknife or a pack of matches if they're halfway bright. So, no. I ain't scared.'

At that Charlie's face relaxed; an expression of almost indescribable relief flowed across it.

'I'll tell you,' she said then. 'I'll tell you everything.' She began to speak and was still speaking when Norma returned an hour later. Norma stopped in the doorway, listening, then slowly unbuttoned her coat and took it off. She put her purse down. And still Charlie's young but somehow old voice droned, on and on, telling it, telling it all.

And by the time she was done, both of them understood just what the stakes were, and how enormous they had become.

9

Winter came with no firm decision made. Irv and Norma began to go to church again, leaving Charlie alone in the house with strict instructions not to answer the telephone if it rang and to go down the cellar if someone drove in while they were gone. Hofferitz's words, *like a parrot in a cage*, haunted Irv. He bought a pile of schoolbooks – in Albany – and took up teaching Charlie himself. Although she was quick, he was not particularly good at it. Norma was a little better. But sometimes the two of them would be sitting at the kitchen table, bent over a history or geography book, and Norma would look up at him with a question in her eyes . . . a question for which Irv had no answer.

The New Year came; February; March. Charlie's birthday. Presents bought in Albany. Like a parrot in a cage. Charlie did not seem entirely to mind, and in some ways, Irv reasoned to himself on nights when he couldn't sleep, perhaps it had been the best thing in the world for her, this period of slow healing, of each day taken in its slow winter course. But what came next? He didn't know.

There was the day in early April after a drenching two-day rain when the damned kindling was so damp he couldn't get the kitchen stove lit.

'Stand back a second,' Charlie said, and he did, automatically, thinking she wanted to look at something in there. He felt something pass him in midair, something tight and hot, and a moment later the kindling was blazing nicely.

Irv stared around at her, wide-eyed, and saw Charlie looking back at him with a kind of nervous, guilty hope on her face.

'I helped you, didn't I?' she said in a voice that was not quite steady. 'It wasn't really bad, was it?'

'No,' he said. 'Not if you can control it, Charlie.'

'I can control the little ones.'

'Just don't do it around Norma, girl. She'd drop her teddies.'

Charlie smiled a little.

Irv hesitated and then said, 'For myself, anytime you want to give me a hand and save me messing around with that damned kindling, you go right ahead. I've never been any good at it.'

'I will,' she said, smiling more now. 'And I'll be careful.'

'Sure. Sure you will,' he said, and for just a moment he saw those men on the porch again, beating at their flaming hair, trying to put it out.

Charlie's healing quickened, but still there were bad dreams and her appetite remained poor. She was what Norma Manders called 'peckish.'

Sometimes she would wake up from these nightmares with shuddering suddenness, not so much pulled from sleep as ejected from it, like a fighter pilot from his plane. This happened to her one night during the second week of

April; at one moment she was asleep, and at the next she was wide awake in her narrow bed in the back room, her body coated with sweat. For a moment the nightmare remained with her, vivid and terrible (the sap was running freely in the maples now, and Irv had taken her with him that afternoon to change the buckets; in her dream they had been sapping again, and she had heard something behind and had looked back to see John Rainbird creeping up on them, flitting from tree to tree, barely visible; his one eye glittered with a baleful lack of mercy, and his gun, the one he had shot her daddy with, was in one hand, and he was gaining). And then it slipped away. Mercifully, she could remember none of the bad dreams for long, and she rarely screamed anymore upon awakening from them, frightening Irv and Norma into her room to see what was wrong.

Charlie heard them talking in the kitchen. She fumbled for the Big Ben on her dresser and brought it close to her face. It was ten o'clock. She had been asleep only an hour and a half.

'—going to do?' Norma asked.

It was wrong to eavesdrop, but how could she help it? And they were talking about her; she knew it.

'I don't know,' Irv said.

'Have you thought anymore about the paper?'

Papers, Charlie thought. *Daddy wanted to talk to the papers. Daddy said it would be all right then.*

'Which one?' Irv asked. 'The Hastings *Bugle*? They can put it right next to the A&P ad and this week's shows at the Bijou.'

'It was what her father was planning to do.'

'Norma,' he said. 'I could take her to New York City. I could take her to the *Times*. And what would happen if four guys pulled guns and started shooting in the lobby?'

Charlie was all ears now. Norma's footfalls crossed the

502

kitchen; there was the rattle of the teapot's lid, and what she said in reply was mostly lost under running water.

Irv said, 'Yeah, I think it might happen. And I tell you what might be even worse, as much as I love her. She might get the drop on *them*. And if it got out of control, like it did at that place where they kep her . . . well, there's pretty nearly eight million people in New York City, Norma. I just feel like I'm too old to take a risk like that.'

Norma's footfalls crossed back to the table again, the old flooring of the farmhouse creaking comfortably beneath them. 'But, Irv, listen to me now,' she said. Norma spoke carefully and slowly, as if she had been thinking this out carefully over a long period of time. 'Even a little paper, even a little weekly like the *Bugle*, they're hooked into those AP tickers. News comes from everyplace these days. Why, just two years ago a little paper in Southern California won the Pulitzer Prize for some news story, and they had a circulation of under fifteen hundred!'

He laughed, and Charlie suddenly knew he had taken her hand across the table. 'You've been studying on this, haven't you?'

'Yes I have, and there's no reason to laugh at me for it, Irv Manders! This is serious, a serious business! We're in a box! How long can we keep her here before somebody finds out? You took her sapping out in the woods just this afternoon—'

'Norma, I wasn't laughin at you, and the child has got to get out sometime—'

'Don't you think I know that? I didn't say no, did I? That's just it! A growing child needs fresh air, exercise. Got to have those things if you're going to have any appetite, and she's—'

'Peckish, I know.'

'Pale and peckish, that's right. So I didn't say no. I was glad to see you take her. But, Irv, what if Johnny Gordon

503

or Ray Parks had been out today and had just happened to drift over to see what you were doing, like they sometimes do?'

'Honey, they didn't.' But Irv sounded uneasy.

'Not this time! Not the time before! But Irv, it can't go on! We been lucky already, and you know it!'

Her footsteps crossed the kitchen again, and then there was the sound of tea being poured.

'Yeah,' Irv said. 'Yeah, I know we have. But . . . thanks, darlin.'

'Welcome,' she said, sitting down again. 'And never mind the buts, either. You know it only takes one person, or maybe two. It'll spread. It'll get *out*, Irv, that we got a little girl up here. Never mind what it's doing to her; what happens if it gets back to *them*?'

In the darkness of the back room, Charlie's arms rashed out in goosebumps.

Slowly, Irv answered her. 'I know what you're saying, Norma. We got to do something, and I keep going over and over it in my head. A little paper . . . well, it's not just *sure* enough. You know we've got to get this story out right if we're going to make that girl safe for the rest of her life. If she's going to be safe, a lot of people have got to know she exists and what she can do – isn't that right? A *lot* of people.'

Norma Manders stirred restlessly but said nothing.

Irv pressed on. 'We got to do it right for her, and we got to do it right for us. Because it could be our lives at stake, too. Me, I've already been shot once. I believe that. I love her like my own, and I know you do, too, but we got to be realists about it, Norma. She could get us killed.'

Charlie felt her face grow hot with shame . . . and with terror. Not for herself but for them. What had she brought on their house?

'And it's not just us or her. You remember what that

504

man Tarkington said. The files he showed us. It's your brother and my nephew Fred and Shelley, and—'

'—and all those people back in Poland,' Norma said.

'Well, maybe he was only bluffing about that. I pray to God he was. It's hard for me to believe anyone could get that low.'

Norma said grimly, 'They've been pretty low already.'

'Anyway,' Irv said, 'we know they'll follow through on as much as they can, the dirty bastards. The shit is going to fly. All I'm saying, Norma, is I don't want the shit to fly to no good purpose. If we're going to make a move, I want it to be a good one. I don't want to go to some country weekly and then have them get wind of it and squash it. They could do it. They could do it.'

'But what does that leave?'

'That,' Irv said heavily, 'is what I keep tryin to figure out. A paper or a magazine, but one they won't think of. It's got to be honest, and it ought to be nationwide. But most of all, it can't have any ties to the government or to the government's ideas.'

'You mean to the Shop,' she said flatly.

'Yeah. That's what I mean.' There was the soft sound of Irv sipping his tea. Charlie lay in her bed, listening, waiting.

. . . it could be our lives at stake, too . . . I've already been shot once . . . I love her like my own, and I know you do, too, but we got to be realists about it, Norma . . . she could get us killed.

(*no please I*)

(*she could get us killed like she got her mother killed*)

(*no please please don't don't say that*)

(*like she got her daddy killed*)

(*please stop*)

Tears rolled across her side-turned face, catching in her ears, wetting the pillowcase.

'Well, we'll think on it some more,' Norma said finally.
'There's an answer to this, Irv. Somewhere.'

'Yeah. I hope so.'

'And in the meantime,' she said, 'we just got to hope no
one knows she's here.' Her voice suddenly kindled with
excitement. 'Irv, maybe if we got a lawyer—'

'Tomorrow,' he said. 'I'm done in, Norma. And no one
knows she's here yet.'

But someone did. And the news had already begun to
spread.

10

Until he was in his late sixties, Dr Hofferitz, an inveterate
bachelor, had slept with his longtime housekeeper, Shirley
McKenzie. The sex part of it had slowly dried up: the last
time, as well as Hofferitz could recall, had been about
fourteen years before, and that had been something of an
anomaly. But the two of them had remained close; in fact,
with the sex gone, the friendship had deepened and had
lost some of that tense prickliness that seems to be at the
center of most sexual relationships. Their friendship had
become of that platonic variety that seems to genuinely
obtain only in the very young and in the very old of the
opposite sex.

Still, Hofferitz held onto his knowledge of the Manderses' 'boarder' for better than three months. Then, one
night in February, after three glasses of wine while he and
Shirley (who had just that January turned seventy-five)
were watching television, he told her the whole story, after
swearing her to complete secrecy.

Secrets, as Cap could have told Dr Hofferitz, are even
more unstable than U-235, and stability lessens propor-
tionately as the secret is told. Shirley McKenzie kept the
secret for almost a month before telling her best girlfriend,

Hortense Barclay. Hortense kept the secret for about ten days before telling *her* best girlfriend, Christine Traegger. Christine told her husband and her best friends (all three of them) almost immediately.

This is how the truth spreads in small towns; and by the night in April when Irv and Norma had their overheard conversation, a good deal of Hastings Glen knew that they had taken in a mysterious girl. Curiosity ran high. Tongues wagged.

Eventually the news reached the wrong pair of ears. A telephone call was made from a scrambler phone.

Shop agents closed in on the Manders farm for the second time on the last day of April; this time they came across the dawn fields through a spring mist, like horrific invaders from Planet X in their bright flame-resistant suits. Backing them up was a National Guard unit who didn't know what the fuck they were doing or why they had been ordered out to the peaceful little town of Hastings Glen, New York.

They found Irv and Norma Manders sitting stunned in their kitchen, a note between them. Irv had found it that morning when he arose at five o'clock to milk the cows. It was one line: *I think I know what to do now. Love, Charlie.*

She had eluded the Shop again – but wherever she was, she was alone.

The only consolation was that this time she didn't have so far to hitch.

11

The librarian was a young man, twenty-six years old, bearded, long-haired. Standing in front of his desk was a little girl in a green blouse and bluejeans. In one hand she held a paper shopping bag. She was woefully thin, and the

507

young man wondered what the hell her mother and father had been feeding her . . . if anything.

He listened to her question carefully and respectfully. Her daddy, she said, had told her that if you had a really hard question, you had to go to the library to find the answer, because at the library they knew the answers to almost all the questions. Behind them, the great lobby of the New York Public Library echoed dimly; outside, the stone lions kept their endless watch.

When she was done, the librarian recapitulated, ticking off the salient points on his fingers.

'Honest.'

She nodded.

'Big . . . that is, nationwide.'

She nodded again.

'No ties to the government.'

For the third time, the thin girl nodded.

'Do you mind my asking why?'

'I' – she paused – 'I have to tell them something.'

The young man considered for several moments. He seemed about to speak, then held up a finger and went and conferred with another librarian. He came back to the little girl and spoke two words.

'Can you give me an address?' she asked.

He found the address and then printed it carefully on a square of yellow paper.

'Thank you,' the girl said, and turned to go.

'Listen,' he said, 'when was the last time you had something to eat, kid? You want a couple of bucks for lunch?'

She smiled – an amazingly sweet and gentle smile. For a moment, the young librarian was almost in love.

'I have money,' she said, and opened the sack so he could see.

The paper bag was filled with quarters.

508

Before he could say anything else – ask her if she had taken a hammer to her piggybank, or what – she was gone.

12

The little girl rode the elevator up to the sixteenth floor of the skyscraper. Several of the men and women who rode with her looked at her curiously – just a small girl in a green blouse and bluejeans, holding a crumpled paper bag in one hand and a Sunkist orange in the other. But they were New Yorkers, and the essence of the New York character is to mind your own business and let other people mind theirs.

She got off the elevator, read the signs, and turned left. Double glass doors gave on a handsome reception area at the end of the hall. Written below the two words the librarian had spoken to her was this motto: 'All the News That Fits.'

Charlie paused outside a moment longer.

'I'm doing it, Daddy,' she whispered. 'Oh, I hope I'm doing it right.'

Charlie McGee tugged open one of the glass doors and went into the offices of *Rolling Stone*, where the librarian had sent her.

The receptionist was a young woman with clear gray eyes. She looked at Charlie for several seconds in silence, taking in the crumpled Shop and Save bag, the orange, the slightness of the girl herself: she was slender almost to the point of emaciation, but tall for a child, and her face had a kind of serene, calm glow. *She's going to be so beautiful*, the receptionist thought.

'What can I do for you, little sister?' the receptionist asked, and smiled.

'I need to see someone who writes for your magazine,'

Charlie said. Her voice was low, but it was clear and firm. 'I have a story I want to tell. And something to show.'

'Just like show-and-tell in school, huh?' the receptionist asked.

Charlie smiled. It was the smile that had so dazzled the librarian. 'Yes,' she said. 'I've been waiting for a long time.'